THE VIKING PORTABLE LIBRARY
MARGARET FULLER

Poet, editor, translator, and literary critic Margaret Fuller, nineteenth-century America's most prominent woman of letters, was born on March 23, 1810, in Cambridgeport, Massachusetts. The eldest child of Timothy and Margarett Crane Fuller, Margaret was schooled at home by her father in classical literature before attending Miss Prescott's Young Ladies' Seminary in Groton. After a period of teaching in Boston and in Providence, Rhode Island, she edited the Transcendentalist journal the *Dial* from 1840 to 1842. As the *Dial*'s first editor, she published fellow Transcendentalists Ralph Waldo Emerson, Theodore Parker, and George Ripley. In 1844 Horace Greeley recruited her as the first literary critic for the *New-York Daily Tribune*. As the *Tribune*'s special European correspondent, Fuller spent her last years in revolutionary Italy, where she met Giovanni Ossoli, with whom she had a son in 1848. Nearly a year after the overthrow of the Roman Republic, Fuller, Ossoli, and their son, Angelo, left Italy. They perished together in a shipwreck off Fire Island, New York, on July 19, 1850. Fuller's best-known books include *Summer on the Lakes* (1844), *Woman in the Nineteenth Century* (1845), and *Papers on Literature and Art* (1846).

Mary Kelley, the John Sloan Dickey Professor of History at Dartmouth College, is the author of *Private Woman, Public Stage: Literary Domesticity in Nineteenth-Century America*. Co-author of *The Limits of Sisterhood: The Beecher Sisters on Women's Rights and Woman's Sphere*, she has recently completed *The Power of Her Sympathy*, an edition of Catharine Maria Sedgwick's autobiography and journal. The project in which she is currently engaged, titled "Intellectual Woman/Woman Intellectual: Gender, Culture, and Authority in Nineteenth-Century America," examines the multifaceted intellectual lives of nineteenth-century women.

Each volume in The Viking Portable Library either presents a representative selection from the works of a single outstanding writer or offers a comprehensive anthology on a special subject. Averaging 700 pages in length and designed for compactness and readability, these books fill a need not met by other compilations. All are edited by distinguished authorities, who have written introductory essays and included much other helpful material.

The Portable

MARGARET FULLER

Edited and with an Introduction by

MARY KELLEY

PENGUIN BOOKS

PENGUIN BOOKS
Published by the Penguin Group
Penguin Books USA Inc., 375 Hudson Street,
New York, New York 10014, U.S.A.
Penguin Books Ltd, 27 Wrights Lane, London W8 5TZ, England
Penguin Books Australia Ltd, Ringwood, Victoria, Australia
Penguin Books Canada Ltd, 10 Alcorn Avenue,
Toronto, Ontario, Canada M4V 3B2
Penguin Books (N.Z.) Ltd, 182-190 Wairau Road,
Auckland 10, New Zealand

Penguin Books Ltd, Registered Offices:
Harmondsworth, Middlesex, England

First published in Penguin Books 1994

1   3   5   7   9   10   8   6   4   2

Margaret Fuller's letters are reprinted from *The Letters of Margaret Fuller,* edited
by Robert N. Hudspeth, volumes I–V, Cornell University Press, 1983, 1984,
1987, 1988.

LIBRARY OF CONGRESS CATALOGING IN PUBLICATION DATA
Fuller, Margaret, 1810–1850.
[Selections. 1994]
The portable Margaret Fuller/edited and with an introduction by Mary Kelley.
p.   cm.
Includes bibliographical references (p.).
ISBN 0 14 01.7665 9
I. Kelley, Mary, 1943–   .   II. Title.
PS2502.K44   1994
818'.309—dc20   93–49079

Printed in the United States of America
Set in Sabon

ACKNOWLEDGMENTS

Colleagues at Dartmouth College and elsewhere have long been generous in supporting my scholarship. Their contributions to this volume have continued that tradition. I learned much from the different perspectives that Sharon O'Brien, Nell Irvin Painter, John Seelye, James Tatum, and Suzanne Zantop brought to the introduction. With their discerning eye for language that obscures more than it enlightens, Susan Macvicar, Judith McGaw, and Larry Tise insisted that I clarify, always clarify, my meaning. Whether they were locating sources, developing bibliographies, or transcribing documents, Daisy Alpert, Pherabe Kolb, Michele-Ann Moninak, Katherine Monteiro, Lynn Rainville, and Susannah Shin each displayed a remarkable commitment to this project. They also brought laughter to the enterprise, an ingredient that lightened many a task. Patricia Carter was indefatigable in locating an original edition of Margaret Fuller's *Woman in the Nineteenth Century*. The American Antiquarian Society granted permission to quote from the letters and journals of Mary Ware Allen, Anna Gale, and Evelina Metcalf. Charles Capper, Fuller's most recent biographer, stood ready to answer questions, large and small. Robert Hudspeth, the editor of Fuller's letters, shared a limitless knowledge of his subject. And Robert Eaton Kelley brought his unrivaled skills as critic and stylist to bear on these pages.

CONTENTS

INTRODUCTION

IN A LETTER THAT SHE WROTE to William Henry Channing late in 1844, Margaret Fuller told her friend that she had completed *Woman in the Nineteenth Century,* the book that made her famous then and now. The final pages of the project behind her, Fuller acknowledged to the Transcendentalist Channing that she "felt a delightful glow as if I had put a good deal of my true life in it, as if, suppose I went away now, the measure of my foot-print would be left on the earth." Priced at fifty cents a copy, the original edition of one thousand sold within two weeks of its publication in 1845. Another edition appeared in England before the end of that year. Whether they celebrated or condemned its contents, reviewers kept *Woman in the Nineteenth Century* in the public eye. Journalist and abolitionist Lydia Maria Child, who hailed the book's "noble aspirations," described its author as a woman of "powerful intellect, comprehensive thought, and thorough education." An anonymous reviewer disagreed most vehemently, saying that the aspirations of *Woman in the Nineteenth Century* were actually heresies. And, having unsexed herself, Margaret Fuller was "no longer a woman."

Why such diametrically opposed responses? Edgar Allan Poe suggested that Fuller's "way of independence, of unmitigated radicalism" made her an idol to some, a villain to others. Still it was Fuller's subject, her claims for *Woman in the Nineteenth Century,* that made her controversial. During a century in which Americans divided the world on the basis of gender and made marriage and motherhood a female's sole occupation, Fuller insisted that women be able to develop their potential, not only as wives and mothers whose lives were defined by domesticity, but as individuals, each of whom had particular inclinations, desires, and talents. "Let them be sea-captains, if you will," Fuller declared. That was not likely without a revolution in the values held by a majority of Fuller's contemporaries.

Woman in the Nineteenth Century appeared at a crucial moment in Margaret Fuller's career as nineteenth-century America's most prominent woman of letters. In the previous decade, Fuller had supported herself as a teacher, instructing students at private schools in Boston and Providence and leading members of Boston's female elite in a series of classes she described as "Conversations." A teacher who left an imprint on her students whatever the setting, Fuller nonetheless identified herself primarily as a writer. The variety of Fuller's publications prior to the appearance of *Woman in the Nineteenth Century* testified to her already expansive intellectual and cultural interests. They included essays of literary criticism, translations of German intellectuals, poems, reviews of contemporary literature, music, and art, and a volume describing her travels West during 1843.

The publication of *Woman in the Nineteenth Century* coincided with Fuller's decision to join the ranks of journalists for Horace Greeley's *New-York Daily Tribune*. The nearly two hundred columns that she published in one of the nation's most widely circulated newspapers reflected her growing interest in social and political issues. Charitable institutions, racial prejudice, penal reform, class relations—all were now included in her literary domain. Two years after she had left her native New England for New York City, Fuller departed for Europe, embarking on yet another journey of discovery. Employed as Greeley's correspondent, she sent dispatches from England, Scotland, and France. Her final destination was Italy. It was also her most notable. In residence in Rome during the Italian Revolution, Fuller provided the *New-York Daily Tribune*'s readers with riveting descriptions of the struggle for a unified and independent Italy.

Margaret Fuller's experiences were shaped by the social and cultural milieu of the early nineteenth century and the individual circumstances of her life. Simultaneously, Fuller the woman played a signal role in shaping those experiences. Most obviously, she did so by the different paths she chose, sometimes yielding to the claims of family and friends, sometimes acting in response to her deeply felt needs and desires. However, the woman of letters did not stop here. Fuller also inscribed herself in her writings. Whether in her autobiographical sketch published posthumously or in her books with characters who resembled her, Fuller left readers with meditations on her life.

Born in Cambridgeport, Massachusetts, in 1810, Fuller was the eldest of Timothy and Margarett Crane Fuller's seven children. Descended from settlers who had left England early in the seventeenth century, both her parents came from relatively modest circumstances. Nonetheless, Timothy's father educated his ten children himself and sent four of five sons to Harvard College; eldest son Timothy became a prominent lawyer. Elected to the Massachusetts legislature in 1813 and to the House of Representatives five years later, Jeffersonian Republican Timothy Sr. also served four terms in Congress. A decade younger than her husband, Margarett taught at a local school before her marriage in the spring of 1809. In Fuller's autobiographical sketch, she described Timothy's devotion to Margarett as "the green spot on which he stood apart from the common-places of a mere bread-winning, bread-bestowing existence." Fuller's memory might well have enlarged that "green spot" had she recalled the unusually strong and intense engagement that her father developed with his children. In this regard, Timothy also stood apart from his contemporaries.

Nowhere was the father's engagement more clearly displayed than in the responsibility that he assumed for his eldest daughter's education. Instructing Fuller as if she were a son preparing for his alma mater, Timothy began schooling her in English and Latin grammar at the age of six. Three years later Fuller was reading Virgil, Cicero, Horace, Livy, and Tacitus. Greek grammar was added to her daily studies, as were French and Italian. Fuller herself counterpointed this relentless study of languages with volumes of Shakespeare, Cervantes, Moliere, Fielding, Smollett, and Scott that filled her father's library. Nonetheless, the classical texts were the decisive influence. In her autobiographical sketch, Fuller recalled that the heroes presented in those pages had impressed her with the importance of "earnest purpose," of "self-command," of "force of expression," all of which constituted the basis of virtue. In saying that she "steadily loved this ideal in my childhood," Fuller highlighted her early identification with the heroes of Greece and Rome. Clearly, she considered these luminaries her companions, their struggles her inspiration. In reading herself into these texts, Fuller laid claim to qualities of character that had been considered the possession of men. Simultaneously, she made the classical heritage and Western culture her own.

Written when she herself was thirty, Fuller's autobiographical sketch is filled with criticism of her father's approach to her education. In his efforts to develop Fuller's precocious intellect as early and as thoroughly as possible, the daughter thought Timothy had subjected her to an overly exacting discipline. His standards had been too exceptional, his judgments too severe. The toll on her had been extreme. In one of the sketch's most moving passages, Fuller charged that she had been denied a "natural childhood." In *Woman in the Nineteenth Century*, however, Fuller praised precisely the same approach. This volume is replete with examples of learned women, some historical, some constructed from Fuller's imagination. None is more impressive than the aptly named Miranda, a figure whose education bears a striking resemblance to Fuller's. Always treating his daughter "as a living mind," Miranda's father insists that she develop judgment, courage, honor, and fidelity, in short, all those virtues celebrated by the Greeks and Romans whose example Fuller's father had set before her. This education had stimulated in Miranda "a dignified sense of self-dependence," a sense of self that Fuller celebrated in *Woman in the Nineteenth Century*. Serene, confident, and decisive, Miranda gave the lie to the idea that women were inherently dependent. Equally important, Miranda's education made her an able participant in "the world of mind." Composed selectively from memories of a complicated childhood, the autobiographical sketch and *Woman in the Nineteenth Century* counterpoint each other, reflecting the lights and shadows of Timothy Fuller's legacy.

If Timothy focused exclusively on the development of Fuller's intellect, Margarett introduced their daughter to other dimensions of the self. The setting was Margarett's garden, a place of many delights. Filled with a dazzling variety of flowers, it was here the daughter recalled that she "felt at home." Instead of being pressed to meet her father's exacting standards, Fuller wistfully recalled that in the garden her "thoughts could lie callow in the nest and only be fed and kept warm, not called to fly or sing before the time." The violets, the lilies, the roses, and the asters awakened deeply felt emotions, "such as I have never dared express to any human being." Her praise for Margarett's approach was unequivocal, although Fuller came to acknowledge the need to develop all dimensions of the self.

Whatever relative importance she ascribed to her father's or her mother's influences in her childhood, Fuller readily acknowledged that her parents shared equally in the decision to change the trajectory of their fourteen-year-old daughter's instruction. Unlike the education of other elite daughters, Fuller's schooling had not combined an academic curriculum with domestic and social accomplishments. Telling Margaret that she had been kept at home "because I took such pleasure in teaching you myself," Timothy nonetheless dispatched his adolescent daughter to Miss Susan Prescott's Young Ladies' Seminary in

Groton, Massachusetts. Concerned that Margaret's education had been one-dimensional, Margarett strongly supported her husband's decision to send their daughter to a school that leavened its academic curriculum with social accomplishments.

One of the nearly four hundred academies and seminaries founded exclusively for women in the years between 1790 and 1830, Miss Prescott's exemplified women's increased educational opportunities in the early republic. In offering history, geography, philosophy, mathematics, and the natural sciences, the seminary was representative of schools for young women. Prescott's decision to include music, sewing, dancing, and drawing in the curriculum was equally typical, as was her emphasis upon manners and morals. Fuller, however, was not a typical student. Her studies had focused upon Latin and Greek, neither of which were taught at the seminary. Not surprisingly, she was very disappointed with the school. Writing to her father ten days after her arrival, she laced her letter with biting commentary: "I feel myself rather degraded from Cicero's oratory to One and two are how many? It is rather a change is it not?" Nonetheless, the most stinging disappointment had nothing to do with Fuller's studies, as revealed in *Summer on the Lakes*. It was there Fuller introduced readers to a character very much like her adolescent self. Keenly intelligent and passionate, the self-dramatizing Mariana captivates the other students at a seminary. Soon, however, Mariana's haughtiness annoys her erstwhile admirers. Her punishment is as swift as it is cruel—public humiliation before the entire school. Anguished that no one has defended her, Mariana calculates an equally cruel revenge. Eventually exposed for spreading discord and reprimanded by the school's headmistress, she emerges a chastened individual. Fuller once claimed Mariana as herself, although there is no evidence that the character in *Summer on the Lakes* was a literal description of either Fuller or her experience at Miss Prescott's. However, there is evidence that Mariana stands as a metaphor for extracurricular lessons Fuller mastered at no small cost. Years later she told Susan Prescott that there were still painful memories of the year spent at her seminary. Yet, she added resolutely, those memories "have had a most powerful effect on my character." She readily acknowledged her debt to her mentor, telling Prescott: "Can I ever forget that to your treatment in that crisis of youth I owe the true life,—the love of Truth and Honor?" Fuller had suppressed the pain for the principle.

Whether the learning took place in her father's library or in Prescott's seminary, Margaret Fuller's education had not been intended to prepare her to become a woman of letters. Presuming that a daughter's existence would be centered in the household, elite families located female education in the context of domesticity. Serving as companion to husband and instructor to children, the educated woman devoted herself to her family. Those daughters who did not marry were expected to remain with their parents or to attach themselves to their siblings' families. There too the educated woman stood ready to serve as companion and teacher. In the decade after she completed her education, the unmarried Fuller did both—providing companionship for her father and instruction for her siblings.

When Fuller returned from Miss Prescott's Seminary in 1825, she was nearly fifteen. During the next decade, Fuller remained with her family in Cambridge and after 1833 in Groton. Not surprisingly, she pursued the studies she had begun with her father. Increasingly, Fuller herself decided upon the content of those studies. There was the reading, always the reading that filled her days. She read widely in Italian literature, taking pleasure in Petrarch, Dante, Berni, and Tasso. Epictetus, Milton, Racine, and de Staël also occupied her, as did the major texts of the Enlightenment. In Germaine de Staël and Maria Edgeworth, Fuller discovered women of letters. Reading them in tandem, Fuller considered their relative merits. "Had you rather be the brilliant de Staël or the useful Edgeworth?" she asked Susan Prescott. Since she was already steeped in English and French Romanticism, it was not surprising that Fuller betrayed a preference for de Staël, author of *Corinne* and a founder of French Romanticism. Whatever her preference, the young Fuller now had models of women who pursued intellectual and cultural pursuits.

Joining her friend James Freeman Clarke in the study of German, the two of them began reading Goethe. Fuller's engagement with the German poet, playwright, and novelist was immediate and intense—in only a few months, she read *Torquato Tasso, Iphigenia, Hermann and Dorothea, Faust,* and *The Elective Affinities.* She preferred "reading Goethe to anybody," she wrote to another friend, saying, "and as I proceed find more and more to learn." *Wilhelm Meisters Lehrjahre* proved the most powerful influence. Reading at a turn in her life when Fuller had taken responsibility for her education, she found the emphasis on self-culture in this novel compelling.

Strikingly, it was at this time that Fuller found the bridge to self-production. She embarked upon a translation of *Torquato Tasso,* Goethe's verse drama about the deeply alienated Renaissance poet. And Fuller herself began to write criticism, poetry, and fiction. In

1834, she published an essay in the *Boston Daily Advertiser*. The next year three articles appeared in Clarke's periodical, the *Western Messenger*. Margaret Fuller had taken command of her education and made it serve ends she had determined. Her career as a woman of letters had begun.

Almost at the moment at which Fuller embarked on that career, it looked as if she would have to cast it aside. In October of 1835, Timothy Fuller died from cholera, leaving his family with slender means of support. The eldest child of Timothy and Margarett lamented she had not been a son: "If I were an eldest son, I could be guardian to my brothers and sister, administer the estate, and really become the head of my family." The constraints of gender that Fuller articulated did not stop her. She resolved to be that son, albeit as a surrogate. The challenges proved formidable—supervising the family's affairs, managing the education of her siblings, and earning herself an income. Simultaneously, Fuller was determined to keep pace with her reading, to publish literary essays, and to begin research for a biography of Goethe. Less than a year after her father's death, she had managed all of this, except earning an income for herself. She resolved this last challenge with her decision to become a teacher, virtually the only occupation that antebellum Americans deemed appropriate for a genteel white woman.

Settling in Boston during the fall of 1836, Fuller developed a series of strategies to support herself as a teacher. She offered German, French, and Italian literature to classes of Boston's elite daughters. Simultaneously, she taught Latin, French, and Italian at Bronson Alcott's coeducational Temple School. Designed as a pedagogical experiment in which teacher and student participated in a Socratic dialogue, Alcott led his charges in conversations on a variety of topics, including biblical interpretation. Seemingly innocent at least in approach, the radical religiosity of the conversations shocked nearly everyone in Boston once they were published. The resulting controversy and the school's precipitous decline in enrollment led to Fuller's resignation in the spring of 1837. The resignation notwithstanding, Fuller's seven months in Boston left an important mark. Writing to a friend shortly after her departure, she said proudly, "I have fulfilled all my engagements faithfully; have acquired more power of attention, self-command, and fortitude; have acted in life as I thought I would in my lonely meditations, and I have gained some knowledge of means." Able to support herself and to meet her most exacting standards in the process, Fuller felt she had proved herself.

Very much in need of an income, Fuller secured another position at Providence, Rhode Island's, Greene Street School. She was paid the exceptional sum of one thousand dollars a year and taught a challenging variety of courses, ranging from natural history to English poetry. Whatever the course, Fuller pressed her female students to pursue the same ends she sought for herself—"activity of mind, accuracy in processes, constant looking for principles, and search after the good and beautiful," as she wrote to a friend. Fuller built upon what she had learned in Boston and made the conventional method of daily recitation secondary to dialogue. "It is all talk," said Fuller's student Mary Ware Allen, who explained Fuller's reasoning: "She says we must *think* as well as *study,* and *talk* as well as *recite.*" In this more participatory model adopted by Fuller, learning took place through engagement between teacher and student.

Beginning with her tenure at Greene Street School, Fuller became increasingly concerned with the issue of women's status in nineteenth-century society. In a journal that she kept as a student at Greene Street School, Mary Ware Allen recounted her teacher's aspirations for America's women: "She spoke upon what woman could do—said she should like to see a woman everything she might be, in intellect and character." The teacher tried to instill those same aspirations in her students. Having heard Fuller describe a young woman who had become a sculptor, Evelina Metcalf made a telling entry in her journal: "It makes me proud when I hear such things as this for it shows what our sex is capable of doing and encourages us to go on improving and doing all we can to show that we are not entirely incapable of intellectual cultivation as some think." Fuller also introduced her students to the Greek poet Sappho, the French Romantic Germaine de Staël, and the English novelist Hannah More, women who had distinguished themselves in literary pursuits. Two of Fuller's former students, Evelina Metcalf and Anna Gale, testified to the influence of such models of female achievement. Telling Anna that she had a talent for literary enterprises, Evelina pressed her to continue their pursuit: "Someday the name of Anna Gale will be even more celebrated than that of Hannah More."

The satisfactions derived from teaching notwithstanding, Fuller found it increasingly difficult to pursue her primary vocation. In the spring of 1838, she told Emerson that she could not sustain both "a worldling and a literary existence," making clear her preference for the latter. Yet, as she admitted to him, "I keep on 'fulfilling all my duties' as the technical phrase is except to myself." Nine months later, she acted on her desires, resigning her position at Greene Street School to focus on her literary career. Within two months she had completed a translation of *Eckermann's Conversations with Goethe,* a volume of meditations recorded by Goethe's devoted secretary. Shortly thereafter, she agreed to be the editor of the newly established Transcendentalist periodical the *Dial.*

Income remained an issue. And Fuller once again showed her inventiveness. Convinced that educated women did not have the opportunity either to integrate or to test their learning, she proposed to remedy that defect with a series of classes, or "Conversations" between herself and other highly educated women. Employing the same pedagogy that she had practiced at Greene Street School, Fuller suggested that she lead participants in a systematization and interrogation of key bodies of knowledge. In a letter that served as a prospectus for the "Conversations," she told her friend Sophia Ripley that the participants could ask, "What were we born to do? How shall we do it?" Fuller anticipated that ultimately the "Conversations" could be a "means of building up the life of thought upon the life of action." No less ambitious than the project itself, Fuller described herself as its "moving spring." In the next five years, Fuller led participants from Boston and environs in a series of "Conversations" that addressed Greek mythology, contemporary definitions of masculinity and femininity, development of the arts, and, not least, female intellectual potential.

Her audience responded enthusiastically. Not surprisingly, the participants were dazzled by Fuller's ability to gather ideas from disparate sources and weave them together in a tapestry of larger meanings. But it was her example as a learned woman, a woman participating in the creation of culture, that struck them most forcibly. Decades later, one of the leaders of the nineteenth-century women's rights movement, Elizabeth Cady Stanton, would remark that Fuller's "Conversations" had been "a vindication of woman's right to think." Confident, articulate, and brilliant, Fuller had exemplified that "vindication." Fuller herself was pleased with the "Conversations." Writing to Emerson shortly after they had begun, she described the participants as all "intelligent" and their approach as "devoutly thoughtful." Concerned that she might be treated as a "paid Corinne," she had been relieved to find that she was seen as "truly a teacher and a guide." The heroine in de Staël's most famous novel, the brilliant improvisator Corinne, had obviously captured Fuller's imagination. Of course, the teacher and guide was paid, receiving ten dollars for the initial series and double that amount thereafter. Fuller's "Conversations" served her well for many reasons. Offered twice a year with as many as thirty-five participants at a time, they provided her with an income for five years. They validated Fuller as a model of *woman thinking*. Perhaps most important, they made her more conscious of every woman's potential in this regard. The "Conversations," then, were a rehearsal for the claim that Fuller would make on behalf of *women thinking* in *Woman in the Nineteenth Century*.

When Fuller left Boston for Providence in the spring of 1837, she had taken away an intangible but valuable possession—a deepened friendship with Ralph Waldo Emerson. Marked by a lively correspondence and by visits with him and his wife, Lidian, at their home in Concord, Fuller's friendship with Emerson had a profound impact on her life. Already familiar with Transcendentalism, Fuller had maintained a certain distance from its tenets until she met Emerson. More than anyone else, he was elaborating a Transcendentalism that spoke to her needs and aspirations. Distinguishing between types of knowledge that derived either from sensory experience or from sources within the self, Emerson claimed superiority for the latter, insisting that intuition (or Reason, as he labelled it) provided the highest truths. In a series of essays that Emerson published during the years in which he and Fuller became friends, he called upon readers to claim their independence from the institutional sources of knowledge, whether religious or secular. "Trust thyself," he declared. Summoning Americans to have confidence in *their* Reason, he told them, "Nothing is at last sacred but the integrity of your own mind." In a letter to William Henry Channing, Fuller acknowledged her debt to Emerson, saying he "makes me think." For Fuller, this was the highest praise. Simultaneously, however, Fuller had a complicated relationship with Emerson. Engaged by his philosophy, she found his person distant. In the same letter in which she praised Emerson, Fuller told Channing that Emerson had disappointed her. The problem was his inability to establish a deeply felt connection with others. Emerson, she said with an almost uncanny perception, "had faith in the Universal, but not in the Individual Man; he met men, not as a brother, but as a critic."

Margaret Fuller was much more than Emerson's disciple. Multidimensional in its concerns, Emersonian Transcendentalism interwove religious, philosophical, and literary preoccupations. Fuller tended to be more focused, emphasizing Transcendentalism's potential for reforming American literary and artistic culture. Certainly, she sympathized with a Theodore Parker or a George Ripley, both of whom sought in Transcendentalism a more vital religion. She did the same with those whose engagement derived from Transcendentalism's philosophical promise. Yet she sought to commit Transcendentalism to another project. Convinced that Americans had become "superficial, irreverent, and more anxious to get a living than to live mentally and morally," she told William Henry Channing that the nation's civilization mirrored the sorry condition of its people. That Fuller invested literature and the arts with the power to reform America and its people suggests the signal role that her exceptionally broad reading had played in the construction of her identity. That reading had provided the means by which Fuller had initially discovered and then made herself anew. Writ large across a rapidly expanding nation, she thought it might have the same impact upon all Americans.

Fuller's candidates to lead this reformation were none other than the members of the " 'Transcendental party,' " as she referred to them in her letter to Channing. Insisting that Transcendentalists conceived the human being "as an immortal soul, and not as a mere comfort-loving inhabitant of earth, or as a subscriber to the social contract," Fuller enlisted in their party and made the *Dial* the vehicle for this reformation. In another letter that she wrote to Channing shortly after she had taken on the editorship of the *Dial*, Fuller underscored her objective: "That this periodical will not aim at leading public opinion, but at stimulating each man to think for himself, to think more deeply and more nobly by letting them see how some minds are kept alive by a wise self-trust."

Both a creed and a call for reformation, Emersonian self-reliance resonated through the pages of the periodical. In the initial issue, Emerson himself celebrated as the *Dial*'s own those who had placed "greater trust in the nature and resources of men, than the laws or the popular opinion will well allow." Farmers, matrons, schoolteachers, ministers, these were the leaders of Emerson's boldly labeled "revolution." Fuller's letters to potential contributors carried the same message. Combining praise with a plea for submissions, Fuller told fellow Transcendentalist Frederic Hedge, "I really hope you will make this the occasion for assailing the public ear with such a succession of melodies that all the stones will advance to form a city of refuge for the just."

The initial volume of the *Dial* reflected the powerful current of individualism that flowed through Transcendentalism. Prominent contributors Emerson, Parker, Ripley, and Alcott each spoke with a distinctive inflection. Simultaneously, however, their voices sounded a similar challenge to conventional opinion. The same radical individualism, the same dissent characterized subsequent volumes edited by Fuller between 1840 and 1842. Fuller's *Dial* was open, speculative, and willing to risk controversy. Perhaps most important, she welcomed experiment in content and form.

In concert with other Transcendentalists, Fuller herself engaged in such experiments. Mystical contemplations, commentaries on Goethe, translations, and essays on critical theory all appeared in the *Dial*. However, Fuller distinguished herself from Emerson, Parker, Ripley, and Alcott: She took women as her subject in a number of her contributions to the *Dial*. Her controversial "The Great Lawsuit," an essay that served as the basis for *Woman in the Nineteenth Century,* is a notable example in this regard. So too is the lesser known but still striking "Bettine Brentano and Her Friend Günderode," an essay on letters exchanged by two German intellectuals.

Presented as a meditation on the promise of female friendship, "Bettine Brentano and Her Friend Günderode" combines selected excerpts from the two women's correspondence along with Fuller's commentary. Based upon Bettine Brentano von Arnim's *Die Günderode,* which itself is a collage of actual and fictionalized letters, Fuller's meditation explored the dynamics of the relationship between Bettine Brentano, a member of a highly successful commercial family, and Karoline von Günderode, a canoness and aspiring poet. The author of *Goethe's Correspondence with a Child,* Brentano had already memorialized her friendship with the exalted Goethe. Using this text as a counterpoint to *Die Günderode,* Fuller informed readers that Brentano's relationship with Goethe had not been one of equals. Obvious differences had contributed to the relationship's hierarchical character. Already one of Europe's most celebrated men of letters when they met, Goethe was more than three decades older than the adolescent Brentano. However, Fuller detected more than structural imbalances in this hierarchy. Insisting that a condescending Goethe had placed their differences on a vertical axis, she suggested that he made Bettine a "tool" for his artistic purposes. Fuller did not idolize this exemplar of self-culture unqualifiedly.

The contrast between the relationships that Brentano established with Goethe and Günderode could not have been more stark. The reasons were telling, according to Fuller. It was not as if Brentano and Günderode were alike. Günderode was also the older and the more cultured participant in the friendship. And yet the same imbalances that had signaled the hierarchical relationship with Goethe had the opposite effect on Brentano and Günderode: "The advantage in years, the higher culture, and greater harmony of Günderode's nature is counterbalanced, by the ready springing impulse, richness, and melody of the other." Placed on a horizontal axis, the differences between them became the ground upon which Brentano and Günderode built an egalitarian relationship. Marked by respect and reciprocity, their bond had made them become "enough to one another to be led to indicate their best thoughts, their fairest visions." Instead of setting Brentano and Günderode apart from each other, the differences had enlarged their self-knowledge, making each of them more fully realized human beings.

The juxtaposition of Brentano's relationships with Goethe and Günderode highlighted the relative superiority of female friendship. Those who read only "Bettine and Her Friend Günderode" might presume that Fuller's decision to celebrate female friendship was based solely on her interpretation of the adolescent Brentano's experiences with Goethe and Günderode. But Fuller's autobiographical sketch suggests that personal experience also shaped her perspective. When Fuller was approaching adolescence, she met Ellen Kilshaw, an English woman who played a role comparable to Günderode's. Described by Fuller as her "first friend," Kilshaw appeared the embodiment of gentility, elegance, and cultivation to the young New Englander. Just as Fuller's mother had done, Kilshaw introduced her friend to a world that stimulated "the sense of beauty, not the mere utilities of life." Ellen Kilshaw became no less than Fuller's " 'angel.' "

The idealization of female friendship that marks the pages of both the essay and the autobiographical sketch testifies to the importance Fuller attached to this bond. Older mentors, classmates, and students took Kilshaw's place during Fuller's adulthood. These women, many of whom participated in Fuller's "Conversations," constituted a female circle of friendship that paralleled the almost exclusively male circle of Transcendentalists. In choosing her most intimate friends, Fuller moved back and forth between these circles, choosing a William Henry Channing from one, a Caroline Sturgis from the other. Regardless of her circle of choice, the individual shared Fuller's intellectual and cultural concerns. Each touched chords in Fuller's emotional self, eliciting a deeply felt intimacy. With these men and women, then, Fuller found it possible to join the rational and the emotional, bringing together the previously separate legacies of her father and mother.

Equally important, a Channing or a Sturgis exemplified that the rational need not be defined as inherently masculine, the emotional as inherently feminine. Instead, both had combined these attributes in a single person. The implications were significant indeed. Antebellum Americans thought that the traits they identified as masculine and feminine were fixed by nature. These individuals suggested a different interpretation. Perhaps the constellation of human attributes that had been linked with either masculinity or femininity had been socially and culturally determined. Perhaps antebellum Americans had arbitrarily identified some traits with men, others with women. If masculinity and femininity had been defined by the culture, then they could be redefined. Alternatives were possible.

Only a few years later Fuller elaborated upon these implications in *Woman in the Nineteenth Century*. Declaring that there was no "wholly masculine man, no purely feminine woman," she aligned herself with the position that the attributes that had been linked to either men or women were actually shared by both sexes. Not one to rely upon declarations alone, Fuller documented her position with illustrations from nature itself: "She sends women to battle, and sets Hercules spinning; she enables women to bear immense burdens, cold, and frost; she enables the man, who feels maternal love, to nourish his infant like a mother." With precedents such as these, it was surely inevitable that "she will make a female Newton, and a male Syren." Rummaging through nature itself, Fuller had based her definitions on the experiences of men and women. She now challenged her readers to do the same from their experience. In the process, they might construct themselves anew. They might become female Newtons and male Syrens.

"Bettine and Her Friend Günderode" appeared in the *Dial*'s seventh issue. The next issue proved to be the last that Fuller edited. By the spring of 1842, the demands of the "Conversations" and the *Dial* had exhausted her. Now so spent that letters were all she was able to write, Fuller decided to resign the editorship. Doing so was "a sad business," she told Emerson. Nonetheless, the resignation freed Fuller to pursue other projects. That she did, taking those who read *Summer on the Lakes* on the journey she had made through Illinois, Wisconsin, and Michigan during the summer of 1843.

When Fuller traveled west that summer, the nineteenth-century system of gender relations, and especially its impact upon women, was at the forefront of her consciousness. Shortly before her departure, she had sent the *Dial* "The Great Lawsuit: Man *versus* Men. Woman *versus* Women," the essay in which she called for the elimination of obstacles to women's participation in the nation's social and political life. She had completed another series of "Conversations," her fourth in as many years. Whatever the topic, the "Conversations" reminded her that women's position relative to men's provided little opportunity to develop intellectual and cultural potential. The very obstacles she had cited in "The Great Lawsuit" made it difficult for women to move toward the self-reliance celebrated by Transcendentalists like herself. Not surprisingly, then, Fuller's increasingly critical perspective on gender relations marked the pages of *Summer on the Lakes*. Indeed, it is this concern that links its seemingly unrelated journal entries, dialogues, tales of disastrous marriages, poems, commentaries on Indians, letters, and historical sketches.

In the intellectual and cultural baggage they carried with them, settlers had brought a conventional system of gender relations. Tucked away in that baggage, asymmetries in those relations were brought out after their arrival in the West. An observant Fuller discerned the resulting strains almost immediately. Westering women, many of whom had been reluctant to leave their communities, had nonetheless followed their husbands, "doing their best for affection's sake." Isolated and lonely in the sparsely settled West, they had had to endure more than their male counterparts. Men had been able to "find assistance in field labor, and recreation with the gun and fishing-rod." Women's "comfortless and laborious indoor life" stood in sharp contrast. Unable to find anyone to assist them with household labor, some became "slatterns," others struggled simply to maintain the "necessary routine of small arrangements." A source of pleasure in the East, the social accomplishments they had cultivated there were almost worthless in this environment: "They can dance, but not draw; talk French, but know nothing of the language of flowers." Little wonder, then, that Fuller concluded "women did not like the change." And yet they still insisted upon schooling their daughters in the same social and cultural practices. Fuller proposed a remedy, suggesting that the next generation be encouraged to develop "strength of body, dexterity, simple tastes, and resources that would fit them to enjoy and refine the western farmer's life."

The remedy chosen by Fuller was telling. She had observed the strains. She had not determined the underlying cause, a system of hierarchical gender relations in which women occupied a dependent position. That determination came only when Fuller enlarged the scope of *Summer on the Lakes*, including figures with no connection to the West. The product of Fuller's imagination, the figure of Mariana appears as a startling lesson in the consequences of female dependence. The same Mariana who served as Fuller's vehicle for the meditation

on her experience at Miss Prescott's meets a sorry fate. A life so full
of promise is destroyed by a disastrous marriage. With nary a thought
in his head, Mariana's suitor, Sylvain, is obviously not the appropriate
partner for this highly intellectual woman. But a devoted Mariana
commits herself nonetheless. Now trapped in a marriage with an increasingly indifferent husband, she becomes a "solitary and wretched
wife." Quickly, very quickly, she dies. Fuller had her reasons for con-
cluding Mariana's narrative so melodramatically. Most notably, it left
Mariana, the woman, less responsible for her death than "the defect
in the position of woman," as Fuller described the female dependence
that marked conventional gender relations. Had Mariana been male
"many resources would have presented themselves." Most important,
she "would have been called by life." She would not have been
"wrecked through the affections only." In short, she would have been
in a position to act for herself.

In the fall and winter after her journey west, Fuller returned to
the life she had left earlier in the year, tutoring several students and
resuming the "Conversations." It was then that she had begun to
weave all her varied documents into the fabric that became *Summer
on the Lakes.* Simultaneously, she did more research on the West and
its inhabitants, reading in the library at the exclusively male Harvard
College. Years later Thomas Wentworth Higginson, one of Fuller's
biographers, recalled her "sitting, day after day, under the covert gaze
of the undergraduates who had never before looked upon a woman
reading within those sacred precincts." Acknowledging to William
Henry Channing that she had much invested in the success of *Summer
on the Lakes,* she explained that "outward success in this way is very
desirable to me, not so much on account of present profit to be derived, as because it would give me advantage in making future bargains, and open the way to ransom more time for writing." Fuller
received an unanticipated return on that investment in an offer from
Horace Greeley, the editor of the *New-York Daily Tribune.* Impressed
with both *Summer on the Lakes* and "The Great Lawsuit," he invited
her to become the literary editor at the *Tribune.* He also suggested
that she expand "The Great Lawsuit." Fuller did both, joining the
ranks of the *Tribune*'s journalists and transforming "The Great Lawsuit" into *Woman in the Nineteenth Century.*

Manifesto, celebration, meditation, and declamation, *Woman in
the Nineteenth Century* begins on a highly optimistic note. Confident
that individual and social perfection was possible, Fuller declared,
"Now, no more a glimmering consciousness, but assurance begins to

be felt and spoken, that the highest ideal man can form of his own powers, is that which he is destined to attain." However, the male dominance that made the prevailing system of gender relations asymmetrical stood as a basic obstacle. (Fuller did acknowledge an equally visible asymmetry based on race, noting the abuse of African Americans in the "monstrous display of slave-dealing and slave-keeping.") Despite asymmetries that highlighted the distance between the real and the ideal, Fuller believed that the achievement of the ideal was inevitable. Comparing America with Europe, Fuller predicted that "this country is as surely destined to elucidate a great moral law, as Europe was to promote the mental culture of man." Nowhere was Fuller's confidence in the power of ideas more apparent. With the Declaration of Independence as her source, Fuller chose equality as the idea, or the "moral law," that constituted America's destiny.

To appreciate Fuller's declaration of rights, one need look only three years hence to America's first women's rights convention. Produced in Seneca Falls, New York, late in the summer of 1848, the convention's Declaration of Sentiments also employed the language of the Declaration of Independence to call for female equality. The Declaration of Sentiments, the conventions that followed almost yearly, and the movement on behalf of women's rights all cast the demand for equality into sharp relief. In their pursuit of female equality, women's rights advocates focused upon structural reforms that provided women control of the property they brought to a marriage and the wages they earned thereafter. They sought equal rights in matters of divorce and custody of children. They championed increased educational opportunity for women. Not least, they advocated female suffrage.

Not surprisingly, Fuller had supported all of these structural reforms. Proclaiming in *Woman in the Nineteenth Century* that she "would have every path laid open to woman as freely as to man," she made the male public world woman's domain. And yet Fuller believed that women had a still more basic need. With an eloquence that bespoke deeply felt conviction, she told her readers, "What woman needs is not as a woman to act or rule, but as a nature to grow, as an intellect to discern, as a soul to live freely and unimpeded, to unfold such powers as were given her when we left our common home." Convinced that structural reforms alone were insufficient to meet this need, Fuller asked that Americans dismantle the system of gender relations that had secured female dependence. Based upon a series of paired oppositions that juxtaposed private and public, household and mar-

ketplace, feminine and masculine, this system of gender relations had
made man the measure for all humanity. Inevitably, that yardstick had
led to the conviction "that woman was made *for man*," as Fuller aptly
described women's position relative to men.

Any project that sought to dismantle this system challenged prevailing definitions of masculinity and femininity. Fuller readily did so,
taking aim at the convention of female fragility. Those who insisted
that this mark of femininity barred women from participation in public
life were illogical at best, hypocritical at worst, she charged, saying
"those who think that physical circumstances of woman would make
a part in the affairs of national government unsuitable, are by no
means those who think it impossible for the negresses to endure field
work, even during pregnancy, or the semptresses to go through their
killing labors." Mention of the "negresses" and "semptresses," who
were invisible to most of Fuller's readers, might well have brought a
shock of recognition. African American field hands and seamstresses
were also women, although those same readers might well dismiss
them as anomalies, as other than women. In an antebellum America
in which gender was used to obscure divisions of race and class, Fuller's white and affluent readers might well presume that only those
who shared their racial and social location were truly women.

Miranda, the female intellectual as imagined by Fuller, was not
so easily dismissed. White and at least middling in social status, her
race and class made her a more familiar figure to readers of *Woman
in the Nineteenth Century*. Nonetheless, Fuller's Miranda did challenge many a premise about femininity. Not least, her almost tangible
strength called into question the idea that women were necessarily
fragile. And yet Mirandas, whether imagined or real, were also dismissed as anomalies, or as Fuller phrased it, as "manly." Apparently,
a woman who exhibited strength was not a woman at all.

In an effort to sever the linkage between femininity and fragility,
Fuller searched past and present. There she located a variety of women
who suited her purposes. Embodying supposedly masculine traits,
these women as presented by Fuller were also feminine. Heroine of
Poland's struggle with Russia in the early nineteenth century, Emily
Plater was a striking example. In leading soldiers into battle, she exhibited the "concentrated resolve," the "stern virtue," necessary for
this supremely masculine enterprise. Yet the Plater that Fuller offered
her readers was also "tender and gentle in an uncommon degree." And
Manon Roland, a prominent participant in the French Revolution,
exemplified the "self-sufficingness, strength, and clear-sightedness"

that one expected in a male revolutionary. But Fuller told her readers that Roland displayed as well a "deep and calm affection."

Abby Kelley was perhaps Fuller's most telling example. A radical abolitionist, Kelley damned Americans, North and South, for the sin of slavery. Delivering her message before "promiscuous" assemblies, as nineteenth-century Americans labeled mixed gatherings of men and women, she spoke with a power that held those assemblies spellbound. Little wonder, then, that Kelley herself was damned. Supposedly a "Jezebel," she embodied the *unwomanly*. And yet the Abby Kelley who appeared in Fuller's pages was *womanly*. There was the "gentleness," the "unpretension," the "womanly calmness." There was the "earnest, fresh, and simple" character that spoke to the nation's need to cleanse itself of slavery's sin. Fuller had transformed Kelley into a heroine to be emulated by Americans, female and male.

In the examples of Plater, Roland, and Kelley, Fuller sought to demonstrate that conventional markers of masculinity and femininity had been integrated, one balancing another in reciprocal relationships. It was precisely this integration that Fuller made the linchpin of her alternative system of gender relations. She promoted the cultivation of intuition, or the affections as they were more commonly known in nineteenth-century America. Describing intuition as the "electrical, the magnetic element," Fuller celebrated this trait of femininity. Nonetheless, she insisted that cultivation of reason, or the intellect, required more emphasis. In this regard, the highly educated figure of Miranda represented a model for Fuller's readers. Nonetheless, society had marked Miranda's supposedly "masculine mind" as unfeminine. It was this ascription that Fuller resisted, in saying "it should be acknowledged that [women] have intellect which needs developing, that they should not be considered complete, if beings of affection and habit alone." In defending a position that was vulnerable to challenge, Fuller appealed to a source that was virtually impossible to challenge in nineteenth-century America. Turning to the sacred, to the source that her readers considered indisputable, she declared that all of women's potential should be cultivated "because the Power who gave a power, by its mere existence, signifies that it must be brought out towards perfection."

Filling the pages of *Woman in the Nineteenth Century* with images of learned women, Fuller buttressed her claims for the significance of female education. Simultaneously, she presented her readers with a female tradition designed to stir their imaginations. Fuller cast a wide net, selecting examples from history, folklore, literature, mythology,

and contemporary society. Those from the last source were perhaps
the most arresting. In describing the accomplishments of Mary Somerville, she asked her readers that if this acclaimed English scientist
"has achieved so much, will any young girl be prevented from seeking
a knowledge of the physical sciences, if she wishes it?" In her tribute
to Maria Edgeworth and Catharine Maria Sedgwick, Fuller cited these
novelists' concern with women's potential. Edgeworth was com-
mended for stressing the need for "cultivation of a clear, independent
judgment, and adherence to its dictates; habits of various and liberal
study and employment, and a capacity for friendship." In building her
tradition of learned women, Fuller reserved special acclaim for Sedgwick, one of antebellum America's most prominent novelists. It is not
surprising that she did so. Sedgwick embodied Fuller's conviction "that
intellect need not absorb or weaken, but rather will refine and invigorate the affections." Describing the novelist as "the clearest, wisest,
and kindliest" commentator on the subject of women's potential, she
highlighted her emphasis upon the "free and careful cultivation of the
powers that have been given, with an aim at moral and intellectual
perfection." Just as Germaine de Staël and Maria Edgeworth had provided the young Fuller with models of learned women, so Fuller now
offered readers similar exemplars.

Margaret Fuller concluded *Woman in the Nineteenth Century* as
she had begun it. Suggesting that the fulfillment of an individual's
potential entailed development of energy and harmony, of power and
beauty, of intellect and love, Fuller employed these already familiar
juxtapositions for an unusual purpose. Differences remained, but they
no longer marked the masculine as superior, the feminine as inferior.
Instead, Fuller's juxtapositions signaled "unison in variety, congeniality in difference." Equally important, the characteristics that had
been designated as either male or female were to be cultivated by members of both sexes. Having sought to have the "conditions of life and
freedom recognized as the same for the daughters and sons of time,"
Fuller had created an alternative system of gender relations that
achieved this purpose.

Little more than two weeks after she had completed *Woman in
the Nineteenth Century*, Fuller's columns began appearing on the front
page of the *New-York Daily Tribune*. Occupying the post of the newspaper's literary editor, Fuller defined her position broadly, reviewing
poetry, theology, fiction, philosophy, and history. Her first column,
which appeared on December 7, 1844, joined Fuller's past with her
present. In reviewing Emerson's second series of *Essays*, Fuller was

generous in her praise. Precisely because he represented "the claims of individual culture in a nation which tends to lay such stress on artificial organization and external results," Emerson was an enormously valuable presence. Yet she also took her friend to task, complaining about a certain aloofness that she detected in the essays. Fuller missed, as readers since have missed, "the glow, uniform yet various in tint, which is given to a body by free circulation of the heart's blood from the hour of birth." In this most public of settings, Fuller acknowledged the conviction she had already voiced in letters to her friends. Emerson's Olympian posture betrayed a bloodless detachment.

A cosmopolitan Fuller kept readers abreast of developments in European literature, introducing them to historians Jules Michelet and Thomas Arnold, novelists Honoré de Balzac and Eugene Sue, and poets Thomas Hood and Percy Shelley. Not least, Fuller recorded women's increasing participation in the world of literature. American writers Caroline Kirkland, Lydia Maria Child, Anna Mowatt, and Lydia Signourney all received notice in Fuller's columns, as did Englishwomen Elizabeth Barrett Browning, Felicia Hemans, and Anna Jameson. Perhaps most strikingly, Fuller defended the then notorious George Sand, praising the French novelist's "fine intuitions," her "bold clear eye," and her "great descriptive powers." In a century that made domesticity almost sacred, Fuller's defense of a woman who criticized marriage, left her husband, and openly engaged in liaisons was courageous indeed. Nonetheless, Fuller reminded readers that "it is her works and not her private life that we are considering." Those novels reflected "a soul so capable of goodness and honor as to depict them most successfully in her ideal forms." Extending her domain to include art and music, Fuller celebrated the New York Philharmonic, the exhibits at the National Academy of Design, and the concerts of Norwegian violist Ole Bull.

In contrast to the *Dial,* whose subscribers had numbered three hundred, the *New-York Daily Tribune* counted more than ten thousand readers. With columns appearing two to three times a week in Greeley's newspaper, Fuller's literary criticism had considerable influence during the years in which the nation struggled to define an authentically American literature. Her sympathetic reviews of Melville, Hawthorne, and Poe advanced their claims to places in that literature. Simultaneously, Fuller supported authors such as Lydia Maria Child, Anna Mowatt, and Caroline Kirkland, all of whom were favorably reviewed in her columns. It has taken more than a century for scholars to heed Fuller's example and consider the claims of women writers alongside those of Melville, Hawthorne, and Poe, who long ago entered the canon of American literature.

Shortly after Fuller joined Greeley at the *Tribune,* he asked her to report on New York City's prisons, almshouses, hospitals, and insane asylums. Published in March of 1845, "Our City's Charities" contained that report and more. Fuller's reasoning can still be heard in debates about social welfare in contemporary America. Concerned that institutions for the destitute did not prepare their inmates for self-support, Fuller suggested that they be trained in various occupations. She extended this reasoning to those incarcerated in the city's penal institutions. Suggesting that simple punishment was not sufficient, she called for rehabilitation as an objective.

Signaled in columns such as "Our City's Charities," Fuller's interest in social and political issues took a sharper focus as she began to consider America's class and race relations. Already familiar with the asymmetries of power in gender relations, Fuller came to see the same configuration in relations of race and class. Telling her readers "that the ark of human hopes has been placed for the present in our charge," she also made America's special destiny the basis for claims on behalf of the nation's disempowered. Sharply criticizing men and women who behaved with condescension toward those less fortunate than themselves, she said the privileged should cultivate a more "expansive nature, a heart alive to affection, and some true notion, however imperfectly developed, of the nature of human brotherhood." The more generous behavior described by Fuller did not challenge the structural relationship between classes. Indeed, it did little except perhaps to obscure sharp conflicts of interest between rich and poor.

However, Fuller did mount a substantive challenge to the racially based slavery that dominated the antebellum South. Not surprisingly, she sought to expose the contradiction between America's promise of equality and the enslavement of African Americans. Employing a parable, she asked her readers to contemplate the words of the anonymous but readily identifiable character of Jesus Christ: "I came hither an uninvited guest, because I read sculptured above the door—'All men born Free and Equal,' and in this dwelling hoped to find myself at home." The institution of slavery made a mockery of the Declaration of Independence, as Fuller's Christ made clear. Written only four months after the annexation of Texas had extended that institution, Fuller's column made her condemnation equally clear.

Entitled simply "Farewell," Fuller's last column as the *Tribune*'s literary editor appeared on August 1, 1846. Acknowledging to her readers that the twenty months spent in New York City had provided her "with a richer and more varied exercise for thought and life than twenty years could in any other part of these United States," she told them that Europe was her next destination. There she hoped "to behold the wonders of art, and the temples of old religion." Twenty months later, Fuller, now a resident of Rome, was living in the midst of the Italian Revolution. Her initial interest in museums and cathedrals had been displaced by her engagement in the struggle for a unified and independent Italy. The twenty months in Europe had provided her as much stimulation as could have been possible in twenty years.

Fuller's European journey had been deferred for more than a decade. Timothy Fuller's death in the fall of 1835 had forced his daughter to decline an invitation to spend a year abroad with Eliza Farrar, one of Fuller's mentors during her early adulthood. On this occasion Quaker merchant Marcus Spring and his wife, Rebecca, extended the invitation. Horace Greeley supplied the income, paying Fuller ten dollars for each of the dispatches that appeared in his *Tribune*. Beginning with "Letters From England" dated August 23, 1846, Fuller sent Greeley a total of thirty-seven dispatches. Those that she sent before her arrival in Italy focused upon England, Scotland, and France. In these dispatches, Fuller engaged a variety of topics, describing coal mines in Newcastle, castles in Scotland, silk weavers in Lyon, and conversations with Wordsworth, Carlyle, and Sand. Increasingly, however, social and political issues dominated her commentaries. One might have thought that Fuller was preparing herself to chronicle the Italian Revolution.

Observer, participant, and historian, Fuller had a complicated relationship with the revolutions that swept across Europe in 1848. However, her commitment to the Italian Revolution was readily apparent. Strongly in support of unification and independence, Fuller envisioned an Italy in which the duchies, principalities, and kingdoms were united and all Italy liberated from foreign domination. More specifically, she identified with the cause of the Roman Republic, an independent government established in the wake of Pope Pius IX's flight from Rome in November of 1848. Fuller's attachment to the ancient city dated from her childhood. In her studies of classical literature, Rome had made an indelible impression upon the young Fuller. "ROME!" she declared in her autobiographical sketch, "stands by itself, a clear Word. The power of will, the dignity of fixed purpose is what it utters."

More immediately, however, Fuller's identification was deeply personal. It was also profound. Shortly after her arrival in Rome during the spring of 1847, Fuller met Giovanni Ossoli, an Italian nobleman ten years her junior. By the fall they had become romantically involved. Within a year they had a son, Angelo. Questions surrounding Fuller's marital status have been debated for more than a century. They remain unanswered today. What is surely more relevant was the deep commitment that Fuller and Ossoli made to each other. Despite the personal and political crises that engulfed them, Fuller wrote her mother that she and Ossoli "have had much joy together." No less relevant was their mutual devotion to their son. Telling her sister Ellen that she had "thought a mother's heart lived in me before," she now recognized "it did not;—I knew nothing about it." She also exulted that Ossoli was "capable of the sacred love, the love passing that of women, he showed it to his father, to Rome, to me, now he loves his child in the same way." Little wonder, then, that Fuller embraced Rome so completely. Writing to Emerson with a passion that bespoke the depth of her commitment, she declared, "Oh Rome, *my* country!" The ancient city had become the touchstone for her life.

Written in the spring of 1848, the opening dispatches on the Italian Revolution mirror the enthusiasm with which Fuller embraced the cause of independence. The revolt in Naples, the creation of a republic in Venice, the uprising in Modena and Parma, and the removal of the Austrians from Milan, all seemed to her a prelude to victory against the forces of despotism. Recording the response of Rome's residents to the revolutionary movements, Fuller shared the elation she described: "Men were seen dancing, women weeping with joy along the street." Eager to help the Milanese in their struggle with Austria, Rome's youth "rushed to enroll themselves in regiments to go to the frontier."

But the defeats of the summer dampened Fuller's ardor. With the forces of revolt in Naples in disarray, Ferdinand II took the opportunity to recall his soldiers from the war with Austria in the north. Pope Pius IX, once a supporter of opposition to the Austrians, reversed himself and ordered his troops to return home. Fuller reported that Piedmont's Charles Albert now stood alone against the Austrians. Decisively defeated in a series of battles during July, Charles Albert abandoned Milan and retreated to Piedmont. Triumphant in the north, the Austrians advanced toward the Papal States. Simultaneously, Pius IX appointed Pellegrino Rossi as his prime minister. Fuller's antipathy to Rossi notwithstanding, he was clearly left with an unenviable task: reconciliation of Austria's demands for a return to the status quo ante

with the increasingly revolutionary sentiments of Rome. His efforts
cost him his life. Rossi's assassination in November of 1848 so frightened the Pope that he fled Rome. When Fuller told her readers that
the Pope had deserted the city, she did nothing to disguise her pleasure.
"No more of him!" she declared. Equally pleased that the Roman
Republic had replaced the Papal States, Fuller's description of the inauguration bordered on ecstasy: "The imposing grandeur of the spectacle to me gave new force to the thought that already swelled my
heart; my nerves thrilled." Fuller's identification was complete. In her
final dispatch, she told her readers, "go where I may, a large part of
my heart will ever remain in Italy."

Based upon a constitutional assembly that had been elected by
universal male suffrage, Rome's experiment in democracy lasted but
one hundred and forty-three days. The French, not the Austrians, were
the invading force that destroyed the Roman Republic. Declaring that
the "Mother of Nations is now at bay against them all," Fuller took
her readers into a city that was being laid waste in the spring of 1849.
She did not spare them the still more devastating toll on Rome's defenders. Appointed director of a hospital during the siege, Fuller spent
every day with those who filled its beds. There she "saw the terrible
agonies of those dying or who needed amputation, felt their mental
pains and longing for the loved ones." At the end of the siege, she told
her readers that "those who were brought into the Hospitals were
generally grievously wounded, very commonly subject for amputation." Fuller's final words, however, spoke not to loss but to a bond
that had been forged. "Remember," she said to her readers, " 'Mankind is one/And beats with one great heart.' "

On New Year's Day of 1848 Fuller had dramatically told her
readers "at this moment, all things bode and declare a new outbreak
of the fire." The fire of revolution blazed across Italy that year. By the
end of the summer of 1849, its flames had been extinguished by the
forces of despotism. Still, Fuller remained confident that the fire would
appear again. "Principles of democracy," she claimed, would battle
with "old powers, no longer legitimate." Perhaps it would take decades, but she felt certain that the outcome would be victory for the
allies of democracy. Europe, she predicted, "is to be under Republican
Government in the next century." Clearly, Fuller's confidence stemmed
from the Italian Revolution, the experience that had so galvanized her,
professionally and personally.

Less than a year after the fall of the Roman Republic, Fuller,
Ossoli, and their son, Angelo, left Italy for America. Sailing on the

Elizabeth on May 17, 1850, they reached Fire Island, New York, sixty-three days later. Only a few hundred yards from shore, the storm-tossed *Elizabeth* was wrecked on a sandbar. Fuller, Ossoli, and Angelo perished. Fuller's death stilled a voice that had challenged her contemporaries to create an America in which all individuals could fulfill their potential. When she told William Henry Channing that she felt as if she had left a footprint on the earth, Fuller had referred only to *Woman in the Nineteenth Century*. The same might be said about everything that came from her pen. Fuller's challenge remained in the words she left behind.

CHRONOLOGY

1810   Sarah Margaret Fuller is born in Cambridgeport, Massachusetts, on May 23.

1818   Meets Ellen Kilshaw, the older friend she describes in her "Autobiographical Sketch."

1824   Begins a year as a student at Miss Prescott's Young Ladies' Seminary in Groton, Massachusetts.

1825   Returns to Cambridge, Massachusetts.

1833   Moves to Groton, Massachusetts, with family and tutors her younger siblings Richard, Arthur, and Lloyd. Translates Goethe's *Torquato Tasso*.

1834   Publishes "In Defense of Brutus," in the *Boston Daily Advertiser & Patriot*.

1835   Timothy Fuller dies from cholera on October 1.

1836   Begins teaching at Bronson Alcott's Temple School in Boston.

1837   Moves to Providence, Rhode Island, to teach at the Greene Street School.

1838   Resigns position at the Greene Street School.

1839   Publishes her translation of *Eckermann's Conversations with Goethe*. Continues research on biography of Goethe. Agrees to edit newly founded Transcendentalist periodical *Dial*. Begins series of classes, or "Conversations," for adult women.

1840   Begins "Autobiographical Sketch." Edits *Dial* from July until July of 1842.

1841   Publishes critical essay "Goethe" in *Dial*.

1842   Publishes "Bettine Brentano and Her Friend Günderode" in *Dial*. Publishes translation of *Correspondence of Fraulein Günderode with Bettine von Arnim*. Resigns editorship of *Dial*.

1843   Publishes "The Great Lawsuit: Man *versus* Men. Woman *versus* Women" in *Dial*. Travels through Illinois, Wisconsin, and Michigan.

1844   Concludes final series of "Conversations." Publishes *Summer on the Lakes, during 1843*. Moves to New York City and begins literary editorship of Horace Greeley's *New-York Daily Tribune*.

1845   Publishes *Woman in the Nineteenth Century*.

1846   Publishes *Papers on Literature and Art*, a collection of previously published essays. Resigns literary editorship and accepts position as a foreign correspondent for the *New-York Daily Tribune*. Sails for Europe with Marcus and Rebecca Spring. Publishes first dispatch in *New-York Daily Tribune* on September 24. Travels in England, Scotland, and France.

1847   Leaves France for Italy in February. Arrives in Rome and meets Giovanni Angelo Ossoli in April. Travels in northern Italy and Switzerland from June to October. Begins residence in Rome in October.

1848   Angelo Ossoli is born in Rieti on September 5. Pellegrino Rossi is assassinated and Pope Pius IX flees from Rome in November.

1849   Roman Republic is proclaimed in February. Siege of Rome by the French begins in April. French invade Rome and restore Pope to power in June. Fuller, Ossoli, and their son, Angelo, move to Florence in November.

1850   Publishes her final dispatch in *New-York Daily Tribune* on February 13. Sails for the United States with Ossoli and Angelo on May 17. Dies in shipwreck off Fire Island on July 19.

A NOTE ON THE TEXTS

Both *Summer on the Lakes, during 1843* (1844) and *Woman in the Nineteenth Century* (1845) have been reprinted from the original editions. The "Autobiographical Sketch" has been drawn from the *Memoirs of Margaret Fuller Ossoli* (1852) compiled by Ralph Waldo Emerson, William Henry Channing, and James Freeman Clarke. Fuller's columns and dispatches have been reprinted without deletions from the *New-York Daily Tribune*. "Bettine Brentano and Her Friend Günderode" has been taken from the second volume of the *Dial*, which appeared in January of 1842. Selections from Margaret Fuller's correspondence have been reprinted from *The Letters of Margaret Fuller* edited by Robert N. Hudspeth. Scholars interested in Margaret Fuller are deeply indebted to Hudspeth. His reconstruction, emendation, and annotation of Fuller's letters are exceptional. Published by Cornell University Press, these five volumes of letters are a model of scholarship.

THE PORTABLE
MARGARET FULLER

AUTOBIOGRAPHICAL
SKETCH

Written at the beginning of the fourth decade of her life, Margaret Fuller's "Autobiographical Sketch" mirrors the ambivalence that Fuller the adult felt about her childhood. Taking her father to task for the intellectual demands he made upon his eldest child, Fuller lamented the considerable strain that had been involved in making her "the heir of all he knew." Nonetheless, she also celebrated the education that Timothy Fuller provided her. Schooled in Latin and Greek, Fuller immersed herself in classical literature during her childhood. Simultaneously, she read widely in the volumes of Shakespeare, Cervantes, Moliere, Fielding, Smollett, and Scott that lined the shelves of her father's library. "Reading," she remembered, "became a habit and a passion." Charged with a powerful intensity, that habit sustained Fuller throughout her life. In the "Autobiographical Sketch," Fuller represented her mother in an entirely different light. Her mother's garden, which had made Fuller "exquisitely happy," had stimulated the daughter's imagination, summoning emotions that Fuller had "never dared express to any human being." Tinged with nostalgia, Fuller's portrayal of her mother's garden is a lyrical tribute to the emotional dimensions of the self. The "Autobiographical Sketch" concludes with Fuller's recollection of another shaping influence on her childhood, the friendship she shared with Ellen Kilshaw. Like reading, friendship became a passionately charged habit that marked Fuller's entire life.

I
YOUTH

PARENTS

My father was a lawyer and a politician. He was a man largely endowed with that sagacious energy, which the state of New England society, for the last half century, has been so well fitted to develop. His father was a clergyman, settled as a pastor in Princeton, Massachusetts, within the bounds of whose parish-farm was Wachuset. His means were small, and the great object of his ambition was to send his sons to college. As a boy, my father was taught to think only of preparing himself for Harvard University, and when there of preparing himself for the profession of Law. As a Lawyer, again, the ends constantly presented were to work for distinction in the community, and for the means of supporting a family. To be an honored citizen, and to have a home on earth, were made the great aims of existence. To open the deeper fountains of the soul, to regard life here as the prophetic entrance to immortality, to develop his spirit to perfection, —motives like these had never been suggested to him, either by fellow-beings or by outward circumstances. The result was a character, in its social aspect, of quite the common sort. A good son and brother, a kind neighbor, an active man of business—in all these outward relations he was but one of a class, which surrounding conditions have made the majority among us. In the more delicate individual relations, he never approached but two mortals, my mother and myself.

His love for my mother was the green spot on which he stood apart from the common-places of a mere bread-winning, bread-bestowing existence. She was one of those fair and flower-like natures, which sometimes spring up even beside the most dusty highways of life—a creature not to be shaped into a merely useful instrument, but bound by one law with the blue sky, the dew, and the frolic birds. Of all persons whom I have known, she had in her most of the angelic, —of that spontaneous love for every living thing, for man, and beast, and tree, which restores the golden age.

DEATH IN THE HOUSE

My earliest recollection is of a death,—the death of a sister, two years younger than myself. Probably there is a sense of childish endearments, such as belong to this tie, mingled with that of loss, of wonder, and mystery; but these last are prominent in memory. I remember coming home and meeting our nursery-maid, her face streaming with tears. That strange sight of tears made an indelible impression. I realize how little I was of stature, in that I looked up to this weeping face;—and it has often seemed since, that—full-grown for the life of this earth, I have looked up just so, at times of threatening, of doubt, and distress, and that just so has some being of the next higher order of existences looked down, aware of a law unknown to me, and tenderly commiserating the pain I must endure in emerging from my ignorance.

She took me by the hand and led me into a still and dark chamber,—then drew aside the curtain and showed me my sister. I see yet that beauty of death! The highest achievements of sculpture are only the reminder of its severe sweetness. Then I remember the house all still and dark,—the people in their black clothes and dreary faces,—the scent of the newly-made coffin,—my being set up in a chair and detained by a gentle hand to hear the clergyman,—the carriages slowly going, the procession slowly doling out their steps to the grave. But I have no remembrance of what I have since been told I did,—insisting, with loud cries, that they should not put the body in the ground. I suppose that my emotion was spent at the time, and so there was nothing to fix that moment in my memory.

I did not then, nor do I now, find any beauty in these ceremonies. What had they to do with the sweet playful child? Her life and death were alike beautiful, but all this sad parade was not. Thus my first experience of life was one of death. She who would have been the companion of my life was severed from me, and I was left alone. This has made a vast difference in my lot. Her character, if that fair face promised right, would have been soft, graceful and lively; it would have tempered mine to a gentler and more gradual course.

OVERWORK

My father,—all whose feelings were now concentrated on me,—instructed me himself. The effect of this was so far good that, not passing through the hands of many ignorant and weak persons as so many do at preparatory schools, I was put at once under discipline of considerable severity, and, at the same time, had a more than ordinarily high standard presented to me. My father was a man of business, even in literature; he had been a high scholar at college, and was warmly attached to all he had learned there, both from the pleasure he had derived in the exercise of his faculties and the associated memories of success and good repute. He was, beside, well read in French literature, and in English, a Queen Anne's man. He hoped to make me the heir of all he knew, and of as much more as the income of his profession enabled him to give me means of acquiring. At the very beginning, he made one great mistake, more common, it is to be hoped, in the last generation, then the warnings of physiologists will permit it to be with the next. He thought to gain time, by bringing forward the intellect as early as possible. Thus I had tasks given me, as many and various as the hours would allow, and on subjects beyond my age; with the additional disadvantage of reciting to him in the evening, after he returned from his office. As he was subject to many interruptions, I was often kept up till very late; and as he was a severe teacher, both from his habits of mind and his ambition for me, my feelings were kept on the stretch till the recitations were over. Thus frequently, I was sent to bed several hours too late, with nerves unnaturally stimulated. The consequence was a premature development of the brain, that made me a "youthful prodigy" by day, and by night a victim of spectral illusions, nightmare, and somnambulism, which at the time prevented the harmonious development of my bodily powers and checked my growth, while, later, they induced continual headache, weakness and nervous affections, of all kinds. As these again reacted on the brain, giving undue force to every thought and every feeling, there was finally produced a state of being both too active and too intense, which wasted my constitution, and will bring me,—even although I have learned to understand and regulate my now morbid temperament,— to a premature grave.

No one understood this subject of health then. No one knew why this child, already kept up so late, was still unwilling to retire. My aunts cried out upon the "spoiled child, the most unreasonable child that ever was,—if brother could but open his eyes to see it,—who was never willing to go to bed." They did not know that, so soon as the light was taken away, she seemed to see colossal faces advancing slowly towards her, the eyes dilating, and each feature swelling loathsomely as they came, till at last, when they were about to close upon her, she started up with a shriek which drove them away, but only to return when she lay down again. They did not know that, when at last she went to sleep, it was to dream of horses trampling over her, and to awake once more in fright; or, as she had just read in her Virgil, of being among trees that dripped with blood, where she walked and walked and could not get out, while the blood became a pool and splashed over her feet, and rose higher and higher, till soon she dreamed it would reach her lips. No wonder the child arose and walked in her sleep, moaning all over the house, till once, when they heard her, and came and waked her, and she told what she had dreamed, her father sharply bid her "leave off thinking of such non-sense, or she would be crazy,"—never knowing that he was himself the cause of all these horrors of the night. Often she dreamed of fol-lowing to the grave the body of her mother, as she had done that of her sister, and woke to find the pillow drenched in tears. These dreams softened her heart too much, and cast a deep shadow over her young days; for then, and later, the life of dreams,—probably because there was in it less to distract the mind from its own earnestness,—has often seemed to her more real, and been remembered with more interest, then that of waking hours.

Poor child! Far remote in time, in thought, from that period, I look back on these glooms and terrors, wherein I was enveloped, and perceived that I had no natural childhood.

BOOKS

Thus passed my first years. My mother was in delicate health, and much absorbed in the care of her younger children. In the house was neither dog nor bird, nor any graceful animated form of existence. I saw no persons who took my fancy, and real life offered no attraction. Thus my already over-excited mind found no relief from without, and was driven for refuge from itself to the world of books. I was taught Latin and English grammar at the same time, and began to read Latin at six years old, after which, for some years, I read it daily. In this branch of study, first by my father, and afterwards by a tutor, I was trained to quite a high degree of precision. I was expected to under-stand the mechanism of the language thoroughly, and in translating to give the thoughts in as few well-arranged words as possible, and without breaks or hesitation,—for with these my father had absolutely no patience.

Indeed, he demanded accuracy and clearness in everything: you must not speak, unless you can make your meaning perfectly intelligible to the person addressed; must not express a thought, unless you can give a reason for it, if required; must not make a statement, unless sure of all particulars—such were his rules. "But," "if," "unless," "I am mistaken," and "it may be so," were words and phrases excluded from the province where he held sway. Trained to great dexterity in artificial methods, accurate, ready, with entire command of his resources, he had no belief in minds that listen, wait, and receive. He had no conception of the subtle and indirect motions of imagination and feeling. His influence on me was great, and opposed to the natural unfolding of my character, which was fervent, of strong grasp, and disposed to infatuation, and self-forgetfulness. He made the common prose world so present to me, that my natural bias was controlled. I did not go mad, as many would do, at being continually roused from my dreams. I had too much strength to be crushed,—and since I must put on the fetters, could not submit to let them impede my motions. My own world sank deep within, away from the surface of my life; in what I did and said I learned to have reference to other minds. But my true life was only the dearer that it was secluded and veiled over by a thick curtain of available intellect, and that coarse, but wearable stuff woven by the ages,—Common Sense.

In accordance with this discipline in heroic common sense, was the influence of those great Romans, whose thoughts and lives were my daily food during those plastic years. The genius of Rome displayed itself in Character, and scarcely needed an occasional wave of the torch of thought to show its lineaments, so marble strong they gleamed in every light. Who, that has lived with those men, but admires the plain force of fact, of thought passed into action? They take up things with their naked hands. There is just the man, and the block he casts before you,—no divinity, no demon, no unfulfilled aim, but just the man and Rome, and what he did for Rome. Everything turns your attention to what a man can become, not by yielding himself freely to impressions, not by letting nature play freely through him, but by a single thought, an earnest purpose, an indomitable will, by hardihood, self-command, and force of expression. Architecture was the art in which Rome excelled, and this corresponds with the feeling these men of Rome excite. They did not grow,—they built themselves up, or were built up by the fate of Rome, as a temple for Jupiter Stator. The ruined Roman sits among the ruins; he flies to no green garden; he does not look to heaven; if his intent is defeated, if he is less than he meant to be, he lives no more. The names which end in "*us*," seem to speak with lyric cadence. That measured cadence,—that tramp and march,—which are not stilted, because they indicate real force, yet which seem so when compared with any other language,—make Latin a study in itself of mighty influence. The language alone, without the literature, would give one the *thought* of Rome. Man present in nature, commanding nature too sternly to be inspired by it, standing like the rock amid the sea, or moving like the fire over the land, either impassive, or irresistible; knowing not the soft mediums or fine flights of life, but by the force which he expresses, piercing to the centre.

We are never better understood than when we speak of a "Roman virtue," a "Roman outline." There is somewhat indefinite, somewhat yet unfulfilled in the thought of Greece, of Spain, of modern Italy; but ROME! it stands by itself, a clear Word. The power of will, the dignity of a fixed purpose is what it utters. Every Roman was an emperor. It is well that the infallible church should have been founded on this rock, that the presumptuous Peter should hold the keys, as the conquering Jove did before his thunderbolts, to be seen of all the world. The Apollo tends flocks with Admetus; Christ teaches by the lonely lake, or plucks wheat as he wanders through the fields some Sabbath morning. They never come to this stronghold; they could not have breathed freely where all became stone as soon as spoken, where divine youth found no horizon for its all-promising glance, but every thought put on, before it dared issue to the day in action, its *toga virilis*.

Suckled by this wolf, man gains a different complexion from that which is fed by the Greek honey. He takes a noble bronze in camps and battle-fields; the wrinkles of council will beseem his brow, and the eye cuts its way like the sword. The Eagle should never have been used as a symbol by any other nation: it belonged to Rome.

The history of Rome abides in mind, of course, more than literature. It was degeneracy for a Roman to use the pen; his life was in the day. The "vaunting" of Rome, like that of the North American Indians, is her proper literature. A man rises; he tells who he is, and what he has done; he speaks of his country and her brave men; he knows that a conquering god is there, whose agent is his own right hand; and he should end like the Indian, "I have no more to say."

It never shocks us that the Roman is self-conscious. One wants no universal truths from him, no philosophy, no creation, but only his life, his Roman life felt in every pulse, realized in every gesture. The universal heaven takes in the Roman only to make us feel his individuality the more. The Will, the Resolve of Man!—it has been expressed,—fully expressed!

I steadily loved this ideal in my childhood, and this is the cause, probably, why I have always felt that man must know how to stand firm on the ground, before he can fly. In vain for me are men more, if they are less than Romans. Dante was far greater than any Roman, yet I feel he was right to take the Mantuan as his guide through hell, and to heaven.

Horace was a great deal to me then, and is so still. Though his words do not abide in memory, his presence does: serene, courtly, of darting hazel eye, a self-sufficient grace, and an appreciation of the world of stern realities, sometimes pathetic, never tragic. He is the natural man of the world; he is what he ought to be, and his darts never fail of their aim. There is a perfume and raciness, too, which makes life a banquet, where the wit sparkles no less that the viands were bought with blood.

Ovid gave me not Rome, nor himself, but a view into the enchanted gardens of Greek mythology. This path I followed, have been following ever since; and now, life half over, it seems to me, as in my childhood, that every thought of which man is susceptible, is intimated there. In those young years, indeed, I did not see what I now see, but loved to creep from amid the Roman pikes to lie beneath this great vine, and see the smiling and serene shapes go by, woven from the finest fibres of all the elements. I knew not why, at that time,—but I loved to get away from the hum of the forum, and the mailed clang of Roman speech, to these shifting shows of nature, these Gods and Nymphs born of the sunbeam, the wave, the shadows on the hill.

As with Rome I antedated the world of deeds, so I lived in those Greek forms the true faith of a refined and intense childhood. So great was the force of reality with which these forms impressed me, that I prayed earnestly for a sign,—that it would lighten in some particular region of the heavens, or that I might find a bunch of grapes in the path, when I went forth in the morning. But no sign was given, and I was left a waif stranded upon the shores of modern life!

Of the Greek language, I knew only enough to feel that the sounds told the same story as the mythology;—that the law of life in that land was beauty, as in Rome it was a stern composure. I wish I had learned as much of Greece as of Rome,—so freely does the mind play in her sunny waters, where there is no chill, and the restraint is from within out; for these Greeks, in an atmosphere of ample grace, could not be impetuous, or stern, but loved moderation as equable life always must, for it is the law of beauty.

With these books I passed my days. The great amount of study exacted of me soon ceased to be a burden, and reading became a habit and a passion. The force of feeling, which, under other circumstances, might have ripened thought, was turned to learn the thoughts of others. This was not a tame state, for the energies brought out by rapid acquisition gave glow enough. I thought with rapture of the all-accomplished man, him of many talents, wide resources, clear sight, and omnipotent will. A Caesar seemed great enough. I did not then know that such men impoverished the treasury to build the palace. I kept their statues as belonging to the hall of my ancestors, and loved to conquer obstacles, and fed my youth and strength for their sake.

Still, though this bias was so great that in the earliest years I learned, in these ways, how the world takes hold of a powerful nature, I had yet other experiences. None of these were deeper then what I found in the happiest haunt of my childish years,—our little garden. Our house, though comfortable, was very ugly, and in a neighborhood which I detested,—every dwelling and its appurtenances having a *mesquin* and huddled look. I liked nothing about us except the tall graceful elms before the house, and the dear little garden behind. Our back door opened on a high flight of steps, by which I went down to a green plot, much injured in my ambitious eyes by the presence of the pump and the tool-house. This opened into a little garden, full of choice flowers and fruit-trees, which was my mother's delight, and was carefully kept. Here I felt at home. A gate opened thence into the fields, —a wooden gate made of boards, in a high, unpainted board wall, and embowered in the clematis creeper. This gate I used to open to see the sunset heaven; beyond this black frame I did not step, for I liked to look at the deep gold behind it. How exquisitely happy I was in its beauty, and how I loved the silvery wreaths of my protecting vine! I never would pluck one of its flowers at that time, I was so jealous of its beauty, but often since I carry off wreaths of it from the wild-wood, and its stands in nature to my mind as the emblem of domestic love.

Of late I have thankfully felt what I owe to that garden, where the best hours of my lonely childhood were spent. Within the house everything was socially utilitarian; my books told of a proud world, but in another temper were the teachings of the little garden. There my thoughts could lie callow in the nest, and only be fed and kept warm, not called to fly or sing before the time. I loved to gaze on the roses, the violets, the lilies, the pinks; my mother's hand had planted them, and they bloomed for me. I culled the most beautiful. I looked at them on every side. I kissed them, I pressed them to my bosom with passionate emotions, such as I have never dared express to any human being. An ambition swelled my heart to be as beautiful, as perfect as they. I have not kept my vow. Yet, forgive, ye wild asters, which gleam so sadly amid the fading grass; forgive me, ye golden autumn flowers, which so strive to reflect the glories of the parting distant sun; and ye silvery flowers, whose moonlight eyes I knew so well, forgive! Living and blooming in your unchecked law, ye know nothing of the blights, the distortions, which beset the human being; and which at such hours it would seem that no glories of free agency could ever repay!

There was, in the house, no apartment appropriated to the purpose of a library, but there was in my father's room a large closet filled with books, and to these I had free access when the task-work of the day was done. Its window overlooked wide fields, gentle slopes, a rich and smiling country, whose aspect pleased without much occupying the eye, while a range of blue hills, rising at about twelve miles distance, allured to reverie. "Distant mountains," says Tieck, "excite the fancy, for beyond them we place the scene of our Paradise." Thus, in the poems of fairy adventure, we climb the rocky barrier, pass fearless its dragon caves, and dark pine forests, and find the scene of enchantment in the vale behind. My hopes were never so definite, but my eye was constantly allured to that distant blue range, and I would sit, lost in fancies, till tears fell on my cheek. I love this sadness; but only in the later years, when the realities of life had taught me moderation, did the passionate emotions excited by seeing them again teach how glorious were the hopes that swelled my heart while gazing on them in those early days.

Melancholy attends on the best joys of a merely ideal life, else I should call most happy the hours in the garden, the hours in the book closet. Here were the best French writers of the last century; for my father had been more than half a Jacobin, in the time when the French Republic cast its glare of promise over the world. Here, too, were the Queen Anne authors, his models, and the English novelists; but among them I found none that charmed me. Smollett, Fielding, and the like, deal too broadly with the coarse actualities of life. The best of their men and women—so merely natural, with the nature found every day—do not meet our hopes. Sometimes the simple picture, warm with life and the light of the common sun, cannot fail to charm,—as in the wedded love of Fielding's Amelia,—but it is a later day, when the mind is trained to comparison, that we learn to prize excellence like this as it deserves. Early youth is prince-like: it will bend only to "the king, my father." Various kinds of excellence please, and leave their impression, but the most commanding, alone, is duly acknowledged at that all-exacting age.

Three great authors it was my fortune to meet at this important period,—all, though of unequal, yet congenial powers,—all of rich and wide, rather than aspiring genius,—all free to the extent of the horizon their eye took in,—all fresh with impulse, racy with experience; never to be lost sight of, or superseded, but always to be apprehended more and more.

Ever memorable is the day on which I first took a volume of SHAKESPEARE in my hand to read. It was on a Sunday.

—This day was punctiliously set apart in our house. We had family prayers, for which there was no time on other days. Our dinners were different, and our clothes. We went to church. My father put some limitations on my reading, but—bless him for the gentleness which has left me a pleasant feeling for the day!—he did not prescribe what was, but only what was *not,* to be done. And the liberty this left was a large one. "You must not read a novel, or a play;" but all other books, the worst, or the best, were open to me. The distinction was merely technical. The day was pleasing to me, as relieving me from the routine of tasks and recitations; it gave me freer play than usual, and there were fewer things occurred in its course, which reminded me of the divisions of time; still the church-going, where I heard nothing that had any connection with my inward life, and these rules, gave me associations with the day of empty formalities, and arbitrary restrictions; but though the forbidden book or walk always seemed more charming then, I was seldom tempted to disobey.—

This Sunday—I was only eight years old—I took from the bookshelf a volume lettered SHAKESPEARE. It was not the first time I had looked at it, but before I had been deterred from attempting to read, by the broken appearance along the page, and preferred smooth narrative. But this time I held in my hand "Romeo and Juliet" long enough to get my eye fastened to the page. It was a cold winter afternoon. I took the book to the parlor fire, and had there been seated an hour or two, when my father looked up and asked what I was reading so intently. "Shakespeare," replied the child, merely raising her eye from the page, "Shakespeare,—that won't do; that's no book for Sunday; go put it away and take another." I went as I was bid, but took no other. Returning to my seat, the unfinished story, the personages to whom I was but just introduced, thronged and burnt my brain. I could not bear it long; such a lure it was impossible to resist. I went and brought the book again. There were several guests present, and I had got half through the play before I again attracted attention. "What is that child about that she don't hear a word that's said to her?" quoth my aunt. "What are you reading?" said my father. "Shakespeare" was again the reply, in a clear, though somewhat impatient, tone "How?" said my father angrily,—then restraining himself before his guests,—"Give me the book and go directly to bed."

Into my little room no care of his anger followed me. Alone, in the dark, I thought only of the scene placed by the poet before my eye, where the free flow of life, sudden and graceful dialogue, and forms, whether grotesque or fair, seen in the broad lustre of his imagination, gave just what I wanted, and brought home the life I seemed born to live. My fancies swarmed like bees, as I contrived the rest of the story;—what all would do, what say, where go. My confinement tortured me. I could not go forth from this prison to ask after these friends; I could not make my pillow of the dreams about them which yet I could not forbear to frame. Thus was I absorbed when my father entered. He felt it right, before going to rest, to reason with me about my disobedience, shown in a way, as he considered, so insolent. I listened, but could not feel interested in what he said, nor turn my mind from what engaged it. He went away really grieved at my impenitence, and quite at a loss to understand conduct in me so unusual.

—Often since I have seen the same misunderstanding between parent and child,—the parent thrusting the morale, the discipline, of life upon the child, when just engrossed by some game of real importance and great leadings to it. That is only a wooden horse to the father,—the child was careering to distant scenes of conquest and crusade, through a country of elsewhere unimagined beauty. None but poets remember their youth; but the father who does not retain poetical apprehension of the world, free and splendid as it stretches out before the child, who cannot read his natural history, and follow out its intimations with reverence, must be a tyrant in his home, and the purest intentions will not prevent his doing much to cramp him. Each new child is a new Thought, and has bearings and discernings, which the Thoughts older in date know not yet, but must learn.—

My attention thus fixed on Shakespeare, I returned to him at every hour I could command. Here was a counterpoise to my Romans, still more forcible than the little garden. My author could read the Roman nature too,—read it in the sternness of Coriolanus, and in the varied wealth of Caesar. But he viewed these men of will as only one kind of men; he kept them in their place, and found I that he, who could understand the Roman, yet expressed in Hamlet a deeper thought.

In CERVANTES, I found far less productive talent,—indeed, a far less powerful genius,—but the same wide wisdom, a discernment piercing the shows and symbols of existence, yet rejoicing in them all, both for their own life, and as signs of the unseen reality. Not that Cervantes philosophized,—his genius was too deeply philosophical for that; he took things as they came before him, and saw their actual relations and bearings. Thus the work he produced was of deep meaning, though he might never have expressed that meaning to himself. It was left implied in the whole. A Coleridge comes and calls Don Quixote the pure Reason, and Sancho the Understanding. Cervantes made no such distinctions in his own mind; but he had seen and suffered enough to bring out all his faculties, and to make him comprehend the higher as well as the lower part of our nature. Sancho is too amusing and sagacious to be contemptible; the Don too noble and clear-sighted towards absolute truth, to be ridiculous. And we are pleased to see manifested in this way, how the lower must follow and serve the higher, despite its jeering mistrust and the stubborn realities which break up the plans of this pure-minded champion.

The effect produced on the mind is nowise that described by Byron:—

"Cervantes smiled Spain's chivalry away," &c.

On the contrary, who is not conscious of a sincere reverence for the Don, prancing forth on his gaunt steed? Who would not rather be he than any of the persons who laugh at him?—Yet the one we would wish to be is thyself, Cervantes, unconquerable spirit! gaining flavor and color like wine from every change, while being carried round the world; in whose eye the serene sagacious laughter could not be dimmed by poverty, slavery, or unsuccessful authorship. Thou art to us still more the Man, though less the Genius, than Shakespeare; thou dost not evade our sight, but, holding the lamp to thine own magic shows, dost enjoy them with us.

My third friend was Molière, one very much lower, both in range and depth, than the others, but, as far as he goes, of the same character. Nothing secluded or partial is there about his genius,—a man of the world, and a man by himself, as he is. It was, indeed, only the poor social world of Paris that he saw, but he viewed it from the foundations of his manhood, and every lightest laugh rings from a clear perception, and teaches life anew.

These men were all alike in this,—they loved the *natural history* of man. Not what he should be, but what he is, was the favorite subject of their thought. Whenever a noble leading opened to the eye new paths of light, they rejoiced; but it was never fancy, but always fact that inspired them. They loved a thorough penetration of the murkiest dens, and most tangled paths of nature; they did not spin from the desires of their own special natures, but reconstructed the world from materials which they collected on every side. Thus their influence upon me was not to prompt me to follow out thought in myself so much as to detect it everywhere, for each of these men is not only a nature, but a happy interpreter of many natures. They taught me to distrust all invention which is not based on a wide experience. Perhaps, too, they taught me to overvalue an outward experience at the expense of inward growth; but all this I did not appreciate till later.

It will be seen that my youth was not unfriended since those great minds came to me in kindness. A moment of action in one's self, however, is worth an age of apprehension through others; not that our deeds are better, but that they produce a renewal of our being. I have had more productive moments and of deeper joy but never hours of more tranquil pleasure than those in which these demi-gods visited me,—and with a smile so familiar, that I imagined the world to be full of such. They did me good, for by them a standard was early given of sight and thought, from which I could never go back, and beneath which I cannot suffer patiently my own life or that of any friend to fall. They did me harm, too, for the child fed with meat instead of milk becomes too soon mature. Expectations and desires were thus early raised, after which I must long toil before they can be realized. How poor the scene around, how tame one's own existence, how meagre and faint every power, with these beings in my mind. Often I must cast them quite aside in order to grow in my small way, and not sink into despair. Certainly I do not wish that instead of these masters I had read baby books, written down to children, and with such ignorant dulness that they blunt the senses and corrupt the tastes of the still plastic human being. But I do wish that I had read no books at all till later,—that I had lived with toys, and played in the open air. Children should not cull the fruits of reflection and observation early, but expand in the sun, and let thoughts come to them. They should not through books antedate their actual experiences, but should take them gradually, as sympathy and interpretation are needed. With me, much of life was devoured in the bud.

FIRST FRIEND

For a few months, this bookish and solitary life was invaded by interest in a living, breathing figure. At church, I used to look around with a feeling of coldness and disdain, which, though I now well understand its causes, seems to my wiser mind as odious as it was unnatural. The puny child sought everywhere for the Roman and Shakespeare figures, and she was met by the shrewd, honest eye, the homely decency, or the smartness of a New England village on Sunday. There was beauty, but I could not see it then; it was not the kind I longed for. In the next pew sat a family who were my especial aversion. There were five daughters, the eldest not above four-and-twenty,—yet they had the old fairy, knowing look, hard, dry, dwarfed, strangers to the All-Fair,—were working-day residents in this beautiful planet. They looked as if their thoughts had never strayed beyond the jobs of the day, and they were glad of it. Their mother was one of those shrunken, faded patterns of woman who have never done anything to keep smooth the cheek and dignify the brow. The father had a Scotch look of shrewd narrowness, and entire self-complacency. I could not endure this family, whose existence contradicted all my visions; yet I could not forbear looking at them.

As my eye one day was ranging about with its accustomed coldness, and the proudly foolish sense of being in a shroud of thoughts that were not their thoughts, it was arrested by a face most fair, and well-known as it seemed at first glance,—for surely I had met her before and waited for her long. But soon I saw that she was a new apparition foreign to that scene, if not to me. Her dress,—the arrangement of her hair, which had the graceful pliancy of races highly cultivated for long,—the intelligent and full picture of her eye, whose reserve was in its self-possession, not in timidity,—all combined to make up a whole impression, which, though too young to understand, I was well prepared to feel.

How wearisome now appears that thorough-bred *millefleur* beauty, the distilled result of ages of European culture! Give me rather the wild heath on the lonely hill-side, than such a rose-tree from the daintily clipped garden. But, then, I had but tasted the cup, and knew not how little it could satisfy; more, more, was all my cry; continued through years, till I had been at the very fountain. Indeed, it was ruby-red, a perfumed draught, and I need not abuse the wine because I prefer water, but merely say I have had enough of it. Then, the first sight, the first knowledge of such a person was intoxication.

She was an English lady, who, by a singular chance, was cast upon this region for a few months. Elegant and captivating, her every look and gesture was tuned to a different pitch from anything I had ever known. She was in various ways "accomplished," as it is called, though to what degree I cannot now judge. She painted in oils;—I had never before seen any one use the brush, and days would not have been too long for me to watch the pictures growing beneath her hand. She played the harp; and its tones are still to me the heralds of the promised land I saw before me then. She rose, she looked, she spoke; and the gentle swaying motion she made all through life has gladdened memory, as the stream does the woods and meadows.

As she was often at the house of one of our neighbors, and afterwards at our own, my thoughts were fixed on her with all the force of my nature. It was my first real interest in my kind, and it engrossed me wholly. I had seen her,—I should see her,—and my mind lay steeped in the visions that flowed from this source. My task-work I went through with, as I have done on similar occasions all my life, aided by pride that could not bear to fail, or be questioned. Could I cease from doing the work of the day, and hear the reason sneeringly given,—"Her head is so completely taken up with ——— that she can do nothing?" Impossible.

Should the first love be blighted, they say, the mind loses its sense of eternity. All forms of existence seem fragile, the prison of time real, for a god is dead. Equally true is this of friendship. I thank Heaven that the first feeling was permitted its free flow. The years that lay between the woman and the girl only brought her beauty into perspective, and enabled me to see her as I did the mountains from my window, and made her presence to me a gate of Paradise. That which she was, that which she brought, that which she might have brought, were mine, and over a whole region of new life I ruled proprietor of the soil in my own right.

Her mind was sufficiently unoccupied to delight in my warm devotion. She could not know what it was to me, but the light cast by the flame through so delicate a vase cheered and charmed her. All who saw admired her in their way; but she would lightly turn her head from their hard or oppressive looks, and fix a glance of full-eyed sweetness on the child, who, from a distance, watched all her looks and motions. She did not say much to me—not much to any one; she spoke in her whole being rather than by chosen words. Indeed, her proper speech was dance or song, and what was less expressive did not greatly interest her. But she saw much, having in its perfection the woman's delicate sense for sympathies and attractions. We walked in the fields, alone. Though others were present, her eyes were gliding over all the field and plain for the objects of beauty to which she was of kin. She was not cold to her seeming companions; a sweet courtesy satisfied them, but it hung about her like her mantle that she wore without thinking of it; her thoughts were free, for these civilized beings can really live two lives at the same moment. With them she seemed to be, but her hand was given to the child at her side; others did not observe me, but to her I was the only human presence. Like a guardian spirit she led me through the fields and groves, and every tree, every bird greeted me, and said, what I felt, "She is the first angel of your life."

One time I had been passing the afternoon with her. She had been playing to me on the harp, and I sat listening in happiness almost unbearable. Some guests were announced. She went into another room to receive them, and I took up her book. It was Guy Mannering, then lately published, and the first of Scott's novels I had ever seen. I opened where her mark lay, and read merely with the feeling of continuing our mutual existence by passing my eyes over the same page where hers had been. It was the description of the rocks on the sea-coast where the little Harry Bertram was lost. I had never seen such places, and my mind was vividly stirred to imagine them. The scene rose before me, very unlike reality, doubtless, but majestic and wild. I was the little Harry Bertram, and had lost her,—all I had to lose,—and sought her vainly in long dark caves that had no end, splashing through the water; while the crags beetled above, threatening to fall and crush the poor child. Absorbed in the painful vision, tears rolled down my cheeks. Just then she entered with light step, and full-beaming eye. When she saw me thus, a soft cloud stole over her face, and clothed every feature with a lovelier tenderness than I had seen there before. She did not question, but fixed on me inquiring looks of beautiful love. I laid my head against her shoulder and wept,—dimly feeling that I must lose her and all,—all who spoke to me of the same things,—that the cold wave must rush over me. She waited till my tears were spent, then rising, took from a little box a bunch of golden amaranths or everlasting flowers, and gave them to me. They were very fragrant. "They came," she said, "from Madeira." These flowers stayed with me seventeen years. "Madeira" seemed to me the fortunate isle, apart in the blue ocean from all of ill or dread. Whenever I saw a sail passing in the distance,—if it bore itself with fulness of beauty certainty,—I felt that it was going to Madeira. Those thoughts are all gone now. No Madeira exists for me now,—no fortunate purple isle,—and all these hopes and fancies are lifted from the sea into the sky. Yet I thank the charms that fixed them here so long,—fixed them till perfumes like those of the golden flowers were drawn from the earth, teaching me to know my birth-place.

I can tell little else of this time,—indeed, I remember little, except the state of feeling in which I lived. For I *lived,* and when this is the case, there is little to tell in the form of thought. We meet—at least those who are true to their instincts meet—a succession of persons through our lives, all of whom have some peculiar errand to us. There is an outer circle, whose existence we perceive, but with whom we stand in no real relation. They tell us the news, they act on us in the offices of society, they show us kindness and aversion; but their influence does not penetrate; we are nothing to them, nor they to us, except as a part of the world's furniture. Another circle, within this, are dear and near to us. We know them and of what kind they are. They are to us not mere facts, but intelligible thoughts of the divine mind. We like to see how they are unfolded; we like to meet them and part from them; we like their action upon us and the pause that succeeds and enables us to appreciate its quality. Often we leave them on our path, and return no more, but we bear them in our memory, tales which have been told, and whose meaning has been felt.

But yet a nearer group there are, beings born under the same star, and bound with us in a common destiny. These are not mere acquaintances, mere friends, but, when we meet, are sharers of our very existence. There is no separation; the same thought is given at the same moment to both,—indeed, it is born of the meeting, and would not otherwise have been called into existence at all. These not only know themselves more, but *are* more for having met, and regions of their being, which would else have laid sealed in cold obstruction, burst into leaf and bloom and song.

The times of these meetings are fated, nor will either party be able ever to meet any other person in the same way. Both seem to rise at a glance into that part of the heavens where the word can be spoken, by which they are revealed to one another and to themselves. The step in being thus gained, can never be lost, nor can it be re-trod; for neither party will be again what the other wants. They are no longer fit to interchange mutual influence, for they do not really need it, and if they think they do, it is because they weakly pine after a past pleasure.

To the inmost circle of relations but few are admitted, because some prejudice or lack of courage has prevented the many from listening to their instincts the first time they manifested themselves. If the voice is one disregarded it becomes fainter each time, till, at last, it is wholly silenced, and the man lives in this world, a stranger to its real life, deluded like the maniac who fancies he has attained his throne, while in reality he is on a bed of musty straw. Yet, if the voice finds a listener and servant the first time of speaking, it is encouraged to more and more clearness. Thus it was with me,—from no merit of mine, but because I had the good fortune to be free enough to yield to my impressions. Common ties had not bound me; there were no traditionary notions in my mind; I believed in nothing merely because others believed in it; I had taken no feelings on trust. Thus my mind was open to their sway.

This woman came to me, a star from the east, a morning star, and I worshipped her. She too was elevated by that worship, and her fairest self called out. To the mind she brought assurance that there was a region congenial with its tendencies and tastes, a region of elegant culture and intercourse, whose object, fulfilled or not, was to gratify the sense of beauty, not the mere utilities of life. In our relation she was lifted to the top of her being. She had known many celebrities, had roused to passionate desire many hearts, and became afterwards a wife; but I do not believe she ever more truly realized her best self than towards the lonely child whose heaven she was, whose eyes she met, and whose possibilities she predicted. "He raised me," said a woman inspired by love, "upon the pedestal of his own high thoughts, and wings came at once, but I did not fly away. I stood there with downcast eyes worthy of his love, for he had made me so."

Thus we do always for those who inspire us to expect from them the best. That which they are able to be, they become, because we demand it of them. "We expect the impossible—and find it."

My English friend went across the sea. She passed into her former life, and into ties that engrossed her days. But she has never ceased to think of me. Her thoughts turn forcibly back to the child who was to her all she saw of the really New World. On the promised coasts she had found only cities, careful men and women, the aims and habits of ordinary life in her own land, without that elegant culture which she, probably, over-estimated, because it was her home. But in the mind of the child she found the fresh prairie, the untrodden forests for which she had longed. I saw in her the storied castles, the fair stately parks and the wind laden with tones from the past, which I desired to know. We wrote to one another for many years;—her shallow and delicate epistles did not disenchant me, nor did she fail to see something of the old poetry in my rude characters and stammering speech. But we must never meet again.

When this friend was withdrawn I fell into a profound depression. I knew not how to exert myself, but lay bound hand and foot. Melancholy enfolded me in an atmosphere, as joy had done. This suffering, too, was out of the gradual and natural course. Those who are really children could not know such love, or feel such sorrow. "I am to blame," said my father, "in keeping her at home so long merely to please myself. She needs to be with other girls, needs play and variety. She does not seem to me really sick, but dull rather. She eats nothing, you say. I see she grows thin. She ought to change the scene."

I was indeed *dull*. The books, the garden, had lost all charm. I had the excuse of headache, constantly, for not attending to my lessons. The light of life was set, and every leaf was withered. At such an early age there are no back or side scenes where the mind, weary and sorrowful, may retreat. Older, we realize the width of the world more, and it is not easy to despair on any point. The effort at thought to which we are compelled relieves and affords a dreary retreat, like hiding in a brick-kiln till the shower be over. But then all joy seemed to have departed with my friend, and the emptiness of our house stood revealed. This I had not felt while I every day expected to see or had seen her, or annoyance and dulness were unnoticed or swallowed up in the one thought that clothed my days with beauty. But now she was gone, and I was roused from habits of reading or reverie to feel the fiery temper of the soul, and to learn that it must have vent, that it would not be pacified by shadows, neither meet without consuming what lay around it. I avoided the table as much as possible, took long walks and lay in bed, or on the floor of my room. I complained of my head, and it was not wrong to do so, for a sense of dulness and suffocation, if not pain, was there constantly.

But when it was proposed that I should go to school, that was a remedy I could not listen to with patience for a moment. The peculiarity of my education had separated me entirely from the girls around, except that when they were playing at active games, I would sometimes go out and join them. I liked violent bodily exercise, which always relieved my nerves. But I had no success in associating with them beyond the mere play. Not only I was not their schoolmate, but my book-life and lonely habits had given a cold aloofness to my whole expression, and veiled my manner with a hauteur which turned all hearts away. Yet, as this reserve was superficial, and rather ignorance than arrogance, it produced no deep dislike. Besides, the girls supposed me really superior to themselves, and did not hate me for feeling it, but neither did they like me, nor wish to have me with them. Indeed, I had gradually given up all such wishes myself; for they seemed to me rude, tiresome, and childish, as I did to them dull and strange. This experience had been earlier, before I was admitted to any real friendship; but now that I had been lifted into the life of mature years, and into just that atmosphere of European life to which I had before been tending, the thought of sending me to school filled me with disgust.

Yet what could I tell my father of such feelings? I resisted all I could, but in vain. He had no faith in medical aid generally, and justly saw that this was no occasion for its use. He thought I needed change of scene, and to be roused to activity by other children. "I have kept you at home," he said, "because I took such pleasure in teaching you myself, and besides I knew that you would learn faster with one who is desirous to aid you. But you will learn fast enough wherever you are, and you ought to be more with others your own age. I shall soon hear that you are better, I trust."

BETTINE BRENTANO
AND HER FRIEND
GÜNDERODE

In the spring of 1840, Margaret Fuller began to solicit contributions for the initial issue of the Dial, *a Transcendentalist periodical that she edited until the middle of 1842. In the two years that she spent as editor, Fuller filled the pages of the* Dial *with the Transcendentalists' claims for radical individualism. In taking women as her subject in a number of contributions, she distinguished herself from her colleagues and left her special mark on the* Dial. *Nowhere was this more apparent than in "Bettine Brentano and Her Friend Günderode," an essay on a series of letters exchanged by two German intellectuals. Combining excerpts from the letters of the two women with commentary, Fuller celebrated the friendship of Bettine Brentano, a member of a highly successful commercial family, and Karoline Günderode, a canoness and aspiring poet. The idealization of female friendship that marks Fuller's essay recalls her portrayal of the relationship with Ellen Kilshaw. Described in the "Autobiographical Sketch" as the dearest of friends, Ellen Kilshaw had played a role similar to Günderode's. "Bettine Brentano and Her Friend Günderode" appeared in the* Dial *in January of 1842. Two months later, Fuller published a translation of* Correspondence of Fraulein Günderode with Bettine von Arnim.

Bettine Brentano's letters to Goethe, published under the title of Goethe's Correspondence with a Child, are already well known among us and met with a more cordial reception from readers in general than could have been expected. Even those who are accustomed to measure the free movements of art by the conventions that hedge the path of daily life, who, in great original creations, seek only intimations of the moral character borne by the author in his private circle, and who, had they been the contemporaries of Shakspeare, would have been shy of visiting the person who took pleasure in the delineation of a Falstaff; —even those whom Byron sneers at as "the garrison people," suffered themselves to be surprised in their intrenchments, by the exuberance and wild, youthful play of Bettine's genius, and gave themselves up to receive her thoughts and feelings in the spirit which led her to express them. They felt that here was one whose only impulse was to *live*,— to unfold and realize her nature, and they forgot to measure what she did by her position in society.

There have been a few exceptions of persons who judged the work unworthily, who showed entire insensibility to its fulness of original thought and inspired fidelity to nature, and vulgarized by their impure looks the innocent vagaries of youthful idolatry. But these have been so few that, this time, the vulgar is not the same with the mob, but the reverse.

If such was its reception from those long fettered by custom, and crusted over by artificial tastes, with what joy was it greeted by those of free intellect and youthful eager heart. So very few printed books are in any wise a faithful transcript of life, that the possession of one really sincere made an era in many minds, unlocking tongues that had long been silent as to what was dearest and most delicate in their experiences, or most desired for the future, and making the common day and common light rise again to their true value, since it was seen how fruitful they had been to this one person. The meteor playing in our sky diffused there an electricity and a light, which revealed unknown attractions in seemingly sluggish substances, and lured many secrets from the dim recesses in which they had been cowering for years, unproductive, cold, and silent.

Yet, while we enjoyed this picture of a mind tuned to its highest pitch by the desire of daily ministering to an idolized object; while we were enriched by the results of the Child's devotion to him, hooted at by the Philistines as the "Old Heathen," but to her poetic apprehension "Jupiter, Apollo, all in one," we must feel that the relation in which she stands to Goethe is not a beautiful one. Idolatries are natural to youthful hearts noble enough for a passion beyond the desire for sympathy or the instinct of dependence, and almost all aspiring natures can recall a period when some noble figure, whether in life or literature, stood for them at the gate of heaven, and represented all the possible glories of nature and art. This worship is, in most instances, a secret worship; the still, small voice constantly rising in the soul to bid them harmonize the discords of the world, and distill beauty from imperfection, for another of kindred nature has done so. This figure whose achievements they admire is their St. Peter, holding for them the keys of Paradise, their model, their excitement to fulness and purity of life, their external conscience. When this devotion is silent, or only spoken out through our private acts, it is most likely to make the stair to heaven, and lead men on till suddenly they find the golden gate will open at their own touch, and they need neither mediator nor idol more. The same course is observable in the religion of nations, where the worship of Persons rises at last into free thought in the minds of Philosophers.

But when this worship is expressed, there must be singular purity and strength of character on the part both of Idol and Idolater, to prevent its degenerating into a mutual excitement of vanity, or mere infatuation.

"Thou art the only one worthy to inspire me;" cries one.

"Thou art the only one capable of understanding my inspiration," smiles back the other.

And clouds of incense rise to hide from both the free breath of heaven!

But if the idol stands there, grim and insensible, the poor votary will oftentimes redouble his sacrifices with passionate fervor, till the scene becomes as sad a farce as that of Juggernaut, and all that is dignified in human nature lies crushed and sullied by one superstitious folly.

An admiration restrained by self-respect; (I do not mean pride, but a sense that one's own soul is, after all, a regal power and a precious possession, which, if not now of as apparent magnificence, is of as high an ultimate destiny as that of another) honors the admirer no less than the admired. But humility is not groveling weakness, neither does bounty consist in prodigality; and the spendthrifts of the soul deserve to famish on husks for many days; for, if they had not wandered so far from the Father, he would have given them bread.

In short we are so admirably constituted, that excess anywhere must lead to poverty somewhere; and though he is mean and cold, who is incapable of free abandonment to a beautiful object, yet if there be not in the mind a counterpoising force, which draws us back to the centre in proportion as we have flown from it, we learn nothing from our experiment, and are not vivified but weakened by our love.

Something of this we feel with regard to Bettine and Goethe. The great poet of her nation, and representative of half a century of as high attainment as mind has ever made, was magnet strong enough to draw

out the virtues of many beings as rich as she. His greatness was a
household word, and the chief theme of pride in the city of her birth.
To her own family he had personally been well known in all the bril-
liancy of his dawn. She had grown up in the atmosphere he had created. Seeing him up there on the mountain, he seemed to her all
beautiful and majestic in the distant rosy light of its snow-peaks. Add
a nature, like one of his own melodies, as subtle, as fluent, and as
productive of minute flowers and mosses, we could not wonder if one
so fitted to receive him, had made of her whole life a fair sculptured
pedestal for this one figure.

All this would be well, or rather, not ill, if he were to her only an
object of thought; but when the two figures are brought into open
relation with one another; it is too unequal. Were Bettine, indeed, a
child, she might bring her basket of flowers and strew them in his path
without expecting even a smile in return. But to say nothing of the
reckoning by years, which the curious have made, we constantly feel
that she is not a child. She is so indeed when compared with him as
to maturity of growth, but she is not so in their relation, and the degree
of knowledge she shows of life and thought compels us to demand
some conscious dignity of her as a woman. The great art where to
stop is not evinced in all passages. Then Goethe is so cold, so repulsive,
diplomatic, and courteously determined not to compromise himself.
Had he assumed truly the paternal attitude, he might have been far
more gentle and tender, he might have fostered all the beauteous blossoms of this young fancy, without ever giving us a feeling of pain and
inequality. But he does not; there is an air as of an elderly guardian
flirting cautiously with a giddy, inexperienced ward, or a Father Confessor, who, instead of through the holy office raising and purifying
the thoughts of the devotee, uses it to gratify his curiosity. We cannot
accuse him of playing with her feelings. He never leads her on. She
goes herself, following the vision which gleams before her. "I will not,"
he says, "wile the little bird from its nest," and he does not. But he is
willing to make a tool of this fresh, fervent being; he is unrelenting as
ever in this. What she offers from the soul the artist receives,—to use
artistically. Indeed we see, that he enjoyed as we do the ceaseless bee-
like hum of gathering from a thousand flowers, but only with the cold
pleasure of an observer; there is no genuine movement of a grateful
sensibility. We often feel that Bettine should perceive this, and that it
should have modified the nature of her offerings. For now there is
nothing kept sacred, and no balance of beauty maintained in her life.
Impatiently she has approached where she was not called, and the

truth and delicacy of spiritual affinities has been violated. She has followed like a slave where she might as a pupil. Observe this, young idolaters. Have you chosen a bright particular star for the object of your vespers? you will not see it best or revere it best by falling prostrate in the dust; but stand erect, though with upturned brow and face pale with devotion.

An ancient author says, "it is the punishment of those who have honored their kings as gods to be expelled from the gods," and we feel this about Bettine, that her boundless abandonment to one feeling must hinder for a time her progress and that her maturer years are likely to lag slowly after the fiery haste of her youth. She lived so long, not for truth, but for a human object, that the plant must have fallen into the dust when its prop was withdrawn, and lain there long before it could economize its juices enough to become a tree where it had been a vine.

We also feel as if she became too self-conscious in the course of this intimacy. There being no response from the other side to draw her out naturally, she hunts about for means to entertain a lordly guest, who brings nothing to the dinner, but a silver fork. Perhaps Goethe would say his questions and answers might be found in his books; that if she knew what he was, she knew what to bring. But the still human little maiden wanted to excite surprise at least if not sympathy by her gifts, and her simplicity was perverted in the effort. We see the fanciful about to degenerate into the fantastic, freedom into lawlessness, and are reminded of the fate of Euphorion in Goethe's great Rune.

Thus we follow the course of this intimacy with the same feelings as the love of Tasso, and, in the history of fiction, of Werther, and George Douglas, as also those of Sappho, Eloisa, and Mlle. de L'Espinasse. There is a hollowness in the very foundation, and we feel from the beginning,

"It will not, nor it cannot come to good."

Yet we cannot but be grateful to circumstances, even if not in strict harmony with our desires, to which we owe some of the most delicate productions of literature, those few pages it boasts which are genuine transcripts of private experience. They are mostly tear-stained; —by those tears have been kept living on the page those flowers, which the poets present to us only when distilled into essences. The few records in this kind that we possess remind us of the tapestries woven by prisoners and exiles, pathetic heir-looms, in noble families.

Of these letters to Goethe some have said they were so pure a product, so free from any air of literature, as to make the reader feel he had never seen a genuine book before.

Another, "She seems a spirit in a mask of flesh, to each man's heart revealing his secret wishes and the vast capacities of the narrowest life."

But the letters to Goethe are not my present subject; and those before me with the same merits give us no cause however trifling for regret. They are letters which passed between Bettine, and the Canoness Günderode, the friend to whom she was devoted several years previous to her acquaintance with Goethe.

The readers of the Correspondence with a Child will remember the history of this intimacy, and of the tragedy with which it closed, as one of the most exquisite passages in the volumes. The filling out of the picture is not unworthy the outline there given.

Günderode was a Canoness in one of the orders described by Mrs. Jameson, living in the house of her order, but mixing freely in the world at her pleasure. But as she was eight or ten years older than her friend, and of a more delicate and reserved nature, her letters describe a narrower range of outward life. She seems to have been intimate with several men of genius and high cultivation, especially in philosophy, as well as with Bettine; these intimacies afforded stimulus to her life, which passed, at the period of writing, either in her little room with her books and her pen, or in occasional visits to her family and to beautiful country-places.

Bettine, belonging to a large and wealthy family of extensive commercial connexions, and seeing at the house of grandmother Me. La Roche, most of the distinguished literati of the time, as well as those noble and princely persons who were proud to do honor to letters, if they did not professedly cultivate them, brings before us a much wider circle. The letters would be of great interest, if only for the distinct pictures they present of the two modes of life; and the two beautiful figures which animate and portray these modes of life are in perfect harmony with them.

I have been accustomed to distinguish the two as Nature and Ideal. Bettine, hovering from object to object, drawing new tides of vital energy from all, living freshly alike in man and tree, loving the breath of the damp earth as well as that of the flower which springs from it, bounding over the fences of society as easily as over the fences of the field, intoxicated with the apprehension of each new mystery, never hushed into silence by the highest, flying and singing like the bird, sobbing with the hopelessness of an infant, prophetic, yet astonished at the fulfilment of each prophecy, restless, fearless, clinging to love, yet unwearied in experiment—is not this the pervasive vital force, cause of the effect which we call nature?

And Günderode, in the soft dignity of each look and gesture, whose lightest word has the silvery spiritual clearness of an angel's lyre, harmonizing all objects into their true relations, drawing from every form of life its eternal meaning, checking, reproving, and clarifying all that was unworthy by her sadness at the possibility of its existence. Does she not meet the wild, fearless bursts of the friendly genius, to measure, to purify, to interpret, and thereby to elevate? As each word of Bettine's calls to enjoy and behold, like a free breath of mountain air, so each of Günderode's comes like the moonbeam to transfigure the landscape, to hush the wild beatings of the heart and dissolve all the sultry vapors of day into the pure dewdrops of the solemn and sacred night.

The action of these two beings upon one another, as representing classes of thoughts, is thus of the highest poetical significance. As persons, their relation is not less beautiful. An intimacy between two young men is heroic. They call one another to combat with the wrongs of life; they buckler one another against the million; they encourage each other to ascend the steps of knowledge; they hope to aid one another in the administration of justice, and the diffusion of prosperity. As the life of man is to be active, they have still more the air of brothers in arms than of fellow students. But the relation between two young girls is essentially poetic. What is more fair than to see little girls, hand in hand, walking in some garden, laughing, singing, chatting in low tones of mystery, cheek to cheek and brow to brow. Hermia and Helena, the nymphs gathering flowers in the vale of Enna, sister Graces and sister Muses rise to thought, and we feel how naturally the forms of women are associated in the contemplation of beauty and the harmonies of affection. The correspondence between very common-place girls is interesting, if they are not foolish sentimentalists, but healthy natures with a common groundwork of real life. There is a fluent tenderness, a native elegance in the arrangement of trifling incidents, a sincere childlike sympathy in aspirations that mark the destiny of woman. She should be the poem, man the poet.

The relation before us presents all that is lovely between woman and woman, adorned by great genius and beauty on both sides. The

advantage in years, the higher culture, and greater harmony of Günderode's nature is counterbalanced, by the ready springing impulse,
richness, and melody of the other.

And not only are these letters interesting as presenting this view
of the interior of German life, and of an ideal relation realized, but
the high state of culture in Germany which presented to the thoughts
of those women themes of poesy and philosophy as readily, as to the
English or American girl come the choice of a dress, the last concert
or assembly, has made them expressions of the noblest aspiration,
filled them with thoughts and oftentimes deep thoughts on the great
subjects. Many of the poetical fragments from the pen of Günderode
are such as would not have been written, had she not been the contemporary of Schelling and Fichte, yet are they native and original, the
atmosphere of thought reproduced in the brilliant and delicate hues of
a peculiar plant. This transfusion of such energies as are manifested
in Goethe, Kant, and Schelling into these private lives is a creation not
less worthy our admiration, than the forms which the muse has given
them to bestow on the world through their immediate working by their
chosen means. These are not less the children of the genius than his
statue or the exposition of his method. Truly, as regards the artist, the
immortal offspring of the Muse,

"Loves where (art) has set its seal,"

are objects of clearer confidence than the lives on which he has
breathed; they are safe as the poet tells us death alone can make the
beauty of the actual; they will ever bloom as sweet and fair as now,
ever thus radiate pure light, nor degrade the prophecy of high moments, by compromise, fits of inanity, or folly, as the living poems do.
But to the universe, which will give time and room to correct the bad
lines in those living poems, it is given to wait as the artist with his
human feelings cannot; though secure that a true thought never dies,
but once gone forth must work and live forever.

We know that cant and imitation must always follow a bold expression of thought in any wise, and reconcile ourself as well as we
can to those insects called by the very birth of the rose to prey upon
its sweetness. But pleasure is unmingled, where thought has done its
proper work and fertilized while it modified each being in its own kind.
Let him who has seated himself beneath the great German oak, and
gazed upon the growth of poesy, of philosophy, of criticism, of historic
painting, of the drama, till the life of the last fifty years seems well

worth man's living, pick up also these little acorns which are dropping gracefully on the earth, and carry them away to be planted in his own home, for in each fairy form may be read the story of the national tree, the promise of future growths as noble.

The talisman of this friendship may be found in Günderode's post-script to one of her letters, "If thou findest Muse, write soon again," I have hesitated whether this might not be, "if thou findest Musse (leisure) write soon again;" then had the letters wound up like one of our epistles here in America. But, in fine, I think there can be no mistake. They waited for the Muse. Here the pure products of public and private literature are on a par. That inspiration which the poet finds in the image of the ideal man, the man of the ages, of whom nations are but features, and Messiahs the voice, the friend finds in the thought of his friend, a nature in whose positive existence and illimitable tendencies he finds the mirror of his desire, and the spring of his conscious growth. For those who write in the spirit of sincerity, write neither to the public nor the individual, but to the soul made manifest in the flesh, and publication or correspondence only furnish them with the occasion for bringing their thoughts to a focus.

The day was made rich to Bettine and her friend by hoarding its treasures for one another. If we have no object of the sort, we cannot live at all in the day, but thoughts stretch out into eternity and find no home. We feel of these two that they were enough to one another to be led to indicate their best thoughts, their fairest visions, and there-fore theirs was a true friendship. They needed not "descend to meet."

Sad are the catastrophes of friendships, for they are mostly un-equal, and it is rare that more than one party keeps true to the original covenant. Happy the survivor if in losing his friend, he loses not the idea of friendship, nor can be made to believe, because those who were once to him the angels of his life, sustaining the aspiration of his nobler nature, and calming his soul by the gleams of pure beauty that for a time were seen in their deeds, in their desires, unexpectedly grieve the spirit, and baffle the trust which had singled them out as types of excellence amid a sullied race, by infirmity of purpose, shallowness of heart and mind, selfish absorption or worldly timidity, that there is no such thing as true intimacy, as harmonious development of mind by mind, two souls prophesying to one another, two minds feeding one another, two human hearts sustaining and pardoning one another! Be not faithless, thou whom I see wandering alone amid the tombs of thy buried loves. The relation thou hast thus far sought in vain is possible even on earth to calm, profound, tender, and unselfish natures; it is assured in heaven, where only chastened spirits can enter,—pilgrims dedicate to Perfection.

As there is no drawback upon the beauty of this intimacy—there being sufficient nearness of age to give Günderode just the advantage needful with so daring a child as Bettine, and a sufficient equality in every other respect—so is every detail of their position attractive and picturesque. There is somewhat fantastic or even silly in some of the scenes with Goethe; there is a slight air of travestie and we feel sometimes as if we saw rather a masque aiming to express nature, than nature's self. Bettine's genius was excited to idealize life for Goethe, and gleams of the actual will steal in and give a taint of the grotesque to the groupes. The aim is to meet as nymph and Apollo, but with sudden change the elderly prime minister and the sentimental maiden are beheld instead. But in the intercourse with Günderode there is no effort; each mind being at equal expense of keeping up its fires. We think with unmingled pleasure of the two seated together beside the stove in Günderode's little room, walking in Madame La Roche's garden, where they *"founded a religion for a young prince,"* or on the Rhine, or in the old castle on the hill, as described in the following beautiful letters.

"She (Günderode) was so timid; a young Canoness, who feared to say grace aloud; she often told me that she trembled when her turn came to pronounce the benedicite;—our communion was sweet,—it was the epoch in which I first became conscious of myself. She had sought me out in Offenbach; she took me by the hand and begged me to visit her in the town; afterwards we came every day together; with her I learned to read my first books with understanding; she wanted to teach me History, but soon saw that I was too busy with the *present,* to be held long by the *past.* How delighted I was to visit her; I could not miss her for a single day; but ran to her every afternoon; when I came to the chapter-gate I peeped through the key-hole of her door, till I was let in. The little apartment was on the ground-floor, looking into the garden; before the window, grew up a silver poplar, up which I climbed to read; at each chapter, I clambered one bough higher, and then read down to her;—she stood at the window and listened, speaking to me above; every now and then she would say; 'Bettine, don't fall.' I now for the first time, know how happy I then was; for all, even the most trifling thing is impressed on my mind as the remembrance of enjoyment. She was as soft and delicate in all her features as a blonde. She had brown hair, but blue eyes, that were shaded by long lashes; when she laughed it was not loud, it was rather a soft, subdued *crooing,* in which joy and cheerfulness distinctly spoke; she did not walk, she *moved,* if one can understand what I mean by this; her dress was a robe which encompassed her with caressing folds; this was owing to the gentleness of her movements. She was tall of stature; her figure was too flowing, for the word slender to express; she was *timid-friendly* and much too yielding to make herself prominent in society. She once dined with all the baronesses at the Royal Primate's table, she wore the black chapter-dress with long train, white collar and cross of the order; some one remarked that she looked amidst the others, like a phantom—a spirit about to melt into air. She read her poems to me and was as well pleased with my applause, as if I had been the great Public; and indeed I was full of lively eagerness to hear them; not that I seized upon the meaning of what I heard, on the contrary, it was to me an 'element unknown' and the smooth verses affected me like the harmony of a strange language, which flatters the ear, though one cannot translate it.

"We laid the plan of a journey,—devised our route and adventures, wrote everything down, pictured all before us— our Fancy was so busy that Reality could hardly have afforded us a better experience. We often read in this fictitious journal and delighted in the sweetest adventures, which we had there met with; invention thus became as it were a *remembrance,* whose relations still continued their connexions with the *present.* Of that which happened in the real world we communicated to each other nothing, the kingdom in which we met sank down like a cloud, parting to receive us to a secret Paradise, there all was new—surprising, but congenial to spirit and heart, and thus the days went by.

"She wished to teach me Philosophy; what she imparted to me, she expected me to comprehend, and to give again in my way under a written form. The Essays which I wrote on these subjects, she read with wonder; they did not contain the most distant idea of what she had communicated; but I maintained that I had so understood it; she called these themes, Revela-

tions, enhanced by the sweetest colorings of an extasied imagination; she collected them carefully, and once wrote to me;
Thou dost not yet understand, how deep these openings lead
into the mine of the mind; but the time will come, when it
will be important to thee; for man often goes through desert
paths—the greater his inclination to penetrate, the more
dreadful is the loneliness of his way, the more endless the
wilderness. But when thou becomest aware how deep thou
hast descended into the spring of thought and how there below, thou findest a new dawn, risest with joy again to the
surface and speakest of thy deep-hid world, then will it be
thy consolation; for thou and the world can never be united;
thou wilt have no other outlet, except back through this
spring, into the magic garden of thy fancy; but it is no fancy,
it is *Truth* which is merely reflected from it. Genius makes
use of Fancy, to impart or instil the Divine, which the mind
of man could not embrace under its ideal form; yes! thou wilt
have no other way of enjoyment in thy life, than that, which
children promise themselves from magic-caverns and deep
fountains, through which one comes to blooming gardens,
wonderful fruits and crystal palaces, where yet unimagined
music sounds, and the sun builds bridges of its rays, upon the
centre of which one may walk with a firm foot. All this in
these pages of thine will form a key, with which thou mayest
perhaps unlock deep-hid kingdoms; therefore, lose nothing
nor contend against that incentive which prompts thee to
write, but learn to *labor in thought,* without which Genius
can never be born in the spirit; when it becomes incarnate in
thee, then wilt thou rejoice in inspiration, even as the dancer
in music."—*Correspondence with a Child.*

These inspired sayings look almost as beautiful in the German-
English of Bettine's translation as in the original. I cannot hope for
equal success in the following extracts from "Die Günderode;" but the
peculiar grace and originality of expression cannot be quite lost. I have
followed as much as possible the idiom of the writer as well as her
truly girlish punctuation. Commas and dashes are the only stops natural to girls; their sentences flow on in little minim ripples, unbroken
as the brook in a green field unless by some slight waterfall or jet of
Ohs and Ahs.

"To Günderode. I did not think that I could be so these beautiful days. In thy letter, line for line, read I nothing mournful, and yet it makes me sad. Thou speakest of thyself as if thou wert wholly other than I,—wholly of other nature. Ah! and yet thou alone standest opposite to me among all men. When we talked together, we were not one; thou wert one way minded, and I another. Certainly I am different from thee; I feel it to-day from every line of they letter; and yet it is so true to me, illuminating the deep ground of thy soul! How is each man a great mystery! Until all is transfigured into the heavenly, how much remains that is not understood! Wholly to be understood—that seems to me the true only metamorphosis; the proper ascension. In the summer-house where we last year saw one another for the first time,—yes, a whole year have we been good friends to one another???!!!!! Thus could I continue to make signs of admiration, of mute surprise of thought, of sighing; or if I knew a sign for shuddering, for tears, I could mark the leaves full of the deepest feelings for which I know no name. The woodbine that then grew over the lattice, blooms this year much more luxuriant. Dost thou remember that was our first word? I said to thee 'this was a very cold winter the Hahnenfuss* has almost all its twigs frozen; the leaves give little shade.' Then saidst thou, the sun gives and the leaves take; what they cannot receive of the light, they must let pass to us; and thou saidst this plant is fairer named Geisblatt, than Hahnenfuss,—because then we think of a pretty goat, who with pleasure eats the fragrant flowers; and that nature offers an ideal life to every creature. And as the elements in undisturbed working produce, sustain, nourish, and fulfil life, so in enjoyment of undisturbed development, is preparing the some-time element in which the ideal of the Spirit may bloom, thrive, and be fulfilled. And then thou saidst that I ought to wear white, if I loved Nature; for as she round about us strewed such lovely flowers, to wear a robe with painted flowers is tasteless,—and we ought to live in harmony with Nature,—otherwise the buds of the human spirit could not bloom out. I thought awhile about thy sayings,—so were we both silent. For it was my place to an-

---

* Hahnenfuss and Geisblatt are German names for the woodbine, Geisblatt, leaf for the goat.

swer, and I did not venture. Thou seemedst to me so full of wisdom; thy thought really seemed to be at one with nature and thy soul to tower above men, as the tree-tops full of fragrant flowers in sunshine, rain, and wind, through night and day, are ever striving up into the air. Indeed thou didst seem to me a lofty tree, inhabited and nourished by the spirits of Nature. And when I heard mine own voice that would answer thee, then was I abashed, as if its tone were not noble enough for thee. I could not say it out, thou wouldst help me; and didst say 'the spirit streams into feeling,—and that goes forth from all which Nature produces. Man has reverence before nature, because she is the mother who nourishes the soul with that which she gives it to feel.' How very much have I thought of thee and on thy words, and thy black eye-lashes that covered thy blue eyes, even as I saw thee that very first time of all; and thy tender gesture, and thy hand that smoothed my hair. I wrote, 'to-day have I seen Günderode, it was a gift from God.' Now read I that again, and I would fain do all for thy love. Do not tell me if thou hast tenderness for other men; I mean to say, be to others as thou wilt, only let that be separate from us. We must be secluded one with another, in nature; we must go hand in hand, and speak with one another not of things, but a great speech;—Let there be nothing about learning,—I cannot use that; what shall I learn which others know already? That may not be entirely lost; but what happens only just for love of us, that would I not neglect to live with thee; when with thee I would put aside all the superfluous world-stuff, for truly all the comme-il-faut is but an injustice that cries to heaven, contradicting the great voice of poesy in us, which points the soul to all which is right. How hateful is that courtesy which ever bows before others, and yet has no real intercourse with any, as if it were discourteous to put aside what does not belong to us. Were nature so perverted, intriguing and irrational as men are, there could not be even a potato ripened,—much less a tree blos-som. All is the pure consequence of magnanimity in nature, —each ear of corn which doubles its seed, bears witness.— Narrow-heartedness will never open its seeds to the light. It blights them in the bud.—Now I begin to feel why I am here; each morning prayed I when I awoke, 'dear God, why was I born;' and now I know; that I may not be so senseless as the others are; that I should walk the true path marked out in my heart; for why has the finger of God stamped it there?— and taken my five senses to school? so that each one may learn the letters, if it were not to confirm this way.—One would attribute wisdom to man, and prescribe it to him as the simple way of nature; but the denial of a great mighty world-mind in us, is ever the consequence of our conventional life with others; till at last one can draw no free breath, nor have a great thought, or great feeling, from mere courtliness and decorum. Let the Devil be grateful for great actions;— they must happen of themselves; if all went on naturally in life.—It is a shame that men should give such things the name of magnanimity; as if an earnest independent life must not perpetually stream out, like electric fire, what they name great actions.—The tiresome race of men cackle like geese; they do not hear the sobs of Love. This must I say, because the night-ingales are sobbing so sweetly above me. Four nightingales are there; also last year were there four. Truly I will never love for I should be abashed before the nightingales, that I could not sing like them. How they breathe out their souls in the art of extasy, in music, and in such a tone, so pure, so innocent, so pure and deep, such as no human soul can pro-duce, either from the voice, or an instrument. Why must man learn to sing, while the nightingale so purely, with such un-alloyed beauty, understands to sing deep into the heart. I have never heard a song of man's that touched me like the night-ingale's. Just now thought I, because I heard them so deeply, I would try whether they would hear me. When they made a pause I raised my voice; Instantly they all four burst out to-gether, as if to say 'leave us our Empire.' Arias, operas, songs, are mere false tendencies of the conventional world; the dec-lamation of a false inspiration. Yet is man carried away by sublime music. Wherefore, if he be not himself sublime? Yes, there is a secret will in the soul to be great, it refreshes like dew to hear one's proper genius in its original speech. Is not that true? Oh we also would be like these tones, which swiftly reach their aim without ever faltering; there embrace they fulness—in each rhythmus a deep mystery of inward forma-tion, as man does not. Surely melodies are God-created be-ings, with a continuous life of their own, each thought living forth out of the soul. Man produces thoughts not—They pro-

duce man.———Ah! there falls a Linden-flower on my nose;
and now it rains a little. Here am I writing stupid stuff, I can
scarcely read it now; it is fast growing dark; how fair nature
spreads out her veil! so light, so transparent. Now begin the
souls of the plants to hover round about; and the oranges in
the grove, and the Linden-fragrance comes streaming wave
over wave. It is now dark; the nightingales become more zealous; they sing indeed in the silence of the moon; ah! we will
do something really great, we will not in vain have met one
another in this world. Let us found a religion for mankind,
and make it well again. A life with God. Thy Mahomet did
a great deal by only two or three rides into heaven; let us ride
a little into heaven.———

"Yesterday I forgot to write to thee, because I sent thy
poem to Clemens; but I first copied it for myself. And wished
to say to thee how beautiful I find it. Through gratitude that
I have thee to my friend, have I neglected it. Thou seest it in
the letter; that it is thy great heart that touches me, and that
I hold myself unworthy to loose thy shoe-ties. Thou choosest
a fair thought, and puttest it in rhyme as a mantle of honor
for Clemens; what a fair virtue hast thou! raising the spirit
from the life of earth. God made the world from nothing,
preached ever the nuns, then would I ask how that was done?
They could not tell me, and bid me be silent. But I went about
and looked at all the growing things, as if I must know out
of what they are made. Now I know he has not made them
out of nothing. He has made them out of the spirit. That learn
I from the Poet; from thee. God is a Poet. Indeed, then I
understand him."

In another letter, after describing her bringing back to town a poor
woman whom she found ill beyond the gates.

"Then came the good doctor Neville and to him I gave the
woman. When I came to the Horse-market, Moritz met me
and said, 'how pale you look, what is the matter.' I am so
very hungry, said I; and it was true; the anxiety about the
woman had made me hungry. Moritz had a pocket full of
dried olives; I like them much. He emptied his pocket into my
glove which I had drawn off to have it filled. Just at that
moment the cuckoo brought Lotte in my way. Moritz went

away, and Lotte came to me and asked, 'how canst thou stand
in the open street hand in hand with Moritz.' That vexed me.
I went into the convent to thee, where I ate my olives and
laid all the stones in a row on the window-sill. In the dusk
thou wast standing beside me, entirely sunk in silence. At last
thou saidst, 'why art thou to-day so silent?' I said 'I am eating
my olives,—that occupies me, but thou also art silent; why
art thou silent?' 'There is a silence of the soul,' saidst thou,
'where all is dead in the breast;' 'is it so in thee?' asked I.
Thou wert silent awhile, and then thou saidst 'It is just so in
me, as out there in the garden; the dusk lies on my soul as on
those bushes. She is colorless, but she knows herself——
but she is colorless,' saidst thou yet again. And this time in a
tone so without vibration, that I looked on thee in the night-
shimmer, wondering and affrighted, for I ventured to speak
no more. I thought what words I could use to thee, I sought
in wide circles round about. Nothing seemed to me suited to
interrupt this silence,—which ever deeper and deeper took
root,—till it streamed through my head like a slumber which
I could no more resist.—I laid my head dreaming on the
window-board and know not how much time passed. Then
came light into the chamber, and when I looked up thou wert
leaning over me, and when I looked inquiringly on thee, then
gavest thou as answer, 'Yes, I feel often as it were a chasm
here in the breast; I may not touch it,—it pains me.' I said
'can I not fill it? this chasm?' 'That also would pain me,' saidst
thou. Then I gave thee my hand and went away.—And long
followed me thy look, it was so still and so profound, and
yet seemed to pass away over me. Oh, as I went home I loved
thee so! In thought I wound my arms about thee so close; I
thought I would bear thee in my arms to the end of the world,
and set thee down on a fair mossy place; there would I serve
thee,—and let nothing touch thee which could give thee
pain.—Yes, so was it in my childish heart; perforce would I
make thee happy, and thought a moment I must succeed; but
I know well that such a thing cannot succeed to me, and that
it is only the illusion of my thoughts, for even as children
cannot separate the far and near, and think they can reach
down the moon with their hand, to comfort the playmate
with, when he is silent and sorrowful,—so was it with me
when I came home, they were all at the tea-table and I was

mute, for I thought of thee, and sat down on a stool by the stove; then went I deep into my heart, and waked there an inner life for my spirit, which might touch thee a little,—for until now thou only hast given me all. And before thee I have never been able to make audible the voice within my breast. Then thought I, when I should be far from thee I should more surely come to myself, because the manifold, indeed the thousand-fold tumult in me makes me dumb, and I cannot find a word for my true self.—And I remembered when we once spoke of the Monologues of Schleiermacher that pleased me not, thou wert of another opinion; and saidst 'if he had said only this single word, "Man shall bring out to the light what dwells in his inmost soul, that he may learn to know himself,"—Schleiermacher would have been eternally divine, and a first greatest spirit.'—Then thought I, when I should be far from thee, would I in letters reveal the entire depth of my nature; only for thee and me; and wholly in its undisturbed truth, even as I perhaps know it not yet; and if I will that thou lovest me, how should I begin other than with my innermost self? Else have I nothing———and from that hour I pursued myself as a spirit, which I would lure into the net for thy sake.

· · ·

From the Rhineland.

"I was a whole hour alone there, seeing the sails pass on the Rhine. I felt a deep longing to be with thee again; for beautiful as it is here, it is sad without echo in the living breast. Man is nothing but the desire to feel himself in another. Before I saw thee I knew nothing; I had often read and heard of friends, yet never knew what a life it would be; for what thought I then of men? Absolutely nothing. I took the watchdog out, that I might have society; but when I had been awhile with thee, and had heard so many things from thee, then looked I on each face as an enigma, and might well have divined many things, or perhaps *have* divined them, for I am really sharp-minded. Truly man does express his being, if the looker-on knows how to put things together,—and neither dissipates his thoughts, nor adds anything from his own fancy; but one is always blind when he seeks to please others, or seem somewhat before them. That have I remarked in myself. If one loves another, it is better to compose oneself, to understand the one beloved. If we wholly forget ourselves and look at him, I believe it is possible to divine the whole hidden man from his outward being. I have recognised this, for of other men I have not understood what they were to me. The most I cannot consider long, because I observe nothing which pleases me, or harmonizes with me; but with thee have I felt like a music, so at home was I at once. I was like a child, which still unborn, is removed form his father-land, sees the light in another, and must by some foreign bird be wafted back over a sea. He finds all new, yet nearest related, and most domestic. So was it always with me when I entered thy apartment. So was it on the old castle ruins yesterday; the smiling meadows, and the merry maidens singing there, the evening light, the passing sails and the butterflies, all was nothing to me, I longed only for thee! for thy little room, for the winter; for the snow without, and the early twilight, and the blazing fire; this sunshine and blooming and shouting tears my heart.—I was delighted when Tonie came up with the carriage, I looked down, and there was a beggar with his two pretty children; laughing and rolling over one another, holding each other close embraced. I said, what are your names? and they answered, Röschen and Bienchen; Röschen is fair, with round red cheeks. And Bienchen is a brunette, with black glancing eyes. They were truly one in two. Home at midnight; a most sweet sleep by the rushing of the Spring-fountains.

"Monday.—I have often re-read thy last letter, I am surprised when I compare it with others which I have received here at the same time,—then must I think that there are destinies in Spirit; as beings can be so remote from one another and so different, that they may meet every day, yet one will never conceive of the other, what he thinks and dreams, and what he feels in thinking and dreaming. Thy whole being with others is dreamy; I well know why; wert thou awake, thou couldst not live among them and be so indulgent; hadst thou been quite awake, they would certainly have driven thee away; the grimaces that they make would certainly have put thee to flight.—I saw the same in a dream myself when I was two years old; and sometimes the dream comes over me again

so that it seems that men are mere frightful larvæ by whom
I am surrounded and who will take from me my senses; even
as in the dream I shut my eyes, that I may not see and perish
with anguish. So thou from thy magnanimity dost shut thy
eyes in life; Thou wouldst not see how it is appointed with
men; Thou wouldst not have an aversion arise against these
who are not thy brothers, for the absurd is neither sister nor
brother. But thou wilt be their sister, so standest thou among
them with dreaming head, smiling in thy sleep, for thou
dreamest them all away as a flickering grotesque masquerade
dance. This read I again to-day in thy letter; for it is now so
still here, that one can think; thou art good to me, for among
all men thou holdest thyself most awake to me. As if shouldst
thou quite open thy eyes thou wouldst venture really to look
upon me. Oh I have often thought that I would never terrify
thy look,—lest thou shouldst indulgently shut thine eyes to
me also, and only peep sideways at me to avoid seeing all my
faults and vices.

"Thou sayest we will trifle together; dost thou know how
I interpret that? I remember what you lately wrote to
Clemens,—'ever new and living is the desire in me to express
my life in a permanent form; in a shape that may be worthy
to advance towards the most excellent, to greet them and
claim community with them. Yes, after this community have
I constantly longed. This is the church, towards which my
spirit constantly makes pilgrimages upon the earth.'—But
now thou sayest, we will trifle,—because thou wouldst remain untouched; because thou findest no community, and yet
thou believest that there is somewhere a height where the air
blows pure, and a longed for shower rains down upon the
soul, making it freer and stronger. But certainly this is not in
philosophy; I do not quote this from Boigt; my own feeling
bears witness to me. Healthful breathing men cannot so narrow themselves. Imagine to thyself a philosopher, living quite
alone on an island, where it should be beautiful as only spring
can be, where all was blooming, free, and living, birds singing,
and all the births of nature perfectly fair, but no creature there
to whom the Philosopher could interpret anything. Dost thou
believe that he would take such flights as those which I cannot
constrain with thee? I believe he would take a bite from a
beautiful apple, rather than make dry wooden scaffoldings for

his own edification from the high cedars of Lebanon. The Philosopher combines, and transposes, and considers, and writes the processes of thought, not to understand himself, that is not the object of this expense, but to let others know how high he has climbed. He does not wish to impart his wisdom to his low-stationed companions, but only the hocus-pocus of his superlatively excellent machine, the triangle which binds together all circles.—But it is only the idle man who has never realized his own being that is taken by this.

· · ·

" 'To know much, to learn much,' saidst thou, 'and then die young.' Why saidst thou that?——With each step in life meets thee some one who has somewhat to ask of thee,—how wilt thou satisfy them all? Say, wilt thou let one pass hungry from thee, who asks thee for alms? No, that wilt thou not! Therefore live with me. I have every day something to ask of thee. Ah! where should I go, if thou wert no more! Never again would I seek the path of happiness.—I would let myself go, and never ask after myself, for only for thy sake do I ask after myself, and I will do all which thou wishest.—Only for thy sake do I live, dost thou hear? I am afraid, for thou art great, I know it; and yet I will not speak to thee thus loudly,—no, thou art not. Thou art a soft child, and because it cannot endure pain, it denies it wholly. I know it, for so hast thou veiled many a loss.—But in thy neighborhood, in the atmosphere of thy spirit, the world seems to me great,—thou not, do not be afraid! But because all life is so pure in thee, each sign so simply received by thee, the spirit must find a place to dilate and become great. Forgive me to-day, but a mirror is before my eyes, and as if some one had withdrawn the veil from it, and I am so sad, I see nothing but clouds in the mirror, and winds are mourning, as if I must forever weep because I think on thee. This evening I was out beside the Maine; then rustled the sedges so wondrously, and because I in loneliness am ever with thee, I asked thee in my soul, 'what is that? does the sedge speak to thee?'—For I will confess it —I should not be willing to be spoken to so,—so mournful, so complaining, I wished to put it from me. Ah Günderode, I am so sad,—was not that cowardly in me that I wished to turn the lamentations of Nature from myself, and address them to thee, as if she talked with thee, when she so wofully moaned in the sedge? Yet I would willingly share all with thee. It is to me happiness, great happiness to take thy pains upon myself; I am strong, I am hard, I feel them not so easily. I can endure tears, and then Hope springs up again so quickly in me, as if all might return again, and better yet than what the soul desires.—Rely on me when it seizes thee, as if it would cast thee into the pit. I will accompany thee every where. No way is too gloomy for me; when thine eye cannot look at the light; it is so mournful.—I am willingly in darkness, dear Günderode. I am not alone there, I am full of new thoughts which will make Day in the soul. Precisely in the darkness rises up to me clear, glittering Peace. Oh despair not of me, though I went in my letters on lonely paths,—truly too much as if I sought myself only. Yet it was not so; I sought thee, I sought intimacy with thee, that I might drink with thee of the fountains of life which flow along our course. I feel it well in thy letter, that thou wilt withdraw from me. That will I not permit. I cannot lay down my pen,—I think thou must spring from the wall, all in armor like Minerva, and must swear to me, must swear to my friendship which is nothing but in thee; from that time forth thou wilt swim in the blue ether, walk with a lofty step like her, with thy crest in the sunlight like her, no more dwelling mournfully in the shadows. Adieu, I go to bed, and go from thee; although I could wait the whole night until thou shouldst show thyself, beautiful as thou art, and in peace, and breathing freedom as it becomes thy spirit, capable of the best and fairest.—Let there be one place of repose to thee in earth, on my breast. Good night, love me, if only a little.—"

To Günderode.

"But this one thing have I kept. God is Poesy. Man created in his image is also a born Poet, but also all are called and few chosen. That must I alas! experience in myself. Yet I too am a Poet, although I can make no rhyme. I feel it when I go into the open air, in the wood, or up on the hill, there lies a rhythmus in my soul according to which I am obliged to think and my mood gives it measure. And then when I am among men, I let myself be carried away by their vulgar street-ballad

measure or metrum, then feel I myself a pitiful person, and
know nothing more but mere stupid stuff. Dost thou not feel
also that stupid men can make one much stupider than one
naturally is? They are not altogether wrong to say I am stupid, but heart which understands me, come only—and I will
give thee a banquet that shall do thee honor. Listen yet a little
further. Every great action is a poem. Is transformation of the
personality into divinity. If an action is not a poem, it is not
great.—Yet great is all which is discerned with the light of
reason,—that is to say—all which thou canst seize in its true
sense, must be great; for certain is it, that every such thought
must have a root which is planted in the ground of wisdom,
and a flower which blooms in divine light. We must pass from
the ground of the soul into the image of God, over and up to
our origin.—Am I not in the right? And if it is true that man
can be such, why should it be otherwise? I understand it not.
All men are other than it would have been so easy to be. They
hang upon what they should not regard, and disdain that
which they should hold fast.—

"Oh I have a longing to be pure from these faults. To enter
the bath, and wash myself from all these corruptions. The
whole world seems to me crazy, and ever I play the fool with
them, and yet there is in me a voice which teaches me better.
Let us then found a religion, I and thou. And let us therein
for a while be both priest and layman, and live wholly in
silence, and live severely in it and develop its laws as a young
king's son is developed,—who sometime shall be the greatest
ruler of the whole world.—So must it be as if he were a Hero,
and through his will could reprove all frailties, and so embrace the whole world that it must grow better.—I believe
also that God has only let the races of kings exist, that they
might display manhood so high before the eyes, that it may
be seen on all sides.—The king has power over all; thus men
who see his public actions perceive how badly he acts, or if
he does anything good how great they themselves might be.
—Then if the king is so that he does all which no other can,
a genial ruler draws his people perforce, to a step whither
they never would have come without him.—We must mould
our religion entirely fit for such a young Ruler; oh wait only!
that has wholly turned me to the East. I shall soon understand
it all now. Ah! I pray thee take a little heart sympathy in it,

—that will animate me so! like God to think it all out of pure nothing. Then am I too a poet. I know the way how we can consider it all. We will walk together here, in Grandmama's garden up and down in these splendid summer days, or in the bosquet which has such dark avenues; we can seem to be only walking, and unfold it all in our conversation; then evenings will I write it all down, and send it into the city to thee by the Jew. And thou shalt put it into a poetic form; so that when men sometime find it, they will have the more reverence and faith in it; this is a fair jest,—yet take it not so; it is my earnest, for wherefore should we not think together over the weal and wants of humanity. Wherefore have we then so many things together already thought over, which others do not consider, but for the benefit of humanity? For every germ which sprouts up, from the earth, or from the spirit, may be expected to bring forth fruit in time,—and I know not why we should not expect a good harvest, which may profit humanity. Humanity, poor humanity! it is like a will-o'-the wisp caught in a net, quite dull and slimy.————Ah God! I shall sleep no more, good night, only I will say our religion must be called the *hovering religion*. That I will tell thee about to-morrow.—

"Yet one law in our religion must I propose for thy consideration, truly a first fundamental law. Namely, man shall always do a great action,—never another. And then I will come to thee and say that each action can and shall be a very greatest. Ah hear! I see already in spirit, when we go into the council what clouds of dust there will be!

" 'Who prays not cannot think.' I shall have that painted on an earthen spoon, with which our disciples shall eat their porridge. On other spoons we might have painted, 'who thinks not, learns not to pray.' The Jew is coming, I must make haste to put our world-revolution in his sack; and we sometime shall be able to say, what wonderful instruments God has chosen to accomplish his aims, like the old nun in Fritzler.—'

To Bettine.

"Best were it we should say thinking is praying; then something good would be expressed,—we should win time; thinking with praying, and praying with thinking.—Thou art mighty cunning, to think of making me rhyme thy unrhymed stuff.—Thy projects are ever uncommonly venturesome like a rope-dancer who feels sure that he can balance himself, or one who has wings and knows he can spread them out, if the hurricane should take him from the height.—For the rest I have understood thee well, notwithstanding the many sweet praises which thou scatterest like grass for the victim, that I am the victim which thou wouldst offer. I feel that thou hast the right,—and know that I am too timid, and cannot what I inly think right, outwardly defend against the reasonings of falsehood. I am mute and ashamed just where others should be ashamed; that goes so far in me that I beg people for forgiveness when they have injured me, for fear they should observe what they have done.—Truly I cannot endure that any one should believe I could distrust him, rather I smile like a child at all which meets me, I cannot endure that those whom I cannot convince of the better, should have the idea that I am better and wiser than they. If two understand one another, to that belongs the living action of a divine third.—Thus recognise I our relation, as a present from the Gods, in which they themselves play the most happy part; but my inner feelings, my inconsequent propositions to display to light, for that lends me neither the blue-eyed Minerva, nor Areus god of the combat, a support.*—I agree with thee it would be better, could I bear myself more manly, and laid not aside this powerful thought of the world, in intercourse with other men. But what wouldst thou have in one so timid, that she fears in the convent to say at table the blessing loud enough to be heard.—Let me alone, and bear with me as I am—if I have not the heart to raise my voice against all madness, yet at least I have never permitted any, the least wave of thy rushing life-blood to dash itself against that hard rock.—It stands dry and untouched by the holy inspirations, and thou canst untroubled let thy life flow thither.—I know thou art grieved that we did not visit Holderlin; before St. Clair went away yesterday he came to see me. Seeing thy thick letter, he was very desirous to hear something from it and the timid one was bold enough to read him the passage where Bettine

* To whom maidens offered up a ram, when they ran for a wager in public.

speaks of Œdipus.—He would copy it, he must copy it, else
had his soul passed; and the timid one was too cowardly to
refuse him. He said, 'I will read it to him; perhaps it will work
like balsam on his soul. If not, still it must be that the highest
excitement produced through his poetic nature should find an
echo in him. I must read it to him.' It will at least win from
him a smile. Now see me already again full of timidity, lest
my boldness displease thee. Yet if my ear did not deceive me,
that hymn on the dove-house was sung for the poor Poet,
that it might make an echo to his broken lute.

"I have now much society distress. This week the second
time must I creep into the black Canoness-robe, in which per-
secutes me my silly timidity. I seem to myself so strangely in
it, it is so unusual to me publicly to maintain a borrowed
dignity, that I must always hang my head and look away
when I am spoken to. Yesterday we dined in a body with the
Primate. I lost my Order-cross. It lay under the stool, I felt it
with the point of my foot, that made me much embarrassed;
and think only, the Primate himself picked it up, and begged
leave to fasten it on my shoulder. But Heaven be praised! our
duenna came up, and took the trouble on herself. I could not
sleep the whole night for this adventure,—it made me blush
to think of it. I went out to ride, and met Moritz in his cab-
riolet; then to the comedy in your box. George took me. The
play was the 'Brother and Sister.'—The house was very empty
on account of the heat. The Frau Rath sat quite alone at my
side. She called into the theatre 'Mr. Berdy, play well, I'm
here,' it made me quite confused. I thought if he answered, a
conversation might arise, in which perhaps I might be called
on to take part.—There were not fifty men in the pit; but
Berdy played extremely well; and the Frau Rath clapped at
each scene so as to make the house echo. Then Berdy would
make her profound bows.—It was very droll, the empty
house,—the boxdoors open on account of the heat, through
which the day shone in. Then came wind,—and played with
the tattered decorations. Then Madame Goethe called to
Berdy, 'ah what a superb wind,'—and fanned herself. It was
just as if she played too. And they seemed in the theatre as if
they were alone, in confidential domestic intercourse. I
thought of the great Poet, who disdained not so simply to
speak out his deep nature.—Yes thou mayst be right,—there

is something great in it. It was awing, even tragic, this void, this silence, the open doors,—the unique mother full of delight, as if her son had built her a throne on which she, far elevated above the dust of the earth, received the homage of Art.—They played admirably, indeed with inspiration, merely on account of the Frau Rath. She knows how to inspire respect.—At the end she called out, 'She was much obliged, and would write about it to her son.'—Then began a conversation, to which the public was very attentive; but which I did not hear because I was sent for."

This little sketch of Goethe's mother will remind the reader of the humorous letter, in which Bettine, writing to him, describes the meeting between this woman of lively simple genius, and her whose mind was "truly an ant-hill of thoughts" the French Corinne, Madame de Staël.

The two following letters passed between the friends while Bettine was at a watering-place, where she became acquainted with the Duke of Gotha. They were written at different times, but give an idea so distinct of the habits and tendencies of the two persons, that they seem to answer one another; therefore I have given them together.

Bettine to Günderode.

"Twice, three times between oaks and beeches and young light bushes, hill up, hill down—then comes one to a rock, —smooth shining basalt-surfaces, catching the sunbeams like a dark magical mirror, between are green moss-seats;—this morning went I thither; it is my usual walk when I am alone, not too long and yet secluded,—there saw I the mist like young down between the rock-clefts floating hither and thither, and above me was it ever more golden, the morning-shadows drew aside, the sun crowned me, it struck back sharply from the black stone, it burned very fiercely, yet oppressed not my forehead; I would willingly wear a crown, if it pressed no harder than the hot August sun, so sat I and sang to the rocks and listened for the echos, and thoughts of empire rose into my head. To govern the world according to the maxims which have been produced in the innermost work shop of my feelings and to drive out Philistines everywhere, such are the wishes that rise to my head in such a hot summer-morning, and to which Boigt's speech of the stars had now given a powerful excitement; he said each feeling, each conception becomes a capacity and a possession; it draws itself back indeed, but at a wholly unexpected hour, it comes forth again, and then I seated myself in a lonely place, and feigned such things out into the blue and came to nothing, except tameless heart-beatings as I thought that I might quiet the shrieking of the Philistines, who stifle by their formulas the voice of the spirit, merely by the government of my feelings; indeed this would be a heavenly compensation for those blows of the rod with which they blindly persecute all inspiration. Günderode I would thou wert a ruler and I thy Kobold; that would be my province and I know certainly that I should be discreet before the pure life-flame. But now, is it a wonder that one is stupid. Thus was I beneath the burning sun, sunk in meditation, chasing on a steed like the wind to all quarters of the globe, and as thy delegate of lofty inspiration set the world to rights commanding hither and thither, sometimes with a stamp of the foot or threatening word to make matters go on quick—meanwhile I had neglected to read thy dramalet which I took out with me, intending to study it really; but now the impetuous motions of my soul I felt compelled to soothe in sleep, as always I do when my temples burn thus from zeal about the future. O goblet of the soul, how artistic-rich and divinely gifted is thy rim made so that it may restrain the rushing floods of life, inevitably else should I have overflowed thee.—My friend, the spaniel, scented me out, he waked me with his barking and wanted me to play with him, he barked so loud that all the rocks groaned and echoed; it seemed as if a whole hunt were out; I must shout too for joy and gayety; he brought me my straw-hat which I had thrown down the steep rock with such graceful leaps—so is it when we wish through love to please any one, we do not measure the dangers of the pit, but trust in our own powers and succeed.—Ah Günderode, it would be much if man would trust his own Genius as this spaniel. He laid his paws on my shoulders when he had brought me back the hat without hurting it; in jest I named him Erodion, thinking he must even so have looked up to the Goddess Immortalita, for he was so noble and fair and bold; men look not easily out so simply great and undisturbed in their own

wise, as animals do. The Duke had followed the barking of
his dog, and now came forth from behind the trees; he asked
why I gave that name to the dog which he calls Cales, this he
said was the name of a charioteer slain before Troy by Di-
omed; I showed him thy poem to explain whence I took the
name Erodion. He sat down on the rock, and read it partly
aloud, making notes with a pencil; I send these to thee, he
has read it with self-collection, and thus truly with love. I
know not how often chance may favor thee so that thou
mayst touch the more delicate strings of the soul; thus will it
rejoice thee. He asked whether I understood the poem; I said
No! but I like to read it because thou art my friend who
educatest me. He said, 'A bud is this little work, carefully
guarded from each foreign influence which the great soul of
the friend embraces, and in this softly folded germ of a yet
undeveloped speech slumber giant powers. The inspiration to
recreate lifts up its wings within thee, full of presentiment,
and because the world is too unclean for such childlike pure
essays to express thy presentiments, so will it not unfold this
unpretending veil which embraces thy far reaching imagination and thy high philosophic spirit.' With surprise I received
the pleasure of this praise. He walked on with me, and as we
went would have me talk of thee, of our life together, of thy
character, of thy form; then have I for the first time reflected
how fair thou art; we saw a well-grown white silver-birch in
the distance, with its hanging boughs, which had grown up
out of a cleft in the midst of the rock, and, softly moved by
the wind, bent downwards toward the valley; to this I involuntarily pointed, as I spoke of thy spirit and thy form; the
Duke said, 'then is the friend like that birch?'—I said, 'yes,'
so would he go with me and look on thee nearer; the path
was so steep and slippery, I thought we could not go; but he
said Cales would find us out a way. 'What sort of hair has
she?'—'Glossy black-brown hair, which flows freely in loose
soft curls on her shoulders.'—'And her eyes?'—'Pallas-eyes,
blue in color, full of fire but also liquid and calm.'—'Her
forehead?'—'Soft and white as ivory, nobly arched and free,
small, yet broad like Plato's; eyelashes that smiling curl-
backward, brows like two black dragons that measuring one
another with sharp look, neither seizing nor leaving one another, proudly raise their crests, then fearfully smooth them

again. Thus watches each brow, defying yet timid, over the
soft glances of her eyes.'—'And the nose and cheek?'—'The
nose has been censured as a little proud and disdainful, but
that is because the nostril trembles with every feeling, hardly
taming the breath, as thoughts rise upwards from the lip,
which swells out fresh and powerful, guarded and gently restrained by the delicate upper lip.' Even the chin must I describe, truly I have not forgotten that Erodion had had his
seat there and left a little hollow, which the finger is pressed
into as poetry full of wisdom expands her spirit. Meanwhile
there stood the birch so gorgeous, so filled with gold, so whispered through, by the sun, by the breeze, so willing to bow
itself gently to the stream of the morning wind, waving its
green waves joyfully into the blue heaven, that I could not
decide, what lay between both, suits one, and not the other.
Cales found with many leaps the way to the birch; the Duke
followed; I remained behind; I could easily have followed, but
I would not in his presence. He cut letters in the bark quite
low down near to the foot and said he wished it might be
called the Friendship-birch, and that he also might be our
friend. I was willing. Ah let him; he will come this winter to
Frankfort, at first a prince forgets easily such a matter among
many other distractions, for he cannot believe it possible that,
if a man but gave himself entirely to one thing, through this
alone the penetration, the force of judgment, the all-sidedness
can arise, for which they are all hunting and fluttering about;
—besides he is sick and has few good days; for such an one
must we fill out from all healing fountains,—Adieu,—To-
morrow morning a great party is formed for a donkey excursion, and to-morrow before noon goes the good Electress
away, and very early, about three o'clock, the Englishmen
wish to climb the hill with us to see the sun rise; the others
did not wish to have Boigt, but I would have him, for else I
am weary, though the others say it makes them weary to have
him there. Early to-morrow comes the carrier-woman, I shall
send this letter by her, though it is not yet so alarmingly long
as my first, but thou art melancholy and I would fain amuse
thee a little, and I know the pretty story of the Duke will
make thee laugh, however thou mayest draw thy lips together.
Grant it may make thee pleasure also? I have copied his declaration of love from thy Immortalita, that from his own hand

belongs to thee; he wrote it for thee. Thou mayst put a value on it; I hear he is celebrated, of noble nature, witty, and on that account much feared by many; he is also very generous and kindly, but many would rather have nothing to do with him, fearing his best friendliness covers a secret satire. How foolish is that, about me might any one make merry as much as he would; it would be pleasant to me, if he enjoyed it.

Paper sent back to Günderode with the preceding letter.

• • •

IMMORTALITA

Dramatis personæ.
Immortalita, a goddess.
Erodion.
Charon.
Hecate.

FIRST SCENE.

A dark cavern at the entrance of the lower world. In the back-ground of this cavern are seen the Styx and Charon's bark passing hither and thither, in the fore-ground a black altar on which fire is burning. The trees and plants at the entrance of the cavern, and indeed all the decorations, and the figures of Hecate and Charon are flame-color and black, the shadows light grey, Immortalita white; Erodion dressed like a Roman youth. A great fiery snake, which has its tail in its mouth, forms a circle out of which Immortalita does not pass.

IMMORTALITA. (*awaking.*) Charon! Charon! Charon!
CHARON. (*stopping his boat.*) Why dost thou call me?
IMMORTALITA. When will the time come?
CHARON. Look at the snake at thy feet, so long as the circle is unbroken the spell lasts also, thou knowest it; then why dost thou ask me?
IMMORTALITA. Unkind old man, if it comforts me yet once again to hear the promise of a better future, why dost thou deny me a friendly word?
CHARON. We are in the land of silence.
IMMORTALITA. Prophesy to me yet once again,—
CHARON. I hate speech.

IMMORTALITA. Speak—speak.

CHARON. Ask Hecate. (*He rows away.*)

IMMORTALITA. (*strewing incense on the altar.*) Hecate, goddess of midnight, discoverer of the future which yet sleeps in the bosom of chaos, mysterious Hecate! Appear.

HECATE. Powerful exorcist,—why callest thou me from out the caves of eternal midnight; this shore is hateful to me; its gloom too full of light; it seems to me that gleams from the land of life have wandered hither.

IMMORTALITA. O Hecate, forgive, and hear my prayer.

HECATE. Pray not; thou art queen here, thou reignest, and knowest it not.

IMMORTALITA. I know it not; and wherefore do I not know it?

HECATE. Because thou canst not see thyself.

IMMORTALITA. Who will show me a mirror in which I may behold myself?

HECATE. Love.

IMMORTALITA. And wherefore Love?

HECATE. Because the infinity of that alone answers to thine.

IMMORTALITA. How far does my kingdom extend?

HECATE. Everywhere, if once beyond that barrier.

IMMORTALITA. How? shall the impenetrable wall that separates my province from the upper world ever fall asunder?

HECATE. It will fall asunder, thou wilt dwell in light, all shall find thee.

IMMORTALITA. O when shall this be?

HECATE. When believing Love tears thee away from night.

IMMORTALITA. When—in hours—or years?

HECATE. Count not by hours—with thee time is not. Look down; the snake winds about as if in pain, but vainly he fixes his teeth more firmly to keep close the imprisoning circle—vain is this resistance; the empire of unbelief, of barbarism, and night must fall to ruins. (*She vanishes.*)

IMMORTALITA. O future—wilt thou but resemble that blessed distant past when I dwelt with the gods in perpetual glory. I smiled on them all, and at my smile their looks lightened as never from the nectar, and Hebe thanked me for her youth, and the ever-blooming Aphrodite for her charms. But separated from me by the darkness of time, before my breath had lent them permanence, they fell from their thrones, those serene Gods, and went back into the elements of life. Jupiter into the power of the primæval heavens, Eros into the hearts of men, Minerva into the minds of the wise, the Muses into the songs of the poets, and I, most unhappy of all, was not permitted to bind the unfading laurel upon the brows of the hero, of the poet. Banished into this kingdom of night, a land of shadows, this gloomy other-side; I must live only for the future.

CHARON. (*passing in his boat with shades.*) Bow yourselves, Shades, this is the queen of Erebus, and that you still live after your earthly life is her work.

CHORUS OF SHADES.

Silent guides us the bark
To the unknown land,
Where the sun never dawns
On the always dark strand,—
Reluctantly we see it go,
No other sphere our looks would know
Than life's bright-colored land.

SAME SCENE.

(*Charon's bark lands. Erodion springs on shore. Immortalita still seen in the back-ground.*)

ERODION. Back, Charon, from this shore, which no shade may tread. Why lookest thou upon me? I am not a shadow like you; a joyful hope, a faith full of visions have kindled the spark of my life to flame.

CHARON. (*aside.*) Surely this must be the youth who bears in himself the golden future. (*He rows away.*)

IMMORTALITA. Yes, thou art he, prophesied to me by Hecate; through thy look will the light of day break into these ancient caverns, and dispel the night.

ERODION. If I am he prophesied to thee, Maiden or Goddess, however thou art named, believe thou fulfillest to me the inmost presentiment of the heart.

IMMORTALITA. Say, who art thou?—what is thy name, and how didst thou find the way to this pathless shore, where neither shades nor men dare wander, but only subterranean Gods.

ERODION. I am unwilling to speak to thee of anything but my love;

indeed to speak of my love is to speak of my life. Then hear me. I am the son of Eros and Aphrodite; the double-union of love and beauty has implanted in my being an idea of bliss which I nowhere find, yet must everywhere foresee and seek. Long was I a stranger upon earth. I could not enjoy its unsubstantial goods, till at last came into my soul a dim presentiment of thee. Everywhere was I accompanied by the Idea reflected from thee, everywhere I followed the trace of the beloved, even when it plunged me down into the realm of dreams, thus guiding me to the gates of the lower world, but never could I press through to thee, an unhappy fate drew me ever back to the upper world.

IMMORTALITA. How, youth, hast thou so loved me that rather than not find me thou wouldst have forsaken Helios and the rosy dawn?

ERODION. So have I loved thee, and without thee the earth no more could give me joy, neither the flowery spring, the sunny day, nor dewy night, which to possess, the gloomy Pluto would willingly resign his sceptre. But as the love of my parents was beyond all other, for they were love itself, so the desire which has drawn me to thee was most powerful, and my faith in finding thee victorious over all obstacles, for my parents knew that the child of love and beauty could find nothing higher than itself, and gave me this faith in thee that my powers might not be exhausted by striving after somewhat higher out of myself.

IMMORTALITA. But how camest thou to me at last? Unwillingly does Charon receive the living into the brittle bark made only for the shades.

ERODION. Once was my longing to see thee so great, that all men have invented to surround thee with uncertainty, seemed to me little and vain. Courage inspired my whole being; my only wish is for her, thought I, and boldly cast from me all the goods of this earth, and steered my bark hitherward to the perilous rock where everything earthly is wrecked. A moment I thought, what if thou shouldst lose all, and find nothing; but high confidence pressed doubt aside, joyously I said to the upper world a last farewell, night embraced me,—a ghastly pause,—and I found myself with thee. The torch of my life still burns the other side of the Stygian water.

IMMORTALITA. The heroes of the former world have already tried this same path, courage enabled them to pass the river, but to love only is it given to found here a permanent empire. The dwellers here say my breath bestows immortal life, then be thou immortal, for thou hast worked in me an inexpressible change; before I lived a mummy life, but thou hast breathed into me a soul. Yes, dear youth, in thy love I behold myself transfigured, I know now who I am, know that the sunny day must fill with light these ancient caverns.

(HECATE *comes from behind the altar.*)

HECATE. Erodion, enter into the snake circle. (*He does so, and the snake vanishes.*) Too long, Immortalita, wert thou in the night of unbelief and barbarism, known by the few, despaired of by the many, confined by a spell within this narrow circle. An oracle, as old as the world, says "believing love will find thee even in the darkness of Erebus, draw thee forth, and found thy throne in everlasting glory, accessible to all." The time is come, but to thee, Erodion, remains yet somewhat to be done.

(*The scene changes into a part of the Elysian garden, faintly illuminated, shadows are seen gliding hither and thither, on one side a rock, in the back-ground the Styx and Charon's bark.*)

HECATE. See, Erodion, this threatening rock is the impassable wall of separation, which divides the realm of mortal life from that of thy mistress; it intercepts from this place the sunbeams, and prevents severed loves from meeting again. Erodion, try to throw down the rock, that thy beloved may ascend on the ruins from the narrow dominion of the lower world, that in future no impassable barrier may separate the land of the dead from that of the living.

(ERODION *strikes the rock, it falls, full daylight shines in.*)

IMMORTALITA. Triumph! the rock is sunken, and from this time it shall be permitted the thoughts of love, the dreams of hope, the inspiration of the poet to descend hither and to return.

HECATE. All hail! Threefold, immortal life will fill the pale realm of shades now thy empire is founded.

IMMORTALITA. Come, Erodion, ascend with me into eternal light, and all love, all nobleness shall share my empire. Thou, Charon, smooth thy brow, be friendly guide to those who would enter my kingdom.

ERODION. Well for me that I faithfully tended as a vestal fire the holy presentiment of my heart; well for me, that I had courage to die to mortality, to live for immortality, to offer up the visible to the invisible.

•   •   •

The following note was written by the hand of the Duke Emil August von Gotha upon the manuscript of Immortalita.

"It is a little thing not worthy thy attention, that I esteem it a gift from heaven to understand thee, thou noble life. Looking down upon the earth, thou mayst, like the sun, give it a fair day; but thou wouldst look in vain for thy peer beneath the stars.

"Like fresh flower-stalks comes the careless life of thy thoughts before the subdued man; his bosom heaves with deep breathings as thy spirit plays round him like loose tresses, just escaped from the band.

"He gazes on thee, a lover! like still roses, and waving lilies hover before him thy thoughts bearing blessings on their glances. Confidential, near the heart are they. They illuminate and beautify his aims and his vocation, and on the silent paths of night are the stars looking from on high, the witnesses of his vow to thee.

"Yet is it a little thing only, not worthy thy attention, that I esteem it as a gift from heaven to understand thee, thou noble life."

The letter of Günderode to Bettine introduces livelier images, and though we may suppose it to exaggerate in playful malice the picture of Bettine's environment, corresponds with what we should imagine to be her habits.

To Bettine.

"It seems to me sometimes quite too absurd, dear Bettine, that thou shouldst with such solemnity declare thyself my scholar when I might as well hold myself thine, yet it gives me much pleasure, and there is also a truth in it if the teacher feels himself stimulated by the scholar; thus may I with some reason call myself thine. Many new insights are brought me by thy opinions and by thy divinations in which I confide, and since thou art so loving as to name thyself my scholar, I may sometime marvel to see over what a bird I have been brooding.

"Thy story of Vostel is quite pleasant; nothing dost thou love better than to take the sins of the world upon thyself— to thee they are no burden, they give thee wings rather for gayety and whim; we may think God himself takes pleasure with thee. But thou wilt never be able to make men esteem thee something better than themselves. Yet however genius makes to itself air and light, it is always ethereal-wise, even when it bears on its pinions all the load of Philisterei. In such matters thou art a born genius, and in these can I only be thy scholar, toiling after thee with diligence. It is an amusing play in the circle that while others complain of thy so called inconsequences I secretly lament that my genius does not lead to such "Careless away over the plains where thou seest no path dug before thee by the boldest pioneers." Yet always do only one thing at a time, do not begin so many all confusedly. In thy chamber it looked like the shore where a fleet lies wrecked. Schlosser wanted two great folios that he lent you now three months ago from the city library and which you have never read. Homer lay open on the ground, and thy canary-bird had not spared it. Thy fairly designed map of the voyages of Odysseus lay near, as well as the shell box with all the Sepia saucers and shells of colors; they have made a brown spot on thy pretty straw carpet, but I have tried to put all once more into order. Thy flageolet which thou couldst not find to take with thee; guess where I found it; in the orange tree box on the balcony; it was buried in the earth up to the mouth-piece; probably thou hast desired on thy return to find a tree of flageolets sprouting up. Liesbet has bountifully watered the tree and the instrument has been all drenched. I have laid it in a cool place that it may dry gradually and not burst, but what to do with the music that lay near by I cannot tell; I put it in the sun, but before human eyes canst thou never show it again. The blue ribbon of thy guitar has been fluttering out of the window to the great delight of the school children opposite ever since thy departure. I chid Liesbet a little for not having shut the window;

she excused herself because it was hid by the green silk curtain, yet whenever the door is open there is a draught. The sedge upon the glass is still green. I have given it fresh water. In thy box where are sowed oats and I know not what else, all has grown up together; I think there are many weeds, but, as I cannot be sure, I have not ventured to pull any thing up. Of books I have found on the floor Ossian,—Sacontala,—the Frankfort Chronicle, the second volume of Hemsterhuis which I took home with me because I have the first already: in Hemsterhuis lay the accompanying philosophical essay, which I pray thee present to me, unless thou hast some special value for it; I have more of the same sort from thee and as thy dislike to philosophy makes thee esteem them so lightly I should like to keep together these studies against thy will, perhaps in time they will become interesting to thee. Siegwart, a romance of the olden day, I found on the harpsichord with the inkstand lying on it; luckily there was little ink, yet wilt thou find thy moonlight composition, over which it has flowed, not easy to decipher. I heard something rattle in a little box in the window sill and had the curiosity to open it, then flew out two butterflies which thou hast put in as chrysalises. Liesbet and I chased them into the balcony where they satisfied their first hunger in the bean blossoms. From under the bed Liesbet swept out Charles the Twelfth, the Bible, and also a glove which belongs not to the hand of a lady, in which was a French poem; this glove seems to have lain under thy pillow; I did not know thou hadst ever busied thyself with writing French poems in the old style. The perfume of the glove is very pleasant and reminds me of something which gives me a notion where its fellow may be, yet be easy about thy treasure, I have fastened it up behind Kranach's Lucretia, and there at thy return it may be found. I saw two letters among many written papers, the seals were unbroken, one was from young Lichtenberg of Darmstadt, the other from Vienna. What acquaintances hast thou there, and how is it possible that one who so seldom receives letters should not be more curious or rather so heedless about them? I left them on thy table. All is now in tolerable order so that thou mayst diligently and comfortably continue thy studies.

"I have with true pleasure described to thee thy chamber,

for it, like an optic mirror, expresses thy apart manner of being, and gives the range of thy whole character; thou has brought together various and strange materials to kindle the sacrificial flame; it is burning; whether the Gods are edified thereby is to me unknown.

"If thou findest Muse, write soon again.—Caroline."

A feeling of faithlessness, almost of remorse, comes over me, on rereading the few extracts for which room could be found here. Surely in their own place these field flowers were beautiful; the dullest observer was pleased to see them enamel the green earth. But here, torn asunder from their proper home, they look as soiled and forlorn as might a bunch of cowslips, dropped by chance in the public street beneath the feet of busy men. Half the purpose of placing them here was to draw attention to the translation of these volumes soon to be published, and now it seems as if the delicate music of the fairy bells cannot possibly make itself heard beside the din of the forge or factory; yet courage! for they tell us it is a property of the simplest tone to cleave straight through a world of mere *noise*.

The acceptance that a book, of the same delicate beauty, and somewhat the same scope met among us, is an encouraging fact. I refer to "Pericles and Aspasia." There, in artistic form, the author has presented what, in these letters, lives and grows before us. Here we find a little circle of intimacies, noble enough to excite and gratify the high desires of heart and mind. Each relation is peculiar, each harmonious with all the rest. The statesman, the philosopher, the enchanting woman of the world, the lay nun, the profuse and petulant nature, for which we know no better name than Alcibiades, all are shown, on the private as well as the public side, with admirable force and distinctness. None could read this book without feeling love, friendship, and the daily business of life to be ennobled and enriched at least for that day. None could fail to feel the eternal leadings of every true relation. Yet, withal, Landor's book is marble-cold compared with the one before us. Those divinely human figures convey to us life as it ought to be, as it might be, but only in statuesque representation. Yet, if cold, it is pure, and earth may cover, but cannot consume the sculptures, as it does the living forms. We are deeply indebted to the book which presents this portraiture of a home, a home in mutually enchained hearts, too wise to expect perfection, too noble to pardon imperfection, worthy to demand the best and—to wait for it. Here are intimacies so rooted in the characters of the parties, that they may endure and deepen through ages. We feel that this book, with all its singular beauty of detail, presents to us but a beginning. How happily is reverence tempered by playfulness, conscious worth by tenderness and knowledge. Yes! all who read this book must be, at least for the day, shamed out of frivolous and vulgar intercourse, intellectual sloth, or distempered care.

The intimacy between Aspasia and Cleone is not unlike this between Bettine and Günderode, in the influences of the two characters upon one another. The two women are both in different ways as remarkable in intellect, as in character, and the intellect of both is feminine in its modification. They study no less than love one another; they cannot flatter, neither make weak exactions; the sentiment is too true to allow of sentimentality. It is founded on no illusion, but a parallelism of lives that was written in the stars.

Without full confidence no friendship can subsist, none without generosity, without unwearied sympathy, and the modesty that permits, when suffering, to receive this balm. But also none can subsist and grow, without mutual stimulus, without an infinite promise, a stern demand of excellence from either side, and revelations of thoughts, not only hoarded from the past, but constantly new-born from intercourse between the two natures. There must be faith in one another, action upon one another, love, patiently to wait for one another.

All these we find in these two friendships. Bettine feels in her friend the same joy and pride which is expressed of Aspasia, where Alcibiades tells us she was accustomed to fly to Pericles with the letters of Cleone, and read them on his shoulder. Cleone regards Aspasia with the same admiration, angelic in its pure humility, though melancholy in its smile, as Günderode does Bettine.

The book of "Günderode" is more poetic than "Pericles and Aspasia," in this, that we see living and changing before us what is only given us as results, of fixed outline, in Landor's book. This breathing life makes us living; that pictured life only commanded us to live.

A few words more in answer to the queries of a friend. Bettine is accused of interpolating passages into these letters from a more advanced period of her existence, and there certainly are pages which look like it. The past seems the canvass on which she paints. The fears of those who loved her best, that the exuberant, but unstable nature could not economize sufficiently to live princely in its later days, are justified by her devotion to the past.

"Bettine!

> *In this fair book from thy letters compiled*
> *Shall the woman be made thus to wait on the child?*
> *Not so the oak gathers his first summer's leaves,*
> *But new strength every year with new branches receives."*

We learn by excess, we thrive on error, but only where reactions and convictions come in their due alternation. The way God leads man is the only way, but man must learn to understand that it is so.— What seems to the youthful aspirant so true as the path Bettine took? Straight forward pursuing her own genius, headlong down precipices, indefatigable up hill, and through bog, in the most important step as the least whimsy, she acted out her nature, would recognise no compromise, knew no society, only the natures "that stood opposite to her" could she see. Here then is one wise, here is one free! Alas no! Heaven has not permitted such manacles to be forged for man without a cause, and the bold outlaw blackens and blasphemes, while the willing prisoner soars and sings.

If any quarrel with the law that "care is taken that the trees grow not up into the heavens," let him watch the progress of such a character as Bettine's, and see the tree which defied the law mar its own growth. Sorrow must alternate with joy, or the character is shallow; patient toil with inspiration, or there is no noble growth; the most ardent imagination must demand and elicit the severest judgment. In the mind of the Child was no patience, no power of adaptation, nothing that fitted her to reach maturity and uphold or reconstruct a world. She must always be a child; the actual world intervened and she became a Phantast. Yet not the less welcome this radiant picture of a peculiar state, that period of keen perception and intuitive glances, which so many know only in some holy dream, or beneath the first illusions of earthly love. Here is the picture of all-promising, all-discerning youth; let some other life join to this a fitting sequel.

Whoever has closely observed the dramatic tendency in man will see that its first demonstrations must be in the way of what the many call falsehood, if only for this reason, that the poetic eye cannot even *see* a fact bare and solitary as it appears to the prose observer. To such a mind the actual only exists as representing the ideal, and each object seen by the bodily eye becomes the centre to a throng of visionary shapes. Even as in the pictures of Magdalens and Madonnas, cherub faces start from every side, created as it were by the expression of the face which occupies the centre, so each new object beheld, each new thought apprehended, brings to the poetic mind accessories natural if not yet realized by nature.

It is from this cause that children, fitted by imagination to appreciate the noblest exhibitions of truth, are often blamed as false or inaccurate, while those of meagre faculties and limited vision are praised for their correctness. Yet, paradoxical as it may seem to the superficial, there is often more hope of truth in the liar than in the truthteller, for the former may learn to prune his fancy and turn romance into its legitimate channels, but the latter will have to feed and train his powers by ways and means yet unknown, before he can comprehend truth in its fulness.

The romantic or dramatic tendency, which leads those who do not absolutely recreate in play or novel, to embellish a narrative of their daily walk, by giving the facts higher coloring, embellishing them by the invention of incidents, rounding and filling out where there were pauses or languors, and casting over all the soft ideal light of the thought derived by the narrator from the passage, which is obvious in many parts of these letters, and makes them poetical still more than historical, may also have induced Bettine to interpolate sentences or even paragraphs. If she has done so, it is not from motives of vanity, but from a poetical growth in herself, since the period of the correspondence, which makes what really happened seem an inadequate expression of what really was. Whatever has been added is in such harmony with the scenes and personages, that you are only led to doubt, because it is too good, because all is said and done with a fulness, which is elsewhere discovered only in that liberty of law which art grants to her votaries.

It is in reference to this that Goethe said with one of his calm ironical smiles, when Richter (I think it was Richter) published his memoirs as "Truth out of my Life," intending to reprove Goethe for his title "Poesy and Truth out of my Life"—"As if the bare truth from the life of such a man could be other than that he was a Philistine."

There comes indeed a time when Poesy and Truth, though twin-born in the thought, can be separate in the expression, and the groundwork, no longer all shot through and interwoven by the bright threads of imagination, appears in clear relief beneath the beautiful patterns emblazoned upon it. But this is in the perfection of the faculties, when reason, imagination, and the perceptive organs are in entire harmony, when the meaning of the great world-poem is so distinctly seen, that details are never unmeaning, because incomplete, nor do we need perpetually to evolve fabrics of art as from a chaos. It is the highest attainment of man to be able to tell the truth, and more hardly achieved by the chronicler than the Phantast.

This much may be granted to the caviller. Bettine has missed her way to this excellence from undue indulgence of one or two powers.

But all the drawbacks are upon her own character; her book is true, and of the rarest excellence, a many-petalled flower on the bosom of nature, from which the dew shall never vanish. Like the flights often seen on a smaller scale in common lives, it attains a perfection which the complete sum of the character entirely misses. Like the sky lark's, these morning songs drop from the clouds which upbear the songster dew from heaven, such as active, lustrous, enduring, prying day shall never boast.

Let us conclude by the last letter addressed to Bettine by Günderode, while meditating her voluntary death. On this subject I have said nothing; it involves too much for the space to let me venture. This letter has the true tone of Günderode's genius, and is no less worthy of attention for the distinct idea it gives of the friend she loved, but not well enough to love to live for her sake.

To Bettine.

"I was obliged to set out on my journey without writing to thee, for my sister who has long been unwell required my presence. Think not I neglect thee, dear Bettine, but the impossibilities of realizing the objects of my thoughts, crowd upon me; I know not how to overcome them, but must let myself be driven where chance wills; resistance brings only loss of time and no success. Thou hast a much more energetic nature than I, indeed than almost any of whom I am able to judge; to me are set, not only through my relations, but also through my character, narrower limits for my activity, therefore it may well happen that things to me impossible may not be so to thee. Bear this in mind while looking into the future. If thou wilt persist to walk the same path of life with me, mightst thou not be obliged to sacrifice to my timidity or rather to my incapacity what thy spirit requires, for I see not how I could follow thee, my wings are not full-grown for such a flight. I pray thee, fix thy eyes betimes on this fact, and think of me as of a being who must leave many things untried to which thou wilt feel thyself impelled. Even if thou shouldst resolve to give up many of thy claims on life, or let me rather say if thou wouldst refuse to let the element which is active within thee work itself clear, rather than thus be divorced from me, thy refusal would be vain. There are laws in the soul which must manifest themselves, else the whole man is ruined; this cannot happen to thee, the life must again and again rise up, for in thee dwells the right of conquest, and that which would perchance only sing me to sleep wakes thee to impetuous freewill existence; for when thou wouldst converse with the stars of heaven and boldly constrain them to answer, I would give myself up rather to their soft shining as the child is soothed by the motion of his cradle. All men are against thee, the whole world wilt thou feel and experience only through the contradiction in thy soul, there is no other possible way for thee to comprehend it. Where wilt thou ever find an action, how much less a nature in harmony with thine, it has never yet been so and will also never be (of myself will I speak to thee by and by). What experience has taught to others, that to which they accommodate themselves, is to thee folly and falsehood.—The actual world has presented itself to thee as a deformed monster, but it did not terrify thee; thou hast at once set thy foot upon it, and although it whirls beneath thee and forever moves itself, thou lettest thyself be borne by it, without ever in thought dreaming the possibility that thou couldst for a moment be at one with it. I speak of to-day, and more yet of the future, I would wish there might come moments into thy life when this flowing together with the energies of other natures might be granted thee. Dost thou remember thy dream in the mountain castle which thou relatedst to me in the night when I waked thee, because thou wert weeping bitterly in thy sleep? It was that a man, who for the good of mankind had done I know not what heroic deed, was brought to the scaffold in consequence of his great deed. The people shouted in its ignorant joy, but in thee rose great desire to ascend to him there on the scaffold, only the blow fell just as thou wert hoping to reach him. Thou canst not have forgotten the dream, for thy painful weeping moved me too, so much that I hardly dared remind thee it was only a dream, and then found this was the very reason of thy being inconsolable, for thou saidst not even in a dream was it granted thee to fulfil the desire of thy soul, how much less would it be so in reality. Then in the night have I jested that I might comfort thee a little, but to-day I feel impelled once more to take up the question whether it was not a misfortune not to have died in the dream with that hero; yes it was a misfortune, for the awaking, the living on after so endured proof of thy inmost dispositions, which can so seldom in actual life be verified and confirmed, must be to thee a triumph, aye a happiness, even though only in a dream, for in dreams the noblest convictions may meet shipwreck as elsewhere. And I agree with thee that it was a trick played by thy demon, yet one with a meaning of wisdom; for, if thou hadst been satisfied in the dream so perhaps had also been satisfied thy longing for great deeds, and what would that have availed thee? would it not have increased that careless self-reliance to which Savigny must positively give the name of arrogance; no, that would not have been, yet would there not have been that exaltation which is now continually renewed by the lightest excitement of that unsatisfied longing.

"I would wish for thee, Bettine (to speak between ourselves, for this may no man hear) that those deeply implanted dispositions might be called forth by destiny, and no trial omitted which either in dream or life might aid gloriously to solve the problem why it has been worth the pain and trouble to have lived. Plans are easily baffled, therefore must we make none. The best way is to find oneself ready for all which offers itself as worthiest to do, and that alone which obliges us to act, the holy principle which springs up of itself on the ground of our conviction, never to violate, but ever to unfold it more and more through our thoughts and actions, so that we at last recognise nothing in ourselves, but the originally divine. There are many who have taken with them great Christmas presents from the Gods, and yet never learn to make use of any of them, to these it suffices to believe themselves raised above the ground of the community, merely because the alphabet of a higher law is stamped within them, yet the spirit has never risen up within them, and they know not how far they are from having realized that nobility of soul, of which they are so proud.—This seems to me the noblest school of

life, constantly to take heed that nothing belies those principles through which our inner being is consecrated, never in
thought nor in deed. From this school the noble man is not
released to the last breath of his life. Thy Ephraim will agree
with me, and is himself a proof of this; I believe also that it
is the highest distinction of destiny to be called to always
severer trials. And one must indeed be able to prophesy the
destiny of a noble man from his dispositions. Thou hast energy and courage enough for severe truth, and at the same
time art the most gladsome nature which hardly can perceive
any injustice that is done towards it. To thee is it a light thing
to bear what others could not at all endure, and yet thou art
not compassionate, it is energy which leads thee to assist others. If I wished briefly to express thy character I would prophesy that hadst thou been a boy, thou wouldst have become a
hero, but as thou art a girl I interpret all these dispositions as
furnishing materials for a future life, preparation for an energetic character which perhaps in a living active time will be
born.—As the sea, so the ages seem to me to have their ebb
and flow. We are now in the time of ebb, where it is indifferent who makes himself valid, because it is not now the hour
for the waves to rise up; the human race sinks its breath, and
whatever of significant occurs in history is only prelude, to
awaken feelings, to practise and collect the faculties to seize
upon a higher potency of spirit. Spirit rules and raises the
world, through this alone life is living, through this alone moment is joined to moment, all else is fleeting shadow, each
man who makes true a moment in time is a great man, and
however forcible are many apparitions in time, I cannot
reckon them among realities because no deep recognition, no
pure will of the absolute spirit bids them rise and rule, but
wholly vulgar motives of passion. Napoleon is an example.
—Yet are such not without use for the human capacities of
the spirit. Partialities and prejudices must be satiated, even let
me say sated, before they can leave free the spirit of the time.
Now what prejudices may not this hero of all have shaken to
pieces,—what will he not satiate even to disgust, how many
will the future time root up with detestation, to which it now
clings with passionate, blind devotion.—Or can it be possible
that after such terrible ghostly destinies, time should not be
given to reflect.—I doubt not of this, all things find their end,

and only that lives which is able to awake life, of this I have said to thee enough, thou wilt understand me. Why should not each one begin his career of life with solemnity and consecration, regarding himself as a development of the divine which is the aim of us all, seeking where and how it may be furthered. Indeed I have now said to thee enough to bring close to thee the thought that the higher powers of the spirit of man must be the only real aim of thy inner contemplation, so that all may be to thee for one purpose, however far thy faculties may be brought into action. Nothing can remain untried in man which his higher ideal nature is capable of producing. For our destiny is the Mother which bears beneath its heart this fruit of the ideal.—Take from these lines all that bears upon the heaped up leaves thou hast sent me, and soothe therewith thy anxiety on my account. Farewell and take my thanks for all thy love."

> *Such Beauty is not given, only lent,*
> *Darts winged by love divine, the speedier spent,*
> *Frail effigies of that most seen Unseen,*
> *What is and must be, yet hath never been;—*
> *O teach the ear to catch that under-tone,*
> *Which draws the heart to know the Unknown, Alone!*
> *I see thee passing, once incarnate Soul,*
> *From sphere to sphere seeking that only goal,*
> *Where thought and love and life together flow,*
> *And the Above smiles back from the Below.*
> *This earthly life to thee was but as glass,*
> *Seeing beyond thy thoughts and wishes pass,*
> *Thou couldst not stay behind to water flowers,*
> *Upon the pathway of these puny Hours*
> *With tears undue.—O solitary flame*
> *We will not stir thee by a human blame,*
> *Ask mercy from the heaven thou teachest us to name.*
>
>   F.

SUMMER ON
THE LAKES

During the summer of 1843, Margaret Fuller journeyed west with her friends James Freeman Clarke and his sister Sarah, who appear, respectively, as J. and S. in chapter 2 of Summer on the Lakes. *Based on the journal that Fuller kept during the four months she spent in Illinois, Wisconsin, and Michigan,* Summer on the Lakes *illustrates her increasing concern with nineteenth-century America's system of gender relations and its impact upon women. Indeed, it is this concern that stitches together the seemingly unrelated journal entries, dialogues, letters, and historical sketches that comprise the volume. Before leaving for the West, Fuller had sent her final contribution to the* Dial. *Entitled "The Great Lawsuit: Man versus Men. Woman versus Women," the essay called for the removal of the obstacles to female participation in the nation's social and political life. More and more, she had come to recognize that these obstacles made it virtually impossible for women to practice the self-reliance that Fuller the Transcendentalist celebrated. Shortly after* Summer on the Lakes *was published in June of 1844, she proudly told her friend William Henry Channing that "there are complimentary notices in the papers and I receive good letters about it." In her letter to Channing, Fuller also claimed identification with Mariana, one of the most arresting characters in* Summer on the Lakes.*

SUMMER ON THE LAKES

Summer days of busy leisure,
Long summer days of dear-bought pleasure,
You have done your teaching well;
Had the scholar means to tell
How grew the vine of bitter-sweet,
What made the path for truant feet,
Winter nights would quickly pass,
Gazing on the magic glass
O'er which the new-world shadows pass;
But, in fault of wizard spell,
Moderns their tale can only tell
In dull words, with a poor reed
Breaking at each time of need.
But those to whom a hint suffices
Mottoes find for all devices,
See the knights behind their shields,
Through dried grasses, blooming fields.

TO A FRIEND

Some dried grass-tufts from the wide flowery plain,
A muscle shell from the lone fairy shore,
Some antlers from tall woods which never more
To the wild deer a safe retreat can yield,
An' eagle's feather which adorned a Brave,
Well-nigh the last of his despairing band,
For such slight gifts wilt thou extend thy hand
When weary hours a brief refreshment crave?
I give you what I can, not what I would,
If my small drinking-cup would hold a flood,
As Scandinavia sung those must contain
With which the giants gods may entertain;
In our dwarf day we drain few drops, and soon must thirst again.

CHAPTER I

Since you are to share with me such foot-notes as may be made on the pages of my life during this summer's wanderings, I should not be quite silent as to this magnificent prologue to the, as yet, unknown drama. Yet I, like others, have little to say where the spectacle is, for once, great enough to fill the whole life, and supersede thought, giving us only its own presence. "It is good to be here," is the best as the simplest expression that occurs to the mind.

We have been here eight days, and I am quite willing to go away. So great a sight soon satisfies, making us content with itself, and with what is less than itself. Our desires, once realized, haunt us again less readily. Having "lived one day" we would depart, and become worthy to live another.

We have not been fortunate in weather, for there cannot be too much, or too warm sunlight for this scene, and the skies have been lowering, with cold, unkind winds. My nerves, too much braced up by such an atmosphere, do not well bear the continual stress of sight and sound. For here there is no escape from the weight of a perpetual creation; all other forms and motions come and go, the tide rises and recedes, the wind, at its mightiest, moves in gales and gusts, but here is really an incessant, an indefatigable motion. Awake or asleep, there is no escape, still this rushing round you and through you. It is in this way I have most felt the grandeur—somewhat eternal, if not infinite.

At times a secondary music rises; the cataract seems to seize its own rhythm and sing it over again, so that the ear and soul are roused by a double vibration. This is some effect of the wind, causing echoes to the thundering anthem. It is very sublime, giving the effect of a spiritual repetition through all the spheres.

When I first came I felt nothing but a quiet satisfaction. I found that drawings, the panorama, &c. had given me a clear notion of the position and proportions of all objects here; I knew where to look for everything, and everything looked as I thought it would.

Long ago, I was looking from a hill-side with a friend at one of the finest sunsets that ever enriched this world. A little cow-boy, trudging along, wondered what we could be gazing at. After spying about some time, he found it could only be the sunset, and looking, too, a moment, he said approvingly "that sun looks well enough;" a speech worthy of Shakespeare's Cloten, or the infant Mercury, up to everything from the cradle, as you please to take it.

Even such a familiarity, worthy of Jonathan, our national hero, in a prince's palace, or "stumping" as he boasts to have done, "up the Vatican stairs, into the Pope's presence, in my old boots," I felt here; it looks really *well enough*, I felt, and was inclined, as you suggested, to give my approbation as to the one object in the world that would not disappoint.

But all great expression, which, on a superficial survey, seems so easy as well as so simple, furnishes, after a while, to the faithful observer its own standard by which to appreciate it. Daily these proportions widened and towered more and more upon my sight, and I got, at last, a proper foreground for these sublime distances. Before coming away, I think I really saw the full wonder of the scene. After awhile it so drew me into itself as to inspire an undefined dread, such as I never knew before, such as may be felt when death is about to usher us into a new existence. The perpetual trampling of the waters seized my senses. I felt that no other sound, however near, could be heard, and would start and look behind me for a foe. I realized the identity of that mood of nature in which these waters were poured down with such absorbing force, with that in which the Indian was shaped on the same soil. For continually upon my mind came, unsought and unwelcome, images, such as never haunted it before, of naked savages stealing behind me with uplifted tomahawks; again and again this illusion recurred, and even after I had thought it over, and tried to shake it off, I could not help starting and looking behind me.

As picture, the Falls can only be seen from the British side. There they are seen in their veils, and at sufficient distance to appreciate the magical effects of these, and the light and shade. From the boat, as you cross, the effects and contrasts are more melodramatic. On the road back from the whirlpool, we saw them as a reduced picture with delight. But what I liked best was to sit on Table Rock, close to the great fall. There all power of observing details, all separate consciousness, was quite lost.

Once, just as I had seated myself there, a man came to take his first look. He walked close up to the fall, and, after looking at it a moment, with an air as if thinking how he could best appropriate it to his own use, he spat into it.

This trait seemed wholly worthy of an age whose love of *utility* is such that the Prince Puckler Muskau suggests the probability of men coming to put the bodies of their dead parents in the fields to fertilize them, and of a country such as Dickens has described; but these will not, I hope, be seen on the historic page to be truly the age or truly the America. A little leaven is leavening the whole mass for other bread.

The whirlpool I like very much. It is seen to advantage after the great falls; it is so sternly solemn. The river cannot look more imperturbable, almost sullen in its marble green, than it does just below the great fall; but the slight circles that mark the hidden vortex, seem to whisper mysteries the thundering voice above could not proclaim,—a meaning as untold as ever.

It is fearful, too, to know, as you look, that whatever has been swallowed by the cataract, is like to rise suddenly to light here, whether up-rooted tree, or body of man or bird.

The rapids enchanted me far beyond what I expected; they are so swift that they cease to seem so; you can think only of their beauty. The fountain beyond the Moss Islands, I discovered for myself, and thought it for some time an accidental beauty which it would not do to leave, lest I might never see it again. After I found it permanent, I returned many times to watch the play of its crest. In the little waterfall beyond, nature seems, as she often does, to have made a study for some larger design. She delights in this,—a sketch within a sketch, a dream within a dream. Wherever we see it, the lines of the great buttress in the fragment of stone, the hues of the waterfall, copied in the flowers that star its bordering mosses, we are delighted; for all the lineaments become fluent, and we mould the scene in congenial thought with its genius.

People complain of the buildings at Niagara, and fear to see it further deformed. I cannot sympathize with such an apprehension: the spectacle is capable to swallow up all such objects; they are not seen in the great whole, more than an earthworm in a wide field.

The beautiful wood on Goat Island is full of flowers; many of the fairest love to do homage here. The Wake Robin and May Apple are in bloom now; the former, white, pink, green, purple, copying the rainbow of the fall, and fit to make a garland for its presiding deity when he walks the land, for they are of imperial size, and shaped like stones for a diadem. Of the May Apple, I did not raise one green tent without finding a flower beneath.

And now farewell, Niagara. I have seen thee, and I think all who come here must in some sort see thee; thou art not to be got rid of as easily as the stars. I will be here again beneath some flooding July moon and sun. Owing to the absence of light, I have seen the rainbow only two or three times by day; the lunar bow not at all. However, the imperial presence needs not its crown, though illustrated by it.

General Porter and Jack Downing were not unsuitable figures here. The former heroically planted the bridges by which we cross to Goat Island, and the Wake-Robin-crowned genius has punished his termerity with deafness, which must, I think, have come upon him when he sank the first stone in the rapids. Jack seemed an acute and entertaining representative of Jonathan, come to look at his great water-privilege. He told us all about the Americanisms of the spectacle; that is to say, the battles that have been fought here. It seems strange that men could fight in such a place; but no temple can still the personal griefs and strifes in the breasts of its visitors.

No less strange is the fact that, in this neighborhood, an eagle should be chained for a plaything. When a child, I used often to stand at a window from which I could see an eagle chained in the balcony of a museum. The people used to poke at it with sticks, and my childish heart would swell with indignation as I saw their insults, and the mien with which they were borne by the monarch-bird. Its eye was dull, and its plumage soiled and shabby, yet, in its form and attitude, all the king was visible, though sorrowful and dethroned. I never saw another of the family till, when passing through the Notch of the White Mountains, at that moment striding before us in all the panoply of sunset, the driver shouted, "Look there!" and following with our eyes his upward-pointing finger, we saw, soaring slow in majestic poise above the highest summit, the bird of Jove. It was a glorious sight, yet I know not that I felt more on seeing the bird in all its natural freedom and royalty, than when, imprisoned and insulted, he had filled my early thoughts with the Byronic "silent rages" of misanthropy.

Now, again, I saw him a captive, and addressed by the vulgar with the language they seem to find most appropriate to such occasions—that of thrusts and blows. Silently, his head averted, he ignored their existence, as Plotinus or Sophocles might that of a modern reviewer. Probably, he listened to the voice of the cataract, and felt that congenial powers flowed free, and was consoled, though his own wing was broken.

The story of the Recluse of Niagara interested me a little. It is wonderful that men do not oftener attach their lives to localities of great beauty—that, when once deeply penetrated, they will let themselves so easily be borne away by the general stream of things, to live any where and any how. But there is something ludicrous in being the hermit of a showplace, unlike St. Francis in his mountain-bed, where none but the stars and rising sun ever saw him.

There is also a "guide to the falls," who wears his title labeled on his hat; otherwise, indeed, one might as soon think of asking for a gentleman usher to point out the moon. Yet why should we wonder at such, either, when we have Commentaries on Shakespeare, and Harmonies of the Gospels?

And now you have the little all I have to write. Can it interest you? To one who has enjoyed the full life of any scene, of any hour, what thoughts can be recorded about it, seem like the commas and semicolons in the paragraph, mere stops. Yet I suppose it is not so to the absent. At least, I have read things written about Niagara, music, and the like, that interested *me*. Once I was moved by Mr. Greenwood's remark, that he could not realize this marvel till, opening his eyes the next morning after he had seen it, his doubt as to the possibility of its being still there, taught him what he had experienced. I remember this now with pleasure, though, or because, it is exactly the opposite to what I myself felt. For all greatness affects different minds, each in "its own particular kind," and the variations of testimony mark the truth of feeling.

I will add a brief narrative of the experience of another here, as being much better than anything I could write, because more simple and individual.

"Now that I have left this 'Earth-wonder,' and the emotions it excited are past, it seems not so much like profanation to analyze my feelings, to recall minutely and accurately the effect of this manifestation of the Eternal. But one should go to such a scene prepared to yield entirely to its influences, to forget one's little self and one's little mind. To see a miserable worm creep to the brink of this falling world of waters, and watch the trembling of its own petty bosom, and fancy that this is made alone to act upon him excites—derision?—No,—pity."

As I rode up to the neighborhood of the falls, a solemn awe imperceptibly stole over me, and the deep sound of the ever-hurrying rapids prepared my mind for the lofty emotions to be experienced. When I reached the hotel, I felt a strange indifference about seeing the aspiration of my life's hopes. I lounged about the rooms, read the stage bills upon the walls, looked over the register, and, finding the name of an acquaintance, sent to see if he was still there. What this hesitation arose from, I know not; perhaps it was a feeling of my unworthiness to enter this temple which nature has erected to its God.

At last, slowly and thoughtfully I walked down to the bridge leading to Goat Island, and when I stood upon this frail support, and saw
a quarter of a mile of tumbling, rushing rapids, and heard their everlasting roar, my emotions overpowered me, a choking sensation rose
to my throat, a thrill rushed through my veins, "my blood ran rippling
to my finger's ends." This was the climax of the effect which the falls
produced upon me—neither the American nor the British fall moved
me as did these rapids. For the magnificence, the sublimity of the latter
I was prepared by descriptions and by paintings. When I arrived in
sight of them I merely felt, "ah, yes, here is the fall, just as I have seen
it in picture." When I arrived at the terrapin bridge, I expected to be
overwhelmed, to retire trembling from this giddy eminence, and gaze
with unlimited wonder and awe upon the immense mass rolling on
and on, but, somehow or other, I thought only of comparing the effect
on my mind with what I had read and heard. I looked for a short
time, and then with almost a feeling of disappointment, turned to go
to the other points of view to see if I was not mistaken in not feeling
any surpassing emotion at this sight. But from the foot of Biddle's
stairs, and the middle of the river, and from below the table rock, it
was still "barren, barren all." And, provoked with my stupidity in
feeling most moved in the wrong place, I turned away to the hotel,
determined to set off for Buffalo that afternoon. But the stage did not
go, and, after nightfall, as there was a splendid moon, I went down
to the bridge, and leaned over the parapet, where the boiling rapids
came down in their might. It was grand, and it was also gorgeous; the
yellow rays of the moon made the broken waves appear like auburn
tresses twining around the black rocks. But they did not inspire me as
before. I felt a foreboding of a mightier emotion to rise up and swallow
all others, and I passed on to the terrapin bridge. Everything was
changed, the misty apparition had taken off its many-colored crown
which it had worn by day, and a bow of silvery white spanned its
summit. The moonlight gave a poetical indefiniteness to the distant
parts of the waters, and while the rapids were glancing in her beams,
the river below the falls was black as night, save where the reflection
of the sky gave it the appearance of a shield of blued steel. No gaping
tourists loitered, eyeing with their glasses, or sketching on cards the
hoary locks of the ancient river god. All tended to harmonize with the
natural grandeur of the scene. I gazed long. I saw how here mutability
and unchangeableness were united. I surveyed the conspiring waters
rushing against the rocky ledge to overthrow it at one mad plunge,
till, like toppling ambition, o'erleaping themselves, they fall on t'other

side, expanding into foam ere they reach the deep channel where they creep submissively away.

Then arose in my breast a genuine admiration, and a humble adoration of the Being who was the architect of this and of all. Happy were the first discoverers of Niagara, those who could come unawares upon this view and upon that, whose feelings were entirely their own. With what gusto does Father Hennepin describe "this great downfall of water," "this vast and prodigious cadence of water, which falls down after a surprising and astonishing manner, insomuch that the universe does not afford its parallel. 'Tis true Italy and Swedeland boast of some such things, but we may well say that they be sorry patterns when compared with this of which we do now speak."

CHAPTER II

THE LAKES

SCENE, STEAMBOAT

—About to leave Buffalo—Baggage coming on board—Passengers bustling for their berths—Little boys persecuting everybody with their newspapers and pamphlets—J., S. and M. huddled up in a forlorn corner, behind a large trunk—A heavy rain falling.

M.   Water, water everywhere. After Niagara one would like a dry strip of existence. And at any rate it is quite enough for me to have it under foot without having it over head in this way.

J.   Ah, do not abuse the gentle element. It is hardly possible to have too much of it, and indeed, if I were obliged to choose amid the four, it would be the one in which I could bear confinement best.

S.   You would make a pretty Undine, to be sure!

J.   Nay, I only offered myself as a Triton, a boisterous Triton of the sounding shell. You, M. I suppose, would be a salamander, rather.

M.   No! that is too equivocal a position, whether in modern mythology, or Hoffman's tales. I should choose to be a gnome.

J.   That choice savors of the pride that apes humility.

M.   By no means; the gnomes are the most important of all the elemental tribes. Is it not they who make the money?

J.   And are accordingly a dark, mean, scoffing,—

M.   You talk as if you had always lived in that wild unprofitable element you are so fond of, where all things glitter, and nothing is gold; all show and no substance. My people work in the secret, and their works praise them in the open light; they remain in the dark because only there such marvels could be bred. You call them mean. They do not spend their energies on their own growth, or their own play, but to feed the veins of mother earth with permanent splendors, very different from what she shows on the surface.

Think of passing a life, not merely in heaping together, but making gold. Of all dreams, that of the alchymist is the most poetical, for he looked at the finest symbol. Gold, says one of our friends, is the hidden light of the earth, it crowns the mineral, as wine the vegetable order, being the last expression of vital energy.

J.   Have you paid for your passage?

M.   Yes! and in gold, not in shells or pebbles.

J.   No really wise gnome would scoff at the water, the beautiful water. "The spirit of man is like the water."

S.   Yes, and like the air and fire, no less.

J.   Yes, but not like the earth, this low-minded creature's chosen dwelling.

M.   The earth is spirit made fruitful,—life. And its heart-beats are told in gold and wine.

J.   Oh! it is shocking to hear such sentiments in these times. I thought that Bacchic energy of yours was long since repressed.

M.   No! I have only learned to mix water with my wine, and stamp upon my gold the heads of kings, or the hieroglyphics of worship. But since I have learnt to mix with water, let's hear what you have to say in praise of your favorite.

J.   From water Venus was born, what more would you have? It is the mother of Beauty, the girdle of earth, and the marriage of nations.

S.   Without any of that high-flown poetry, it is enough, I think, that it is the great artist, turning all objects that approach it to picture.

J.   True, no object that touches it, whether it be the cart that ploughs the wave for sea-weed, or the boat or plank that rides upon it, but is brought at once from the demesne of coarse utilities into that of picture. All trades, all callings, become picturesque by the water's side, or on the water. The soil, the slovenliness is washed out of every calling by its touch. All river-crafts, sea-crafts, are picturesque, are poetical. Their very slang is poetry.

M. The reasons for that are complex.

J. The reason is, that there can be no plodding, groping words and motions, on my water as there are on your earth. There is no time, no chance for them where all moves so rapidly, though so smoothly, everything connected with water must be like itself, forcible, but clear. That is why sea-slang is so poetical; there is a word for everything and every act, and a thing and an act for every word. Seamen must speak quick and bold, but also with utmost precision. They cannot reef and brace other than in a Homeric dialect—therefore,—(Steamboat bell rings.) But I must say a quick good-by.

M. What, going, going back to earth after all this talk upon the other side. Well, that is nowise Homeric, but truly modern.

J. is borne off without time for any reply, but a laugh—at himself, of course.

S. and *M.* retire to their state-rooms to forget the wet, the chill and steamboat smell in their just-bought new world of novels.

Next day, when we stopped at Cleveland, the storm was just clearing up; ascending the bluff, we had one of the finest views of the lake that could have been wished. The varying depths of these lakes give to their surface a great variety of coloring, and beneath this wild sky and changeful lights, the waters presented kaleidoscopic varieties of hues, rich, but mournful. I admire these bluffs of red, crumbling earth. Here land and water meet under very different auspices from those of the rock-bound coast to which I have been accustomed. There they meet tenderly to challenge, and proudly to refuse, though not in fact repel. But here they meet to mingle, are always rushing together, and changing places; a new creation takes place beneath the eye.

The weather grew gradually clearer, but not bright; yet we could see the shore and appreciate the extent of these noble waters.

Coming up the river St. Clair, we saw Indians for the first time. They were camped out on the bank. It was twilight, and their blanketed forms, in listless groups or stealing along the bank, with a lounge and a stride so different in its wildness from the rudeness of the white settler, gave me the first feeling that I really approached the West.

The people on the boat were almost all New Englanders, seeking their fortunes. They had brought with them their habits of calculation, their cautious manners, their love of polemics. It grieved me to hear these immigrants who were to be the fathers of a new race, all, from the old man down to the little girl, talking not of what they should do, but of what they should get in the new scene. It was to them a prospect, not of the unfolding nobler energies, but of more ease, and larger accumulation. It wearied me, too, to hear Trinity and Unity discussed in the poor, narrow doctrinal way on these free waters; but that will soon cease, there is not time for this clash of opinions in the West, where the clash of material interests is so noisy. They will need the spirit of religion more than ever to guide them, but will find less time than before for its doctrine. This change was to me, who am tired of the war of words on these subjects, and believe it only sows the wind to reap the whirlwind, refreshing, but I argue nothing from it; there is nothing real in the freedom of thought at the West, it is from the position of men's lives, not the state of their minds. So soon as they have time, unless they grow better meanwhile, they will cavil and criticise, and judge other men by their own standard, and outrage the law of love every way, just as they do with us.

We reached Mackinaw the evening of the third day, but, to my great disappointment, it was too late and too rainy to go ashore. The beauty of the island, though seen under the most unfavorable circumstances, did not disappoint my expectations. But I shall see it to more purpose on my return.

As the day has passed dully, a cold rain preventing us from keeping out in the air, my thoughts have been dwelling on a story told when we were off Detroit, this morning, by a fellow passenger, and whose moral beauty touched me profoundly.

Some years ago, said Mrs. L., my father and mother stopped to dine at Detroit. A short time before dinner my father met in the hall Captain P., a friend of his youthful days. He had loved P. extremely, as did many who knew him, and had not been surprised to hear of the distinction and popular esteem which his wide knowledge, talents, and noble temper commanded, as he went onward in the world. P. was every way fitted to succeed; his aims were high, but not too high for his powers, suggested by an instinct of his own capacities, not by an ideal standard drawn from culture. Though steadfast in his course, it was not to overrun others, his wise self-possession was no less for them than himself. He was thoroughly the gentleman, gentle because manly, and was a striking instance that where there is strength for sincere courtesy, there is no need of other adaptation to the character of others, to make one's way freely and gracefully through the crowd.

My father was delighted to see him, and after a short parley in the hall—"We will dine together," he cried, "then we shall have time to tell all our stories."

P. hesitated a moment, then said, "My wife is with me."

"And mine with me," said my father, "that's well; they, too, will have an opportunity of getting acquainted and can entertain one another, if they get tired of our college stories."

P. acquiesced, with a grave bow, and shortly after they all met in the dining-room. My father was much surprised at the appearance of Mrs. P. He had heard that his friend married abroad, but nothing further, and he was not prepared to see the calm, dignified P. with a woman on his arm, still handsome, indeed, but whose coarse and imperious expression showed as low habits of mind as her exaggerated dress and gesture did of education. Nor could there be a greater contrast to my mother, who, though understanding her claims and place with the certainty of a lady, was soft and retiring in an uncommon degree.

However, there was no time to wonder or fancy; they sat down, and P. engaged in conversation, without much vivacity, but with his usual ease. The first quarter of an hour passed well enough. But soon it was observable that Mrs. P. was drinking glass after glass of wine, to an extent few gentlemen did, even then, and soon that she was actually excited by it. Before this, her manner had been brusque, if not contemptuous towards her new acquaintance; now it became, towards my mother especially, quite rude. Presently she took up some slight remark made by my mother, which, though it did not naturally mean anything of the sort, could be twisted into some reflection upon England, and made it a handle, first of vulgar sarcasm, and then, upon my mother's defending herself with some surprise and gentle dignity, hurled upon her a volley of abuse, beyond Billingsgate.

My mother, confounded, feeling scenes and ideas presented to her mind equally new and painful, sat trembling; she knew not what to do, tears rushed into her eyes. My father, no less distressed, yet unwilling to outrage the feelings of his friend by doing or saying what his indignation prompted, turned an appealing look on P.

Never, as he often said, was the painful expression of that sight effaced from his mind. It haunted his dreams and disturbed his waking thoughts. P. sat with his head bent forward, and his eyes cast down, pale, but calm, with a fixed expression, not merely of patient wo, but of patient shame, which it would not have been thought possible for that noble countenance to wear, "yet," said my father, "it became him. At other times he was handsome, but then beautiful, though of a beauty saddened and abashed. For a spiritual light borrowed from the worldly perfection of his mien that illustration by contrast, which the penitence of the Magdalen does from the glowing earthliness of her charms."

Seeing that he preserved silence, while Mrs. P. grew still more exasperated, my father rose and led his wife to her own room. Half an hour had passed, in painful and wondering surmises, when a gentle knock was heard at the door, and P. entered equipped for a journey. "We are just going," he said, and holding out his hand, but without looking at them, "Forgive."

They each took his hand, and silently pressed it, then he went without a word more.

Some time passed and they heard now and then of P., as he passed from one army station to another, with his uncongenial companion, who became, it was said, constantly more degraded. Whoever mentioned having seen them, wondered at the chance which had yoked him to such a woman, but yet more at the silent fortitude with which he bore it. Many blamed him for enduring it, apparently without efforts to check her; others answered that he had probably made such at an earlier period, and finding them unavailing, had resigned himself to despair, and was too delicate to meet the scandal that, with such a resistance as such a woman could offer, must attend a formal separation.

But my father, who was not in such haste to come to conclusions, and substitute some plausible explanation for the truth, found something in the look of P. at that trying moment to which none of these explanations offered a key. There was in it, he felt, a fortitude, but not the fortitude of the hero, a religious submission, above the penitent, if not enkindled with the enthusiasm of the martyr.

I have said that my father was not one of those who are ready to substitute specious explanations for truth, and those who are thus abstinent rarely lay their hand on a thread without making it a clue. Such an one, like the dexterous weaver, lets not one color go, till he finds that which matches it in the pattern; he keeps on weaving, but chooses his shades, and my father found at last what he wanted to make out the pattern for himself. He met a lady who had been intimate with both himself and P. in early days, and finding she had seen the latter abroad, asked if she knew the circumstances of the marriage. "The circumstances of the act I know," she said, "which sealed the misery of our friend, though as much in the dark as any one about the motives that led to it."

We were quite intimate with P. in London, and he was our most delightful companion. He was then in the full flower of the varied accomplishments, which set off his fine manners and dignified character, joined, towards those he loved, with a certain soft willingness which gives the desirable chivalry to a man. None was more clear of choice where his personal affections were not touched, but where they were, it cost him pain to say no, on the slightest occasion. I have thought this must have had some connexion with the mystery of his misfortunes.

One day he called on me, and, without any preface, asked if I would be present next day at his marriage. I was so surprised, and so unpleasantly surprised, that I did not at first answer a word. We had been on terms so familiar, that I thought I knew all about him, yet had never dreamed of his having an attachment, and, though I had never inquired on the subject, yet this reserve, where perfect openness had been supposed, and really, on my side, existed, seemed to me a kind of treachery. Then it is never pleasant to know that a heart, on which we have some claim, is to be given to another. We cannot tell how it will affect our own relations with a person; it may strengthen or it may swallow up other affections; the crisis is hazardous, and our first thought, on such an occasion, is too often for ourselves, at least, mine was. Seeing me silent, he repeated his question.

To whom, said I, are you to be married?

That, he replied, I cannot tell you. He was a moment silent, then continued with an impassive look of cold self-possession, that affected me with strange sadness.

"The name of the person you will hear, of course, at the time, but more I cannot tell you. I need, however, the presence, not only of legal, but of respectable and friendly witnesses. I have hoped you and your husband would do me this kindness. Will you?"

Something in his manner made it impossible to refuse. I answered before I knew I was going to speak, "We will," and he left me.

I will not weary you with telling how I harassed myself and my husband, who was, however, scarce less interested, with doubts and conjectures. Suffice it that, next morning, P. came and took us in a carriage to a distant church. We had just entered the porch when a cart, such as fruit and vegetables are brought to market in, drove up, containing an elderly woman and a young girl. P. assisted them to alight, and advanced with the girl to the altar.

The girl was neatly dressed and quite handsome, yet something in her expression displeased me the moment I looked upon her. Meanwhile the ceremony was going on, and, at its close, P. introduced us to the bride, and we all went to the door.

Good-by, Fanny, said the elderly woman. The new-made Mrs. P. replied without any token of affection or emotion. The woman got into the cart and drove away.

From that time I saw but little of P. or his wife. I took our mutual friends to see her, and they were civil to her for his sake. Curiosity was very much excited, but entirely baffled; no one, of course, dared speak to P. on the subject, and no other means could be found of solving the riddle.

He treated his wife with grave and kind politeness, but it was always obvious that they had nothing in common between them. Her manners and tastes were not at that time gross, but her character showed itself hard and material. She was fond of riding, and spent much time so. Her style in this, and in dress, seemed the opposite of P.'s; but he indulged all her wishes, while, for himself, he plunged into his own pursuits.

For a time he seemed, if not happy, not positively unhappy; but, after a few years, Mrs. P. fell into the habit of drinking, and then such scenes as you witnessed grew frequent. I have often heard of them, and always that P. sat, as you describe him, his head bowed down and perfectly silent all through, whatever might be done or whoever be present, and always his aspect has inspired such sympathy that no person has questioned him or resented her insults, but merely got out of the way, so soon as possible.

Hard and long penance, said my father, after some minutes musing, for an hour of passion, probably for his only error.

Is that your explanation? said the lady. O, improbable. P. might err, but not be led beyond himself.

I know his cool gray eye and calm complexion seemed to say so, but a different story is told by the lip that could tremble, and showed what flashes might pierce those deep blue heavens; and when these over intellectual beings do swerve aside, it is to fall down a precipice, for their narrow path lies over such. But he was not one to sin without making a brave atonement, and that it had become a holy one, was written on that downcast brow.

The fourth day on these waters, the weather was milder and brighter, so that we could now see them to some purpose. At night was clear moon, and, for the first time, from the upper deck, I saw one of the great steamboats come majestically up. It was glowing with lights, looking many-eyed and sagacious; in its heavy motion it seemed a dowager queen, and this motion, with its solemn pulse, and determined sweep, becomes these smooth waters, especially at night, as much as the dip of the sailship the long billows of the ocean.

But it was not so soon that I learned to appreciate the lake scenery; it was only after a daily and careless familiarity that I entered into its beauty, for nature always refuses to be seen by being stared at. Like Bonaparte, she discharges her face of all expression when she catches the eye of impertinent curiosity fixed on her. But he who has gone to sleep in childish ease on her lap, or leaned an aching brow upon her breast, seeking there comfort with full trust as from a mother, will see all a mother's beauty in the look she bends upon him. Later, I felt that I had really seen these regions, and shall speak of them again.

In the afternoon we went on shore at the Manitou islands, where the boat stops to wood. No one lives here except woodcutters for the steamboats. I had thought of such a position, from its mixture of profound solitude with service to the great world, as possessing an ideal beauty. I think so still, after seeing the woodcutters and their slovenly huts.

In times of slower growth, man did not enter a situation without a certain preparation or adaptedness to it. He drew from it, if not to the poetical extent, at least, in some proportion, its moral and its meaning. The woodcutter did not cut down so many trees a day, that the hamadryads had not time to make their plaints heard; the shepherd tended his sheep, and did no jobs or chores the while; the idyl had a chance to grow up, and modulate his oaten pipe. But now the poet must be at the whole expense of the poetry in describing one of these positions; the worker is a true Midas to the gold he makes. The poet must describe, as the painter sketches Irish peasant girls and Danish fishwives, adding the beauty, and leaving out the dirt.

I come to the west prepared for the distaste I must experience at its mushroom growth. I know that where "go ahead" is the only motto, the village cannot grow into the gentle proportions that successive lives, and the gradations of experience involuntarily give. In older countries the house of the son grew from that of the father, as naturally as new joints on a bough. And the cathedral crowned the whole as naturally as the leafy summit the tree. This cannot be here. The march of peaceful is scarce less wanton than that of warlike invasion. The old landmarks are broken down, and the land, for a season, bears none, except of the rudeness of conquest and the needs of the day, whose bivouac fires blacken the sweetest forest glades. I have come prepared to see all this, to dislike it, but not with stupid narrowness to distrust or defame. On the contrary, while I will not be so obliging as to confound ugliness with beauty, discord with harmony, and laud and be contented with all I meet, when it conflicts with my best desires and tastes, I trust by reverent faith to woo the mighty meaning of the scene, perhaps to foresee the law by which a new order, a new poetry is to be evoked from this chaos, and with a curiosity as ardent, but not so selfish as that of Macbeth, to call up the apparitions of future kings from the strange ingredients of the witch's caldron. Thus, I will not grieve that all the noble trees are gone already from this island to feed this caldron, but believe it will have Medea's virtue, and reproduce them in the form of new intellectual growths, since centuries cannot again adorn the land with such.

On this most beautiful beach of smooth white pebbles, interspersed with agates and cornelians, for those who know how to find them, we stepped, not like the Indian, with some humble offering, which, if no better than an arrow-head or a little parched corn, would, he judged, please the Manitou, who looks only at the spirit in which it is offered. Our visit was so far for a religious purpose that one of our party went to inquire the fate of some Unitarian tracts left among the woodcutters a year or two before. But the old Manitou, though, daunted like his children by the approach of the fire-ships which he probably considered demons of a new dynasty, he had suffered his woods to be felled to feed their pride, had been less patient of an encroachment, which did not to him seem so authorized by the law of the strongest, and had scattered those leaves as carelessly as the others of that year.

But S. and I, like other emigrants, went not to give, but to get, to rifle the wood of flowers for the service of the fire-ship. We returned with a rich booty, among which was the uva ursi, whose leaves the Indians smoke, with the kinnick-kinnick, and which had then just put forth its highly-finished little blossoms, as pretty as those of the blueberry.

Passing along still further, I thought it would be well if the crowds assembled to stare from the various landings were still confined to the kinnick-kinnick, for almost all had tobacco written on their faces, their cheeks rounded with plugs, their eyes dull with its fumes. We reached Chicago on the evening of the sixth day, having been out five days and a half, a rather longer passage than usual at a favorable season of the year.

There can be no two places in the world more completely thoroughfares than this place and Buffalo. They are the two correspondent
valves that open and shut all the time, as the life-blood rushes from
east to west, and back again from west to east.

Since it is their office thus to be the doors, and let in and out, it
would be unfair to expect from them much character of their own. To
make the best provisions for the transmission of produce is their office,
and the people who live there are such as are suited for this; active,
complaisant, inventive, business people. There are no provisions for
the student or idler; to know what the place can give, you should be
at work with the rest, the mere traveller will not find it profitable to
loiter there as I did.

Since circumstances made it necessary for me so to do, I read all
the books I could find about the new region, which now began to
become real to me. All the books about the Indians, a paltry collection,
truly, yet which furnished material for many thoughts. The most
narrow-minded and awkward recital still bears some lineaments of the
great features of this nature, and the races of men that illustrated them.

Catlin's book is far the best. I was afterwards assured by those
acquainted with the regions he describes, that he is not to be depended
on for the accuracy of his facts, and, indeed, it is obvious, without the
aid of such assertions, that he sometimes yields to the temptation of
making out a story. They admitted, however, what from my feelings
I was sure of, that he is true to the spirit of the scene, and that a far
better view can be got from him than from any source at present
existing, of the Indian tribes of the far west, and of the country where
their inheritance lay.

Murray's travels I read, and was charmed by their accuracy and
clear broad tone. He is the only Englishman that seems to have traversed these regions, as man, simply, not as John Bull. He deserves to
belong to an aristocracy, for he showed his title to it more when left
without a guide in the wilderness, than he can at the court of Victoria.
He has, himself, no poetic force at description, but it is easy to make
images from his hints. Yet we believe the Indian cannot be looked at
truly except by a poetic eye. The Pawnees, no doubt, are such as he
describes them, filthy in their habits, and treacherous in their character,
but some would have seen, and seen truly, more beauty and dignity
than he does with all his manliness and fairness of mind. However,
his one fine old man is enough to redeem the rest, and is perhaps the
relic of a better day, a Phocion among the Pawnees.

Schoolcraft's Algic Researches is a valuable book, though a worse use could hardly have been made of such fine material. Had the mythological or hunting stories of the Indians been written down exactly as they were received from the lips of the narrators, the collection could not have been surpassed in interest, both for the wild charm they carry with them, and the light they throw on a peculiar modification of life and mind. As it is, though the incidents have an air of originality and pertinence to the occasion, that gives us confidence that they have not been altered, the phraseology in which they were expressed has been entirely set aside, and the flimsy graces, common to the style of annuals and souvenirs, substituted for the Spartan brevity and sinewy grasp of Indian speech. We can just guess what might have been there, as we can detect the fine proportions of the Brave whom the bad taste of some white patron has arranged in frock-coat, hat, and pantaloons.

The few stories Mrs. Jameson wrote out, though to these also a sentimental air has been given, offend much less in that way than is common in this book. What would we give for a completely faithful version of some among them. Yet with all these drawbacks we cannot doubt from internal evidence that they truly ascribe to the Indian a delicacy of sentiment and of fancy that justifies Cooper in such inventions as his Uncas. It is a white man's view of a savage hero, who would be far finer in his natural proportions; still, through a masquerade figure, it implies the truth.

Irving's books I also read, some for the first, some for the second time, with increased interest, now that I was to meet such people as he received his materials from. Though the books are pleasing from their grace and luminous arrangement, yet, with the exception of the Tour to the Prairies, they have a stereotype, second-hand air. They lack the breath, the glow, the charming minute traits of living presence. His scenery is only fit to be glanced at from dioramic distance; his Indians are academic figures only. He would have made the best of pictures, if he could have used his own eyes for studies and sketches; as it is, his success is wonderful, but inadequate.

McKenney's Tour to the Lakes is the dullest of books, yet faithful and quiet, and gives some facts not to be met with elsewhere.

I also read a collection of Indian anecdotes and speeches, the worst compiled and arranged book possible, yet not without clues of some value. All these books I read in anticipation of a canoe-voyage on Lake Superior as far as the Pictured Rocks, and, though I was afterwards compelled to give up this project, they aided me in judging of what I afterwards saw and heard of the Indians.

In Chicago I first saw the beautiful prairie flowers. They were in their glory the first ten days we were there—

"The golden and the flame-like flowers."

The flame-like flower I was taught afterwards, by an Indian girl, to call "Wickapee;" and she told me, too, that its splendors had a useful side, for it was used by the Indians as a remedy for an illness to which they were subject.

Beside these brilliant flowers, which gemmed and gilt the grass in a sunny afternoon's drive near the blue lake, between the low oak-wood and the narrow beach, stimulated, whether sensuously by the optic nerve, unused to so much gold and crimson with such tender green, or symbolically through some meaning dimly seen in the flow-ers, I enjoyed a sort of fairyland exultation never felt before, and the first drive amid the flowers gave me anticipation of the beauty of the prairies.

At first, the prairie seemed to speak of the very desolation of dull-ness. After sweeping over the vast monotony of the lakes to come to this monotony of land, with all around a limitless horizon,—to walk, and walk, and run, but never climb, oh! it was too dreary for any but a Hollander to bear. How the eye greeted the approach of a sail, or the smoke of a steamboat; it seemed that any thing so animated must come from a better land, where mountains gave religion to the scene.

The only thing I liked at first to do, was to trace with slow and unexpecting step the narrow margin of the lake. Sometimes a heavy swell gave it expression; at others, only its varied coloring, which I found more admirable every day, and which gave it an air of mirage instead of the vastness of ocean. Then there was a grandeur in the feeling that I might continue that walk, if I had any seven-leagued mode of conveyance to save fatigue, for hundreds of miles without an obstacle and without a change.

But after I had rode out, and seen the flowers and seen the sun set with that calmness seen only in the prairies, and the cattle winding slowly home to their homes in the "island groves"—peacefullest of sights—I began to love because I began to know the scene, and shrank no longer from "the encircling vastness."

It is always thus with the new form of life; we must learn to look at it by its own standard. At first, no doubt my accustomed eye kept saying, if the mind did not, What! no distant mountains? what, no valleys? But after a while I would ascend the roof of the house where we lived, and pass many hours, needing no sight but the moon reigning in the heavens, or starlight falling upon the lake, till all the lights were out in the island grove of men beneath my feet, and felt nearer heaven that there was nothing but this lovely, still reception on the earth; no towering mountains, no deep tree-shadows, nothing but plain earth and water bathed in light.

Sunset, as seen from that place, presented most generally, low-lying, flaky clouds, of the softest serenity, "like," said S., "the Buddhist tracts."

One night a star shot madly from its sphere, and it had a fair chance to be seen, but that serenity could not be astonished.

Yes! it was a peculiar beauty of those sunsets and moonlights on the levels of Chicago which. Chamouny or the Trosachs could not make me forget.

Notwithstanding all the attractions I thus found out by degrees on the flat shores of the lake, I was delighted when I found myself really on my way into the country for an excursion of two or three weeks. We set forth in a strong wagon, almost as large, and with the look of those used elsewhere for transporting caravans of wild beas-teses, loaded with every thing we might want, in case nobody would give it to us—for buying and selling were no longer to be counted on—with a pair of strong horses, able and willing to force their way through mud holes and amid stumps, and a guide, equally admirable as marshal and companion, who knew by heart the country and its history, both natural and artificial, and whose clear hunter's eye needed neither road nor goal to guide it to all the spots where beauty best loves to dwell.

Add to this the finest weather, and such country as I had never seen, even in my dreams, although these dreams had been haunted by wishes for just such an one, and you may judge whether years of dullness might not, by these bright days, be redeemed, and a sweetness be shed over all thoughts of the West.

The first day brought us through woods rich in the moccasin flower and lupine, and plains whose soft expanse was continually touched with expression by the slow moving clouds which

"Sweep over with their shadows, and beneath
The surface rolls and fluctuates to the eye;

> *Dark hollows seem to glide along and chase*
> *The sunny ridges,"*

to the banks of the Fox river, a sweet and graceful stream. We reached Geneva just in time to escape being drenched by a violent thunder shower, whose rise and disappearance threw expression into all the features of the scene.

Geneva reminds me of a New England village, as indeed there, and in the neighborhood, are many New Englanders of an excellent stamp, generous, intelligent, discreet, and seeking to win from life its true values. Such are much wanted, and seem like points of light among the swarms of settlers, whose aims are sordid, whose habits thoughtless and slovenly.

With great pleasure we heard, with his attentive and affectionate congregation, the Unitarian clergyman, Mr. Conant, and afterward visited him in his house, where almost everything bore traces of his own handywork or that of his father. He is just such a teacher as is wanted in this region, familiar enough with the habits of those he addresses to come home to their experience and their wants; earnest and enlightened enough to draw the important inferences from the life of every day.

A day or two we remained here, and passed some happy hours in the woods that fringe the stream, where the gentlemen found a rich booty of fish.

Next day, travelling along the river's banks, was an uninterrupted pleasure. We closed our drive in the afternoon at the house of an English gentleman, who has gratified, as few men do, the common wish to pass the evening of an active day amid the quiet influences of country life. He showed us a bookcase filled with books about this country; these he had collected for years, and become so familiar with the localities that, on coming here at last, he sought and found, at once, the very spot he wanted, and where he is as content as he hoped to be, thus realizing Wordsworth's description of the wise man, who "sees what he foresaw."

A wood surrounds the house, through which paths are cut in every direction. It is, for this new country, a large and handsome dwelling; but round it are its barns and farm yard, with cattle and poultry. These, however, in the framework of wood, have a very picturesque and pleasing effect. There is that mixture of culture and rudeness in the aspect of things as gives a feeling of freedom, not of confusion.

I wish it were possible to give some idea of this scene as viewed by the earliest freshness of dewy dawn. This habitation of man seemed like a nest in the grass, so thoroughly were the buildings and all the objects of human care harmonized with what was natural. The tall trees bent and whispered all around, as if to hail with sheltering love the men who had come to dwell among them.

The young ladies were musicians, and spoke French fluently, having been educated in a convent. Here in the prairie, they had learned to take care of the milk-room, and kill the rattlesnakes that assailed their poultry yard. Beneath the shade of heavy curtains you looked out from the high and large windows to see Norwegian peasants at work in their national dress. In the wood grew, not only the flowers I had before seen, and wealth of tall, wild roses, but the splendid blue spiderwort, that ornament of our gardens. Beautiful children strayed there, who were soon to leave these civilized regions for some really wild and western place, a post in the buffalo country. Their no less beautiful mother was of Welsh descent, and the eldest child bore the name of Gwynthleon. Perhaps there she will meet with some young descendants of Madoc, to be her friends; at any rate, her looks may retain that sweet, wild beauty, that is soon made to vanish from eyes which look too much on shops and streets, and the vulgarities of city "parties."

Next day we crossed the river. We ladies crossed on a little footbridge, from which we could look down the stream, and see the wagon pass over at the ford. A black thunder cloud was coming up. The sky and waters heavy with expectation. The motion of the wagon, with its white cover, and the laboring horses, gave just the due interest to the picture, because it seemed as if they would not have time to cross before the storm came on. However, they did get across, and we were a mile or two on our way before the violent shower obliged us to take refuge in a solitary house upon the prairie. In this country it is as pleasant to stop as to go on, to lose your way as to find it, for the variety in the population gives you a chance for fresh entertainment in every hut, and the luxuriant beauty makes every path attractive. In this house we found a family "quite above the common," but, I grieve to say, not above false pride, for the father, ashamed of being caught barefoot, told us a story of a man, one of the richest men, he said, in one of the eastern cities, who went barefoot, from choice and taste.

Near the door grew a Provence rose, then in blossom. Other families we saw had brought with them and planted the locust. It was pleasant to see their old home loves, brought into connection with their new splendors. Wherever there were traces of this tenderness of feeling, only too rare among Americans, other things bore signs also of prosperity and intelligence, as if the ordering mind of man had some idea of home beyond a mere shelter, beneath which to eat and sleep.

No heaven need wear a lovelier aspect than earth did this afternoon, after the clearing up of the shower. We traversed the blooming plain, unmarked by any road, only the friendly track of wheels which tracked, not broke the grass. Our stations were not from town to town, but from grove to grove. These groves first floated like blue islands in the distance. As we drew nearer, they seemed fair parks, and the little log houses on the edge, with their curling smokes, harmonized beautifully with them.

One of these groves, Ross's grove, we reached just at sunset. It was of the noblest trees I saw during this journey, for the trees generally were not large or lofty, but only of fair proportions. Here they were large enough to form with their clear stems pillars for grand cathedral aisles. There was space enough for crimson light to stream through upon the floor of water which the shower had left. As we slowly plashed through, I thought I was never in a better place for vespers.

That night we rested, or rather tarried at a grove some miles beyond, and there partook of the miseries so often jocosely portrayed, of bedchambers for twelve, a milk dish for universal handbasin, and expectations that you would use and lend your "hankercher" for a towel. But this was the only night, thanks to the hospitality of private families, that we passed thus, and it was well that we had this bit of experience, else might we have pronounced all Trollopian records of the kind to be inventions of pure malice.

With us was a young lady who showed herself to have been bathed in the Britannic fluid, wittily described by a late French writer, by the impossibility she experienced of accommodating herself to the indecorums of the scene. We ladies were to sleep in the bar-room, from which its drinking visiters could be ejected only at a late hour. The outer door had no fastening to prevent their return. However, our host kindly requested we would call him, if they did, as he had "conquered them for us," and would do so again. We had also rather hard couches; (mine was the supper table,) but we yankees, born to rove, were altogether too much fatigued to stand upon trifles, and slept as sweetly as we would in the "bigly bower" of any baroness. But I think England sat up all night, wrapped in her blanket shawl, and with a neat lace cap upon her head; so that she would have looked perfectly the lady, if any one had come in; shuddering and listening. I know

that she was very ill next day, in requital. She watched, as her parent
country watches the seas, that nobody may do wrong in any case, and
deserved to have met some interruption, she was so well prepared.
However, there was none, other than from the nearness of some
twenty sets of powerful lungs, which would not leave the night to a
deadly stillness. In this house we had, if not good beds, yet good tea,
good bread, and wild strawberries, and were entertained with most
free communications of opinion and history from our hosts. Neither
shall any of us have a right to say again that we cannot find any who
may be willing to hear all we may have to say. "A's fish that comes
to the net," should be painted on the sign at Papaw grove.

CHAPTER III

In the afternoon of this day we reached the Rock river, in whose neighborhood we proposed to make some stay, and crossed at Dixon's ferry.

This beautiful stream flows full and wide over a bed of rocks,
traversing a distance of near two hundred miles, to reach the Mississippi. Great part of the country along its banks is the finest region of
Illinois, and the scene of some of the latest romance of Indian warfare.
To these beautiful regions Black Hawk returned with his band "to
pass the summer," when he drew upon himself the warfare in which
he was finally vanquished. No wonder he could not resist the longing,
unwise though its indulgence might be, to return in summer to this
home of beauty.

Of Illinois, in general, it has often been remarked that it bears the
character of country which has been inhabited by a nation skilled like
the English in all the ornamental arts of life, especially in landscape
gardening. That the villas and castles seem to have been burnt, the
enclosures taken down, but the velvet lawns, the flower gardens, the
stately parks, scattered at graceful intervals by the decorous hand of
art, the frequent deer, and the peaceful herd of cattle that make picture
of the plain, all suggest more of the masterly mind of man, than the
prodigal, but careless, motherly love of nature. Especially is this true
of the Rock river country. The river flows sometimes through these
parks and lawns, then betwixt high bluffs, whose grassy ridges are
covered with fine trees, or broken with crumbling stone, that easily
assumes the forms of buttress, arch and clustered columns. Along the

face of such crumbling rocks, swallows' nests are clustered, thick as cities, and eagles and deer do not disdain their summits. One morning, out in the boat along the base of these rocks, it was amusing, and affecting too, to see these swallows put their heads out to look at us. There was something very hospitable about it, as if man had never shown himself a tyrant near them. What a morning that was! Every sight is worth twice as much by the early morning light. We borrow something of the spirit of the hour to look upon them.

The first place where we stopped was one of singular beauty, a beauty of soft, luxuriant wildness. It was on the bend of the river, a place chosen by an Irish gentleman, whose absenteeship seems of the wisest kind, since for a sum which would have been but a drop of water to the thirsty fever of his native land, he commands a residence which has all that is desirable, in its independence, its beautiful retirement, and means of benefit to others.

His park, his deer-chase, he found already prepared; he had only to make an avenue through it. This brought us by a drive, which in the heat of noon seemed long, though afterwards, in the cool of morning and evening, delightful, to the house. This is, for that part of the world, a large and commodious dwelling. Near it stands the log-cabin where its master lived while it was building, a very ornamental accessory.

In front of the house was a lawn, adorned by the most graceful trees. A few of these had been taken out to give a full view of the river, gliding through banks such as I have described. On this bend the bank is high and bold, so from the house or the lawn the view was very rich and commanding. But if you descended a ravine at the side to the water's edge, you found there a long walk on the narrow shore, with a wall above of the richest hanging wood, in which they said the deer lay hid. I never saw one, but often fancied that I heard them rustling, at daybreak, by these bright clear waters, stretching out in such smiling promise, where no sound broke the deep and blissful seclusion, unless now and then this rustling, or the plash of some fish a little gayer than the others; it seemed not necessary to have any better heaven, or fuller expression of love and freedom than in the mood of nature here.

Then, leaving the bank, you would walk far and far through long grassy paths, full of the most brilliant, also the most delicate flowers. The brilliant are more common on the prairie, but both kinds loved this place.

Amid the grass of the lawn, with a profusion of wild strawberries, we greeted also a familiar love, the Scottish harebell, the gentlest, and most touching form of the flower-world.

The master of the house was absent, but with a kindness beyond thanks had offered us a resting place there. Here we were taken care of by a deputy, who would, for his youth, have been assigned the place of a page in former times, but in the young west, it seems he was old enough for a steward. Whatever be called his function, he did the honors of the place so much in harmony with it, as to leave the guests free to imagine themselves in Elysium. And the three days passed here were days of unalloyed, spotless happiness.

There was a peculiar charm in coming here, where the choice of location, and the unobtrusive good taste of all the arrangements, showed such intelligent appreciation of the spirit of the scene, after seeing so many dwellings of the new settlers, which showed plainly that they had no thought beyond satisfying the grossest material wants. Sometimes they looked attractive, the little brown houses, the natural architecture of the country, in the edge of the timber. But almost always when you came near, the slovenliness of the dwelling and the rude way in which objects around it were treated, when so little care would have presented a charming whole, were very repulsive. Seeing the traces of the Indians, who chose the most beautiful sites for their dwellings, and whose habits do not break in on that aspect of nature under which they were born, we feel as if they were the rightful lords of a beauty they forbore to deform. But most of these settlers do not see it at all; it breathes, it speaks in vain to those who are rushing into its sphere. Their progress is Gothic, not Roman, and their mode of cultivation will, in the course of twenty, perhaps ten, years, obliterate the natural expression of the country.

This is inevitable, fatal; we must not complain but look forward to a good result. Still, in travelling through this country, I could not but be struck with the force of a symbol. Wherever the hog comes, the rattlesnake disappears; the omnivorous traveller, safe in its stupidity, willingly and easily makes a meal of the most dangerous of reptiles, and one whom the Indian looks on with a mystic awe. Even so the white settler pursues the Indian, and is victor in the chase. But I shall say more upon the subject by-and-by.

While we were here we had one grand thunder storm, which added new glory to the scene.

One beautiful feature was the return of the pigeons every afternoon to their home. Every afternoon they came sweeping across the

lawn, positively in clouds, and with a swiftness and softness of winged
motion, more beautiful than anything of the kind I ever knew. Had I
been a musician, such as Mendelsohn, I felt that I could have impro-
vised a music quite peculiar, from the sound they made, which should
have indicated all the beauty over which their wings bore them. I will
here insert a few lines left at this house, on parting, which feebly indicate some of the features.

> *Familiar to the childish mind were tales*
>   *Of rock-girt isles amid a desert sea,*
> *Where unexpected stretch the flowery vales*
>   *To soothe the shipwrecked sailor's misery.*
> *Fainting, he lay upon a sandy shore,*
> *And fancied that all hope of life was o'er;*
> *But let him patient climb the frowning wall,*
> *Within, the orange glows beneath the palm tree tall,*
> *And all that Eden boasted waits his call.*
>
> *Almost these tales seem realized to-day,*
> *When the long dullness of the sultry way,*
> *Where "independent" settlers' careless cheer*
> *Made us indeed feel we were "strangers" here,*
> *Is cheered by sudden sight of this fair spot,*
> *On which "improvement" yet has made no blot,*
> *But Nature all-astonished stands, to find*
> *Her plan protected by the human mind.*
>
> *Blest be the kindly genius of the scene;*
>   *The river, bending in unbroken grace,*
> *The stately thickets, with their pathways green,*
>   *Fair lonely trees, each in its fittest place.*
> *Those thickets haunted by the deer and fawn;*
> *Those cloudlike flights of birds across the lawn;*
> *The gentlest breezes here delight to blow,*
> *And sun and shower and star are emulous to deck the show.*
>
> *Wondering, as Crusoe, we survey the land;*
> *Happier than Crusoe we, a friendly band;*
> *Blest be the hand that reared this friendly home,*
> *The heart and mind of him to whom we owe*
> *Hours of pure peace such as few mortals know;*
> *May he find such, should he be led to roam;*

Be tended by such ministering sprites—
Enjoy such gaily childish days, such hopeful nights!
And yet, amid the goods to mortals given,
To give those goods again is most like heaven.

                    Hazelwood, Rock River, June 30th, 1843

The only really rustic feature was of the many coops of poultry near the house, which I understood it to be one of the chief pleasures of the master to feed.

Leaving this place, we proceeded a day's journey along the beautiful stream, to a little town named Oregon. We called at a cabin, from whose door looked out one of those faces which, once seen, are never forgotten; young, yet touched with many traces of feeling, not only possible, but endured; spirited, too, like the gleam of a finely tempered blade. It was a face that suggested a history, and many histories, but whose scene would have been in courts and camps. At this moment their circles are dull for want of that life which is waning unexcited in this solitary recess.

The master of the house proposed to show us a "short cut," by which we might, to especial advantage, pursue our journey. This proved to be almost perpendicular down a hill, studded with young trees and stumps. From these he proposed, with a hospitality of service worthy an Oriental, to free our wheels whenever they should get entangled, also, to be himself the drag, to prevent our too rapid descent. Such generosity deserved trust; however, we women could not be persuaded to render it. We got out and admired, from afar, the process. Left by our guide—and prop! we found ourselves in a wide field, where, by playful quips and turns, an endless "creek," seemed to divert itself with our attempts to cross it. Failing in this, the next best was to whirl down a steep bank, which feat our charioteer performed with an air not unlike that of Rhesus, had he but been as suitably furnished with chariot and steeds!

At last, after wasting some two or three hours on the "short cut," we got out by following an Indian trail,—Black Hawk's! How fair the scene through which it led! How could they let themselves be conquered, with such a country to fight for!

Afterwards, in the wide prairie, we saw a lively picture of nonchalance, (to speak in the fashion of dear Ireland.) There, in the wide sunny field, with neither tree nor umbrella above his head, sat a pedler, with his pack, waiting apparently for customers. He was not disappointed. We bought, what hold in regard to the human world, as unmarked, as mysterious, and as important an existence, as the infusoria to the natural, to wit, pins. This incident would have delighted those modern sages, who, in imitation of the sitting philosophers of ancient Ind, prefer silence to speech, waiting to going, and scornfully smile in answer to the motions of earnest life,

> *"Of itself will nothing come,*
> *That ye must still be seeking?"*

However, it seemed to me to-day, as formerly on these sublime occasions, obvious that nothing would come, unless something would go; now, if we had been as sublimely still as the pedler, his pins would have tarried in the pack, and his pockets sustained an aching void of pence!

Passing through one of the fine, park-like woods, almost clear from underbrush and carpeted with thick grasses and flowers, we met, (for it was Sunday,) a little congregation just returning from their service, which had been performed in a rude house in its midst. It had a sweet and peaceful air, as if such words and thoughts were very dear to them. The parents had with them all their little children; but we saw no old people; that charm was wanting, which exists in such scenes in older settlements, of seeing the silver bent in reverence beside the flaxen head.

At Oregon, the beauty of the scene was of even a more sumptuous character than at our former "stopping place." Here swelled the river in its boldest course, interspersed by halcyon isles on which nature had lavished all her prodigality in tree, vine, and flower, banked by noble bluffs, three hundred feet high, their sharp ridges as exquisitely definite as the edge of a shell; their summits adorned with those same beautiful trees, and with buttresses of rich rock, crested with old hemlocks, which wore a touching and antique grace amid the softer and more luxuriant vegetation. Lofty natural mounds rose amidst the rest, with the same lovely and sweeping outline, showing everywhere the plastic power of water,—water, mother of beauty, which, by its sweet and eager flow, had left such lineaments as human genius never dreamt of.

Not far from the river was a high crag, called the Pine Rock, which looks out, as our guide observed, like a helmet above the brow of the country. It seems as if the water left here and there a vestige of forms and materials that preceded its course, just to set off its new and richer designs.

The aspect of this country was to me enchanting, beyond any I have ever seen, from its fullness of expression, its bold and impassioned sweetness. Here the flood of emotion has passed over and marked everywhere its course by a smile. The fragments of rock touch it with a wildness and liberality which give just the needed relief. I should never be tired here, though I have elsewhere seen country of more secret and alluring charms, better calculated to stimulate and suggest. Here the eye and heart are filled.

How happy the Indians must have been here! It is not long since they were driven away, and the ground, above and below, is full of their traces.

"The earth is full of men."

You have only to turn up the sod to find arrowheads and Indian pottery. On an island, belonging to our host, and nearly opposite his house, they loved to stay, and, no doubt; enjoyed its lavish beauty as much as the myriad wild pigeons that now haunt its flower-filled shades. Here are still the marks of their tomahawks, the troughs in which they prepared their corn, their caches.

A little way down the river is the site of an ancient Indian village, with its regularly arranged mounds. As usual, they had chosen with the finest taste. It was one of those soft shadowy afternoons when we went there, when nature seems ready to weep, not from grief, but from an overfull heart. Two prattling, lovely little girls, and an African boy, with glittering eye and ready grin, made our party gay; but all were still as we entered their little inlet and trod those flowery paths. They may blacken Indian life as they will, talk of its dirt, its brutality, I will ever believe that the men who chose that dwelling-place were able to feel emotions of noble happiness as they returned to it, and so were the women that received them. Neither were the children sad or dull, who lived so familiarly with the deer and the birds, and swam that clear wave in the shadow of the Seven Sisters. The whole scene suggested to me a Greek splendor, a Greek sweetness, and I can believe that an Indian brave, accustomed to ramble in such paths, and be bathed by such sunbeams, might be mistaken for Apollo, as Apollo was for him by West. Two of the boldest bluffs are called the Deer's Walk, (not because deer do *not* walk there,) and the Eagle's Nest. The latter I visited one glorious morning; it was that of the fourth of July, and certainly I think I had never felt so happy that I was born in America. Wo to all country folks that never saw this spot, never swept an enraptured gaze over the prospect that stretched beneath. I do believe Rome and Florence are suburbs compared to this capital of nature's art.

The bluff was decked with great bunches of a scarlet variety of the milkweed, like cut coral, and all starred with a mysterious-looking dark flower, whose cup rose lonely on a tall stem. This had, for two or three days, disputed the ground with the lupine and phlox. My companions disliked, I liked it.

Here I thought of, or rather saw, what the Greek expresses under the form of Jove's darling, Ganymede, and the following stanzas took form.

GANYMEDE TO HIS EAGLE,

SUGGESTED BY A WORK OF THORWALDSEN'S
Composed on the height called the Eagle's Nest, Oregon,
Rock River, July 4th, 1843.

Upon the rocky mountain stood the boy,
  A goblet of pure water in his hand,
His face and form spoke him one made for joy,
  A willing servant to sweet love's command,
But a strange pain was written on his brow,
And thrilled throughout his silver accents now—

"My bird," he cries, "my destined brother friend,
  O whither fleets to-day thy wayward flight?
Hast thou forgotten that I here attend,
  From the full noon until this sad twilight?
A hundred times, at least, from the clear spring,
  Since the full noon o'er hill and valley glowed,
I've filled the vase which our Olympian king
  Upon my care for thy sole use bestowed;
That at the moment when thou should'st descend,
A pure refreshment might thy thirst attend.

Hast thou forgotten earth, forgotten me,
  Thy fellow bondsman in a royal cause,
Who, from the sadness of infinity,
  Only with thee can know that peaceful pause
In which we catch the flowing strain of love,
Which binds our dim fates to the throne of Jove?

Before I saw thee, I was like the May,
  Longing for summer that must mar its bloom,
Or like the morning star that calls the day,
  Whose glories to its promise are the tomb;
And as the eager fountain rises higher
  To throw itself more strongly back to earth,
Still, as more sweet and full rose my desire,
  More fondly it reverted to its birth,
For, what the rosebud seeks tells not the rose,
The meaning foretold by the boy the man cannot disclose.

I was all Spring, for in my being dwelt
  Eternal youth, where flowers are the fruit,
Full feeling was the thought of what was felt,
  Its music was the meaning of the lute;
But heaven and earth such life will still deny,
For earth, divorced from heaven, still asks the question
  Why?

Upon the highest mountains my young feet
  Ached, that no pinions from their lightness grew,
My starlike eyes the stars would fondly greet,
  Yet win no greeting from the circling blue;
Fair, self-subsistent each in its own sphere,
  They had no care that there was none for me;
Alike to them that I was far or near,
  Alike to them, time and eternity.

But, from the violet of lower air,
  Sometimes an answer to my wishing came,
Those lightning births my nature seemed to share,
  They told the secrets of its fiery frame,
The sudden messengers of hate and love,
The thunderbolts that arm the hand of Jove,
And strike sometimes the sacred spire, and strike the sacred grove.

Come in a moment, in a moment gone,
They answered me, then left me still more lone,
They told me that the thought which ruled the world,
As yet no sail upon its course had furled,
That the creation was but just begun,
New leaves still leaving from the primal one,
But spoke not of the goal to which my rapid wheels would run.

Still, still my eyes, though tearfully, I strained
To the far future which my heart contained,
And no dull doubt my proper hope profaned.

At last, O bliss, thy living form I spied,
  Then a mere speck upon a distant sky,
Yet my keen glance discerned its noble pride,
  And the full answer of that sun-filled eye;
I knew it was the wing that must upbear
My earthlier form into the realms of air.

Thou knowest how we gained that beauteous height,
Where dwells the monarch of the sons of light,
Thou knowest he declared us two to be
The chosen servants of his ministry,
Thou as his messenger, a sacred sign
Of conquest, or with omen more benign,
To give its due weight to the righteous cause,
To express the verdict of Olympian laws.

And I to wait upon the lonely spring,
  Which slakes the thirst of bards to whom 'tis given
The destined dues of hopes divine to sing,
  And weave the needed chain to bind to heaven.
Only from such could be obtained a draught
For him who in his early home from Jove's own cup has quaffed.

To wait, to wait, but not to wait too long,
Till heavy grows the burthen of a song;
O bird! too long hast thou been gone to-day,
My feet are weary of their frequent way,
The spell that opes the spring my tongue no more can say.

If soon thou com'st not, night will fall around,
My head with a sad slumber will be bound,
And the pure draught be spilt upon the ground.

Remember that I am not yet divine,
Long years of service to the fatal Nine
Are yet to make a Delphian vigor mine.

O, make them not too hard, thou bird of Jove,
Answer the stripling's hope, confirm his love,
Receive the service in which he delights,

And bear him often to the serene heights,
Where hands that were so prompt in serving thee,
Shall be allowed the highest ministry,
And Rapture live with bright Fidelity.

The afternoon was spent in a very different manner. The family, whose guests we were, possessed a gay and graceful hospitality that gave zest to each moment. They possessed that rare politeness which, while fertile in pleasant expedients to vary the enjoyment of a friend, leaves him perfectly free the moment he wishes to be so. With such hosts, pleasure may be combined with repose. They lived on the bank opposite the town, and, as their house was full, we slept in the town, and passed three days with them, passing to and fro morning and evening in their boats. (To one of these, called the Fairy, in which a sweet little daughter of the house moved about lighter than any Scotch Ellen ever sung, I should indite a poem, if I had not been guilty of rhyme on the very last page.) At morning this was very pleasant; at evening, I confess I was generally too tired with the excitements of the day to think it so.

Their house—a double log cabin—was, to my eye, the model of a Western villa. Nature had laid out before it grounds which could not be improved. Within, female taste had veiled every rudeness—availed itself of every sylvan grace.

In this charming abode what laughter, what sweet thoughts, what pleasing fancies, did we not enjoy! May such never desert those who reared it and made us so kindly welcome to all its pleasures!

Fragments of city life were dexterously crumbled into the dish prepared for general entertainment. Ice creams followed the dinner drawn by the gentlemen from the river, and music and fireworks wound up the evening of days spent on the Eagle's Nest. Now they had prepared a little fleet to pass over to the Fourth of July celebration, which some queer drumming and fifing, from the opposite bank, had announced to be "on hand."

We found the free and independent citizens there collected beneath the trees, among whom many a round Irish visage dimpled at the usual puffs of Ameriky.

The orator was a New Englander, and the speech smacked loudly of Boston, but was received with much applause, and followed by a plentiful dinner, provided by and for the Sovereign People, to which Hail Columbia served as grace.

Returning, the gay flotilla hailed the little flag which the children had raised from a log-cabin, prettier than any president ever saw, and drank the health of their country and all mankind, with a clear conscience.

Dance and song wound up the day. I know not when the mere local habitation has seemed to me to afford so fair a chance of happiness as this. To a person of unspoiled tastes, the beauty alone would afford stimulus enough. But with it would be naturally associated all kinds of wild sports, experiments, and the studies of natural history. In these regards, the poet, the sportsman, the naturalist, would alike rejoice in this wide range of untouched loveliness.

Then, with a very little money, a ducal estate may be purchased, and by a very little more, and moderate labor, a family be maintained upon it with raiment, food and shelter. The luxurious and minute comforts of a city life are not yet to be had without effort disproportionate to their value. But, where there is so great a counterpoise, cannot these be given up once for all? If the houses are imperfectly built, they can afford immense fires and plenty of covering; if they are small, who cares?—with such fields to roam in. In winter, it may be borne; in summer, is of no consequence. With plenty of fish, and game, and wheat, can they not dispense with a baker to bring "muffins hot" every morning to the door for their breakfast?

Here a man need not take a small slice from the landscape, and fence it in from the obtrusions of an uncongenial neighbor, and there cut down his fancies to miniature improvements which a chicken could run over in ten minutes. He may have water and wood and land enough, to dread no incursions on his prospect from some chance Vandal that may enter his neighborhood. He need not painfully economise and manage how he may use it all; he can afford to leave some of it wild, and to carry out his own plans without obliterating those of nature.

Here, whole families might live together, if they would. The sons might return from their pilgrimages to settle near the parent hearth; the daughters might find room near their mother. Those painful separations, which already desecrate and desolate the Atlantic coast, are not enforced here by the stern need of seeking bread; and where they are voluntary, it is no matter. To me, too, used to the feelings which haunt a society of struggling men, it was delightful to look upon a scene where nature still wore her motherly smile and seemed to promise room not only for those favored or cursed with the qualities best adapting for the strifes of competition, but for the delicate, the thoughtful, even the indolent or eccentric. She did not say, Fight or starve; nor even, Work or cease to exist; but, merely showing that the apple was a finer fruit than the wild crab, gave both room to grow in the garden.

A pleasant society is formed of the families who live along the banks of this stream upon farms. They are from various parts of the world, and have much to communicate to one another. Many have cultivated minds and refined manners, all a varied experience, while they have in common the interests of a new country and a new life. They must traverse some space to get at one another, but the journey is through scenes that make it a separate pleasure. They must bear inconveniences to stay in one another's houses; but these, to the well-disposed, are only a source of amusement and adventure.

The great drawback upon the lives of these settlers, at present, is the unfitness of the women for their new lot. It has generally been the choice of the men, and the women follow, as women will, doing their best for affection's sake, but too often in heartsickness and weariness. Beside it frequently not being a choice or conviction of their own minds that it is best to be here, their part is the hardest, and they are least fitted for it. The men can find assistance in field labor, and recreation with the gun and fishing-rod. Their bodily strength is greater, and enables them to bear and enjoy both these forms of life.

The women can rarely find any aid in domestic labor. All its various and careful tasks must often be performed, sick or well, by the mother and daughters, to whom a city education has imparted neither the strength nor skill now demanded.

The wives of the poorer settlers, having more hard work to do than before, very frequently become slatterns; but the ladies, accustomed to a refined neatness, feel that they cannot degrade themselves by its absence, and struggle under every disadvantage to keep up the necessary routine of small arrangements.

With all these disadvantages for work, their resources for pleasure are fewer. When they can leave the housework, they have not learnt to ride, to drive, to row, alone. Their culture has too generally been that given to women to make them "the ornaments of society." They can dance, but not draw; talk French, but know nothing of the language of flowers; neither in childhood were allowed to cultivate them, lest they should tan their complexions. Accustomed to the pavement of Broadway, they dare not tread the wildwood paths for fear of rattlesnakes!

Seeing much of this joylessness, and inaptitude, both of body and mind, for a lot which would be full of blessings for those prepared for it, we could not but look with deep interest on the little girls, and hope they would grow up with the strength of body, dexterity, simple tastes, and resources that would fit them to enjoy and refine the western farmer's life.

But they have a great deal to war with in the habits of thought acquired by their mothers from their own early life. Everywhere the fatal spirit of imitation, of reference to European standards, penetrates, and threatens to blight whatever of original growth might adorn the soil.

If the little girls grow up strong, resolute, able to exert their faculties, their mothers mourn over their want of fashionable delicacy. Are they gay, enterprising, ready to fly about in the various ways that teach them so much, these ladies lament that "they cannot go to school, where they might learn to be quiet." They lament the want of "education" for their daughters, as if the thousand needs which call out their young energies, and the language of nature around, yielded no education.

Their grand ambition for their children, is to send them to school in some eastern city, the measure most likely to make them useless and unhappy at home. I earnestly hope that, ere long, the existence of good schools near themselves, planned by persons of sufficient thought to meet the wants of the place and time, instead of copying New York or Boston, will correct this mania. Instruction the children want to enable them to profit by the great natural advantages of their position; but methods copied from the education of some English Lady Augusta, are as ill suited to the daughter of an Illinois farmer, as satin shoes to climb the Indian mounds. An elegance she would diffuse around her, if her mind were opened to appreciate elegance; it might be of a kind new, original, enchanting, as different from that of the city belle as that of the prairie torchflower from the shopworn article that touches the cheek of that lady within her bonnet.

To a girl really skilled to make home beautiful and comfortable, with bodily strength to enjoy plenty of exercise, the woods, the streams, a few studies, music, and the sincere and familiar intercourse, far more easily to be met here than elsewhere, would afford happiness enough. Her eyes would not grow dim, nor her cheeks sunken, in the absence of parties, morning visits, and milliner's shops.

As to music, I wish I could see in such places the guitar rather than the piano, and good vocal more than instrumental music.

The piano many carry with them, because it is the fashionable instrument in the eastern cities. Even there, it is so merely from the habit of imitating Europe, for not one in a thousand is willing to give the labor requisite to ensure any valuable use of the instrument.

But, out here, where the ladies have so much less leisure, it is still less desirable. Add to this, they never know how to tune their own instruments, and as persons seldom visit them who can do so, these pianos are constantly out of tune, and would spoil the ear of one who began by having any.

The guitar, or some portable instrument which requires less practice, and could be kept in tune by themselves, would be far more desirable for most of these ladies. It would give all they want as a household companion to fill up the gaps of life with a pleasant stimulus or solace, and be sufficient accompaniment to the voice in social meetings.

Singing in parts is the most delightful family amusement, and those who are constantly together can learn to sing in perfect accord. All the practice it needs, after some good elementary instruction, is such as meetings by summer twilight, and evening firelight naturally suggest. And, as music is an universal language, we cannot but think a fine Italian duet would be as much at home in the log cabin as one of Mrs. Gore's novels.

The sixth July we left this beautiful place. It was one of those rich days of bright sunlight, varied by the purple shadows of large sweeping clouds. Many a backward look we cast, and left the heart behind.

Our journey to-day was no less delightful than before, still all new, boundless, limitless. Kinmont says, that limits are sacred; that the Greeks were in the right to worship a god of limits. I say, that what is limitless is alone divine, that there was neither wall nor road in Eden, that those who walked there lost and found their way just as we did, and that all the gain from the Fall was that we had a wagon to ride in. I do not think, either, that even the horses doubted whether this last was any advantage.

Everywhere the rattlesnake-weed grows in profusion. The antidote survives the bane. Soon the coarser plantain, the "white man's footstep," shall take its place.

We saw also the compass plant, and the western tea plant. Of some of the brightest flowers an Indian girl afterwards told me the medicinal virtues. I doubt not those students of the soil knew a use to every fair emblem, on which we could only look to admire its hues and shape.

After noon we were ferried by a girl, (unfortunately not of the most picturesque appearance) across the Kishwaukie, the most graceful stream, and on whose bosom rested many full-blown water-lilies, twice as large as any of ours. I was told that, *en revanche,* they were scentless, but I still regret that I could not get at one of them to try.

Query, did the lilied fragrance which, in the miraculous times, accompanied visions of saints and angels, proceed from water or garden lilies?

Kishwaukie is, according to tradition, the scene of a famous battle, and its many grassy mounds contain the bones of the valiant. On these waved thickly the mysterious purple flower, of which I have spoken before. I think it springs from the blood of the Indians, as the hyacinth did from that of Apollo's darling.

The ladies of our host's family at Oregon, when they first went there, after all the pains and plagues of building and settling, found their first pastime in opening one of these mounds, in which they found, I think, three of the departed, seated in the Indian fashion.

One of these same ladies, as she was making bread one winter morning, saw from the window a deer directly before the house. She ran out, with her hands covered with dough, calling the others, and they caught him bodily before he had time to escape.

Here (at Kishwaukie) we received a visit from a ragged and barefoot, but bright-eyed gentleman, who seemed to be the intellectual loafer, the walking Will's coffeehouse of the place. He told us many charming snake stories; among others, of himself having seen seventeen young ones reënter the mother snake, on the intrusion of a visiter.

This night we reached Belvidere, a flourishing town in Boon county, where was the tomb, now despoiled, of Big Thunder. In this later day we felt happy to find a really good hotel.

From this place, by two days of very leisurely and devious journeying, we reached Chicago, and thus ended a journey, which one at least of the party might have wished unending.

I have not been particularly anxious to give the geography of the scene, inasmuch as it seemed to me no route, nor series of stations, but a garden interspersed with cottages, groves and flowery lawns, through which a stately river ran. I had no guidebook, kept no diary, do not know how many miles we travelled each day, nor how many in all. What I got from the journey was the poetic impression of the country at large; it is all I have aimed to communicate.

The narrative might have been made much more interesting, as life was at the time, by many piquant anecdotes and tales drawn from private life. But here courtesy restrains the pen, for I know those who received the stranger with such frank kindness would feel ill requited by its becoming the means of fixing many spy-glasses, even though the scrutiny might be one of admiring interest, upon their private homes.

For many of these, too, I was indebted to a friend, whose property they more lawfully are. This friend was one of those rare beings who are equally at home in nature and with man. He knew a tale of all that ran and swam, and flew, or only grew, possessing that extensive familiarity with things which shows equal sweetness of sympathy and playful penetration. Most refreshing to me was his unstudied lore, the unwritten poetry which common life presents to a strong and gentle mind. It was a great contrast to the subtleties of analysis, the philosophic strainings of which I had seen too much. But I will not attempt to transplant it. May it profit others as it did me in the region where it was born, where it belongs. The evening of our return to Chicago the sunset was of a splendor and calmness beyond any we saw at the West. The twilight that succeeded was equally beautiful; soft, pathetic, but just so calm. When afterwards I learned this was the evening of Allston's death, it seemed to me as if this glorious pageant was not without connection with that event; at least, it inspired similar emotions,—a heavenly gate closing a path adorned with shows well worthy Paradise.

> Farewell, ye soft and sumptuous solitudes!
> Ye fairy distances, ye lordly woods,
> Haunted by paths like those that Poussin knew,
> When after his all gazers eyes he drew;
> I go,—and if I never more may steep
> An eager heart in your enchantments deep,
> Yet ever to itself that heart may say,
> Be not exacting; thou hast lived one day;
> Hast looked on that which matches with thy mood,
> Impassioned sweetness of full being's flood,
> Where nothing checked the bold yet gentle wave,
> Where nought repelled the lavish love that gave.
> A tender blessing lingers o'er the scene,
> Like some young mother's thought, fond, yet serene,
> And through its life new-born our lives have been.
> Once more farewell,—a sad, a sweet farewell;
> And, if I never must behold you more,
> In other worlds I will not cease to tell
> The rosary I here have numbered o'er;
> And bright-haired Hope will lend a gladdened ear,

And Love will free him from the grasp of Fear,
And Gorgon critics, while the tale they hear,
Shall dew their stony glances with a tear,
If I but catch one echo from your spell;—
And so farewell,—a grateful, sad farewell!

CHAPTER IV

CHICAGO AGAIN

Chicago had become interesting to me now, that I knew it as the portal to so fair a scene. I had become interested in the land, in the people, and looked sorrowfully on the lake on which I must soon embark, to leave behind what I had just begun to enjoy.

Now was the time to see the lake. The July moon was near its full, and night after night it rose in a cloudless sky above this majestic sea. The heat was excessive, so that there was no enjoyment of life, except in the night, but then the air was of that delicious temperature, worthy of orange groves. However, they were not wanted;—nothing was, as that full light fell on the faintly rippling waters which then seemed boundless.

A poem received shortly after, from a friend in Massachusetts, seemed to say that the July moon shone there not less splendid, and may claim insertion here.

TRIFORMIS

I.
So pure her forehead's dazzling white,
  So swift and clear her radiant eyes,
Within the treasure of whose light
  Lay undeveloped destinies,—
Of thoughts repressed such hidden store
  Was hinted by each flitting smile,
I could but wonder and adore,
  Far off, in awe, I gazed the while.

I gazed at her, as at the moon,
*   Hanging in lustrous twilight skies,*
Whose virgin crescent, sinking soon,
*   Peeps through the leaves before it flies.*
Untouched Diana, flitting dim,
*   While sings the wood its evening hymn.*

II.

Again we met. O joyful meeting!
*   Her radiance now was all for me,*
Like kindly airs her kindly greeting,
*   So full, so musical, so free.*
Within romantic forest aisles,
*   Within romantic paths we walked,*
I bathed me in her sister smiles,
*   I breathed her beauty as we talked.*

So full-orbed Cynthia walks the skies,
*   Filling the earth with melodies,*
Even so she condescends to kiss
*   Drowsy Endymions, coarse and dull,*
Or fills our waking souls with bliss,
*   Making long nights too beautiful.*

III.

O fair, but fickle lady-moon,
*   Why must thy full form ever wane?*
O love! O friendship! why so soon
*   Must your sweet light recede again?*
I wake me in the dead of night,
*   And start,—for through the misty gloom*
Red Hecate stares—a boding sight!—
*   Looks in, but never fills my room.*

Thou music of my boyhood's hour!
*   Thou shining light on manhood's way!*
No more dost thou fair influence shower
*   To move my soul by night or day.*
O strange! that while in hall and street
*   Thy hand I touch, thy grace I meet,*
Such miles of polar ice should part
*   The slightest touch of mind and heart!*

> *But all thy love has waned, and so*
> *I gladly let thy beauty go.*

Now that I am borrowing, I will also give a letter received at this time, and extracts from others from an earlier traveller, and in a different region of the country from that I saw, which, I think, in different ways, admirably descriptive of the country.

"And you, too, love the Prairies, flying voyager of a summer hour; but *I* have only there owned the wild forest, the wide-spread meadows; there only built my house, and seen the livelong day the thoughtful shadows of the great clouds color, with all-transient browns, the untrampled floor of grass; there has Spring pranked the long smooth reaches with those golden flowers, whereby became the fields a sea too golden to o'erlast the heats. Yes! and with many a yellow bell she gilded our unbounded path, that sank in the light swells of the varied surface, skirted the untilled barrens, nor shunned the steep banks of rivers darting merrily on. There has the white snow frolicsomely strown itself, till all that vast, outstretched distance glittered like a mirror in which only the heavens were reflected, and among these drifts our steps have been curbed. Ah! many days of precious weather are on the Prairies!

"You have then found, after many a weary hour, when Time has locked your temples as in a circle of heated metal, some cool, sweet, swift-gliding moments, the iron ring of necessity ungirt, and the fevered pulses at rest. You have also found this where fresh nature suffers no ravage, amid those bowers of wild-wood, those dream-like, bee-sung, murmuring and musical plains, swimming under their hazy distances, as if there, in that warm and deep back ground, stood the fairy castle of our hopes, with its fountains, its pictures, its many mystical figures in repose. Ever could we rove over those sunny distances, breathing that modulated wind, eyeing those so well-blended, imaginative, yet thoughtful surfaces, and above us wide—wide a horizon effortless and superb as a young divinity.

"I was a prisoner where you glide, the summer's pensioned guest, and my chains were the past and the future, darkness and blowing sand. There, very weary, I received from the distance a sweet emblem of an incorruptible, lofty and pervasive nature, but was I less weary? I was a prisoner, and you, plains, were my prison bars.

"Yet never, O never, beautiful plains, had I any feeling for you but profoundest gratitude, for indeed ye are only fair, grand and majestic, while I had scarcely a right there. Now, ye stand in that past day, grateful images of unshattered repose, simple in your tranquillity, strong in your self-possession, yet ever musical and springing as the footsteps of a child.

"Ah! that to some poet, whose lyre had never lost a string, to whom mortality, kinder than is her custom, had vouchsafed a day whose down had been untouched,—that to him these plains might enter, and flow forth in airy song. And you, forests, under whose symmetrical shields of dark green the colors of the fawns move, like the waters of the river under its spears,—its cimeters of flag, where, in gleaming circles of steel, the breasts of the wood-pigeons flash in the playful sunbeam, and many sounds, many notes of no earthly music, come over the well-relieved glades,—should not your depth pass into that poet's heart,—in your depths should he not fuse his own?"

The other letters show the painter's eye, as this the poet's heart.

SPRINGFIELD, ILLINOIS, MAY 20, 1840

"Yesterday morning I left Griggsville, my knapsack at my back, pursued my journey all day on foot, and found so new and great delight in this charming country, that I must needs tell you about it. Do you remember our saying once, that we never found the trees tall enough, the fields green enough. Well, the trees are for once tall, and fair to look upon, and one unvarying carpet of the tenderest green covers these marvellous fields, that spread out their smooth sod for miles and miles, till they even reach the horizon. But, to begin my day's journey. Griggsville is situated on the west side of the Illinois river, on a high prairie; between it and the river is a long range of bluffs which reaches a hundred miles north and south, then a wide river bottom, and then the river. It was a mild, showery morning, and I directed my steps toward the bluffs. They are covered with forest, not like our forests, tangled and impassable, but where the trees stand fair and apart from one another, so that you might ride every where about on horseback, and the tops of the hills are generally bald, and covered with green turf, like our pastures. Indeed, the whole country reminds me perpetually of one that has been carefully cultivated by a civilized people, who had been suddenly removed from the earth, with all the works of their hands, and the land given again into nature's keeping. The solitudes are not savage; they have not that dreary, stony loneliness that used to affect me in our own country; they never repel; there are no lonely heights, no isolated spots, but all is gentle, mild, inviting,— all is accessible. In following this winding, hilly road for four or five miles, I think I counted at least a dozen new kinds of wild flowers,

not timid, retiring little plants like ours, but bold flowers of rich colors,
covering the ground in abundance. One very common flower resembles
our cardinal flower, though not of so deep a color, another is very like
rocket or phlox, but smaller and of various colors, white, blue and
purple. Beautiful white lupines I find too, violets white and purple.
The vines and parasites are magnificent. I followed on this road till I
came to the prairie which skirts the river, and this, of all the beauties
of this region, is the most peculiar and wonderful. Imagine a vast and
gently-swelling pasture of the brightest green grass, stretching away
from you on every side, behind, toward these hills I have described,
in all other directions, to a belt of tall trees, all growing up with noble
proportions, from the generous soil. It is an unimagined picture of
abundance and peace. Somewhere about, you are sure to see a huge
herd of cattle, often white, and generally brightly marked, grazing. All
looks like the work of man's hand, but you see no vestige of man,
save perhaps an almost imperceptible hut on the edge of the prairie.
Reaching the river, I ferried myself across, and then crossed over to
take the Jacksonville railroad, but, finding there was no train, passed
the night at a farm house. And here may find its place this converse
between the solitary old man and the young traveller.

SOLITARY

My son, with weariness thou seemest spent,
And toiling on the dusty road all day,
Weary and pale, yet with inconstant step,
Hither and thither turning,—seekest thou
To find aught lost, or what dark care pursues thee?
If thou art weary, rest, if hungry, eat.

TRAVELLER

Oh rather, father, let me ask of thee
What is it I do seek, what thing I lack?
These many days I've left my father's hall,
Forth driven by insatiable desire,
That, like the wind, now gently murmuring,
Enticed me forward with its own sweet voice
Through many-leaved woods, and valleys deep,
Yet ever fled before me. Then with sound

Stronger than hurrying tempest, seizing me,
Forced me to fly its power. Forward still,
Bound by enchanted ties, I seek its source.
Sometimes it is a something I have lost,
Known long since, before I bent my steps
Toward this beautiful broad plane of earth.
Sometimes it is a spirit yet unknown,
In whose dim-imaged features seem to smile
The dear delight of these high-mansioned thoughts,
That sometimes visit me. Like unto mine
Her lineaments appear, but beautiful,
As of a sister in a far-off world,
Waiting to welcome me. And when I think
To reach and clasp the figure, it is gone,
And some ill-omened ghastly vision comes
To bid beware, and not too curiously
Demand the secrets of that distant world,
Whose shadow haunts me.—On the waves below
But now I gazed, warmed with the setting sun,
Who sent his golden streamers to my feet,
It seemed a pathway to a world beyond,
And I looked round, if that my spirit beckoned
That I might follow it.

SOLITARY

Dreams, all, my son. Yes, even so I dreamed,
And even so was thwarted. You must learn
To dream another long and troublous dream,
The dream of life. And you shall think you wake,
And think the shadows substance, love and hate,
Exchange and barter, joy, and weep, and dance,
And this too shall be dream.

TRAVELLER

Oh who can say
Where lies the boundary? What solid things
That daily mock our senses, shall dissolve
Before the might within; while shadowy forms

> Freeze into stark reality, defying
> The force and will of man. These forms I see,
> They may go with me through eternity,
> And bless or curse with ceaseless company,
> While yonder man, that I met yesternight,
> Where is he now? He passed before my eyes,
> He is gone, but these stay with me ever.
>
> That night the young man rested with the old,
> And, grave or gay, in laughter or in tears,
> They wore the night in converse. Morning came,
> The dreamer took his solitary way;
> And, as he pressed the old man's hand, he sighed,
> Must this too be a dream?

Afterwards, of the rolling prairie. "There was one of twenty miles in extent, not flat, but high and rolling, so that when you arrived at a high part, by gentle ascents, the view was beyond measure grand; as far as the eye could reach, nothing but the green, rolling plain, and at a vast distance, groves, all looking gentle and cultivated, yet all uninhabited. I think it would impress you, as it does me, that these scenes are truly sublime. I have a sensation of vastness which I have sought in vain among high mountains. Mountains crowd one sensation on another, till all is excitement, all is surprise, wonder, enchantment. Here is neither enchantment or disappointment, but expectation fully realized. I have always had an attachment for a plain. The Roman Campagna is a prairie. Peoria is in a most lovely situation. In fact I am so delighted that I am as full of superlatives as the Italian language. I could, however, find fault enough, if you ask what I dislike."

But no one did ask; it is not worth while where there is so much to admire. Yet the following is a good statement of the shadow side.

"As to the boasts about the rapid progress here, give me rather the firm fibre of a slow and knotty growth. I could not help thinking as much when I was talking to E. the other day, whom I met on board the boat. He quarrelled with Boston for its slowness; said it was a bad place for a young man. He could not make himself felt, could not see the effects of his exertions as he could here.—To be sure he could not. Here he comes, like a yankee farmer, with all the knowledge that our hard soil and laborious cultivation could give him, and what wonder if he is surprised at the work of his own hands, when he comes to such a soil as this. But he feeds not so many mouths, though he tills more acres. The plants he raises have not so exquisite a form, the vegetables so fine a flavor. His cultivation becomes more negligent, he is not so good a farmer. Is not this a true view? It strikes me continually. The traces of a man's hand in a new country are rarely productive of beauty. It is a cutting down of forest trees to make zigzag fences."

The most picturesque objects to be seen from Chicago on the inland side were the lines of Hoosier wagons. These rude farmers, the large first product of the soil, travel leisurely along, sleeping in their wagons by night, eating only what they bring with them. In the town they observe the same plan, and trouble no luxurious hotel for board and lodging. In the town they look like foreign peasantry, and contrast well with the many Germans, Dutch, and Irish. In the country it is very pretty to see them prepared to "camp out" at night, their horses taken out of harness, and they lounging under the trees, enjoying the evening meal.

On the lake side it is fine to see the great boats come panting it from their rapid and marvellous journey. Especially at night the motion of their lights is very majestic.

When the favorite boats, the Great Western and Illinois, are going out, the town is thronged with people from the south and farther west, to go in them. These moonlight nights I would hear the French rippling and fluttering familiarly amid the rude ups and downs of the Hoosier dialect.

At the hotel table were daily to be seen new faces, and new stories to be learned. And any one who has a large acquaintance may be pretty sure of meeting some of them here in the course of a few days.

Among those whom I met was Mrs. Z., the aunt of an old schoolmate, to whom I impatiently hastened, as soon as the meal was over, to demand news of Mariana. The answer startled me. Mariana, so full of life, was dead. That form, the most rich in energy and coloring of any I had ever seen, had faded from the earth. The circle of youthful associations had given way in the part, that seemed the strongest. What I now learned of the story of this life, and what was by myself remembered, may be bound together in this slight sketch.

At the boarding-school to which I was too early sent, a fond, a proud, and timid child, I saw among the ranks of the gay and graceful, bright or earnest girls, only one who interested my fancy or touched my young heart; and this was Mariana. She was, on the father's side, of Spanish Creole blood, but had been sent to the Atlantic coast, to receive a school education under the care of her aunt, Mrs. Z.

This lady had kept her mostly at home with herself, and Mariana had gone from her house to a day-school; but the aunt, being absent for a time in Europe, she had now been unfortunately committed for some time to the mercies of a boarding-school.

A strange bird she proved there,—a lonely swallow that could not make for itself a summer. At first, her schoolmates were captivated with her ways; her love of wild dances and sudden song, her freaks of passion and of wit. She was always new, always surprising, and, for a time, charming.

But, after awhile, they tired of her. She could never be depended on to join in their plans, yet she expected them to follow out hers with their whole strength. She was very loving, even infatuated in her own affections, and exacted from those who had professed any love for her, the devotion she was willing to bestow.

Yet there was a vein of haughty caprice in her character; a love of solitude, which made her at times wish to retire entirely, and at these times she would expect to be thoroughly understood, and let alone, yet to be welcomed back when she returned. She did not thwart others in their humors, but she never doubted of great indulgence from them.

Some singular habits she had which, when new, charmed, but, after acquaintance, displeased her companions. She had by nature the same habit and power of excitement that is described in the spinning dervishes of the East. Like them, she would spin until all around her were giddy, while her own brain, instead of being disturbed, was excited to great action. Pausing, she would declaim verse of others or her own; act many parts, with strange catch-words and burdens that seemed to act with mystical power on her own fancy, sometimes stimulating her to convulse the hearer with laughter, sometimes to melt him to tears. When her power began to languish, she would spin again till fired to recommence her singular drama, into which she wove figures from the scenes of her earlier childhood, her companions, and the dignitaries she sometimes saw, with fantasies unknown to life, unknown to heaven or earth.

This excitement, as may be supposed, was not good for her. It oftenest came on in the evening, and often spoiled her sleep. She would wake in the night, and cheat her restlessness by inventions that teazed, while they sometimes diverted her companions.

She was also a sleep-walker; and this one trait of her case did somewhat alarm her guardians, who, otherwise, showed the same profound stupidity as to this peculiar being, usual in the overseers of the young. They consulted a physician, who said she would outgrow it, and prescribed a milk diet.

Meantime, the fever of this ardent and too early stimulated nature was constantly increased by the restraints and narrow routine of the boarding school. She was always devising means to break in upon it. She had a taste which would have seemed ludicrous to her mates, if they had not felt some awe of her, from a touch of genius and power that never left her, for costume and fancy dresses, always some sash twisted about her, some drapery, something odd in the arrangement of her hair and dress, so that the methodical preceptress dared not let her go out without a careful scrutiny and remodelling, whose soberizing effects generally disappeared the moment she was in the free air.

At last, a vent for her was found in private theatricals. Play followed play, and in these and the rehearsals she found entertainment congenial with her. The principal parts, as a matter of course, fell to her lot; most of the good suggestions and arrangements came from her, and for a time she ruled masterly and shone triumphant.

During these performances the girls had heightened their natural bloom with artificial red; this was delightful to them—it was something so out of the way. But Mariana, after the plays were over, kept her carmine saucer on the dressing-table, and put on her blushes regularly as the morning.

When stared and jeered at, she at first said she did it because she thought it made her look prettier; but, after a while, she became quite petulant about it,—would make no reply to any joke, but merely kept on doing it.

This irritated the girls, as all eccentricity does the world in general, more than vice or malignity. They talked it over among themselves, till they got wrought up to a desire of punishing, once for all, this sometimes amusing, but so often provoking nonconformist.

Having obtained the leave of the mistress, they laid, with great glee, a plan one evening, which was to be carried into execution next day at dinner.

Among Mariana's irregularities was a great aversion to the meal-time ceremonial. So long, so tiresome she found it, to be seated at a certain moment, to wait while each one was served at so large a table, and one where there was scarcely any conversation; from day to day it became more heavy to her to sit there, or go there at all. Often as possible she excused herself on the ever-convenient plea of headache, and was hardly ever ready when the dinner-bell rang.

To-day it found her on the balcony, lost in gazing on the beautiful prospect. I have heard her say afterwards, she had rarely in her life been so happy,—and she was one with whom happiness was a still rapture. It was one of the most blessed summer days; the shadows of great white clouds empurpled the distant hills for a few moments only to leave them more golden; the tall grass of the wide fields waved in the softest breeze. Pure blue were the heavens, and the same hue of pure contentment was in the heart of Mariana.

Suddenly on her bright mood jarred the dinner bell. At first rose her usual thought, I will not, cannot go; and then the *must,* which daily life can always enforce, even upon the butterflies and birds, came, and she walked reluctantly to her room. She merely changed her dress, and never thought of adding the artificial rose to her cheek.

When she took her seat in the dining-hall, and was asked if she would be helped, raising her eyes, she saw the person who asked her was deeply rouged, with a bright glaring spot, perfectly round, in either cheek. She looked at the next, same apparition! She then slowly passed her eyes down the whole line, and saw the same, with a suppressed smile distorting every countenance. Catching the design at once, she deliberately looked along her own side of the table, at every schoolmate in turn; every one had joined in the trick. The teachers strove to be grave, but she saw they enjoyed the joke. The servants could not suppress a titter.

When Warren Hastings stood at the bar of Westminster Hall—when the Methodist preacher walked through a line of men, each of whom greeted him with a brickbat or a rotten egg, they had some preparation for the crisis, and it might not be very difficult to meet it with an impassive brow. Our little girl was quite unprepared to find herself in the midst of a world which despised her, and triumphed in her disgrace.

She had ruled, like a queen, in the midst of her companions; she had shed her animation through their lives, and loaded them with prodigal favors, nor once suspected that a powerful favorite might not be loved. Now, she felt that she had been but a dangerous plaything in the hands of those whose hearts she never had doubted.

Yet, the occasion found her equal to it, for Mariana had the kind of spirit, which, in a better cause, had made the Roman matron truly say of her deathwound, "It is not painful, Poetus." She did not blench—she did not change countenance. She swallowed her dinner with apparent composure. She made remarks to those near her, as if she had no eyes.

The wrath of the foe of course rose higher, and the moment they were freed from the restraints of the dining-room, they all ran off, gaily calling, and sarcastically laughing, with backward glances, at Mariana, left alone.

She went alone to her room, locked the door, and threw herself on the floor in strong convulsions. These had sometimes threatened her life, as a child, but of later years, she had outgrown them. School-hours came, and she was not there. A little girl, sent to her door, could get no answer. The teachers became alarmed, and broke it open. Bitter was their penitence and that of her companions at the state in which they found her. For some hours, terrible anxiety was felt; but, at last, nature, exhausted, relieved herself by a deep slumber.

From this Mariana rose an altered being. She made no reply to the expressions of sorrow from her companions, none to the grave and kind, but undiscerning comments of her teacher. She did not name the source of her anguish, and its poisoned dart sank deeply in. It was this thought which stung her so. What, not one, not a single one, in the hour of trial, to take my part, not one who refused to take part against me. Past words of love, and caresses, little heeded at the time, rose to her memory, and gave fuel to her distempered thoughts. Beyond the sense of universal perfidy, of burning resentment, she could not get. And Mariana, born for love, now hated all the world.

The change, however, which these feelings made in her conduct and appearance bore no such construction to the careless observer. Her gay freaks were quite gone, her wildness, her invention. Her dress was uniform, her manner much subdued. Her chief interest seemed now to lie in her studies, and in music. Her companions she never sought, but they, partly from uneasy remorseful feelings, partly that they really liked her much better now that she did not oppress and puzzle them, sought her continually. And here the black shadow comes upon her life, the only stain upon the history of Mariana.

They talked to her, as girls, having few topics, naturally do, of one another. And the demon rose within her, and spontaneously, with-out design, generally without words of positive falsehood, she became a genius of discord among them. She fanned those flames of envy and jealousy which a wise, true word from a third will often quench for-ever; by a glance, or a seemingly light reply, she planted the seeds of dissension, till there was scarce a peaceful affection, or sincere intimacy in the circle where she lived, and could not but rule, for she was one whose nature was to that of the others as fire to clay.

It was at this time that I came to the school, and first saw Mari-ana. Me she charmed at once, for I was a sentimental child, who, in my early ill health, had been indulged in reading novels, till I had no eyes for the common greens and browns of life. The heroine of one of these, "The Bandit's Bride," I immediately saw in Mariana. Surely the Bandit's Bride had just such hair, and such strange, lively ways, and such a sudden flash of the eye. The Bandit's Bride, too, was born to be "misunderstood" by all but her lover. But Mariana, I was determined, should be more fortunate, for, until her lover appeared, I myself would be the wise and delicate being who could understand her.

It was not, however, easy to approach her for this purpose. Did I offer to run and fetch her handkerchief, she was obliged to go to her room, and would rather do it herself. She did not like to have people turn over for her the leaves of the music book as she played. Did I approach my stool to her feet, she moved away, as if to give me room. The bunch of wild flowers which I timidly laid beside her plate was left there.

After some weeks my desire to attract her notice really preyed upon me, and one day meeting her alone in the entry, I fell upon my knees, and kissing her hand, cried, "O Mariana, do let me love you, and try to love me a little." But my idol snatched away her hand, and, laughing more wildly than the Bandit's Bride was ever described to have done, ran into her room. After that day her manner to me was not only cold, but repulsive; I felt myself scorned, and became very unhappy.

Perhaps four months had passed thus, when, one afternoon, it became obvious that something more than common was brewing. Dismay and mystery were written in many faces of the older girls; much whispering was going on in corners.

In the evening, after prayers, the principal bade us stay; and, in a grave, sad voice, summoned forth Mariana to answer charges to be made against her.

Mariana came forward, and leaned against the chimney-piece. Eight of the older girls came forward, and preferred against her charges, alas, too well-founded, of calumny and falsehood.

My heart sank within me, as one after the other brought up their proofs, and I saw they were too strong to be resisted. I could not bear the thought of this second disgrace of my shining favorite. The first had been whispered to me, though the girls did not like to talk about it. I must confess, such is the charm of strength to softer natures, that neither of these crises could deprive Mariana of hers in my eyes.

At first, she defended herself with self-possession and eloquence. But when she found she could no more resist the truth, she suddenly threw herself down, dashing her head, with all her force, against the iron hearth, on which a fire was burning, and was taken up senseless.

The affright of those present was great. Now that they had perhaps killed her, they reflected it would have been as well, if they had taken warning from the former occasion, and approached very carefully a nature so capable of any extreme. After awhile she revived, with a faint groan, amid the sobs of her companions. I was on my knees by the bed, and held her cold hand. One of those most aggrieved took it from me to beg her pardon, and say it was impossible not to love her. She made no reply.

Neither that night, nor for several days, could a word be obtained from her, nor would she touch food; but, when it was presented to her, or any one drew near for any cause, she merely turned away her head, and gave no sign. The teacher saw that some terrible nervous affection had fallen upon her, that she grew more and more feverish. She knew not what to do.

Meanwhile a new revolution had taken place in the mind of the passionate, but nobly-tempered child. All these months nothing but the sense of injury had rankled in her heart. She had gone on in one mood, doing what the demon prompted, without scruple and without fear.

But, at the moment of detection, the tide ebbed, and the bottom of her soul lay revealed to her eye. How black, how stained and sad. Strange, strange that she had not seen before the baseness and cruelty of falsehood, the loveliness of truth. Now, amid the wreck, uprose the moral nature which never before had attained the ascendant. "But," she thought, "too late, sin is revealed to me in all its deformity, and, sin-defiled, I will not, cannot live. The main-spring of life is broken."

And thus passed slowly by her hours in that black despair of which only youth is capable. In older years men suffer more dull pain, as each sorrow that comes drops its leaden weight into the past, and, similar features of character bringing similar results, draws up a heavy burden buried in those depths. But only youth has energy, with fixed unwinking gaze, to contemplate grief, to hold it in the arms and to the heart, like a child which makes it wretched, yet is indubitably its own.

The lady who took charge of this sad child had never well understood her before, but had always looked on her with great tenderness. And now love seemed, when all around were in greatest distress, fearing to call in medical aid, fearing to do without it, to teach her where the only balm was to be found that could have healed this wounded spirit.

One night she came in, bringing a calming draught. Mariana was sitting, as usual, her hair loose, her dress the same robe they had put on her at first, her eyes fixed vacantly upon the whited wall. To the proffers and entreaties of her nurse she made no reply.

The lady burst into tears, but Mariana did not seem even to observe it.

The lady then said, "O my child, do not despair, do not think that one great fault can mar a whole life. Let me trust you, let me tell you the griefs of my sad life. I will tell to you, Mariana, what I never expected to impart to any one."

And so she told her tale: it was one of pain, of shame, borne, not for herself, but for one near and dear as herself. Mariana knew the lady, knew the pride and reserve of her nature; she had often admired to see how the cheek, lovely, but no longer young, mantled with the deepest blush of youth, and the blue eyes were cast down at any little emotion. She had understood the proud sensibility of the character. She fixed her eyes on those now raised to hers, bright with fast falling tears. She heard the story to the end, and then, without saying a word, stretched out her hand for the cup.

She returned to life, but it was as one who has passed through the valley of death. The heart of stone was quite broken in her. The fiery life fallen from flame to coal. When her strength was a little restored, she had all her companions summoned, and said to them; "I deserved to die, but a generous trust has called me back to life. I will be worthy of it, nor ever betray the truth, or resent injury more. Can you forgive the past?"

And they not only forgave, but, with love and earnest tears, clasped in their arms the returning sister. They vied with one another in offices of humble love to the humbled one; and, let it be recorded as an instance of the pure honor of which young hearts are capable, that these facts, known to forty persons, never, so far as I know, transpired beyond those walls.

It was not long after this that Mariana was summoned home. She went thither a wonderfully instructed being, though in ways those who had sent her forth to learn little dreamed of.

Never was forgotten the vow of the returning prodigal. Mariana could not resent, could not play false. The terrible crisis, which she so early passed through, probably prevented the world from hearing much of her. A wild fire was tamed in that hour of penitence at the boarding school, such as has oftentimes wrapped court and camp in its destructive glow.

But great were the perils she had yet to undergo, for she was one of those barks which easily get beyond soundings, and ride not lightly on the plunging billow.

Her return to her native climate seconded the effects of inward revolutions. The cool airs of the north had exasperated nerves too susceptible for their tension. Those of the south restored her to a more soft and indolent state. Energy gave place to feeling, turbulence to intensity of character.

At this time love was the natural guest, and he came to her under a form that might have deluded one less ready for delusion.

Sylvain was a person well proportioned to her lot in years, family, and fortune. His personal beauty was not great, but of a noble character. Repose marked his slow gesture, and the steady gaze of his large brown eye, but it was a repose that would give way to a blaze of energy when the occasion called. In his stature, expression, and heavy coloring, he might not unfitly be represented by the great magnolias that inhabit the forests of that climate. His voice, like everything about him, was rich and soft, rather than sweet or delicate.

Mariana no sooner knew him than she loved, and her love, lovely as she was, soon excited his. But, oh! it is a curse to woman to love first, or most. In so doing she reverses the natural relations, and her heart can never, never be satisfied with what ensues.

Mariana loved first, and loved most, for she had most force and variety to love with. Sylvain seemed, at first, to take her to himself, as the deep southern night might some fair star. But it proved not so.

Mariana was a very intellectual being, and she needed companionship. This she could only have with Sylvain, in the paths of passion and action. Thoughts he had none, and little delicacy of sentiment. The gifts she loved to prepare of such for him, he took with a sweet, but indolent smile; he held them lightly, and soon they fell from his grasp. He loved to have her near him, to feel the glow and fragrance of her nature, but cared not to explore the little secret paths whence that fragrance was collected.

Mariana knew not this for a long time. Loving so much, she imagined all the rest, and, where she felt a blank, always hoped that further communion would fill it up. When she found this could never be; that there was absolutely a whole province of her being to which nothing in his answered, she was too deeply in love to leave him. Often after passing hours together, beneath the southern moon, when, amid the sweet intoxication of mutual love, she still felt the desolation of solitude, and a repression of her finer powers, she had asked herself, can I give him up? But the heart always passionately answered, no! I may be miserable with him, but I cannot live without him.

And the last miserable feeling of these conflicts was, that if the lover, soon to be the bosom friend, could have dreamed of these conflicts, he would have laughed, or else been angry, even enough to give her up.

Ah weakness of the strong. Of these strong only where strength is weakness. Like others she had the decisions of life to make, before she had light by which to make them. Let none condemn her. Those who have not erred as fatally, should thank the guardian angel who gave them more time to prepare for judgment, but blame no children who thought at arm's length to find the moon. Mariana, with a heart capable of highest Eros, gave it to one who knew love only as a flower or plaything, and bound her heartstrings to one who parted his as lightly as the ripe fruit leaves the bough. The sequel could not fail. Many console themselves for the one great mistake with their children, with the world. This was not possible to Mariana. A few months of domestic life she still was almost happy. But Sylvain then grew tired. He wanted business and the world; of these she had no knowledge, for them no faculties. He wanted in her the head of his house; she to make her heart his home. No compromise was possible between natures of such unequal poise, and which had met only on one or two points. Through all its stages she

> *"felt*
> *The agonizing sense*
> *Of seeing love from passion melt*
> *Into indifference;*
> *The fearful shame that, day by day,*
> *Burns onward, still to burn,*
> *To have thrown her precious heart away,*
> *And met this black return,"*

till death at last closed the scene. Not that she died of one downright blow on the heart. That is not the way such cases proceed. I cannot detail all the symptoms, for I was not there to watch them, and aunt Z. was neither so faithful an observer or narrator as I have shown myself in the school-day passages; but, generally, they were as follows.

Sylvain wanted to go into the world, or let it into his house. Mariana consented; but, with an unsatisfied heart, and no lightness of character, she played her part ill there. The sort of talent and facility she had displayed in early days, were not the least like what is called out in the social world by the desire to please and to shine. Her excitement had been muse-like, that of the improvisatrice, whose kindling fancy seeks to create an atmosphere round it, and makes the chain through which to set free its electric sparks. That had been a time of wild and exuberant life. After her character became more tender and concentrated, strong affection or a pure enthusiasm might still have called out beautiful talents in her. But in the first she was utterly disappointed. The second was not roused within her thought. She did not expand into various life, and remained unequal; sometimes too passive, sometimes too ardent, and not sufficiently occupied with what occupied those around her to come on the same level with them and embellish their hours.

Thus she lost ground daily with her husband, who, comparing her with the careless shining dames of society, wondered why he had found her so charming in solitude.

At intervals, when they were left alone, Mariana wanted to open her heart, to tell the thoughts of her mind. She was so conscious of secret riches within herself, that sometimes it seemed, could she but reveal a glimpse of them to the eye of Sylvain, he would be attracted near her again, and take a path where they could walk hand in hand. Sylvain, in these intervals, wanted an indolent repose. His home was his castle. He wanted no scenes too exciting there. Light jousts and plays were well enough, but no grave encounters. He liked to lounge, to sing, to read, to sleep. In fine, Sylvain became the kind, but preoccupied husband, Mariana, the solitary and wretched wife. He was off continually, with his male companions, on excursions or affairs of pleasure. At home Mariana found that neither her books nor music would console her.

She was of too strong a nature to yield without a struggle to so dull a fiend as despair. She looked into other hearts, seeking whether she could there find such home as an orphan asylum may afford. This she did rather because the chance came to her, and it seemed unfit not to seize the proffered plank, than in hope, for she was not one to double her stakes, but rather with Cassandra power to discern early the sure course of the game. And Cassandra whispered that she was one of those

"Whom men love not, but yet regret,"

And so it proved. Just as in her childish days, though in a different form, it happened betwixt her and these companions. She could not be content to receive them quietly, but was stimulated to throw herself too much into the tie, into the hour, till she filled it too full for them. Like Fortunio, who sought to do homage to his friends by building a fire of cinnamon, not knowing that its perfume would be too strong for their endurance, so did Mariana. What she wanted to tell, they did not wish to hear; a little had pleased, so much overpowered, and they preferred the free air of the street, even, to the cinnamon perfume of her palace.

However, this did not signify; had they staid, it would not have availed her! It was a nobler road, a higher aim she needed now; this did not become clear to her.

She lost her appetite, she fell sick, had fever. Sylvain was alarmed, nursed her tenderly; she grew better. Then his care ceased, he saw not the mind's disease, but left her to rise into health and recover the tone of her spirits, as she might. More solitary than ever, she tried to raise herself, but she knew not yet enough. The weight laid upon her young life was a little too heavy for it. One long day she passed alone, and the thoughts and presages came too thick for her strength. She knew not what to do with them, relapsed into fever, and died.

Notwithstanding this weakness, I must ever think of her as a fine sample of womanhood, born to shed light and life on some palace home. Had she known more of God and the universe, she would not have given way where so many have conquered. But peace be with her; she now, perhaps, has entered into a larger freedom, which is knowledge. With her died a great interest in life to me. Since her I have never seen a Bandit's Bride. She, indeed, turned out to be only a merchant's.—Sylvain is married again to a fair and laughing girl, who will not die, probably, till their marriage grows a "golden marriage."

Aunt Z. had with her some papers of Mariana's, which faintly shadow forth the thoughts that engaged her in the last days. One of these seems to have been written when some faint gleam had been thrown across the path, only to make its darkness more visible. It seems to have been suggested by remembrance of the beautiful ballad, *Helen of Kirconnel Lee,* which once she loved to recite, and in tones that would not have sent a chill to the heart from which it came.

                                                "Death
Opens her sweet white arms, and whispers Peace;
Come, say thy sorrows in this bosom! This
Will never close against thee, and my heart,
Though cold, cannot be colder much than man's."

    "I wish I were where Helen lies,"
A lover in the times of old,
    Thus vents his grief in lonely sighs,
And hot tears from a bosom cold.

    But, mourner for thy martyred love,
Could'st thou but know what hearts must feel,
    Where no sweet recollections move,
Whose tears a desert fount reveal.

    When "in thy arms burd Helen fell,"
She died, sad man, she died for thee,
    Nor could the films of death dispel
Her loving eye's sweet radiancy.

    Thou wert beloved, and she had loved,
Till death alone the whole could tell,
    Death every shade of doubt removed,
And steeped the star in its cold well.

    On some fond breast the parting soul
Relies,—earth has no more to give;
    Who wholly loves has known the whole,
The wholly loved doth truly live.

    But some, sad outcasts from this prize,
Wither down to a lonely grave,
    All hearts their hidden love despise,
And leave them to the whelming wave.

    They heart to heart have never pressed,
Nor hands in holy pledge have given,
    By father's love were ne'er caressed,
Nor in a mother's eye saw heaven.

    A flowerless and fruitless tree,
A dried up stream, a mateless bird,
    They live, yet never living be,
They die, their music all unheard.

I wish I were where Helen lies,
For there I could not be alone;
But now, when this dull body dies,
The spirit still will make its moan.

Love passed me by, nor touched my brow;
Life would not yield one perfect boon;
And all too late it calls me now,
O all too late, and all too soon.

If thou couldst the dark riddle read
Which leaves this dart within my breast,
Then might I think thou lov'st indeed,
Then were the whole to thee confest.

Father, they will not take me home,
To the poor child no heart is free;
In sleet and snow all night I roam;
Father,—was this decreed by thee?

I will not try another door,
To seek what I have never found;
Now, till the very last is o'er,
Upon the earth I'll wander round.

I will not hear the treacherous call
That bids me stay and rest awhile,
For I have found that, one and all,
They seek me for a prey and spoil.

They are not bad, I know it well;
I know they know not what they do;
They are the tools of the dread spell
Which the lost lover must pursue.

In temples sometimes she may rest,
In lonely groves, away from men,
There bend the head, by heats distrest,
Nor be by blows awoke again.

Nature is kind, and God is kind,
And, if she had not had a heart,
Only that great discerning mind,
She might have acted well her part.

> *But oh this thirst, that none can still,*
> *Save those unfounden waters free;*
> *The angel of my life should fill*
> *And soothe me to Eternity!*

It marks the defect in the position of woman that one like Mariana should have found reason to write thus. To a man of equal power, equal sincerity, no more!—many resources would have presented themselves. He would not have needed to seek, he would have been called by life, and not permitted to be quite wrecked through the affections only. But such women as Mariana are often lost, unless they meet some man of sufficiently great soul to prize them.

Van Artevelde's Elena, though in her individual nature unlike my Mariana, is like her in a mind whose large impulses are disproportioned to the persons and occasions she meets, and which carry her beyond those reserves which mark the appointed lot of woman. But, when she met Van Artevelde, he was too great not to revere her rare nature, without regard to the stains and errors of its past history; great enough to receive her entirely and make a new life for her; man enough to be a lover! But as such men come not so often as once an age, their presence should not be absolutely needed to sustain life.

At Chicago I read again Philip Van Artevelde, and certain passages in it will always be in my mind associated with the deep sound of the lake, as heard in the night. I used to read a short time at night, and then open the blind to look out. The moon would be full upon the lake, and the calm breath, pure light, and the deep voice harmonized well with the thought of the Flemish hero. When will this country have such a man? It is what she needs; no thin Idealist, no coarse Realist, but a man whose eye reads the heavens while his feet step firmly on the ground, and his hands are strong and dexterous for the use of human implements. A man religious, virtuous and—sagacious; a man of universal sympathies, but self-possessed; a man who knows the region of emotion, though he is not its slave; a man to whom this world is no mere spectacle, or fleeting shadow, but a great solemn game to be played with good heed, for its stakes are of eternal value, yet who, if his own play be true, heeds not what he loses by the falsehood of others. A man who hives from the past, yet knows that its honey can but moderately avail him; whose comprehensive eye scans the present, neither infatuated by its golden lures, nor chilled by its many ventures; who possesses prescience, as the wise man must, but not so far as to be driven mad to-day by the gift which discerns to-morrow. When there is such a man for America, the thought which urges her on will be expressed.

Now that I am about to leave Illinois, feelings of regret and admiration come over me, as in parting with a friend whom we have not had the good sense to prize and study, while hours of association, never perhaps to return, were granted. I have fixed my attention almost exclusively on the picturesque beauty of this region; it was so new, so inspiring. But I ought to have been more interested in the housekeeping of this magnificent state, in the education she is giving her children, in their prospects.

Illinois is, at present, a by-word of reproach among the nations, for the careless, prodigal course, by which, in early youth, she has endangered her honor. But you cannot look about you there, without seeing that there are resources abundant to retrieve, and soon to retrieve, far greater errors, if they are only directed with wisdom.

Might the simple maxim, that honesty is the best policy be laid to heart! Might a sense of the true aims of life elevate the tone of politics and trade, till public and private honor become identical! Might the western man in that crowded and exciting life which develops his faculties so fully for to-day, not forget that better part which could not be taken from him! Might the western woman take that interest and acquire that light for the education of the children, for which she alone has leisure!

This is indeed the great problem of the place and time. If the next generation be well prepared for their work, ambitious of good and skilful to achieve it, the children of the present settlers may be leaven enough for the mass constantly increasing by emigration. And how much is this needed where those rude foreigners can so little understand the best interests of the land they seek for bread and shelter. It would be a happiness to aid in this good work, and interweave the white and golden threads into the fate of Illinois. It would be a work worthy the devotion of any mind.

In the little that I saw, was a large proportion of intelligence, activity, and kind feeling; but, if there was much serious laying to heart of the true purposes of life, it did not appear in the tone of conversation.

Having before me the Illinois guide-book, I find there mentioned, as a "visionary," one of the men I should think of as able to be a truly valuable settler in a new and great country—Morris Birkbeck, of England. Since my return, I have read his journey to, and letters from, Illinois. I see nothing promised there that will not surely belong to the man who knows how to seek for it.

Mr. Birkbeck was an enlightened philanthropist, the rather that he did not wish to sacrifice himself to his fellow men, but to benefit them with all he had, and was, and wished. He thought all the creatures of a divine love ought to be happy and ought to be good, and that his own soul and his own life were not less precious than those of others; indeed, that to keep these healthy, was his only means of a healthy influence.

But his aims were altogether generous. Freedom, the liberty of law, not license; not indolence, work for himself and children and all men, but under genial and poetic influences;—these were his aims. How different from those of the new settlers in general! And into his mind so long ago shone steadily the two thoughts, now so prevalent in thinking and aspiring minds, of "Resist not evil," and "Every man his own priest, and the heart the only true church."

He has lost credit for sagacity from accidental circumstances. It does not appear that his position was ill chosen, or his means disproportioned to his ends, had he been sustained by funds from England, as he had a right to expect. But through the profligacy of a near relative, commissioned to collect these dues, he was disappointed of them, and his paper protested and credit destroyed in our cities, before he became aware of his danger.

Still, though more slowly and with more difficulty, he might have succeeded in his designs. The English farmer might have made the English settlement a model for good methods and good aims to all that region, had not death prematurely cut short his plans.

I have wished to say these few words, because the veneration with which I have been inspired for his character by those who knew him well, makes me impatient of this careless blame being passed from mouth to mouth and book to book. Success is no test of a man's endeavor, and Illinois will yet, I hope, regard this man, who knew so well what *ought* to be, as one of her true patriarchs, the Abraham of a promised land.

He was one too much before his time to be soon valued; but the time is growing up to him, and will understand his mild philanthropy and clear, large views.

I subjoin the account of his death, given me by a friend, as expressing, in fair picture, the character of the man.

"Mr. Birkbeck was returning from the seat of government,

whither he had been on public business, and was accompanied by his son Bradford, a youth of sixteen or eighteen. It was necessary to cross a ford, which was rendered difficult by the swelling of the stream. Mr. B.'s horse was unwilling to plunge into the water, so his son offered to go first, and he followed. Bradford's horse had just gained footing on the opposite shore, when he looked back and perceived his father was dismounted, struggling in the water, and carried down by the current.

"Mr. Birkbeck could not swim; Bradford could; so he dismounted, and plunged into the stream to save his father. He got to him before he sank, held him up above water, and told him to take hold of his collar, and he would swim ashore with him. Mr. B. did so, and Bradford exerted all his strength to stem the current and reach the shore at a point where they could land; but, encumbered by his own clothing and his father's weight, he made no progress; and when Mr. B. perceived this, he, with his characteristic calmness and resolution, gave up his hold of his son, and, motioning to him to save himself, resigned himself to his fate. His son reached the shore, but was too much overwhelmed by his loss to leave it. He was found by some travellers, many hours after, seated on the margin of the stream, with his head in his hands, stupefied with grief.

"The body was found, and on the countenance was the sweetest smile; and Bradford said, 'just so he smiled upon me when he let go and pushed me away from him.' "

Many men can choose the right and best on a great occasion, but not many can, with such ready and serene decision, lay aside even life, when it is right and best. This little narrative touched my imagination in very early youth, and often has come up, in lonely vision, that face, serenely smiling above the current which bore him away to another realm of being.

CHAPTER V

WISCONSIN

A territory, not yet a state; still, nearer the acorn than we were.

It was very pleasant coming up. These large and elegant boats are so well arranged that every excursion may be a party of pleasure.

There are many fair shows to see on the lake and its shores, almost always new and agreeable persons on board, pretty children playing about, ladies singing, (and if not very well, there is room to keep out of the way.) You may see a great deal here of Life, in the London sense, if you know a few people; or if you do not, and have the tact to look about you without seeming to stare.

We came to Milwaukie, where we were to pass a fortnight or more.

This place is most beautifully situated. A little river, with romantic banks, passes up through the town. The bank of the lake is here a bold bluff, eighty feet in height. From its summit, you enjoyed a noble outlook on the lake. A little narrow path wound along the edge of the lake below. I liked this walk much. Above me this high wall of rich earth, garlanded on its crest with trees, the long ripples of the lake coming up to my feet. Here, standing in the shadow, I could appreciate better its magnificent changes of color, which are the chief beauties of the lake-waters; but these are indescribable.

It was fine to ascend into the lighthouse, above this bluff, and watch from thence the thunder-clouds which so frequently rose over the lake, or the great boats coming in. Approaching the Milwaukie pier, they made a bend, and seemed to do obeisance in the heavy style of some dowager duchess entering a circle she wishes to treat with especial respect.

These boats come in and out every day, and still afford a cause for general excitement. The people swarm down to greet them, to receive and send away their packages and letters. To me they seemed such mighty messengers, to give, by their noble motion, such an idea of the power and fullness of life, that they were worthy to carry despatches from king to king. It must be very pleasant for those who have an active share in carrying on the affairs of this great and growing world to see them come in. It must be very pleasant to those who have dearly loved friends at the next station. To those who have neither business nor friends, it sometimes gives a desolating sense of insignificance.

The town promises to be, some time, a fine one, as it is so well situated; and they have good building material—a yellow brick, very pleasing to the eye. It seems to grow before you, and has indeed but just emerged from the thickets of oak and wild roses. A few steps will take you into the thickets, and certainly I never saw so many wild roses, or of so beautiful a red. Of such a color were the first red ones the world ever saw, when, says the legend, Venus flying to the assistance of Adonis, the rosebushes kept catching her to make her stay, and the drops of blood the thorns drew from her feet, as she tore herself away, fell on the white roses, and turned them this beautiful red.

I will here insert, though with no excuse, except that it came to memory at the time, this description of Titian's Venus and Adonis.

"This picture has that perfect balance of lines and forms that it would, (as was said of all Raphael's) 'seen at any distance have the air of an ornamental design.' It also tells its story at the first glance, though, like all beautiful works, it gains by study.

"On one side slumbers the little God of Love, as an emblem, I suppose, that only the love of man is worth embodying, for surely Cytherea's is awake enough. The quiver of Cupid, suspended to a tree, gives sportive grace to the scene which softens the tragedy of a breaking tie. The dogs of Adonis pull upon his hand; he can scarce forbear to burst from the detaining arms of Beauty herself, yet he waits a moment to coax her—to make an unmeaning promise. 'A moment, a moment, my love, and I will return; a moment only.' Adonis is not beautiful, except in his expression of eager youth. The Queen of Beauty does not choose Apollo. Venus herself is very beautiful; especially the body is lovely as can be; and the soft, imploring look, gives a conjugal delicacy to the face which purifies the whole picture. This Venus is not as fresh, as moving and breathing as Shakespeare's, yet lovelier to the mind if not to the sense. 'Tis difficult to look at this picture without indignation, because it is, in one respect, so true. Why must women always try to detain and restrain what they love? Foolish beauty; let him go; it is thy tenderness that has spoiled him. Be less lovely—less feminine; abandon thy fancy for giving thyself wholly; cease to love so well, and any Hercules will spin among thy maids, if thou wilt. But let him go this time; thou canst not keep him. Sit there, by thyself, on that bank, and, instead of thinking how soon he will come back, think how thou may'st love him no better than he does thee, for the time has come."

It was soon after this moment that the poor Queen, hearing the frightened hounds, apprehended the rash huntsman's danger, and, flying through the woods, gave their hue to the red roses.

To return from the Grecian isles to Milwaukie. One day, walking along the river's bank in search of a waterfall to be seen from one ravine, we heard tones from a band of music, and saw a gay troop shooting at a mark, on the opposite bank. Between every shot the band played; the effect was very pretty.

On this walk we found two of the oldest and most gnarled hemlocks that ever afforded study for a painter. They were the only ones we saw; they seemed the veterans of a former race.

At Milwaukie, as at Chicago, are many pleasant people, drawn together from all parts of the world. A resident here would find great piquancy in the associations,—those he met having such dissimilar histories and topics. And several persons I saw evidently transplanted from the most refined circles to be met in this country. There are lures enough in the West for people of all kinds;—the enthusiast and the cunning man; the naturalist, and the lover who needs to be rich for the sake of her he loves.

The torrent of emigration swells very strongly towards this place. During the fine weather, the poor refugees arrive daily, in their national dresses, all travel-soiled and worn. The night they pass in rude shantees, in a particular quarter of the town, then walk off into the country—the mothers carrying their infants, the fathers leading the little children by the hand, seeking a home where their hands may maintain them.

One morning we set off in their track, and travelled a day's journey into this country,—fair, yet not, in that part which I saw, comparable, in my eyes, to the Rock River region. It alternates rich fields, proper for grain, with oak openings, as they are called; bold, various and beautiful were the features of the scene, but I saw not those majestic sweeps, those boundless distances, those heavenly fields; it was not the same world.

Neither did we travel in the same delightful manner. We were now in a nice carriage, which must not go off the road, for fear of breakage, with a regular coachman, whose chief care was not to tire his horses, and who had no taste for entering fields in pursuit of wild flowers, or tempting some strange wood path in search of whatever might befall. It was pleasant, but almost as tame as New England.

But charming indeed was the place where we stopped. It was in the vicinity of a chain of lakes, and on the bank of the loveliest little stream, called the Bark river, which flowed in rapid amber brightness, through fields, and dells, and stately knolls, of most idyllic beauty.

The little log cabin where we slept, with its flower garden in front, disturbed the scene no more than a stray lock on the fair cheek. The hospitality of that house I may well call princely; it was the boundless hospitality of the heart, which, if it has no Aladdin's lamp to create a palace for the guest, does him still higher service by the freedom of its bounty up to the very last drop of its powers.

Sweet were the sunsets seen in the valley of this stream, though here, and, I grieve to say, no less near the Rock River, the fiend, who has ever liberty to tempt the happy in this world, appeared in the shape of mosquitoes, and allowed us no bodily to enjoy our mental peace.

One day we ladies gave, under the guidance of our host, to visiting all the beauties of the adjacent lakes—Nomabbin, Silver, and Pine Lakes. On the shore of Nomabbin had formerly been one of the finest Indian villages. Our host said that, one day, as he was lying there beneath the bank, he saw a tall Indian standing at gaze on the knoll. He lay a long time, curious to see how long the figure would maintain its statue-like absorption. But, at last, his patience yielded, and, in moving, he made a slight noise. The Indian saw him, gave a wild, snorting sound of indignation and pain, and strode away.

What feelings must consume their heart at such moments! I scarcely see how they can forbear to shoot the white man where he stands.

But the power of fate is with the white man, and the Indian feels it. This same gentleman told of his travelling through the wilderness with an Indian guide. He had with him a bottle of spirit which he meant to give him in small quantities, but the Indian, once excited, wanted the whole at once. I would not, said Mr. ———, give it him, for I thought if he got really drunk, there was an end to his services as a guide. But he persisted, and at last tried to take it from me. I was not armed; he was, and twice as strong as I. But I knew an Indian could not resist the look of a white man, and I fixed my eye steadily on his. He bore it for a moment, then his eye fell; he let go the bottle. I took his gun and threw it to a distance. After a few moments' pause, I told him to go and fetch it, and left it in his hands. From that moment he was quite obedient, even servile, all the rest of the way.

This gentleman, though in other respects of most kindly and liberal heart, showed the aversion that the white man soon learns to feel for the Indian on whom he encroaches, the aversion of the injurer for him he has degraded. After telling the anecdote of his seeing the Indian gazing at the seat of his former home,

> "A thing for human feelings the most trying,"

and which, one would think, would have awakened soft compassion —almost remorse—in the present owner of that fair hill, which contained for the exile the bones of his dead, the ashes of his hopes,—he observed, "They cannot be prevented from straggling back here to their old haunts. I wish they could. They ought not to be permitted to drive away *our* game." OUR game—just heavens!

The same gentleman showed, on a slight occasion, the true spirit of the sportsman, or, perhaps I might say of Man, when engaged in any kind of chase. Showing us some antlers, he said, "This one belonged to a majestic creature. But this other was the beauty. I had been lying a long time at watch, when at last I heard them come crackling along. I lifted my head cautiously, as they burst through the trees. The first was a magnificent fellow; but then I saw coming one, the prettiest, the most graceful I ever beheld—there was something so soft and beseeching in its look. I chose him at once; took aim, and shot him dead. You see the antlers are not very large; it was young, but the prettiest creature!"

In the course of this morning's drive, we visited the gentlemen on their fishing party. They hailed us gaily, and rowed ashore to show us what fine booty they had. No disappointment there, no dull work. On the beautiful point of land from which we first saw them, lived a contented woman, the only one I heard of out there. She was English, said she had seen so much suffering in her own country that the hardships of this seemed as nothing to her. But the others—even our sweet and gentle hostess—found their labors disproportioned to their strength, if not to their patience; and, while their husbands and brothers enjoyed the country in hunting or fishing, they found themselves confined to a comfortless and laborious indoor life. But it need not be so long.

This afternoon, driving about on the banks of these lakes, we found the scene all of one kind of loveliness; wide, graceful woods, and then these fine sheets of water, with fine points of land jutting out boldly into them. It was lovely, but not striking or peculiar.

All woods suggest pictures. The European forest, with its long glades and green sunny dells, naturally suggested the figures of armed knight on his proud steed, or maiden, decked in gold and pearl, pricking along them on a snow white palfrey. The green dells, of weary Palmer sleeping there beside the spring with his head upon his wallet. Our minds, familiar with such figures, people with them the New England woods, wherever the sunlight falls down a longer than usual cart-track, wherever a cleared spot has lain still enough for the trees to look friendly, with their exposed sides cultivated by the light, and the grass to look velvet warm, and be embroidered with flowers. These western woods suggest a different kind of ballad. The Indian legends have, often, an air of the wildest solitude, as has the one Mr. Lowell has put into verse, in his late volume. But I did not see those wild woods; only such as suggest little romances of love and sorrow, like this:

A maiden sat beneath the tree,
Tear-bedewed her pale cheeks be,
And she sigheth heavily.

From forth the wood into the light,
A hunter strides with carol light,
And a glance so bold and bright.

He careless stopped and eyed the maid;
"Why weepest thou?" he gently said,
"I love thee well; be not afraid."

He takes her hand, and leads her on;
She should have waited there alone,
For he was not her chosen one.

He leans her head upon his breast,
She knew 't was not her home of rest,
But ah! she had been sore distrest.

The sacred stars looked sadly down;
The parting moon appeared to frown,
To see thus dimmed the diamond crown.

Then from the thicket starts a deer,
The huntsman, seizing on his spear,
Cries, "Maiden, wait thou for me here."

She sees him vanish into night,
She starts from sleep in deep affright,
For it was not her own true knight.

Though but in dream Gunhilda failed;
Though but a fancied ill assailed,
Though she but fancied fault bewailed.

Yet thought of day makes dream of night:
She is not worthy of the knight,
The inmost altar burns not bright.

If loneliness thou canst not bear,
Cannot the dragon's venom dare,
Of the pure meed thou shouldst despair.

Now sadder that lone maiden sighs,
Far bitterer tears profane her eyes,
Crushed in the dust her heart's flower lies.

On the bank of Silver Lake we saw an Indian encampment. A shower threatened us, but we resolved to try if we could not visit it before it came on. We crossed a wide field on foot, and found them amid the trees on a shelving bank; just as we reached them the rain began to fall in torrents, with frequent thunder claps, and we had to take refuge in their lodges. These were very small, being for temporary use, and we crowded the occupants much, among whom were several sick, on the damp ground, or with only a ragged mat between them and it. But they showed all the gentle courtesy which marks them towards the stranger, who stands in any need; though it was obvious that the visit, which inconvenienced them, could only have been caused by the most impertinent curiosity, they made us as comfortable as their extreme poverty permitted. They seemed to think we would not like to touch them: a sick girl in the lodge where I was, persisted in moving so as to give me the dry place; a woman with the sweet melancholy eye of the race, kept off the children and wet dogs from even the hem of my garment.

Without, their fires smouldered, and black kettles, hung over them on sticks, smoked and seethed in the rain. An old theatrical looking Indian stood with arms folded, looking up to the heavens, from which the rain dashed and the thunder reverberated; his air was French-Roman, that is, more romanesque than Roman. The Indian ponies, much excited, kept careering through the wood, around the encampment, and now and then halting suddenly, would thrust in their intelligent, though amazed, phizzes, as if to ask their masters when this awful pother would cease, and then, after a moment, rush and trample off again.

At last we got off, well wetted, but with a picturesque scene for memory. At a house where we stopped to get dry, they told us that this wandering band (of Pottawattamies,) who had returned on a visit, either from homesickness, or need of relief, were extremely destitute. The women had been there to see if they could barter their head bands with which they club their hair behind into a form not unlike a Grecian knot, for food. They seemed, indeed, to have neither food, utensils, clothes, nor bedding; nothing but the ground, the sky, and their own strength. Little wonder if they drove off the game!

Part of the same band I had seen in Milwaukie, on a begging dance. The effect of this was wild and grotesque. They wore much paint and feather head-dresss. "Indians without paint are poor coots," said a gentleman who had been a great deal with, and really liked, them; and I like the effect of the paint on them; it reminds of the gay fantasies of nature. With them in Milwaukie, was a chief, the finest Indian figure I saw, more than six feet in height, erect, and of a sullen, but grand gait and gesture. He wore a deep red blanket, which fell in large folds from his shoulders to his feet, did not join in the dance, but slowly strode about through the streets, a fine sight, not a French-Roman, but a real Roman. He looked unhappy, but listlessly unhappy, as if he felt it was of no use to strive or resist.

While in the neighborhood of these lakes, we visited also a foreign settlement of great interest. Here were minds, it seemed, to "comprehend the trusts," of their new life; and if they can only stand true to them, will derive and bestow great benefits therefrom.

But sad and sickening to the enthusiast who comes to these shores, hoping the tranquil enjoyment of intellectual blessings, and the pure happiness of mutual love, must be a part of the scene that he encounters at first. He has escaped from the heartlessness of courts, to encounter the vulgarity of a mob; he has secured solitude, but it is a lonely, a deserted solitude. Amid the abundance of nature he cannot, from petty, but insuperable obstacles, procure, for a long time, comforts, or a home.

But let him come sufficiently armed with patience to learn the new spells which the new dragons require, (and this can only be done on the spot,) he will not finally be disappointed of the promised treasure; the mob will resolve itself into men, yet crude, but of good dispositions, and capable of good character; the solitude will become sufficiently enlivened and home grow up at last from the rich sod.

In this transition state we found one of these homes. As we approached it seemed the very Eden which earth might still afford to a pair willing to give up the hackneyed pleasures of the world, for a better and more intimate communion with one another and with beauty: the wild road led through wide beautiful woods, to the wilder and more beautiful shores of the finest lake we saw. On its waters, glittering in the morning sun, a few Indians were paddling to and fro in their light canoes. On one of those fair knolls I have so often mentioned, stood the cottage, beneath trees which stooped as if they yet felt brotherhood with its roof tree. Flowers waved, birds fluttered round, all had the sweetness of a happy seclusion; all invited on entrance to cry, All hail ye happy ones! to those who inhabited it.

But on entrance to those evidently rich in personal beauty, talents, love, and courage, the aspect of things was rather sad. Sickness had been with them, death, care, and labor; these had not yet blighted them, but had turned their gay smiles grave. It seemed that hope and joy had given place to resolution. How much, too, was there in them, worthless in this place, which would have been so valuable elsewhere. Refined graces, cultivated powers, shine in vain before field laborers, as laborers are in this present world; you might as well cultivate heliotropes to present to an ox. Oxen and heliotropes are both good, but not for one another.

With them were some of the old means of enjoyment, the books, the pencil, the guitar; but where the wash-tub and the axe are so constantly in requisition, there is not much time and pliancy of hand for these.

In the inner room the master of the house was seated; he had been sitting there long, for he had injured his foot on ship-board, and his farming had to be done by proxy. His beautiful young wife was his only attendant and nurse, as well as a farm housekeeper; how well she performed hard and unaccustomed duties, the objects of her care shewed; everything that belonged to the house was rude but neatly arranged; the invalid, confined to an uneasy wooden chair, (they had not been able to induce any one to bring them an easy chair from the town,) looked as neat and elegant as if he had been dressed by the valet of a duke. He was of northern blood, with clear full blue eyes, calm features, a tempering of the soldier, scholar, and man of the world, in his aspect; whether that various intercourses had given himself that thorough-bred look never seen in Americans, or that it was inherited from a race who had known all these disciplines. He formed a great but pleasing contrast to his wife, whose glowing complexion and dark mellow eye bespoke an origin in some climate more familiar with the sun. He looked as if he could sit there a great while patiently, and live on his own mind, biding his time; she, as if she could bear anything for affection's sake, but would feel the weight of each moment as it passed.

Seeing the album full of drawings and verses which bespoke the circle of elegant and affectionate intercourse they had left behind, we could not but see that the young wife sometimes must need a sister, the husband a companion, and both must often miss that electricity which sparkles from the chain of congenial minds.

For man, a position is desirable in some degree proportioned to his education. Mr. Birkbeck was bred a farmer, but these were nurslings of the court and city; they may persevere, for an affectionate courage shone in their eyes, and, if so, become true lords of the soil, and informing geniuses to those around; then, perhaps, they will feel that they have not paid too dear for the tormented independence of the new settler's life. But, generally, damask roses will not thrive in the wood, and a ruder growth, if healthy and pure, we wish rather to see there.

I feel very differently about these foreigners from Americans; American men and women are inexcusable if they do not bring up children so as to be fit for vicissitudes; that is the meaning of our star, that here all men being free and equal, all should be fitted for freedom and an independence by his own resources wherever the changeful wave of our mighty stream may take him. But the star of Europe brought a different horoscope, and to mix destinies breaks the thread of both. The Arabian horse will not plough well, nor can the plough-horse be rode to play the jeered. But a man is a man wherever he goes, and something precious cannot fail to be gained by one who knows how to abide by a resolution of any kind, and pay the cost without a murmur.

Returning, the fine carriage at last fulfilled its threat of breaking down. We took refuge in a farm house. Here was a pleasant scene. A rich and beautiful estate, several happy families, who had removed together, and formed a natural community, ready to help and enliven one another. They were farmers at home, in western New York, and both men and women knew how to work. Yet even here the women did not like the change, but they were willing, "as it might be best for the young folks." Their hospitality was great, the housefull of women and pretty children seemed all of one mind.

Returning to Milwaukie much fatigued, I entertained myself for a day or two with reading. The book I had brought with me was in strong contrast with the life around me. Very strange was this vision of an exalted and sensitive existence, which seemed to invade the next sphere, in contrast with the spontaneous, instinctive life, so healthy and so near the ground I had been surveying. This was the German book entitled:

Die Scherin von Prevorst.—Eröffnungen über das innere Leben des Menschen und über das hereinragen einer Geisterwelt in die unsere. Mitgetheilt von Justinus Kerner.

The Seeress of Prevorst.—Revelations concerning the inward life of man, and the projection of a world of spirits into ours, communicated by Justinus Kerner.

This book, published in Germany some twelve years since, and which called forth there plenteous dews of admiration, as plenteous hail-storms of jeers and scorns, I never saw mentioned till some year or two since, in any English publication. Then a playful, but not sarcastic account of it, in the Dublin Magazine, so far excited my curiosity that I procured the book intending to read it so soon as I should have some leisure days, such as this journey has afforded.

Dr. Kerner, its author, is a man of distinction in his native land, both as a physician and a thinker, though always on the side of reverence, marvel, and mysticism. He was known to me only through two or three little poems of his in Catholic legends, which I much admired for the fine sense they showed of the beauty of symbols.

He here gives a biography, mental and physical, of one of the most remarkable cases of high nervous excitement that the age, so interested in such, yet affords, with all its phenomena of clairvoyance and susceptibility of magnetic influences. I insert some account of this biography at the request of many who have been interested by slight references to it. The book, a thick and heavy volume, written with true German patience, some would say clumsiness, has not, probably, and may not be translated into other languages. As to my own mental position on these subjects it may be briefly expressed by a dialogue between several persons who honor me with a portion of friendly confidence and of criticism, and myself expressed as *Free Hope*. The others may be styled *Old Church, Good Sense*, and *Self-Poise*.

Good Sense. I wonder you can take any interest in such observations or experiments. Don't you see how almost impossible it is to make them with any exactness, how entirely impossible to know anything about them unless made by yourself, when the least leaven of credulity, excited fancy, to say nothing of willing or careless imposture, spoils the whole loaf. Beside, allowing the possibility of some clear glimpses into a higher state of being, what do we want of it now? All around us lies what we neither understand nor use. Our capacities, our instincts for this our present sphere are but half developed. Let us confine ourselves to that till the lesson be learned; let us be completely natural, before we trouble ourselves with the supernatural. I never see any of these things but I long to get away and lie under a green tree and let the wind blow on me. There is marvel and charm enough in that for me.

Free Hope. And for me also. Nothing is truer than the Wordsworthian creed, on which Carlyle lays such stress, that we need only look on the miracle of every day, to sate ourselves with thought and admiration every day. But how are our faculties sharpened to do it? Precisely by apprehending the infinite results of every day.

Who sees the meaning of the flower uprooted in the ploughed field? The ploughman who does not look beyond its boundaries and does not raise his eyes from the ground? No—but the poet who sees that field in its relations with the universe, and looks oftener to the sky than on the ground. Only the dreamer shall understand realities, though, in truth, his dreaming must not be out of proportion to his waking!

The mind, roused powerfully by this existence, stretches of itself into what the French sage calls the "aromal state." From the hope thus gleaned it forms the hypothesis, under whose banner it collects its facts.

Long before these slight attempts were made to establish as a science what is at present called animal magnetism, always, in fact men were occupied more or less with this vital principle, principle of flux and influx, dynamic of our mental mechanics, human phase of electricity. Poetic observation was pure, there was no quackery in its free course, as there is so often in this wilful tampering with the hidden springs of life, for it is tampering unless done in a patient spirit and with severe truth; yet it may be, by the rude or greedy miners, some good ore is unearthed. And some there are who work in the true temper, patient and accurate in trial, not rushing to conclusions, feeling there is a mystery, not eager to call it by name, till they can know it as a reality: such may learn, such may teach.

Subject to the sudden revelations, the breaks in habitual existence caused by the aspect of death, the touch of love, the flood of music, I never lived, that I remember, what you call a common natural day. All my days are touched by the supernatural, for I feel the pressure of hidden causes, and the presence, sometimes the communion, of unseen powers. It needs not that I should ask the clairvoyant whether "a spirit-world projects into ours." As to the specific evidence, I would not tarnish my mind by hasty reception. The mind is not, I know, a highway, but a temple, and its doors should not be carelessly left open.

Yet it were sin, if indolence or coldness excluded what had a claim to enter; and I doubt whether, in the eyes of pure intelligence, an ill-grounded hasty rejection be not a greater sign of weakness than an ill-grounded and hasty faith.

I will quote, as my best plea, the saying of a man old in years, but not in heart, and whose long life has been distinguished by that clear adaptation of means to ends which gives the credit of practical wisdom. He wrote to his child, "I have lived too long, and seen too much to be *in*credulous." Noble the thought, no less so its frank expression, instead of saws of caution, mean advices, and other modern instances. Such was the romance of Socrates when he bade his disciples "sacrifice a cock to Æsculapius."

Old Church. You are always so quick-witted and voluble, Free Hope, you don't get time to see how often you err, and even, perhaps, sin and blaspheme. The Author of all has intended to confine our knowledge within certain boundaries, has given us a short span of time for a certain probation, for which our faculties are adapted. By wild speculation and intemperate curiosity we violate his will and incur dangerous, perhaps fatal, consequences. We waste our powers, and, becoming morbid and visionary, are unfitted to obey positive precepts, and perform positive duties.

Free Hope. I do not see how it is possible to go further beyond the results of a limited human experience than those do who pretend to settle the origin and nature of sin, the final destiny of souls, and the whole plan of the causal spirit with regard to them. I think those who take your view, have not examined themselves, and do not know the ground on which they stand.

I acknowledge no limit, set up by man's opinion, as to the capacities of man. "Care is taken," I see it, "that the trees grow not up into heaven," but, to me it seems, the more vigorously they aspire the better. Only let it be a vigorous, not a partial or sickly aspiration. Let not the tree forget its root.

So long as the child insists on knowing where its dead parent is, so long as bright eyes weep at mysterious pressures, too heavy for the life, so long as that impulse is constantly arising which made the Roman emperor address his soul in a strain of such touching softness, vanishing from the thought, as the column of smoke from the eye, I know of no inquiry which the impulse of man suggests that is forbidden to the resolution of man to pursue. In every inquiry, unless sustained by a pure and reverent spirit, he gropes in the dark, or falls headlong.

Self-Poise. All this may be very true, but what is the use of all this straining? Far-sought is dear-bought. When we know that all is in each, and that the ordinary contains the extraordinary, why should we play the baby, and insist upon having the moon for a toy when a tin dish will do as well. Our deep ignorance is a chasm that we can only fill up by degrees, but the commonest rubbish will help us as well as shred silk. The God Brahma, while on earth, was set to fill up a valley, but he had only a basket given him in which to fetch earth for this purpose; so is it with us all. No leaps, no starts will avail us, by patient crystallization alone the equal temper of wisdom is attainable. Sit at home and the spirit-world will look in at your window with moonlit eyes; run out to find it, and rainbow and golden cup will have vanished and left you the beggarly child you were. The better part of wisdom is a sublime prudence, a pure and patient truth that will receive nothing it is not sure it can permanently lay to heart. Of our study there should be in proportion two-thirds of rejection to one of acceptance. And, amid the manifold infatuations and illusions of this world of emotion, a being capable of clear intelligence can do no better service than to hold himself upright, avoid nonsense, and do what chores lie in his way, acknowledging every moment that primal truth, which no fact exhibits, nor, if pressed by too warm a hope, will even indicate. I think, indeed, it is part of our lesson to give a formal consent to what is farcical, and to pick up our living and our virtue amid what is so ridiculous, hardly deigning a smile, and certainly not vexed. The work is done through all, if not by every one.

Free Hope. Thou art greatly wise, my friend, and ever respected by me, yet I find not in your theory or your scope, room enough for the lyric inspirations, or the mysterious whispers of life. To me it seems that it is madder never to abandon oneself, than often to be infatuated; better to be wounded, a captive, and a slave, than always to walk in armor. As to magnetism, that is only a matter of fancy. You sometimes need just such a field in which to wander vagrant, and if it bear a higher name, yet it may be that, in last result, the trance of Pythagoras might be classed with the more infantine transports of the Seeress of Prevorst.

What is done interests me more than what is thought and supposed. Every fact is impure, but every fact contains in it the juices of life. Every fact is a clod, from which may grow an amaranth or a palm.

Do you climb the snowy peaks from whence come the streams, where the atmosphere is rare, where you can see the sky nearer, from which you can get a commanding view of the landscape? I see great disadvantages as well as advantages in this dignified position. I had rather walk myself through all kinds of places, even at the risk of being robbed in the forest, half drowned at the ford, and covered with dust in the street.

I would beat with the living heart of the world, and understand all the moods, even the fancies or fantasies, of nature. I dare to trust to the interpreting spirit to bring me out all right at last—to establish truth through error.

Whether this be the best way is of no consequence, if it be the one individual character points out.

> *For one, like me, it would be vain*
> *From glittering heights the eyes to strain;*
> *I the truth can only know,*
> *Tested by life's most fiery glow.*
> *Seeds of thought will never thrive*
> *Till dews of love shall bid them live.*

Let me stand in my age with all its waters flowing round me. If they sometimes subdue, they must finally upbear me, for I seek the universal—and that must be the best.

The Spirit, no doubt, leads in every movement of my time: if I seek the How, I shall find it, as well as if I busied myself more with the Why.

Whatever is, is right, if only men are steadily bent to make it so, by comprehending and fulfilling its design.

May not I have an office, too, in my hospitality and ready sympathy? If I sometimes entertain guests who cannot pay with gold coin, with "fair rose nobles," that is better than to lose the chance of entertaining angels unawares.

You, my three friends, are held in heart-honor, by me. You, especially, Good-Sense, because where you do not go yourself, you do not object to another's going, if he will. You are really liberal. You, Old Church, are of use, by keeping unforgot the effigies of old religion, and reviving the tone of pure Spenserian sentiment, which this time is apt to stifle in its childish haste. But you are very faulty in censuring and wishing to limit others by your own standard. You, Self-Poise, fill a priestly office. Could but a larger intelligence of the vocations of others, and a tender sympathy with their individual natures be added, had you more of love, or more of apprehensive genius, (for either would give you the needed expansion and delicacy) you would command my entire reverence. As it is, I must at times deny and oppose you, and so must others, for you tend, by your influence, to exclude us from our full, free life. We must be content when you censure, and rejoiced when you approve; always admonished to good by your whole being, and sometimes by your judgment. And so I pass on to interest myself and others in the memoir of the Seherin von Prevorst.

Aside from Löwenstein, a town of Wirtemberg, on mountains whose highest summit is more than eighteen hundred feet above the level of the sea, lies in romantic seclusion, surrounded on all sides by woods and hills, the hamlet of Prevorst.

Its inhabitants number about four hundred and fifty, most of whom support themselves by wood-cutting, and making charcoal, and collecting wood seed.

As is usual with those who live upon the mountains, these are a vigorous race, and generally live to old age without sickness. Diseases that infest the valley, such as ague, never touch them; but they are subject in youth to attacks upon the nerves, which one would not expect in so healthy a class. In a town situated near to, and like Prevorst, the children were often attacked with a kind of St. Vitus's dance. They would foresee when it would seize upon them, and, if in the field, would hasten home to undergo the paroxysms there. From these they rose, as from magnetic sleep, without memory of what had happened.

Other symptoms show the inhabitants of this region very susceptible to magnetic and sidereal influences.

On this mountain, and indeed in the hamlet of Prevorst, was, in 1801, a woman born, in whom a peculiar inner life discovered itself from early childhood. Frederica Hauffe, whose father was gamekeeper of this district of forest, was, as the position and solitude of her birthplace made natural, brought up in the most simple manner. In the keen mountain air and long winter cold, she was not softened by tenderness either as to dress or bedding, but grew up lively and blooming; and while her brothers and sisters, under the same circumstances, were subject to rheumatic attacks, she remained free from them. On the other hand, her peculiar tendency displayed itself in her dreams. If anything affected her painfully, if her mind was excited by reproof, she had instructive warning, or prophetic dreams.

While yet quite young, her parents let her go, for the advantages of instruction, to her grand-father, Johann Schmidgall, in Löwenstein.

Here were discovered in her the sensibility to magnetic and ghostly influences, which, the good Kerner assures us, her grand-parents deeply lamented, and did all in their power to repress. But, as it appears that her grandfather, also, had seen a ghost, and there were evidently legends in existence about the rooms in which the little Frederika saw ghosts, and spots where the presence of human bones caused her sudden shivering, we may be allowed to doubt whether indirect influence was not more powerful than direct repression upon these subjects.

There is the true German impartiality with regard to the scene of appearance for these imposing visiters; sometimes it is "a room in the Castle of Löwenstein, long disused," à la Radcliffe, sometimes "a deserted kitchen."

This "solemn, unhappy gift," brought no disturbance to the childish life of the maiden, she enjoyed life with more vivacity than most of her companions. The only trouble she had was the extreme irritability of the optic nerve, which, though without inflammation of the eyes, sometimes confined her to a solitary chamber. "This," says Dr. K. "was probably a sign of the development of the spiritual in the fleshly eye."

Sickness of her parents at last called her back to the lonely Prevorst, where, by trouble and watching beside sick beds, her feelings were too much excited, so that the faculty for prophetic dreams and the vision of spirits increased upon her.

From her seventeenth to her nineteenth year, when every outward relation was pleasant for her, this inward life was not so active, and she was distinguished from other girls of her circle only by the more intellectual nature, which displayed itself chiefly in the eyes, and by a greater liveliness which, however, never passed the bounds of grace and propriety.

She had none of the sentimentality so common at that age, and it can be proved that she had never an attachment, nor was disappointed in love, as has been groundlessly asserted.

In her nineteenth year, she was by her family betrothed to Herr H. The match was desirable on account of the excellence of the man, and the sure provision it afforded for her comfort through life.

But, whether from presentiment of the years of suffering that were before her, or from other hidden feelings, of which we only know with certainty that, if such there were, they were not occasioned by another attachment, she sank into a dejection, inexplicable to her family;

passed whole days in weeping; scarcely slept for some weeks, and thus the life of feeling which had been too powerful in her childhood was called up anew in full force.

On the day of her solemn betrothal, took place, also, the funeral of T., the preacher of Oberstenfeld, a man of sixty and more years, whose preaching, instruction, and character, (he was goodness itself,) had had great influence upon her life. She followed the dear remains, with others, to the church-yard. Her heart till then so heavy, was suddenly relieved and calmed, as she stood beside the grave. She remained there long, enjoying her new peace, and when she went away found herself tranquil, but indifferent to all the concerns of this world. Here began the period, not indeed as yet of sickness, but of her peculiar inward life, which knew afterward no pause.

Later, in somnambulic state, she spoke of this day in the following verses. The deceased had often appeared to her as a shape of light, protecting her from evil spirits.

(These are little simple rhymes; they are not worth translating into verse, though, in the original, they have a childish grace.)

> *What was once so dark to me,*
> *I see now clearly.*
> > *In that day*
> *When I had given in marriage myself away,*

> *I stood quite immersed in thee,*
> *Thou angel figure above thy grave mound.*
> *Willingly would I have exchanged with thee,*
> *Willingly given up to thee my earthly luck,*
> *Which those around praised as the blessing of heaven.*

> *I prayed upon thy grave*
> *For one blessing only,*
> > *That the wings of this angel*
> > *Might henceforward*
> > *On the hot path of life,*
> > *Waft around me the peace of heaven.*
> *There standest thou, angel, now; my prayer was heard.*

She was, in consequence of her marriage, removed to Kürnbach, a place on the borders of Würtemberg and Baden. Its position is low, gloomy, shut in by hills; opposite in all the influences of earth and atmosphere to those of Prevorst and its vicinity.

Those of electrical susceptibility are often made sick or well by change of place. Papponi, (of whom Amoretti writes,) a man of such susceptibility, was cured of convulsive attacks by change of place. Pennet could find repose while in one part of Calabria, only by wrapping himself in an oil-cloth mantle, thus, as it were, isolating himself. That great sense of sidereal and imponderable influences, which afterward manifested itself so clearly in the Seherin, probably made this change of place very unfavorable to her. Later, it appeared, that the lower she came down from the hills, the more she suffered from spasms, but on the heights her tendency to the magnetic state was the greatest.

But also mental influences were hostile to her. Already withdrawn from the outward life, she was placed, where, as consort and housekeeper to a laboring man, the calls on her care and attention were incessant. She was obliged hourly to forsake her inner home, to provide for an outer, which did not correspond with it.

She bore this seven months, though flying to solitude, whenever outward relations permitted. But longer it was not possible to conceal the inward verity by an outward action, "the body sank beneath the attempt, and the spirit took refuge in the inner circle."

One night she dreamed that she awoke and found the dead body of the preacher T. by her side; that at the same time her father, and two physicians were considering what should be done for her in a severe sickness. She called out that "the dead friend would help her; she needed no physician." Her husband, hearing her cry out in sleep, woke her.

This dream was presage of a fever, which seized her next morning. It lasted fourteen days with great violence, and was succeeded by attacks of convulsion and spasm. This was the beginning of that state of bodily suffering and mental exaltation in which she passed the remaining seven years of her life.

She seems to have been very injudiciously treated in the first stages of her illness. Bleeding was resorted to, as usual in cases of extreme suffering where the nurses know not what else to do, and, as usual, the momentary relief was paid for by an increased nervousness, and capacity for suffering.

Magnetic influences from other persons were of frequent use to her, but they were applied without care as to what characters and constitutions were brought into connexion with hers, and were probably in the end just as injurious to her as the loss of blood. At last she became so weak, so devoid of all power in herself, that her life seemed entirely dependent on artificial means and the influence of other men.

There is a singular story of a woman in the neighborhood, who visited her once or twice, apparently from an instinct that she should injure her, and afterwards, interfered in the same way, and with the same results, in the treatment of her child.

This demoniacal impulse and power, which were ascribed to the Canidias of ancient superstition, may be seen subtly influencing the members of every-day society. We see persons led, by an uneasy impulse, towards the persons and the topics where they are sure they can irritate and annoy. This is constantly observable among children, also in the closest relations between grown up people who have not yet the government of themselves, neither are governed by the better power.

There is also an interesting story of a quack who treated her with amulets, whose parallel may be found in the action of such persons in common society. It is an expression of the power that a vulgar and self-willed nature will attain over one delicate, poetical, but not yet clear within itself; outwardly it yields to a power which it inwardly disclaims.

A touching little passage is related of a time in the first years, when she seemed to be better, so much so as to receive an evening visit from some female friends. They grew merry and began to dance; she remained sad and thoughtful. When they stopped, she was in the attitude of prayer. One of her intimates, observing this, began to laugh. This affected her so much, that she became cold and rigid like a corpse. For some time they did not hear her breathe, and, when she did, it was with a rattling noise. They applied mustard poultices, and used foot and hand baths; she was brought back to life, but to a state of great suffering.

She recognized as her guardian spirit, who sometimes magnetized her or removed from her neighborhood substances that were hurtful to her, her grandmother; thus coinciding with the popular opinion that traits reappear in the third generation.

Now began still greater wonders; the second sight, numerous and various visits from spirits and so forth.

The following may be mentioned in connection with theories and experiments current among ourselves.

"A friend, who was often with her at this time, wrote to me (Kerner): When I, with my finger, touch her *on the forehead between the eyebrows,* she says each time something that bears upon the state of my soul. Some of these sentences I record.

"Keep thy soul so that thou mayst bear it in thy hands."

"When thou comest into a world of bustle and folly, hold the Lord fast in thy heart."

"If any seek to veil from thee thy true feeling, pray to God for grace."

"Permit not thyself to stifle the light that springs up within thyself."

"Think often of the cross of Jesus; go forth and embrace it."

"As the dove found a resting-place in Noah's ark, so wilt thou, also, find a resting-place which God has appointed for thee."

When she was put under the care of Kerner, she had been five years in this state, and was reduced to such weakness, that she was, with difficulty, sustained from hour to hour.

He thought at first it would be best to take no notice of her magnetic states and directions, and told her he should not, but should treat her with regard to her bodily symptoms, as he would any other invalid.

"At this time she fell every evening into magnetic sleep, and gave orders about herself; to which, however, those round her no longer paid attention.

"I was now called in. I had never seen this woman, but had heard many false or perverted accounts of her condition. I must confess that I shared the evil opinion of the world as to her illness; that I advised to pay no attention to her magnetic situation, and the orders she gave in it; in her spasms, to forbear the laying of hands upon her; to deny her the support of persons of stronger nerves; in short, to do all possible to draw her out of the magnetic state, and to treat her with attention, but with absolutely none but the common medical means.

"These views were shared by my friend, Dr. Off, of Löwenstein, who continued to treat her accordingly. But without good results. Hemorrhage, spasms, night-sweats continued. Her gums were scorbutically affected, and bled constantly; she lost all her teeth. Strengthening remedies affected her like being drawn up from her bed by force; she sank into a fear of all men, and a deadly weakness. Her death was to be wished, but it came not. Her relations, in despair, not knowing themselves what they could do with her, brought her, almost against my will, to me at Weinsburg.

"She was brought hither an image of death, perfectly emaciated, unable to raise herself. Every three or four minutes, a teaspoonful of nourishment must be given her, else she fell into faintness or convulsion. Her somnambulic situation alternated with fever, hemorrhage, and night-sweats. Every evening, about seven o'clock, she fell into magnetic sleep. She then spread out her arms, and found herself, from that moment, in a clairvoyant state; but only when she brought them back upon her breast, did she begin to speak. (Kerner mentions that her child, too, slept with its hands and feet crossed.) In this state her eyes were shut, her face calm and bright. As she fell asleep, the first night after her arrival, she asked for me, but I bade them tell her that I now, and in future, should speak to her only when awake.

"After she awoke, I went to her and declared, in brief and earnest terms, that I should pay no attention to what she said in sleep, and that her somnambulic state, which had lasted so long to the grief and trouble of her family, must now come to an end. This declaration I accompanied by an earnest appeal, designed to awaken a firm will in her to put down the excessive activity of brain that disordered her whole system. Afterwards, no address was made to her on any subject when in her sleep-waking state. She was left to lie unheeded. I pursued a homœopathic treatment of her case. But the medicines constantly produced effects opposite to what I expected. She now suffered less from spasm and somnambulism, but with increasing marks of weakness and decay. All seemed as if the end of her sufferings drew near. It was too late for the means I wished to use. Affected so variously and powerfully by magnetic means in the first years of her illness, she had now no life more, so thoroughly was the force of her own organization exhausted, but what she borrowed from others. In her now more infrequent magnetic trance, she was always seeking the true means of her cure. It was touching to see how, retiring within herself, she sought for help. The physician who had aided her so little with his drugs, must often stand abashed before this inner physician, perceiving it to be far better skilled than himself."

After some weeks forbearance, Kerner did ask her in her sleep what he should do for her. She prescribed a magnetic treatment, which was found of use. Afterwards, she described a machine, of which there is a drawing in this book, which she wished to have made for her use; it was so, and she derived benefit from it. She had indicated such a machine in the early stages of her disease, but at that time no one attended to her. By degrees she grew better under this treatment, and lived at Weinsberg, nearly two years, though in a state of great weakness, and more in the magnetic and clairvoyant than in the natural human state.

How his acquaintance with her affected the physician, he thus expresses:

"During those last months of her abode on the earth, there remained to her only the life of a sylph. I have been interested to record, not a journal of her sickness, but the mental phenomena of such an almost disembodied life. Such may cast light on the period when also our Psyche may unfold her wings, free from bodily bonds, and the hindrances of space and time. I give facts; each reader may interpret them in his own way.

"The manuals of animal magnetism and other writings have proposed many theories by which to explain such. All these are known to me. I shall make no reference to them, but only, by use of parallel facts here and there, show that the phenomena of this case recall many in which there is nothing marvellous, but which are manifestly grounded in our common existence. Such apparitions cannot too frequently, if only for moments, flash across that common existence, as electric lights from the higher world.

"Frau H. was, previous to my magnetic treatment, in so deep a somnambulic life, that she was, in fact, never rightly awake, even when she seemed to be; or rather, let us say, she was at all times more awake than others are; for it is strange to term sleep this state which is just that of the clearest wakefulness. Better to say she was immersed in the inward state.

"In this state and the consequent excitement of the nerves, she had almost wholly lost organic force, and received it only by transmission from those of stronger condition, principally from their eyes and the ends of the fingers. The atmosphere and nerve communications of others, said she, bring me the life which I need; they do not feel it; these effusions on which I live, would flow from them and be lost, if my nerves did not attract them; only in this way can I live.

"She often assured us that others did not suffer by loss of what they imparted to her; but it cannot be denied that persons were weakened by constant intercourse with her, suffered from contraction in the limbs, trembling, &c. They were weakened also in the eyes and pit of the stomach. From those related to her by blood, she could draw more benefit than from others, and, when very weak, from them only; probably on account of a natural affinity of temperament. She could not bear to have around her nervous and sick persons; those from whom she could gain nothing made her weaker.

"Even so it is remarked that flowers soon lose their beauty near the sick, and suffer peculiarly under the contact or care of some persons.

"Other physicians, beside myself, can vouch that the presence of some persons affected her as a pabulum vitæ, while, if left with certain others or alone, she was sure to grow weaker.

"From the air, too, she seemed to draw a peculiar ethereal nourishment of the same sort; she could not remain without an open window in the severest cold of winter.*

"The spirit of things, about which we have no perception, was sensible to her, and had influence on her; she showed this sense of the spirit of metals, plants, animals, and men. Imponderable existences, such as the various colors of the ray, showed distinct influences upon her. The electric fluid was visible and sensible to her when it was not to us. Yea! what is incredible! even the written words of men she could discriminate by touch.†

"These experiments are detailed under their several heads in the book.

"From her eyes flowed a peculiar spiritual light which impressed even those who saw her for a very short time. She was in each relation more spirit than human.

"Should we compare her with anything human, we would say she was as one detained at the moment of dissolution, betwixt life and death; and who is better able to discern the affairs of the world that lies before, than that behind him.

"She was often in situations when one who had, like her, the power of discerning spirits, would have seen her own free from the body, which at all times enveloped it only as a light veil. She saw herself often out of the body; saw herself double. She would say, "I seem out of myself, hover above my body, and think of it as something apart from myself. But it is not a pleasant feeling, because I still sympathize with my body. If only my soul were bound more firmly to the

---

* Near us, this last winter, a person who suffered, and finally died, from spasms like those of the Seherin, also found relief from having the windows open, while the cold occasioned great suffering to his attendants.

† Facts of the same kind are asserted of late among ourselves, and believed, though "incredible."

nerve-spirit, it might be bound more closely with the nerves themselves; but the bond of my nerve-spirit is always becoming looser."

She makes a distinction between spirit as the pure intelligence; soul, the ideal of this individual man; and nerve-spirit, the dynamic of his temporal existence. Of this feeling of double identity, an invalid, now wasting under nervous disease, often speaks to me. He has it when he first awakes from sleep. Blake, the painter, whose life was almost as much a series of trances as that of our Seherin, in his designs of the Resurrection, represents spirits as rising from, or hovering over, their bodies in the same way.

Often she seemed quite freed from her body, and to have no more sense of its weight.

As to artificial culture, or dressing, (dressur,) Frau H. had nothing of it. She had learned no foreign tongue, neither history, nor geography, nor natural philosophy, nor any other of those branches now imparted to those of her sex in their schools. The Bible and hymn-book were, especially in the long years of her sickness, her only reading: her moral character was throughout blameless; she was pious without fanaticism. Even her long suffering, and the peculiar manner of it, she recognized as the grace of God; as she expresses in the following verses:

> Great God! how great is thy goodness,
> To me thou hast given faith and love,
> Holding me firm in the distress of my sufferings.
>
> In the darkness of my sorrow,
> I was so far led away,
> As to beg for peace in speedy death.
>
> But then came to me the mighty strong faith;
> Hope came; and came eternal love;
> They shut my earthly eyelids.
> When, O bliss!
>
> Dead lies my bodily frame,
> But in the inmost mind a light burns up,
> Such as none knows in the waking life.
> Is it a light? no! but a sun of grace!

Often in the sense of her sufferings, while in the magnetic trance, she made prayers in verse, of which this is one:

Father, hear me!
Hear my prayer and supplication.
Father, I implore thee,
Let not thy child perish!
Look on my anguish, my tears.

Shed hope into my heart, and still its longing,
Father, on thee I call; have pity!
Take something from me, the sick one, the poor one.

Father, I leave thee not,
Though sickness and pain consume me.
If I the spring's light,
See only through the mist of tears,
Father, I leave thee not.

These verses lose their merit of a touching simplicity in an un-rhymed translation; but they will serve to show the habitual temper of her mind.

"As I was a maker of verses," continues Dr. Kerner, "it was easy to say, Frau H. derived this talent from my magnetic influence; but she made these little verses before she came under my care." Not without deep significance was Apollo distinguished as being at once the God of poesy, of prophecy, and the medical art. Sleep-waking develops the powers of seeing, healing, and poesy. How nobly the ancients understood the inner life; how fully is it indicated in their mysteries?

I know a peasant maiden, who cannot write, but who, in the magnetic state, speaks in measured verse.

Galen was indebted to his nightly dreams for a part of his medical knowledge.

The calumnies spread about Frau H. were many and gross; this she well knew. As one day she heard so many of these as to be much affected by them, we thought she would express her feelings that night in the magnetic sleep, but she only said "they can affect my body, but not my spirit." Her mind, raised above such assaults by the consciousness of innocence, maintained its tranquillity and dwelt solely on spiritual matters.

Once in her sleep-waking she wrote thus:

When the world declares of me
Such cruel ill in calumny,

And to your ears it finds a way,
Do you believe it, yea or nay?

I answered:

To us thou seemest true and pure,
Let others view it as they will;
We have our assurance still
If our own sight can make us sure.

People of all kinds, to my great trouble, were always pressing to see her. If we refused them access to the sick room, they avenged themselves by the invention of all kinds of falsehoods.

She met all with an equal friendliness, even when it cost her bodily pain, and those who defamed her, she often defended. There came to her both good and bad men. She felt the evil in men clearly, but would not censure; lifted up a stone to cast at no sinner, but was rather likely to awake, in the faulty beings she suffered near her, faith in a spiritual life which might make them better.

Years before she was brought to me, the earth, with its atmosphere, and all that is about and upon it, human beings not excepted, was no more for her. She needed, not only a magnetizer, not only a love, an earnestness, an insight, such as scarce lies within the capacity of any man, but also what no mortal could bestow upon her, another heaven, other means of nourishment, other air than that of this earth. She belonged to the world of spirits, living here herself, as more than half spirit. She belonged to the state after death, into which she had advanced more than half way.

It is possible she might have been brought back to an adaptation for this world in the second or third year of her malady; but, in the fifth, no mode of treatment could have effected this. But by care she was aided to a greater harmony and clearness of the inward life; she enjoyed at Weinsberg, as she after said, the richest and happiest days of this life, and to us her abode here remains a point of light.

As to her outward form, we have already said it seemed but a thin veil about her spirit. She was little, her features of an oriental cast, her eye had the penetrating look of a seer's eye, which was set off by the shade of long dark eyelashes. She was a light flower that only lived on rays.

Eschenmayer writes thus of her in his "Mysteries."

"Her natural state was a mild, friendly earnestness, always disposed to prayer and devotion; her eye had a highly spiritual expression, and remained, notwithstanding her great sufferings, always bright and clear. Her look was penetrating, would quickly change in the conversation, seem to give forth sparks, and remain fixed on some one place,—this was a token that some strange apparition fettered it,—then would she resume the conversation. When I first saw her, she was in a situation which showed that her bodily life could not long endure, and that recovery to the common natural state was quite impossible. Without visible derangement of the functions, her life seemed only a wick glimmering in the socket. She was, as Kerner truly describes her, like one arrested in the act of dying and detained in the body by magnetic influences. Spirit and soul seemed often divided, and the spirit to have taken up its abode in other regions, while the soul was yet bound to the body."

I have given these extracts as being happily expressive of the relation between the physician and the clairvoyant, also of her character.

It seems to have been one of singular gentleness, and grateful piety, simple and pure, but not at all one from which we should expect extraordinary development of brain in any way; yet the excitement of her temperament from climate, scenery, the influence of traditions which evidently flowed round her, and a great constitutional impressibility did develop in her brain the germs both of poetic creation and science.

I say poetic creation, for, to my mind, the ghosts she saw were projections of herself into objective reality. The Hades she imagines is based in fact, for it is one of souls, who, having neglected their opportunities for better life, find themselves left forlorn, helpless, seeking aid from beings still ignorant and prejudiced, perhaps much below themselves in natural powers. Having forfeited their chance of direct access to God, they seek mediation from the prayers of men. But in the coloring and dress* of these ghosts, as also in their manner and mode of speech, there is a great deal which seems merely fanciful—local and peculiar.

To me, these interviews represent only prophecies of her mind; yet, considered in this way, they are, if not ghostly, spiritual facts of high beauty, and which cast light on the state of the soul after its separation from the body. Her gentle patience with them, her steady reference to a higher cause, her pure joy, when they became white in

* The women ghosts all wear veils, put on the way admired by the Italian poets, of whom, however, she could know nothing.

the light of happiness obtained through aspiration, are worthy of a more than half enfranchised angel.

As to the stories of mental correspondence and visits to those still engaged in this world, such as are told of her presentiment of her father's death, and connexion with him in the last moments, these are probably pure facts. Those who have sufficient strength of affection to be easily disengaged from external impressions and habits, and who dare trust their mental impulses are familiar with such.

Her invention of a language seems a simply natural motion of the mind when left to itself. The language we habitually use is so broken, and so hackneyed by ages of conventional use, that, in all deep states of being, we crave one simple and primitive in its stead. Most persons make one more or less clear from looks, tones, and symbols:—this woman, in the long leisure of her loneliness, and a mind bent upon itself, attempted to compose one of letters and words. I look upon it as no gift from without, but a growth from her own mind.

Her invention of a machine, of which she made a drawing, her power of drawing correctly her life-circle, and sun-circle, and the mathematical feeling she had of her existence, in correspondent sections of the two, are also valuable as mental facts. These figures describe her history and exemplify the position of mathematics toward the world of creative thought.

Every fact of mental existence ought to be capable of similar demonstration. I attach no especial importance to her circles:—we all live in such; all who observe themselves have the same sense of exactness and harmony in the revolutions of their destiny. But few attend to what is simple and invariable in the motions of their minds, and still fewer seek out means clearly to express them to others.

Gœthe has taken up these facts in his Wanderjahre, where he speaks of his Macaria; also, one of these persons who are compensated for bodily infirmity by a more concentrated and acute state of mind, and consequent accesses of wisdom, as being bound to a star. When she was engaged by a sense of these larger revolutions, she seemed to those near her on the earth, to be sick; when she was, in fact, lower, but better adapted to the details and variations of an earthly life, these said she was well. Macaria knew the sun and life circles, also, the lives of spirit and soul, as did the forester's daughter of Prevorst.

Her power of making little verses was one of her least gifts. Many excitable persons possess this talent at versification, as all may possess it. It is merely that a certain exaltation of feeling raises the mode of expression with it, in the same way as song differs from speech. Verses of this sort do not necessarily demand the high faculties that constitute the poet,—the creative powers. Many verses, good ones, are personal or national merely. Ballads, hymns, love-lyrics, have often no claim differing from those of common prose speech, to the title of poems, except a greater keenness and terseness of expression.

The verses of this Seherin are of the simplest character, the natural garb for the sighs or aspirations of a lonely heart. She uses the shortest words, the commonest rhymes, and the verses move us by their nature and truth alone.

The most interesting of these facts to me, are her impressions from minerals and plants. Her impressions coincide with many ancient superstitions.

The hazel woke her immediately and gave her more power, therefore the witch with her hazel wand, probably found herself superior to those around her. We may also mention, in reference to witchcraft, that Dr. K. asserts that, in certain moods of mind, she had no weight, but was upborne upon water, like cork, thus confirming the propriety, and justice of our forefathers' ordeal for witchcraft!

The laurel produced on her the highest magnetic effect, therefore the Sibyls had good reasons for wearing it on their brows.

"The laurel had on her, as on most sleep-wakers, a distinguished magnetic effect. We thus see why the priestess at Delphi, previous to uttering her oracles, shook a laurel tree, and then seated herself on a tripod covered with laurel boughs. In the temple of Æsculapius, and others, the laurel was used to excite sleep and dream."

From grapes she declared impressions, which corresponded with those caused by the wines made from them. Many kinds were given her, one after the other, by the person who raised them, and who gives a certificate as to the accuracy of her impressions, and his belief that she could not have derived them from any cause, but that of the touch.

She prescribed vegetable substances to be used in her machine, (as a kind of vapor bath,) and with good results to herself.

She enjoyed contact with minerals, deriving from those she liked a sense of concentrated life. Her impressions of the precious stones, corresponded with many superstitions of the ancients, which led to the preference of certain gems for amulets, on which they had engraved talismanic figures.

The ancients, in addition to their sense of the qualities that distinguish the diamond above all gems, venerated it as a talisman against wild beasts, poison, and evil spirits, thus expressing the natural influence of what is so enduring, bright, and pure. Townshend, speaking of the effect of gems on one of his sleep-wakers, said, she loved the diamond so much that she would lean her forehead towards it, whenever it was brought near her.

It is observable that these sleep-wakers, in their prescriptions, resemble the ancient sages, who culled only simples for the sick. But if they have this fine sense, also, for the qualities of animal and mineral substances, there is no reason why they should not turn bane to antidote, and prescribe at least homeopathic doses of poison, to restore the diseased to health.

The Seherin ascribed different states to the right and left sides of every body, even of the lady moon. The left is most impressible. Query: Is this the reason why the left hand has been, by the custom of nations, so almost disused, because the heart is on the left side?

She also saw different sights in the left from the right eye. In the left, the bodily state of the person; in the right, his real or destined self, how often unknown to himself, almost always obscured or perverted by his present ignorance or mistake. She had also the gift of second sight. She saw the coffins of those about to die. She saw in mirrors, cups of water; in soap-bubbles, the coming future.

We are here reminded of many beautiful superstitions and legends; of the secret pool in which the daring may, at mid-moon of night, read the future; of the magic globe, on whose pure surface Britomart sees her future love, whom she must seek, arrayed in knightly armor, through a difficult and hostile world.

> *A looking-glass, right wondrously aguized,*
> *Whose virtues through the wyde world soon were solemnized.*
>   *It vertue had to show in perfect sight,*
> *Whatever thing was in the world contayned,*
>   *Betwixt the lowest earth and hevens hight;*
> *So that it to the looker appertayned,*
>   *Whatever foe had wrought, or friend had fayned,*
> *Herein discovered was, ne ought mote pas,*
>   *Ne ought in secret from the same remayned;*
> *Forthy it round and hollow shaped was,*
> *Like to the world itselfe, and seemed a World of Glas.*
>   *Faerie Queene, Book III.*

Such mirrors had Cornelius Agrippa and other wizards. The soap-bubble is such a globe; only one had need of second sight or double sight to see the pictures on so transitory a mirror. Perhaps it is some vague expectation of such wonders, that makes us so fond of blowing them in childish years. But, perhaps, it is rather as a prelude to the occupation of our lives, blowing bubbles where all things may be seen, that, "to the looker appertain," if we can keep them long enough or look quick enough.

In short, were this biography of no other value, it would be most interesting as showing how the floating belief of nations, always no doubt shadowing forth in its imperfect fashion the poetic facts with their scientific exposition, is found to grow up anew in a simple, but high-wrought nature.

The fashioning spirit, working upwards from the clod to man, proffers as its last, highest essay, the brain of man. In the lowest zoöphyte it aimed at this; some faint rudiments may there be discerned: but only in man has it perfected that immense galvanic battery that can be loaded from above, below, and around;—that engine, not only of perception, but of conception and consecutive thought,—whose right hand is memory, whose life is idea, the crown of nature, the platform from which spirit takes wing.

Yet, as gradation is the beautiful secret of nature, and the fashioning spirit, which loves to develop and transcend, loves no less to moderate, to modulate, and harmonize, it did not mean by thus drawing man onward to the next state of existence, to destroy his fitness for this. It did not mean to destroy his sympathies with the mineral, vegetable, and animal realms, of whose components he is in great part composed; which were the preface to his being, of whom he is to take count, whom he should govern as a reasoning head of a perfectly arranged body. He was meant to be the historian, the philosopher, the poet, the king of this world, no less than the prophet of the next.

These functions should be in equipoise, and when they are not, when we see excess either on the natural (so called as distinguished from the spiritual,) or the spiritual side, we feel that the law is transgressed. And, if it be the greatest sorrow to see brain merged in body, to see a man more hands or feet than head, so that we feel he might, with propriety, be on all fours again, or even crawl like the serpent; it is also sad to see the brain, too much excited on some one side, which we call madness, or even unduly and prematurely, so as to destroy in its bloom, the common human existence of the person, as in the case before us, and others of the poetical and prophetical existence.

We would rather minds should foresee less and see more surely, that death should ensue by gentler gradation, and the brain be the governor and interpreter, rather than the destroyer, of the animal life. But, in cases like this, where the animal life is prematurely broken up, and the brain prematurely exercised, we may as well learn what we can from it, and believe that the glimpses thus caught, if not as precious as the full view, are bright with the same light, and open to the same scene.

There is a family character about all the German ghosts. We find the same features in these stories as in those related by Jung Stilling and others. They bear the same character as the pictures by the old masters, of a deep and simple piety. She stands before as, this piety, in a full, high-necked robe, a simple, hausfrauish cap, a clear, straightforward blue eye. These are no terrible, gloomy ghosts with Spanish mantle or Italian dagger. We feel quite at home with them, and sure of their good faith.

To the Seherin, they were a real society, constantly inspiring good thoughts. The reference to them in these verses, written in her journal shortly before her death, is affecting, and shows her deep sense of their reality. She must have felt that she had been a true friend to them, by refusing always, as she did, requests she thought wrong, and referring them to a Saviour.

> Farewell, my friends,
> All farewell,
> God bless you for your love—
> Bless you for your goodness.
>   All farewell!
>
> And you, how shall I name you?
>   Who have so saddened me,
> I will name you also—Friends;
> You have been discipline to me.
>   Farewell! farewell!
>
> Farewell! you my dear ones,
> Soon will you know*
> How hard have been my sufferings
>   In the Pilgrim land.
>   Farewell!

* The physician thought she here referred to the examination of her body that would take place after her death. The brain was found to be sound, though there were marks of great disease elsewhere.

> *Let it not grieve you;*
> *That my woes find an end;*
> *Farewell, dear ones,*
> *Till the second meeting;*
> *Farewell! Farewell!*

In this journal her thoughts dwell much upon those natural ties which she was not permitted to enjoy. She thought much of her children, and often fancied she had saw the one who had died, growing in the spirit land. Any allusion to them called a sweet smile on her face when in her trance.

Other interesting poems are records of these often beautiful visions, especially of that preceding her own death; the address to her life-circle, the thought of which is truly great, (this was translated in the Dublin Magazine,) and descriptions of her earthly state as an imprisonment. The story of her life, though stained like others, by partialities, and prejudices, which were not justly distinguished from what was altogether true and fair, is a poem of so pure a music, presents such gentle and holy images, that we sympathize fully in the love and gratitude Kerner and his friends felt towards her, as the friend of their best life. She was a St. Theresa in her way.

His address to her, with which his volume closes, may thus be translated in homely guise. In the original it has no merit, except as uttering his affectionate and reverent feeling towards his patient, the peasant girl,—"the sick one, the poor one." But we like to see how, from the mouths of babes and sucklings, praise may be so perfected as to command this reverence from the learned and worldly-wise.

> *Farewell; the debt I owe thee*
> *Ever in heart I bear;*
> *My soul sees, since I know thee,*
> *The spirit depths so clear.*
>
> *Whether in light or shade,*
> *Thy soul now dwelling hath;*
> *Be, if my faith should fade,*
> *The guide upon my path.*
>
> *Livest thou in mutual power,*
> *With spirits blest and bright,*
> *O be, in death's dark hour,*
> *My help to heaven's light.*

> *Upon thy grave is growing,*
> *The plant by thee beloved,* *
> *St. Johns-wort golden glowing,*
> *Like St. John's thoughts of love.*
>
> *Witness of sacred sorrow,*
> *Whene'er thou meet'st my eye,*
> *O flower, from thee I borrow,*
> *Thoughts for eternity.*
>
> *Farewell! the woes of earth*
> *No more my soul affright;*
> *Who knows their temporal birth*
> *Can easy bear their weight.*

I do confess this is a paraphrase, not a translation, also, that in the other extracts, I have taken liberties with the original for the sake of condensation, and clearness. What I have written must be received as a slight and conversational account of the work.

Two or three other remarks, I had forgotten, may come in here.

The glances at the spirit-world have none of that large or universal significance, none of that value from philosophical analogy, that is felt in any picture by Swedenborg, or Dante, of permanent relations. The mind of the forester's daughter was exalted and rapidly developed; still the wild cherry tree bore no orange; she was not transformed into a philosophic or poetic organization.

Yet many of her untaught notions remind of other seers of a larger scope. She, too, receives this life as one link in a long chain; and thinks that immediately after death, the meaning of the past life will appear to us as one word.

She tends to a belief in the aromal state, and in successive existences on this earth; for behind persons she often saw another being, whether their form in the state before or after this, I know not; behind a woman a man, equipped for fight, and so forth. Her perception of character, even in cases of those whom she saw only as they passed her window, was correct.

Kerner aims many a leaden sarcasm at those who despise his credulity. He speaks of those sages as men whose brain is a glass table, incapable of receiving the electric spark, and who will not believe,

---

* She received great benefit from decoctions of this herb, and often prescribed it to others.

because, in their mental isolation, they are incapable of feeling these facts.

Certainly, I think he would be dull, who could see no meaning or beauty in the history of the forester's daughter of Prevorst. She lived but nine-and-twenty years, yet, in that time, had traversed a larger portion of the field of thought than all her race before, in their many and long lives.

Of the abuses to which all these magical implements are prone, I have an instance, since leaving Milwaukie, in the journal of a man equally sincere, but not equally inspired, led from Germany hither by signs and wonders, as a commissioned agent of Providence, who, indeed, has arranged every detail of his life with a minuteness far beyond the promised care of the sparrow. He props himself by spiritual aid from a maiden now in this country, who was once an attendant on the Seeress, and who seems to have caught from her the contagion of trance, but not its revelations.

Do not blame me that I have written so much about Germany and Hades, while you were looking for news of the West. Here, on the pier, I see disembarking the Germans, the Norwegians, the Swedes, the Swiss. Who knows how much of old legendary lore, of modern wonder, they have already planted amid the Wisconsin forests? Soon, soon their tales of the origin of things, and the Providence which rules them, will be so mingled with those of the Indian, that the very oak trees will not know them apart,—will not know whether itself be a Runic, a Druid, or a Winnebago oak.

Some seeds of all growths that have ever been known in this world might, no doubt, already be found in these Western wilds, if we had the power to call them to life.

I saw, in the newspaper, that the American Tract Society boasted of their agents' having exchanged, at a Western cabin door, tracts for the Devil on Two Sticks, and then burnt that more entertaining than edifying volume. No wonder, though, they study it there. Could one but have the gift of reading the dreams dreamed by men of such various birth, various history, various mind, it would afford much more extensive amusement than did the chambers of one Spanish city!

Could I but have flown at night through such mental experiences, instead of being shut up in my little bedroom at the Milwaukie boarding house, this chapter would have been worth reading. As it is, let us hasten to a close.

Had I been rich in money, I might have built a house, or set up in business, during my fortnight's stay at Milwaukie, matters move on there at so rapid a rate. But, being only rich in curiosity, I was obliged to walk the streets and pick up what I could in casual intercourse. When I left the street, indeed, and walked on the bluffs, or sat beside the lake in their shadow, my mind was rich in dreams congenial to the scene, some time to be realized, though not by me.

A boat was left, keel up, half on the sand, half in the water, swaying with each swell of the lake. It gave a picturesque grace to that part of the shore, as the only image of inaction—only object of a pensive character to be seen. Near this I sat, to dream my dreams and watch the colors of the lake, changing hourly, till the sun sank. These hours yielded impulses, wove webs, such as life will not again afford.

Returning to the boarding house, which was also a boarding school, we were sure to be greeted by gay laughter.

This school was conducted by two girls of nineteen and seventeen years; their pupils were nearly as old as themselves; the relation seemed very pleasant between them. The only superiority—that of superior knowledge—was sufficient to maintain authority—all the authority that was needed to keep daily life in good order.

In the West, people are not respected merely because they are old in years; people there have not time to keep up appearances in that way; when they cease to have a real advantage in wisdom, knowledge, or enterprise, they must stand back, and let those who are oldest in character "go ahead," however few years they may count. There are no banks of established respectability in which to bury the talent there; no napkin of precedent in which to wrap it. What cannot be made to pass current, is not esteemed coin of the realm.

To the windows of this house, where the daughter of a famous "Indian fighter," i.e. fighter against the Indians, was learning French and the piano, came wild, tawny figures, offering for sale their baskets of berries. The boys now, instead of brandishing the tomahawk, tame their hands to pick raspberries.

Here the evenings were much lightened by the gay chat of one of the party, who, with the excellent practical sense of mature experience, and the kindest heart, united a naiveté and innocence such as I never saw in any other who had walked so long life's tangled path. Like a child, she was everywhere at home, and like a child, received and bestowed entertainment from all places, all persons. I thanked her for making me laugh, as did the sick and poor, whom she was sure to find out in her briefest sojourn in any place, for more substantial aid.

Happy are those who never grieve, and so often aid and enliven their fellow men!

This scene, however, I was not sorry to exchange for the much celebrated beauties of the Island of Mackinaw.

CHAPTER VI

MACKINAW

Late at night we reached this island, so famous for its beauty, and to which I proposed a visit of some length. It was the last week in August, when a large representation from the Chippewa and Ottowa tribes are here to receive their annual payments from the American government. As their habits make travelling easy and inexpensive to them, neither being obliged to wait for steamboats, or write to see whether hotels are full, they come hither by thousands, and those thousands in families, secure of accommodation on the beach, and food from the lake, to make a long holiday out of the occasion. There were near two thousand encamped on the island already, and more arriving every day.

As our boat came in, the captain had some rockets let off. This greatly excited the Indians, and their yells and wild cries resounded along the shore. Except for the momentary flash of the rockets, it was perfectly dark, and my sensations as I walked with a stranger to a strange hotel, through the midst of these shrieking savages, and heard the pants and snorts of the departing steamer, which carried away all my companions, were somewhat of the dismal sort; though it was pleasant, too, in the way that everything strange is; everything that breaks in upon the routine that so easily incrusts us.

I had reason to expect a room to myself at the hotel, but found none, and was obliged to take up my rest in the common parlor and eating-room, a circumstance which ensured my being an early riser.

With the first rosy streak, I was out among my Indian neighbors, whose lodges honey-combed the beautiful beach, that curved away in long, fair outline on either side the house. They were already on the alert, the children creeping out from beneath the blanket door of the lodge; the women pounding corn in their rude mortars, the young men playing on their pipes. I had been much amused, when the strain proper to the Winnebago courting flute was played to me on another instrument, at any one fancying it a melody; but now, when I heard the notes in their true tone and time, I thought it not unworthy comparison, in its graceful sequence, and the light flourish, at the close, with the sweetest bird-songs; and this, like the bird-song, is only practised to allure a mate. The Indian, become a citizen and a husband, no more thinks of playing the flute than one of the "settled down" members of our society would of choosing the "purple light of love" as dye-stuff for a surtout.

Mackinaw has been fully described by able pens, and I can only add my tribute to the exceeding beauty of the spot and its position. It is charming to be on an island so small that you can sail round it in an afternoon, yet large enough to admit of long secluded walks through its gentle groves. You can go round it in your boat; or, on foot, you can tread its narrow beach, resting, at times, beneath the lofty walls of stone, richly wooded, which rise from it in various architectural forms. In this stone, caves are continually forming, from the action of the atmosphere; one of these is quite deep, and with a fragment left at its mouth, wreathed with little creeping plants, that looks, as you sit within, like a ruined pillar.

The arched rock surprised me, much as I had heard of it, from the perfection of the arch. It is perfect whether you look up through it from the lake, or down through it to the transparent waters. We both ascended and descended, no very easy matter, the steep and crumbling path, and rested at the summit, beneath the trees, and at the foot upon the cool mossy stones beside the lapsing wave. Nature has carefully decorated all this architecture with shrubs that take root within the crevices, and small creeping vines. These natural ruins may vie for beautiful effect with the remains of European grandeur, and have, beside, a charm as of a playful mood in nature.

The sugar-loaf rock is a fragment in the same kind as the pine rock we saw in Illinois. It has the same air of a helmet, as seen from an eminence at the side, which you descend by a long and steep path. The rock itself may be ascended by the bold and agile. Half way up is a niche, to which those, who are neither, can climb by a ladder. A very handsome young officer and lady who were with us did so, and then, facing round, stood there side by side, looking in the niche, if not like saints or angels wrought by pious hands in stone, as romantically, if not as holily, worthy the gazer's eye.

The woods which adorn the central ridge of the island are very full in foliage, and, in August, showed the tender green and pliant leaf of June elsewhere. They are rich in beautiful mosses and the wild raspberry.

From Fort Holmes, the old fort, we had the most commanding view of the lake and straits, opposite shores, and fair islets. Mackinaw, itself, is best seen from the water. Its peculiar shape is supposed to have been the origin of its name, Michilimackinac, which means the Great Turtle. One person whom I saw, wished to establish another etymology, which he fancied to be more refined; but, I doubt not, this is the true one, both because the shape might suggest such a name, and that the existence of an island in this commanding position, which did so, would seem a significant fact to the Indians. For Henry gives the details of peculiar worship paid to the Great Turtle, and the oracles received from this extraordinary Apollo of the Indian Delphos.

It is crowned most picturesquely, by the white fort, with its gay flag. From this, on one side, stretches the town. How pleasing a sight, after the raw, crude, staring assemblage of houses, everywhere else to be met in this country, an old French town, mellow in its coloring, and with the harmonious effect of a slow growth, which assimilates, naturally, with objects round it. The people in its streets, Indian, French, half-breeds, and others, walked with a leisure step, as of those who live a life of taste and inclination, rather than of the hard press of business, as in American towns elsewhere.

On the other side, along the fair, curving beach, below the white houses scattered on the declivity, clustered the Indian lodges, with their amber brown matting, so soft, and bright of hue, in the late afternoon sun. The first afternoon I was there, looking down from a near height, I felt that I never wished to see a more fascinating picture. It was an hour of the deepest serenity; bright blue and gold, rich shadows. Every moment the sunlight fell more mellow. The Indians were grouped and scattered among the lodges; the women preparing food, in the kettle or frying-pan, over the many small fires; the children, half-naked, wild as little goblins, were playing both in and out of the water. Here and there lounged a young girl, with a baby at her back, whose bright eyes glanced, as if born into a world of courage and of joy, instead of ignominious servitude and slow decay. Some girls were cutting wood, a little way from me, talking and laughing, in the low musical tone, so charming in the Indian women. Many bark canoes were upturned upon the beach, and, by that light, of almost the same amber as the lodges. Others, coming in, their square sails set, and with almost ar- rowy speed, though heavily laden with dusky forms, and all the apparatus of their household. Here and there a sail-boat glided by, with a different, but scarce less pleasing motion.

It was a scene of ideal loveliness, and these wild forms adorned it, as looking so at home in it. All seemed happy, and they were happy that day, for they had no firewater to madden them, as it was Sunday, and the shops were shut.

From my window, at the boarding house, my eye was constantly attracted by these picturesque groups. I was never tired of seeing the canoes come in, and the new arrivals set up their temporary dwellings. The women ran to set up the tent-poles, and spread the mats on the ground. The men brought the chests, kettles, &c.; the mats were then laid on the outside, the cedar boughs strewed on the ground, the blanket hung up for a door, and all was completed in less than twenty minutes. Then they began to prepare the night meal, and to learn of their neighbors the news of the day.

The habit of preparing food out of doors, gave all the gipsy charm and variety to their conduct. Continually I wanted Sir Walter Scott to have been there. If such romantic sketches were suggested to him, by the sight of a few gipsies, not a group near one of these fires but would have furnished him material for a separate canvass. I was so taken up with the spirit of the scene, that I could not follow out the stories suggested by these weather-beaten, sullen, but eloquent figures.

They talked a great deal, and with much variety of gesture, so that I often had a good guess at the meaning of their discourse. I saw that, whatever the Indian may be among the whites, he is anything but taciturn with his own people. And he often would declaim, or narrate at length, as indeed it is obvious, that these tribes possess great power that way, if only from the fables taken from their stores, by Mr. Schoolcraft.

I liked very much to walk or sit among them. With the women I held much communication by signs. They are almost invariably coarse and ugly, with the exception of their eyes, with a peculiarly awkward gait, and forms bent by burthens. This gait, so different from the steady and noble step of the men, marks the inferior position they occupy. I had heard much eloquent contradiction of this. Mrs. Schoolcraft had maintained to a friend, that they were in fact as nearly on a par with their husbands as the white woman with hers. "Although," said she, "on account of inevitable causes, the Indian woman is subjected to many hardships of a peculiar nature, yet her position, compared with that of the man, is higher and freer than that of the white woman. Why will people look only on one side? They either exalt the

Red man into a Demigod or degrade him into a beast. They say that he compels his wife to do all the drudgery, while he does nothing but hunt and amuse himself; forgetting that, upon his activity and power of endurance as a hunter, depends the support of his family; that this is labor of the most fatiguing kind, and that it is absolutely necessary that he should keep his frame unbent by burdens and unworn by toil, that he may be able to obtain the means of subsistence. I have witnessed scenes of conjugal and parental love in the Indian's wigwam from which I have often, often thought the educated white man, proud of his superior civilization, might learn an useful lesson. When he returns from hunting, worn out with fatigue, having tasted nothing since dawn, his wife, if she is a good wife, will take off his moccasons and replace them with dry ones, and will prepare his game for their repast, while his children will climb upon him, and he will caress them with all the tenderness of a woman; and in the evening the Indian wigwam is the scene of the purest domestic pleasures. The father will relate for the amusement of the wife, and for the instruction of the children, all the events of the day's hunt, while they will treasure up every word that falls, and thus learn the theory of the art, whose practice is to be the occupation of their lives."

Mrs. Grant speaks thus of the position of woman amid the Mohawk Indians:

"Lady Mary Montague says, that the court of Vienna was the paradise of old women, and that there is no other place in the world where a woman past fifty excites the least interest. Had her travels extended to the interior of North America, she would have seen another instance of this inversion of the common mode of thinking. Here a woman never was of consequence, till she had a son old enough to fight the battles of his country. From that date she held a superior rank in society; was allowed to live at ease, and even called to consultations on national affairs. In savage and warlike countries, the reign of beauty is very short, and its influence comparatively limited. The girls in childhood had a very pleasing appearance; but excepting their fine hair, eyes, and teeth, every external grace was soon banished by perpetual drudgery, carrying burdens too heavy to be borne, and other slavish employments considered beneath the dignity of the men. These walked before erect and graceful, decked with ornaments which set off to advantage the symmetry of their well-formed persons, while the poor women followed, meanly attired, bent under the weight of the children and utensils, which they carried everywhere with them, and disfigured and degraded by ceaseless toils. They were very early married, for a Mohawk had no other servant but his wife, and, whenever he commenced hunter, it was requisite he should have some one to carry his load, cook his kettle, make his moccasons, and, above all, produce the young warriors who were to succeed him in the honors of the chase and of the tomahawk. Wherever man is a mere hunter, woman is a mere slave. It is domestic intercourse that softens man, and elevates woman; and of that there can be but little, where the employments and amusements are not in common; the ancient Caledonians honored the fair; but then it is to be observed, they were fair huntresses, and moved in the light of their beauty to the hill of roes; and the culinary toils were entirely left to the rougher sex. When the young warrior made his appearance, it softened the cares of his mother, who well knew that, when he grew up, every deficiency in tenderness to his wife would be made up in superabundant duty and affection to her. If it were possible to carry filial veneration to excess, it was done here; for all other charities were absorbed in it. I wonder this system of depressing the sex in their early years, to exalt them when all their juvenile attractions were flown, and when mind alone can distinguish them, has not occurred to our modern reformers. The Mohawks took good care not to admit their women to share their prerogatives, till they approved themselves good wives and mothers."

The observations of women upon the position of woman are always more valuable than those of men; but, of these two, Mrs. Grant's seems much nearer the truth than Mrs. Schoolcraft's, because, though her opportunities for observation did not bring her so close, she looked more at both sides to find the truth.

Carver, in his travels among the Winnebagoes, describes two queens, one nominally so, like Queen Victoria; the other invested with a genuine royalty, springing from her own conduct.

In the great town of the Winnebagoes, he found a queen presiding over the tribe, instead of a sachem. He adds, that, in some tribes, the descent is given to the female line in preference to the male, that is, a sister's son will succeed to the authority, rather than a brother's son.

The position of this Winnebago queen, reminded me forcibly of Queen Victoria's.

"She sat in the council, but only asked a few questions, or gave some trifling directions in matters relative to the state, for women are never allowed to sit in their councils, except they happen to be invested with the supreme authority, and then it is not customary for them to make any formal speeches, as the chiefs do. She was a very ancient woman, small in stature, and not much distinguished by her dress from several young women that attended her. These, her attendants, seemed greatly pleased whenever I showed any tokens of respect to their queen, especially when I saluted her, which I frequently did to acquire her favor."

The other was a woman, who being taken captive, found means to kill her captor, and make her escape, and the tribe were so struck with admiration at the courage and calmness she displayed on the occasion, as to make her chieftainess in her own right.

Notwithstanding the homage paid to women, and the consequence allowed her in some cases, it is impossible to look upon the Indian women, without feeling that they *do* occupy a lower place than women among the nations of European civilization. The habits of drudgery expressed in their form and gesture, the soft and wild but melancholy expression of their eye, reminded me of the tribe mentioned by Mackenzie, where the women destroy their female children, whenever they have a good opportunity; and of the eloquent reproaches addressed by the Paraguay woman to her mother, that she had not, in the same way, saved her from the anguish and weariness of her lot.

More weariness than anguish, no doubt, falls to the lot of most of these women. They inherit submission, and the minds of the generality accommodate themselves more or less to any posture. Perhaps they suffer less than their white sisters, who have more aspiration and refinement, with little power of self-sustenance. But their place is certainly lower, and their share of the human inheritance less.

Their decorum and delicacy are striking, and show that when these are native to the mind, no habits of life make any difference. Their whole gesture is timid, yet self-possessed. They used to crowd round me, to inspect little things I had to show them, but never press near; on the contrary, would reprove and keep off the children. Anything they took from my hand, was held with care, then shut or folded, and returned with an air of lady-like precision. They would not stare, however curious they might be, but cast sidelong glances.

A locket that I wore, was an object of untiring interest; they seemed to regard it as a talisman. My little sun-shade was still more fascinating to them; apparently they had never before seen one. For an umbrella they entertain profound regard, probably looking upon it as the most luxurious superfluity a person can possess, and therefore a badge of great wealth. I used to see an old squaw, whose sullied skin and coarse, tanned locks, told that she had braved sun and storm, without a doubt or care, for sixty years at the least, sitting gravely at

the door of her lodge, with an old green umbrella over her head, happy
for hours together in the dignified shade. For her happiness pomp came
not, as it so often does, too late; she received it with grateful enjoyment.

One day, as I was seated on one of the canoes, a woman came
and sat beside me, with her baby in its cradle set up at her feet. She
asked me by a gesture, to let her take my sun-shade, and then to show
her how to open it. Then she put it into her baby's hand, and held it
over its head, looking at me the while with a sweet, mischievous laugh,
as much as to say, "you carry a thing that is only fit for a baby;" her
pantomime was very pretty. She, like the other women, had a glance,
and shy, sweet expression in the eye; the men have a steady gaze.

That noblest and loveliest of modern Preux, Lord Edward Fitzgerald, who came through Buffalo to Detroit and Mackinaw, with
Brant, and was adopted into the Bear tribe by the name of Eghnidal,
was struck, in the same way, by the delicacy of manners in the women.
He says, "Notwithstanding the life they lead, which would make most
women rough and masculine, they are as soft, meek and modest, as
the best brought up girls in England. Somewhat coquettish too! Imagine the manners of Mimi in a poor *squaw,* that has been carrying packs
in the woods all her life."

McKenney mentions that the young wife, during the short bloom
of her beauty, is an object of homage and tenderness to her husband.
One Indian woman, the Flying Pigeon, a beautiful, an excellent
woman, of whom he gives some particulars, is an instance of the power
uncommon characters will always exert of breaking down the barriers
custom has erected round them. She captivated by her charms, and
inspired with reverence for her character, her husband and son. The
simple praise with which the husband indicates the religion, the judgment, and the generosity he saw in her, are as satisfying as Count
Zinzendorf's more labored eulogium on his "noble consort." The conduct of her son, when, many years after her death, he saw her picture
at Washington, is unspeakably affecting. Catlin gives anecdotes of the
grief of a chief for the loss of a daughter, and the princely gifts he
offers in exchange for her portrait, worthy not merely of European,
but of Troubadour sentiment. It is also evident that, as Mrs. Schoolcraft says, the women have great power at home. It can never be
otherwise, men being dependent upon them for the comfort of their
lives. Just so among ourselves, wives who are neither esteemed nor
loved by their husbands, have great power over their conduct by the
friction of every day, and over the formation of their opinions by the

daily opportunities so close a relation affords, of perverting testimony and instilling doubts. But these sentiments should not come in brief flashes, but burn as a steady flame, then there would be more women worthy to inspire them. This power is good for nothing, unless the woman be wise to use it aright. Has the Indian, has the white woman, as noble a feeling of life and its uses, as religious a self-respect, as worthy a field of thought and action, as man? If not, the white woman, the Indian woman, occupies an inferior position to that of man. It is not so much a question of power, as of privilege.

The men of these subjugated tribes, now accustomed to drunkenness and every way degraded, bear but a faint impress of the lost grandeur of the race. They are no longer strong, tall, or finely proportioned. Yet as you see them stealing along a height, or striding boldly forward, they remind you of what *was* majestic in the red man.

On the shores of lake Superior, it is said, if you visit them at home, you may still see a remnant of the noble blood. The Pillagers—(Pilleurs)—a band celebrated by the old travellers, are still existant there.

"Still some, 'the eagles of their tribe,' may rush."

I have spoken of the hatred felt by the white man for the Indian: with white women it seems to amount to disgust, to loathing. How I could endure the dirt, the peculiar smell of the Indians, and their dwellings, was a great marvel in the eyes of my lady acquaintance; indeed, I wonder why they did not quite give me up, as they certainly looked on me with great distaste for it. "Get you gone, you Indian dog," was the felt, if not the breathed, expression towards the hapless owners of the soil. All their claims, all their sorrows quite forgot, in abhorrence of their dirt, their tawny skins, and the vices the whites have taught them.

A person who had seen them during great part of a life, expressed his prejudices to me with such violence, that I was no longer surprised that the Indian children threw sticks at him, as he passed. A lady said, "do what you will for them, they will be ungrateful. The savage cannot be washed out of them. Bring up an Indian child and see if you can attach it to you." The next moment, she expressed, in the presence of one of those children whom she was bringing up, loathing at the odor left by one of her people, and one of the most respected, as he passed through the room. When the child is grown she will consider it basely ungrateful not to love her, as it certainly will not; and this will be cited as an instance of the impossibility of attaching the Indian.

Whether the Indian could, by any efforts of love and intelligence from the white man, have been civilized and made a valuable ingredient in the new state, I will not say; but this we are sure of; the French Catholics, at least, did not harm them, nor disturb their minds merely to corrupt them. The French they loved. But the stern Presbyterian, with his dogmas and his task-work, the city circle and the college, with their niggard concessions and unfeeling stare, have never tried the experiment. It has not been tried. Our people and our government have sinned alike against the first-born of the soil, and if they are the fated agents of a new era, they have done nothing—have invoked no god to keep them sinless while they do the hest of fate.

Worst of all, when they invoke the holy power only to mask their iniquity; when the felon trader, who, all the week, has been besotting and degrading the Indian with rum mixed with red pepper, and damaged tobacco, kneels with him on Sunday before a common altar, to tell the rosary which recalls the thought of him crucified for love of suffering men, and to listen to sermons in praise of "purity"!!

My savage friends, cries the old fat priest, you must, above all things, aim at *purity*.

Oh, my heart swelled when I saw them in a Christian church. Better their own dog-feasts and bloody rites than such mockery of that other faith.

"The dog," said an Indian, "was once a spirit; he has fallen for his sin, and was given by the Great Spirit, in this shape, to man, as his most intelligent companion. Therefore we sacrifice it in highest honor to our friends in this world,—to our protecting geniuses in another."

There was religion in that thought. The white man sacrifices his own brother, and to Mammon, yet he turns in loathing fron the dog-feast.

"You say," said the Indian of the South to the missionary, "that Christianity is pleasing to God. How can that be?—Those men at Savannah are Christians."

Yes! slave-drivers and Indian traders are called Christians, and the Indian is to be deemed less like the Son of Mary than they! Wonderful is the deceit of man's heart!

I have not, on seeing something of them in their own haunts, found reason to change the sentiments expressed in the following lines, when a deputation of the Sacs and Foxes visited Boston in 1837, and were, by one person at least, received in a dignified and courteous manner.

GOVERNOR EVERETT
RECEIVING THE INDIAN CHIEFS,

NOVEMBER, 1837.

Who says that Poesy is on the wane,
And that the Muses tune their lyres in vain?
'Mid all the treasures of romantic story,
When thought was fresh and fancy in her glory,
Has ever Art found out a richer theme,
More dark a shadow, or more soft a gleam,
Than fall upon the scene, sketched carelessly,
In the newspaper column of to-day?

American romance is somewhat stale.
Talk of the hatchet, and the faces pale,
Wampum and calumets and forests dreary,
Once so attractive, now begins to weary.
Uncas and Magawisca please us still,
Unreal, yet idealized with skill;
But every poetaster scribbling witling,
From the majestic oak his stylus whittling,
Has helped to tire us, and to make us fear
The monotone in which so much we hear
Of "stoics of the wood," and "men without a tear."

Yet Nature, ever buoyant, ever young,
If let alone, will sing as erst she sung;
The course of circumstance gives back again
The Picturesque, erewhile pursued in vain;
Shows us the fount of Romance is not wasted—
The lights and shades of contrast not exhausted.

Shorn of his strength, the Samson now must sue
    For fragments from the feast his fathers gave,
The Indian dare not claim what is his due,
    But as a boon his heritage must crave;
His stately form shall soon be seen no more
Through all his father's land, th' Atlantic shore,
Beneath the sun, to us so kind, they melt,

More heavily each day our rule is felt;
The tale is old,—we do as mortals must:
Might makes right here, but God and Time are just.

So near the drama hastens to its close,
On this last scene awhile your eyes repose;
The polished Greek and Scythian meet again,
The ancient life is lived by modern men—

The savage through our busy cities walks,—
He in his untouched grandeur silent stalks.
Unmoved by all our gaieties and shows,
Wonder nor shame can touch him as he goes;
He gazes on the marvels we have wrought,
But knows the models from whence all was brought;
In God's first temples he has stood so oft,
And listened to the natural organ loft—
Has watched the eagle's flight, the muttering thunder heard,
Art cannot move him to a wondering word;
Perhaps he sees that all this luxury
Brings less food to the mind than to the eye;
Perhaps a simple sentiment has brought
More to him than your arts had ever taught.
What are the petty triumphs Art has given,
To eyes familiar with the naked heaven?

All has been seen—dock, railroad, and canal,
Fort, market, bridge, college, and arsenal,
Asylum, hospital, and cotton mill,
The theatre, the lighthouse, and the jail.
The Braves each novelty, reflecting, saw,
And now and then growled out the earnest yaw.
And now the time is come, 't is understood,
When, having seen and thought so much, a talk may do some good.

A well-dressed mob have thronged the sight to greet,
And motley figures throng the spacious street;
Majestical and calm through all they stride,
Wearing the blanket with a monarch's pride;
The gazers stare and shrug, but can't deny
Their noble forms and blameless symmetry.

If the Great Spirit their morale has slighted,
And wigwam smoke their mental culture blighted,
Yet the physique, at least, perfection reaches,
In wilds where neither Combe nor Spursheim teaches;
Where whispering trees invite man to the chase,
And bounding deer allure him to the race.

Would thou hadst seen it! That dark, stately band,
Whose ancestors enjoyed all this fair land,
Whence they, by force or fraud, were made to flee,
Are brought, the white man's victory to see.
Can kind emotions in their proud hearts glow,
As through these realms, now decked by Art, they go?
The church, the school, the railroad and the mart—
Can these a pleasure to their minds impart?
All once was theirs—earth, ocean, forest, sky—
How can they joy in what now meets the eye?
Not yet Religion has unlocked the soul,
Nor Each has learned to glory in the Whole!

Must they not think, so strange and sad their lot,
That they by the Great Spirit are forgot?
From the far border to which they are driven,
They might look up in trust to the clear heaven;
But here—what tales doth every object tell
Where Massasoit sleeps—where Philip fell!

We take our turn, and the Philosopher
Sees through the clouds a hand which cannot err,
An unimproving race, with all their graces
And all their vices, must resign their places;
And Human Culture rolls its onward flood
Over the broad plains steeped in Indian blood.

Such thoughts steady our faith; yet there will rise
Some natural tears into the calmest eyes—
Which gaze where forest princes haughty go,
Made for a gaping crowd a raree show.

But this a scene seems where, in courtesy,
The pale face with the forest prince could vie,
For One presided, who, for tact and grace,

In any age had held an honored place,—
In Beauty's own dear day, had shone a polished Phidian vase!

Oft have I listened to his accents bland,
    And owned the magic of his silvery voice,
In all the graces which life's arts demand,
    Delighted by the justness of his choice.
Not his the stream of lavish, fervid thought,—
The rhetoric by passion's magic wrought;
Not his the massive style, the lion port,
Which with the granite class of mind assort;
But, in a range of excellence his own,
With all the charms to soft persuasion known,
Amid our busy people we admire him—"elegant and lone."

He scarce needs words, so exquisite the skill
Which modulates the tones to do his will,
That the mere sound enough would charm the ear,
And lap in its Elysium all who hear.
The intellectual paleness of his cheek,
    The heavy eyelids and slow, tranquil smile,
The well cut lips from which the graces speak,
    Fit him alike to win or to beguile;
Then those words so well chosen, fit, though few,
Their linked sweetness as our thoughts pursue,
We deem them spoken pearls, or radiant diamond dew.

And never yet did I admire the power
    Which makes so lustrous every threadbare theme—
Which won for Lafayette one other hour,
    And e'en on July Fourth could cast a gleam—
As now, when I behold him play the host,
With all the dignity which red men boast—
With all the courtesy the whites have lost;—
Assume the very hue of savage mind,
Yet in rude accents show the thought refined;—
Assume the naiveté of infant age,
And in such prattle seem still more a sage;
The golden mean with tact unerring seized,
A courtly critic shone, a simple savage pleased;
The stoic of the woods his skill confessed,
As all the Father answered in his breast,

> To the sure mark the silver arrow sped,
> The man without a tear a tear has shed;
> And thou hadst wept, hadst thou been there, to see
> How true one sentiment must ever be,
> In court or camp, the city or the wild,
> To rouse the Father's heart, you need but name his Child.
>
> 'T was a fair scene—and acted well by all;
> So here's a health to Indian braves so tall—
> Our Governor and Boston people all!

I will copy the admirable speech of Governor Everett on that oc-casion, as I think it the happiest attempt ever made to meet the Indian in his own way, and catch the tone of his mind. It was said, in the newspapers, that Keokuck did actually shed tears when addressed as a father. If he did not with his eyes, he well might in his heart.

EVERETT'S SPEECH.

Chiefs and warriors of the Sauks and Foxes, you are welcome to our hall of council.

Brothers! you have come a long way from home to visit your white brethren; we rejoice to take you by the hand.

Brothers! we have heard the names of your chiefs and war-riors; our brothers, who have travelled into the West, have told us a great deal of the Sauks and Foxes; we rejoice to see you with our own eyes, and take you by the hand.

Brothers! we are called the Massachusetts. This is the name of the red men that once lived here. Their wigwams filled yonder field; their council fire was kindled on this spot. They were of the same great race as the Sauks and Misquakuiks.

Brothers! when our fathers came over the great waters, they were a small band. The red man stood upon the rock by the seaside, and saw our fathers. He might have pushed them into the water and drowned them. But he stretched out his arm to our fathers and said, "Welcome, white men!" Our fathers were hungry, and the red men gave them corn and venison. Our fathers were cold, and the red man wrapped them up in his blanket. We are now numerous and powerful, but we re-member the kindness of the red man to our fathers. Brothers, you are welcome; we are glad to see you.

Brothers! our faces are pale, and your faces are dark; but

our hearts are alike. The Great Spirit has made his children of different colors, but he loves them all.

Brothers! you dwell between the Mississippi and the Missouri. They are mighty rivers. They have one branch far East in the Alleghanies, and the other far West in the Rocky Mountains; but they flow together at last into one great stream, and run down together into the sea. In like manner, the red man dwells in the West, and the white man in the East, by the great waters; but they are all one branch, one family; it has many branches and one head.

Brothers! as you entered our council house, you beheld the image of our great Father Washington. It is a cold stone—it cannot speak. But he was the friend of the red man, and bad his children live in peace with their red brethren. He is gone to the world of spirits. But his words have made a very deep print in our hearts, like the step of a strong buffalo on the soft clay of the prairie.

Brother! I perceive your little son between your knees. God preserve his life, my brother. He grows up before you like the tender sapling by the side of the mighty oak. May the oak and the sapling flourish a long time together. And when the mighty oak is fallen to the ground, may the young tree fill its place in the forest, and spread out its branches over the tribe like the parent trunk.

Brothers! I make you a short talk, and again bid you welcome to our council hall.

Not often have they been addressed with such intelligence and tact. The few who have not approached them with sordid rapacity, but from love to them, as men, and souls to be redeemed, have most frequently been persons intellectually too narrow, too straightly bound in sects or opinions, to throw themselves into the character or position of the Indians, or impart to them anything they can make available. The Christ shown them by these missionaries, is to them but a new and more powerful Manito; the signs of the new religion, but the fetiches that have aided the conquerors.

Here I will copy some remarks made by a discerning observer, on the methods used by the missionaries, and their natural results.

"Mr. ———— and myself had a very interesting conversation, upon the subject of the Indians, their character, capabilities, &c. After ten years' experience among them, he was forced to acknowledge, that the results of the missionary·efforts had produced nothing calculated to encourage. He thought that there was an intrinsic disability in them, to rise above, or go beyond the sphere in which they had so long moved. He said, that even those Indians who had been converted, and who had adopted the habits of civilization, were very little improved in their real character; they were as selfish, as deceitful, and as indolent, as those who were still heathens. They had repaid the kindnesses of the missionaries with the basest ingratitude, killing their cattle and swine, and robbing them of their harvests, which they wantonly destroyed. He had abandoned the idea of effecting any general good to the Indians. He had conscientious scruples, as to promoting an enterprise so hopeless, as that of missions among the Indians, by sending accounts to the east, that might induce philanthropic individuals to contribute to their support. In fact, the whole experience of his intercourse with them, seemed to have convinced him of the irremediable degradation of the race. Their fortitude under suffering, he considered the result of physical and mental insensibility; their courage, a mere animal excitement, which they found it necessary to inflame, before daring to meet a foe. They have no constancy of purpose; and are, in fact, but little superior to the brutes, in point of moral development. It is not astonishing, that one looking upon the Indian character, from Mr. ———'s point of view, should entertain such sentiments. The object of his intercourse with them was, to make them apprehend the mysteries of a theology, which, to the most enlightened, is an abstruse, metaphysical study; and it is not singular they should prefer their pagan superstitions, which address themselves more directly to the senses. Failing in the attempt to christianize, before civilizing them, he inferred, that, in the intrinsic degradation of their faculties, the obstacle was to be found."

Thus the missionary vainly attempts, by once or twice holding up the cross, to turn deer and tigers into lambs; vainly attempts to convince the red man that a heavenly mandate takes from him his broad lands. He bows his head, but does not at heart acquiesce. He cannot. It is not true; and if it were, the descent of blood through the same channels, for centuries, had formed habits of thought not so easily to be disturbed.

Amalgamation would afford the only true and profound means of civilization. But nature seems, like all else, to declare, that this race is fated to perish. Those of mixed blood fade early, and are not generally a fine race. They lose what is best in either type, rather than enhance the value of each, by mingling. There are exceptions, one or two such I know of, but this, it is said, is the general rule.

A traveller observes, that the white settlers, who live in the woods, soon become sallow, lanky, and dejected; the atmosphere of the trees does not agree with Caucasian lungs; and it is, perhaps, in part, an instinct of this, which causes the hatred of the new settlers towards trees. The Indian breathed the atmosphere of the forests freely; he loved their shade. As they are effaced from the land, he fleets too; a part of the same manifestation, which cannot linger behind its proper era.

The Chippewas have lately petitioned the state of Michigan, that they may be admitted as citizens; but this would be vain, unless they could be admitted, as brothers, to the heart of the white man. And while the latter feels that conviction of superiority, which enabled our Wisconsin friend to throw away the gun, and send the Indian to fetch it, he had need to be very good, and very wise, not to abuse his position. But the white man, as yet, is a half-tamed pirate, and avails himself, as much as ever, of the maxim, "Might makes right." All that civilization does for the generality, is to cover up this with a veil of subtle evasions and chicane, and here and there to rouse the individual mind to appeal to heaven against it.

I have no hope of liberalizing the missionary, of humanizing the sharks of trade, of infusing the conscientious drop into the flinty bosom of policy, of saving the Indian from immediate degradation, and speedy death. The whole sermon may be preached from the text, "Needs be that offences must come, yet wo them by whom they come." Yet, ere they depart, I wish there might be some masterly attempt to reproduce, in art or literature, what is proper to them, a kind of beauty and grandeur, which few of the every-day crowd have hearts to feel, yet which ought to leave in the world its monuments, to inspire the thought of genius through all ages. Nothing in this kind has been done masterly; since it was Clevengers's ambition, 'tis pity he had not opportunity to try fully his powers. We hope some other mind may be bent upon it, ere too late.

At present the only lively impress of their passage through the world is to be found in such books as Catlin's and some stories told by the old travellers, of which I purpose a brief account.

First, let me give another brief tale of the power exerted by the white man over the savage in a trying case, but, in this case, it was righteous, was moral power.

We were looking over McKenney's trip to the Lakes, and, on observing the picture of Key-way-no-wut, or the Going Cloud, Mr. B. observed "Ah, that is the fellow I came near having a fight with," and he detailed at length the circumstances. This Indian was a very desperate character, and whom all the Leech lake band stood in fear of. He would shoot down any Indian who offended him, without the least hesitation, and had become quite the bully of that part of the tribe. The trader at Leech lake warned Mr. B. to beware of him, and said that he once, when he (the trader) refused to give up to him his stock of wild rice, went and got his gun and tomahawk, and shook the tomahawk over his head, saying "*Now,* give me your wild rice." The trader complied with his exaction, but not so did Mr. B. in the adventure which I am about to relate. Key-way-no-wut came frequently to him with furs, wishing him to give for them cotton cloth, sugar, flour, &c. Mr. B. explained to him that he could not trade for furs, as he was sent there as a teacher, and that it would be like putting his hand into the fire to do so, as the traders would inform against him, and he would be sent out of the country. At the same time, he *gave* him the articles which he wished. Key-way-no-wut found this a very convenient way of getting what he wanted, and followed up this sort of game, until, at last, it became insupportable. One day the Indian brought a very large otter skin, and said "I want to get for this ten pounds of sugar, and some flour and cloth," adding, "I am not like other Indians, *I* want to pay for what I get. Mr. B. found that he must either be robbed of all he had by submitting to these exactions, or take a stand at once. He thought, however, he would try to avoid a scrape, and told his customer he had not so much sugar to spare. "Give me then," said he, "what you can spare," and Mr. B. thinking to make him back out, told him he would give him five pounds of sugar for his skin. "Take it," said the Indian. He left the skin, telling Mr. B. to take good care of it. Mr. B. took it at once to the trader's store, and related the circumstance, congratulating himself that he had got rid of the Indian's exactions. But, in about a month, Key-way-no-wut appeared bringing some dirty Indian sugar, and said "I have brought back the sugar that I borrowed of you, and I want my otter skin back." Mr. B. told him, "I *bought* an otter skin of you, but if you will return the other articles you have got for it, perhaps I can get it for you." "Where is the skin?" said he very quickly, "what have you done with it?" Mr. B. replied it was in the trader's store, where he (the Indian) could not get it. At this information he was furious, laid his hands on his knife and tomahawk, and commanded Mr. B. to bring it at once.

Mr. B. found this was the crisis, where he must take a stand or be "rode over rough shod" by this man; his wife, who was present was much alarmed, and begged he would get the skin for the Indian, but he told her that "either he or the Indian would soon be master of his house, and if she was afraid to see it decided which was to be so, she had better retire." He turned to Key-way-no-wut, and addressed him in a stern voice as follows: "I will *not* give you the skin. How often have you come to my house, and I have shared with you what I had. I gave you tobacco when you were well, and medicine when you were sick, and you never went away from my wigwam with your hands empty. And this is the way you return my treatment to you. I had thought you were a man and a chief, but you are not, you are nothing but an old woman. Leave this house, and never enter it again." Mr. B. said he expected the Indian would attempt his life when he said this, but that he had placed himself in a position so that he could defend himself, and he looked straight into the Indian's eye, and like other wild beasts he quailed before the glance of mental and moral courage. He calmed down at once, and soon began to make apologies. Mr. B. then told him kindly, but firmly, that, if he wished to walk in the same path with him, he must walk as straight as the crack on the floor before them; adding that he would not walk with anybody who would jostle him by walking so crooked as he had done. He was perfectly tamed, and Mr. B. said he never had any more trouble with him.

The conviction here livingly enforced of the superiority on the side of the white man, was thus expressed by the Indian orator at Mackinaw while we were there. After the customary compliments about sun, dew, &c., "This," said he, "is the difference between the white and the red man; the white man looks to the future and paves the way for posterity." This is a statement uncommonly refined for an Indian; but one of the gentlemen present, who understood the Chippeway, vouched for it as a literal rendering of his phrases; and he did indeed touch the vital point of difference. But the Indian, if he understands, cannot make use of his intelligence. The fate of his people is against it, and Pontiac and Philip have no more chance, than Julian in the times of old.

Now that I am engaged on this subject, let me give some notices of writings upon it, read either at Mackinaw or since my return.

Mrs. Jameson made such good use of her brief visit to these regions, as leaves great cause to regret she did not stay longer and go farther; also, that she did not make more use of her acquaintance with, indeed, adoption by, the Johnson family. Mr. Johnson seems to have been almost the only white man who knew how to regard with due intelligence and nobleness, his connexion with the race. Neither French or English, of any powers of sympathy, or poetical apprehension, have lived among the Indians without high feelings of enjoyment. Perhaps no luxury has been greater, than that experienced by the persons, who, sent either by trade or war, during the last century, into these majestic regions, found guides and shelter amid the children of the soil, and recognized in a form so new and of such varied, yet simple, charms, the tie of brotherhood.

But these, even Sir William Johnston, whose life, surrounded by the Indians in his castle on the Mohawk, is described with such vivacity by Mrs. Grant, have been men better fitted to enjoy and adapt themselves to this life, than to observe and record it. The very faculties that made it so easy for them to live in the present moment, were likely to unfit them for keeping its chronicle. Men, whose life is full and instinctive, care little for the pen. But the father of Mrs. Schoolcraft seems to have taken pleasure in observation and comparison, and to have imparted the same tastes to his children. They have enough of European culture to have a standard, by which to judge their native habits and inherited lore.

By the premature death of Mrs. Schoolcraft was lost a mine of poesy, to which few had access, and from which Mrs. Jameson would have known how to coin a series of medals for the history of this ancient people. We might have known in clear outline, as now we shall not, the growths of religion and philosophy, under the influences of this climate and scenery, from such suggestions as nature and the teachings of the inward mind presented.

Now we can only gather that they had their own theory of the history of this globe; had perceived a gap in its genesis, and tried to fill it up by the intervention of some secondary power, with moral sympathies. They have observed the action of fire and water upon this earth; also that the dynasty of animals has yielded to that of man. With these animals they have profound sympathy, and are always trying to restore to them their lost honors. On the rattlesnake, the beaver, and the bear, they seem to look with a mixture of sympathy and veneration, as on their fellow settlers in these realms. There is something that appeals powerfully to the imagination in the ceremonies they observe, even in case of destroying one of these animals. I will say more of this by-and-by.

The dog they cherish as having been once a spirit of high intelligence; and now in its fallen and imprisoned state, given to man as his special companion. He is therefore to them a sacrifice of peculiar worth: whether to a guardian spirit or a human friend. Yet nothing would be a greater violation than giving the remains of a sacrificial feast to the dogs, or even suffering them to touch the bones.

Similar inconsistences may be observed in the treatment of the dog by the white man. He is the most cherished companion in the familiar walks of many men; his virtues form the theme of poetry and history; the nobler races present grand traits, and are treated with proportionate respect. Yet the epithets dog and hound, are there set apart to express the uttermost contempt.

Goethe, who abhorred dogs, has selected that animal for the embodiment of the modern devil, who, in earlier times, chose rather the form of the serpent.

There is, indeed, something that peculiarly breaks in on the harmony of nature, in the bark of the dog, and that does not at all correspond with the softness and sagacity observable in his eye. The baying the moon, I have been inclined to set down as an unfavorable indication; but, since Fourier has found out that the moon is dead, and "no better than carrion;" and the Greeks have designated her as Hecate, the deity of suicide and witchcraft, the dogs are perhaps in the right.

They have among them the legend of the carbuncle, so famous in oriental mythos. Adair states that they believe this fabulous gem may be found on the spot where the rattlesnake has been destroyed.

If they have not the archetypal man, they have the archetypal animal, "the grandfather of all beavers;" to them, who do not know the elephant, this is the symbol of wisdom, as the rattlesnake and bear of power.

I will insert here a little tale about the bear, which has not before appeared in print, as representing their human way of looking on these animals, even when engaged in their pursuit. To me such stories give a fine sense of the lively perceptions and exercise of fancy, enjoyed by them in their lives of woodcraft:

MUCKWA, OR THE BEAR

A young Indian, who lived a great while ago, when he was quite young killed a bear; and the tribe from that circumstance called him Muckwa. As he grew up he became an expert hunter, and his favorite game was the bear, many of which he killed. One day he started off to a river far remote from the lodges of his tribe, and where berries and grapes were very plenty, in pursuit of bears. He hunted all day but found nothing; and just at night he came to some lodges which he thought to be those of some of his tribe. He approached the largest of them, lifted the curtain at its entrance, and went in, when he perceived the inmates to be bears, who were seated around the fire smoking. He said nothing, but seated himself also and smoked the pipe which they offered him, in silence. An old grey bear, who was the chief, ordered supper to be brought for him, and after he had eaten it, addressed him as follows: "My son, I am glad to see you come among us in a friendly manner. You have been a great hunter, and all the she-bears of our tribe tremble when they hear your name. But cease to trouble us, and come and live with me; we have a very pleasant life, living upon the fruits of the earth; and in the winter, instead of being obliged to hunt and travel through the deep snow, we sleep soundly until the sun unchains the streams, and makes the tender buds put forth for our subsistence. I will give you my daughter for a wife, and we will live happily together." Muckwa was inclined to accept the old bear's offer; but when he saw the daughter, who came and took off his wet moccasons, and gave him dry ones, he thought that he had never seen any Indian woman so beautiful. He accepted the offer of the chief of the bears, and lived with his wife very happily for some time. He had by her two sons, one of whom was like an Indian, and the other like a bear. When the bear-child was oppressed with heat, his mother would take him into the deep cool caves, while the Indian-child would shiver with cold, and cry after her in vain. As the autumn advanced, the bears began to go out in search of acorns, and then the she-bear said to Muckwa, "Stay at home here and watch our house, while I go to gather some nuts." She departed and was gone for some days with her people. By-and-by Muckwa became tired of staying at home, and thought that he would go off to a distance and resume his favorite bear-hunting. He accordingly started off, and at last came to a grove of lofty oaks, which were full of large acorns. He found signs of bear, and soon espied a fat she-bear on the top of a tree. He shot at her with a good aim, and she fell, pierced by his unerring arrow. He went up to her, and found it was his sister-in-law, who reproached him with his cruelty, and told him to return to his own people. Muckwa returned quietly home, and pretended not to have left his lodge. However, the old chief understood, and was disposed to kill him in revenge; but his wife found means to avert her father's anger. The winter season now coming on, Muckwa prepared to accompany his wife into winter quarters; they selected a large tamarack tree, which was hollow, and lived there comfortably until a party of hunters discovered their retreat. The she-bear told Muckwa to remain quietly in the tree, and that she would decoy off the hunters. She came out of the hollow, jumped from a bough of the tree, and escaped unharmed, although the hunters shot after her. Some time after, she returned to the tree, and told Muckwa that he had better go back to his own people. "Since you have lived among us," said she, "we have nothing but ill-fortune; you have killed my sister; and now your friends have followed your footsteps to our retreats to kill us. The Indian and the bear cannot live in the same lodge, for the Master of Life has appointed for them different habitations." So Muckwa returned with his son to his own people; but he never after would shoot a she-bear, for fear that he should kill his wife.

I admire this story for the *savoir faire,* the nonchalance, the Vivian Greyism of Indian life. It is also a poetical expression of the sorrows of unequal relations; those in which the Master of Life was not consulted. Is it not pathetic; the picture of the mother carrying off the child that was like herself into the deep, cool caves, while the other, shivering with cold, cried after her in vain? The moral, too, of Muckwa's return to the bear lodges, thinking to hide his sin by silence, while it was at once discerned by those connected with him, is fine.

We have a nursery tale, of which children never weary, of a little boy visiting a bear house and holding intercourse with them on terms as free as Muckwa did. So, perhaps, the child of Norman-Saxon blood, no less than the Indian, finds some pulse of the Orson in his veins.

As they loved to draw the lower forms of nature up to them, divining their histories, and imitating their ways, in their wild dances and paintings; even so did they love to look upward and people the atmosphere that enfolds the earth, with fairies and manitoes. The sister, obliged to leave her brother on the earth, bids him look up at evening, and he will see her painting her face in the west.

All places, distinguished in any way by nature, aroused the feelings of worship, which, however ignorant, are always elevating. See as instances in this kind, the stories of Nanabojou, and the Winnebago Prince, at the falls of St. Anthony.

As with the Greeks, beautiful legends grow up which express the aspects of various localities. From the distant sand-banks in the lakes, glittering in the sun, come stories of enchantresses combing, on the shore, the long golden hair of a beautiful daughter. The Lorelei of the Rhine, with her syren song, and the sad events that follow, is found on the lonely rocks of Lake Superior.

The story to which I now refer, may be found in a book called Life on the Lakes, or, a Trip to the Pictured Rocks. There are two which purport to be Indian tales; one is simply a romantic narrative, connected with a spot at Mackinaw, called Robinson's Folly. This, no less than the other, was unknown to those persons I saw on the island; but as they seem entirely beyond the powers of the person who writes them down, and the other one has the profound and original meaning of Greek tragedy, I believe they must be genuine legends.

The one I admire is the story of a young warrior, who goes to keep, on these lonely rocks, the fast which is to secure him vision of his tutelary spirit. There the loneliness is broken by the voice of sweet music from the water. The Indian knows well that to break the fast, which is the crisis of his life, by turning his attention from seeking the Great Spirit, to any lower object, will deprive him through life of heavenly protection, probably call down the severest punishment.

But the temptation is too strong for him; like the victims of the Lorelei, he looks, like them beholds a maiden of unearthly beauty, to him the harbinger of earthly wo.

The development of his fate, that succeeds; of love, of heart-break, of terrible revenge, which back upon itself recoils, may vie with anything I have ever known of stern tragedy, is altogether unlike any other form, and with all the peculiar expression we see lurking in the Indian eye. The demon is not frightful and fantastic, like those that haunt the German forest; but terribly human, as if of full manhood, reared in the shadow of the black forests. An Indian sarcasm vibrates through it, which, with Indian fortitude, defies the inevitable torture.

The Indian is steady to that simple creed, which forms the basis of all this mythology; that there is a God, and a life beyond this; a right and wrong which each man can see, betwixt which each man should choose; that good brings with it its reward and vice its punishment. Their moral code, if not refined as that of civilized nations, is clear and noble in the stress laid upon truth and fidelity. And all unprejudiced observers bear testimony that the Indians, until broken from their old anchorage by intercourse with the whites, who offer them, instead, a religion of which they furnish neither interpretation nor example, were singularly virtuous, if virtue be allowed to consist in a man's acting up to his own ideas of right.

Old Adair, who lived forty years among the Indians; not these tribes, indeed, but the southern Indians, does great justice to their religious aspiration. He is persuaded that they are Jews, and his main object is to identify their manifold ritual, and customs connected with it, with that of the Jews. His narrative contains much that is worthless, and is written in the most tedious manner of the folios. But his devotion to the records of ancient Jewry, has really given him power to discern congenial traits elsewhere, and for the sake of what he has expressed of the noble side of Indian character, we pardon him our having to wade through so many imbecilities.

An infidel, he says, is, in their language, "one who has shaken hands with the accursed speech;" a religious man, "one who has shaken hands with the beloved speech." If this be a correct definition, we could wish Adair more religious.

He gives a fine account of their methods of purification. These show a deep reliance on the sustaining Spirit. By fasting and prayer they make ready for all important decisions and actions. Even for the war path, on which he is likely to endure such privations, the brave prepares by a solemn fast. His reliance is on the spirit in which he goes forth.

We may contrast with the opinion of the missionary, as given on a former page, the testimony of one, who knew them as Adair did, to their heroism under torture.

He gives several stories, illustrative both of their courage, fortitude, and resource in time of peril, of which I will cite only the two first.

The Shawano Indians took a Muskohge warrior, known by the name of "Old Scrany;" they bastinadoed him in the usual manner, and condemned him to the fiery torture. He underwent a great deal, without showing any concern; his countenance and behavior were as if he suffered not the least pain, and was formed beyond the common laws of nature. He told them, with a bold voice, that he was a very noted warrior, and gained most of his martial preferments at the expense of their nation, and was desirous of showing them in the act of dying that he was still as much their superior, as when he headed his gallant countrymen against them. That, although he had fallen into their hands, in forfeiting the protection of the divine power, by some impurity or other, yet he had still so much virtue remaining, as would enable him to punish himself more exquisitely than all their despicable, ignorant crowd could possibly do, if they gave him liberty by untying him, and would hand to him one of the red hot gun-barrels out of the fire. The proposal, and his method of address, appeared so exceedingly bold and uncommon, that his request was granted. Then he suddenly seized one end of the red hot barrel, and, brandishing it from side to side, he found his way through the armed and surprised multitude, and leaped down a prodigious steep and high bank into a branch of the river, dived through it, ran over a small island, passed the other branch amidst a shower of bullets, and, though numbers of his eager enemies were in close pursuit of him, he got to a bramble swamp, and in that naked, mangled condition, reached his own country. He proved a sharp thorn in their side afterwards, to the day of his death.

The Shawano also captivated a warrior of the Anantooiah, and put him to the stake, according to their usual cruel solemnities. Having unconcernedly suffered much sharp torture, he told them with scorn, they did not know how to punish a noted enemy, therefore he was willing to teach them, and would confirm the truth of his assertion, if they allowed him the opportunity. Accordingly he requested of them a pipe and some tobacco, which was given him; as soon as he lighted it, he sat down, naked as he was, on the women's burning torches, that were within his circle, and continued smoking his pipe without the least discomposure. On this a head warrior leaped up, and said they had seen, plain enough, that he was a warrior, and not afraid of dying; nor should he have died, but that he was both spoiled by the fire, and devoted to it by their laws; however, though he was a very dangerous enemy, and his nation a treacherous people, it should appear they paid a regard to bravery, even in one, who was marked over the body with war streaks at the cost of many lives of their beloved kindred. And then, by way of favor, he, with his friendly tomahawk, put an end to all his pains: though this merciful but bloody instrument was ready some minutes before it gave the blow, yet, I was assured, the spectators could not perceive the sufferer to change, either his posture, or his steady, erect countenance in the least.

Some stories as fine, but longer, follow. In reference to which Adair says, "The intrepid behavior of these red stoics, their surprising contempt of and indifference to life or death, instead of lessening, helps to confirm our belief of that supernatural power, which supported the great number of primitive martyrs, who sealed the christian faith with their blood. The Indians have as much belief and expectation of a future state, as the greater part of the Israelites seem to have. But the christians of the first centuries, may justly be said to exceed even the most heroic American Indians, for they bore the bitterest persecution with steady patience, in imitation of their divine leader Messiah, in full confidence of divine support and of a glorious recompense of reward; and, instead of even wishing for revenge on their cruel enemies and malicious tormentors, (which is the chief principle that actuates the Indians,) they not only forgave them, but, in the midst of their cere love, and unabated fervor. And not only men of different condi-

and died praying for their tormentors: the Indian women and children,

and their young men untrained to war, are incapable of displaying the

Thus impartially looks the old trader. I meant to have inserted
other passages, that of the encampment at Yowanne, and the horse
race to which he challenged them, to show how well he could convey
in his garrulous fashion the whole presence of Indian life. That of
Yowanne, especially, takes my fancy much, by its wild and subtle air,
and the old-nurse fashion in which every look and gesture is detailed.
His enjoyment, too, at outwitting the Indians in their own fashion is
contagious. There is a fine history of a young man driven by a presentiment to run upon his death. But I find, to copy these stories, as
they stand, would half fill this little book, and compression would spoil
them, so I must wait some other occasion.

The story, later, of giving an Indian liquid fire to swallow, I give
at full length, to show how a kindhearted man and one well disposed
towards them, can treat them, and view his barbarity as a joke. It is
not then so much wonder, if the trader, with this same feeling that
they may be treated, (as however brutes should not be,) brutally, mixes
red pepper and damaged tobacco with the rum, intending in their fever
to fleece them of all they possess.

Like Murray and Henry, he has his great Indian chief, who represents what the people should be, as Pericles and Phocion what the
Greek people should be. If we are entitled to judge by its best fruits
of the goodness of the tree, Adair's Red Shoes, and Henry's Wawatam,
should make us respect the first possessors of our country, and doubt
whether we are in all ways worthy to fill their place. Of the whole
tone of character, judgment may be formed by what is said of the
death of Red Shoes.

"This chief, by his several transcendent qualities had arrived at
the highest pitch of the red glory. . . .

"He was murdered, for the sake of a French reward, by one of
his own countrymen. He had the misfortune to be taken very sick on
the road, and to lodge apart from the camp, according to their custom.
A Judas, tempted by the high reward of the French for killing him,
officiously pretended to take great care of him. While Red Shoes kept
his face toward him, the barbarian had such feelings of awe and pity
that he had not power to perpetrate his wicked design; but when he

turned his back, then gave the fatal shot. In this manner fell this valuable brave man, by hands that would have trembled to attack him on an equality."

Adair, with all his sympathy for the Indian, mixes quite unconsciously some white man's views of the most decided sort. For instance, he recommends that the tribes be stimulated as much as possible to war with each other, that they may the more easily and completely be kept under the dominion of the whites, and he gives the following record of brutality as quite a jocose and adroit procedure.

"I told him, on his importuning me further, that I had a full bottle of the water of *ane hoome,* 'bitter ears,' meaning long pepper, of which he was ignorant. We were of opinion that his eager thirst for liquor, as well as his ignorance of the burning quality of the pepper, would induce the bacchanal to try it. He accordingly applauded my generous disposition, and said his heart had all along told him I would not act beneath the character I bore among his country people. The bottle was brought, I laid it on the table, and then told him, as he was spitting very much, (a general custom among the Indians when they are eager for anything,) if I drank it all at one sitting it would cause me to spit in earnest, as I used it only when I ate, and then very moderately; but though I loved it, if his heart was very poor for it, I should be silent, and not the least grudge him for pleasing his mouth. He said, 'your heart is honest, indeed; I thank you, for it is good to my heart, and makes it greatly to rejoice.' Without any further ceremony he seized the bottle, uncorked it, and swallowed a large quantity of the burning liquid, till he was nearly strangled. He gasped for a considerable time, and as soon as he recovered his breath, he said *Hah,* and soon after kept stroking his throat with his right hand. When the violence of this burning draught was pretty well over, he began to flourish away in praise of the strength of the liquor and bounty of the giver. He then went to his companion and held the liquor to his mouth according to custom, till he took several hearty swallows. This Indian seemed rather more sensible of its fiery quality than the other, for it suffocated him for a considerable time; but as soon as he recovered his breath, he tumbled about the floor like a drunken person. In this manner they finished the whole bottle, into which two others had been decanted. The burning liquor so highly inflamed their bodies, that one of the Choctaws, to cool his inward parts, drank water till he almost burst; the other, rather than bear the ridicule of the people, and the inward fire that distracted him, drowned himself the second night after in a broad and shallow clay hole. . . .

"There was an incident similar, which happened among the Cherokees. When all the liquor was expended the Indians went home, leading with them, at my request, those that were drunk. One, however, soon came back, and earnestly importuned me for more Nawahti, which signifies both physic and spirituous liquor. They, as they are now become great liars, suspect all others of being infected with their own disposition and principles. The more I excused myself, the more anxious he grew, so as to become offensive. I then told him I had only one quarter of a bottle of strong physic, which sick people might drink in small quantities, for the cure of inward pains: and, laying it down before him, I declared I did not on any account choose to part with it, but as his speech had become very long and troublesome, he might do just as his heart directed him concerning it. He took it up, saying, his heart was very poor for physic, but he would cure it, and make it quite straight. The bottle contained three gills of strong spirits of turpentine, which, in a short time he drank off. Such a quantity would have demolished me or any white person. The Indians, in general, are either capable of suffering exquisite pain longer than we are, or of showing more constancy and composure in their torments. The troublesome visiter soon tumbled down and foamed prodigiously. I then sent for some of his relations to carry him home. They came; I told them he drank greedily, and too much of the physic. They said, it was his usual custom, when the red people bought the English physic. They gave him a decoction of proper herbs and roots, the next day sweated him, repeated the former draught, and he got well. As these turpentine spirits did not inebriate him, but only inflamed his intestines, he well remembered the burning quality of my favorite physic, and cautioned the rest from ever teasing me for any physic I had concealed in any sort of bottles for my own use; otherwise they might be sure it would spoil them like the eating of fire."

We are pleased to note that the same white man, who so resolutely resisted the encroachments of Key-way-no-wut, devised a more humane expedient in a similar dilemma.

Mr. B. told me that, when he first went into the Indian country, they got the taste of his peppermint, and, after that, colics prevailed among them to an alarming extent, till Mrs. B. made a strong decoction of flagroot, and gave them in place of their favorite medicine. This effected, as might be supposed, a radical cure.

I am inclined to recommend Adair to the patient reader, if such may be found in these United States, with the assurance that, if he will have tolerance for its intolerable prolixity and dryness, he will find, on rising from the book, that he has partaken of an infusion of real Indian bitters, such as may not be drawn from any of the more attractive memoirs on the same subject.

Another book of interest, from its fidelity and candid spirit, though written without vivacity, and by a person neither of large mind nor prepared for various inquiry, is Carver's Travels, "for three years throughout the interior parts of America, for more than five thousand miles."

He set out from Boston in "June, 1786, and proceeded, by way of Albany and Niagara, to Michilimackinac, a fort situated between the Lakes Huron and Michigan, and distant from Boston 1300 miles."

It is interesting to follow his footsteps in these localities, though they be not bold footsteps.

He mentions the town of the Sacs, on the Wisconsin, as the largest and best built he saw, "composed of ninety houses, each large enough for several families. These are built of hewn plank, neatly jointed, and covered with bark so compactly as to keep out the most penetrating rains. Before the doors are placed comfortable sheds, in which the inhabitants sit, when the weather will permit, and smoke their pipes. The streets are regular and spacious. In their plantations, which lie adjacent to their houses, and which are neatly laid out, they raise great quantities of Indian corn, beans and melons."

Such settlements compare very well with those which were found on the Mohawk. It was of such that the poor Indian was thinking, whom our host saw gazing on the shore of Nomabbin lake.

He mentions the rise and fall of the lake-waters, by a tide of three feet, once in seven years,—a phenomenon not yet accounted for.

His view of the Indian character is truly impartial. He did not see it so fully drawn out by circumstances as Henry did, (of whose narrative we shall presently speak,) but we come to similar results from the two witnesses. They are in every feature Romans, as described by Carver, and patriotism their leading impulse. He deserves the more credit for the justice he is able to do them, that he had undergone the terrors of death at their hands, when present at the surrender of one of the forts, and had seen them in that mood which they express by drinking the blood and eating the hearts of their enemies, yet is able to understand the position of their minds, and allow for their notions of duty.

No selfish views, says he, influence their advice, or obstruct their consultations.

Let me mention here the use they make of their vapor baths.

"When about to decide on some important measure, they go into them, thus cleansing the skin and carrying off any peccant humors, so that the body may, as little as possible, impede the mind by any ill conditions."

They prepare the bath for one another when any arrangement is to be made between families, on the opposite principle to the whites, who make them drunk before bargaining with them. The bath serves them instead of a cup of coffee, to stimulate the thinking powers.

He mentions other instances of their kind of delicacy, which, if different from ours, was, perhaps, more rigidly observed.

Lovers never spoke of love till the daylight was quite gone.

"If an Indian goes to visit any particular person in a family, he mentions for whom his visit is intended, and the rest of the family, immediately retiring to the other end of the hut or tent, are careful not to come near enough to interrupt them during the whole of the conversation."

In cases of divorce, which was easily obtained, the advantage rested with the woman. The reason given is indeed contemptuous toward her, but a chivalric direction is given to the contempt.

"The children of the Indians are always distinguished by the name of the mother, and, if a woman marries several husbands, and has issue by each of them, they are called after her. The reason they give for this is, that, 'as their offspring are indebted to the father for the soul, the invisible part of their essence, and to the mother for their corporeal and apparent part, it is most rational that they should be distinguished by the name of the latter, from whom they indubitably derive their present being.' "

This is precisely the division of functions made by Ovid, as the father sees Hercules perishing on the funeral pyre.

> *"Nee nisi materna Vulcanum parte potentem*
> *Sentiet. Eternuin est a me quod traxit et expers*
> *Atque immune necis, nullaqe domabile flamma."*

He is not enough acquainted with natural history to make valuable observations. He mentions, however, as did my friend, the Indian girl, that those splendid flowers, the Wickapee and the root of the Wake-Robin, afford valuable medicines. Here, as in the case of the Lobelia, nature has blazoned her drug in higher colors than did ever quack doctor.

He observes some points of resemblance between the Indians and

Tartars, but they are trivial, and not well considered. He mentions that the Tartars have the same custom, with some of these tribes, of shaving all the head except a tuft on the crown. Catlin says this is intended to afford a convenient means by which to take away the scalp; for they consider it a great disgrace to have the foeman neglect this, as if he considered the conquest, of which the scalp is the certificate, no addition to his honors.

"The Tartars," he says, "had a similar custom of sacrificing the dog; and among the Kamschatkans was a dance resembling the dog-dance of our Indians."

My friend, who joined me at Mackinaw, happened, on the homeward journey, to see a little Chinese girl, who had been sent over by one of the missions, and observed that, in features, complexion, and gesture, she was a counterpart to the little Indian girls she had just seen playing about on the lake shore.

The parentage of these tribes is still an interesting subject of speculation, though, if they be not created for this region, they have become so assimilated to it as to retain little trace of any other. To me it seems most probable, that a peculiar race was bestowed on each region, as the lion on one latitude and the white bear on another. As man has two natures—one, like that of the plants and animals, adapted to the uses and enjoyments of this planet, another, which presages and demands a higher sphere—he is constantly breaking bounds, in proportion as the mental gets the better of the mere instinctive existence. As yet, he loses in harmony of being what he gains in height and extension; the civilized man is a larger mind, but a more imperfect nature than the savage.

It is pleasant to meet, on the borders of these two states, one of those persons who combines some of the good qualities of both; not, as so many of these adventurers do, the rapaciousness and cunning of the white, with the narrowness and ferocity of the savage, but the sentiment and thoughtfulness of the one, with the boldness, personal resource, and fortitude of the other.

Such a person was Alexander Henry, who left Quebec in 1760, for Mackinaw and the Sault St. Marie, and remained in those regions, of which he has given us a most lively account, sixteen years.

His visit to Mackinaw was premature; the Indians were far from satisfied; they hated their new masters. From the first, the omens were threatening, and before many months passed, the discontent ended in the seizing of the fort at Mackinaw and massacre of its garrison; on which occasion Henry's life was saved by a fine act of Indian chivalry.

Wawatam, a distinguished chief, had found himself drawn, by strong affinity, to the English stranger. He had adopted him as a brother, in the Indian mode. When he found that his tribe had determined on the slaughter of the whites, he obtained permission to take Henry away with him, if he could. But not being able to prevail on him, as he could not assign the true reasons, he went away deeply saddened, but not without obtaining a promise that his brother should not be injured. The reason he was obliged to go, was, that his tribe felt his affections were so engaged, that his self-command could not be depended on to keep their secret. Their promise was not carefully observed, and, in consequence of the baseness of a French Canadian in whose house Henry took refuge,—baseness such as has not, even by their foes, been recorded of any Indian, his life was placed in great hazard. But Wawatam returned in time to save him. The scene in which he appears, accompanied by his wife—who seems to have gone hand in hand with him in this matter—lays down all his best things in a heap, in the middle of the hall, as a ransom for the captive, and his little, quiet speech, are as good as the Iliad. They have the same simplicity, the same lively force and tenderness.

Henry goes away with his adopted brother, and lives for some time among the tribe. The details of this life are truly interesting. One time he is lost for several days while on the chase. The description of these weary, groping days, the aspect of natural objects and of the feelings thus inspired, and the mental change after a good night's sleep, form a little episode worthy the epic muse. He stripped off the entire bark of a tree for a coverlet in the snow-storm, going to sleep with "the most distracted thoughts in the world, while the wolves around seemed to know the distress to which he was reduced;" but he waked in the morning another man, clear-headed, able to think out the way to safety.

When living in the lodge, he says: "At one time much scarcity of food prevailed. We were often twenty-four hours without eating; and when in the morning we had no victuals for the day before us, the custom was to black our faces with grease and charcoal, and exhibit, through resignation, a temper as cheerful as in the midst of plenty." This wise and dignified proceeding reminds one of a charming expression of what is best in French character, as described by Rigolette, in the Mysteries of Paris, of the household of Père Cretu and Ramonette.

He bears witness to much virtue among them. Their superstitions, as described by him, seem childlike and touching. He gives with much

humor, traits that show their sympathy with the lower animals, such
as I have mentioned. He speaks of them as, on the whole, taciturn,
because their range of topics is so limited, and seems to have seen
nothing of their talent for narration. Catlin, on the contrary, describes
them as lively and garrulous, and says, that their apparent taciturnity
among the whites is owing to their being surprised at what they see,
and unwilling, from pride, to show that they are so, as well as that
they have little to communicate on their side, that they think will be
valuable.

After peace was restored, and Henry lived long at Mackinaw and
the Sault St. Marie, as a trader, the traits of his biography and intercourse with the Indians, are told in the same bold and lively style. I
wish I had room for many extracts, as the book is rare.

He made a journey one winter on snow shoes, to Prairie du Chien,
which is of romantic interest as displaying his character. His companions could not travel nearly so fast as he did, and detained him on the
way. Provisions fell short; soon they were ready to perish of starvation.
Apprehending this, on a long journey, in the depth of winter, broken
by no hospitable station, Henry had secreted some chocolate. When
he saw his companions ready to lie down and die, he would heat
water, boil in it a square of this, and give them. By the heat of the
water and the fancy of nourishment, they would be revived, and induced to proceed a little further. At last they saw antlers sticking up
from the ice, and found the body of an elk, which had sunk in and
been frozen there, and thus preserved to save their lives. On this "and
excellent soup" made from bones they found they were sustained to
their journey's end; thus furnishing, says Henry, one other confirma-
tion of the truth, that "despair was not made for man;" this expression, and his calm consideration for the Canadian woman that was
willing to betray him to death, denote the two sides of a fine character.

He gives an interesting account of the tribe called "The Weepers,"
on account of the rites with which they interrupt their feasts in honor
of their friends.

He gives this humorous notice of a chief, called "The Great
Road."

"The chief, to whose kindly reception we were so much indebted,
was of a complexion rather darker than that of the Indians in general.
His appearance was greatly injured by the condition of his hair, and
this was the result of an extraordinary superstition.

"The Indians universally fix upon a particular object as sacred to
themselves—as the giver of prosperity and as their preserver from evil.

The choice is determined either by a dream or some strong predilection of fancy, and usually falls upon an animal, part of an animal, or something else which is to be met with by land, or by water; but the Great Road had made choice of his hair, placing, like Samson, all his safety in this portion of his proper substance! His hair was the fountain of all his happiness; it was his strength and his weapon—his spear and his shield. It preserved him in battle, directed him in the chase, watched over him in the march, and gave length of days to his wives and children. Hair, of a quality like this, was not to be profaned by the touch of human hands. I was assured that it never had been cut nor combed from his childhood upward, and that when any part of it fell from his head, he treasured that part with care; meanwhile, it did not escape all care, even while growing on the head, but was in the especial charge of a spirit, who dressed it while the owner slept. The spirit's style of hair-dressing was peculiar, the hair being matted into ropes, which spread in all directions."

I insert the following account of a visit from some Indians to him at Mackinaw, with a design to frighten him, and one to Carver, for the same purpose, as very descriptive of Indian manners:

"At two o'clock in the afternoon, the Chippeways came to my house, about sixty in number, and headed by Mina-va-va-na, their chief. They walked in single file, each with his tomahawk in one hand, and scalping knife in the other. Their bodies were naked, from the waist upwards, except in a few examples, where blankets were thrown loosely over the shoulders. Their faces were painted with charcoal, worked up with grease; their bodies with white clay in patterns of various fancies. Some had feathers thrust through their noses, and their heads decorated with the same. It is unnecessary to dwell on the sensations with which I beheld the approach of this uncouth, if not frightful, assemblage.

"Looking out, I saw about twenty naked young Indians, the most perfect in their shape, and by far the handsomest I had ever seen, coming towards me, and dancing as they approached to the music of their drums. At every ten or twelve yards they halted, and set up their yells and cries.

"When they reached my tent I asked them to come in, which, without deigning to make me any answer, they did. As I observed they were painted red and black, as they are when they go against an enemy, and perceived that some parts of the war-dance were intermixed with their other movements, I doubted not but they were set on by the hostile chief who refused my salutation. I therefore determined to sell my life as dearly as possible. To this purpose I received them sitting on my chest, with my gun and pistols beside me; and ordered my men to keep a watchful eye on them, and be also on their guard.

"The Indians being entered, they continued their dance alternately, singing at the same time of their heroic exploits, and the superiority of their race over every other people. To enforce their language, though it was uncommonly nervous and expressive, and such as would of itself have carried terror to the firmest heart; at the end of every period they struck their war-clubs against the poles of my tent with such violence, that I expected every moment it would have tumbled upon us. As each of them in dancing round passed by me, they placed their right hands over their eyes, and coming close to me, looked me steadily in the face, which I could not construe into a token of friendship. My men gave themselves up for lost; and I acknowledge for my own part, that I never found my apprehensions more tumultuous on any occasion."

He mollified them, however, in the end by presents.

It is pity that Lord Edward Fitzgerald did not leave a detailed account of his journey through the wilderness, where he was pilot of an unknown course for twenty days, as Murray and Henry have of theirs. There is nothing more interesting than to see the civilized man thus thrown wholly on himself and his manhood, and *not* found at fault.

McKenney and Hall's book upon the Indians is a valuable work. The portraits of the chiefs alone would make a history, and they are beautifully colored.

Most of the anecdotes may be found again in Drake's Book of the Indians; which will afford a useful magazine to their future historian.

I shall, however, cite a few of them, as especially interesting to myself.

Of Guess, the inventor of the Cherokee alphabet, it was observable in the picture, and observed in the text, that his face had an oriental cast. The same, we may recall, was said of that of the Seeress of Prevorst, and the circumstance presents pleasing analogies. Intellect dawning through features still simple and national, presents very different apparitions from the "expressive" and "historical" faces of a broken and cultured race, where there is always more to divine than to see.

Of the picture of the Flying Pigeon, the beautiful and excellent woman mentioned above, a keen observer said, "If you cover the forehead, you would think the face that of a Madonna, but the forehead is still savage; the perceptive faculties look so sharp, and the forehead not moulded like a European forehead." This is very true; in her the moral nature was most developed, and the effect of a higher growth upon her face is entirely different from that upon Guess.

His eye is inturned, while the proper Indian eye gazes steadily, as if on a distant object. That is half the romance of it, that it makes you think of dark and distant places in the forest.

Guess always preferred inventing his implements to receiving them from others: and, when considered as mad by his tribe, while bent on the invention of his alphabet, contented himself with teaching it to his little daughter; an unimpeachable witness.

Red Jacket's face, too, is much more intellectual than almost any other. But, in becoming so, it loses nothing of the peculiar Indian stamp, but only carries these traits to their perfection. Irony, discernment, resolution, and a deep smouldering fire, that disdains to flicker where it cannot blaze, may there be read. Nothing can better represent the sort of unfeelingness the whites have towards the Indians, than their conduct towards his remains. He had steadily opposed the introduction of white religion, or manners, among the Indians. He believed that for them to break down the barriers was to perish. On many occasions he had expressed this with all the force of his eloquence. He told the preachers, "if the Great Spirit had meant your religion for the red man, he would have given it to them. What they (the missionaries) tell us, we do not understand; and the light they ask for us, makes the straight and plain path trod by our fathers dark and dreary."

When he died, he charged his people to inter him themselves. "Dig my grave yourselves, and let not the white man pursue me there." In defiance of this last solemn request, and the invariable tenor of his life, the missionaries seized the body and performed their service over it, amid the sullen indignation of his people, at what, under the circumstances, was sacrilege.

Of Indian religion a fine specimen is given in the conduct of one of the war chiefs, who, on an important occasion, made a vow to the sun of entire renunciation in case he should be crowned with success. When he was so, he first went through a fast, and sacrificial dance, involving great personal torment, and lasting several days; then, distributing all his property, even his lodges, and mats, among the tribe, he and his family took up their lodging upon the bare ground, beneath the bare sky.

The devotion of the Stylites and the hair-cloth saints, is in act, though not in motive, less noble, because this great chief proposed to go on in common life, where he had lived as a prince—a beggar.

The memoir by Corn Plant of his early days is beautiful.

Very fine anecdotes are told of two of the Western chiefs, father and son, who had the wisdom to see the true policy toward the whites, and steadily to adhere to it.

A murder having taken place in the jurisdiction of the father, he delivered himself up, with those suspected, to imprisonment. One of his companions chafed bitterly under confinement. He told the chief, if they ever got out, he would kill him, and did so. The son, then a boy, came in his rage and sorrow, to this Indian, and insulted him in every way. The squaw, angry at this, urged her husband "to kill the boy at once." But he only replied with "the joy of the valiant," "He will be a great Brave," and then delivered himself up to atone for his victim, and met his death with the noblest Roman composure.

This boy became rather a great chief than a great brave, and the anecdotes about him are of signal beauty and significance.

There is a fine story of an old mother, who gave herself to death instead of her son. The son, at the time, accepted the sacrifice, seeing, with Indian coolness, that it was better she should give up her few solitary and useless days, than he a young existence full of promise. But he could not abide by this view, and after suffering awhile all the anguish of remorse, he put himself solemnly to death in the presence of the tribe, as the only atonement he could make. His young wife stood by, with her child in her arms, commanding her emotions, as he desired, for, no doubt, it seemed to her also, a sacred duty.

But the finest story of all is that of Petalesharro, in whose tribe at the time, and not many years since, the custom of offering human sacrifices still subsisted. The fire was kindled, the victim, a young female captive, bound to the stake, the tribe assembled round. The young brave darted through them, snatched the girl from her peril, placed her upon his horse, and both had vanished before the astonished spectators had thought to interpose.

He placed the girl in her distant home, and then returned. Such is the might of right, when joined with courage, that none ventured a word of resentment or question. His father, struck by truth, endeavored, and with success, to abolish the barbarous custom in the tribe. On a later occasion, Petalesharro again offered his life, if required, but it was not.

This young warrior visiting Washington, a medal was presented him in honor of these acts. His reply deserves sculpture: "When I did it, I knew not that it was good. I did it in ignorance. This medal makes me know that it was good."

The recorder, through his playful expressions of horror at a declaration so surprising to the civilized Good, shows himself sensible to the grand simplicity of heroic impulse it denotes. Were we, too, so good, as to need a medal to show us that we are!

The half-breed and half-civilized chiefs, however handsome, look vulgar beside the pure blood. They have the dignity of neither race.

The death of Oseola, (as described by Catlin,) presents a fine picture in the stern, warlike kind, taking leave with kindness, as a private friend, of the American officers; but, as a foe in national regards, he raised himself in his dying bed, and painted his face with the tokens of eternal enmity.

The historian of the Indians should be one of their own race, as able to sympathize with them, and possessing a mind as enlarged and cultivated as John Ross, and with his eye turned to the greatness of the past, rather than the scanty promise of the future. Hearing of the wampum belts, supposed to have been sent to our tribes by Montezuma, on the invasion of the Spaniard, we feel that an Indian who could glean traditions familiarly from the old men, might collect much that we could interpret.

Still, any clear outline, even of a portion of their past, is not to be hoped, and we shall be well contented if we can have a collection of genuine fragments, that will indicate as clearly their life, as a horse's head from the Parthenon the genius of Greece.

Such, to me, are the stories I have cited above. And even European sketches of this greatness, distant and imperfect though they be, yet convey the truth, if made in a sympathizing spirit. Adair's Red Shoes, Murray's old man, Catlin's noble Mandan chief, Henry's Wa-wa-tam, with what we know of Philip, Pontiac, Tecumseh and Red Jacket, would suffice to give the ages a glimpse at what was great in Indian life and Indian character.

We hope, too, there will be a national institute, containing all the remains of the Indians—all that has been preserved by official intercourse at Washington, Catlin's collection, and a picture gallery as complete as can be made, with a collection of skulls from all parts of the country. To this should be joined the scanty library that exists on the subject.

I have not mentioned Mackenzie's Travels. He is an accurate observer, but sparing in his records, because his attention was wholly bent on his own objects. This circumstance gives a heroic charm to his scanty and simple narrative. Let what will happen, or who will go back, he cannot; he must find the sea, along those frozen rivers, through those starving countries, among tribes of stinted men, whose habitual interjection was "edui, it is hard, uttered in a querulous tone," distrusted by his followers, deserted by his guides, on, on he goes, till he sees the sea, cold, lowering, its strand bristling with foes; but he does see it.

His few observations, especially on the tribes who lived on fish, and held them in such superstitious observance, give a lively notion of the scene.

A little pamphlet has lately been published, giving an account of the massacre at Chicago, which I wish much I had seen while there, as it would have imparted an interest to spots otherwise barren. It is written with animation, and in an excellent style, telling just what we want to hear, and no more. The traits given of Indian generosity are as characteristic as those of Indian cruelty. A lady, who was saved by a friendly chief holding her under the waters of the lake, while the balls were whizzing around, received also, in the heat of the conflict, a reviving draught from a squaw, who saw she was exhausted; and, as she lay down, a mat was hung up between her and the scene of butchery, so that she was protected from the sight, though she could not be from sounds, full of horror.

I have not wished to write sentimentally about the Indians, however moved by the thought of their wrongs and speedy extinction. I know that the Europeans who took possession of this country, felt themselves justified by their superior civilization and religious ideas. Had they been truly civilized or Christianized, the conflicts which sprang from the collision of the two races, might have been avoided; but this cannot be expected in movements made by masses of men. The mass has never yet been humanized, though the age may develop a human thought.

Since those conflicts and differences did arise, the hatred which sprang, from terror and suffering, on the European side, has naturally warped the whites still farther from justice.

The Indian, brandishing the scalps of his friends and wife, drinking their blood and eating their hearts, is by him viewed as a fiend, though, at a distant day, he will no doubt be considered as having acted the Roman or Carthaginian part of heroic and patriotic self-defence, according to the standard of right and motives prescribed by his religious faith and education. Looked at by his own standard, he is virtuous when he most injures his enemy, and the white, if he be really the superior in enlargement of thought, ought to cast aside his inherited prejudices enough to see this,—to look on him in pity and brotherly goodwill, and do all he can to mitigate the doom of those who survive his past injuries.

In McKenney's book, is proposed a project for organizing the Indians under a patriarchal government, but it does not look feasible, even on paper. Could their own intelligent men be left to act unimpeded in their behalf, they would do far better for them than the white thinker, with all his general knowledge. But we dare not hope the designs of such will not always be frustrated by the same barbarous selfishness they were in Georgia. There was a chance of seeing what might have been done, now lost forever.

Yet let every man look to himself how far this blood shall be required at his hands. Let the missionary, instead of preaching to the Indian, preach to the trader who ruins him, of the dreadful account which will be demanded of the followers of Cain, in a sphere where the accents of purity and love come on the ear more decisively than in ours. Let every legislator take the subject to heart, and if he cannot undo the effects of past sin, try for that clear view and right sense that may save us from sinning still more deeply. And let every man and every woman, in their private dealings with the subjugated race, avoid all share in embittering, by insult or unfeeling prejudice, the captivity of Israel.

CHAPTER VII

SAULT ST. MARIE

Nine days I passed alone at Mackinaw, except for occasional visits from kind and agreeable residents at the fort, and Mr. and Mrs. A. Mr. A., long engaged in the fur-trade, is gratefully remembered by many travellers. From Mrs. A., also, I received kind attentions, paid in the vivacious and graceful manner of her nation.

The society at the boarding house entertained, being of a kind entirely new to me. There were many traders from the remote stations, such as La Pointe, Arbre Croche,—men who had become half wild and wholly rude, by living in the wild; but good-humored, observing, and with a store of knowledge to impart, of the kind proper to their place.

There were two little girls here, that were pleasant companions for me. One gay, frank, impetuous, but sweet and winning. She was an American, fair, and with bright brown hair. The other, a little French Canadian, used to join me in my walks, silently take my hand, and sit at my feet when I stopped in beautiful places. She seemed to understand without a word; and I never shall forget her little figure, with its light, but pensive motion, and her delicate, grave features, with the pale, clear complexion and soft eye. She was motherless, and much left alone by her father and brothers, who were boatmen. The two little girls were as pretty representatives of Allegro and Penseroso, as one would wish to see.

I had been wishing that a boat would come in to take me to the Sault St. Marie, and several times started to the window at night in hopes that the pant and dusky-red light crossing the waters belonged to such an one; but they were always boats for Chicago or Buffalo, till, on the 28th of August, Allegro, who shared my plans and wishes, rushed in to tell me that the General Scott had come, and, in this little steamer, accordingly, I set off the next morning.

I was the only lady, and attended in the cabin by a Dutch girl and an Indian woman. They both spoke English fluently, and entertained me much by accounts of their different experiences.

The Dutch girl told me of a dance among the common people at Amsterdam, called the shepherd's dance. The two leaders are dressed as shepherd and shepherdess; they invent to the music all kinds of movements, descriptive of things that may happen in the field, and the rest were obliged to follow. I have never heard of any dance which gave such free play to the fancy as this. French dances merely describe the polite movements of society; Spanish and Neapolitan, love; the beautiful Mazurkas, &c., are warlike or expressive of wild scenery. But in this one is great room both for fun and fancy.

The Indian was married, when young, by her parents, to a man she did not love. He became dissipated, and did not maintain her. She left him, taking with her their child; for whom and herself she earns a subsistence by going as chambermaid in these boats. Now and then, she said, her husband called on her, and asked if he might live with her again; but she always answered, no. Here she was far freer than she would have been in civilized life.

I was pleased by the nonchalance of this woman, and the perfectly national manner she had preserved after so many years of contact with all kinds of people. The two women, when I left the boat, made me presents of Indian work, such as travellers value, and the manner of the two was characteristic of their different nations. The Indian brought me hers, when I was alone, looked bashfully down when she gave it, and made an almost sentimental little speech. The Dutch girl brought hers in public, and, bridling her short chin with a self-complacent air, observed she had *bought* it for me. But the feeling of affectionate regard was the same in the minds of both.

Island after island we passed, all fairly shaped and clustering friendly, but with little variety of vegetation.

In the afternoon the weather became foggy, and we could not proceed after dark. That was as dull an evening as ever fell.

The next morning the fog still lay heavy, but the captain took me out in his boat on an exploring expedition, and we found the remains of the old English fort on Point St. Joseph's. All around was so wholly unmarked by anything but stress of wind and weather, the shores of these islands and their woods so like one another, wild and lonely, but nowhere rich and majestic, that there was some charm in the remains of the garden, the remains even of chimneys and a pier. They gave feature to the scene.

Here I gathered many flowers, but they were the same as at Mackinaw.

The captain, though he had been on this trip hundreds of times, had never seen this spot, and never would, but for this fog, and his desire to entertain me. He presented a striking instance how men, for the sake of getting a living, forget to live. It is just the same in the most romantic as the most dull and vulgar places. Men get the harness on so fast, that they can never shake it off, unless they guard against this danger from the very first. In Chicago, how many men, who never found time to see the prairies or learn anything unconnected with the business of the day, or about the country they were living in!

So this captain, a man of strong sense and good eyesight, rarely found time to go off the track or look about him on it. He lamented, too, that there had been no call which induced him to develop his powers of expression, so that he might communicate what he had seen, for the enjoyment or instruction of others.

This is a common fault among the active men, the truly living, who could tell what life is. It should not be so. Literature should not be left to the mere literati—eloquence to the mere orator. Every Cæsar should be able to write his own commentary. We want a more equal, more thorough, more harmonious development, and there is nothing to hinder from it the men of this country, except their own supineness, or sordid views.

When the weather did clear, our course up the river was delightful. Long stretched before us the island of St. Joseph's, with its fair woods of sugàr maple. A gentleman on board, who belongs to the Fort at the Sault, said their pastime was to come in the season of making sugar, and pass some time on this island,—the days at work, and the evening in dancing and other amusements.

I wished to extract here Henry's account of this, for it was just the same sixty years ago as now, but have already occupied too much room with extracts. Work of this kind done in the open air, where everything is temporary, and every utensil prepared on the spot, gives life a truly festive air. At such times, there is labor and no care—energy with gaiety, gaìety of the heart.

I think with the same pleasure of the Italian vintage, the Scotch harvest-home, with its evening dance in the barn, the Russian cabbage-feast even, and our huskings and hop-gatherings—the hop-gatherings where the groups of men and girls are pulling down and filling baskets with the gay festoons, present as graceful pictures as the Italian vintage.

I should also like to insert Henry's descriptions of the method of catching trout and white fish, the delicacies of this region, for the same reason as I want his account of the Gens de Terre, the savages among savages, and his tales, dramatic, if not true, of cannibalism.

I have no less grieved to omit Carver's account of the devotion of a Winnebago prince at the Falls of St. Anthony, which he describes with a simplicity and intelligence, that are very pleasing.

I take the more pleasure in both Carver and Henry's power of appreciating what is good in the Indian character, that both had run the greatest risk of losing their lives during their intercourse with the Indians, and had seen them in their utmost exasperation, with all its revolting circumstances.

I wish I had a thread long enough to string on it all these beads that take my fancy; but, as I have not, I can only refer the reader to the books themselves, which may be found in the library of Harvard College, if not elsewhere.

How pleasant is the course along a new river, the sight of new shores; like a life, would but life flow as fast, and upbear us with as full a stream. I hoped we should come in sight of the rapids by daylight; but the beautiful sunset was quite gone, and only a young moon trembling over the scene, when we came within hearing of them.

I sat up long to hear them merely. It was a thoughtful hour. These two days, the 29th and 30th August, are memorable in my life; the latter is the birth-day of a near friend. I pass them alone, approaching Lake Superior; but I shall not enter into that truly wild and free region; shall not have the canoe voyage, whose daily adventure, with the camping out at night beneath the stars, would have given an interlude of such value to my existence. I shall not see the Pictured Rocks, their chapels and urns. It did not depend on me; it never has, whether such things shall be done or not.

My friends! may they see, and do, and be more, especially those who have before them a greater number of birthdays, and of a more healthy and unfettered existence:

TO EDITH, ON HER BIRTHDAY

If the same star our fates together bind,
Why are we thus divided, mind from mind?
If the same law one grief to both impart,
How could'st thou grieve a trusting mother's heart?

Our aspiration seeks a common aim,
Why were we tempered of such differing frame?
—But 'tis too late to turn this wrong to right;
Too cold, too damp, too deep, has fallen the night.

And yet, the angel of my life replies,
Upon that night a Morning Star shall rise,
Fairer than that which ruled the temporal birth,
Undimmed by vapors of the dreamy earth;

It says, that, where a heart thy claim denies,
Genius shall read its secret ere it flies;
The earthly form may vanish from thy side,
Pure love will make thee still the spirit's bride.

And thou, ungentle, yet much loving child,
Whose heart still shows the "untamed haggard wild,"
A heart which justly makes the highest claim,
Too easily is checked by transient blame;

Ere such an orb can ascertain its sphere,
The ordeal must be various and severe;

My prayers attend thee, though the feet may fly,
I hear thy music in the silent sky.

I should like, however, to hear some notes of earthly music to-night. By the faint moonshine I can hardly see the banks; how they look I have no guess, except that there are trees, and, now and then, a light lets me know there are homes with their various interests. I should like to hear some strains of the flute from beneath those trees, just to break the sound of the rapids.

When no gentle eyebeam charms;
No fond hope the bosom warms;
Of thinking the lone mind is tired—
Nought seems bright to be desired;

Music, be thy sails unfurled,
Bear me to thy better world;
O'er a cold and weltering sea,
Blow thy breezes warm and free;

By sad sighs they ne'er were chilled,
By sceptic spell were never stilled;
Take me to that far-off shore,
Where lovers meet to part no more;
There doubt, and fear and sin are o'er,
The star of love shall set no more.

With the first light of dawn I was up and out, and then was glad I had not seen all the night before; it came upon me with such power in its dewy freshness. O! they are beautiful indeed, these rapids! The grace is so much more obvious than the power. I went up through the old Chippeway burying ground to their head, and sat down on a large stone to look. A little way off was one of the home lodges, unlike in shape to the temporary ones at Mackinaw, but these have been described by Mrs. Jameson. Women, too, I saw coming home from the woods, stooping under great loads of cedar boughs, that were strapped upon their backs. But in many European countries women carry great loads, even of wood, upon their backs. I used to hear the girls singing and laughing as they were cutting down boughs at Mackinaw; this part of their employment, though laborious, gives them the pleasure of being a great deal in the free woods.

I had ordered a canoe to take me down the rapids, and presently I saw it coming, with the two Indian canoe-men in pink calico shirts, moving it about with their long poles, with a grace and dexterity worthy fairy land. Now and then they cast the scoop-net; all looked just as I had fancied, only far prettier.

When they came to me, they spread a mat in the middle of the canoe; I sat down, and in less than four minutes we had descended the rapids, a distance of more than three quarters of a mile. I was somewhat disappointed in this being no more of an exploit than I found it. Having heard such expressions used as of "darting," or, "shooting down," these rapids, I had fancied there was a wall of rock somewhere, where descent would somehow be accomplished, and that there would come some one gasp of terror and delight, some sensation entirely new to me; but I found myself in smooth water, before I had time to feel anything but the buoyant pleasure of being carried so lightly through this surf amid the breakers. Now and then the Indians spoke to one another in a vehement jabber, which, however, had no tone that expressed other than pleasant excitement. It is, no doubt, an act of wonderful dexterity to steer amid these jagged rocks, when one rude touch would tear a hole in the birch canoe; but these men are evidently so used to doing it, and so adroit, that the silliest person could not feel afraid. I should like to have come down twenty times, that I might have had leisure to realize the pleasure. But the fog which had detained us on the way, shortened the boat's stay at the Sault, and I wanted my time to walk about.

While coming down the rapids, the Indians caught a white-fish for my breakfast; and certainly it was the best of breakfasts. The white-fish I found quite another thing caught on this spot, and cooked immediately, from what I had found it at Chicago or Mackinaw. Before, I had had the bad taste to prefer the trout, despite the solemn and eloquent remonstrances of the Habitués, to whom the superiority of white-fish seemed a cardinal point of faith.

I am here reminded that I have omitted that indispensable part of a travelling journal, the account of what we found to eat. I cannot hope to make up, by one bold stroke, all my omissions of daily record; but that I may show myself not destitute of the common feelings of humanity, I will observe that he whose affections turn in summer towards vegetables, should not come to this region, till the subject of diet be better understood; that of fruit, too, there is little yet, even at the best hotel tables; that the prairie chickens require no praise from me, and that the trout and white-fish are worthy the transparency of the lake waters.

In this brief mention I by no means mean to give myself an air of superiority to the subject. If a dinner in the Illinois woods, on dry bread and drier meat, with water from the stream that flowed hard by, pleased me best of all, yet at one time, when living at a house where nothing was prepared for the table fit to touch, and even the bread could not be partaken of without a headache in consequence, I learnt to understand and sympathize with the anxious tone in which fathers of families, about to take their innocent children into some scene of wild beauty, ask first of all, "Is there a good table?" I shall ask just so in future. Only those whom the Powers have furnished small travelling cases of ambrosia, can take exercise all day, and be happy without even bread morning or night.

Our voyage back was all pleasure. It was the fairest day. I saw the river, the islands, the clouds to the greatest advantage.

On board was an old man, an Illinois farmer, whom I found a most agreeable companion. He had just been with his son, and eleven other young men, on an exploring expedition to the shores of lake Superior. He was the only old man of the party, but he had enjoyed, most of any, the journey. He had been the counsellor and playmate, too, of the young ones. He was one of those parents,—why so rare? —who understand and live a new life in that of their children, instead of wasting time and young happiness in trying to make them conform to an object and standard of their own. The character and history of each child may be a new and poetic experience to the parent, if he will let it. Our farmer was domestic, judicious, solid; the son, inventive, enterprising, superficial, full of follies, full of resources, always liable to failure, sure to rise above it. The father conformed to, and learnt from, a character he could not change, and won the sweet from the bitter.

His account of his life at home, and of his late adventures among the Indians, was very amusing, but I want talent to write it down. I have not heard the slang of these people intimately enough. There is a good book about Indiana, called the New Purchase, written by a person who knows the people of the country well enough to describe them in their own way. It is not witty, but penetrating, valuable for its practical wisdom and good-humored fun.

There were many sportsman stories told, too, by those from Illinois and Wisconsin. I do not retain any of these well enough, nor any that I heard earlier, to write them down, though they always interested me from bringing wild, natural scenes before the mind. It is pleasant for the sportsman to be in countries so alive with game; yet it is so plenty that one would think shooting pigeons or grouse would seem more like slaughter, than the excitement of skill to a good sportsman. Hunting the deer is full of adventure, and needs only a Scrope to describe it to invest the western woods with *historic* associations.

How pleasant it was to sit and hear rough men tell pieces out of their own common lives, in place of the frippery talk of some fine circle with its conventional sentiment, and timid, second-hand criticism. Free blew the wind, and boldly flowed the stream, named for Mary mother mild.

A fine thunder shower came on in the afternoon. It cleared at sunset, just as we came in sight of beautiful Mackinaw, over which a rainbow bent in promise of peace.

I have always wondered, in reading travels, at the childish joy travellers felt at meeting people they knew, and their sense of loneliness when they did not, in places where there was everything new to occupy the attention. So childish, I thought, always to be longing for the new in the old, and the old in the new. Yet just such sadness I felt, when I looked on the island, glittering in the sunset, canopied by the rainbow, and thought no friend would welcome me there; just such childish joy I felt, to see unexpectedly on the landing, the face of one whom I called friend.

The remaining two or three days were delightfully spent, in walking or boating, or sitting at the window to see the Indians go. This was not quite so pleasant as their coming in, though accomplished with the same rapidity; a family not taking half an hour to prepare for departure, and the departing canoe a beautiful object. But they left behind, on all the shore, the blemishes of their stay—old rags, dried boughs, fragments of food, the marks of their fires. Nature likes to cover up and gloss over spots and scars, but it would take her some time to restore that beach to the state it was in before they came.

S. and I had a mind for a canoe excursion, and we asked one of the traders to engage us two good Indians, that would not only take us out, but be sure and bring us back, as we could not hold converse with them. Two others offered their aid, beside the chief's son, a fine looking youth of about sixteen, richly dressed in blue broadcloth, scarlet sash and leggins, with a scarf of brighter red than the rest, tied around his head, its ends falling gracefully on one shoulder. They thought it, apparently, fine amusement to be attending two white women; they carried us into the path of the steamboat, which was going out, and paddled with all their force,—rather too fast, indeed, for there was something of a swell on the lake, and they sometimes threw water into the canoe. However, it flew over the waves, light as a sea-gull. They would say, "Pull away," and "Ver' warm," and, after these words, would laugh gaily. They enjoyed the hour, I believe, as much as we.

The house where we lived belonged to the widow of a French trader, an Indian by birth, and wearing the dress of her country. She spoke French fluently, and was very ladylike in her manners. She is a great character among them. They were all the time coming to pay her homage, or to get her aid and advice; for she is, I am told, a shrewd woman of business. My companion carried about her sketch-book with her, and the Indians were interested when they saw her using her pencil, though less so than about the sun-shade. This lady of the tribe wanted to borrow the sketches of the beach, with its lodges and wild groups, "to show to the *savages*," she said.

Of the practical ability of the Indian women, a good specimen is given by McKenney, in an amusing story of one who went to Washington, and acted her part there in the "first circles," with a tact and sustained dissimulation worthy of Cagliostro. She seemed to have a thorough love of intrigue for its own sake, and much dramatic talent. Like the chiefs of her nation, when on an expedition among the foe, whether for revenge or profit, no impulses of vanity or wayside seductions had power to turn her aside from carrying out her plan as she had originally projected it.

Although I have little to tell, I feel that I have learnt a great deal of the Indians, from observing them even in this broken and degraded condition. There is a language of eye and motion which cannot be put into words, and which teaches what words never can. I feel acquainted with the soul of this race; I read its nobler thought in their defaced figures. There *was* a greatness, unique and precious, which he who does not feel will never duly appreciate the majesty of nature in this American continent.

I have mentioned that the Indian orator, who addressed the agents on this occasion, said, the difference between the white man and the red man is this: "the white man no sooner came here, than he thought of preparing the way for his posterity; the red man never thought of this." I was assured this was exactly his phrase; and it defines the true difference. We get the better because we do

> *"Look before and after."*

But, from the same cause, we

> *"Pine for what is not."*

The red man, when happy, was thoroughly happy; when good, was simply good. He needed the medal, to let him know that he *was* good.

These evenings we were happy, looking over the old-fashioned garden, over the beach, over the waters and pretty island opposite, beneath the growing moon; we did not stay to see it full at Mackinaw. At two o'clock, one night, or rather morning, the Great Western came snorting in, and we must go; and Mackinaw, and all the north-west summer, is now to me no more than picture and dream;—

> *"A dream within a dream."*

These last days at Mackinaw have been pleasanter than the "lonesome" nine, for I have recovered the companion with whom I set out from the East, one who sees all, prizes all, enjoys much, interrupts never.

At Detroit we stopped for half a day. This place is famous in our history, and the unjust anger at its surrender is still expressed by almost every one who passes there. I had always shared the common feeling on this subject; for the indignation at a disgrace to our arms that seemed so unnecessary, has been handed down from father to child, and few of us have taken the pains to ascertain where the blame lay. But now, upon the spot, having read all the testimony, I felt convinced that it should rest solely with the government, which, by neglecting to sustain General Hull, as he had a right to expect they would, compelled him to take this step, or sacrifice many lives, and of the defenceless inhabitants, not of soldiers, to the cruelty of a savage foe, for the sake of his reputation.

I am a woman, and unlearned in such affairs; but, to a person with common sense and good eyesight, it is clear, when viewing the location, that, under the circumstances, he had no prospect of suc-

cessful defence, and that to attempt it would have been an act of
vanity, not valor.

I feel that I am not biased in this judgment by my personal relations, for I have always heard both sides, and, though my feelings had
been moved by the picture of the old man sitting down, in the midst
of his children, to a retired and despoiled old age, after a life of honor
and happy intercourse with the public, yet tranquil, always secure that
justice must be done at last, I supposed, like others, that he deceived
himself, and deserved to pay the penalty for failure to the responsibility
he had undertaken. Now on the spot, I change, and believe the country
at large must, ere long, change from this opinion. And I wish to add
my testimony, however trifling its weight, before it be drowned in the
voice of general assent, that I may do some justice to the feelings which
possessed me here and now.

A noble boat, the Wisconsin, was to be launched this afternoon,
the whole town was out in many-colored array, the band playing. Our
boat swept round to a good position, and all was ready but—the
Wisconsin, which could not be made to stir. This was quite a disappointment. It would have been an imposing sight.

In the boat many signs admonished that we were floating east-
ward. A shabbily dressed phrenologist laid his hand on every head
which would bend, with half-conceited, half-sheepish expression, to
the trial of his skill. Knots of people gathered here and there to discuss
points of theology. A bereaved lover was seeking religious consolation
in—Butler's Analogy, which he had purchased for that purpose. However, he did not turn over many pages before his attention was drawn
aside by the gay glances of certain damsels that came on board at
Detroit, and, though Butler might afterwards be seen sticking from his
pocket, it had not weight to impede him from many a feat of lightness
and liveliness. I doubt if it went with him from the boat. Some there
were, even, discussing the doctrines of Fourier. It seemed pity they
were not going to, rather than from, the rich and free country where
it would be so much easier, than with us, to try the great experiment
of voluntary association, and show, beyond a doubt, that "an ounce
of prevention is worth a pound of cure," a maxim of the "wisdom of
nations," which has proved of little practical efficacy as yet.

Better to stop before landing at Buffalo, while I have yet the advantage over some of my readers.

THE BOOK TO THE READER

WHO OPENS, AS AMERICAN READERS OFTEN DO,
AT THE END, WITH DOGGEREL SUBMISSION.

To see your cousin in her country home,
If at the time of blackberries you come,
"Welcome, my friends," she cries with ready glee,
"The fruit is ripened, and the paths are free.
But, madam, you will tear that handsome gown;
The little boy be sure to tumble down;
And, in the thickets where they ripen best,
The matted ivy, too, its bower has drest.
And then, the thorns your hands are sure to rend,
Unless with heavy gloves you will defend;
Amid most thorns the sweetest roses blow,
Amid most thorns the sweetest berries grow."

If, undeterred, you to the fields must go,
    You tear your dresses and you scratch your hands;
But, in the places where the berries grow,
    A sweeter fruit the ready sense commands,
Of wild, gay feelings, fancies springing sweet—
Of bird-like pleasures, fluttering and fleet.

Another year, you cannot go yourself,
    To win the berries from the thickets wild,
And housewife skill, instead, has filled the shelf
    With blackberry jam, "by best receipts compiled,—
Not made with country sugar, for too strong
The flavors that to maple juice belong;
But foreign sugar, nicely mixed 'to suit
The taste,' spoils not the fragrance of the fruit."

" 'T is pretty good," half-tasting, you reply,
"I scarce should know it from fresh blackberry.
But the best pleasure such a fruit can yield,
Is to be gathered in the open field;
If only as an article of food,
Cherry or crab-apple are quite as good;
And, for occasions of festivity,
West India sweetmeats you had better buy."

Thus, such a dish of homely sweets as these
In neither way may chance the taste to please.

Yet try a little with the evening-bread;
Bring a good needle for the spool of thread;
Take fact with fiction, silver with the lead,
And, at the mint, you can get gold instead;
In fine, read me, even as you would be read.

WOMAN IN THE
NINETEENTH CENTURY

A landmark in the history of feminism, Margaret Fuller's Woman in the Nineteenth Century *continues to speak to us nearly one hundred and fifty years after its publication. "Let them be sea captains, if you will," Fuller declared in one of the volume's most controversial statements. That declaration signaled Fuller's challenge to the nineteenth-century system of gender relations that divided the world into public and private, marketplace and household, and masculine and feminine. Convinced that women and men should be freed from these restrictive categories, Fuller offered her readers an alternative world in which members of both sexes were able to develop individual potential. Nonetheless, her major concern was women's subordinate position within this system of gender relations. With the Declaration of Independence as her source, Fuller made female equality the rallying cry of* Woman in the Nineteenth Century. *Joining other women's rights advocates who called for structural reforms, she supported increased educational opportunity, equal rights in divorce and custody of children, and female suffrage. Simultaneously, however, Fuller distinguished herself from the prevailing emphasis upon structural reforms. Believing that "what woman needs is not as a woman to act or rule, but as a nature to grow, as an intellect to discern, as a soul to live freely and unimpeded, to unfold such powers as were given her when we left our common home," Fuller sought to dismantle the entire system of gender relations. In the decidedly radical approach that characterizes* Woman in the Nineteenth Century, *she contested prevailing definitions of masculinity and femininity. She severed the linkage between femininity and fragility. And she offered readers a women's history filled with learned individuals. In her effort to have the*

"conditions of life and freedom recognized as the same for the daugh-
ters and sons of time," Fuller created an alternative system of gender
relations that made this possible.

PREFACE

The following essay is a reproduction, modified and expanded, of an article published in "The Dial, Boston, July, 1843," under the title of "The Great Lawsuit. Man versus Men: Woman versus Women."

This article excited a good deal of sympathy, and still more interest. It is in compliance with wishes expressed from many quarters, that it is prepared for publication in its present form.

Objections having been made to the former title, as not sufficiently easy to be understood, the present has been substituted as expressive of the main purpose of the essay; though, by myself, the other is preferred, partly for the reason others do not like it, *i. e.,* that it requires some thought to see what it means, and might thus prepare the reader to meet me on my own ground. Beside, it offers a larger scope, and is, in that way, more just to my desire. I meant, by that title, to intimate the fact that, while it is the destiny of Man, in the course of the Ages, to ascertain and fulfil the law of his being, so that his life shall be seen, as a whole, to be that of an angel or messenger, the action of prejudices and passions, which attend, in the day, the growth of the individual, is continually obstructing the holy work that is to make the earth a part of heaven. By Man I mean both man and woman: these are the two halves of one thought. I lay no especial stress on the welfare of either. I believe that the development of the one cannot be effected without that of the other. My highest wish is that this truth should be distinctly and rationally apprehended, and the conditions of life and freedom recognized as the same for the daughters and the sons of time; twin exponents of a divine thought.

I solicit a sincere and patient attention from those who open the following pages at all. I solicit of women that they will lay it to heart to ascertain what is for them the liberty of law. It is for this, and not for any, the largest, extension of partial privileges that I seek. I ask them, if interested by these suggestions, to search their own experience and intuitions for better, and fill up with fit materials the trenches that hedge them in. From men I ask a noble and earnest attention to any thing that can be offered on this great and still obscure subject, such as I have met from many with whom I stand in private relations.

And may truth, unpolluted by prejudice, vanity, or selfishness, be granted daily more and more, as the due inheritance, and only valuable conquest for us all!

November, 1844.

WOMAN IN THE
NINETEENTH CENTURY

Frailty, thy name is WOMAN.
The Earth waits for her Queen.

The connection between these quotations may not be obvious, but it is strict. Yet would any contradict us, if we made them applicable to the other side, and began also

Frailty, thy name is MAN.
The Earth waits for its King.

Yet man, if not yet fully installed in his powers, has given much earnest of his claims. Frail he is indeed, how frail! how impure! Yet often has the vein of gold displayed itself amid the baser ores, and Man has appeared before us in princely promise worthy of his future.

If, oftentimes, we see the prodigal son feeding on the husks in the fair field no more his own, anon, we raise the eyelids, heavy from bitter tears, to behold in him the radiant apparition of genius and love, demanding not less than the all of goodness, power and beauty. We see that in him the largest claim finds a due foundation. That claim is for no partial sway, no exclusive possession. He cannot be satisfied with any one gift of life, any one department of knowledge or telescopic peep at the heavens. He feels himself called to understand and aid nature, that she may, through his intelligence, be raised and interpreted; to be a student of, and servant to, the universe-spirit; and king of his planet, that as an angelic minister, he may bring it into conscious harmony with the law of that spirit.

In clear triumphant moments, many times, has rung through the spheres the prophecy of his jubilee, and those moments, though past in time, have been translated into eternity by thought; the bright signs they left hang in the heavens, as single stars or constellations, and, already, a thickly sown radiance consoles the wanderer in the darkest night. Other heroes since Hercules have fulfilled the zodiac of beneficent labors, and then given up their mortal part to the fire without a murmur; while no God dared deny that they should have their reward

> *Siquis tamen, Hercule, siquis*
> *Forte Deo doliturus erit, data præmia nollet,*
> *Sed meruise dari sciet, invitus que probabit,*
> *Assensere Dei.*

Sages and lawgivers have bent their whole nature to the search for truth, and thought themselves happy if they could buy, with the sacrifice of all temporal ease and pleasure, one seed for the future Eden. Poets and priests have strung the lyre with the heartstrings, poured out their best blood upon the altar, which, reared anew from age to age shall at last sustain the flame pure enough to rise to highest heaven. Shall we not name with as deep a benediction those who, if not so immediately, or so consciously, in connection with the eternal truth, yet, led and fashioned by a divine instinct, serve no less to develope and interpret the open secret of love passing into life, energy creating for the purpose of happiness; the artist whose hand, drawn by a pre-existent harmony to a certain medium, moulds it to forms of life more highly and completely organized than are seen elsewhere, and, by carrying out the intention of nature, reveals her meaning to those who are not yet wise enough to divine it; the philosopher who listens steadily for laws and causes, and from those obvious, infers those yet unknown; the historian who, in faith that all events must have their reason and their aim, records them, and thus fills archives from which the youth of prophets may be fed. The man of science dissects the statements, tests the facts, and demonstrates order, even where he cannot its purpose.

Lives, too, which bear none of these names, have yielded tones of no less significance. The candlestick set in a low place has given light as faithfully, where it was needed, as that upon the hill. In close alleys, in dismal nooks, the Word has been read as distinctly, as when shown by angels to holy men in the dark prison. Those who till a spot of earth scarcely larger than is wanted for a grave, have deserved that the sun should shine upon its sod till violets answer.

So great has been, from time to time, the promise, that, in all ages, men have said the gods themselves came down to dwell with them; that the All-Creating wandered on the earth to taste, in a limited nature, the sweetness of virtue; that the All-Sustaining incarnated himself to guard, in space and time, the destinies of this world; that heavenly genius dwelt among the shepherds, to sing to them and teach them how to sing. Indeed

> *Der stets den Hirten gnadig sich bewies.*

"He has constantly shown himself favorable to shepherds."

And the dwellers in green pastures and natural students of the stars were selected to hail, first among men, the holy child, whose life and death were to present the type of excellence, which has sustained the heart of so large a portion of mankind in these later generations.

Such marks have been made by the footsteps of *man,* (still alas! to be spoken of as the *ideal* man,) wherever he has passed through the wilderness of *men,* and whenever the pigmies stepped in one of those they felt dilate within the breast somewhat that promised nobler stature and purer blood. They were impelled to forsake their evil ways of decrepit scepticism, and covetousness of corruptible possessions. Conviction flowed in upon them. They, too, raised the cry; God is living, now, to-day; and all beings are brothers, for they are his children. Simple words enough, yet which only angelic nature, can use or hear in their full free sense.

These were the triumphant moments, but soon the lower nature took its turn, and the era of a truly human life was postponed.

Thus is man still a stranger to his inheritance, still a pleader, still a pilgrim. Yet his happiness is secure in the end. And now, no more a glimmering consciousness, but assurance begins to be felt and spoken, that the highest ideal man can form of his own powers, is that which he is destined to attain. Whatever the soul knows how to seek, it cannot fail to obtain. This is the law and the prophets. Knock and it shall be opened, seek and ye shall find. It is demonstrated; it is a maxim. Man no longer paints his proper nature in some form and says, "Prometheus had it; it is God-like;" but "Man must have it; it is human." However disputed by many, however ignorantly used, or falsified by those who do receive it, the fact of an universal, unceasing revelation has been too clearly stated in words to be lost sight of in thought, and sermons preached from the text, "Be ye perfect," are the only sermons of a pervasive and deep-searching influence.

But, among those who meditate upon this text, there is a great difference of view, as to the way in which perfection shall be sought.

Through the intellect, say some. Gather from every growth of life its seed of thought; look behind every symbol for its law; if thou canst *see* clearly, the rest will follow.

Through the life, say others. Do the best thou knowest to-day. Shrink not from frequent error in this gradual fragmentary state. Follow thy light for as much as it will show thee, be faithful as far as thou canst, in hope that faith presently will lead to sight. Help others, without blaming their need of thy help. Love much and be forgiven.

It needs not intellect, needs not experience, says a third. If you took the true way, your destiny would be accomplished in a purer and more natural order. You would not learn through facts of thought or action, but express through them the certainties of wisdom. In quietness yield thy soul to the causal soul. Do not disturb thy apprenticeship by premature effort; neither check the tide of instruction by methods of thy own. Be still, seek not, but wait in obedience. Thy commission will be given.

Could we indeed say what we want, could we give a description of the child that is lost, he would be found. As soon as the soul can affirm clearly that a certain demonstration is wanted, it is at hand. When the Jewish prophet described the Lamb, as the expression of what was required by the coming era, the time drew nigh. But we say not, see not as yet, clearly, what we would. Those who call for a more triumphant expression of love, a love that cannot be crucified, show not a perfect sense of what has already been given. Love has already been expressed, that made all things new, that gave the worm its place and ministry as well as the eagle; a love to which it was alike to descend into the depths of hell, or to sit at the right hand of the Father.

Yet, no doubt, a new manifestation is at hand, a new hour in the day of man. We cannot expect to see any one sample of completed being, when the mass of men still lie engaged in the sod, or use the freedom of their limbs only with wolfish energy. The tree cannot come to flower till its root be free from the cankering worm, and its whole growth open to air and light. While any one is base, none can be entirely free and noble. Yet something new shall presently be shown of the life of man, for hearts crave, if minds do not know how to ask it.

Among the strains of prophecy, the following, by an earnest mind of a foreign land, written some thirty years ago, is not yet outgrown; and it has the merit of being a positive appeal from the heart, instead of a critical declaration what man should *not* do.

"The ministry of man implies, that he must be filled from the divine fountains which are being engendered through all eternity, so that, at the mere name of his master, he may be able to cast all his enemies into the abyss; that he may deliver all parts of nature from the barriers that imprison them; that he may purge the terrestrial atmosphere from the poisons that infect it; that he may preserve the bodies of men from the corrupt influences that surround, and the maladies that afflict them; still more, that he may keep their souls pure from the malignant insinuations which pollute, and the gloomy images that obscure them; that he may restore its serenity to the Word, which false words of men fill with mourning and sadness; that he may satisfy the desires of the angels, who await from him the development of the marvels of nature; that, in fine, his world may be filled with God, as eternity is."*

Another attempt we will give, by an obscure observer of our own day and country, to draw some lines of the desired image. It was suggested by seeing the design of Crawford's Orpheus, and connecting with the circumstance of the American, in his garret at Rome, making choice of this subject, that of Americans here at home, showing such ambition to represent the character, by calling their prose and verse "Orphic sayings"—"Orphics." We wish we could add that they have shown that musical apprehension of the progress of nature through her ascending gradations which entitled them so to do, but their attempts are frigid, though sometimes grand; in their strain we are not warmed by the fire which fertilized the soil of Greece.

Orpheus was a law-giver by theocratic commission. He understood nature, and made her forms move to his music. He told her secrets in the form of hymns, nature as seen in the mind of God. His soul went forth toward all beings, yet could remain sternly faithful to a chosen type of excellence. Seeking what he loved, he feared not death nor hell, neither could any shape of dread daunt his faith in the power of the celestial harmony that filled his soul.

It seemed significant of the state of things in this country, that the sculptor should have represented the seer at the moment when he was obliged with his hand to shade his eyes.

> Each Orpheus must to the depths descend,
> For only thus the Poet can be wise,
> Must make the sad Persephone his friend,

* St. Martin.

And buried love to second life arise;
  Again his love must lose through too much love,
Must lose his life by living life too true,
  For what he sought below is passed above,
Already done is all that he would do;
  Must tune all being with his single lyre,
Must melt all rocks free from their primal pain,
  Must search all nature with his one soul's fire,
Must bind anew all forms in heavenly chain.
  If he already sees what he must do,
Well may he shade his eyes from the far-shining view.

A better comment could not be made on what is required to perfect man, and place him in that superior position for which he was designed, than by the interpretation of Bacon upon the legends of the Syren coast. When the wise Ulysses passed, says he, he caused his mariners to stop their ears with wax, knowing there was in them no power to resist the lure of that voluptuous song. But he, the much experienced man, who wished to be experienced in all, and use all to the service of wisdom, desired to hear the song that he might understand its meaning. Yet, distrusting his own power to be firm in his better purpose, he caused himself to be bound to the mast, that he might be kept secure against his own weakness. But Orpheus passed unfettered, so absorbed in singing hymns to the gods that he could not even hear those sounds of degrading enchantment.

Meanwhile not a few believe, and men themselves have expressed the opinion, that the time is come when Eurydice is to call for an Orpheus, rather than Orpheus for Eurydice: that the idea of Man, however imperfectly brought out, has been far more so than that of Woman, that she, the other half of the same thought, the other chamber of the heart of life, needs now to take her turn in the full pulsation, and that improvement in the daughters will best aid in the reformation of the sons of this age.

It should be remarked that, as the principle of liberty is better understood, and more nobly interpreted, a broader protest is made in behalf of Woman. As men become aware that few men have had a fair chance, they are inclined to say that no women have had a fair chance. The French Revolution, that strangely disguised angel, bore witness in favor of woman, but interpreted her claims no less ignorantly than those of man. Its idea of happiness did not rise beyond outward enjoyment, unobstructed by the tyranny of others. The title

it gave was citoyen, citoyenne, and it is not unimportant to woman
that even this species of equality was awarded her. Before, she could
be condemned to perish on the scaffold for treason, not as a citizen,
but as a subject. The right with which this title then invested a human
being, was that of bloodshed and license. The Goddess of Liberty was
impure. As we read the poem addressed to her not long since, by
Beranger, we can scarcely refrain from tears as painful as the tears of
blood that flowed when "such crimes were committed in her name."
Yes! man, born to purify and animate the unintelligent and the cold,
can, in his madness, degrade and pollute no less the fair and the chaste.
Yet truth was prophesied in the ravings of that hideous fever, caused
by long ignorance and abuse. Europe is conning a valued lesson from
the blood-stained page. The same tendencies, farther unfolded, will
bear good fruit in this country.

Yet, by men in this country, as by the Jews, when Moses was
leading them to the promised land, every thing has been done that
inherited depravity could do, to hinder the promise of heaven from its
fulfilment. The cross here as elsewhere, has been planted only to be
blasphemed by cruelty and fraud. The name of the Prince of Peace has
been profaned by all kinds of injustice toward the Gentile whom he
said he came to save. But I need not speak of what has been done
towards the red man, the black man. Those deeds are the scoff of the
world; and they have been accompanied by such pious words that the
gentlest would not dare to intercede with "Father, forgive them, for
they know not what they do."

Here, as elsewhere, the gain of creation consists always in the
growth of individual minds, which live and aspire, as flowers bloom
and birds sing, in the midst of morasses; and in the continual development of that thought, the thought of human destiny, which is given
to eternity adequately to express, and which ages of failure only seemingly impede. Only seemingly, and whatever seems to the contrary,
this country is as surely destined to elucidate a great moral law, as
Europe was to promote the mental culture of man.

Though the national independence be blurred by the servility of
individuals, though freedom and equality have been proclaimed only
to leave room for a monstrous display of slave-dealing and slave-
keeping; though the free American so often feels himself free, like the
Roman, only to pamper his appetites and his indolence through the
misery of his follow beings, still it is not in vain, that the verbal statement has been made, "All men are born free and equal." There it
stands, a golden certainty wherewith to encourage the good, to shame

the bad. The new world may be called clearly to perceive that it incurs the utmost penalty, if it reject or oppress the sorrowful brother. And, if men are deaf, the angels hear. But men cannot be deaf. It is inevitable that an external freedom, an independence of the encroachments of other men, such as has been achieved for the nation, should be so also for every member of it. That which has once been clearly conceived in the intelligence cannot fail sooner or later to be acted out. It has become a law as irrevocable as that of the Medes in their ancient dominion; men will privately sin against it, but the law, as expressed by a leading mind of the age,

> *Tutti fatti a sembianza d'un Solo,*
> *Figli tutti d'un solo riscatto,*
> *In qual'ora, in qual parte del suolo*
> *Trascorriamo quest' aura vital,*
> *Siam fratelli, siam stretti ad un patto:*
> *Maladetto colui che lo infrange,*
> *Che s'innalza sul fiacco che piange*
> *Che contrista uno spirto immortal.* *

> *All made in the likeness of the One,*
> *-   All children of one ransom,*
> *In whatever hour, in whatever part of the soil,*
> *   We draw this vital air,*
> *We are brothers; we must be bound by one compact,*
> *   Accursed he who infringes it,*
> *Who raises himself upon the weak who weep,*
> *   Who saddens an immortal spirit.*

This law cannot fail of universal recognition. Accursed be he who willingly saddens an immortal spirit, doomed to infamy in later, wiser ages, doomed in future stages of his own being to deadly penance, only short of death. Accursed be he who sins in ignorance, if that ignorance be caused by sloth.

We sicken no less at the pomp than the strife of words. We feel that never were lungs so puffed with the wind of declamation, on moral and religious subjects, as now. We are tempted to implore these

* Manzoni.

"word-heroes," these word-Catos, word-Christs, to beware of cant*
above all things; to remember that hypocrisy is the most hopeless as
well as the meanest of crimes, and that those must surely be polluted
by it, who do not reserve a part of their morality and religion for
private use. Landor says that he cannot have a great deal of mind who
cannot afford to let the larger part of it lie fallow, and what is true of
genius is not less so of virtue. The tongue is a valuable member, but
should appropriate but a small part of the vital juices that are needful
all over the body. We feel that the mind may "grow black and rancid
in the smoke" even "of altars." We start up from the harangue to go
into our closet and shut the door. There inquires the spirit, "Is this
rhetoric the bloom of healthy blood or a false pigment artfully laid
on?" And yet again we know where is so much smoke, must be some
fire; with so much talk about virtue and freedom, must be mingled
some desire for them; that it cannot be in vain that such have become
the common topics of conversation among men, rather than schemes
for tyranny and plunder, that the very newspapers see it best to proclaim themselves Pilgrims, Puritans, Heralds of Holiness. The king that
maintains so costly a retinue cannot be a mere boast, or Carabbas
fiction. We have waited here long in the dust; we are tired and hungry,
but the triumphal procession must appear at last.

Of all its banners, none has been more steadily upheld, and under
none have more valor and willingness for real sacrifices been shown,
than that of the champions of the enslaved African. And this band it
is, which, partly from a natural following out of principles, partly
because many women have been prominent in that cause, makes, just
now, the warmest appeal in behalf of woman.

Though there has been a growing liberality on this subject, yet
society at large is not so prepared for the demands of this party, but
that they are and will be for some time, coldly regarded as the Jacobins
of their day.

"Is it not enough," cries the irritated trader, "that you have done
all you could to break up the national union, and thus destroy the
prosperity of our country, but now you must be trying to break up
family union, to take my wife away from the cradle and the kitchen
hearth to vote at polls, and preach from a pulpit? Of course, if she

* Dr. Johnson's one piece of advice should be written on every door; "Clear
your mind of cant." But Byron, to whom it was so acceptable, in clearing away the
noxious vine, shook down the building. Sterling's emendation is worthy of honor:
"Realize your cant, not cast it off."

does such things, she cannot attend to those of her own sphere. She is happy enough as she is. She has more leisure than I have, every means of improvement, every indulgence."

"Have you asked her whether she was satisfied with these *indulgences?*"

"No, but I know she is. She is too amiable to wish what would make me unhappy, and too judicious to wish to step beyond the sphere of her sex. I will never consent to have our peace disturbed by any such discussions."

" 'Consent—you?' it is not consent from you that is in question, it is assent from your wife."

"Am not I the head of my house?"

"You are not the head of your wife. God has given her a mind of her own."

"I am the head and she the heart."

"God grant you play true to one another then. I suppose I am to be grateful that you did not say she was only the hand. If the head represses no natural pulse of the heart, there can be no question as to your giving your consent. Both will be of one accord, and there needs but to present any question to get a full and true answer. There is no need of precaution, of indulgence, or consent. But our doubt is whether the heart does consent with the head, or only obeys its decrees with a passiveness that precludes the exercise of its natural powers, or a repugnance that turns sweet qualities to bitter, or a doubt that lays waste the fair occasions of life. It is to ascertain the truth, that we propose some liberating measures."

Thus vaguely are these questions proposed and discussed at present. But their being proposed at all implies much thought and suggests more. Many women are considering within themselves, what they need that they have not, and what they can have, if they find they need it. Many men are considering whether women are capable of being and having more than they are and have, *and,* whether, if so, it will be best to consent to improvement in their condition.

This morning, I open the Boston "Daily Mail," and find in its "poet's corner," a translation of Schiller's "Dignity of Woman." In the advertisement of a book on America, I see in the table of contents this sequence, "Republican Institutions. American Slavery. American Ladies."

I open the *"Deutsche Schnellpost,"* published in New-York, and find at the head of a column, *Juden-und Frauen-emancipation in Ungarn.* Emancipation of Jews and Women in Hungary.

The past year has seen action in the Rhode-Island legislature, to secure married women rights over their own property, where men showed that a very little examination of the subject could teach them much; an article in the Democratic Review on the same subject more largely considered, written by a woman, impelled, it is said, by glaring wrong to a distinguished friend having shown the defects in the existing laws, and the state of opinion from which they spring; and an answer from the revered old man, J. Q. Adams, in some respects the Phocion of his time, to an address made him by some ladies. To this last I shall again advert in another place.

These symptoms of the times have come under my view quite accidentally: one who seeks, may, each month or week, collect more.

The numerous party, whose opinions are already labelled and adjusted too much to their mind to admit of any new light, strive, by lectures on some model-woman of bride-like beauty and gentleness, by writing and lending little treatises, intended to mark out with precision the limits of woman's sphere, and woman's mission, to prevent other than the rightful shepherd from climbing the wall, or the flock from using any chance to go astray.

Without enrolling ourselves at once on either side, let us look upon the subject from the best point of view which to-day offers. No better, it is to be feared, than a high house-top. A high hill-top, or at least a cathedral spire, would be desirable.

It may well be an Anti-Slavery party that pleads for woman, if we consider merely that she does not hold property on equal terms with men; so that, if a husband dies without making a will, the wife, instead of taking at once his place as head of the family, inherits only a part of his fortune, often brought him by herself, as if she were a child, or ward only, not an equal partner.

We will not speak of the innumerable instances in which profligate and idle men live upon the earnings of industrious wives; or if the wives leave them, and take with them the children, to perform the double duty of mother and father, follow from place to place, and threaten to rob them of the children, if deprived of the rights of a husband, as they call them, planting themselves in their poor lodgings, frightening them into paying tribute by taking from them the children, running into debt at the expense of these otherwise so overtasked helots. Such instances count up by scores within my own memory. I have seen the husband who had stained himself by a long course of low vice, till his wife was wearied from her heroic forgiveness, by finding that his treachery made it useless, and that if she would provide bread for herself and her children, she must be separate from his ill fame. I have known this man come to instal himself in the chamber of a woman who loathed him and say she should never take food without his company. I have known these men steal their children whom they knew they had no means to maintain, take them into dissolute company, expose them to bodily danger, to frighten the poor woman, to whom, it seems, the fact that she alone had borne the pangs of their birth, and nourished their infancy, does not give an equal right to them. I do believe that this mode of kidnapping, and it is frequent enough in all classes of society, will be by the next age viewed as it is by Heaven now, and that the man who avails himself of the shelter of men's laws to steal from a mother her own children, or arrogate any superior right in them, save that of superior virtue, will bear the stigma he deserves, in common with him who steals grown men from their mother land, their hopes, and their homes.

I said, we will not speak of this now, yet I have spoken, for the subject makes me feel too much. I could give instances that would startle the most vulgar and callous, but I will not, for the public opinion of their own sex is already against such men, and where cases of extreme tyranny are made known, there is private action in the wife's favor. But she ought not to need this, nor, I think, can she long. Men must soon see that, on their own ground, that woman is the weaker party, she ought to have legal protection, which would make such oppression impossible. But I would not deal with "atrocious instances" except in the way of illustration, neither demand from men a partial redress in some one matter, but go to the root of the whole. If principles could be established, particulars would adjust themselves aright. Ascertain the true destiny of woman, give her legitimate hopes, and a standard within herself; marriage and all other relations would by degrees be harmonized with these.

But to return to the historical progress of this matter. Knowing that there exists in the minds of men a tone of feeling towards women as towards slaves, such as is expressed in the common phrase, "Tell that to women and children," that the infinite soul can only work through them in already ascertained limits; that the gift of reason, man's highest prerogative, is allotted to them in much lower degree; that they must be kept from mischief and melancholy by being constantly engaged in active labor, which is to be furnished and directed by those better able to think, &c. &c.; we need not multiply instances, for who can review the experience of last week without recalling words which imply, whether in jest or earnest, these views or views like these;

knowing this, can we wonder that many reformers think that measures are not likely to be taken in behalf of women, unless their wishes could be publicly represented by women?

That can never be necessary, cry the other side. All men are privately influenced by women; each has his wife, sister, or female friends, and is too much biased by these relations to fail of representing their interests, and, if this is not enough, let them propose and enforce their wishes with the pen. The beauty of home would be destroyed, the delicacy of the sex be violated, the dignity of halls of legislation degraded by an attempt to introduce them there. Such duties are inconsistent with those of a mother; and then we have ludicrous pictures of ladies in hysterics at the polls, and senate chambers filled with cradles.

But if, in reply, we admit as truth that woman seems destined by nature rather for the inner circle, we must add that the arrangements of civilized life have not been, as yet, such as to secure it to her. Her circle, if the duller, is not the quieter. If kept from "excitement," she is not from drudgery. Not only the Indian squaw carries the burdens of the camp, but the favorites of Louis the Fourteenth accompany him in his journeys, and the washerwoman stands at her tub and carries home her work at all seasons, and in all states of health. Those who think the physical circumstances of woman would make a part in the affairs of national government unsuitable, are by no means those who think it impossible for the negresses to endure field work, even during pregnancy, or the sempstresses to go through their killing labors.

As to the use of the pen, there was quite as much opposition to woman's possessing herself of that help to free agency, as there is now to her seizing on the rostrum or the desk; and she is likely to draw, from a permission to plead her cause that way, opposite inferences to what might be wished by those who now grant it.

As to the possibility of her filling with grace and dignity, any such position, we should think those who had seen the great actresses, and heard the Quaker preachers of modern times, would not doubt, that woman can express publicly the fulness of thought and creation, without losing any of the peculiar beauty of her sex. What can pollute and tarnish is to act thus from any motive except that something needs to be said or done. Women could take part in the processions, the songs, the dances of old religion; no one fancied their delicacy was impaired by appearing in public for such a cause.

As to her home, she is not likely to leave it more than she now does for balls, theatres, meetings for promoting missions, revival meetings, and others to which she flies, in hope of an animation for her existence, commensurate with what she sees enjoyed by men. Governors of ladies' fairs are no less engrossed by such a change, than the Governor of the state by his; presidents of Washingtonian societies no less away from home than presidents of conventions. If men look straitly to it, they will find that, unless their lives are domestic, those of the women will not be. A house is no home unless it contain food and fire for the mind as well as for the body. The female Greek, of our day, is as much in the street as the male to cry, What news? We doubt not it was the same in Athens of old. The women, shut out from the market place, made up for it at the religious festivals. For human beings are not so constituted that they can live without expansion. If they do not get it one way, they must another, or perish.

As to men's representing women fairly at present, while we hear from men who owe to their wives not only all that is comfortable or graceful, but all that is wise in the arrangement of their lives, the frequent remark, "You cannot reason with a woman," when from those of delicacy, nobleness, and poetic culture, the contemptuous phrase "women and children," and that in no light sally of the hour, but in works intended to give a permanent statement of the best experiences, when not one man, in the million, shall I say? no, not in the hundred million, can rise above the belief that woman was made *for man*, when such traits as these are daily forced upon the attention, can we feel that man will always do justice to the interests of woman? Can we think that he takes a sufficiently discerning and religious view of her office and destiny, *ever* to do her justice, except when prompted by sentiment, accidentally or transiently, that is, for the sentiment will vary according to the relations in which he is placed. The lover, the poet, the artist, are likely to view her nobly. The father and the philosopher have some chance of liberality; the man of the world, the legislator for expediency, none.

Under these circumstances, without attaching importance, in themselves, to the changes demanded by the champions of woman, we hail them as signs of the times. We would have every arbitrary barrier thrown down. We would have every path laid open to woman as freely as to man. Were this done and a slight temporary fermentation allowed to subside, we should see crystallizations more pure and of more various beauty. We believe the divine energy would pervade nature to a degree unknown in the history of former ages, and that no discordant collision, but a ravishing harmony of the spheres would ensue.

Yet, then and only then, will mankind be ripe for this, when inward and outward freedom for woman as much as for man shall be acknowledged as a right, not yielded as a concession. As the friend of the negro assumes that one man cannot by right, hold another in bondage, so should the friend of woman assume that man cannot, by right, lay even well-meant restrictions on woman. If the negro be a soul, if the woman be a soul, appareled in flesh, to one Master only are they accountable. There is but one law for souls, and if there is to be an interpreter of it, he must come not as man, or son of man, but as son of God.

Were thought and feeling once so far elevated that man should esteem himself the brother and friend, but nowise the lord and tutor of woman, were he really bound with her in equal worship, arrangements as to function and employment would be of no consequence. What woman needs is not as a woman to act or rule, but as a nature to grow, as an intellect to discern, as a soul to live freely and unimpeded, to unfold such powers as were given her when we left our common home. If fewer talents were given her, yet if allowed the free and full employment of these, so that she may render back to the giver his own with usury, she will not complain; nay I dare to say she will bless and rejoice in her earthly birth-place, her earthly lot. Let us consider what obstructions impede this good era, and what signs give reason to hope that it draws near.

I was talking on this subject with Miranda, a woman, who, if any in the world could, might speak without heat and bitterness of the position of her sex. Her father was a man who cherished no sentimental reverence for woman, but a firm belief in the equality of the sexes. She was his eldest child, and came to him at an age when he needed a companion. From the time she could speak and go alone, he addressed her not as a plaything, but as a living mind. Among the few verses he ever wrote was a copy addressed to this child, when the first locks were cut from her head, and the reverence expressed on this occasion for that cherished head, he never belied. It was to him the temple of immortal intellect. He respected his child, however, too much to be an indulgent parent. He called on her for clear judgment, for courage, for honor and fidelity; in short, for such virtues as he knew. In so far as he possessed the keys to the wonders of this universe, he allowed free use of them to her, and by the incentive of a high expectation, he forbade, as far as possible, that she should let the privilege lie idle.

Thus this child was early led to feel herself a child of the spirit. She took her place easily, not only in the world of organized being, but in the world of mind. A dignified sense of self-dependence was given as all her portion, and she found it a sure anchor. Herself securely anchored, her relations with others were established with equal security. She was fortunate in a total absence of those charms which might have drawn to her bewildering flatteries, and in a strong electric nature, which repelled those who did not belong to her; and attracted those who did. With men and women her relations were noble, affectionate without passion, intellectual without coldness. The world was free to her, and she lived freely in it. Outward adversity came, and inward conflict, but that faith and self-respect had early been awakened which must always lead at last, to an outward serenity and an inward peace.

Of Miranda I had always thought as an example, that the restraints upon the sex were insuperable only to those who think them so, or who noisily strive to break them. She had taken a course of her own, and no man stood in her way. Many of her acts had been unusual, but excited no uproar. Few helped, but none checked her, and the many men, who knew her mind and her life, showed to her confidence, as to a brother, gentleness as to a sister. And not only refined, but very coarse men approved and aided one in whom they saw resolution and clearness of design. Her mind was often the leading one, always effective.

When I talked with her upon these matters, and had said very much what I have written, she smilingly replied: "and yet we must admit that I have been fortunate, and this should not be. My good father's early trust gave the first bias, and the rest followed of course. It is true that I have had less outward aid, in after years, than most women, but that is of little consequence. Religion was early awakened in my soul, a sense that what the soul is capable to ask it must attain, and that, though I might be aided and instructed by others, I must depend on myself as the only constant friend. This self dependence, which was honored in me, is deprecated as a fault in most women. They are taught to learn their rule from without, not to unfold it from within.

"This is the fault of man, who is still vain, and wishes to be more important to woman than, by right, he should be."

"Men have not shown this disposition toward you," I said.

"No! because the position I early was enabled to take was one of self-reliance. And were all women as sure of their wants as I was, the result would be the same. But they are so overloaded with precepts by guardians, who think that nothing is so much to be dreaded for a woman as originality of thought or character, that their minds are impeded by doubts till they lose their chance of fair free proportions. The difficulty is to get them to the point from which they shall naturally develope self-respect, and learn self-help.

"Once I thought that men would help to forward this state of things more than I do now. I saw so many of them wretched in the connections they had formed in weakness and vanity. They seemed so glad to esteem women whenever they could.

"The soft arms of affection," said one of the most discerning spirits, "will not suffice for me, unless on them I see the steel bracelets of strength."

But early I perceived that men never, in any extreme of despair, wished to be women. On the contrary they were ever ready to taunt one another at any sign of weakness, with,

Art thou not like the women, who—

The passage ends various ways, according to the occasion and rhetoric of the speaker. When they admired any woman they were inclined to speak of her as "above her sex." Silently I observed this, and feared it argued a rooted scepticism, which for ages had been fastening on the heart, and which only an age of miracles could eradicate. Ever I have been treated with great sincerity; and I look upon it as a signal instance of this, that an intimate friend of the other sex said, in a fervent moment, that I "deserved in some star to be a man." He was much surprised when I disclosed my view of my position and hopes, when I declared my faith that the feminine side, the side of love, of beauty, of holiness, was now to have its full chance, and that, if either were better, it was better now to be a woman, for even the slightest achievement of good was furthering an especial work of our time. He smiled incredulous. "She makes the best she can of it," thought he. "Let Jews believe the pride of Jewry, but I am of the better sort, and know better."

Another used as highest praise, in speaking of a character in literature, the words "a manly woman."

So in the noble passage of Ben Jonson:

> I meant the day-star should not brighter ride,
> 	Nor shed like influence from its lucent seat;
> I meant she should be courteous, facile, sweet,
> 	Free from that solemn vice of greatness, pride;
> I meant each softest virtue there should meet,

> *Fit in that softer bosom to abide,*
> *Only a learned and a manly soul,*
> *I purposed her, that should with even powers,*
> *The rock, the spindle, and the shears control*
> *Of destiny, and spin her own free hours.*

"Methinks," said I, "you are too fastidious in objecting to this. Jonson in using the word 'manly' only meant to heighten the picture of this, the true, the intelligent fate, with one of the deeper colors." "And yet," said she, "so invariable is the use of this word where a heroic quality is to be described, and I feel so sure that persistence and courage are the most womanly no less than the most manly qualities, that I would exchange these words for others of a larger sense at the risk of marring the fine tissue of the verse. Read, 'a heavenward and instructed soul,' and I should be satisfied. Let it not be said, wherever there is energy or creative genius, 'She has a masculine mind.' "

This by no means argues a willing want of generosity toward woman. Man is as generous toward her, as he knows how to be.

Wherever she has herself arisen in national or private history, and nobly shone forth in any form of excellence, men have received her, not only willingly, but with triumph. Their encomiums indeed, are always, in some sense, mortifying; they show too much surprise. Can this be you? he cries to the transfigured Cinderella; well I should never have thought it, but I am very glad. We will tell every one that you have "*surpassed your sex.*"

In every-day life the feelings of the many are stained with vanity. Each wishes to be lord in a little world, to be superior at least over one; and he does not feel strong enough to retain a life-long ascendancy over a strong nature. Only a Theseus could conquer before he wed the Amazonian Queen. Hercules wished rather to rest with Dejanira, and received the poisoned robe, as a fit guerdon. The tale should be interpreted to all those who seek repose with the weak.

But not only is man vain and fond of power, but the same want of development, which thus affects him morally, prevents his intellectually discerning the destiny of woman. The boy wants no woman, but only a girl to play ball with him, and mark his pocket handkerchief.

Thus, in Schiller's Dignity of Woman, beautiful as the poem is, there is no "grave and perfect man," but only a great boy to be softened and restrained by the influence of girls. Poets, the elder brothers of their race, have usually seen farther; but what can you expect of every-day men, if Schiller was not more prophetic as to what women must be? Even with Richter, one foremost thought about a wife was that she would "cook him something good." But as this is a delicate subject, and we are in constant danger of being accused of slighting what are called "the functions," let me say in behalf of Miranda and myself, that we have high respect for those who cook something good, who create and preserve fair order in houses, and prepare therein the shining raiment for worthy inmates, worthy guests. Only these "functions" must not be a drudgery, or enforced necessity, but a part of life. Let Ulysses drive the beeves home while Penelope there piles up the fragrant loaves; they are both well employed if these be done in thought and love, willingly. But Penelope is no more meant for a baker or weaver solely, than Ulysses for a cattle-herd.

The sexes should not only correspond to and appreciate, but prophesy to one another. In individual instances this happens. Two persons love in one another the future good which they aid one another to unfold. This is imperfectly or rarely done in the general life. Man has gone but little way; now he is waiting to see whether woman can keep step with him, but instead of calling out, like a good brother, "you can do it, if you only think so," or impersonally; "any one can do what he tries to do;" he often discourages with school-boy brag: "Girls can't do that; girls can't play ball." But let any one defy their taunts, break through and be brave and secure, they rend the air with shouts.

This fluctuation was obvious in a narrative I have lately seen, the story of the life of Countess Emily Plater, the heroine of the last revolution in Poland. The dignity, the purity, the concentrated resolve, the calm, deep enthusiasm, which yet could, when occasion called, sparkle up a holy, an indignant fire, make of this young maiden the figure I want for my frontispiece. Her portrait is to be seen in the book, a gentle shadow of her soul. Short was the career—like the maid of Orleans, she only did enough to verify her credentials, and then passed from a scene on which she was, probably, a premature apparition.

When the young girl joined the army where the report of her exploits had preceded her, she was received in a manner that marks the usual state of feeling. Some of the officers were disappointed at her quiet manners; that she had not the air and tone of a stage-heroine. They thought she could not have acted heroically unless in buskins; had no idea that such deeds only showed the habit of her mind. Others talked of the delicacy of her sex, advised her to withdraw from perils and dangers, and had no comprehension of the feelings within her breast that made this impossible. The gentle irony of her reply to these self-constituted tutors, (not one of whom showed himself her equal in conduct or reason,) is as good as her indignant reproof at a later period to the general, whose perfidy ruined all.

But though, to the mass of these men, she was an embarrassment and a puzzle, the nobler sort viewed her with a tender enthusiasm worthy of her. "Her name," said her biographer, "is known throughout Europe. I paint her character that she may be as widely loved."

With pride, he shows her freedom from all personal affections; that, though tender and gentle in an uncommon degree, there was no room for a private love in her consecrated life. She inspired those who knew her with a simple energy of feeling like her own. We have seen, they felt, a woman worthy the name, capable of all sweet affections, capable of stern virtue.

It is a fact worthy of remark, that all these revolutions in favor of liberty have produced female champions that share the same traits, but Emily alone has found a biographer. Only a near friend could have performed for her this task, for the flower was reared in feminine seclusion, and the few and simple traits of her history before her appearance in the field could only have been known to the domestic circle. Her biographer has gathered them up with a brotherly devotion.

No! man is not willingly ungenerous. He wants faith and love, because he is not yet himself an elevated being. He cries, with sneering skepticism, Give us a sign. But if the sign appears, his eyes glisten, and he offers not merely approval, but homage.

The severe nation which taught that the happiness of the race was forfeited through the fault of a woman, and showed its thought of what sort of regard man owed her, by making him accuse her on the first question to his God; who gave her to the patriarch as a handmaid, and by the Mosaical law, bound her to allegiance like a serf; even they greeted, with solemn rapture, all great and holy women as heroines, prophetesses, judges in Israel; and if they made Eve listen to the serpent, gave Mary as a bride to the Holy Spirit. In other nations it has been the same down to our day. To the woman who could conquer, a triumph was awarded. And not only those whose strength was recommended to the heart by association with goodness and beauty, but those who were bad, if they were steadfast and strong, had their claims allowed. In any age a Semiramis, an Elizabeth of England, a Catharine of Russia, makes her place good, whether in a large or small circle. How has a little wit, a little genius, been celebrated in a woman! What

an intellectual triumph was that of the lonely Aspasia, and how heart-
ily acknowledged! She, indeed, met a Pericles. But what annalist, the
rudest of men, the most plebeian of husbands, will spare from his page
one of the few anecdotes of Roman women—Sappho! Eloisa! The
names are of threadbare celebrity. Indeed they were not more suitably
met in their own time than the Countess Colonel Plater on her first
joining the army. They had much to mourn, and their great impulses
did not find due scope. But with time enough, space enough, their
kindred appear on the scene. Across the ages, forms lean, trying to
touch the hem of their retreating robes. The youth here by my side
cannot be weary of the fragments from the life of Sappho. He will not
believe they are not addressed to himself, or that he to whom they
were addressed could be ungrateful. A recluse of high powers devotes
himself to understand and explain the thought of Eloisa; he asserts her
vast superiority in soul and genius to her master; he curses the fate
that cast his lot in another age than hers. He could have understood
her: he would have been to her a friend, such as Abelard never could.
And this one woman he could have loved and reverenced, and she,
alas! lay cold in her grave hundreds of years ago. His sorrow is truly
pathetic. These responses that come too late to give joy are as tragic
as any thing we know, and yet the tears of later ages glitter as they
fall on Tasso's prison bars. And we know how elevating to the captive
is the security that somewhere an intelligence must answer to his.

The man habitually most narrow towards women will be flushed,
as by the worst assault on Christianity, if you say it has made no
improvement in her condition. Indeed, those most opposed to new acts
in her favor, are jealous of the reputation of those which have been
done.

We will not speak of the enthusiasm excited by actresses, improv-
isatrici, female singers, for here mingles the charm of beauty and grace;
but female authors, even learned women, if not insufferably ugly and
slovenly, from the Italian professor's daughter, who taught behind the
curtain, down to Mrs. Carter and Madame Dacier, are sure of an
admiring audience, and what is far better, chance to use what they
have learned, and to learn more, if they can once get a platform on
which to stand.

But how to get this platform, or how to make it of reasonably
easy access is the difficulty. Plants of great vigor will almost always
struggle into blossom, despite impediments. But there should be en-
couragement, and a free genial atmosphere for those of more timid
sort, fair play for each in its own kind. Some are like the little, delicate

flowers which love to hide in the dripping mosses, by the sides of mountain torrents, or in the shade of tall trees. But others require an open field, a rich and loosened soil, or they never show their proper hues.

It may be said that man does not have his fair play either; his energies are repressed and distorted by the interposition of artificial obstacles. Ay, but he himself has put them there; they have grown out of his own imperfections. If there *is* a misfortune in woman's lot, it is in obstacles being interposed by men, which do *not* mark her state; and, if they express her past ignorance, do not her present needs. As every man is of woman born, she has slow but sure means of redress, yet the sooner a general justness of thought makes smooth the path, the better.

Man is of woman born, and her face bends over him in infancy with an expression he can never quite forget. Eminent men have delighted to pay tribute to this image, and it is an hacknied observation, that most men of genius boast some remarkable development in the mother. The rudest tar brushes off a tear with his coat-sleeve at the hallowed name. The other day, I met a decrepit old man of seventy, on a journey, who challenged the stage-company to guess where he was going. They guessed aright, "To see your mother." "Yes," said he, "she is ninety-two, but has good eye-sight still, they say. I have not seen her these forty years, and I thought I could not die in peace without." I should have liked his picture painted as a companion piece to that of a boisterous little boy, whom I saw attempt to declaim at a school exhibition—

> *O that those lips had language. Life has passed*
> *With me but roughly since I heard thee last.*

He got but very little way before sudden tears shamed him from the stage.

Some gleams of the same expression which shone down upon his infancy, angelically pure and benign, visit man again with hopes of pure love, of a holy marriage. Or, if not before, in the eyes of the mother of his child they again are seen, and dim fancies pass before his mind, that woman may not have been born for him alone, but have come from heaven, a commissioned soul, a messenger of truth and love; that she can only make for him a home in which he may lawfully repose, in so far as she is

True to the kindred points of Heaven and home.

In gleams, in dim fancies, this thought visits the mind of common men. It is soon obscured by the mists of sensuality, the dust of routine, and he thinks it was only some meteor, or ignis fatuus that shone. But, as a Rosicrucian lamp, it burns unwearied, though condemned to the solitude of tombs; and to its permanent life, as to every truth, each age has in some form borne witness. For the truths, which visit the minds of careless men only in fitful gleams, shine with radiant clearness into those of the poet, the priest, and the artist.

Whatever may have been the domestic manners of the ancients, the idea of woman was nobly manifested in their mythologies and poems, where she appears as Sita in the Ramayana, a form of tender purity, as the Egyptian Isis,* of divine wisdom never yet surpassed. In Egypt, too, the Sphinx, walking the earth with lion tread, looked out upon its marvels in the calm, inscrutable beauty of a virgin's face, and the Greek could only add wings to the great emblem. In Greece, Ceres and Proserpine, significantly termed "the great goddesses," were seen seated, side by side. They needed not to rise for any worshipper or any change; they were prepared for all things, as those initiated to their mysteries knew. More obvious is the meaning of these three forms, the Diana, Minerva, and Vesta. Unlike in the expression of their beauty, but alike in this,—that each was self-sufficing. Other forms were only accessories and illustrations, none the complement to one like these. Another might, indeed, be the companion, and the Apollo and Diana set off one another's beauty. Of the Vesta, it is to be observed, that not only deep-eyed, deep-discerning Greece, but ruder Rome, who represents the only form of good man, (the always busy warrior), that could be indifferent to woman, confided the permanence of its glory to a tutelary goddess, and her wisest legislator spoke of meditation as a nymph.

Perhaps in Rome the neglect of woman was a reaction on the manners of Etruria, where the priestess Queen, warrior Queen, would seem to have been so usual a character.

An instance of the noble Roman marriage, where the stern and calm nobleness of the nation was common to both, we see in the historic page through the little that is told us of Brutus and Portia. Shakspeare has seized on the relation in its native lineaments, harmonizing the particular with the universal; and, while it is conjugal

* For an adequate description of the Isis, see Appendix A.

love, and no other, making it unlike the same relation, as seen in Cymbeline, or Othello, even as one star differeth from another in glory.

> *By that great vow*
> *Which did incorporate and make us one,*
> *Unfold to me, yourself, your half,*
> *Why you are heavy.*
>   *Dwell I but in the suburbs*
> *Of your good pleasure? If it be no more,*
> *Portia is Brutus' harlot, not his wife.*

Mark the sad majesty of his tone in answer. Who would not have lent a life-long credence to that voice of honor?

> *You are my true and honorable wife,*
> *As dear to me as are the ruddy drops*
> *That visit this sad heart.*

It is the same voice that tells the moral of his life in the last words—

> *Countrymen,*
> *My heart doth joy, that yet in all my life,*
> *I found no man but he was true to me.*

It was not wonderful that it should be so.

Shakspeare, however, was not content to let Portia rest her plea for confidence on the essential nature of the marriage bond;

> *I grant I am a woman; but withal,*
> *A woman that lord Brutus took to wife.*
> *I grant I am a woman; but withal,*
> *A woman well reputed—Cato's daughter.*
> *Think you I am no stronger than my sex,*
> *Being so fathered and so husbanded?*

And afterwards in the very scene where Brutus is suffering under that "insupportable and touching loss," the death of his wife, Cassius pleads—

> Have you not love enough to bear with me,
> When that rash humor which my mother gave me
> Makes me forgetful?
Brutus.—*Yes, Cassius; and henceforth,*
> *When you are over-earnest with your Brutus,*
> *He'll think your mother chides and leave you so.*

As indeed it was a frequent belief among the ancients, as with our Indians, that the *body* was inherited from the mother, the *soul* from the father. As in that noble passage of Ovid, already quoted, where Jupiter, as his divine synod are looking down on the funeral pyre of Hercules, thus triumphs—

> *Nie nisi* maternâ *Vulcanum parte potentem.*
> *Sentiet. Aeternum est, à me quod traxit, et expers*
> *At que immune necis, nullaque domabile flamma*
> *Idque ego defunctum terrâ cœlestibus oris*
> *Accipiam, cunctisque meum lætabile factum*
> *Dis fore confido.*

> *The part alone of gross* maternal *frame*
> *Fire shall devour, while that from me he drew*
> *Shall live immortal and its force renew;*
> *That, when he's dead, I'll raise to realms above;*
> *Let all the powers the righteous act approve.*

It is indeed a god speaking of his union with an earthly woman, but it expresses the common Roman thought as to marriage, the same which permitted a man to lend his wife to a friend, as if she were a chattel.

> *She dwelt but in the suburbs of his good pleasure.*

Yet the same city as I have said leaned on the worship of Vesta, the Preserver, and in later times was devoted to that of Isis. In Sparta, thought, in this respect as in all others, was expressed in the characters of real life, and the women of Sparta were as much Spartans as the men. The citoyen, citoyenne of France was here actualized. Was not the calm equality they enjoyed as honorable as the devotion of chivalry? They intelligently shared the ideal life of their nation.

Like the men they felt

> *Honor gone, all's gone,*
> *Better never have been born.*

They were the true friends of men. The Spartan, surely, would not
think that he received only his body from his mother. The sage, had
he lived in that community, could not have thought the souls of "vain
and foppish men will be degraded after death, to the forms of women,
and, if they do not there make great efforts to retrieve themselves, will
become birds."

(By the way it is very expressive of the hard intellectuality of the
merely *mannish* mind, to speak thus of birds, chosen always by the
feminine poet as the symbols of his fairest thoughts.)

We are told of the Greek nations in general, that woman occupied
there an infinitely lower place than man. It is difficult to believe this
when we see such range and dignity of thought on the subject in the
mythologies, and find the poets producing such ideals as Cassandra,
Iphiginia, Antigone, Macaria, where Sibylline priestesses told the oracle of the highest god, and he could not be content to reign with a
court of fewer than nine muses. Even victory wore a female form.

But whatever were the facts of daily life, I cannot complain of the
age and nation, which represents its thought by such a symbol as I see
before me at this moment. It is a zodiac of the busts of gods and
goddesses, arranged in pairs. The circle breathes the music of a heavenly order. Male and female heads are distinct in expression, but equal
in beauty, strength and calmness. Each male head is that of a brother
and a king—each female of a sister and a queen. Could the thought,
thus expressed, be lived out, there would be nothing more to be desired. There would be unison in variety, congeniality in difference.

Coming nearer our own time, we find religion and poetry no less
true in their revelations. The rude man, just disengaged from the sod,
the Adam, accuses woman to his God, and records her disgrace to
their posterity. He is not ashamed to write that he could be drawn
from heaven by one beneath him, one made, he says, from but a small
part of himself. But in the same nation, educated by time, instructed
by a succession of prophets, we find woman in as high a position as
she has ever occupied. No figure that has ever arisen to greet our eyes
has been received with more fervent reverence than that of the Madonna. Heine calls her the *Dame du Comptoir* of the Catholic church,
and this jeer well expresses a serious truth.

And not only this holy and significant image was worshipped by
the pilgrim, and the favorite subject of the artist, but it exercised an

immediate influence on the destiny of the sex. The empresses who embraced the cross, converted sons and husbands. Whole calendars of female saints, heroic dames of chivalry, binding the emblem of faith on the heart of the best-beloved, and wasting the bloom of youth in separation and loneliness, for the sake of duties they thought it religion to assume, with innumerable forms of poesy, trace their lineage to this one. Nor, however imperfect may be the action, in our day, of the faith thus expressed, and though we can scarcely think it nearer this ideal, than that of India or Greece was near their ideal, is it in vain that the truth has been recognized, that woman is not only a part of man, bone of his bone, and flesh of his flesh, born that men might not be lonely, but that women are in themselves possessors of and possessed by immortal souls. This truth undoubtedly received a greater outward stability from the belief of the church that the earthly parent of the Saviour of souls was a woman.

The assumption of the Virgin, as painted by sublime artists, Petrarch's Hymn to the Madonna,* cannot have spoken to the world wholly without result, yet, oftentimes those who had ears heard not.

See upon the nations the influence of this powerful example. In Spain look only at the ballads. Woman in these is "very woman;" she is the betrothed, the bride, the spouse of man, there is on her no hue of the philosopher, the heroine, the savante, but she looks great and noble; why? because she is also, through her deep devotion, the betrothed of heaven. Her upturned eyes have drawn down the light that casts a radiance round her. See only such a ballad as that of "Lady Teresa's Bridal."

Where the Infanta, given to the Moorish bridegroom, calls down the vengeance of Heaven on his unhallowed passion, and thinks it not too much to expiate by a life in the cloister, the involuntary stain upon her princely youth.† It was this constant sense of claims above those of earthly love or happiness that made the Spanish lady who shared this spirit, a guerdon to be won by toils and blood and constant purity, rather than a chattel to be bought for pleasure and service.

Germany did not need to *learn* a high view of woman; it was inborn in that race. Woman was to the Teuton warrior his priestess, his friend, his sister, in truth, a wife. And the Christian statues of noble pairs, as they lie above their graves in stone, expressing the meaning of all the by-gone pilgrimage by hands folded in mutual prayer, yield

---

* Appendix, B.
† Appendix, C.

not a nobler sense of the place and powers of woman, than belonged
to the altvater day. The holy love of Christ which summoned them,
also, to choose "the better part, that which could not be taken from
them," refined and hallowed in this nation a native faith, thus showing
that it was not the warlike spirit alone that left the Latins so barbarous
in this respect.

But the Germans, taking so kindly to this thought, did it the more
justice. The idea of woman in their literature is expressed both to a
greater height and depth than elsewhere.

I will give as instances the themes of three ballads.

One is upon a knight who had always the name of the Virgin on
his lips. This protected him all his life through, in various and beautiful
modes, both from sin and other dangers, and, when he died, a plant
sprang from his grave, which so gently whispered the Ave Maria that
none could pass it by with an unpurified heart.

Another is one of the legends of the famous Drachenfels. A
maiden, one of the earliest converts to Christianity, was carried by the
enraged populace to this dread haunt of "the dragon's fabled brood,"
to be their prey. She was left alone, but unafraid, for she knew in
whom she trusted. So, when the dragons came rushing towards her,
she showed them a crucifix and they crouched reverently at her feet.
Next day the people came, and seeing these wonders, are all turned
to the faith which exalts the lowly.

The third I have in mind is another of the Rhine legends. A youth
is sitting with the maid he loves on the shore of an isle, her fairy
kingdom, then perfumed by the blossoming grape vines, which draped
its bowers. They are happy; all blossoms with them, and life promises
its richest wine. A boat approaches on the tide; it pauses at their feet.
It brings, perhaps, some joyous message, fresh dew for their flowers,
fresh light on the wave. No! it is the usual check on such great happiness. The father of the Count departs for the crusade; will his son
join him, or remain to rule their domain, and wed her he loves? Neither of the affianced pair hesitate a moment. "I must go with my
father." "Thou must go with thy father." It was one thought, one
word. "I will be here again," he said, "when these blossoms have
turned to purple grapes." "I hope so," she sighed, while the prophetic
sense said "no."

And there she waited, and the grapes ripened, and were gathered
into the vintage, and he came not. Year after year passed thus, and no
tidings; yet still she waited.

He, meanwhile, was in a Moslem prison. Long he languished there without hope, till, at last, his patron saint appeared in vision and announced his release, but only on condition of his joining the monastic order for the service of the saint.

And so his release was effected, and a safe voyage home given. And once more he sets sail upon the Rhine. The maiden, still watching beneath the vines, sees at last the object of all this patient love approach. Approach, but not to touch the strand to which she, with outstretched arms, has rushed. He dares not trust himself to land, but in low, heart-broken tones, tells her of heaven's will; and that he, in obedience to his vow, is now on his way to a convent on the river bank, there to pass the rest of his earthly life in the service of the shrine. And then he turns his boat, and floats away from her and hope of any happiness in this world, but urged, as he believes, by the breath of heaven.

The maiden stands appalled, but she dares not murmur, and cannot hesitate long. She also bids them prepare her boat. She follows her lost love to the convent gate, requests an interview with the abbot, and devotes her Elysian isle, where vines had ripened their ruby fruit in vain for her, to the service of the monastery where her love was to serve. Then, passing over to the nunnery opposite, she takes the veil, and meets her betrothed at the altar; and for a life long union, if not the one they had hoped in earlier years.

Is not this sorrowful story of a lofty beauty? Does it not show a sufficiently high view of woman, of marriage? This is commonly the chivalric, still more the German view.

Yet, wherever there was a balance in the mind of man of sentiment, with intellect, such a result was sure. The Greek Xenophon has not only painted as a sweet picture of the domestic woman, in his Economics, but in the Cyropedia has given, in the picture of Panthea, a view of woman which no German picture can surpass, whether lonely and quiet with veiled lids, the temple of a vestal loveliness, or with eyes flashing, and hair flowing to the free wind, cheering on the hero to fight for his God, his country, or whatever name his duty might bear at the time. This picture I shall copy by and by. Yet Xenophon grew up in the same age with him who makes Iphigenia say to Achilles—

> *Better a thousand women should perish than one man cease*
>   *to see the light.*

This was the vulgar Greek sentiment. Xenophon, aiming at the ideal man, caught glimpses of the ideal woman also. From the figure of a Cyrus, the Pantheas stand not afar. They do not in thought; they would not in life.

I could swell the catalogue of instances far beyond the reader's patience. But enough have been brought forward to show that, though there has been great disparity betwixt the nations as between individuals in their culture on this point, yet the idea of woman has always cast some rays and often been forcibly represented.

Far less has woman to complain that she has not had her share of power. This, in all ranks of society, except the lowest, has been hers to the extent that vanity would crave, far beyond what wisdom would accept. In the very lowest, where man, pressed by poverty, sees in woman only the partner of toils and cares, and cannot hope, scarcely has an idea of, a comfortable home, he often maltreats her, and is less influenced by her. In all ranks, those who are gentle and uncomplaining, too candid to intrigue, too delicate to encroach, suffer much. They suffer long, and are kind; verily, they have their reward. But wherever man is sufficiently raised above extreme poverty or brutal stupidity, to care for the comforts of the fireside, or the bloom and ornament of life, woman has always power enough, if she choose to exert it, and is usually disposed to do so, in proportion to her ignorance and childish vanity. Unacquainted with the importance of life and its purposes, trained to a selfish coquetry and love of petty power, she does not look beyond the pleasure of making herself felt at the moment, and governments are shaken and commerce broken up to gratify the pique of a female favorite. The English shopkeeper's wife does not vote, but it is for her interest that the politician canvasses by the coarsest flattery. France suffers no woman on her throne, but her proud nobles kiss the dust at the feet of Pompadour and Dubarry; for such flare in the lighted foreground where a Roland would modestly aid in the closet. Spain, (that same Spain which sang of Ximena and the Lady Teresa,) shuts up her women in the care of duennas, and allows them no book but the Breviary, but the ruin follows only the more surely from the worthless favorite of a worthless queen. Relying on mean precautions, men indeed cry peace, peace, where there is no peace.

It is not the transient breath of poetic incense that women want; each can receive that from a lover. It is not life-long sway; it needs but to become a coquette, a shrew, or a good cook, to be sure of that. It is not money, nor notoriety, nor the badges of authority that men have appropriated to themselves. If demands, made in their behalf, lay stress on any of these particulars, those who make them have not searched deeply into the need. It is for that which at once includes these and precludes them; which would not be forbidden power, lest there be temptation to steal and misuse it; which would not have the mind perverted by flattery from a worthiness of esteem. It is for that which is the birthright of every being capable to receive it,—the freedom, the religious, the intelligent freedom of the universe, to use its means; to learn its secret as far as nature has enabled them, with God alone for their guide and their judge.

Ye cannot believe it, men; but the only reason why women ever assume what is more appropriate to you, is because you prevent them from finding out what is fit for themselves. Were they free, were they wise fully to develop the strength and beauty of woman; they would never wish to be men, or manlike. The well-instructed moon flies not from her orbit to seize on the glories of her partner. No; for she knows that one law rules, one heaven contains, one universe replies to them alike. It is with women as with the slave.

> *Vor dem Sklaven, wenn er die Kette bricht,*
> *Vor dem freien Menschen erzittert nicht.*

Tremble not before the free man, but before the slave who has chains to break.

In slavery, acknowledged slavery, women are on a par with men. Each is a work-tool, an article of property, no more! In perfect freedom, such as is painted in Olympus, in Swedenborg's angelic state, in the heaven where there is no marrying nor giving in marriage, each is a purified intelligence, an enfranchised soul,—no less!

> *Jene himmlische Gestalten*
> *Sie fragen nicht nach Mann und Weib,*
> *Und keine kleider, keine Falten*
> *Umgeben den verklarten Leib.*

The child who sang this was a prophetic form, expressive of the longing for a state of perfect freedom, pure love. She could not remain here, but was transplanted to another air. And it may be that the air of this earth will never be so tempered that such can bear it long. But, while they stay, they must bear testimony to the truth they are constituted to demand.

That an era approaches which shall approximate nearer to such a temper than any has yet done, there are many tokens, indeed so many, that only a few of the most prominent can here be enumerated.

The reigns of Elizabeth of England and Isabella of Castile foreboded this era. They expressed the beginning of the new state, while they forwarded its progress. These were strong characters and in harmony with the wants of their time. One showed that this strength did not unfit a woman for the duties of a wife and a mother, the other that it could enable her to live and die alone, a wide energetic life, a courageous death. Elizabeth is certainly no pleasing example. In rising above the weakness, she did not lay aside the weaknesses ascribed to her sex; but her strength must be respected now, as it was in her own time.

Elizabeth and Mary Stuart seem types, moulded by the spirit of the time, and placed upon an elevated platform to show to the coming ages, woman such as the conduct and wishes of man in general is likely to make her, lovely even to allurement, quick in apprehension and weak in judgment, with grace and dignity of sentiment, but no principle; credulous and indiscreet, yet artful; capable of sudden greatness or of crime, but not of a steadfast wisdom, or self-restraining virtue; and woman half-emancipated and jealous of her freedom, such as she has figured before and since in many a combative attitude, mannish, not equally manly, strong and prudent more than great or wise; able to control vanity, and the wish to rule through coquetry and passion, but not to resign these dear deceits, from the very foundation, as unworthy a being capable of truth and nobleness. Elizabeth, taught by adversity, put on her virtues as armor, more than produced them in a natural order from her soul. The time and her position called on her to act the wise sovereign, and she was proud that she could do so, but her tastes and inclinations would have led her to act the weak woman. She was without magnanimity of any kind.

We may accept as an omen for ourselves, that it was Isabella who furnished Columbus with the means of coming hither. This land must pay back its debt to woman, without whose aid it would not have been brought into alliance with the civilized world.

A graceful and meaning figure is that introduced to us by Mr. Prescott, in the Conquest of Mexico, in the Indian girl Marina, who accompanied Cortes, and was his interpreter in all the various difficulties of his career. She stood at his side, on the walls of the besieged palace, to plead with her enraged countrymen. By her name he was known in New Spain, and, after the conquest, her gentle intercession was often of avail to the conquered. The poem of the Future may be read in some features of the story of "Malinche."

The influence of Elizabeth on literature was real, though, by sympathy with its finer productions, she was no more entitled to give name to an era than Queen Anne. It was simply that the fact of having a female sovereign on the throne affected the course of a writer's thoughts. In this sense, the presence of a woman on the throne always makes its mark. Life is lived before the eyes of men, by which their imaginations are stimulated as to the possibilities of woman. "We will die for our King, Maria Theresa," cry the wild warriors, clashing their swords, and the sounds vibrate through the poems of that generation. The range of female character in Spenser alone might content us for one period. Britomart and Belphœbe have as much room on the canvass as Florimel; and where this is the case, the haughtiest amazon will not murmur that Una should be felt to be the fairest type.

Unlike as was the English Queen to a fairy queen, we may yet conceive that it was the image of *a* queen before the poet's mind, that called up this splendid court of women. Shakspeare's range is also great; but he has left out the heroic characters, such as the Macaria of Greece, the Britomart of Spenser. Ford and Massinger have, in this respect, soared to a higher flight of feeling than he. It was the holy and heroic woman they most loved, and if they could not paint an Imogen, a Desdemona, a Rosalind, yet, in those of a stronger mould, they showed a higher ideal, though with so much less poetic power to embody it, than we see in Portia or Isabella. The simple truth of Cordelia, indeed, is of this sort. The beauty of Cordelia is neither male nor female; it is the beauty of virtue.

The ideal of love and marriage rose high in the mind of all the Christian nations who were capable of grave and deep feeling. We may take as examples of its English aspect, the lines,

> *I could not love thee, dear, so much,*
> *Loved I not honor more.*

Or the address of the Commonwealth's man to his wife, as she looked out from the Tower window to see him for the last time, on his way to the scaffold. He stood up in the cart, waved his hat, and cried, "To Heaven, my love, to Heaven, and leave you in the storm?"

Such was the love of faith and honor, a love which stopped, like Colonel Hutchinson's, "on this side idolatry," because it was religious.

The meeting of two such souls Donne describes as giving birth to an "abler soul."

Lord Herbert wrote to his love,

> *Were not our souls immortal made,*
> *Our equal loves can make them such.*

In the "Broken Heart" of Ford, Penthea, a character which engages my admiration even more deeply than the famous one of Calanthe, is made to present to the mind the most beautiful picture of what these relations should be in their purity. Her life cannot sustain the violation of what she so clearly felt.

Shakspeare, too, saw that, in true love as in fire, the utmost ardor is coincident with the utmost purity. It is a true lover that exclaims in the agony of Othello,

> *If thou art false, O then Heaven mocks itself.*

The son, framed like Hamlet, to appreciate truth in all the beauty of relations, sinks into deep melancholy, when he finds his natural expectations disappointed. He has no mother. She to whom he gave the name, disgraces from his heart's shrine all the sex.

> *Frailty, thy name is woman.*

It is because a Hamlet could find cause to say so, that I have put the line, whose stigma has never been removed, at the head of my work. But, as a lover, surely a Hamlet would not have so far mistook, as to have finished with such a conviction. He would have felt the faith of Othello, and that faith could not, in his more dispassionate mind, have been disturbed by calumny.

In Spain, this thought is arrayed in a sublimity, which belongs to the sombre and passionate genius of the nation. Calderon's Justina resists all the temptation of the Demon, and raises her lover, with her, above the sweet lures of mere temporal happiness. Their marriage is vowed at the stake; their souls are liberated together by the martyr flame into "a purer state of sensation and existence."

In Italy, the great poets wove into their lives an ideal love which answered to the highest wants. It included those of the intellect and the affections, for it was a love of spirit for spirit. It was not ascetic, or superhuman, but, interpreting all things, gave their proper beauty to details of the common life, the common day; the poet spoke of his love, not as a flower to place in his bosom, or hold carelessly in his hand, but as a light towards which he must find wings to fly, or "a stair to heaven." He delighted to speak of her, not only as the bride of his heart, but the mother of his soul; for he saw that, in cases where the right direction had been taken, the greater delicacy of her frame, and stillness of her life, left her more open to spiritual influx than man is. So he did not look upon her as betwixt him and earth, to serve his temporal needs, but, rather, betwixt him and heaven, to purify his affections and lead him to wisdom through love. He sought, in her, not so much the Eve, as the Madonna.

In these minds the thought, which gleams through all the legends of chivalry, shines in broad intellectual effulgence, not to be misinterpreted, and their thought is reverenced by the world, though it lies so far from the practice of the world as yet, so far, that it seems as though a gulf of death yawned between.

Even with such men, the practice was, often, widely different from the mental faith. I say mental, for if the heart were thoroughly alive with it, the practice could not be dissonant. Lord Herbert's was a marriage of convention, made for him at fifteen; he was not discontented with it, but looked only to the advantages it brought of perpetuating his family on the basis of a great fortune. He paid, in act, what he considered a dutiful attention to the bond; his thoughts travelled elsewhere; and while forming a high ideal of the companionship of minds in marriage, he seems never to have doubted that its realization must be postponed to some other state of being. Dante, almost immediately after the death of Beatrice, married a lady chosen for him by his friends, and Boccaccio, in describing the miseries that attended, in this case,

> *The form of an union where union is none,*

speaks as if these were inevitable to the connection, and the scholar and poet, especially, could expect nothing but misery and obstruction in a domestic partnership with woman.

Centuries have passed since, but civilized Europe is still in a transition state about marriage; not only in practice, but in thought. It is idle to speak with contempt of the nations where polygamy is an institution, or seraglios a custom, when practices far more debasing haunt, well nigh fill, every city and every town. And so far as union of one with one is believed to be the only pure form of marriage, a great majority of societies and individuals are still doubtful whether the earthly bond must be a meeting of souls, or only supposes a contract of convenience and utility. Were woman established in the rights of an immortal being, this could not be. She would not, in some countries, be given away by her father, with scarcely more respect for her feelings than is shown by the Indian chief, who sells his daughter for a horse, and beats her if she runs away from her new home. Nor, in societies where her choice is left free, would she be perverted, by the current of opinion that seizes her, into the belief that she must marry, if it be only to find a protector, and a home of her own.

Neither would man, if he thought the connection of permanent importance, form it so lightly. He would not deem it a trifle, that he was to enter into the closest relations with another soul, which, if not eternal in themselves, must eternally affect his growth.

Neither, did he believe woman capable of friendship,* would he, by rash haste, lose the chance of finding a friend in the person who might, probably, live half a century by his side. Did love, to his mind, stretch forth into infinity, he would not miss his chance of its revelations, that he might, the sooner, rest from his weariness by a bright fireside, and secure a sweet and graceful attendant "devoted to him alone." Were he a step higher, he would not carelessly enter into a relation where he might not be able to do the duty of a friend, as well as a protector from external ill, to the other party, and have a being in his power pining for sympathy, intelligence and aid, that he could not give.

What deep communion, what real intercourse is implied by the sharing the joys and cares of parentage, when any degree of equality is admitted between the parties! It is true that, in a majority of instances, the man looks upon his wife as an adopted child, and places her to the other children in the relation of nurse or governess, rather than of parent. Her influence with them is sure, but she misses the education which should enlighten that influence, by being thus treated. It is the order of nature that children should complete the education, moral and mental, of parents, by making them think what is needed for the best culture of human beings, and conquer all faults and impulses that interfere with their giving this to these dear objects, who represent the world to them. Father and mother should assist one another to learn what is required for this sublime priesthood of nature. But, for this, a religious recognition of equality is required.

* See Appendix D, Spinoza's view.

Where this thought of equality begins to diffuse itself, it is shown in four ways.

The household partnership. In our country, the woman looks for a "smart but kind" husband; the man for a "capable, sweet-tempered" wife.

The man furnishes the house; the woman regulates it. Their relation is one of mutual esteem, mutual dependence. Their talk is of business, their affection shows itself by practical kindness. They know that life goes more smoothly and cheerfully to each for the other's aid; they are grateful and content. The wife praises her husband as a "good provider;" the husband, in return, compliments her as a "capital housekeeper." This relation is good, as far as it goes.

Next comes a closer tie, which takes the two forms, either of mutual idolatry, or of intellectual companionship. The first, we suppose, is to no one a pleasing subject of contemplation. The parties weaken and narrow one another; they lock the gate against all the glories of the universe, that they may live in a cell together. To themselves they seem the only wise, to all others steeped in infatuation; the gods smile as they look forward to the crisis of cure; to men, the woman seems an unlovely syren; to women, the man an effeminate boy.

The other form, of intellectual companionship, has become more and more frequent. Men engaged in public life, literary men, and artists, have often found in their wives companions and confidants in thought no less than in feeling. And as the intellectual development of woman has spread wider and risen higher, they have, not unfrequently, shared the same employment. As in the case of Roland and his wife, who were friends in the household and in the nation's councils, read, regulated home affairs, or prepared public documents together, indifferently.

It is very pleasant, in letters begun by Roland, and finished by his wife, to see the harmony of mind, and the difference of nature; one thought, but various ways of treating it.

This is one of the best instances of a marriage of friendship. It was only friendship, whose basis was esteem; probably neither party knew love, except by name.

Roland was a good man, worthy to esteem, and be esteemed; his wife as deserving of admiration, as able to do without it. Madame Roland is the fairest specimen we have yet of her class, as clear to discern her aim, as valiant to pursue it, as Spenser's Britomart; austerely set apart from all that did not belong to her, whether as woman or as mind. She is an antetype of a class to which the coming time will afford a field, the Spartan matron, brought by the culture of the age of Books to intellectual consciousness and expansion.

Self-sufficingness, strength, and clear-sightedness were, in her, combined with a power of deep and calm affection. She, too, would have given a son or husband the device for his shield, "Return with it or upon it;" and this, not because she loved little, but much. The page of her life is one of unsullied dignity.

Her appeal to posterity is one against the injustice of those who committed such crimes in the name of Liberty. She makes it in behalf of herself and her husband. I would put beside it, on the shelf, a little volume, containing a similar appeal from the verdict of contemporaries to that of mankind, made by Godwin in behalf of his wife, the celebrated, the, by most men, detested, Mary Wolstonecraft. In his view, it was an appeal from the injustice of those who did such wrong in the name of virtue.

Were this little book interesting for no other cause, it would be so for the generous affection evinced under the peculiar circumstances. This man had courage to love and honor this woman in the face of the world's sentence, and of all that was repulsive in her own past history. He believed he saw of what soul she was, and that the impulses she had struggled to act out were noble, though the opinions to which they had led might not be thoroughly weighed. He loved her, and he defended her for the meaning and tendency of her inner life. It was a good fact.

Mary Wolstonecraft, like Madame Dudevant, (commonly known as George Sand,) in our day, was a woman whose existence better proved the need of some new interpretation of woman's rights, than any thing she wrote. Such beings as these, rich in genius, of most tender sympathies, capable of high virtue and a chastened harmony, ought not to find themselves, by birth, in a place so narrow, that, in breaking bonds, they become outlaws. Were there as much room in the world for such, as in Spenser's poem for Britomart, they would not run their heads so wildly against the walls, but prize their shelter rather. They find their way, at last, to light and air, but the world will not take off the brand it has set upon them. The champion of the Rights of Woman found, in Godwin, one who would plead that cause like a brother. He who delineated with such purity of traits the form of woman in the Marguerite, of whom the weak St. Leon could never learn to be worthy, a pearl indeed whose price was above rubies, was not false in life to the faith by which he had hallowed his romance. He acted as he wrote, like a brother. This form of appeal rarely fails to touch the basest man. "Are you acting towards other women in the way you would have men act towards your sister?" George Sand smokes, wears male attire, wishes to be addressed as "Mon frère;"— perhaps, if she found those who were as brothers, indeed, she would not care whether she were brother or sister.*

* Since writing the above, I have read with great satisfaction, the following sonnets addressed to George Sand by a woman who has precisely the qualities that the author of Simon and Indiana lacks. It is such a woman, so unblemished in character, so high in aim, and pure in soul, that should address this other, as noble in nature, but clouded by error, and struggling with circumstances. It is such women that will do such justice. They are not afraid to look for virtue and reply to nspiration, among those who have *not* "dwelt in decencies forever." It is a source of pride and happiness to read this address from the heart of Elizabeth Barrett.

> TO GEORGE SAND
> A DESIRE
> *Thou large-brained woman and large-hearted man,*
> *Self-called George Sand! whose soul, amid the lions*
> *Of thy tumultuous senses moans defiance,*
> *And answers roar for roar, as spirits can:*
> *I would some mild miraculous thunder ran*
> *Above the applauded circus, in appliance*
> *Of thine own nobler nature's strength and science,*
> *Drawing two pinions, white as wings of swan,*
> *From the strong shoulders, to amaze the place*
> *With holier light! that thou to woman's claim,*
> *And man's might join, beside, the angel's grace*
> *Of a pure genius sanctified from blame;*
> *Till child and maiden pressed to thine embrace,*
> *To kiss upon thy lips a stainless fame.*

> TO THE SAME
> A RECOGNITION
> *True genius, but true woman! dost deny*
> *Thy woman's nature with a manly scorn,*
> *And break away the gauds and armlets worn*
> *By weaker women in captivity?*
> *Ah, vain denial! that revolted cry*
> *Is sobbed in by a woman's voice forlorn:—*
> *Thy woman's hair, my sister, all unshorn,*
> *Floats back dishevelled strength in agony,*
> *Disproving thy man's name, and while before*

We rejoice to see that she, who expresses such a painful contempt for men in most of her works, as shows she must have known great wrong from them, depicting in "La Roche Mauprat," a man raised by the workings of love, from the depths of savage sensualism, to a moral and intellectual life. It was love for a pure object, for a steadfast woman, one of those who, the Italian said, could make the stair to heaven.

This author, beginning like the many in assault upon bad institutions, and external ills, yet deepening the experience through comparative freedom, sees at last, that the only efficient remedy must come from individual character. These bad institutions, indeed, it may always be replied, prevent individuals from forming good character, therefore we must remove them. Agreed, yet keep steadily the higher aim in view. Could you clear away all the bad forms of society, it is vain, unless the individual begin to be ready for better. There must be a parallel movement in these two branches of life. And all the rules left by Moses availed less to further the best life than the living example of one Messiah.

Still, still the mind of the age struggles confusedly with these problems, better discerning as yet the ill it can no longer bear, than the good by which it may supersede it. But women, like Sand, will speak now and cannot be silenced; their characters and their eloquence alike foretell an era when such as they shall easier learn to lead true lives. But though such forebode, not such shall be the parents of it.* Those who would reform the world must show that they do not speak in the heat of wild impulse; their lives must be unstained by passionate error; they must be severe lawgivers to themselves. They must be religious students of the divine purpose with regard to man, if they would not confound the fancies of a day with the requisitions of eternal good. Their liberty must be the liberty of law and knowledge. But, as to the transgressions against custom which have caused such outcry against

---

> *The world thou burnest in a poet-fire,*
> *We see thy woman-heart beat evermore*
> *Through the large flame. Beat purer, heart, and higher,*
> *Till God unsex thee on the spirit-shore;*
> *To which alone unsexing, purely aspire.*

This last sonnet seems to have been written after seeing the picture of Sand, which represents her in a man's dress, but with long loose hair, and an eye whose mournful fire is impressive even in the caricatures.

* Appendix, E.

those of noble intention, it may be observed, that the resolve of Eloisa to be only the mistress of Abelard, was that of one who saw in practice around her, the contract of marriage made the seal of degradation. Shelley feared not to be fettered, unless so to be was to be false. Wherever abuses are seen, the timid will suffer; the bold will protest. But society has a right to outlaw them till she has revised her law; and this she must be taught to do, by one who speaks with authority, not in anger or haste.

If Godwin's choice of the calumniated authoress of the "Rights of Woman," for his honored wife, be a sign of a new era, no less so is an article to which I have alluded some pages back, published five or six years ago in one of the English Reviews, where the writer, in doing full justice to Eloisa, shows his bitter regret that she lives not now to love him, who might have known better how to prize her love than did the egotistical Abelard.

These marriages, these characters, with all their imperfections, express an onward tendency. They speak of aspiration of soul, of energy of mind, seeking clearness and freedom. Of a like promise are the tracts lately published by Goodwyn Barmby, (the European Pariah, as he calls himself,) and his wife Catharine. Whatever we may think of their measures, we see in them wedlock; the two minds are wed by the only contract that can permanently avail, of a common faith and a common purpose.

We might mention instances, nearer home, of minds, partners in work and in life, sharing together, on equal terms, public and private interests, and which wear not, on any side, the aspect of offence shown by those last-named: persons who steer straight onward, yet, in our comparatively free life, have not been obliged to run their heads against any wall. But the principles which guide them might, under petrified and oppressive institutions, have made them warlike, paradoxical, and in some sense, Pariahs. The phenomena are different, the law is the same, in all these cases. Men and women have been obliged to build up their house anew from the very foundation. If they found stone ready in the quarry, they took it peaceably, other wise they alarmed the country by pulling down old towers to get materials.

These are all instances of marriage as intellectual companionship. The parties meet mind to mind, and a mutual trust is produced, which can buckler them against a million. They work together for a common purpose, and, in all these instances, with the same implement, the pen. The pen and the writing-desk furnish forth as naturally the retirement of woman as of man.

A pleasing expression, in this kind, is afforded by the union in the names of the Howitts. William and Mary Howitt we heard named together for years, supposing them to be brother and sister; the equality of labors and reputation, even so, was auspicious; more so, now we find them man and wife. In his late work on Germany, Howitt mentions his wife, with pride, as one among the constellation of distinguished English-women, and in a graceful simple manner.

Our pleasure, indeed, in this picture, is marred by the vulgar apparition which has of late displaced the image, which we had from her writings cherished of a pure and gentle Quaker poetess. The surprise was painful as that of the little sentimentalist in the tale of "L'Amie Inconnue" when she found her correspondent, the poetess, the "adored Araminta," scolding her servants in Welsh, and eating toasted cheese and garlic. Still, we cannot forget what we have thought of the partnership in literature and affection between the Howitts, the congenial pursuits and productions, the pedestrian tours where the married pair showed that marriage, on a wide enough basis, does not destroy the "inexhaustible" entertainment which lovers found in one another's company.

In naming these instances, I do not mean to imply that community of employment is essential to union of husband and wife, more than to the union of husbands and wife, more than to the union of friends. Harmony exists in difference, no less than in likeness, if only the same key-note govern both parts. Woman the poem, man the poet! Woman the heart, man the head! Such divisions are only important when they are never to be transcended. If nature is never bound down, nor the voice of inspiration stifled, that is enough. We are pleased that women should write and speak, if they feel the need of it, from having something to tell; but silence for ages would be no misfortune, if that silence be from divine command, and not from man's tradition.

While Goetz Von Berlichingen rides to battle, his wife is busy in the kitchen; but difference of occupation does not prevent that community of inward life, that perfect esteem, with which he says—

Whom God loves, to him gives he such a wife.

Manzoni thus dedicates his "Adelchi."

"To his beloved and venerated wife, Enrichetta Luigia Blondel, who, with conjugal affection and maternal wisdom, has preserved a virgin mind, the author dedicates this 'Adelchi,' grieving that he could not, by a more splendid and more durable monument, honor the dear name, and the memory of so many virtues."

The relation could not be fairer, or more equal, if she, too, had written poems. Yet the position of the parties might have been the reverse as well; the woman might have sung the deeds, given voice to the life of the man, and beauty would have been the result, as we see, in pictures of Arcadia, the nymph singing to the shepherds, or the shepherd, with his pipe, alluring the nymphs; either makes a good picture. The sounding lyre requires, not muscular strength, but energy of soul to animate the hand which would control it. Nature seems to delight in varying the arrangements, as if to show that she will be fettered by no rule, and we must admit the same varieties that she admits.

The fourth and highest grade of marriage union, is the religious, which may be expressed as pilgrimage towards a common shrine. This includes the others; home sympathies and household wisdom, for these pilgrims must know how to assist each other along the dusty way; intellectual communion, for how sad it would be on such a journey to have a companion to whom you could not communicate thoughts and aspirations as they sprang to life; who would have no feeling for the prospects that open, more and more glorious as we advance; who would never see the flowers that may be gathered by the most industrious traveller. It must include all these. Such a fellow-pilgrim Count Zinzendorf seems to have found in his Countess, of whom he thus writes:

"Twenty-five years' experience has shown me that just the help-mate whom I have, is the only one that could suit my vocation. Who else could have so carried through my family affairs? Who lived so spotlessly before the world? Who so wisely aided me in my rejection of a dry morality? Who so clearly set aside the Pharisaism which, as years passed, threatened to creep in among us? Who so deeply discerned as to the spirits of delusion, which sought to bewilder us? Who would have governed my whole economy so wisely, richly, and hospitably, when circumstances commanded? Who have taken indifferently the part of servant or mistress, without, on the one side, affecting an especial spirituality; on the other, being sullied by any worldly pride? Who, in a community where all ranks are eager to be on a level, would, from wise and real causes, have known how to maintain inward and outward distinctions? Who, without a murmur, have seen her husband encounter such dangers by land and sea? Who undertaken with him, and *sustained* such astonishing pilgrimages? Who, amid such

difficulties, always held up her head and supported me? Who found
such vast sums of money, and acquitted them on her own credit? And,
finally, who, of all human beings, could so well understand and interpret to others my inner and outer being as this one, of such nobleness
in her way of thinking, such great intellectual capacity, and free from
the theological perplexities that enveloped me!"

Let any one peruse, with all their power, the lineaments of this
portrait, and see if the husband had not reason, with this air of solemn
rapture and conviction, to challenge comparison? We are reminded of
the majestic cadence of the line whose feet step in the just proportions
of Humanity,

> *Daughter of God and Man, accomplished Eve!*

An observer* adds this testimony:

"We may, in many marriages, regard it as the best arrangement,
if the man has so much advantage over his wife, that she can, without
much thought of her own, be, by him, led and directed as by a father.
But it was not so with the Count and his consort. She was not made
to be a copy; she was an original; and, while she loved and honored
him, she thought for herself, on all subjects, with so much intelligence,
that he could and did look on her as sister and friend also."

Compare with this refined specimen of a religiously civilized life,
the following imperfect sketch of a North American Indian, and we
shall see that the same causes will always produce the same results.
The Flying Pigeon (Ratchewaine) was the wife of a barbarous chief,
who had six others, but she was his only true wife, because the only
one of a strong and pure character, and, having this, inspired a veneration, as like as the mind of the man permitted, to that inspired by
the Countess Zinzendorf. She died when her son was only four years
old, yet left on his mind a feeling of reverent love worthy the thought
of Christian chivalry. Grown to manhood, he shed tears on seeing her
portrait.

THE FLYING PIGEON

"Ratchewaine was chaste, mild, gentle in her disposition, kind, generous, and devoted to her husband. A harsh word was never known

* Spangenberg.

to proceed from her mouth; nor was she ever known to be in a passion. Mahaskah used to say of her, after her death, that her hand was shut, when those, who did not want, came into her presence; but when the really poor came in, it was like a strainer full of holes, letting all she held in it pass through. In the exercise of generous feeling she was uniform. It was not indebted for its exercise to whim, or caprice, or partiality. No matter of what nation the applicant for her bounty was, or whether at war or peace with her nation; if he were hungry, she fed him; if naked, she clothed him; and if houseless, she gave him shelter. The continued exercise of this generous feeling kept her poor. And she has been known to give away her last blanket—all the honey that was in the lodge, the last bladder of bear's oil, and the last piece of dried meat.

"She was scrupulously exact in the observance of all the religious rites which her faith imposed upon her. Her conscience is represented to have been extremely tender. She often feared that her acts were displeasing to the Great Spirit, when she would blacken her face, and retire to some lone place, and fast and pray."

To these traits should be added, but for want of room, anecdotes which show the quick decision and vivacity of her mind. Her face was in harmony with this combination. Her brow is as ideal and the eyes and lids as devout and modest as the Italian pictures of the Madonna, while the lower part of the face has the simplicity and childish strength of the Indian race. Her picture presents the finest specimen of Indian beauty we have ever seen.

Such a woman is the sister and friend of all beings, as the worthy man is their brother and helper.

With like pleasure we survey the pairs wedded on the eve of missionary effort. They, indeed, are fellow pilgrims on a well-made road, and whether or no they accomplish all they hope for the sad Hindoo, or the nearer savage, we feel that, in the burning waste, their love is like to be a healing dew, in the forlorn jungle, a tent of solace to one another. They meet, as children of one Father, to read together one book of instruction.

We must insert in this connection the most beautiful picture presented by ancient literature of wedded love under this noble form.

It is from the romance in which Xenophon, the chivalrous Greek, presents his ideal of what human nature should be.

The generals of Cyrus had taken captive a princess, a woman of unequalled beauty, and hastened to present her to the prince as the part of the spoil he would think most worthy of his acceptance.

Cyrus visits the lady, and is filled with immediate admiration by the modesty and majesty with which she receives him. He finds her name is Panthea, and that she is the wife of Abradatus, a young king whom she entirely loves. He protects her as a sister, in his camp, till he can restore her to her husband.

After he first transports of joy at this re-union, the heart of Panthea is bent on showing her love and gratitude to her magnanimous and delicate protector. And as she has nothing so precious to give as the aid of Abradatus, that is what she most wishes to offer. Her husband is of one soul with her in this, as in all things.

The description of her grief and self-destruction, after the death which ensued upon this devotion, I have seen quoted, but never that of their parting when she sends him forth to battle. I shall copy both. If they have been read by any of my readers, they may be so again with profit in this connexion, for never were the heroism of a true woman, and the purity of love, in a true marriage, painted in colors more delicate or more lively.

"The chariot of Abradatus, that had four perches and eight horses, was completely adorned for him; and when he was going to put on his linen corslet, which was a sort of armor used by those of his country, Panthea brought him a golden helmet, and arm-pieces, broad bracelets for his wrists, a purple habit that reached down to his feet, and hung in folds at the bottom, and a crest dyed of a violet color. These things she had made unknown to her husband, and by taking the measure of his armor. He wondered when he saw them, and inquired thus of Panthea: 'And have you made me these arms, woman, by destroying your own ornaments?' 'No, by Jove,' said Panthea, 'not what is the most valuable of them; for it is you, if you appear to others to be what I think you, that will be my greatest ornament.' And, saying that, she put on him the armor, and, though she endeavored to conceal it, the tears poured down her cheeks. When Abradatus, who was before a man of fine appearance, was set out in those arms, he appeared the most beautiful and noble of all, especially, being likewise so by nature. Then, taking the reins from the driver, he was just preparing to mount the chariot, when Panthea, after she had desired all that were there to retire, thus said:

"'O Abradatus! if ever there was a woman who had a greater regard to her husband than to her own soul, I believe you know that I am such an one; what need I therefore speak of things in particular? for I reckon that my actions have convinced you more than any words I can now use. And yet, though I stand thus affected towards you, as you know I do, I swear by this friendship of mine and yours, that I certainly would rather choose to be put under ground jointly with you, approving yourself a brave man, than to live with you in disgrace and shame; so much do I think you and myself worthy of the noblest things. Then I think that we both lie under great obligations to Cyrus, that, when I was a captive, and chosen out for himself, he thought fit to treat me neither as a slave, nor, indeed, as a woman of mean account, but he took and kept me for you, as if I were his brother's wife. Besides, when Araspes, who was my guard, went away from him, I promised him, that, if he would allow me to send for you, you would come to him, and approve yourself a much better and more faithful friend than Araspes.'

"Thus she spoke; and Abradatus being struck with admiration at her discourse, laying his hand gently on her head, and lifting up his eyes to heaven, made this prayer: 'Do thou, O greatest Jove! grant me to appear a husband worthy of Panthea, and a friend worthy of Cyrus, who has done us so much honor!'

"Having said this, he mounted the chariot by the door of the driver's seat; and, after he had got up, when the driver shut the door, Panthea, who had now no other way to salute him, kissed the seat of the chariot. The chariot then moved, and she, unknown to him, followed, till Abradatus turning about, and seeing her, said: 'Take courage, Panthea! Fare you happily and well, and now go your ways.' On this her women and servants carried her to her conveyance, and, laying her down, concealed her by throwing the covering of a tent over her. The people, though Abradatus and his chariot made a noble spectacle, were not able to look at him till Panthea was gone."

After the battle—

"Cyrus calling to some of his servants, 'Tell me,' said he, 'has any one seen Abradatus? for I admire that he now does not appear.' One replied, 'My sovereign, it is because he is not living, but died in the battle as he broke in with his chariot on the Egyptians. All the rest, except his particular companions, they say, turned off when they saw the Egyptians' compact body. His wife is now said to have taken up his dead body, to have placed it in the carriage that she herself was conveyed in, and to have brought it hither to some place on the river Pactolus, and her servants are digging a grave on a certain elevation. They say that his wife, after setting him out with all the ornaments she has, is sitting on the ground with his head on her knees.' Cyrus, hearing this, gave himself a blow on the thigh, mounted his horse at a leap, and taking with him a thousand horse, rode away to this scene of affliction; but gave orders to Gadatas and Gobryas to take with them all the rich ornaments proper for a friend and an excellent man deceased, and to follow after him; and whoever had herds of cattle with him, he ordered them to take both oxen, and horses, and sheep in good number, and to bring them away to the place where, by inquiry, they should find him to be, that he might sacrifice these to Abradatus.

"As soon as he saw the woman sitting on the ground, and the dead body there lying, he shed tears at the afflicting sight, and said: 'Alas! thou brave and faithful soul, hast thou left us, and art thou gone?' At the same time he took him by the right hand, and the hand of the deceased came away, for it had been cut off, with a sword, by the Egyptians. He, at the sight of this, became yet much more concerned than before. The woman shrieked out in a lamentable manner, and, taking the hand from Cyrus, kissed it, fitted it to its proper place again, as well as she could, and said, 'The rest, Cyrus, is in the same condition, but what need you see it? And I know that I was not one of the least concerned in these his sufferings, and, perhaps, you were not less so, for I, fool that I was! frequently exhorted him to behave in such a manner as to appear a friend to you, worthy of notice; and I know he never thought of what he himself should suffer, but of what he should do to please you. He is dead, therefore,' said she, 'without reproach, and I, who urged him on, sit here alive.' Cyrus, shedding tears for some time in silence, then spoke—'He has died, woman, the noblest death; for he has died victorious! do you adorn him with these things that I furnish you with.' (Gobryas and Gadatas were then come up and had brought rich ornaments in great abundance with them.) 'Then,' said he, 'be assured that he shall not want respect and honor in all other things: but, over and above, multitudes shall concur in raising him a monument that shall be worthy of us, and all the sacrifices shall be made him that are proper to be made in honor of a brave man. You shall not be left destitute, but, for the sake of your modesty and every other virtue, I will pay you all other honors, as well as place those about you who will conduct you wherever you please. Do you but make it known to me where it is that you desire to be conveyed to.' And Panthea replied, 'Be confident, Cyrus,' said she, 'I will not conceal from you to whom it is that I desire to go.'

"He, having said this, went away with great pity for her that she should have lost such a husband, and for the man that he should have left such a wife behind him, never to see her more. Panthea then gave orders for her servants to retire, 'Till such time,' said she, 'as I shall have lamented my husband, as I please.' Her nurse she bid to stay, and gave orders that, when she was dead, she would wrap her and her husband up in one mantle together. The nurse, after having repeatedly begged her not to do this, and meeting with no success, but observing her to grow angry, sat herself down, breaking out into tears. She, being before-hand provided with a sword, killed herself, and, laying her head down on her husband's breast, she died. The nurse set up a lamentable cry, and covered them both as Panthea had directed.

"Cyrus, as soon as he was informed of what the woman had done, being struck with it, went to help her if he could. The servants, three in number, seeing what had been done, drew their swords and killed themselves, as they stood at the place where she had ordered them. And the monument is now said to have been raised by continuing the mount on to the servants; and on a pillar above, they say, the names of the man and woman were written in Syriac letters.

"Below were three pillars, and they were inscribed thus, 'Of the servants.' Cyrus, when he came to this melancholy scene, was struck with admiration of the woman, and, having lamented over her, went away. He took care, as was proper, that all the funeral rites should be paid them in the noblest manner, and the monument, they say, was raised up to a very great size."

These be the ancients, who, so many assert had no idea of the dignity of woman, or of marriage. Such love Xenophon could paint as subsisting between those who after death "would see one another never more." Thousands of years have passed since, and with the reception of the cross, the nations assume the belief that those who part thus, may meet again and forever, if spiritually fitted to one another, as Abradatus and Panthea were, and yet do we see such marriages among them? If at all, how often?

I must quote two more short passages from Xenophon, for he is a writer who pleases me well.

Cyrus receiving the Armenians whom he had conquered.

"Tigranes," said he, "at what rate would you purchase the regaining of your wife?" Now Tigranes happened to be *but lately married*, and had a very great love for his wife," (that clause perhaps sounds *modern*.)

"Cyrus," said he, "I would ransom her at the expense of my life."

"Take then your own to yourself," said he.

When they came home, one talked of Cyrus' wisdom, another of his patience and resolution, another of his mildness. One spoke of his beauty and the smallness of his person, and, on that, Tigranes asked his wife, "And do you, Armenian dame, think Cyrus handsome?" "Truly," said she, "I did not look at him." "At whom, then, did you look?" said Tigranes. "At him who said that, to save me from servitude, he would ransom me at the expense of his own life."

From the Banquet.—

Socrates, who observed her with pleasure, said, "This young girl has confirmed me in the opinion I have had, for a long time, that the female sex are nothing inferior to ours, excepting only in strength of body, or, perhaps, in steadiness of judgment."

In the Economics, the manner in which the husband gives counsel to his young wife, presents the model of politeness and refinement. Xenophon is thoroughly the gentleman, gentle in breeding and in soul. All the men he describes are so, while the shades of manner are distinctly marked. There is the serene dignity of Socrates, with gleams of playfulness thrown across its cool religious shades, the princely mildness of Cyrus, and the more domestic elegance of the husband in the Economics.

There is no way that men sin more against refinement, as well as discretion, than in their conduct towards their wives. Let them look at the men of Xenophon. Such would know how to give counsel, for they would know how to receive it. They would feel that the most intimate relations claimed most, not least, of refined courtesy. They would not suppose that confidence justified carelessness, nor the reality of affection want of delicacy in the expression of it.

Such men would be too wise to hide their affairs from the wife and then expect her to act as if she knew them. They would know that if she is expected to face calamity with courage, she must be instructed and trusted in prosperity, or, if they had failed in wise confidence such as the husband shows in the Economics, they would be ashamed of anger or querulous surprise at the results that naturally follow.

Such men would not be exposed to the bad influence of bad wives, for all wives, bad or good, loved or unloved, inevitably influence their husbands, from the power their position not merely gives, but necessitates, of coloring evidence and infusing feelings in hours when the patient, shall I call him? is off his guard. Those who understand the wife's mind, and think it worth while to respect her springs of action, know better where they are. But to the bad or thoughtless man who lives carelessly and irreverently so near another mind, the wrong he does daily back upon himself recoils. A Cyrus, an Abradatus knows where he stands.

But to return to the thread of my subject.

Another sign of the times is furnished by the triumphs of female authorship. These have been great and constantly increasing. Women have taken possession of so many provinces for which men had pronounced them unfit, that though these still declare there are some inaccessible to them, it is difficult to say just *where* they must stop.

The shining names of famous women have cast light upon the path of the sex, and many obstructions have been removed. When a Montague could learn better than her brother, and use her lore afterward to such purpose, as an observer, it seemed amiss to hinder woman from preparing themselves to see, or from seeing all they could, when prepared. Since Somerville has achieved so much, will any young girl be prevented from seeking a knowledge of the physical sciences, if she wishes it? De Stael's name was not so clear of offence; she could not forget the woman in the thought; while she was instructing you as a mind, she wished to be admired as a woman; sentimental tears often dimmed the eagle glance. Her intellect too, with all its splendor, trained in a drawing-room, fed on flattery, was tainted and flawed; yet its beams make the obscurest school-house in New-England warmer and lighter to the little rugged girls, who are gathered together on its wooden bench. They may never through life hear her name, but she is not the less their benefactress.

The influence has been such, that the aim certainly is, now, in arranging school instruction for girls, to give them as fair a field as boys. As yet, indeed, these arrangements are made with little judgment or reflection; just as the tutors of Lady Jane Grey, and other distinguished women of her time, taught them Latin and Greek, because they knew nothing else themselves, so now the improvement in the education of girls is to be made by giving them young men as teachers, who only teach what has been taught themselves at college, while methods and topics need revision for these new subjects, which could better be made by those who had experienced the same wants. Women are, often, at the head of these institutions, but they have, as yet, seldom been thinking women, capable to organize a new whole for the wants of the time, and choose persons to officiate in the departments. And when some portion of instruction is got of a good sort from the school, the far greater proportion which is infused from the general atmosphere of society contradicts its purport. Yet books and a little elementary instruction are not furnished, in vain. Women are better aware how great and rich the universe is, not so easily blinded by narrowness or partial views of a home circle. "Her mother did so before her," is no longer a sufficient excuse. Indeed, it was never received as an excuse to mitigate the severity of censure, but was adduced as a reason, rather, why there should be no effort made for reformation.

Whether much or little has been done or will be done, whether women will add to the talent of narration, the power of systematizing, whether they will carve marble, as well as draw and paint, is not important. But that it should be acknowledged that they have intellect which needs developing, that they should not be considered complete, if beings of affection and habit alone, is important.

Yet even this acknowledgment, rather conquered by woman than proffered by man, has been sullied by the usual selfishness. So much is said of women being better educated, that they may become better companions and mothers *for men.* They should be fit for such companionship, and we have mentioned, with satisfaction, instances where it has been established. Earth knows no fairer, holier relation than that of a mother. It is one which, rightly understood, must both promote and require the highest attainments. But a being of infinite scope must not be treated with an exclusive view to any one relation. Give the soul free course, let the organization, both of body and mind, be freely developed, and the being will be fit for any and every relation to which it may be called. The intellect, no more than the sense of hearing, is to be cultivated merely that she may be a more valuable companion to man, but because the Power who gave a power, by its mere existence, signifies that it must be brought out towards perfection.

In this regard of self-dependence, and a greater simplicity and fulness of being, we must hail as a preliminary the increase of the class contemptuously designated as old maids.

We cannot wonder at the aversion with which old bachelors and old maids have been regarded. Marriage is the natural means of forming a sphere, of taking root on the earth; it requires more strength to do this without such an opening; very many have failed, and their imperfections have been in every one's way. They have been more partial, more harsh, more officious and impertinent than those compelled by severer friction to render themselves endurable. Those, who have a more full experience of the instincts, have a distrust, as to whether they can be thoroughly human and humane, such as is hinted in the saying, "Old maids' and bachelors' children are well cared for," which derides at once their ignorance and their presumption.

Yet the business of society has become so complex, that it could now scarcely be carried on without the presence of these despised auxiliaries; and detachments from the army of aunts and uncles are wanted to stop gaps in every hedge. They rove about, mental and moral Ishmaelites, pitching their tents amid the fixed and ornamented homes of men.

In a striking variety of forms, genius of late, both at home and abroad, has paid its tribute to the character of the Aunt, and the Uncle, recognizing in these personages the spiritual parents, who had supplied defects in the treatment of the busy or careless actual parents.

They also gain a wider, if not so deep experience. Those who are not intimately and permanently linked with others, are thrown upon themselves, and, if they do not there find peace and incessant life, there is none to flatter them that they are not very poor and very mean.

A position which so constantly admonishes, may be of inestimable benefit. The person may gain, undistracted by other relationships, a closer communion with the one. Such a use is made of it by saints and sybils. Or she may be one of the lay sisters of charity, a Canoness, bound by an inward vow! Or the useful drudge of all men, the Martha, much sought, little prized! Or the intellectual interpreter of the varied life she sees; the Urania of a half-formed world's twilight.

Or she may combine all these. Not "needing to care that she may please a husband," a frail and limited being, her thoughts may turn to the centre, and she may, by steadfast contemplation entering into the secret of truth and love, use it for the use of all men, instead of a chosen few, and interpret through it all the forms of life. It is possible, perhaps, to be at once a priestly servant, and a loving muse.

Saints and geniuses have often chosen a lonely position in the faith that if, undisturbed by the pressure of near ties, they would give themselves up to the inspiring spirit, it would enable them to understand and reproduce life better than actual experience could.

How many old maids take this high stand, we cannot say: it is an unhappy fact, that too many who have come before the eye are gossips rather, and not always good-natured gossips. But if these abuse, and none make the best of their vocation, yet it has not failed to produce some good results. It has been seen by others, if not by themselves, that beings, likely to be left alone, need to be fortified and furnished within themselves, and education and thought have tended more and more to regard these beings as related to absolute Being, as well as to other men. It has been seen that, as the breaking of no bond ought to destroy a man, so ought the missing of none to hinder him from growing. And thus a circumstance of the time, which springs rather from its luxury than its purity, has helped to place women on the true platform.

Perhaps the next generation, looking deeper into this matter, will find that contempt is put upon old maids, or old women at all, merely because they do not use the elixir which would keep them always young. Under its influence a gem brightens yearly which is only seen to more advantage through the fissures Time makes in the casket.* No one thinks of Michael Angelo's Persican Sibyl, or St. Theresa, or Tasso's Leonora, or the Greek Electra, as an old maid, more than of Michael Angelo or Canova as old bachelors, though all had reached the period in life's course appointed to take that degree.

See a common woman at forty; scarcely has she the remains of beauty, of any soft poetic grace which gave her attraction as woman, which kindled the hearts of those who looked on her to sparkling thoughts, or diffused round her a roseate air of gentle love. See her, who was, indeed, a lovely girl, in the coarse full-blown dahlia flower of what is commonly called matron-beauty, fat, fair, and forty, show-ily dressed, and with manners as broad and full as her frill or satin cloak. People observe, "how well she is preserved;" "she is a fine woman still," they say. This woman, whether as a duchess in dia-monds, or one of our city dames in mosaics, charms the poet's heart no more, and would look much out of place kneeling before the Ma-donna. She "does well the honors of her house," "leads society," is, in short, always spoken and thought of upholstery-wise.

Or see that care-worn face, from which every soft line is blotted, those faded eyes from which lonely tears have driven the flashes of fancy, the mild white beam of a tender enthusiasm. This woman is not so ornamental to a tea party; yet she would please better, in picture. Yet surely she, no more than the other, looks as a human being should at the end of forty years. Forty years! have they bound those brows with no garland? shed in the lamp no drop of ambrosial oil?

Not so looked the Iphigenia in Aulis. Her forty years had seen her in anguish, in sacrifice, in utter loneliness. But those pains were borne for her father and her country; the sacrifice she had made pure for herself and those around her. Wandering alone at night in the vestal solitude of her imprisoning grove, she has looked up through its "living summits" to the stars, which shed down into her aspect their own lofty melody. At forty she would not misbecome the marble.

* Appendix, F.

Not so looks the Persica. She is withered, she is faded; the drapery
that enfolds her has, in its dignity an angularity, too, that tells of age,
of sorrow, of a stern composure to the *must*. But her eye, that torch
of the soul, is untamed, and in the intensity of her reading, we see a
soul invincibly young in faith and hope. Her age is her charm, for it
is the night of the Past that gives this beacon fire leave to shine. Wither
more and more, black Chrysalid! thou dost but give the winged beauty
time to mature its splendors.

Not so looked Victoria Colonna, after her life of a great hope,
and of true conjugal fidelity. She had been, not merely a bride, but a
wife, and each hour had helped to plume the noble bird. A coronet of
pearls will not shame her brow; it is white and ample, a worthy altar
for love and thought.

Even among the North American Indians, a race of men as completely engaged in mere instinctive life as almost any in the world, and
where each chief, keeping many wives as useful servants, of course
looks with no kind eye on celibacy in woman, it was excused in the
following instance mentioned by Mrs. Jameson. A woman dreamt in
youth that she was betrothed to the Sun. She built her a wigwam apart,
filled it with emblems of her alliance, and means of an independent
life. There she passed her days, sustained by her own exertions, and
true to her supposed engagement.

In any tribe, we believe, a woman, who lived as if she was betrothed to the Sun, would be tolerated, and the rays which made her
youth blossom sweetly, would crown her with a halo in age.

There is, on this subject, a nobler view than heretofore, if not the
noblest, and improvement here must coincide with that in the view
taken of marriage.

We must have units before we can have union, says one of the
ripe thinkers of the times.

If larger intellectual resources begin to be deemed needful to
woman, still more is a spiritual dignity in her, or even the mere assumption of it, looked upon with respect. Joanna Southcote and
Mother Anne Lee are sure of a band of disciples; Ecstatica, Dolorosa,
of enraptured believers who will visit them in their lowly huts, and
wait for days to revere them in their trances. The foreign noble tra-
verses land and sea to hear a few words from the lips of the lowly
peasant girl, whom he believes especially visited by the Most High.
Very beautiful, in this way, was the influence of the invalid of St.
Petersburg, as described by De Maistre.

Mysticism, which may be defined as the brooding soul of the

world, cannot fail of its oracular promise as to woman. "The mothers"—"The mother of all things," are expressions of thought which lead the mind towards this side of universal growth. Whenever a mystical whisper was heard, from Behmen down to St. Simon, sprang up the thought, that, if it be true, as the legend says, that humanity withers through a fault committed by and a curse laid upon woman, through her pure child, or influence, shall the new Adam, the redemption, arise. Innocence is to be replaced by virtue, dependence by a willing submission, in the heart of the Virgin Mother of the new race.

The spiritual tendency is towards the elevation of woman, but the intellectual by itself is not so. Plato sometimes seems penetrated by that high idea of love, which considers man and woman as the twofold expression of one thought. This the angel of Swedenborg, the angel of the coming age, cannot surpass, but only explain more fully. But then again Plato, the man of intellect, treats woman in the Republic as property, and, in the Timæus, says that man, if he misuse the privileges of one life, shall be degraded into the form of woman, and then, if he do not redeem himself, into that of a bird. This, as I said above, expresses most happily how anti-poetical is this state of mind. For the poet, contemplating the world of things, selects various birds as the symbols of his most gracious and ethereal thoughts, just as he calls upon his genius, as muse, rather than as God. But the intellect, cold, is ever more masculine than feminine; warmed by emotion, it rushes towards mother earth, and puts on the forms of beauty.

The electrical, the magnetic element in woman has not been fairly brought out at any period. Every thing might be expected from it; she has far more of it than man. This is commonly expressed by saying that her intuitions are more rapid and more correct. You will often see men of high intellect absolutely stupid in regard to the atmospheric changes, the fine invisible links which connect the forms of life around them, while common women, if pure and modest, so that a vulgar self do not overshadow the mental eye, will seize and delineate these with unerring discrimination.

Women who combine this organization with creative genius, are very commonly unhappy at present. They see too much to act in conformity with those around them, and their quick impulses seem folly to those who do not discern the motives. This is an usual effect of the apparition of genius, whether in man or woman, but is more frequent with regard to the latter, because a harmony, an obvious order and self-restraining decorum, is most expected from her.

Then women of genius, even more than men, are likely to be

enslaved by an impassioned sensibility. The world repels them more rudely, and they are of weaker bodily frame.

Those, who seem overladen with electricity, frighten those around them. "When she merely enters the room, I am what the French call *herissé*," said a man of petty feelings and worldly character of such a woman, whose depth of eye and powerful motion announced the conductor of the mysterious fluid.

Wo to such a woman who finds herself linked to such a man in bonds too close. It is the cruellest of errors. He will detest her with all the bitterness of wounded self-love. He will take the whole prejudice of manhood upon himself, and to the utmost of his power imprison and torture her by its imperious rigors.

Yet, allow room enough, and the electric fluid will be found to invigorate and embellish, not destroy life. Such women are the great actresses, the songsters. Such traits we read in a late searching, though too French analysis of the character of Mademoiselle Rachel, by a modern La Rochefoucoult. The Greeks thus represent the muses; they have not the golden serenity of Apollo; they are *over*-flowed with thought; there is something tragic in their air. Such are the Sibyls of Guercino, the eye is over-full of expression, dilated and lustrous; it seems to have drawn the whole being into it.

Sickness is the frequent result of this over-charged existence. To this region, however misunderstood, or interpreted with presumptuous carelessness, belong the phenomena of magnetism, or mesmerism, as it is now often called, where the trance of the Ecstatica purports to be produced by the agency of one human being on another, instead of, as in her case, direct from the spirit.

The worlding has his sneer at this as at the services of religion. "The churches can always be filled with women." "Show me a man in one of your magnetic states, and I will believe."

Women are, indeed, the easy victims both of priest-craft and self-delusion, but this would not be, if the intellect was developed in proportion to the other powers. They would, then, have a regulator, and be more in equipoise, yet must retain the same nervous susceptibility, while their physical structure is such as it is.

It is with just that hope, that we welcome every thing that tends to strengthen the fibre and develope the nature on more sides. When the intellect and affections are in harmony; when intellectual consciousness is calm and deep; inspiration will not be confounded with fancy.

> Then, "she who advances
> With rapturous, lyrical glances,
> Singing the song of the earth, singing
> Its hymn to the Gods,"

will not be pitied, as a madwoman, nor shrunk from as unnatural.

The Greeks, who saw every thing in forms, which we are trying to ascertain as law, and classify as cause, embodied all this in the form of Cassandra. Cassandra was only unfortunate in receiving her gift too soon. The remarks, however, that the world still makes in such cases, are well expressed by the Greek dramatist.

In the Trojan Dames, there are fine touches of nature with regard to Cassandra. Hecuba shows that mixture of shame and reverence that prosaic kindred always do towards the inspired child, the poet, the elected sufferer for the race.

When the herald announces that Cassandra is chosen to be the mistress of Agamemnon, Hecuba answers, with indignation, betraying the pride and faith she involuntarily felt in this daughter.

> Hec. *The maiden of Phoebus, to whom the golden haired*
> *Gave as a privilege a virgin life!*
> Tal. *Love of the inspired maiden hath pierced him.*
> Hec. *Then cast away, my child, the sacred keys, and from thy*
> *person*
> *The consecrated garlands which thou wearest.*

Yet, when a moment after, Cassandra appears, singing, wildly, her inspired song, Hecuba calls her, "My *frantic* child."

Yet how graceful she is in her tragic *raptus*, the chorus shows.

> Chor. *How sweetly at thy house's ills thou smil'st,*
> *Chanting what, haply, thou wilt not show true.*

If Hecuba dares not trust her highest instinct about her daughter, still less can the vulgar mind of the herald Talthybius, a man not without feeling, but with no princely, no poetic blood, abide the wild prophetic mood which insults all his prejudices.

> Tal. *The venerable, and that accounted wise,*
> *Is nothing better than that of no repute,*

For the greatest king of all the Greeks,
The dear son of Atreus, is possessed with the love
Of this madwoman. I, indeed, am poor,
Yet, I would not receive her to my bed.

The royal Agamemnon could see the beauty of Cassandra, HE was not afraid of her prophetic gifts.

The best topic for a chapter on this subject in the present day, would be the history of the Seeress of Prevorst, the best observed subject of magnetism in our present times, and who, like her ancestresses of Delphos, was roused to ecstacy or phrenzy by the touch of the laurel.

I observe in her case, and in one known to me here, that, what might have been a gradual and gentle disclosure of remarkable powers, was broken and jarred into disease by an unsuitable marriage. Both these persons were unfortunate in not understanding what was involved in this relation, but acted ignorantly as their friends desired. They thought that this was the inevitable destiny of woman. But when engaged in the false position, it was impossible for them to endure its dissonances, as those of less delicate perceptions can, and the fine flow of life was checked and sullied. They grew sick, but, even so, learnt and disclosed more than those in health are wont to do.

In such cases, worldlings sneer, but reverent men learn wondrous news, either from the person observed, or by thoughts caused in themselves by the observation. Fenelon learns from Guyon, Kerner, from his Seeress, what we fain would know. But to appreciate such disclosures one must be a child, and here the phrase, "women and children" may, perhaps, be interpreted aright, that only little children shall enter into the kingdom of heaven.

All these motions of the time, tides that betoken a waxing moon, overflow upon our land. The world, at large, is readier to let woman learn and manifest the capacities of her nature than it ever was before, and here is a less encumbered field and freer air than any where else. And it ought to be so; we ought to pay for Isabella's jewels.

The names of nations are feminine—religion, virtue, and victory are feminine. To those who have a superstition, as to outward reigns, it is not without significance that the name of the queen of our motherland should at this crisis be Victoria—Victoria the First. Perhaps to us it may be given to disclose the era thus outwardly presaged.

Another Isabella too at this time ascends the throne. Might she open a new world to her sex! But, probably, these poor little women are, least of any, educated to serve as examples or inspirers for the rest. The Spanish queen is younger; we know of her that she sprained her foot the other day, dancing in her private apartments; of Victoria, that she reads aloud, in a distinct voice and agreeable manner, her addresses to parliament on certain solemn days, and, yearly, that she presents to the nation some new prop of royalty. These ladies have, very likely, been trained more completely to the puppet life than any other. The queens, who have been queens indeed, were trained by adverse circumstances to know the world around them and their own powers.

It is moving, while amusing, to read of the Scottish peasant measuring the print left by the queen's foot as she walks, and priding himself on its beauty. It is so natural to wish to find what is fair and precious in high places, so astonishing to find the Bourbon a glutton, or the Guelph a dullard or gossip.

In our own country, women are, in many respects, better situated than men. Good books are allowed, with more time to read them. They are not so early forced into the bustle of life, nor so weighed down by demands for outward success. The perpetual changes, incident to our society, make the blood circulate freely through the body politic, and, if not favorable at present to the grace and bloom of life, they are so to activity, resource, and would be to reflection, but for a low materialist tendency, from which the women are generally exempt in themselves, though its existence, among the men, has a tendency to repress their impulses and make them doubt their instincts, thus, often, paralyzing their action during the best years.

But they have time to think, and no traditions chain them, and few conventionalities compared with what must be met in other nations. There is no reason why they should not discover that the secrets of nature are open, the revelations of the spirit waiting for whoever will seek them. When the mind is once awakened to this consciousness, it will not be restrained by the habits of the past, but fly to seek the seeds of a heavenly future.

Their employments are more favorable to meditation than those of men.

Woman is not addressed religiously here, more than elsewhere. She is told she should be worthy to be the mother of a Washington, or the companion of some good man. But in many, many instances, she has already learnt that all bribes have the same flaw; that truth and good are to be sought solely for their own sakes. And, already, an ideal sweetness floats over many forms, shines in many eyes.

Already deep questions are put by young girls on the great theme: What shall I do to enter upon the eternal life?

Men are very courteous to them. They praise them often, check them seldom. There is chivalry in the feeling towards "the ladies," which gives them the best seats in the stage-coach, frequent admission, not only to lectures of all sorts, but to courts of justice, halls of legislature, reform conventions. The newspaper editor "would be better pleased that the Lady's Book should be filled up exclusively by ladies. It would then, indeed, be a true gem, worthy to be presented by young men to the mistresses of their affections." Can gallantry go further?

In this country is venerated, wherever seen, the character which Goethe spoke of as Ideal, which he saw actualized in his friend and patroness, the Grande Duchess Amelia. "The excellent woman is she, who, if the husband dies, can be a father to the children." And this, if read aright, tells a great deal.

Women who speak in public, if they have a moral power, such as has been felt from Angelina Grimke and Abby Kelly; that is, if they speak for conscience' sake, to serve a cause which they hold sacred, invariably subdue the prejudices of their hearers, and excite an interest proportionate to the aversion with which it had been the purpose to regard them.

A passage in a private letter so happily illustrates this, that it must be inserted here.

Abby Kelly in the Town-House of ———.

"The scene was not unheroic—to see that woman, true to humanity and her own nature, a centre of rude eyes and tongues, even gentlemen feeling licensed to make part of a species of mob around a female out of her sphere. As she took her seat in the desk amid the great noise, and in the throng, full, like a wave, of something to ensue, I saw her humanity in a gentleness and unpretension, tenderly open to the sphere around her, and, had she not been supported by the power of the will of genuineness and principle, she would have failed. It led her to prayer, which, in woman especially, is childlike; sensibility and will going to the side of God and looking up to him; and humanity was poured out in aspiration.

"She acted like a gentle hero, with her mild decision and womanly calmness. All heroism is mild and quiet and gentle, for it is life and possession, and combativeness and firmness show a want of actualness. She is as earnest, fresh, and simple as when she first entered the crusade. I think she did much good, more than the men in her place could do, for woman feels more as being and reproducing, this brings the subject more into home relations. Men speak through, and mostly from intellect, and this addresses itself in others, which creates and is combative."

Not easily shall we find elsewhere, or before this time, any written observations on the same subject, so delicate and profound.

The late Dr. Channing, whose enlarged and tender and religious nature, shared every onward impulse of his time, though his thoughts followed his wishes with a deliberative caution, which belonged to his habits and temperament, was greatly interested in these expectations for women. His own treatment of them was absolutely and thoroughly religious. He regarded them as souls, each of which had a destiny of its own, incalculable to other minds, and whose leading it must follow, guided by the light of a private conscience. He had sentiment, delicacy, kindness, taste; but they were all pervaded and ruled by this one thought, that all beings had souls, and must vindicate their own inheritance. Thus all beings were treated by him with an equal, and sweet, though solemn, courtesy. The young and unknown, the woman and the child, all felt themselves regarded with an infinite expectation, from which there was no reaction to vulgar prejudice. He demanded of all he met, to use his favorite phrase, "great truths."

His memory, every way dear and reverend, is, by many, especially cherished for this intercourse of unbroken respect.

At one time, when the progress of Harriet Martineau through this country, Angelina Grimke's appearance in public, and the visit of Mrs. Jameson had turned his thoughts to this subject, he expressed high hopes as to what the coming era would bring to woman. He had been much pleased with the dignified courage of Mrs. Jameson in taking up the defence of her sex, in a way from which women usually shrink, because, if they express themselves on such subjects with sufficient force and clearness to do any good, they are exposed to assaults whose vulgarity makes them painful. In intercourse with such a woman, he had shared her indignation at the base injustice, in many respects, and in many regions, done to the sex; and been led to think of it far more than ever before. He seemed to think that he might some time write upon the subject. That his aid is withdrawn from the cause is a subject of great regret, for, on this question as on others, he would have known how to sum up the evidence and take, in the noblest spirit, middle ground. He always furnished a platform on which opposing parties could stand, and look at one another under the influence of his mildness and enlightened candor.

Two younger thinkers, men both, have uttered noble prophecies, auspicious for woman. Kinmont, all whose thoughts tended towards the establishment of the reign of love and peace, thought that the inevitable means of this would be an increased predominance given to the idea of woman. Had he lived longer, to see the growth of the peace party, the reforms in life and medical practice which seek to substitute water for wine and drugs, pulse for animal food, he would have been confirmed in his view of the way in which the desired changes are to be effected.

In this connection, I must mention Shelley, who, like all men of genius, shared the feminine development, and, unlike many, knew it. His life was one of the first pulse-beats in the present reform-growth, He, too, abhorred blood and heat, and, by his system and his song, tended to reinstate a plant-like gentleness in the development of energy. In harmony with this, his ideas of marriage were lofty, and, of course, no less so of woman, her nature, and destiny.

For woman, if, by a sympathy as to outward condition she is led to aid the enfranchisement of the slave, must be no less so, by inward tendency, to favor measures which promise to bring the world more thoroughly and deeply into harmony with her nature. When the lamb takes place of the lion as the emblem of nations, both women and men will be as children of one spirit, perpetual learners of the word and doers thereof, not hearers only.

A writer in the New-York Pathfinder, in two articles headed "Femality," has uttered a still more pregnant word than any we have named. He views woman truly from the soul, and not from society, and the depth and leading of his thoughts are proportionably remarkable. He views the feminine nature as a harmonizer of the vehement elements, and this has often been hinted elsewhere; but what he expresses most forcibly is the lyrical, the inspiring, and inspired apprehensiveness of her being.

This view being identical with what I have before attempted to indicate, as to her superior susceptibility to magnetic or electric influence, I will now try to express myself more fully.

There are two aspects of woman's nature, represented by the ancients as Muse and Minerva. It is the former to which the writer in the Pathfinder looks. It is the latter which Wordsworth has in mind, when he says—

With a placid brow,
Which woman ne'er should forfeit, keep they vow.

The especial genius of woman I believe to be electrical in movement, intuitive in function, spiritual in tendency. She excels not so easily in classification, or re-creation, as in an instinctive seizure of causes, and a simple breathing out of what she receives that has the singleness of life, rather than the selecting and energizing of art.

More native is it to her to be the living model of the artist than to set apart from herself any one form in objective reality; more native to inspire and receive the poem, than to create it. In so far as soul is in her completely developed, all soul is the same; but as far as it is modified in her as woman, it flows, it breathes, it sings, rather than deposits soil, or finishes work, and that which is especially feminine flushes, in blossom, the face of earth, and pervades, like air and water, all this seeming solid globe, daily renewing and purifying its life. Such may be the especially feminine element, spoken of as Femality. But it is no more the order of nature that it should be incarnated pure in any form, than that the masculine energy should exist unmingled with it in any form.

Male and female represent the two sides of the great radical dualism. But, in fact, they are perpetually passing into one another. Fluid hardens to solid, solid rushes to fluid. There is no wholly masculine man, no purely feminine woman.

History jeers at the attempts of physiologists to bind great original laws by the forms which flow from them. They make a rule; they say from observation, what can and cannot be. In vain! Nature provides exceptions to every rule. She sends women to battle, and sets Hercules spinning; she enables woman to bear immense burdens, cold, and frost; she enables the man, who feels maternal love, to nourish his infant like a mother. Of late she plays still gayer pranks. Not only she deprives organizations, but organs, of a necessary end. She enables people to read with the top of the head, and see with the pit of the stomach. Presently she will make a female Newton, and a male Syren.

Man partakes of the feminine in the Apollo, woman of the masculine as Minerva.

What I mean by the Muse is the unimpeded clearness of the intuitive powers which a perfectly truthful adherence to every admonition of the higher instincts would bring to a finely organized human being. It may appear as prophecy or as poesy. It enabled Cassandra to foresee the results of actions passing round her; the Seeress to behold the true character of the person through the mask of his customary life. (Sometimes she saw a feminine form behind the man, sometimes the reverse.) It enabled the daughter of Linnæus to see the soul of the flower exhaling from the flower.* It gave a man, but a poet man, the power of which he thus speaks: "Often in my contemplation of nature, radiant intimations, and as it were sheaves of light appear before me as to the facts of cosmogony in which my mind has, perhaps, taken especial part." He wisely adds, "but it is necessary with earnestness to verify the knowledge we gain by these flashes of light." And none should forget this. Sight must be verified by life before it can deserve the honors of piety and genius. Yet sight comes first, and of this sight of the world of causes, this approximation to the region of primitive motions, women I hold to be especially capable. Even without equal freedom with the other sex, they have already shown themselves so, and should these faculties have free play, I believe they will open new, deeper and purer sources of joyous inspiration than have as yet refreshed the earth.

Let us be wise and not impede the soul. Let her work as she will. Let us have one creative energy, one incessant revelation. Let it take what form it will, and let us not bind it by the past to man or woman, black or white. Jove sprang from Rhea, Pallas from Jove. So let it be.

If it has been the tendency of these remarks to call woman rather to the Minerva side,—if I, unlike the more generous writer, have spoken from society no less than the soul,—let it be pardoned! It is love that has caused this, love for many incarcerated souls, that might be freed, could the idea of religious self-dependence be established in them, could the weakening habit of dependence on others be broken up.

Proclus teaches that every life has, in its sphere, a totality or wholeness of the animating powers of the other spheres; having only, as its own characteristic, a predominance of some one power. Thus Jupiter comprises, within himself, the other twelve powers, which stand thus: The first triad is *demiurgic* or *fabricative*, i.e., Jupiter, Neptune, Vulcan; the second, *defensive*, Vesta, Minerva, Mars; the third, *vivific*, Ceres, Juno, Diana; and the fourth, Mercury, Venus, Apollo, *elevating and harmonic*. In the sphere of Jupiter, energy is predominant—with Venus, beauty; but each comprehends and apprehends all the others.

---

* The daughter of Linnaeus states, that, while looking steadfastly at the red lily, she saw its spirit hovering above it, as a red flame. It is true, this, like many fair spirit-stories, may be explained away as an optical illusion, but its poetic beauty and meaning would, even then, make it valuable, as an illustration of the spiritual fact.

When the same community of life and consciousness of mind begins among men, humanity will have, positively and finally, subjugated its brute elements and Titanic childhood; criticism will have perished; arbitrary limits and ignorant censure be impossible; all will have entered upon the liberty of law, and the harmony of common growth.

Then Apollo will sing to his lyre what Vulcan forges on the anvil, and the Muse weave anew the tapestries of Minerva.

It is, therefore, only in the present crisis that the preference is given to Minerva. The power of continence must establish the legitimacy of freedom, the power of self-poise the perfection of motion.

Every relation, every gradation of nature is incalculably precious, but only to the soul which is poised upon itself, and to whom no loss, no change, can bring dull discord, for it is in harmony with the central soul.

If any individual live too much in relations, so that he becomes a stranger to the resources of his own nature, he falls, after a while, into a distraction, or imbecility, from which he can only be cured by a time of isolation, which gives the renovating fountains time to rise up. With a society it is the same. Many minds, deprived of the traditionary or instinctive means of passing a cheerful existence, must find help in self-impulse, or perish. It is therefore that, while any elevation, in the view of union, is to be hailed with joy, we shall not decline celibacy as the great fact of the time. It is one from which no vow, no arrangement, can at present save a thinking mind. For now the rowers are pausing on their oars; they wait a change before they can pull together. All tends to illustrate the thought of a wise cotemporary. Union is only possible to those who are units. To be fit for relations in time, souls, whether of man or woman, must be able to do without them in the spirit.

It is therefore that I would have woman lay aside all thought, such as she habitually cherishes, of being taught and led by men. I would have her, like the Indian girl, dedicate herself to the Sun, the Sun of Truth, and go no where if his beams did not make clear the path. I would have her free from compromise, from complaisance, from helplessness, because I would have her good enough and strong enough to love one and all beings, from the fulness, not the poverty of being.

Men, as at present instructed, will not help this work, because they also are under the slavery of habit. I have seen with delight their poetic impulses. A sister is the fairest ideal, and how nobly Wordsworth, and even Byron, have written of a sister.

There is no sweeter sight than to see a father with his little daughter. Very vulgar men become refined to the eye when leading a little girl by the hand. At that moment the right relation between the sexes seems established, and you feel as if the man would aid in the noblest purpose, if you ask him in behalf of his little daughter. Once two fine figures stood before me, thus. The father of very intellectual aspect, his falcon eye softened by affection as he looked down on his fair child, she the image of himself, only more graceful and brilliant in expression. I was reminded of Southey's Kehama; when lo, the dream was rudely broken. They were talking of education, and he said,

"I shall not have Maria brought too forward. If she knows too much, she will never find a husband; superior women hardly ever can."

"Surely," said his wife, with a blush, "you wish Maria to be as good and wise as she can, whether it will help her to marriage or not."

"No," he persisted, "I want her to have a sphere and a home, and some one to protect her when I am gone."

It was a trifling incident, but made a deep impression. I felt that the holiest relations fail to instruct the unprepared and perverted mind. If this man, indeed, could have looked at it on the other side, he was the last that would have been willing to have been taken himself for the home and protection he could give, but would have been much more likely to repeat the tale of Alcibiades with his phials.

But men do *not* look at both sides, and women must leave off asking them and being influenced by them, but retire within themselves, and explore the groundwork of life till they find their peculiar secret. Then, when they come forth again, renovated and baptized, they will know how to turn all dross to gold, and will be rich and free though they live in a hut, tranquil, if in a crowd. Then their sweet singing shall not be from passionate impulse, but the lyrical overflow of a divine rapture, and a new music shall be evolved from this many-chorded world.

Grant her, then, for a while, the armor and the javelin. Let her put from her the press of other minds and meditate in virgin loneliness. The same idea shall re-appear in due time as Muse, or Ceres, the all-kindly patient Earth-Spirit.

Among the throng of symptoms which denote the present tendency to a crisis in the life of woman, which resembles the change from girlhood with its beautiful instincts, but unharmonized thoughts, its blind pupilage and restless seeking, to self-possessed, wise, and graceful womanhood, I have attempted to select a few.

One of prominent interest is the unison of three male minds, upon the subject, which, for width of culture, power of self-concentration and dignity of aim, take rank as the prophets of the coming age, while their histories and labors are rooted in the past.

Swedenborg came, he tells us, to interpret the past revelation and unfold a new. He announces the new church that is to prepare the way for the New Jerusalem, a city built of precious stones, hardened and purified by secret processes in the veins of earth through the ages.

Swedenborg approximated to that harmony between the scientific and poetic lives of mind, which we hope from the perfected man. The links that bind together the realms of nature, the mysteries that accompany her births and growths, were unusually plain to him. He seems a man to whom insight was given at a period when the mental frame was sufficiently matured to retain and express its gifts.

His views of woman are, in the main, satisfactory. In some details, we may object to them as, in all his system, there are still remains of what is arbitrary and seemingly groundless; fancies that show the marks of old habits, and a nature as yet not thoroughly leavened with the spiritual leaven. At least so it seems to me now. I speak reverently, for I find such reason to venerate Swedenborg, from an imperfect knowledge of his mind, that I feel one more perfect might explain to me much that does not now secure my sympathy.

His idea of woman is sufficiently large and noble to interpose no obstacle to her progress. His idea of marriage is consequently sufficient. Man and woman share an angelic ministry, the union is from one to one, permanent and pure.

As the New Church extends its ranks, the needs of woman must be more considered.

Quakerism also establishes woman on a sufficient equality with man. But though the original thought of Quakerism is pure, its scope is too narrow, and its influence, having established a certain amount of good and made clear some truth, must, by degrees, be merged in one of wider range.* The mind of Swedenborg appeals to the various nature of man and allows room for æsthetic culture and the free expression of energy.

As apostle of the new order, of the social fabric that is to rise from love, and supersede the old that was based on strife, Charles Fourier comes next, expressing, in an outward order, many facts of which

---

* In worship at stated periods, in daily expression, whether by word or deed, the Quakers have placed woman on the same platform with man. Can any one assert that they have reason to repent this?

Swedenborg saw the secret springs. The mind of Fourier, though grand and clear, was, in some respects, superficial. He was a stranger to the highest experiences. His eye was fixed on the outward more than the inward needs of man. Yet he, too, was a seer of the divine order, in its musical expression, if not in its poetic soul. He has filled one department of instruction for the new era, and the harmony in action, and freedom for individual growth he hopes shall exist; and if the methods he proposes should not prove the true ones, yet his fair propositions shall give many hints, and make room for the inspiration needed for such.

He, too, places woman on an entire equality with man, and wishes to give to one as to the other that independence which must result from intellectual and practical development.

Those who will consult him for no other reason, might do so to see how the energies of woman may be made available in the pecuniary way. The object of Fourier was to give her the needed means of self help, that she might dignify and unfold her life for her own happiness, and that of society. The many, now, who see their daughters liable to destitution, or vice to escape from it, may be interested to examine the means, if they have not yet soul enough to appreciate the ends he proposes.

On the opposite side of the advancing army, leads the great apostle of individual culture, Goethe. Swedenborg makes organization and union the necessary results of solitary thought. Fourier, whose nature was, above all, constructive, looked to them too exclusively. Better institutions, he thought, will make better men. Goethe expressed, in every way, the other side. If one man could present better forms, the rest could not use them till ripe for them.

Fourier says, As the institutions, so the men! All follies are excusable and natural under bad institutions.

Goethe thinks, As the man, so the institutions! There is no excuse for ignorance and folly. A man can grow in any place, if he will.

Ay! but Goethe, bad institutions are prison walls and impure air that make him stupid, so that he does not will.

And thou, Fourier, do not expect to change mankind at once, or even "in three generations" by arrangement of groups and series, or flourish of trumpets for attractive industry. If these attempts are made by unready men, they will fail.

Yet we prize the theory of Fourier no less than the profound suggestion of Goethe. Both are educating the age to a clearer consciousness of what man needs, what man can be, and better life must ensue.

Goethe, proceeding on his own track, elevating the human being in the most imperfect states of society, by continual efforts at self-culture, takes as good care of women as of men. His mother, the bold, gay Frau Aja, with such playful freedom of nature; the wise and gentle maiden, known in his youth, over whose sickly solitude "the Holy Ghost brooded as a dove;" his sister, the intellectual woman *par excellence*: the Duchess Amelia; Lili, who combined the character of the woman of the world with the lyrical sweetness of the shepherdess, on whose chaste and noble breast flowers and gems were equally at home; all these had supplied abundant suggestions to his mind, as to the wants and the possible excellencies of woman. And, from his poetic soul, grew up forms new and more admirable than life has yet produced, for whom his clear eye marked out paths in the future.

In Faust, we see the redeeming power, which, at present, upholds woman, while waiting for a better day, in Margaret. The lovely little girl, pure in instinct, ignorant in mind, is misled and profaned by man abusing her confidence.* To the Mater *Dolorosa* she appeals for aid. It is given to the soul, if not against outward sorrow; and the maiden, enlightened by her sufferings, refusing to receive temporal salvation by the aid of an evil power, obtains the eternal in its stead.

In the second part, the intellectual man, after all his manifold strivings, owes to the interposition of her whom he had betrayed *his* salvation. She intercedes, this time herself a glorified spirit, with the Mater *Gloriosa*.

Leonora, too, is woman, as we see her now, pure, thoughtful, refined by much acquaintance with grief.

Iphigenia he speaks of in his journals as his "daughter," and she is the daughter† whom a man will wish, even if he has chosen his wife from very mean motives. She is the virgin, steadfast soul, to whom falsehood is more dreadful than any other death.

But it is to Wilhelm Meister's Apprenticeship and Wandering

---

* As Faust says, her only fault was a "Kindly delusion,"—"ein guter wahn."
† Goethe was as false to his ideas in practice, as Lord Herbert. And his punishment was the just and usual one of connections formed beneath the standard of right, from the impulses of the baser self. Iphigenia was the worthy daughter of his mind, but the son, child of his degrading connection in actual life, corresponded with that connection. This son, on whom Goethe vainly lavished so much thought and care, was like his mother, and like Goethe's attachment for his mother, "This young man," says a late well informed writer, (M. Henri Blaze,) "Wieland, with good reason, called the son of the servant, *der Sohn der Magd*. He inherited from his father only his name and his *physique*."

Years that I would especially refer, as these volumes contain the sum of the Sage's observations during a long life, as to what man should do, under present circumstances, to obtain mastery over outward, through an initiation into inward life, and severe discipline of faculty.

As Wilhelm advances in the upward path he becomes acquainted with better forms of woman by knowing how to seek, and how to prize them when found. For the weak and immature man will, often, admire a superior woman, but he will not be able to abide by a feeling, which is too severe a tax on his habitual existence. But, with Wilhelm, the gradation is natural and expresses ascent in the scale of being. At first he finds charm in Mariana and Philina, very common forms of feminine character, not without redeeming traits, no less than charms, but without wisdom or purity. Soon he is attended by Mignon, the finest expression ever yet given to what I have called the lyrical element in woman. She is a child, but too full-grown for this man; he loves, but cannot follow her; yet is the association not without an enduring influence. Poesy has been domesticated in his life, and, though he strives to bind down her heavenward impulse, as art or apothegm, these are only the tents, beneath which he may sojourn for a while, but which may be easily struck, and carried on limitless wanderings.

Advancing into the region of thought, he encounters a wise philanthropy in Natalia, (instructed, let us observe, by an *uncle*,) practical judgment and the outward economy of life in Theresa, pure devotion in the Fair Saint.

Farther and last he comes to the house of Macaria, the soul of a star, *i. e.* a pure and perfected intelligence embodied in feminine form, and the centre of a world whose members revolve harmoniously round her. She instructs him in the archives of a rich human history, and introduces him to the contemplation of the heavens.

From the hours passed by the side of Mariana to these with Macaria, is a wide distance for human feet to traverse. Nor has Wilhelm travelled so far, seen and suffered so much in vain. He now begins to study how he may aid the next generation; he sees objects in harmonious arrangement, and from his observations deduces precepts by which to guide his course as a teacher and a master, "help-full, comfort-full."

In all these expressions of woman, the aim of Goethe is satisfactory to me. He aims at a pure self-subsistence, and free development of any powers with which they may be gifted by nature as much for them as for men. They are units, addressed as souls. Accordingly the meeting between man and woman, as represented by him, is equal and noble, and, if he does not depict marriage, he makes it possible.

In the Macaria, bound with the heavenly bodies in fixed revolutions, the centre of all relations, herself unrelated, he expresses the Minerva side of feminine nature. It was not by chance that Goethe gave her this name. Macaria, the daughter of Hercules, who offered herself as a victim for the good of her country, was canonized by the Greeks, and worshipped as the Goddess of true Felicity. Goethe has embodied this Felicity as the Serenity that arises from Wisdom, a Wisdom, such as the Jewish wise man venerated, alike instructed in the designs of heaven, and the methods necessary to carry them into effect upon earth.

Mignon is the electrical, inspired, lyrical nature. And wherever it appears we echo in our aspirations that of the child,

> *So let me seem until I be:—*
> *Take not the white robe away.*
>
>   *   *   *   **
>
> *Though I lived without care and toil,*
> *Yet felt I sharp pain enough,*
> *Make me again forever young.*

All these women, though we see them in relations, we can think of as unrelated. They all are very individual, yet seem, nowhere, restrained. They satisfy for the present, yet arouse an infinite expectation.

The economist Theresa, the benevolent Natalia, the fair Saint, have chosen a path, but their thoughts are not narrowed to it. The functions of life to them are not ends, but suggestions.

Thus, to them, all things are important, because none is necessary. Their different characters have fair play, and each is beautiful in its minute indications, for nothing is enforced or conventional, but every thing, however slight, grows from the essential life of the being.

Mignon and Theresa wear male attire when they like, and it is graceful for them to do so, while Macaria is confined to her arm-chair behind the green curtain, and the Fair Saint could not bear a speck of dust on her robe.

All things are in their places in this little world, because all is natural and free, just as "there is room for everything out of doors." Yet all is rounded in by natural harmony, which will always arise where Truth and Love are sought in the light of Freedom.

Goethe's book bodes an era of freedom like its own of "extraordinary generous seeking," and new revelations. New individualities shall be developed in the actual world, which shall advance upon it as gently as the figures come out upon his canvass.

I have indicated on this point the coincidence between his hopes and those of Fourier, though his are directed by an infinitely higher and deeper knowledge of human nature. But, for our present purpose, it is sufficient to show how surely these different paths have conducted to the same end two earnest thinkers. In some other place I wish to point out similar coincidences between Goethe's model school and the plans of Fourier, which may cast light upon the page of prophecy.

Many women have observed that the time drew nigh for a better care of the sex, and have thrown out hints that may be useful. Among these may be mentioned—

Miss Edgeworth, who, although restrained by the habits of her age and country, and belonging more to the eighteenth than the nineteenth century, has done excellently as far as she goes. She had a horror of sentimentalism, and the love of notoriety, and saw how likely women, in the early stages of culture, were to aim at these. Therefore she bent her efforts to recommending domestic life. But the methods she recommends are such as will fit a character for any position to which it may be called. She taught a contempt of falsehood, no less in its most graceful, than in its meanest apparitions; the cultivation of a clear, independent judgment, and adherence to its dictates; habits of various and liberal study and employment, and a capacity for friendship. Her standard of character is the same for both sexes. Truth, honor, enlightened benevolence, and aspiration after knowledge. Of poetry, she knows nothing, and her religion consists in honor and loyalty to obligations once assumed, in short, in "the great idea of duty which holds us upright." Her whole tendency is practical.

Mrs. Jameson is a sentimentalist, and, therefore, suits us ill in some respects, but she is full of talent, has a just and refined perception of the beautiful, and a genuine courage when she finds it necessary. She does not appear to have thought out, thoroughly, the subject on which we are engaged, and her opinions, expressed as opinions, are sometimes inconsistent with one another. But from the refined perception of character, admirable suggestions are given in her "Women of Shakspeare," and "Loves of the Poets."

But that for which I most respect her is the decision with which she speaks on a subject which refined women are usually afraid to approach, for fear of the insult and scurril jest they may encounter; but on which she neither can nor will restrain the indignation of a full heart. I refer to the degradation of a large portion of women into the sold and polluted slaves of men, and the daring with which the legislator and man of the world lifts his head beneath the heavens, and says "this must be; it cannot be helped; it is a necessary accompaniment of *civilization*."

So speaks the *citizen*. Man born of woman, the father of daughters, declares that he will and must buy the comforts and commercial advantages of his London, Vienna, Paris, New-York, by conniving at the moral death, the damnation, so far as the action of society can insure it, of thousands of women for each splendid metropolis.

O men! I speak not to you. It is true that your wickedness (for you must not deny that, at least, nine thousand out of the ten fall through the vanity you have systematically flattered, or the promises you have treacherously broken;) yes, it is true that your wickedness is its own punishment. Your forms degraded and your eyes clouded by secret sin; natural harmony broken and fineness of perception destroyed in your mental and bodily organization; God and love shut out from your hearts by the foul visitants you have permitted there; incapable of pure marriage; incapable of pure parentage; incapable of worship; oh wretched men, your sin is its own punishment! You have lost the world in losing yourselves. Who ruins another has admitted the worm to the root of his own tree, and the fuller ye fill the cup of evil, the deeper must be your own bitter draught. But I speak not to you—you need to teach and warn one another. And more than one voice rises in earnestness. And all that *women* say to the heart that has once chosen the evil path, is considered prudery, or ignorance, or perhaps, a feebleness of nature which exempts from similar temptations.

But to you, women, American women, a few words may not be addressed in vain. One here and there may listen.

You know how it was in the Oriental clime. One man, if wealth permitted, had several wives and many hand-maidens. The chastity and equality of genuine marriage, with "the thousand decencies that flow," from its communion, the precious virtues that gradually may be matured, within its enclosure, were unknown.

But this man did not wrong according to his light. What he did, he might publish to God and Man; it was not a wicked secret that hid in vile lurking-places and dens, like the banquets of beasts of prey.

Those women were not lost, not polluted in their own eyes, nor those of others. If they were not in a state of knowledge and virtue, they were at least in one of comparative innocence.

You know how it was with the natives of this continent. A chief had many wives whom he maintained and who did his household work; those women were but servants, still they enjoyed the respect of others and their own. They lived together in peace. They knew that a sin against what was in their nation esteemed virtue, would be as strictly punished in man as in woman.

Now pass to the countries where marriage is between one and one. I will not speak of the Pagan nations, but come to those which own the Christian rule. We all know what that enjoins; there is a standard to appeal to.

See now, not the mass of the people, for we all know that it is a proverb and a bitter jest to speak of the "down-trodden million." We know that, down to our own time, a principle never had so fair a chance to pervade the mass of the people, but that we must solicit its illustration from select examples.

Take the Paladin, take the Poet. Did *they* believe purity more impossible to man than to woman? Did they wish woman to believe that man was less amenable to higher motives, that pure aspirations would not guard him against bad passions, that honorable employments and temperate habits would not keep him free from slavery to the body. O no! Love was to them a part of heaven, and they could not even wish to receive its happiness, unless assured of being worthy of it. Its highest happiness to them was, that it made them wish to be worthy. They courted probation. They wished not the title of knight, till the banner had been upheld in the heats of battle, amid the rout of cowards.

I ask of you, young girls—I do not mean *you*, whose heart is that of an old coxcomb, though your locks have not yet lost their sunny tinge. Not of you whose whole character is tainted with vanity, inherited or taught, who have early learnt the love of coquettish excitement, and whose eyes rove restlessly in search of a "conquest" or a "beau." You who are ashamed *not* to be seen by others the mark of the most contemptuous flattery or injurious desire. To such I do not speak. But to thee, maiden, who, if not so fair, art yet of that unpolluted nature which Milton saw when he dreamed of Comus and the Paradise. Thou, child of an unprofaned wedlock, brought up amid the teachings of the woods and fields, kept fancy-free by useful employment and a free flight into the heaven of thought, loving to please only those whom thou wouldst not be ashamed to love; I ask of thee, whose cheek has not forgotten its blush nor thy heart its lark-like hopes, if he whom thou mayst hope the Father will send thee, as the companion of life's toils and joys, is not to thy thought pure? Is not manliness to thy thought purity, *not* lawlessness? Can his lips speak falsely? Can he do, in secret, what he could not avow to the mother that bore him? O say, dost thou not look for a heart free, open as thine own, all whose thoughts may be avowed, incapable of wronging the innocent, or still farther degrading the fallen. A man, in short, in whom brute nature is entirely subject to the impulses of his better self.

Yes! it was thus that thou didst hope, for I have many, many times seen the image of a future life, of a destined spouse, painted on the tablets of a virgin heart.

It might be that she was not true to these hopes. She was taken into what is called "the world," froth and scum as it mostly is on the social caldron. There, she saw fair woman carried in the waltz close to the heart of a being who appeared to her a Satyr. Being warned by a male friend that he was in fact of that class, and not fit for such familiar nearness to a chaste being, the advised replied that "women should know nothing about such things." She saw one fairer given in wedlock to a man of the same class. "Papa and mamma said that 'all men were faulty, at some time in their lives; they had a great many temptations. Frederick would be so happy at home; he would not want to do wrong." She turned to the married women; they, oh tenfold horror! laughed at her supposing "men were like women." Sometimes, I say, she was not true and either sadly accommodated herself to "woman's lot," or acquired a taste for satyr-society, like some of the Nymphs, and all the Bacchanals of old. But to these who could not and would not accept a mess of pottage, or a Circe cup, in lieu of their birthright, and to these others who have yet their choice to make, I say, Courage! I have some words of cheer for you. A man, himself of unbroken purity, reported to me the words of a foreign artist, that "the world would never be better till men subjected themselves to the same laws they had imposed on women;" that artist, he added, was true to the thought. The same was true of Canova, the same of Beethoven. "Like each other demi-god, they kept themselves free from stain," and Michael Angelo, looking over here from the loneliness of his century, might meet some eyes that need not shun his glance.

In private life, I am assured by men who are not so sustained and occupied by the worship of pure beauty, that a similar consecration is possible, is practiced. That many men feel that no temptation can be too strong for the will of man, if he invokes the aid of the Spirit instead of seeking extenuation from the brute alliances of his nature. In short, what the child fancies is really true, though almost the whole world declares it a lie. Man is a child of God; and if he seek His guidance to keep the heart with diligence, it will be so given that all the issues of life may be pure. Life will then be a temple.

> The temple round
> Spread green the pleasant ground;
> The fair colonnade
> Be of pure marble pillars made;
> Strong to sustain the roof,
>   Time and tempest proof,
> Yet, amidst which, the lightest breeze
>   Can play as it please;
>   The audience hall
>   Be free to all
>   Who revere
> The Power worshipped here,
>   Sole guide of youth
>   Unswerving Truth:
>   In the inmost shrine
>   Stands the image divine,
>   Only seen
> By those whose deeds have worthy been—
>   Priestlike clean.
> Those, who initiated are,
>   Declare,
>   As the hours
> Usher in varying hopes and powers;
>   It changes its face,
>   It changes its age,
>   Now a young beaming Grace,
>   Now Nestorian Sage:
>   But, to the pure in heart,
>   This shape of primal art
>   In age is fair,
>   In youth seems wise,
>   Beyond compare,
>   Above surprise;
> What it teaches native seems

> *Its new lore our ancient dreams;*
> *Incense rises from the ground,*
> *Music flows around;*
> *Firm rest the feet below, clear gaze the eyes above,*
> *When Truth to point the way through Life assumes the wand of*
> *Love;*
> *But, if she cast aside the robe of green,*
> *Winter's silver sheen,*
> *White, pure as light,*
> *Makes gentle shroud as worthy weed as bridal robe had been.**

We are now in a transition state, and but few steps have yet been taken. From polygamy, Europe passed to the marriage *de convenance.* This was scarcely an improvement. An attempt was then made to substitute genuine marriage, (the mutual choice of souls inducing a permanent union,) as yet baffled on every side by the haste, the ignorance, or the impurity of man.

Where man assumes a high principle to which he is not yet ripened; it will happen, for a long time, that the few will be nobler than before; the many worse. Thus now. In the country of Sidney and Milton, the metropolis is a den of wickedness, and a stye of sensuality; in the country of Lady Russell, the custom of English Peeresses, of selling their daughters to the highest bidder, is made the theme and jest of fashionable novels by unthinking children who would stare at the idea of sending them to a Turkish slave dealer, though the circumstances of the bargain are there less degrading, as the will and thoughts of the person sold are not so degraded by it, and it is not done in defiance of an acknowledged law of right in the land and the age.

I must here add that I do not believe there ever was put upon record more depravation of man, and more despicable frivolity of thought and aim in woman, than in the novels which purport to give the picture of English fashionable life, which are read with such favor in our drawing rooms, and give the tone to the manners of some cir-

---

* *(As described by the historian.)*

The temple of Juno is like what the character of woman should be.
Columns! graceful decorums, attractive yet sheltering.
Porch! noble inviting aspect of the life.
Kaos! receives the worshippers. See here the statue of the Divinity.
Ophistodomos! Sanctuary where the most precious possessions were
kept safe from the hand of the spoiler and the eye of the world.

cles. Compared with the hardhearted cold folly there described, crime is hopeful, for it, at least, shows some power remaining in the mental constitution.

To return: Attention has been awakened among men to the stains of celibacy, and the profanations of marriage. They begin to write about it and lecture about it. It is the tendency now to endeavor to help the erring by showing them the physical law. This is wise and excellent; but forget not the better half. Cold bathing and exercise will not suffice to keep a life pure, without an inward baptism and noble and exhilarating employment for the thoughts and the passions. Early marriages are desirable, but if, (and the world is now so out of joint that there are a hundred thousand chances to one against it,) a man does not early, or at all, find the person to whom he can be united in the marriage of souls, will you give him in the marriage *de convenance*, or if not married, can you find no way for him to lead a virtuous and happy life? Think of it well, ye who think yourselves better than pagans, for many of *them* knew this sure way.*

To you, women of America, it is more especially my business to address myself on this subject, and my advice may be classed under three heads:

Clear your souls from the taint of vanity.

Do not rejoice in conquests, either that your power to allure may be seen by other women, or for the pleasure of rousing passionate feelings that gratify your love of excitement.

It must happen, no doubt, that frank and generous women will excite love they do not reciprocate, but, in nine cases out of ten, the woman has, half consciously, done much to excite. In this case she shall not be held guiltless, either as to the unhappiness or injury to the lover. Pure love, inspired by a worthy object, must ennoble and bless, whether mutual or not; but that which is excited by coquettish attraction of any grade of refinement, must cause bitterness and doubt, as

---

* The Persian sacred books, the Desatir, describe the great and holy prince Ky Khosrou, as being "an angel, and the son of an angel," one to whom the Supreme says, "Thou are not absent from before me for one twinkling of an eye. I am never out of thy heart. And I am contained in nothing but in thy heart, and in a heart like thy heart. And I am nearer unto thee than thou art to thyself." This Prince had in his Golden Seraglio three ladies of surpassing beauty, and all four, in this royal monastery, passed their lives, and left the world, as virgins.

The Persian people had no scepticism when the history of such a mind was narrated. They were Catholics.

to the reality of human goodness, so soon as the flush of passion is over. And that you may avoid all taste for these false pleasures

> *Steep the soul*
> *In one pure love, and it will last thee long.*

The love of truth, the love of excellence, which, whether you clothe them in the person of a special object or not, will have power to save you from following Duessa, and lead you in the green glades where Una's feet have trod.

It was on this one subject that a venerable champion of good, the last representative of the spirit which sanctified the revolution and gave our country such a sunlight of hope in the eyes of the nations, the same who lately in Boston offered anew to the young men the pledge taken by the young men of his day, offered, also, his counsel, on being addressed by the principal of a girl's school, thus:

REPLY OF MR. ADAMS

Mr. Adams was so deeply affected by the address of Miss Foster, as to be for some time inaudible. When heard, he spoke as follows:

"This is the first instance in which a lady has thus addressed me personally; and I trust that all the ladies present will be able sufficiently to enter into my feelings to know, that I am more affected by this honor, than by any other I could have received.

"You have been pleased, Madam, to allude to the character of my father, and the history of my family, and their services to the country. It is indeed true, that from the existence of the Republic as an independent nation, my father and myself have been in the public service of the country, almost without interruption. I came into the world, as a person having personal responsibilities, with the Declaration of Independence, which constituted us a nation. I was a child at that time, and had then perhaps the greatest of blessings that can be bestowed on man—a mother who was anxious and capable to form her children to what they ought to be. From that mother I derived whatever instruction—religious especially, and moral—has pervaded a long life; I will not say perfectly, and as it ought to be; but I will say, because it is justice only to the memory of her whom I revere, that if, in the course of my life, there has been any imperfection, or deviation from what she taught me, the fault is mine, and not hers.

"With such a mother, and such other relations with the sex, of sister, wife, and daughter, it has been the perpetual instruction of my life to love and revere the female sex. And in order to carry that sentiment of love and reverence to its highest degree of perfection, I know of nothing that exists in human society better adapted to produce that result, than institutions of the character that I have now the honor to address.

"I have been taught, as I have said, through the course of my life, to love and to revere the female sex; but I have been taught, also— and that lesson has perhaps impressed itself on my mind even more strongly, it may be, than the other—I have been taught not to flatter them. It is not unusual in the intercourse of man with the other sex— and especially for young men—to think, that the way to win the hearts of ladies is by flattery.—To love and to revere the sex, is what I think the duty of man; but *not to flatter them;* and this I would say to the young ladies here; and if they, and others present, will allow me, with all the authority which nearly four score years may have with those who have not yet attained one score—I would say to them what I have no doubt they say to themselves, and are taught here, not to take the flattery of men as proof of perfection.

"I am now, however, I fear, assuming too much of a character that does not exactly belong to me. I therefore conclude, by assuring you, Madam, that your reception of me has affected me, as you perceive, more than I can express in words; and that I shall offer my best prayers, till my latest hour, to the Creator of us all, that this institution especially, and all others of a similar kind, designed to form the female mind to wisdom and virtue, may prosper to the end of time."

It will be interesting to add here the character of Mr. Adams's mother, as drawn by her husband, the first John Adams, in a family letter* written just before his death.

"I have reserved for the last the life of Lady Russell. This I have not yet read, because I read it more than forty years ago. On this hangs a tale which you ought to know and communicate it to your children. I bought the life and letters of Lady Russell, in the year 1775, and sent it to your grandmother, with an express intent and desire, that she should consider it a mirror in which to contemplate herself; for, at that time, I thought it extremely probable, from the daring and dangerous career I was determined to run, that she would one day find herself in the situation of Lady Russell, her husband without a head.

* Journal and Correspondence of Miss Adams, vol. i. p. 246.

This lady was more beautiful than Lady Russell, had a brighter genius, more information, a more refined taste, and, at least, her equal in the virtues of the heart; equal fortitude and firmness of character, equal resignation to the will of Heaven, equal in all the virtues and graces of the christian life. Like Lady Russell, she never, by word or look, discouraged me from running all hazards for the salvation of my country's liberties; she was willing to share with me, and that her children should share with us both, in all the dangerous consequences we had to hazard."

Will a woman who loves flattery or an aimless excitement, who wastes the flower of her mind on transitory sentiments, ever be loved with a love like that, when fifty years trial have entitled to the privileges of "the golden marriage?"

Such was the love of the iron-handed warrior for her, not his hand-maid, but his help-meet:

"Whom God loves, to him gives he such a wife."

I find the whole of what I want in this relation, in the two epithets by which Milton makes Adam address *his* wife.

In the intercourse of every day he begins:

> *Daughter of God and man, accomplished Eve.* *

In a moment of stronger feeling,

> *Daughter of God and man,* IMMORTAL *Eve.*

What majesty in the cadence of the line; what dignity, what reverence in the attitude, both of giver and receiver!

The woman who permits, in her life, the alloy of vanity; the woman who lives upon flattery, coarse or fine, shall never be thus addressed. She is *not* immortal as far as her will is concerned, and every woman who does so creates miasma, whose spread is indefinite. The hand, which casts into the waters of life a stone of offence, knows not how far the circles thus caused, may spread their agitations.

A little while since, I was at one of the most fashionable places of public resort. I saw there many women, dressed without regard to the season or the demands of the place, in apery, or, as it looked, in mockery of European fashions. I saw their eyes restlessly courting attention. I saw the way in which it was paid, the style of devotion, almost an

* See Appendix, H.

open sneer, which it pleased those ladies to receive from men whose expression marked their own low position in the moral and intellectual world. Those women went to their pillows with their heads full of folly, their hearts of jealousy, or gratified vanity: those men, with the low opinion they already entertained of woman confirmed. These were American *ladies;* i. e., they were of that class who have wealth and leisure to make full use of the day, and confer benefits on others. They were of that class whom the possession of external advantages makes of pernicious example to many, if these advantages be misused.

Soon after, I met a circle of women, stamped by society as among the most degraded of their sex. "How," it was asked of them, "did you come here?" for, by the society that I saw in the former place, they were shut up in a prison. The causes were not difficult to trace: love of dress, love of flattery, love of excitement. They had not dresses like the other ladies, so they stole them; they could not pay for flattery by distinctions, and the dower of a worldly marriage, so they paid by the profanation of their persons. In excitement, more and more madly sought from day to day, they drowned the voice of conscience.

Now I ask you, my sisters, if the women at the fashionable house be not answerable for those women being in the prison?

As to position in the world of souls, we may suppose the women of the prison stood fairest, both because they had misused less light, and because loneliness and sorrow had brought some of them to feel the need of better life, nearer truth and good. This was no merit in them, being an effect of circumstance, but it was hopeful. But you, my friends, (and some of you I have already met,) consecrate yourselves without waiting for reproof, in free love and unbroken energy, to win and to diffuse a better life. Offer beauty, talents, riches, on the altar; thus shall ye keep spotless your own hearts, and be visibly or invisibly the angels to others.

I would urge upon those women who have not yet considered this subject, to do so. Do not forget the unfortunates who dare not cross your guarded way. If it do not suit you to act with those who have organized measures of reform, then hold not yourself excused from acting in private. Seek out these degraded women, give them tender sympathy, counsel, employment. Take the place of mothers, such as might have saved them originally.

If you can do little for those already under the ban of the world, and the best considered efforts have often failed, from a want of strength in those unhappy ones to bear up against the sting of shame and the prejudices of the world, which makes them seek oblivion again in their old excitements, you will at least leave a sense of love and justice in their hearts that will prevent their becoming utterly imbittered and corrupt. And you may learn the means of prevention for those yet uninjured. There will be found in a diffusion of mental culture, simple tastes, best taught by your example, a genuine self-respect, and above all, what the influence of man tends to hide from woman, the love and fear of a divine, in preference to a human tribunal.

But suppose you save many who would have lost their bodily innocence (for as to mental, the loss of that is incalculably more general,) through mere vanity and folly; there still remain many, the prey and spoil of the brute passions of man. For the stories frequent in our newspapers outshame antiquity, and vie with the horrors of war.

As to this, it must be considered that, as the vanity and proneness to seduction of the imprisoned women represented a general degradation in their sex; so do these acts a still more general and worse in the male. Where so many are weak it is natural there should be many lost, where legislators admit that ten thousand prostitutes are a fair proportion to one city, and husbands tell their wives that it is folly to expect chastity from men, it is inevitable that there should be many monsters of vice.

I must in this place mention, with respect and gratitude, the conduct of Mrs. Child in the case of Amelia Norman. The action and speech of this lady was of straight-forward nobleness, undeterred by custom or cavil from duty towards an injured sister. She showed the case and the arguments the counsel against the prisoner had the assurance to use in their true light to the public. She put the case on the only ground of religion and equity. She was successful in arresting the attention of many who had before shrugged their shoulders, and let sin pass as necessarily a part of the company of men. They begin to ask whether virtue is not possible, perhaps necessary, to man as well as to woman. They begin to fear that the perdition of a woman must involve that of a man. This is a crisis. The results of this case will be important.

In this connection I must mention Eugene Sue, the French novelist, several of whose works have been lately transplanted among us, as having the true spirit of reform as to women. Like every other French writer, he is still tainted with the transmissions of the old regime. Still falsehood may be permitted for the sake of advancing truth, evil as the way to good. Even George Sand, who would trample on every graceful decorum, and every human law for the sake of a sincere life, does not see that she violates it by making her heroines able to tell falsehoods in a good cause. These French writers need ever to be confronted by the clear perception of the English and German mind, that the only good man, consequently the only good reformer, is he

> *Who bases good on good alone, and owes*
> *To virtue every triumph that he knows.*

Still, Sue has the heart of a reformer, and especially towards women, he sees what they need, and what causes are injuring them. From the histories of Fleur de Marie and La Louve, from the lovely and independent character of Rigolette, from the distortion given to Matilda's mind, by the present views of marriage, and from the truly noble and immortal character of the "hump-backed Sempstress" in the "Wandering Jew," may be gathered much that shall elucidate doubt and direct inquiry on this subject. In reform, as in philosophy, the French are the interpreters to the civilized world. Their own attainments are not great, but they make clear the past, and break down barriers to the future.

Observe that the good man of Sue is pure as Sir Charles Grandison.

Apropos to Sir Charles, women are accustomed to be told by men that the reform is to come *from them*. "You," say the men, "must frown upon vice, you must decline the attentions of the corrupt, you must not submit to the will of your husband when it seems to you unworthy, but give the laws in marriage, and redeem it from its present sensual and mental pollutions."

This seems to us hard. Men have, indeed, been, for more than a hundred years, rating women for countenancing vice. But at the same time, they have carefully hid from them its nature, so that the preference often shown by women for bad men, arises rather from a confused idea that they are bold and adventurous, acquainted with regions which women are forbidden to explore, and the curiosity that ensues, than a corrupt heart in the woman. As to marriage it has been inculcated on women for centuries, that men have not only stronger passions than they, but of a sort that it would be shameful for them to share or even understand. That, therefore, they must "confide in their husbands," i. e., submit implicitly to their will. That the least appearance of coldness or withdrawal, from whatever cause, in the wife is wicked, because liable to turn her husband's thoughts to illicit indulgence; for a man is so constituted that he must indulge his passions or die!

Accordingly a great part of women look upon men as a kind of wild beasts, but "suppose they are all alike;" the unmarried are assured by the married that, "if they knew men as they do," i. e., by being married to them, "they would not expect continence or self-government from them."

I might accumulate illustrations on this theme, drawn from acquaintance with the histories of women, which would startle and grieve all thinking men, but I forbear. Let Sir Charles Grandison preach to his own sex, or if none there be, who feels himself able to speak with authority from a life unspotted in will or deed, let those who are convinced of the practicability and need of a pure life, as the foreign artist was, advise the others, and warn them by their own example, if need be.

The following passage from a female writer on female affairs, expresses a prevalent way of thinking on this subject.

"It may be that a young woman, exempt from all motives of vanity, determines to take for a husband a man who does not inspire her with a very decided inclination. Imperious circumstances, the evident interest of her family, or the danger of a suffering celibacy, may explain such a resolution. If, however, she were to endeavor to surmount a personal repugnance, we should look upon this as *injudicious*. Such a rebellion of nature marks the limit that the influence of parents, or the self-sacrifice of the young girl, should never pass. *We shall be told that this repugnance is an affair of the imagination;* it may be so; but imagination is a power which it is temerity to brave; and its antipathy is more difficult to conquer than its preference."*

Among ourselves, the exhibition of such a repugnance from a woman who had been given in marriage "by advice of friends," was treated by an eminent physician as sufficient proof of insanity. If he had said sufficient cause for it, he would have been nearer right.

It has been suggested by men who were pained by seeing bad men admitted, freely, to the society of modest women, thereby encouraged to vice by impunity, and corrupting the atmosphere of homes; that there should be a senate of the matrons in each city and town, who should decide what candidates were fit for admission to their houses and the society of their daughters.†

Such a plan might have excellent results, but it argues a moral

---

* Madame Necker de Saussure.
† See Goethe's Tasso. "A synod of good women should decide,"—if the golden age is to be restored.

dignity and decision, which does not yet exist, and needs to be induced by knowledge and reflection. It has been the tone to keep women ignorant on these subjects, or when they were not, to command that they should seem so. "It is indelicate," says the father or husband, "to inquire into the private character of such an one. It is sufficient that I do not think him unfit to visit you." And so, this man, who would not tolerate these pages in his house, "unfit for family reading," because they speak plainly, introduces there a man whose shame is written on his brow, as well as the open secret of the whole town, and, presently, if *respectable* still, and rich enough, gives him his daughter to wife. The mother affects ignorance, "supposing he is no worse than most men." The daughter *is* ignorant; something in the mind of the new spouse seems strange to her, but she supposes it is "woman's lot" not to be perfectly happy in her affections; she has always heard, "men could not understand women," so she weeps alone, or takes to dress and the duties of the house. The husband, of course, makes no avowal, and dreams of no redemption.

"In the heart of every young woman," says the female writer, above quoted, addressing herself to the husband, "depend upon it, there is a fund of exalted ideas; she conceals, represses, without succeeding in smothering them. *So long as these ideas in your wife are directed to* YOU, *they are, no doubt, innocent,* but take care that they be not accompanied with *too much* pain. In other respects, also, spare her delicacy. Let all the antecedent parts of your life, if there are such, which would give her pain, be concealed from her; *her happiness and her respect for you would suffer from this misplaced confidence.* Allow her to retain that flower of purity, *which should distinguish her in your eyes from every other woman.*" We should think so, truly, under this canon. Such a man must esteem purity an exotic that could only be preserved by the greatest care. Of the degree of mental intimacy possible, in such a marriage, let every one judge for himself!

On this subject, let every woman, who has once begun to think, examine herself, see whether she does not suppose virtue possible and necessary to man, and whether she would not desire for her son a virtue which aimed at a fitness for a divine life, and involved, if not asceticism, that degree of power over the lower self, which shall "not exterminate the passions, but keep them chained at the feet of reason." The passions, like fire, are a bad master; but confine them to the hearth and the altar, and they give life to the social economy, and make each sacrifice meet for heaven.

When many women have thought upon this subject, some will be fit for the Senate, and one such Senate in operation would affect the morals of the civilized world.

At present I look to the young. As preparatory to the Senate, I should like to see a society of novices, such as the world has never yet seen, bound by no oath, wearing no badge. In place of an oath they should have a religious faith in the capacity of man for virtue; instead of a badge, should wear in the heart a firm resolve not to stop short of the destiny promised him as a son of God. Their service should be action and conservatism, not of old habits, but of a better nature, enlightened by hopes that daily grow brighter.

If sin was to remain in the world, it should not be by their connivance at its stay, or one moment's concession to its claims.

They should succor the oppressed, and pay to the upright the reverence due in hero-worship by seeking to emulate them. They would not denounce the willingly bad, but they could not be with them, for the two classes could not breathe the same atmosphere.

They would heed no detention from the time-serving, the worldly and the timid.

They could love no pleasures that were not innocent and capable of good fruit.

I saw, in a foreign paper, the title now given to a party abroad, "Los Exaltados." Such would be the title now given these children by the world: Los Exaltados, Las Exaltadas; but the world would not sneer always, for from them would issue a virtue by which it would, at last, be exalted too.

I have in my eye a youth and a maiden whom I look to as the nucleus of such a class. They are both in early youth, both as yet uncontaminated, both aspiring, without rashness, both thoughtful, both capable of deep affection, both of strong nature and sweet feelings, both capable of large mental development. They reside in different regions of earth, but their place in the soul is the same. To them I look, as, perhaps, the harbingers and leaders of a new era, for never yet have I known minds so truly virgin, without narrowness or ignorance.

When men call upon women to redeem them, they mean such maidens. But such are not easily formed under the present influences of society. As there are more such young men to help give a different tone, there will be more such maidens.

The English novelist, D'Israeli, has, in his novel of the "Young Duke," made a man of the most depraved stock be redeemed by a woman who despises him when he has only the brilliant mask of fortune and beauty to cover the poverty of his heart and brain, but knows how to encourage him when he enters on a better course. But this woman was educated by a father who valued character in women.

Still there will come now and then, one who will, as I hope of my young Exaltada, be example and instruction to the rest. It was not the opinion of woman current among Jewish men that formed the character of the mother of Jesus.

Since the sliding and backsliding men of the world, no less than the mystics declare that, as through woman man was lost, so through woman must man be redeemed, the time must be at hand. When she knows herself indeed as "accomplished," still more as "immortal Eve," this may be.

As an immortal, she may also know and inspire immortal love, a happiness not to be dreamed of under the circumstances advised in the last quotation. Where love is based on concealment, it must, of course, disappear when the soul enters the scene of clear vision!

And, without this hope, how worthless every plan, every bond, every power!

"The giants," said the Scandinavian Saga, "had induced Loke, (the spirit that hovers between good and ill,) to steal for them Iduna, (Goddess of Immortality,) and her apples of pure gold. He lured her out, by promising to show, on a marvellous tree he had discovered, apples beautiful as her own, if she would only take them with her for a comparison. Thus, having lured her beyond the heavenly domain, she was seized and carried away captive by the powers of misrule.

As now the gods could not find their friend Iduna, they were confused with grief; indeed they began visibly to grow old and gray. Discords arose, and love grew cold. Indeed, Odur, spouse of the goddess of love and beauty, wandered away and returned no more. At last, however, the gods, discovering the treachery of Loke, obliged him to win back Iduna from the prison in which she sat mourning. He changed himself into a falcon, and brought her back as a swallow, fiercely pursued by the Giant King, in the form of an eagle. So she strives to return among us, light and small as a swallow. We must welcome her form as the speck on the sky that assures the glad blue of Summer. Yet one swallow does not make a summer. Let us solicit them in flights and flocks!

Returning from the future to the present, let us see what forms Iduna takes, as she moves along the declivity of centuries to the valley where the lily flower may concentrate all its fragrance.

It would seem as if this time were not very near to one fresh from books, such as I have of late been—no: *not* reading, but sighing over. A crowd of books having been sent me since my friends knew me to be engaged in this way, on Woman's "Sphere," Woman's "Mission," and Woman's "Destiny," I believe that almost all that is extant of formal precept has come under my eye. Among these I read with refreshment, a little one called "The Whole Duty of Woman," "indited by a noble lady at the request of a noble lord," and which has this much of nobleness, that the view it takes is a religious one. It aims to fit woman for heaven, the main bent of most of the others is to fit her to please, or, at least, not to disturb a husband.

Among these I select as a favorable specimen, the book I have already quoted, "The Study* of the Life of Woman, by Madame Necker de Saussure, of Geneva, translated from the French." This book was published at Philadelphia, and has been read with much favor here. Madame Necker is the cousin of Madame de Stael, and has taken from her works the motto prefixed to this.

"Cette vie n'a quelque prix que si elle sert a' l'education morale de notre cœur."

Mde. Necker is, by nature, capable of entire consistency in the application of this motto, and, therefore, the qualifications she makes, in the instructions given to her own sex, show forcibly the weight which still paralyzes and distorts the energies of that sex.

The book is rich in passages marked by feeling and good suggestions, but taken in the whole the impression it leaves is this:

Woman is, and *shall remain* inferior to man and subject to his will, and, in endeavoring to aid her, we must anxiously avoid any thing that can be misconstrued into expression of the contrary opinion, else the men will be alarmed, and combine to defeat our efforts.

The present is a good time for these efforts, for men are less occupied about women than formerly. Let us, then, seize upon the occasion, and do what we can to make our lot tolerable. But we must sedulously avoid encroaching on the territory of man. If we study natural history, our observations may be made useful, by some male naturalist; if we draw well, we may make our services acceptable to the artists. But our names must not be known, and, to bring these labors to any result, we must take some man for our head, and be his hands.

The lot of woman is sad. She is constituted to expect and need a happiness that cannot exist on earth. She must stifle such aspirations

---

* This title seems to be incorrectly translated from the French. I have not seen the original.

within her secret heart, and fit herself, as well as she can, for a life of resignations and consolations.

She will be very lonely while living with her husband. She must not expect to open her heart to him fully, or that, after marriage, he will be capable of the refined service of love. The man is not born for the woman, only the woman for the man. "Men cannot understand the hearts of women." The life of woman must be outwardly a well-intentioned, cheerful dissimulation of her real life.

Naturally, the feelings of the mother, at the birth of a female child, resemble those of the Paraguay woman, described by Southey as lamenting in such heart-breaking tones that her mother did not kill her the hour she was born. "Her mother, who knew what the life of a woman must be;"—or those women seen at the north by Sir A. Mackenzie, who performed this pious duty towards female infants whenever they had an opportunity.

"After the first delight, the young mother experiences feelings a little different, according as the birth of a son or a daughter has been announced.

"Is it a son? A sort of glory swells at this thought the heart of the mother; she seems to feel that she is entitled to gratitude. She has given a citizen, a defender to her country. To her husband an heir of his name, to herself a protector. And yet the contrast of all these fine titles with this being, so humble, soon strikes her. At the aspect of this frail treasure, opposite feelings agitate her heart; she seems to recognize in him *a nature superior to her own,* but subjected to a low condition, and she honors a future greatness in the object of extreme compassion. Somewhat of that respect and adoration for a feeble child, of which some fine pictures offer the expression in the features of the happy Mary, seem reproduced with the young mother who has given birth to a son.

"Is it a daughter? There is usually a slight degree of regret; so deeply rooted is the idea of the superiority of man in happiness and dignity, and yet, as she looks upon this child, she is more and more *softened* towards it—a deep sympathy—a sentiment of identity with this delicate being takes possession of her; an extreme pity for so much weakness, a more pressing need of prayer stirs her heart. Whatever sorrows she may have felt, she dreads for her daughter; but she will guide her to become much wiser, much better than herself. And then the gayety, the frivolity of the young woman have their turn. This little creature is a flower to cultivate, a doll to decorate."

Similar sadness at the birth of a daughter I have heard mothers express not unfrequently.

As to this living so entirely for men, I should think when it was proposed to women they would feel, at least, some spark of the old spirit of races allied to our own. If he is to be my bridegroom *and lord*, cries Brunhilda,* he must first be able to pass through fire and water. I will serve at the banquet, says the Walkyrie, but only him who, in the trial of deadly combat, has shown himself a hero.

If women are to be bond-maids, let it be to men superior to women in fortitude, in aspiration, in moral power, in refined sense of beauty! You who give yourselves "to be supported," or because "one must love something," are they who make the lot of the sex such that mothers are sad when daughters are born.

It marks the state of feeling on this subject that it was mentioned, as a bitter censure on a woman who had influence over those younger than herself. "She makes those girls want to see heroes?"

"And will that hurt them?"

"Certainly; how *can* you ask? They will find none, and so they will never be married."

"*Get* married" is the usual phrase, and the one that correctly indicates the thought, but the speakers, on this occasion, were persons too outwardly refined to use it. They were ashamed of the word, but not of the thing. Madame Necker, however, sees good possible in celibacy.

Indeed, I know not how the subject could be better illustrated, than by separating the wheat from the chaff in Madame Neckar's book; place them in two heaps and then summon the reader to choose; giving him first a near-sighted glass to examine the two; it might be a christian, an astronomical, or an artist glass, any kind of good glass to obviate acquired defects in the eye. I would lay any wager on the result.

But time permits not here a prolonged analysis. I have given the clues for fault-finding.

As a specimen of the good take the following passage, on the phenomena of what I have spoken of, as the lyrical or electric element in woman.

"Women have been seen to show themselves poets in the most pathetic pantomimic scenes, where all the passions were depicted full

---

* See the Nibelungen Lays.

of beauty; and these poets used a language unknown to themselves, and the performance once over, their inspiration was a forgotten dream. Without doubt there is an interior development to beings so gifted, but their sole mode of communication with us is their talent. They are, in all besides, the inhabitants of another planet."

Similar observations have been made by those who have seen the women at Irish wakes, or the funeral ceremonies of modern Greece or Brittany, at times when excitement gave the impulse to genius; but, apparently, without a thought that these rare powers belonged to no other planet, but were a high development of the growth of this, and might by wise and reverent treatment, be made to inform and embellish the scenes of every day. But, when woman has her fair chance, they will do so, and the poem of the hour will vie with that of the ages. I come now with satisfaction to my own country, and to a writer, a female writer, whom I have selected as the clearest, wisest, and kindliest, who has as yet, used pen here on these subjects. This is Miss Sedgwick.

Miss Sedgwick, though she inclines to the private path, and wishes that, by the cultivation of character, might should vindicate right, sets limits nowhere, and her objects and inducements are pure. They are the free and careful cultivation of the powers that have been given, with an aim at moral and intellectual perfection. Her speech is moderate and sane, but never palsied by fear or sceptical caution.

Herself a fine example of the independent and beneficent existence that intellect and character can give to woman, no less than man, if she know how to seek and prize it; also that the intellect need not absorb or weaken, but rather will refine and invigorate the affections, the teachings of her practical good sense come with great force, and cannot fail to avail much. Every way her writings please me both as to the means and the ends. I am pleased at the stress she lays on observance of the physical laws, because the true reason is given. Only in a strong and clean body can the soul do its message fitly.

She shows the meaning of the respect paid to personal neatness both in the indispensable form of cleanliness, and of that love of order and arrangement, that must issue from a true harmony of feeling.

The praises of cold water seem to me an excellent sign in the age. They denote a tendency to the true life. We are now to have, as a remedy for ills, not orvietan, or opium, or any quack medicine, but plenty of air and water, with due attention to warmth and freedom in dress, and simplicity of diet.

Every day we observe signs that the natural feelings on these subjects are about to be reinstated, and the body to claim care as the abode and organ of the soul, not as the tool of servile labor, or the object of voluptuous indulgence.

A poor woman who had passed through the lowest grades of ignominy, seemed to think she had never been wholly lost, "for," said she, "I would always have good under-clothes;" and, indeed, who could doubt that this denoted the remains of private self-respect in the mind?

A woman of excellent sense said, "it might seem childish, but to her one of the most favorable signs of the times, was that the ladies had been persuaded to give up corsets."

Yes! let us give up all artificial means of distortion. Let life be healthy, pure, all of a piece. Miss Sedgwick, in teaching that domestics must have the means of bathing as much as their mistresses, and time, too, to bathe, has symbolized one of the most important of human rights.

Another interesting sign of the time is the influence exercised by two women, Miss Martineau and Miss Barrett, from their sick rooms. The lamp of life which, if it had been fed only by the affections, depended on precarious human relations, would scarce have been able to maintain a feeble glare in the lonely prison, now shines far and wide over the nations, cheering fellow sufferers and hallowing the joy of the healthful.

These persons need not health or youth, or the charms of personal presence, to make their thoughts available. A few more such, and old woman* shall not be the synonyme for imbecility, nor old maid a term of contempt, nor woman be spoken of as a reed shaken in the wind.

It is time, indeed, that men and women both should cease to grow old in any other way than as the tree does, full of grace and honor. The hair of the artist turns white, but his eyes shines clearer than ever, and we feel that age brings him maturity, not decay. So would it be with all were the springs of immortal refreshment but unsealed within the soul, then like these women they would see, from the onely chamber window, the glories of the universe; or, shut in darkness, be visited by angels.

I now touch on my own place and day, and, as I write, events are occurring that threaten the fair fabric approached by so long an avenue. Week before last the Gentile was requested to aid the Jew to return to Palestine, for the Millennium, the reign of the Son of Mary,

* An apposite passage is quoted in Appendix F.

was near. Just now, at high and solemn mass, thanks were returned to the Virgin for having delivered O'Connell from unjust imprisonment, in requital of his having consecrated to her the league formed in behalf of Liberty on Tara's Hill. But, last week brought news which threatens that a cause identical with the enfranchisement of Jews, Irish, women, ay, and of Americans in general, too, is in danger, for the choice of the people threatens to rivet the chains of slavery and the leprosy of sin permanently on this nation, through the annexation of Texas!

Ah! if this should take place, who will dare again to feel the throb of heavenly hope, as to the destiny of this country? The noble thought that gave unity to all our knowledge, harmony to all our designs;— the thought that the progress of history had brought on the era, the tissue of prophecies pointed out the spot, where humanity was, at last, to have a fair chance to know itself, and all men be born free and equal for the eagle's flight, flutters as if about to leave the breast, which, deprived of it, will have no more a nation, no more a home on earth.

Women of my country!—Exaltadas! if such there be,—Women of English, old English nobleness, who understand the courage of Boadicea, the sacrifice of Godiva, the power of Queen Emma to tread the red hot iron unharmed. Women who share the nature of Mrs. Hutchinson, Lady Russell, and the mothers of our own revolution: have you nothing to do with this? You see the men, how they are willing to sell shamelessly, the happiness of countless generations of fellow-creatures, the honor of their country, and their immortal souls, for a money market and political power. Do you not feel within you that which can reprove them, which can check, which can convince them? You would not speak in vain; whether each in her own home, or banded in unison.

Tell these men that you will not accept the glittering baubles, spacious dwellings, and plentiful service, they mean to offer you through these means. Tell them that the heart of women demands nobleness and honor in man, and that, if they have not purity, have not mercy, they are no longer fathers, lovers, husbands, sons of yours.

This cause is your own, for as I have before said, there is a reason why the foes of African slavery seek more freedom for women; but put it not upon that ground, but on the ground of right.

If you have a power, it is a moral power. The films of interest are not so close around you as around the men. If you will but think, you cannot fail to wish to save the country from this disgrace. Let not slip the occasion, but do something to lift off the curse incurred by Eve.

You have heard the women engaged in the abolition movement accused of boldness, because they lifted the voice in public, and lifted the latch of the stranger. But were these acts, whether performed judiciously or no, *so* bold as to dare before God and man to partake the fruits of such offence as this?

You hear much of the modesty of your sex. Preserve it by filling the mind with noble desires that shall ward off the corruptions of vanity and idleness. A profligate woman, who left her accustomed haunts and took service in a New York boarding-house, said "she had never heard talk so vile at the Five Points, as from the ladies at the boarding-house." And why? Because they were idle; because, having nothing worthy to engage them, they dwelt, with unnatural curiosity, on the ill they dared not go to see.

It will not so much injure your modesty to have your name, by the unthinking, coupled with idle blame, as to have upon your soul the weight of not trying to save a whole race of women from the scorn that is put upon *their* modesty.

Think of this well! I entreat, I conjure you, before it is too late. It is my belief that something effectual might be done by women, if they would only consider the subject, and enter upon it in the true spirit, a spirit gentle, but firm, and which feared the offence of none, save One who is of purer eyes than to behold iniquity.

And now I have designated in outline, if not in fulness, the stream which is ever flowing from the heights of my thought.

In the earlier tract, I was told, I did not make my meaning sufficiently clear. In this I have consequently tried to illustrate it in various ways, and may have been guilty of much repetition. Yet, as I am anxious to leave no room for doubt, I shall venture to retrace, once more, the scope of my design in points, as was done in old-fashioned sermons.

Man is a being of two-fold relations, to nature beneath, and intelligences above him. The earth is his school, if not his birth-place: God his object: life and thought, his means of interpreting nature, and aspiring to God.

Only a fraction of this purpose is accomplished in the life of any one man. Its entire accomplishment is to be hoped only from the sum of the lives of men, or man considered as a whole.

As this whole has one soul and one body, any injury or obstruction to a part, or to the meanest member, affects the whole. Man can never be perfectly happy or virtuous, till all men are so.

To address man wisely, you must not forget that his life is partly animal, subject to the same laws with nature.

But you cannot address him wisely unless you consider him still more as soul, and appreciate the conditions and destiny of soul.

The growth of man is two-fold, masculine and feminine.

As far as these two methods can be distinguished they are so as Energy and Harmony.

Power and Beauty.

Intellect and Love.

Or by some such rude classification, for we have not language primitive and pure enough to express such ideas with precision.

These two sides are supposed to be expressed in man and woman, that is, as the more and less, for the faculties have not been given pure to either, but only in preponderance. There are also exceptions in great number, such as men of far more beauty than power, and the reverse. But as a general rule, it seems to have been the intention to give a preponderance on the one side, that is called masculine, and on the other, one that is called feminine.

There cannot be a doubt that, if these two developments were in perfect harmony, they would correspond to and fulfil one another, like hemispheres, or the tenor and bass in music.

But there is no perfect harmony in human nature; and the two parts answer one another only now and then, or, if there be a persistent consonance, it can only be traced, at long intervals, instead of discoursing an obvious melody.

What is the cause of this?

Man, in the order of time, was developed first; as energy comes before harmony; power before beauty.

Woman was therefore under his care as an elder. He might have been her guardian and teacher.

But as human nature goes not straight forward, but by excessive action and then reaction in an undulated course, he misunderstood and abused his advantages, and became her temporal master instead of her spiritual sire.

On himself came the punishment. He educated woman more as a servant than a daughter, and found himself a king without a queen.

The children of this unequal union showed unequal natures, and, more and more, men seemed sons of the hand-maid, rather than princes.

At last there were so many Ishmaelites that the rest grew frightened and indignant. They laid the blame on Hagar, and drove her forth into the wilderness.

But there were none the fewer Ishmaelites for that.

At last men became a little wiser, and saw that the infant Moses was, in every case, saved by the pure instincts of woman's breast. For, as too much adversity is better for the moral nature than too much prosperity, woman, in this respect, dwindled less than man, though in other respects, still a child in leading strings.

So man did her more and more justice, and grew more and more kind.

But yet, his habits and his will corrupted by the past, he did not clearly see that woman was half himself, that her interests were identical with his, and that, by the law of their common being, he could never reach his true proportions while she remained in any wise shorn of hers.

And so it has gone on to our day; both ideas developing, but more slowly than they would under a clearer recognition of truth and justice, which would have permitted the sexes their due influence on one another, and mutual improvement from more dignified relations.

Wherever there was pure love, the natural influences were, for the time, restored.

Wherever the poet or artist gave free course to his genius, he saw the truth, and expressed it in worthy forms, for these men especially share and need the feminine principle. The divine birds need to be brooded into life and song by mothers.

Wherever religion (I mean the thirst for truth and good, not the love of sect and dogma,) had its course, the original design was apprehended in its simplicity, and the dove presaged sweetly from Dodona's oak.

I have aimed to show that no age was left entirely without a witness of the equality of the sexes in function, duty and hope.

Also that, when there was unwillingness or ignorance, which prevented this being acted upon, women had not the less power for their want of light and noble freedom. But it was power which hurt alike them and those against whom they made use of the arms of the servile; cunning, blandishment, and unreasonable emotion.

That now the time has come when a clearer vision and better action are possible. When man and woman may regard one another as brother and sister, the pillars of one porch, the priests of one worship.

I have believed and intimated that this hope would receive an ampler fruition, than ever before, in our own land.

And it will do so if this land carry out the principles from which sprang our national life.

I believe that, at present, women are the best helpers of one another.

Let them think; let them act; till they know what they need.

We only ask of men to remove arbitrary barriers. Some would like to do more. But I believe it needs for woman to show herself in her native dignity, to teach them how to aid her; their minds are so encumbered by tradition.

When Lord Edward Fitzgerald travelled with the Indians, his manly heart obliged him at once, to take the packs from the squaws and carry them. But we do not read that the red men followed his example, though they are ready enough to carry the pack of the white woman, because she seems to them a superior being.

Let woman appear in the mild majesty of Ceres, and rudest churls will be willing to learn from her.

You ask, what use will she make of liberty, when she has so long been sustained and restrained?

I answer; in the first place, this will not be suddenly given. I read yesterday a debate of this year on the subject of enlarging women's rights over property. It was a leaf from the class book that is preparing for the needed instruction. The men learned visibly as they spoke. The champions of woman saw the fallacy of arguments, on the opposite side, and were startled by their own convictions. With their wives at home, and the readers of the paper, it was the same. And so the stream flows on; thought urging action, and action leading to the evolution of still better thought.

But, were this freedom to come suddenly, I have no fear of the consequences. Individuals might commit excesses, but there is not only in the sex a reverence for decorums and limits inherited and enhanced from generation to generation, which many years of other life could not efface, but a native love, in woman as woman, of proportion, of "the simple art of not too much," a Greek moderation, which would create immediately a restraining party, the natural legislators and instructors of the rest, and would gradually establish such rules as are needed to guard, without impeding, life.

The Graces would lead the choral dance, and teach the rest to regulate their steps to the measure of beauty.

But if you ask me what offices they may fill; I reply—any. I do not care what case you put; let them be sea-captains, if you will. I do not doubt there are women well fitted for such an office, and, if so, I should be glad to see them in it, as to welcome the maid of Saragossa, or the maid of Missolonghi, or the Suliote heroine, or Emily Plater.

I think women need, especially at this juncture, a much greater range of occupation than they have, to rouse their latent powers. A party of travellers lately visited a lonely hut on a mountain. There they found an old woman that told them she and her husband had lived there forty years. "Why," they said, "did you choose so barren a spot?" She "did not know; *it was the man's notion.*"

And, during forty years, she had been content to act, without knowing why, upon "the man's notion." I would not have it so.

In families that I know, some little girls like to saw wood, others to use carpenters' tools. Where these tastes are indulged, cheerfulness and good humor are promoted. Where they are forbidden, because "such things are not proper for girls," they grow sullen and mischievous.

Fourier had observed these wants of women, as no one can fail to do who watches the desires of little girls, or knows the ennui that haunts grown women, except where they make to themselves a serene little world by art of some kind. He, therefore, in proposing a great variety of employments, in manufactures or the care of plants and animals, allows for one third of woman, as likely to have a taste for masculine pursuits, one third of men for feminine.

Who does not observe the immediate glow and serenity that is diffused over the life of women, before restless or fretful, by engaging in gardening, building, or the lowest department of art. Here is something that is not routine, something that draws forth life toward the infinite.

I have no doubt, however, that a large proportion of women would give themselves to the same employments as now, because there are circumstances that must lead them. Mothers will delight to make the nest soft and warm. Nature would take care of that; no need to clip the wings of any bird that wants to soar and sing, or finds in itself the strength of pinion for a migratory flight unusual to its kind. The difference would be that *all* need not be constrained to employments, for which *some* are unfit.

I have urged upon the sex self-subsistence in its two forms of self-reliance and self-impulse, because I believe them to be the needed means of the present juncture.

I have urged on woman independence of man, not that I do not think the sexes mutually needed by one another, but because in woman this fact has led to an excessive devotion, which has cooled love, degraded marriage, and prevented either sex from being what it should be to itself or the other.

I wish woman to live, *first* for God's sake. Then she will not make an imperfect man her god, and thus sink to idolatry. Then she will not take what is not fit for her from a sense of weakness and poverty. Then, if she finds what she needs in man embodied, she will know how to love, and be worthy of being loved.

By being more a soul, she will not be less woman, for nature is perfected through spirit.

Now there is no woman, only an overgrown child.

That her hand may be given with dignity, she must be able to stand alone. I wish to see men and women capable of such relations as are depicted by Landor in his Pericles and Aspasia, where grace is the natural garb of strength, and the affections are calm, because deep. The softness is that of a firm tissue, as when

> *The gods approve*
> *The depth, but not the tumult of the soul,*
> *A fervent, not ungovernable love.*

A profound thinker has said, "no married woman can represent the female world, for she belongs to her husband. The idea of woman must be represented by a virgin."

But that is the very fault of marriage, and of the present relation between the sexes, that the woman does belong to the man, instead of forming a whole with him. Were it otherwise, there would be no such limitation to the thought.

Woman, self-centred, would never be absorbed by any relation; it would be only an experience to her as to man. It is a vulgar error that love, *a* love to woman is her whole existence; she also is born for Truth and Love in their universal energy. Would she but assume her inheritance, Mary would not be the only virgin mother. Not Manzoni alone would celebrate in his wife the virgin mind with the maternal wisdom and conjugal affections. The soul is ever young, ever virgin.

And will not she soon appear? The woman who shall vindicate their birthright for all women; who shall teach them what to claim, and how to use what they obtain? Shall not her name be for her era Victoria, for her country and life Virginia? Yet predictions are rash; she herself must teach us to give her the fitting name.

An idea not unknown to ancient times has of late been revived, that, in the metamorphoses of life, the soul assumes the form, first of man, then of woman, and takes the chances, and reaps the benefits of either lot. Why then, say some, lay such emphasis on the rights or needs of woman? What she wins not, as woman, will come to her as man.

That makes no difference. It is not woman, but the law of right, the law of growth, that speaks in us, and demands the perfection of each being in its kind, apple as apple, woman as woman. Without adopting your theory I know that I, a daughter, live through the life of man; but what concerns me now is, that my life be a beautiful, powerful, in a word, a complete life in its kind. Had I but one more moment to live, I must wish the same.

Suppose, at the end of your cycle, your great world-year, all will be completed, whether I exert myself or not (and the supposition is *false*,) but suppose it true, am I to be indifferent about it? Not so! I must beat my own pulse true in the heart of the world; for *that* is virtue, excellence, health.

Thou, Lord of Day! didst leave us to-night so calmly glorious, not dismayed that cold winter is coming, not postponing thy beneficence to the fruitful summer! Thou didst smile on thy day's work when it was done, and adorn thy down-going as thy up-rising, for thou art loyal, and it is thy nature to give life, if thou canst, and shine at all events!

I stand in the sunny noon of life. Objects no longer glitter in the dews of morning, neither are yet softened by the shadows of evening. Every spot is seen, every chasm revealed. Climbing the dusty hill, some fair effigies that once stood for symbols of human destiny have been broken; those I still have with me, show defects in this broad light. Yet enough is left, even by experience, to point distinctly to the glories of that destiny; faint, but not to be mistaken streaks of the future day. I can say with the bard,

Though many have suffered shipwreck, still beat noble hearts.

Always the soul says to us all: Cherish your best hopes as a faith, and abide by them in action. Such shall be the effectual fervent means to their fulfilment,

For the Power to whom we bow
Has given its pledge that, if not now,

They of pure and stedfast mind,
By faith exalted, truth refined,
Shall hear all music loud and clear,
Whose first notes they ventured here.
Then fear not thou to wind the horn,
Though elf and gnome thy courage scorn;
Ask for the Castle's King and Queen;
Though rabble rout may rush between,
Beat thee senseless to the ground,
In the dark beset thee round;
Persist to ask and it will come,
Seek not for rest in humbler home;
So shalt thou see what few have seen,
The palace home of King and Queen.

15th *November,* 1844.

APPENDIX

A

Apparition of the goddess Isis to her votary, from Apuleius.

"Scarcely had I closed my eyes, when behold (I saw in a dream) a divine form emerging from the middle of the sea, and raising a countenance venerable, even to the gods themselves. Afterwards, the whole of the most splendid image seemed to stand before me, having gradually shaken off the sea. I will endeavor to explain to you its admirable form, if the poverty of human language will but afford me the power of an appropriate narration; or if the divinity itself, of the most luminous form, will supply me with a liberal abundance of fluent diction. In the first place, then, her most copious and long hairs, being gradually intorted, and promiscuously scattered on her divine neck, were softly defluous. A multiform crown, consisting of various flowers, bound the sublime summit of her head. And in the middle of the crown, just on her forehead, there was a smooth orb resembling a mirror, or rather a white refulgent light, which indicated that she was the moon. Vipers rising up after the manner of furrows, environed the crown on the right hand and on the left, and Cerealian ears of corn were also extended from above. Her garment was of many colors, and woven from the finest flax, and was at one time lucid with a white splendor, at another yellow from the flower of crocus, and at another flaming with a rosy redness. But that which most excessively dazzled my sight, was a very black robe, fulgid with a dark splendor, and which, spreading round and passing under her right side, and ascending to her left shoulder, there rose protuberant, like the centre of a shield, the dependent part of her robe falling in many folds, and having small knots of fringe, gracefully flowing in its extremities. Glittering stars were dispersed through the embroidered border of the robe, and through the whole of its surface, and the full moon, shining in the middle of the stars, breathed forth flaming fires. A crown, wholly consisting of flowers and fruits of every kind, adhered with indivisible connexion to the border of conspicuous robe, in all its undulating motions.

"What she carried in her hands also consisted of things of a very different nature. Her right hand bore a brazen rattle, through the narrow lamina of which, bent like a belt, certain rods passing, produced a sharp triple sound through the vibrating motion of her arm. An oblong vessel, in the shape of a boat, depended from her left hand, on the handle of which, in that part which was conspicuous, an asp raised its erect head and largely swelling neck. And shoes, woven from the leaves of the victorious palm tree, covered her immortal feet. Such, and so great a goddess, breathing the fragrant odour of the shores of Arabia the happy, deigned thus to address me."

The foreign English of the translator, Thomas Taylor, gives the description the air of being, itself, a part of the Mysteries. But its majestic beauty requires no formal initiation to be enjoyed.

B

I give this, in the original, as it does not bear translation. Those who read Italian will judge whether it is not a perfect description of a perfect woman.

LODI E PREGHIERE A MARIA

Vergine bella che di sol vestita,
Coronata di stelle, al sommo Sole

Piacesti si, che'n te sua luce ascose;
Amor mi spinge a dir di te parole:
Ma non so 'ncominciar senza tu' aita,
E di Colui che amando in te si pose.
Invoco lei che ben sempre rispose,
Chi la chiamò con fede.
Vergine, s'a mercede
Miseria extrema dell' smane cose
Giammai ti volse, al mio prego t'inchina:
Soccorri alla mia guerra;
Bench' i' sia terra, e tu del ciel Regina.

Vergine saggia, e del bel numero una
Delle beate vergini prudenti;
Anzi la prima, e con più chiara lampa;
O saldo scudo dell' afflitte gente
Contra colpi di Morte e di Fortuna,
Sotto' l qual si trionfa, non pur scampa:
O refrigerio alcieco ardor ch' avvampa
Qui fra mortali sciocchi,
Vergine, que' begli occhi
Che vider tristi la spietata stampa
Ne' dolci membri del tuo caro figlio,
Volgi al mio dubbio stato;
Che sconsigliato a te vien per consiglio.

Vergine pura, d'ogni parte intera,
Del tuo parto gentil figliuola e madre;
Che allumi questa vita, e l'altra adorni;
Per te il tuo Figlio e quel del sommo Padre,
O finestra del ciel lucente altera,
Venne a salvarne in su gli estremi giorni,
E fra tutt'i terreni altri soggiorni
Sola tu fusti eletta,
Vergine benedetta;
Che 'l pianto d' Eva in allegrezza torni';
Fammi; che puoi; della sua grazia degno,
Senza fine o beata,
Già coronata nel superno regno.

Vergine santa d'ogni grazia piena;
Che per vera e altissima umiltate

Salisti al ciel, onde miei preghi ascolti;
Tu partoristi il fonte di pietate,
  E di giustizia il Sol, che rasserena
Il secol pien d'errori oscuri e folti:
  Tre dolci e eari nomi ha' in te raccolti,
Madre, Figliuola, e Sposa;
  Vergine gloriosa,
Donna del Re che nostri lacci ha sciolti,
  E fatto 'l mondo libero e felice;
Nelle cui sante piaghe
  Prego ch'appaghe il cor, vera beatrice.

Vergine sola al mondo senza esempio,
Che 'l ciel di tue bellezze innamorasti,
  Cui nè prima fu simil, nè seconda;
Santi pensieri, atti pietosi e casti
  Al vero Dio sacrato, e vivo tempio
Fecero in tua virginita feconda.
  Per te può la mia vita esser gioconda,
S' a' tuoi preghi, o MARIA
  Vergine dolce, e pia,
Ove 'l fallo abbondò, la grazia abbonda.
  Con le ginocchia della mente inchine
Prego che sia mia scorta;
  E la mia torta via drizzi a buon fine.

Vergine chiara, e stabile in eterno,
Di questo tempestoso mare stella;
  D'ogni fedel nocchier fidata guida;
Pon mente in che terribile procella
  I mi ritrovo sol senza governo,
Ed ho gia' da vicin l'ultime strida:
  Ma pur' in te l'anima mia si fida;
Peccatrice; i' nol nego,
  Vergine: ma te prego
Che 'l tuo nemico del mia mal non rida:
  Ricorditi che fece il peccar nostro
Prender Dio, per scamparne,
  Umana carne al tuo virginal christro.

Vergine, quante lagrime ho già sparte,
Quante lusinghe, e quanti preghi indarno,

Pur per mia pena, e per mio grave danno!
Da poi ch' i' nacqui in su la riva d' Arno;
   Cercando or questa ed or quell altra parte,
Non è stata mia vita altro ch' affanno.
   Mortal bellezza, atti, e parole m' hanno
Tutta ingombrata l'alma.
   Vergine sacra, ed alma,
Non tardar; ch' i' non forse all' ultim 'ann,
   I di miei piu correnti che saetta,
Fra miserie e peccati
   Sonsen andati, e sol Morte n'aspetta.

   Vergine, tale è terra, e posto ha in doglia
Lo mio cor; che vivendo in pianto il tenne;
   E di mille miei mali un non sapea;
E per saperlo, pur quel che n'avvenne,
   Fora avvenuto: ch' ogni altra sua voglia
Era a me morte, ed a lei fama rea
   Or tu, donna del ciel, tu nostra Dea,
Se dir lice, e conviensi;
   Vergine d'alti sensi,
Tu vedi il tutto; e quel che non potea
   Far altri, è nulla a e la tua gran virtute;
Pon fine al mio dolore;
   Ch'a te onore ed a me fia salute.

   Vergine, in cui ho tutta mia speranza
Che possi e vogli al gran bisogno aitarme;
   Non mi lasciare in su l'estremo passo:
Non guardar me, ma chi degnò crearme;
   No'l mio valor, ma l'alta sua sembianza;
Che in me ti mova a curar d'uorm si basso.
   Medusa, e l'error mio io han fatto un sasso
D'umor vano stillante;
   Vergine, tu di sante
Lagrime, e pie adempi 'l mio cor lasso;
   Ch' almen l'ultimo pianto sia divoto,
     Senza terrestro limo;
Come fu'l primo non d'insania voto.

   Vergine umana, e nemica d'orgoglio,
Del comune principio amor t'induca;

> *Miserere d' un cor contrito umile;*
> *Che se poca mortal terra caduca*
>   *Amar con si mirabil fede soglio;*
> *Che devro far di te cosa gentile?*
>   *Se dal mio stato assai misero, e vile*
> *Per le tue man resurgo,*
>   *Vergine; è' sacro, e purgo*
> *Al tuo nome e pens ieri e'ngegno, e stile;*
>   *La lingua, e'l cor, le lagrime, e i sospiri,*
> *Scorgimi al miglior guado;*
>   *E prendi in grado i cangiati desiri.*
>
> *Il di s'appressa, e non pote esser lunge;*
>   *Si corre il tempo, e vola,*
> *Vergine uuica, e sola;*
>   *E'l cor' or conscienza, or morte punge.*
> *Raccommandami al tuo Figliuol, verace*
>   *Uomo, e verace Dio;*
> *Ch accolga l mio spirto ultimo in pace.*

As the Scandinavian represented Frigga the Earth, or World mother, knowing all things, yet never herself revealing them, though ready to be called to counsel by the gods. It represents her in action, decked with jewels and gorgeously attended. But, says the Mythos, when she ascended the throne of Odin, her consort (Haaven) she left with mortals, her friend, the Goddess of Sympathy, to protect them in her absence.

Since, Sympathy goes about to do good. Especially she devotes herself to the most valiant and the most oppressed. She consoled the Gods in some degree even for the death of their darling Baldur. Among the heavenly powers she has no consort.

C

"THE WEDDING OF THE LADY THERESA"
FROM LOCKHART'S SPANISH BALLADS.

> *'Twas when the fifth Alphonso in Leon held his sway,*
>   *King Abdalla of Toledo an embassy did send;*
> *He asked his sister for a wife, and in an evil day*
>   *Alphonso sent her, for he feared Abdalla to offend;*

He feared to move his anger, for many times before
He had received in danger much succor from the Moor.

Sad heart had fair Theresa, when she their paction knew;
   With streaming tears she heard them tell she 'mong the Moors
      must go;
That she, a Christian damsel, a Christian firm and true,
   Must wed a Moorish husband, it well might cause her wo;
But all her tears and all her prayers they are of small avail;
   At length she for her fate prepares, a victim sad and pale.

The king hath sent his sister to fair Toledo town,
   Where then the Moor Abdalla his royal state did keep;
When she drew near, the Moslem from his golden throne came
   down,
   And courteously received her, and bade her cease to weep;
With loving words he pressed her to come his bower within;
With kisses he caressed her, but still she feared the sin.

"Sir King, Sir King, I pray thee,"—'twas thus Theresa spake,
   "I pray thee, have compassion, and do to me no wrong;
For sleep with thee I may not, unless the vows I break,
   Whereby I to the holy church of Christ my Lord belong;
For thou hast sworn to serve Mahoun, and if this thing should
   be,
The curse of God it must bring down upon thy realm and thee.

"The angel of Christ Jesu, to whom my heavenly Lord
   Hath given my soul in keeping, is ever by my side;
If thou dost me dishonor, he will unsheath his sword,
   And smite thy body fiercely, at the crying of thy bride;
Invisible he standeth; his sword like fiery flame,
Will penetrate thy bosom, the hour that sees my shame."

The Moslem heard her with a smile; the earnest words she said,
   He took for bashful maiden's wile, and drew her to his bower:
In vain Theresa prayed and strove,—she pressed Abdalla's bed,
   Perforce received his kiss of love, and lost her maiden flower.
A woful woman there she lay, a loving lord beside,
And earnestly to God did pray, her succor to provide.

The angel of Christ Jesu her sore complaint did hear,
   And plucked his heavenly weapon from out his sheath unseen,
He waved the brand in his right hand, and to the King came

near,
And drew the point o'er limb and joint, beside the weeping
    Queen:
A mortal weakness from the stroke upon the King did fall;
He could not stand when daylight broke, but on his knees must
    crawl.

Abdalla shuddered inly, when he this sickness felt,
    And called upon his barons, his pillow to come nigh;
"Rise up," he said "my liegemen," as round his bed they knelt,
    "And take this Christian lady, else certainly I die;
Let gold be in your girdles, and precious stones beside,
    And swiftly ride to Leon, and render up my bride."

When they were come to Leon, Theresa would not go
    Into her brother's dwelling, where her maiden years were
    spent;
But o'er her downcast visage a white veil she did throw,
    And to the ancient nunnery of Las Huelgas went.
There, long, from worldly eyes retired, a holy life she led;
There she, an aged saint, expired; there sleeps she with the dead.

D

The following extract from Spinoza is worthy of attention, as expressing the view which a man of the largest intellectual scope may take of woman, if that part of his life to which her influence appeals, has been left unawakened.

He was a man of the largest intellect, of unsurpassed reasoning powers, yet he makes a statement false to history, for we well know how often men and women have ruled together without difficulty, and one in which very few men even at the present day, I mean men who are thinkers, like him, would acquiesce.

I have put in contrast with it three expressions of the latest literature.

1st. From the poems of W. E. Channing, a poem called "Reverence," equally remarkable for the deep wisdom of its thought and the beauty of its utterance, and containing as fine a description of one class of women as exists in literature.

In contrast with this picture of woman, the happy Goddess of Beauty, the wife, the friend, "the summer queen," I add one by the author of "Festus," of a woman of the muse, the sybil kind, which seems painted from living experience.

And thirdly, I subjoin Eugene Sue's description of a wicked, but able woman of the practical sort, and appeal to all readers whether a species that admits of three such varieties is so easily to be classed away, or kept within prescribed limits, as Spinoza, and those who think like him, believe.

SPINOZA. TRACTATUS POLITICI, DE DEMOCRATIA CAPUT XI

"Perhaps some one will here ask, whether the supremacy of man over woman is attributable to nature or custom? For if it be human institutions alone to which this fact is owing, there is no reason why we should exclude women from a share in government. Experience, however, most plainly teaches that it is woman's weakness which places her under the authority of man. Since it has nowhere happened that men and women ruled together; but wherever men and women are found the world over, there we see the men ruling and the women ruled, and in this order of things men and women live together in peace and harmony. The Amazons, it is true, are reputed formerly to have held the reins of government, but they drove men from their dominions; the male of their offspring they invariably destroyed, permitting their daughters alone to live. Now if women were by nature upon an equality with men, if they equalled men in fortitude, in genius (qualities which give to men might, and consequently, right) it surely would be the case, that among the numerous and diverse nations of the earth, some would be found where both sexes ruled conjointly, and others where the men were ruled by the women, and so educated as to be mentally inferior: since this state of things no where exists, it is perfectly fair to infer that the rights of women are not equal to those of men; but that women must be subordinate, and therefore cannot have an equal, far less a superior place in the government. If, too, we consider the passions of men—how the love men feel towards women is seldom any thing but lust and impulse, and much less a reverence for qualities of soul than an admiration of physical beauty, observing, too, how men are afflicted when their sweethearts favor other wooers, and other things of the same character,—we shall see at a glance that it would be, in the highest degree, detrimental to peace and harmony, for men and women to possess an equal share in government."

"REVERENCE"

> As an ancestral heritage revere
> All learning, and all thought. The painter's fame
> Is thine, whate'er thy lot, who honorest grace.
> And need enough in this low time, when they,
> Who seek to captivate the fleeting notes
> Of heaven's sweet beauty, must despair almost,
> So heavy and obdurate show the hearts
> Of their companions. Honor kindly then
> Those who bear up in their so generous arms
> The beautiful ideas of matchless forms;
> For were these not portrayed, our human fate,—
> Which is to be all high, majestical,
> To grow to goodness with each coming age,
> Till virtue leap and sing for joy to see
> So noble, virtuous men,—would brief decay;
> And the green, festering slime, oblivious, haunt
> About our common fate. Oh honor them!
>
> But what to all true eyes has chiefest charm,
> And what to every breast where beats a heart
> Framed to one beautiful emotion,—to
> One sweet and natural feeling, lends a grace
> To all the tedious walks of common life,
> This is fair woman,—woman, whose applause
> Each poet sings,—woman the beautiful.
> Not that her fairest brow, or gentlest form
> Charm us to tears; not that the smoothest cheek,
> Where ever rosy tints have made their home,
> So rivet us on her; but that she is
> The subtle, delicate grace,—the inward grace,
> For words too excellent; the noble, true,
> The majesty of earth; the summer queen:
> In whose conceptions nothing but what's great
> Has any right. And, O! her love for him,
> Who does but his small part in honoring her;
> Discharging a sweet office, sweeter none,
> Mother and child, friend, counsel and repose;—
> Nought matches with her, nought has leave with her
> To highest human praise. Farewell to him

Who reverences not with an excess
Of faith the beauteous sex; all barren he
Shall live a living death of mockery.

Ah! had but words the power, what could we say
Of woman! We, rude men, of violent phrase,
Harsh action, even in repose inwardly harsh;
Whose lives walk blustering on high stilts, removed
From all the purely gracious influence
Of mother earth. To single from the host
Of angel forms one only, and to her
Devote our deepest heart and deepest mind
Seems almost contradiction. Unto her
We owe our greatest blessings, hours of cheer,
Gay smiles, and sudden tears, and more than these
A sure perpetual love. Regard her as
She walks along the vast still earth; and see!
Before her flies a laughing troop of joys,
And by her side treads old experience,
With never-failing voice admonitory;
The gentle, though infallible, kind advice,
The watchful care, the fine regardfulness,
Whatever mates with what we hope to find,
All consummate in her—the summer queen.

To call past ages better than what now
Man is enacting on life's crowded stage,
Cannot improve our worth; and for the world
Blue is the sky as ever, and the stars
Kindle their crystal flames at soft-fallen eve
With the same purest lustre that the east
Worshipped. The river gently flows through fields
Where the broad-leaved corn spreads out, and loads
Its ear as when the Indian tilled the soil.
The dark green pine,—green in the winter's cold,
Still whispers meaning emblems, as of old;
The cricket chirps, and the sweet, eager birds
In the sad woods crowd their thick melodies;
But yet, to common eyes, life's poetry
Something has faded, and the cause of this
May be that man, no longer at the shrine
Of woman, kneeling with true reverence,

In spite of field, wood, river, stars and sea
Goes most disconsolate. A babble now,
A huge and wind-swelled babble, fills the place
Of that great adoration which of old
Man had for woman. In these days no more
Is love the pith and marrow of man's fate.

Thou who in early years feelest awake
To finest impulses from nature's breath,
And in thy walk hearest such sounds of truth
As on the common ear strike without heed,
Beware of men around thee. Men are foul,
With avarice, ambition and deceit;
The worst of all, ambition. This is life
Spent in a feverish chase for selfish ends,
Which has no virtue to redeem its toil
But one long, stagnant hope to raise the self.
The miser's life to this seems sweet and fair;
Better to pile the glittering coin, than seek
To overtop our brothers and our loves.
Merit in this? Where lies it, though thy name
Ring over distant lands, meeting the wind
Even on the extremest verge of the wide world.
Merit in this? Better be hurled abroad
On the vast whirling tide, than in thyself
Concentred, feed upon thy own applause.
Thee shall the good man yield no reverence;
But, while the idle, dissolute crowd are loud
In voice to send thee flattery, shall rejoice
That he has scaped thy fatal doom, and known
How humble faith in the good soul of things
Provides amplest enjoyment. O my brother,
If the Past's counsel any honor claim
From thee, go read the history of those
Who a like path have trod, and see a fate
Wretched with fears, changing like leaves at noon,
When the new wind sings in the white birch wood.
Learn from the simple child the rule of life,
And from the movements of the unconscious tribes
Of animal nature, those that bend the wing
Or cleave the azure tide, content to be,

What the great frame provides,—freedom and grace.
Thee, simple child, do the swift winds obey,
And the white waterfalls with their bold leaps
Follow thy movements. Tenderly the light
Thee watches, girding with a zone of radiance,
And all the swinging herbs love thy soft steps.

DESCRIPTION OF ANGELA,
FROM ''FESTUS''

I loved her for that she was beautiful,
And that to me she seemed to be all nature
And all varieties of things in one;
Would set at night in clouds of tears, and rise
All light and laughter in the morning; fear
No petty customs nor appearances,
But think what others only dreamed about;
And say what others did but think; and do
What others would but say; and glory in
What others dared but do; it was these which won me;
And that she never schooled within her breast
One thought or feeling, but gave holiday
To all; and that she told me all her woes
And wrongs and ills; and so she made them mine
In the communion of love; and we
Grew like each other, for we loved each other;
She, mild and generous as the sun in spring;
And I, like earth, all budding out with love.
                    *   *   *
The beautiful are never desolate:
For some one always loves them; God or man;
If man abandons, God Himself takes them:
And thus it was. She whom I once loved died,
The lightning loathes its cloud; the soul its clay.
Can I forget that hand I took in mine,
Pale as pale violets; that eye, where mind
And matter met alike divine?—ah, no!
May God that moment judge me when I do!
Oh! she was fair; her nature once all spring
And deadly beauty, like a maiden sword,

Startlingly beautiful. I see her now!
Wherever thou art thy soul is in my mind;
Thy shadow hourly lengthens o'er my brain
And peoples all its pictures with thyself;
Gone, not forgotten; passed, not lost; thou wilt shine
In heaven like a bright spot in the sun!
She said she wished to die, and so she died,
For, cloudlike, she poured out her love, which was
Her life, to freshen this parched heart. It was thus;
I said we were to part, but she said nothing;
There was no discord; it was music ceased,
Life's thrilling, bursting, bounding joy. She sate,
Like a house-god, her hands fixed on her knee,
And her dark hair lay loose and long behind her,
Through which her wild bright eye flashed like a flint;
She spake not, moved not, but she looked the more,
As if her eye were action, speech, and feeling.
I felt it all, and came and knelt beside her,
The electric touch solved both our souls together;
Then came the feeling which unmakes, undoes;
Which tears the sealike soul up by the roots,
And lashes it in scorn against the skies.

*   *   *

It is the saddest and the sorest sight,
One's own love weeping. But why call on God?
But that the feeling of the boundless bounds
All feeling; as the welkin does the world;
It is this which ones us with the whole and God.
Then first we wept; then closed and clung together;
And my heart shook this building of my breast
Like a live engine booming up and down:
She fell upon me like a snow-wreath thawing.
Never were bliss and beauty, love and wo,
Ravelled and twined together into madness,
As in that one wild hour to which all else
The past, is but a picture. That alone
Is real, and forever there in front.

*   *   *

After that I left her,
And only saw her once again alive.

"Mother Saint Perpetua, the superior of the convent, was a tall woman, of about forty years, dressed in dark gray serge, with a long rosary hanging at her girdle; a white mob cap, with a long black veil, surrounded her thin wan face with its narrow hooded border. A great number of deep transverse wrinkles plowed her brow, which resembled yellowish ivory in color and substance. Her keen and prominent nose was curved like the hooked beak of a bird of prey; her black eye was piercing and sagacious; her face was at once intelligent, firm, and cold.

"For comprehending and managing the material interests of the society, Mother Saint Perpetua could have vied with the shrewdest and most wily lawyer. When women are possessed of what is called *business talent,* and when they apply thereto the sharpness of perception, the indefatigable perseverance, the prudent dissimulation, and above all, the correctness and rapidity of judgment at first sight, which are peculiar to them, they arrive at prodigious results.

"To mother Saint Perpetua, a woman of a strong and solid head, the vast monied business of the society was but child's play. None better than she understood how to buy depreciated properties, to raise them to their original value, and sell them to advantage; the average purchase of rents, the fluctuations of exchange, and the current prices of shares in all the leading speculations, were perfectly familiar to her. Never had she directed her agents to make a single false speculation, when it had been the question how to invest funds, with which good souls were constantly endowing the society of Saint Mary. She had established in the house a degree of order, of discipline, and, above all, of economy, that were indeed remarkable; the constant aim of all her exertions being, not to enrich herself, but the community over which she presided; for the spirit of association, when it is directed to an object of *collective selfishness,* gives to corporations all the faults and vices of individuals."

E

The following is an extract from a letter addressed to me by one of the monks of the 19th century. A part I have omitted, because it does not express my own view, unless with qualifications which I could not make, except by full discussion of the subject.

"Woman in the 19th century should be a pure, chaste, holy being.

"This state of being in woman is no more attained by the expansion of her intellectual capacity, than by the augmentation of her physical force.

"Neither is it attained by the increase or refinement of her love for man, or for any object whatever, or for all objects collectively; but

"This state of being is attained by the reference of all her powers and all her actions to the source of Universal Love, whose constant requisition is a pure, chaste and holy life.

"So long as woman looks to man (or to society) for that which she needs, she will remain in an indigent state, for he himself is indigent of it, and as much needs it as she does.

"So long as this indigence continues, all unions or relations constructed between man and woman are constructed in indigence, and can produce only indigent results or unhappy consequences.

"The unions now constructing, as well as those in which the parties constructing them were generated, being based on self-delight, or lust, can lead to no more happiness in the 20th, than is found in the 19th century.

"It is not amended institutions, it is not improved education, it is not another selection of individuals for union, that can meliorate the sad result, but the *basis* of the union must be changed.

"If in the natural order Woman and Man would adhere strictly to physiological or natural laws, in physical chastity, a most beautiful amendment of the human race, and human condition, would in a few generations adorn the world.

"Still, it belongs to Woman in the spiritual order, to devote herself wholly to her eternal husband, and become the Free Bride of the One who alone can elevate her to her true position, and reconstruct her a pure, chaste, and holy being."

F

I have mislaid an extract from "The Memoirs of an American Lady" which I wished to use on this subject, but its import is, briefly, this:

Observing of how little consequence the Indian women are in youth, and how much in age, because in that trying life, good counsel and sagacity are more prized than charms, Mrs. Grant expresses a wish that Reformers would take a hint from observation of this circumstance.

In another place she says: "The misfortune of our sex is, that young women are not regarded as the material from which old women must be made."

I quote from memory, but believe the weight of the remark is retained.

G

EURIPIDES. SOPHOCLES.

As many allusions are made in the foregoing pages to characters of women drawn by the Greek dramatists, which may not be familiar to the majority of readers, I have borrowed from the papers of Miranda, some notes upon them. I trust the girlish tone of apostrophizing rapture may be excused. Miranda was very young at the time of writing, compared with her present mental age. *Now*, she would express the same feelings, but in a worthier garb—if she expressed them at all.

"Iphigenia! Antigone! you were worthy to live! *We* are fallen on evil times, my sisters! our feelings have been checked; our thoughts questioned; our forms dwarfed and defaced by a bad nurture. Yet hearts, like yours, are in our breasts, living, if unawakened; and our minds are capable of the same resolves. You, we understand at once, those who stare upon us pertly in the street, we cannot—could never understand.

"You knew heroes, maidens, and your fathers were kings of men. You believed in your country, and the gods of your country. A great occasion was given to each, whereby to test her character.

"You did not love on earth; for the poets wished to show us the force of woman's nature, virgin and unbiassed. You were women; not wives, or lovers, or mothers. Those are great names, but we are glad to see *you* in untouched flower.

"Were brothers so dear, then, Antigone? We have no brothers. We see no men into whose lives we dare look steadfastly, or to whose destinies we look forward confidently. We care not for their urns; what inscription could we put upon them? They live for petty successes; or to win daily the bread of the day. No spark of kingly fire flashes from their eyes.

"None! are there *none?*

"It is a base speech to say it. Yes! there are some such; we have sometimes caught their glances. But rarely have they been rocked in the same cradle as we, and they do not look upon us much; for the time is not yet come.

"Thou art so grand and simple! we need not follow thee; thou dost not need our love.

"But, sweetest Iphigenia; who knew *thee*, as to me thou art known. I was not born in vain, if only for the heavenly tears I have shed with thee. She will be grateful for them. I have understood her wholly; as a friend should, better than she understood herself.

"With what artless art the narrative rises to the crisis. The conflicts in Agamemnon's mind, and the imputations of Menelaus give us, at once, the full image of him, strong in will and pride, weak in virtue, weak in the noble powers of the mind that depend on imagination. He suffers, yet it requires the presence of his daughter to make him feel the full horror of what he is to do.

> *Ah me! that breast, those cheeks, those golden tresses!*

"It is her beauty, not her misery, that makes the pathos. This is noble. And then, too, the injustice of the gods, that she, this creature of unblemished loveliness, must perish for the sake of a worthless woman. Even Menelaus feels it, the moment he recovers from his wrath.

> *What hath she to do,*
> *The virgin daughter, with my Helena!*
>   *   *   Its former reasonings now*
> *My soul foregoes.*   *   *   *   *
>   *For it is not just*
> *That thou shouldst groan, but my affairs go pleasantly,*
> *That those of thy house should die, and mine see the light.*

"Indeed the overwhelmed aspect of the king of men might well move him.

> Men. *Brother, give me to take thy right hand,*
> Aga. *I give it, for the victory is thine, and I am wretched.*
>   *I am, indeed, ashamed to drop the tear,*
>   *And not to drop the tear I am ashamed.*

"How beautifully is Iphigenia introduced; beaming more and more softly on us with every touch of description. After Clytemnestra has given Orestes (then an infant,) out of the chariot, she says:

> Ye females, in your arms,
> Receive her, for she is of tender age.
> Sit here by my feet, my child,
> By thy mother, Iphigenia, and show
> These strangers how I am blessed in thee,
> And here address thee to thy father.
> Iphi. Oh mother, should I run, wouldst thou be angry?
> And embrace my father breast to breast?

"With the same sweet timid trust she prefers the request to himself, and as he holds her in his arms, he seems as noble as Guido's Archangel; as if he never could sink below the trust of such a being!

"The Achilles, in the first scene, is fine. A true Greek hero; not too good; all flushed with the pride of youth; but capable of god-like impulses. At first, he thinks only of his own wounded pride, (when he finds Iphigenia has been decoyed to Anlis under the pretext of becoming his wife;) but the grief of the queen soon makes him superior to his arrogant chafings. How well he says:—

> Far as a young man may, *I will repress*
> *So great a wrong.*

"By seeing him here, we understand why he, not Hector, was the hero of the Iliad. The beautiful moral nature of Hector was early developed by close domestic ties, and the cause of his country. Except in a purer simplicity of speech and manner, he might be a modern and a christian. But Achilles is cast in the largest and most vigorous mould of the earlier day: his nature is one of the richest capabilities, and therefore less quickly unfolds its meaning. The impression it makes at the early period is only of power and pride; running as fleetly with his armor on, as with it off; but sparks of pure lustre are struck, at moments, from the mass of ore. Of this sort is his refusal to see the beautiful virgin he has promised to protect. None of the Grecians must have the right to doubt his motives. How wise and prudent, too, the advice he gives as to the queen's conduct! He will not show himself, unless needed. His pride is the farthest possible remote from vanity. His thoughts are as free as any in our own time.

> The prophet? what is he? a man
> Who speaks 'mong many falsehoods, but few truths,

> *Whene'er chance leads him to speak true; when false,*
> *The prophet is no more.*

"Had Agamemnon possessed like clearness of sight, the virgin would not have perished, but also, Greece would have had no religion and no national existence.

"When, in the interview with Agamemnon, the Queen begins her speech, in the true matrimonial style, dignified though her gesture be, and true all she says, we feel that truth, thus sauced with taunts, will not touch his heart, nor turn him from his purpose. But when Iphigenia begins her exquisite speech, as with the breathings of a lute,

> *Had I, my father, the persuasive voice*
> *Of Orpheus, &c.*
>   *Compel me not*
> *What is beneath to view. I was the first*
> *To call thee father; me thou first didst call*
> *Thy child: I was the first that on thy knees*
> *Fondly caressed thee, and from thee received*
> *The fond caress: this was thy speech to me:—*
> *"Shall I, my child, e'er see thee in some house*
> *Of splendor, happy in thy husband, live*
> *And flourish, as becomes my dignity?"*
> *My speech to thee was, leaning 'gainst thy cheek,*
> *(Which with my hand I now caress:) "And what*
> *Shall I then do for thee? shall I receive*
> *My father when grown old, and in my house*
> *Cheer him with each fond office, to repay*
> *The careful nurture which he gave my youth?"*
> *These words are in my memory deep impressed,*
> *Thou hast forgot them and will kill thy child.*

"Then she adjures him by all the sacred ties, and dwells pathetically on the circumstance which had struck even Menelaus.

> *If Paris be enamored of his bride,*
> *His Helen, what concerns it me? and how*
> *Comes he to my destruction?*
>   *Look upon me;*
> *Give me a smile, give me a kiss, my father;*

> *That if my words persuade thee not, in death*
> *I may have this memorial of thy love.*

"Never have the names of father and daughter been uttered with a holier tenderness than by Euripides, as in this most lovely passage, or in the 'Supplicants,' after the voluntary death of Evadne; Iphis says

> *What shall this wretch now do? Should I return*
> *To my own house?—sad desolation there*
> *I shall behold, to sink my soul with grief.*
> *Or go I to the house of Capaneus?*
> *That was delightful to me, when I found*
> *My daughter there; but she is there no more:*
> *Oft would she kiss my cheek, with fond caress*
> *Oft soothe me. To a father, waxing old,*
> *Nothing is dearer than a daughter! sons*
> *Have spirits of higher pitch, but less inclined*
> *To sweet endearing fondness. Lead me then,*
> *Instantly lead me to my house, consign*
> *My wretched age to darkness, there to pine*
> *And waste away.*
>   *Old age,*
> *Struggling with many griefs, O how I hate thee!*

"But to return to Iphigenia,—how infinitely melting is her appeal to Orestes, whom she holds in her robe.

> *My brother, small assistance canst thou give*
> *Thy friends; yet for thy sister with thy tears*
> *Implore thy father that she may not die:*
> *Even infants have a sense of ills; and see,*
> *My father! silent though he be, he sues*
> *To thee: be gentle to me; on my life*
> *Have pity: thy two children by this beard*
> *Entreat thee, thy dear children: one is yet*
> *An infant, one to riper years arrived.*

"The mention of Orestes, then an infant, all through, though slight, is of a domestic charm that prepares the mind to feel the tragedy of his after lot. When the Queen says

> *Dost thou sleep,*
> *My son? The rolling chariot hath subdued thee;*
> *Wake to thy sister's marriage happily.*

"We understand the horror of the doom which makes this cherished child a parricide. And so when Iphigenia takes leave of him after her fate is by herself accepted.

> Iphi. *To manhood train Orestes,*
> Cly. *Embrace him, for thou ne'er shalt see him more.*
> Iphi. (To Orestes.) *Far as thou couldst, thou didst assist*
> *thy friends.*

"We know not how to blame the guilt of the maddened wife and mother. In her last meeting with Agamemnon, as in her previous expostulations and anguish, we see that a straw may turn the balance, and make her his deadliest foe. Just then, came the the suit of Ægisthus, then, when every feeling was uprooted or lacerated in her heart.

"Iphigenia's moving address has no further effect than to make her father turn at bay and brave this terrible crisis. He goes out, firm in resolve; and she and her mother abandon themselves to a natural grief.

"Hitherto nothing has been seen in Iphigenia, except the young girl, weak, delicate, full of feeling and beautiful as a sunbeam on the full green tree. But, in the next scene, the first impulse of that passion which makes and unmakes us, though unconfessed even to herself, though hopeless and unreturned, raises her at once into the heroic woman, worthy of the goddess who demands her.

"Achilles appears to defend her, whom all others clamorously seek to deliver to the murderous knife. She sees him, and fired with thoughts, unknown before, devotes herself at once for the country which has given birth to such a man.

> *To be too fond of life*
> *Becomes not me; nor for myself alone,*
> *But to all Greece, a blessing didst thou bear me.*
> *Shall thousands, when their country's injured, lift*
> *Their shields; shall thousands grasp the oar, and dare,*
> *Advancing bravely 'gainst the foe, to die*
> *For Greece? And shall my life, my single life,*
> *Obstruct all this? Would this be just? What word*

> *Can we reply? Nay more, it is not right*
> *That he with all the Grecians should contest*
> *In fight, should die,* and for a woman. No:
> *More than a thousand women is one man*
> *Worthy to see the light of day.*
>   * *   *   *   for Greece I give my life.*
> *Slay me; demolish Troy: for these shall be*
> *Long time my monuments, my children these,*
> *My nuptials and my glory.*

"This sentiment marks woman, when she loves enough to feel what a creature of glory and beauty a true *man* would be, as much in our own time as that of Euripides. Cooper makes the weak Hetty say to her beautiful sister:

" 'Of course, I don't compare you with Harry. A handsome man is always far handsomer than any woman.' True, it was the sentiment of the age, but it was the first time Iphigenia had felt it. In Agamemnon she saw *her father,* to him she could prefer her claim. In Achilles she saw *a man,* the crown of creation, enough to fill the world with his presence, were all other beings blotted from its spaces.*

"The reply of Achilles is as noble. Here is his bride, he feels it now, and all his vain vauntings are hushed.

> *Daughter of Agamemnon, highly blessed*
> *Some god would make me, if I might attain*
> *Thy nuptials. Greece in thee I happy deem,*
> *And thee in Greece.   *   **
> * *   *   * in thy thought*
> *Revolve this well; death is a dreadful thing.*

"How sweet is her reply, and then the tender modesty with which she addresses him here and elsewhere as '*stranger.*'

---

* Men do not often reciprocate this pure love.

> *Her prentice han' she tried on man,*
> *And then she made the lasses o',*

Is a fancy, not a feeling, in their more frequently passionate and strong, than noble or tender natures.

> *Reflecting not on any, thus I speak:*
> *Enough of wars and slaughters from the charms*
> *Of Helen rise; but die not thou for me,*
> *O Stranger, nor distain thy sword with blood,*
> *But let me save my country if I may.*
> Achilles. *O glorious spirit! nought have I 'gainst this*
> *To urge, since such thy will, for what thou sayst*
> *Is generous. Why should not the truth be spoken?*

"But feeling that human weakness may conquer yet, he goes to wait at the altar, resolved to keep his promise of protection thoroughly.

"In the next beautiful scene she shows that a few tears might overwhelm her in his absence. She raises her mother beyond weeping them, yet her soft purity she cannot impart.

> Iphi. *My father, and thy husband do not hate:*
> Cly. *For thy dear sake fierce contests must he bear.*
> Iphi. *For Greece reluctant me to death he yields;*
> Cly. *Basely, with guile unworthy Atreus' son.'*

"This is truth incapable of an answer and Iphigenia attempts none.

"She begins the hymn which is to sustain her,

> *Lead me; mine the glorious fate,*
> *To o'erturn the Phrygian state.*

"After the sublime flow of lyric heroism, she suddenly sinks back into the tenderer feeling of her dreadful fate.

> *O my country, where these eyes*
> *Opened on Pelasgic skies!*
> *O ye virgins, once my pride,*
> *In Mycenæ who abide!*
> CHORUS.
> *Why of Perseus name the town,*
> *Which Cyclopean ramparts crown?*
> IPHIGENIA.
> *Me you rear'd a beam of light,*
> *Freely now I sink in night.*

"*Freely;* as the messenger afterwards recounts it.

*   *   *

> *Imperial Agamemnon, when he saw*
> *His daughter, as a victim to the grave,*
> *Advancing, groan'd, and bursting into tears,*
> *Turned from the sight his head, before his eyes,*
> *Holding his robe. The virgin near him stood,*
> *And thus addressed him: "Father, I to thee*
> *Am present; for my country, and for all*
> *The land of Greece, I freely give myself*
> *A victim: to the altar let them lead me,*
> *Since such the oracle. If aught on me*
> *Depends, be happy, and obtain the prize*
> *Of glorious conquest, and revisit safe*
> *Your country. Of the Grecians, for this cause,*
> *Let no one touch me; with intrepid spirit*
> *Silent will I present my neck." She spoke,*
> *And all that heard revered the noble soul*
> *And virtue of the virgin.*

"How quickly had the fair bud bloomed up into its perfection. Had she lived a thousand years, she could not have surpassed this. Goethe's Iphigenia, the mature woman, with its myriad delicate traits, never surpasses, scarcely equals what we know of her in Euripides.

"Can I appreciate this work in a translation? I think so, impossible as it may seem to one who can enjoy the thousand melodies, and words in exactly the right place and cadence of the original. They say you can see the Apollo Belvidere in a plaster cast, and I cannot doubt it, so great the benefit conferred on my mind, by a transcript thus imperfect. And so with these translations from the Greek. I can divine the original through this veil, as I can see the movements of a spirited horse by those of his coarse grasscloth muffler. Beside, every translator who feels his subject is inspired, and the divine Aura informs even his stammering lips.

"Iphigenia is more like one of the women Shakspeare loved than the others; she is a tender virgin, ennobled and strengthened by sentiment more than intellect, what they call a woman *par excellence.*

"Macaria is more like one of Massinger's women. She advances boldly, though with the decorum of her sex and nation:

Macaria. *Impute not boldness to me that I come*
Before you, strangers; this my first request
I urge; for silence and a chaste reserve
Is woman's genuine praise, and to remain
Quiet within the house. But I come forth,
Hearing thy lamentations, Iolaus:
Though charged with no commission, yet perhaps,
I may be useful.

"Her speech when she offers herself as the victim, is reasonable, as one might speak to-day. She counts the cost all through. Iphigenia is too timid and delicate to dwell upon the loss of earthly bliss, and the due experience of life, even as much as Jeptha's daughter did, but Macaria is explicit, as well befits the daughter of Hercules.

Should these die, myself
Preserved, of prosperous future could I form
One cheerful hope?
A poor forsaken virgin who would deign
To take in marriage? Who would wish for sons
From one so wretched? Better then to die,
Than bear such undeserved miseries:
One less illustrious this might more beseem.

        *   *   *

I have a soul that unreluctantly
Presents itself, and I proclaim aloud
That for my brothers and myself I die.
I am not fond of life, but think I gain
An honorable prize to die with glory.

"Still nobler when Iolaus proposes rather that she shall draw lots with her sisters.

By lot I will not die, for to such death
No thanks are due, or glory—name it not.
If you accept me, if my offered life
Be grateful to you, willingly I give it
For these, but by constraint I will not die.

"Very fine are her parting advice and injunctions to them all:

> *Farewell! revered old man, farewell! and teach*
> *These youths in all things to be wise, like thee,*
> *Naught will avail them more.*

"Macaria has the clear Minerva eye: Antigone's is deeper, and more capable of emotion, but calm. Iphigenia's, glistening, gleaming with angel truth, or dewy as a hidden violet.

"I am sorry that Tennyson, who spoke with such fitness of all the others in his 'Dream of fair women,' has not of Iphigenia. Of her alone he has not made a fit picture, but only of the circumstances of the sacrifice. He can never have taken to heart this work of Euripides, yet he was so worthy to feel it. Of Jeptha's daughter, he has spoken as he would of Iphigenia, both in her beautiful song, and when

> *I heard Him, for He spake, and grief became*
> *A solemn scorn of ills.*

> *It comforts me in this one thought to dwell*
> *That I subdued me to my father's will;*
> *Because the kiss he gave me, ere I fell,*
> *Sweetens the spirit still.*

> *Moreover it is written, that my race*
> *Hewed Ammon, hip and thigh from Arroer*
> *Or Arnon unto Minneth. Here her face*
> *Glow'd as I look'd on her.*

> *She locked her lips; she left me where I stood;*
> *"Glory to God," she sang, and past afar,*
> *Thridding the sombre boskage of the woods,*
> *Toward the morning-star.*

"In the 'Trojan dames' there are fine touches of nature with regard to Cassandra. Hecuba shows that mixture of shame and reverence, that prose kindred always do, towards the inspired child, the poet, the elected sufferer for the race.

"When the herald announces that she is chosen to be the mistress of Agamemnon, Hecuba answers indignant, and betraying the involuntary pride and faith she felt in this daughter.

> *The virgin of Apollo, whom the God,*
> *Radiant with golden locks, allowed to live*

> *In her pure vow of maiden chastity?*
Tal. *With love the raptured virgin smote his heart.*
Hec. *Cast from thee, O my daughter, cast away*
> *Thy sacred wand, rend off the honored wreaths,*
> *The splendid ornaments that grace thy brows.*

"Yet the moment Cassandra appears, singing wildly her inspired song, Hecuba calls her

> *My frantic child.*

"Yet how graceful she is in her tragic phrenzy, the chorus shows—

> *How sweetly at thy house's ills thou smil'st,*
> *Chanting what haply thou wilt not show true?*

"But if Hecuba dares not trust her highest instinct about her daughter, still less can the vulgar mind of the herald (a man not without tenderness of heart, but with no princely, no poetic blood,) abide the wild prophetic mood which insults his prejudices both as to country and decorums of the sex. Yet Agamemnon, though not a noble man, is of large mould and could admire this strange beauty which excited distaste in common minds.

> Tal. *What commands respect, and is held high*
> *As wise, is nothing better than the mean*
> *Of no repute: for this most potent king*
> *Of all the Grecians, the much honored son*
> *Of Atreus, is enamored with his prize,*
> *This frantic raver. I am a poor man,*
> *Yet would I not receive her to my bed.*

"Cassandra answers with a careless disdain,

> *This is a busy slave.*

"With all the lofty decorum of manners among the ancients, how free was their intercourse, man to man, how full the mutual understanding between prince and 'busy slave!' Not here in adversity only, but in the pomp of power, it was so. Kings were approached with ceremonious obeisance, but not hedged round with etiquette, they could see and know their fellows.

"The Andromache here is just as lovely as that of the Iliad.

"To her child whom they are about to murder, the same that was frightened at the 'glittering plume.'

> *Dost thou weep,*
> *My son? Hast thou a sense of thy ill fate?*
> *Why dost thou clasp me with thy hands, why hold*
> *My robes, and shelter thee beneath my wings,*
> *Like a young bird? No more my Hector comes,*
> *Returning from the tomb; he grasps no more*
> *His glittering spear, bringing protection to thee.*
>
>   *   *   *
>
>   *   *   O soft embrace,*
> *And to thy mother dear. O fragrant breath!*
> *In vain I swathed thy infant limbs, in vain*
> *I gave thee nurture at this breast, and toiled,*
> *Wasted with care. If ever, now embrace,*
> *Now clasp thy mother; throw thine arms around*
> *My neck and join thy cheek, thy lips to mine.*

"As I look up I meet the eyes of Beatrice Cenci. Beautiful one, these woes, even, were less than thine, yet thou seemest to understand them all. Thy clear melancholy gaze says, they, at least, had known moments of bliss, and the tender relations of nature had not been broken and polluted from the very first. Yes! the gradations of wo are all but infinite: only good can be infinite.

"Certainly the Greeks knew more of real home intercourse, and more of woman than the Americans. It is in vain to tell me of outward observances. The poets, the sculptors always tell the truth. In proportion as a nation is refined, women *must* have an ascendancy, it is the law of nature.

"Beatrice! thou wert not 'fond of life,' either, more than those princesses. Thou wert able to cut it down in the full flower of beauty, as an offering to *the best* known to thee. Thou wert not so happy as to die for thy country or thy brethren, but thou wert worthy of such an occasion.

"In the days of chivalry woman was habitually viewed more as an ideal, but I do not know that she inspired a deeper and more home-

felt reverence than Iphigenia in the breast of Achilles, or Macaria in
that of her old guardian, Iolaus.

"We may, with satisfaction, add to these notes the words to which
Haydn has adapted his magnificent music in 'The Creation.'

" 'In native worth and honor clad, with beauty, courage, strength
adorned, erect to heaven, and tall, he stands, a Man!—the lord and
king of all! The large and arched front sublime of wisdom deep declares the seat, and in his eyes with brightness shines the soul, the
breath and image of his God. With fondness leans upon his breast the
partner for him formed, a woman fair, and graceful spouse. Her softly
smiling virgin looks, of flowery spring the mirror, bespeak him love,
and joy and bliss.'

"Whoever has heard this music must have a mental standard as
to what man and woman should be. Such was marriage in Eden, when
'erect to heaven *he* stood,' but since, like other institutions, this must
be not only reformed, but revived, may be offered as a picture of
something intermediate,—the seed of the future growth,—"

H

THE SACRED MARRIAGE

And has another's life as large a scope?
It may give due fulfilment to thy hope,
And every portal to the unknown may ope.

If, near this other life, thy inmost feeling
Trembles with fateful prescience of revealing
The future Deity, time is still concealing.

If thou feel thy whole force drawn more and more
To launch that other bark on seas without a shore;
And no still secret must be kept in store;

If meannesses that dim each temporal deed,
The dull decay that mars the fleshly weed,
And flower of love that seems to fall and leave no seed—

Hide never the full presence from thy sight
Of mutual aims and tasks, ideals bright,
Which feed their roots to-day on all this seeming blight.

Twin stars that mutual circle in the heaven,
Two parts for spiritual concord given,
Twin Sabbaths that inlock the Sacred Seven;

Still looking to the centre for the cause,
Mutual light giving to draw out the powers,
And learning all the other groups by cognizance of one another's
    laws:

The parent love the wedded love includes,
The one permits the two their mutual moods,
The two each other know mid myriad multitudes;

With child-like intellect discerning love,
And mutual action energizing love,
In myriad forms affiliating love.

A world whose seasons bloom from pole to pole,
A force which knows both starting-point and goal,
Home in Heaven,—the Union in the Soul.

NEW-YORK DAILY TRIBUNE
COLUMNS

Margaret Fuller left her native New England for New York City in 1844. Joining the ranks of journalists at Horace Greeley's New-York Daily Tribune, *she became that newspaper's first literary editor. Widely read in European literature and deeply committed to the development of an authentically American literature, Fuller was an ideal choice. She kept the* Tribune's *readers informed about developments in European literature, introducing them to contemporary poets, novelists, and historians. Simultaneously, she championed the claims of America's writers, female as well as male. In the nearly two hundred columns that Fuller published in Greeley's* Tribune, *she demonstrated an increasing concern with social and political issues. Subjects such as class relations, penal reform, racial prejudice, and social welfare were analyzed with striking originality. In Fuller's final column as the* Tribune's *literary editor, she told her readers that the previous twenty months had challenged her "with a richer and more varied exercise for thought and life than twenty years could in any other part of these United States." Her readers might well have responded that Fuller had offered them a similar challenge.*

EMERSON'S ESSAYS:
SECOND SERIES

DECEMBER 7, 1844

AT THE DISTANCE OF THREE YEARS this volume follows the first series of Essays, which have already made to themselves a circle of readers, attentive, thoughtful, more and more intelligent, and this circle is a large one if we consider the circumstances of this country, and of England, also, at this time.

In England it would seem there are a larger number of persons waiting for an invitation to calm thought and sincere intercourse than among ourselves. Copies of Mr. Emerson's first published little volume called "Nature," have there been sold by thousands in a short time, while one edition has needed seven years to get circulated here. Several of his Orations and Essays from "The Dial" have also been republished there, and met with a reverent and earnest response.

We suppose that while in England the want of such a voice is as great as here, a larger number are at leisure to recognize that want; a far larger number have set foot in the speculative region and have ears refined to appreciate these melodious accents.

Our people, heated by a partisan spirit, necessarily occupied in these first stages by bringing out the material resources of the land, not generally prepared by early training for the enjoyment of books that require attention and reflection, are still more injured by a large majority of writers and speakers, who lend all their efforts to flatter corrupt tastes and mental indolence, instead of feeling it their prerogative and their duty to admonish the community of the danger and arouse it to nobler energy. The aim of the writer or lecturer is not to say the best he knows in as few and well-chosen words as he can, making it his first aim to do justice to the subject. Rather he seeks to beat out a thought as thin as possible, and to consider what the audience will be most willing to receive.

The result of such a course is inevitable. Literature and Art must become daily more degraded; Philosophy cannot exist. A man who feels within his mind some spark of genius, or a capacity for the exercises of talent, should consider himself as endowed with a sacred commission. He is the natural priest, the shepherd of the people. He must raise his mind as high as he can toward the heaven of truth, and try to draw up with him those less gifted by nature with ethereal lightness. If he does not so, but rather employs his powers to flatter them in their poverty, and to hinder aspiration by useless words, and a mere seeming of activity, his sin is great, he is false to God, and false to man.

Much of this sin indeed is done ignorantly. The idea that literature calls men to the genuine hierarchy is almost forgotten. One, who finds himself able, uses his pen, as he might a trowel, solely to procure himself bread, without having reflected on the position in which he thereby places himself.

Apart from the troop of mercenaries, there is one, still larger, of those who use their powers merely for local and temporary ends, aiming at no excellence other than many conduce to these. Among these, rank persons of honor and the best intentions, but they neglect the lasting for the transient, as a man neglects to furnish his mind that he may provide the better for the house in which his body is to dwell for a few years.

When these sins and errors are prevalent, and threaten to become more so, how can we sufficiently prize and honor a mind which is quite pure from such? When, as in the present case, we find a man whose only aim is the discernment and interpretation of the spiritual laws by which we live and move and have our being, all whose objects are permanent, and whose every word stands for a fact.

If only as a representative of the claims of individual culture in a nation which tends to lay such stress on artificial organization and external results, Mr. Emerson would be invaluable here. History will inscribe his name as a father of the country, for he is one who pleads her cause against herself.

If New-England may be regarded as a chief mental focus to the New World, and many symptoms seem to give her this place, as to other centres the characteristics of heart and lungs to the body politic; if we may believe, as the writer does believe, that what is to be acted out in the country at large is, most frequently, first indicated there, as all the phenomena of the nervous system in the fantasies of the brain, we may hail as an auspicious omen the influence Mr. Emerson has there obtained, which is deep-rooted, increasing, and, over the younger portion of the community, far greater than that of any other person.

His books are received there with a more ready intelligence than elsewhere, partly because his range of personal experience and illustration applies to that region, partly because he has prepared the way for his books to be read by his great powers as a speaker.

The audience that waited for years upon the lectures, a part of which is incorporated into these volumes of Essays, was never large, but it was select, and it was constant. Among the hearers were some, who though, attracted by the beauty of character and manner, they were willing to hear the speaker through, always went away discontented. They were accustomed to an artificial method, whose scaffolding could easily be retraced, and desired an obvious sequence of logical inferences. They insisted there was nothing in what they had heard, because they could not give a clear account of its course and purport. They did not see that Pindar's odes might be very well arranged for their own purpose, and yet not bear translating into the methods of Mr. Locke.

Others were content to be benefited by a good influence without a strict analysis of its means. "My wife says it is about the elevation of human nature, and so it seems to me;" was a fit reply to some of the critics. Many were satisfied to find themselves excited to congenial thought and nobler life, without an exact catalogue of the thoughts of the speaker.

Those who believed no truth could exist, unless encased by the burrs of opinion, went away utterly baffled. Sometimes they thought he was on their side, then presently would come to something on the other. He really seemed to believe there were two sides to every subject, and even to intimate higher ground from which each might be seen to have an infinite number of sides or bearings, an impertinence not to be endured! The partisan heard but once and returned no more.

But some there were, simple souls, whose life had been, perhaps, without clear light, yet still a search after truth for its own sake, who were able to receive what followed on the suggestion of a subject in a natural manner, as a stream of thought. These recognized, beneath the veil of words, the still small voice of conscience, the vestal fires of lone religious hours, and the mild teachings of the summer woods.

The charm of the elocution, too, was great. His general manner was that of the reader, occasionally rising into direct address or invocation in passages where tenderness or majesty demanded more energy. At such times both eye and voice called on a remote future to give a worthy reply. A future which shall manifest more largely the universal soul as it was then manifest to this soul. The tone of the voice was a grave body tone, full and sweet rather than sonorous, yet flexible and haunted by many modulations, as even instruments of wood and brass seem to become after they have been long played on with skill and taste; how much more so the human voice! In the more expressive passages it uttered notes of silvery clearness, winning, yet still more commanding. The words uttered in those tones, floated awhile above us, then took root in the memory like winged seed.

In the union of an even rustic plainness with lyric inspirations, religious dignity with philosophic calmness, keen sagacity in details with boldness of view, we saw what brought to mind the early poets and legislators of Greece—men who taught their fellows to plow and avoid moral evil, sing hymns to the gods and watch the metamorphoses of nature. Here in civic Boston was such a man—one who could see man in his original grandeur and his original childishness, rooted in simple nature, raising to the heavens the brow and eyes of a poet.

And these lectures seemed not so much lectures as grave didactic poems, theogonies, perhaps, adorned by odes when some Power was in question whom the poet had best learned to serve, and with eclogues wisely portraying in familiar tongue the duties of man to man and "harmless animals."

Such was the attitude in which the speaker appeared to that portion of the audience who have remained permanently attached to him.—They value his words as the signets of reality; receive his influence as a help and incentive to a nobler discipline than the age, in its general aspect, appears to require; and do not fear to anticipate the verdict of posterity in claiming for him the honors of greatness, and, in some respects, of a Master.

In New-England he thus formed for himself a class of readers, who rejoice to study in his books what they already know by heart. For, though the thought has become familiar, its beautiful garb is always fresh and bright in hue.

A similar circle of like-minded the books must and do form for themselves, though with a movement less directly powerful, as more distant from its source.

The Essays have also been obnoxious to many charges. To that of obscurity, or want of perfect articulation. Of "Euphuism," as an excess of fancy in proportion to imagination, and an inclination, at times, to subtlety at the expense of strength, has been styled. The human heart complains of inadequacy, either in the nature or experience of the writer, to represent its full vocation and its deeper needs. Sometimes it speaks of this want as "under-development" or a want of expansion which may yet be remedied; sometimes doubts whether "in this mansion there be either hall or portal to receive the loftier of the Passions." Sometimes the soul is deified at the expense of nature, then again nature at that of man, and we are not quite sure that we can make a true harmony by balance of the statements.—This writer has never written one good work, if such a work be one where the whole commands more attention than the parts. If such an one be produced only where, after an accumulation of materials, fire enough be applied to fuse the whole into one new substance. This second series is superior in this respect to the former, yet in no one essay is the main stress so obvious as to produce on the mind the harmonious effect of a noble river or a tree in full leaf. Single passages and sentences engage our attention too much in proportion. These essays, it has been justly said, tire like a string of mosaics or a house built of medals. We miss what we expect in the work of the great poet, or the great philosopher, the liberal air of all the zones: the glow, uniform yet various in tint, which is given to a body by free circulation of the heart's blood from the hour of birth. Here is, undoubtedly, the man of ideas, but we want the ideal man also; want the heart and genius of human life to interpret it, and here our satisfaction is not so perfect. We doubt this friend raised himself too early to the perpendicular and did not lie along the ground long enough to hear the secret whispers of our parent life. We could wish he might be thrown by conflicts on the lap of mother earth, to see if he would not rise again with added powers.

All this we may say, but it cannot excuse us from benefiting by the great gifts that have been given, and assigning them their due place.

Some painters paint on a red ground. And this color may be supposed to represent the ground work most immediately congenial to most men, as it is the color of blood and represents human vitality. The figures traced upon it are instinct with life in its fulness and depth.

But other painters paint on a gold ground. And a very different, but no less natural, because also a celestial beauty, is given to their works who choose for their foundation the color of the sunbeam, which nature has preferred for her most precious product, and that which will best bear the test of purification, gold.

If another simile may be allowed, another no less apt is at hand. Wine is the most brilliant and intense expression of the powers of earth.—It is her potable fire, her answer to the sun. It exhilirates, it inspires, but then it is liable to fever and intoxicate too the careless partaker.

Mead was the chosen drink of the Northern gods. And this essence of the honey of the mountain bee was not thought unworthy to revive the souls of the valiant who had left their bodies on the fields of strife below.

Nectar should combine the virtues of the ruby wine, the golden mead, without their defects or dangers.

Two high claims our writer can vindicate on the attention of his contemporaries. One from his sincerity. You have his thought just as it found place in the life of his own soul. Thus, however near or relatively distant its approximation to absolute truth, its action on you cannot fail to be healthful. It is a part of the free air.

He belongs to that band of whom there may be found a few in every age, and who now in known human history may be counted by hundreds, who worship the one God only, the God of Truth. They worship, not saints, nor creeds, nor churches, nor reliques, nor idols in any form. The mind is kept open to truth, and life only valued as a tendency toward it. This must be illustrated by acts and words of love, purity and intelligence. Such are the salt of the earth; let the minutest crystal of that salt be willingly by us held in solution.

The other is through that part of his life, which, if sometimes obstructed or chilled by the critical intellect, is yet the prevalent and the main source of his power. It is that by which he imprisons his hearer only to free him again as a "liberating God" (to use his own words). But indeed let us use them altogether, for none other, ancient or modern, can more worthily express how, making present to us the courses and destinies of nature, he invests himself with her serenity and animates us with her joy.

"Poetry was all written before time was, and whenever we are so finely organized that we can penetrate into that region where the air is music, we hear those primal warblings, and attempt to write them down, but we lose ever and anon a word, or a verse, and substitute something of our own, and thus miswrite the poem. The men of more delicate ear write down these cadences more faithfully, and these transcripts, though imperfect, become the songs of the nations."

"As the eyes of Lyncæus were said to see through the earth, so the poet turns the world to glass, and shows us all things in their right series and procession. For, through that better perception, he stands one step nearer to things, and sees the flowing or metamorphosis; perceives that thought is multiform; that within the form of every creature is a force impelling it to ascend into a higher form; and following with his eyes the life, uses the forms which express that life, and so the speech flows with the flowing of nature."

Thus have we in a brief and unworthy manner indicated some

views of these books. The only true criticism of these, or any good books, may be gained by making them the companions of our lives. Does every accession of knowledge or a juster sense of beauty make us prize them more? Then they are good, indeed, and more immortal than mortal. Let that test be applied to these; essays which will lead to great and complete poems—somewhere.

OUR CITY CHARITIES
Visit to Bellevue Alms House, to the
Farm School, The Asylum for
the Insane, and Penitentiary
on Blackwell's Island

MARCH 19, 1845

THE ASPECT OF NATURE WAS SAD; what is worse, it was dull and dubious, when we set forth on these visits. The sky was leaden and lowering, the air unkind and piercing, the little birds sat mute and astonished at the departure of the beautiful days which had lured them to premature song. It was a suitable day for such visits. The pauper establishments that belong to a great city take the place of the skeleton at the banquets of old. They admonish us of stern realities, which must bear the same explanation as the frequent blight of Nature's bloom. They should be looked at by all, if only for their own sakes, that they may not sink listlessly into selfish ease, in a world so full of disease. They should be looked at by all who wish to enlighten themselves as to the means of aiding their fellow creatures in any way, public or private. For nothing can really be done till the right principles are discovered, and it would seem they still need to be discovered or elucidated, so little is done, with a great deal of desire in the heart of the community to do what is right. Such visits are not yet calculated to encourage and exhilarate, as does the story of the Prodigal Son; they wear a grave aspect and suit the grave mood of a cold Spring day.

At the Alms House there is every appearance of kindness in the guardians of the poor, and there was a greater degree of cleanliness and comfort than we had expected. But the want of suitable and sufficient employment is a great evil. The persons who find here either a permanent or temporary refuge have scarcely any occupation provided except to raise vegetables for the establishment, and prepare clothing for themselves. The men especially have the most vagrant, degraded air, and so much indolence must tend to confirm them in every bad habit. We were told that, as they are under no strict discipline, their labor at the various trades could not be made profitable; yet surely the means of such should be provided, even at some expense. Employments of various kinds must be absolutely needed, if only to counteract the bad affects of such a position. Every establishment in aid of the poor should be planned with a view to their education. There should be instruction, both practical and in the use of books, openings to a better intercourse than they can obtain from their miserable homes, correct notions as to cleanliness, diet, and fresh air. A great deal of pains would be lost in their case, as with all other arrangements for the good of the many, but here and there the seed would fall into the right places, and some members of the downtrodden million, rising a little from the mud, would raise the whole body with them.

As we saw old women enjoying their dish of gossip and their dish of tea, and mothers able for a while to take care in peace of their poor little children, we longed and hoped for that genius, who shall teach how to make, of these establishments, places of rest and instruction, not of degradation.

The causes which make the acceptance of public charity so much more injurious to the receiver than that of private are obvious, but surely not such that the human mind which has just invented the magnetic telegraph and Anastatic printing, may not obviate them. A deeper religion at the heart of Society would devise such means. Why should it be that the poor may still feel themselves men; paupers not? The poor man does not feel himself injured but benefited by the charity of the doctor who gives him back the bill he is unable to pay, because the doctor is acting from intelligent sympathy—from love. Let Society do the same. She might raise the man, who is accepting her bounty, instead of degrading him.

Indeed, it requires great nobleness and faith in human nature, and God's will concerning it, for the officials not to take the tone toward these under their care, which their vices and bad habits prompt, but which must confirm them in the same. Men treated with respect are reminded of self-respect, and if there is a sound spot left in the character, the healthy influence spreads.

We were sorry to see mothers with their newborn infants exposed to the careless scrutiny of male visitors. In the hospital, those who had children scarce a day old were not secure from the gaze of the stranger. This cannot be pleasant to them, and, if they have not refinement to dislike it, those who have should teach it to them. But we suppose there is no woman who has entirely lost sight of the feelings of girlhood as not to dislike the scrutiny of strangers at a time which is sacred, if any in life is. Women they may like to see, even strangers, if they can approach them with delicacy.

In the yard of the hospital, we saw a little Dutch girl, a dwarf, who would have suggested a thousand poetical images and fictions to the mind of Victor Hugo or Sir Walter Scott. She had been brought here to New York, as we understood, by some showman and then deserted, so that this place was her only refuge. No one could communicate with her or know her feelings, but she showed what they were, by running to the gate whenever it was opened, though treated with familiar kindness and seeming pleased by it. She had a large head, ragged dark hair, a glowering wizard eye, an uncouth yet pleasant smile, like an old child;—she wore a gold ring, and her complexion was as yellow as gold, if not as bright; altogether she looked like a gnome, more than any attempt we have ever known to embody in Art that fabled inhabitant of the mines and secret caves of earth.

From the Alms House we passed in an open boat to the Farm School. We were unprepared to find this, as we did, only a school upon a small farm, instead of one in which study is associated with labor. The children are simply taken care of and taught the common English branches till they are twelve years old, when they are bound out to various kinds of work. We think this plan very injudicious. It is bad enough for the children of rich parents, not likely in after life to bear a hard burden, and who are, at any rate, supplied with those various excitements required to develope the character in the earliest years; it is bad enough, we say, for these to have no kind of useful labor mingled with their plays and studies. Even these children would expand more, and be more variously called forth, and better prepared for common life, if another course were pursued. But, in schools like this at the farm, where the children, on leaving it, will be at once called on for adroitness and readiness of mind and body, and where the absence of natural ties and the various excitements that rise from them inevitably give to life a mechanical routine calculated to cramp and still the character, it would be peculiarly desirable to provide various occupations, and such as are calculated to prepare for common life. As to economy of time, there is never time lost, by mingling other pursuits with the studies of children; they have vital energy enough for many things at once, and learn more from books when their attention is quickened by other kinds of culture.

Some of these children were pretty, and they were healthy and well-grown, considering the general poverty or vice of the class from which they were taken. That terrible scourge, opthalmia, disfigured many among them. This disease, from some cause not yet detected, has been prevalent here for many years. We trust it may yield to the change of location next summer. There is not water enough here to give the children decent advantages as to bathing. This, too, will be remedied by the change. The Principal, who has been almost all his life connected with this establishment and that at Bellevue, seemed to feel a lively interest in his charge. He has arranged the dormitories with excellent judgment, both as to ventilation and neatness. This, alone, is a great advantage these children have over those of poor families living at home. They may pass the night in healthy sleep, and have thereby a chance for innocent and active days.

We saw with pleasure the little children engaged in the kind of drill they so much enjoy, of gesticulation regulated by singing. It was also pretty to see the babies sitting in a circle and the nurses in the midst feeding them, alternately, with a spoon. It seemed like a nest full of little birds, each opening its bill as the parent returns from her flight.

Hence we passed to the Asylum for the Insane. Only a part of this building is completed, and it is well known that the space is insufficient. Twice as many are inmates here as can be properly accommodated. A tolerable degree, however, of order and cleanliness is preserved. We could not but observe the vast difference between the appearance of the insane here and at Bloomingdale, or other Institutions where the number of attendants and nature of the arrangements permit them to be the objects of individual treatment; that is, where the wants and difficulties of each patient can be distinctly and carefully attended to. At Bloomingdale, the shades of character and feeling were nicely kept up, decorum of manners preserved, and the insane showed in every way that they felt no violent separation betwixt them and the rest of the world, and might easily return to it. The eye, though bewildered, seemed lively, and the tongue prompt. But here, insanity appeared in its more stupid, wild, or despairing forms. They crouched in corners; they had no eye for the stranger, no heart for hope, no habitual expectation of light. Just as at the Farm School, where the children show by their uninformed features and mechanical movements that they are treated by wholesale, so do these poor sufferers.

It is an evil incident to public establishments, and which only a more intelligent public attention can obviate.

One figure we saw, here also, of high poetical interest. It was a woman seated on the floor, in the corner of her cell, with a shawl wrapped gracefully around her head and chest, like a Nun's veil. Her hair was grey, her face attenuated and very pallid, her eyes large, open, fixed and bright with a still fire. She never moved them nor ceased chanting the service of the Church. She was a Catholic, who became insane while preparing to be a Nun. She is surely a Nun now in her heart; and a figure from which a painter might study for some of the most consecrated subjects.

Passing to the Penitentiary, we entered on one of the gloomiest scenes that deforms this great metropolis. Here are the twelve hundred, who receive the punishment due to the vices of so large a portion of the rest. And under what circumstances! Never was punishment treated more simply as a social convenience, without regard to pure right, or a hope of reformation.

Public attention is now so far awake to the state of the Penitentiary that it cannot be long, we trust, before proper means of classification are devised, a temporary asylum provided for those who leave this purgatory, even now, unwilling to return to the inferno from which it has for a time kept them, and means presented likely to lead some, at least, among the many, who seem hardened, to better views and hopes. It must be that the more righteous feeling which has shown itself in regard to the prisons at Sing Sing and elsewhere, must take some effect as to the Penitentiary also. The present Superintendant enters into the necessity of such improvements, and, should he remain there, will do what he can to carry them into effect.

The want of proper matrons, or any matrons, to take the care so necessary for the bodily or mental improvement or even decent condition of the seven hundred women assembled here, is an offence that cries aloud. It is impossible to take the most cursory survey of this assembly of women; especially it is impossible to see them in the Hospital, where the circumstances are a little more favorable, without seeing how many there are in whom the feelings of innocent childhood are not dead, who need only good influences and steady aid to raise them from the pit of infamy and wo into which they have fallen. And, if there was not one that could be helped, at least, Society owes them the insurance of a decent condition while here. We trust that interest on this subject will not slumber.

The recognized principles of all such institutions which have any higher object than the punishment of fault, (and we believe few among us are so ignorant as to avow that as the only object, though they may, from want of thought, act as if it were,) are—Classification as the first step, that the bad may not impede those who wish to do well; 2d. Instruction, practical, oral, and by furnishing books which may open entirely new hopes and thoughts to minds oftener darkened than corrupted; 3d. A good Sanitary system, which promotes self-respect, and through health and purity of body, the same in mind.

In visiting the Tombs the other day, we found the air in the upper galleries unendurable, and felt great regret that those confined there should be constantly subjected to it. Give the free breath of Heaven to all who are still permitted to breathe.—We cannot, however, wonder at finding this barbarity in a prison, having been subjected to it at the most fashionable places of public resort. Dr. Griscom has sent us his excellent lecture on the health of New-York, which we recommend to all who take a vital interest in the city where they live, and have intellect to discern that a cancer on the body must in time affect the head and heart also. We thought, while reading, that it was not surprising typhus fever and opthalmia should be bred in the cellars, while the families of those who live in palaces breathe such infected air at public places, and receive their visitors on New Year's day by candlelight. (That was a sad omen for the New Year—did they mean to class themselves among those who love darkness rather than light?)

We hope to see that two thousand poor people, and the poor children, better situated in their new abode, when we visit them again. The Insane Asylum will gain at once by enlargement of accommodations; but more attendance is also necessary, and, for that purpose, the best persons should be selected. We saw, with pleasure, tame pigeons walking about among the most violent of the insane, but we also saw two attendants with faces brutal and stolid. Such a charge is too delicate to be intrusted to any but excellent persons. Of the Penitentiary we shall write again. All criticism, however imperfect, should be welcome. There is no reason why New York should not become a model for other States in these things. There is wealth enough, intelligence, and good desire enough, and surely, need enough. If she be not the best cared for city in the world, she threatens to surpass in corruption London and Paris. Such bane as is constantly poured into her veins demands powerful antidotes.

But nothing effectual can be achieved while both measures and men are made the sport of political changes. It is a most crying and shameful evil, which does not belong to our institutions, but is a careless distortion of them, that the men and measures are changed in these institutions with changes from Whig to Democrat, from Democrat to Whig. Churches, School, Colleges, the care of the Insane, and suffering Poor, should be preserved from the uneasy tossings of this delirium. The Country, the State, should look to it that only those fit for such officers should be chosen for such, apart from all considerations of political party. Let this be thought of; for without an absolute change in this respect no permanent good whatever can be effected; and farther, let not economy but utility be the rule of expenditure, for, here, parsimony is the worst prodigality.

PREVALENT IDEA THAT POLITENESS IS TOO GREAT A LUXURY TO BE GIVEN TO THE POOR

MAY 31, 1845

A FEW DAYS AGO, a lady, crossing in one of the ferry boats that ply from this city, saw a young boy, poorly dressed, sitting with an infant in his arms on one of the benches. She observed that the child looked sickly and coughed. This, as the day was raw, made her anxious in its behalf, and she went to the boy and asked whether he was alone there with the baby, and if he did not think the cold breeze dangerous for it. He replied that he was sent out with the child to take care of it, and that his father said the fresh air from the water would do it good.

While he made this simple answer, a number of persons had collected around to listen, and one of them, a well-dressed woman, addressed the boy in a string of such questions and remarks as these:

"What is your name? Where do you live? Are you telling us the truth? It's a shame to have that baby out in such weather; you'll be the death of it. (To the bystanders:) I would go and see his mother and tell her about it, if I was sure he had told us the truth about where he lived. How do you expect to get back? Here, (in the rudest voice,) somebody says you have not told the truth as to where you live."

The child, whose only offence consisted in taking care of the little one in public, and answering when he was spoken to, began to shed tears at the accusations thus grossly preferred against him. The by-standers stared at both; but among them all there was not one with sufficiently clear notions of propriety and moral energy to say to this impudent questioner, "Woman! do you suppose, because you wear a handsome shawl, and that boy a patched jacket, that you have any right to speak to him at all, unless he wishes it, far less to prefer against him those rude accusations. Your vulgarity is unendurable; leave the place or alter your manner."

Many such instances have we seen of insolent rudeness or more insolent affability founded on no apparent grounds, except an apparent difference in pecuniary position, for no one can suppose in such cases the offending party has really enjoyed the benefit of refined education and society, but all present let them pass as matters of course. It was sad to see how the poor would endure—mortifying to see how the purse-proud dared offend. An excellent man who was, in his early years, a missionary to the poor, used to speak afterwards with great shame of the manner in which he had conducted himself towards them.—"When I recollect," said he, "the freedom with which I entered their houses, inquired into all their affairs, commented on their conduct and disputed their statements I wonder I was never horsewhipped and feel that I ought to have been; it would have done me good, for I needed as severe a lesson on the universal obligations of politeness in its only genuine form of respect for man as man, and delicate sympathy with each in his peculiar position."

Charles Lamb, who was indeed worthy to be called a human being from those refined sympathies, said, "You call him a gentleman: does his washerwoman find him so?" We may say, if she did so, she found him a man, neither treating her with vulgar abruptness, nor giving himself airs of condescending liveliness, but treating her with that genuine respect which a feeling of equality inspires.

To doubt the veracity of another is an insult which in most civilized communities must in the so-called higher classes be atoned for by blood, but, in those same communities, the same men will, with the utmost lightness, doubt the truth of one who wears a ragged coat, and thus do all they can to injure and degrade him by assailing his self-respect, and breaking the feeling of personal honor—a wound to which hurts a man as a wound to its bark does a tree.

Then how rudely are favors conferred, just as a bone is thrown to a dog. A gentleman indeed will not do that without accompanying signs of sympathy and regard. Just as this woman said, "If you have told the truth I will go and see your mother," are many acts performed on which the actors pride themselves as kind and charitable.

All men might learn from the French in these matters. That people, whatever be their faults, are really well-bred, and many acts might be quoted from their romantic annals, where gifts were given from rich to poor with a graceful courtesy, equally honorable and delightful to the giver and the receiver.

In Catholic countries there is more courtesy, for charity is there a duty, and must be done for God's sake; there is less room for a man to give himself the Pharisaical tone about it. A rich man is not so surprised to find himself in contact with a poor one; nor is the custom of kneeling on the open pavement, the silk robe close to the beggar's rags, without profit. The separation by pews, even on the day when all meet nearest, is as bad for the manners as the soul.

Blessed be he or she who has passed through this world, not only with an open purse and willingness to render the aid of mere outward benefits, but with an open eye and open heart, ready to cheer the downcast, and enlighten the dull by words of comfort and looks of love. The wayside charities are the most valuable both as to sustaining hope and diffusing knowledge, and none can render them who has not an expansive nature, a heart alive to affection, and some true notion, however imperfectly developed, of the nature of human brotherhood.

Such an one can never sauce the given meat with taunts, freeze the bread by a cold glance of doubt, or plunge the man who asked for his hand deeper back into the mud by any kind of rudeness.

In the little instance with which we begun, no help was asked, unless by the sight of the timid little boy's old jacket. But the license which this seemed to the well-clothed woman to give to rudeness was so characteristic of a deep fault now existing, that a volume of comments might follow and a host of anecdotes be drawn from almost any one's experience in exposition of it. These few words, perhaps, may awaken thought in those who have drawn tears from others eyes through an ignorance brutal, but not hopelessly so, if they are willing to rise above it.

NARRATIVE OF THE LIFE OF
FREDERICK DOUGLASS,
An American Slave, Written by Himself

JUNE 10, 1845

FREDERICK DOUGLASS has been for some time a prominent member of the Abolition party. He is said to be an excellent speaker—can speak from a thorough personal experience—and has upon the audience, beside, the influence of a strong character and uncommon talents. In the book before us he has put into the story of his life the thoughts, the feelings and the adventures that have been so affecting through the living voice; nor are they less so from the printed page. He has had the courage to name the persons, times and places, thus exposing himself to obvious danger, and setting the seal on his deep convictions as to the religious need of speaking the whole truth. Considered merely as a narrative, we have never read one more simple, true, coherent, and warm with genuine feeling. It is an excellent piece of writing, and on that score to be prized as a specimen of the powers of the Black Race, which Prejudice persists in disputing. We prize highly all evidence of this kind, and it is becoming more abundant. The Cross of the Legion of Honor has just been conferred in France on Dumas and Soulié, both celebrated in the paths of light literature. Dumas, whose father was a General in the French Army, is a Mulatto; Soulié, a Quadroon. He went from New-Orleans, where, though to the eye a white man, yet, as known to have African blood in his veins, he could never have enjoyed the privileges due to a human being. Leaving the Land of Freedom, he found himself free to develope the powers that God had given.

Two wise and candid thinkers,—the Scotchman, Kinmont, prematurely lost to this country, of which he was so faithful and generous a student, and the late Dr. Channing,—both thought that the African Race had in them a peculiar element, which, if it could be assimilated with those imported among us from Europe, would give to genius a development, and to the energies of character a balance and harmony beyond what has been seen heretofore in the history of the world. Such an element is indicated in their lowest estate by a talent for melody, a ready skill at imitation and adaptation, an almost indestructible elasticity of nature. It is to be remarked in the writings both of Soulié and Dumas, full of faults but glowing with plastic life and fertile in invention. The same torrid energy and saccharine fulness may be felt in the writings of this Douglass, though his life being one of action or resistance, was less favorable to such powers than one of a more joyous flow might have been.

The book is prefaced by two communications,—one from Garrison, and one from Wendell Phillips. That from the former is in his usual overemphatic style. His motives and his course have been noble and generous. We look upon him with high respect, but he has indulged in violent invective and denunciation till he has spoiled the temper of his mind. Like a man who has been in the habit of screaming himself hoarse to make the deaf hear, he can no longer pitch his voice on a key agreeable to common ears. Mr. Phillips's remarks are equally decided, without this exaggeration in the tone. Douglass himself seems very just and temperate. We feel that his view, even of those who have injured him most, may be relied upon. He knows how to allow for motives and influences. Upon the subject of Religion, he speaks with great force, and not more than our own sympathies can respond to. The inconsistencies of Slaveholding professors of religion cry to Heaven. We are not disposed to detest, or refuse communion with them. Their blindness is but one form of that prevalent fallacy which substitutes a creed for a faith, a ritual for a life. We have seen too much of this system of atonement not to know that those who adopt it often began with good intentions, and are, at any rate, in their mistakes worthy of the deepest pity. But that is no reason why the truth should not be uttered, trumpet-tongued, about the thing. "Bring no more vain oblations"; sermons must daily be preached anew on that text. Kings, five hundred years ago, built Churches with the spoils of War; Clergymen to-day command Slaves to obey a Gospel which they will not allow them to read, and call themselves Christians amid the curses of their fellow men.—The world ought to get on a little faster than that, if there be really any principle of improvement in it. The Kingdom of Heaven may not at the beginning have dropped seed larger than a mustard-seed, but even from that we had a right to expect a fuller growth than can be believed to exist, when we read such a book as this of Douglass. Unspeakably affecting is the fact that he never saw his mother at all by day-light.

"I do not recollect of ever seeing my mother by the light of day. She was with me in the night. She would lie down with me, and get me to sleep, but long before I waked she was gone."

The [*Narrative*] presents a suitable answer to the hacknied argument drawn by the defender of Slavery from the songs of the Slave, and is also a good specimen of the powers of observation and manly heart of the writer. We wish that everyone may read his book and see what a mind might have been stifled in bondage,—what a man may be subjected to the insults of spendthrift dandies, or the blows of mercenary brutes, in whom there is no whiteness except of the skin, no humanity except in the outward form, and of whom the Avenger will not yet fail to demand—"Where is thy brother?"

ASYLUM FOR
DISCHARGED FEMALE CONVICTS

JUNE 19, 1845

THE LADIES OF THE PRISON ASSOCIATION have been, for some time, engaged in the endeavor to procure funds for establishing this asylum. They have met, thus far, with little success; but, touched by the position of several women, who, on receiving their discharge, were anxiously waiting in hope there would be means provided to save them from return to their former suffering and polluted life, they have taken a house and begun their good work in faith that Heaven must take heed that such an enterprise may not fail, and touch the hearts of men to aid it.

They have taken a house and secured the superintendence of an excellent woman. There are already six women under her care. But this house is unprovided with furniture or the means of securing food for body and mind to these unfortunates during the brief novitiate which gives them so much to learn and unlearn.

The object is to lend a helping hand to the many who show a desire of reformation, but have hitherto been inevitably repelled into infamy by the lack of funds to procure them honest employment, and a temporary refuge till it can be procured. Efforts will be made to instruct them how to break up bad habits and begin a healthy course for body and mind.

The house has in it scarcely any thing; it is a true Lasarus establishment, asking for the crumbs that fall from the rich man's table. Old furniture would be acceptable clothes, books, that are no longer needed by their owners.

Such a statement we make in appealing to the poor, though they are, usually, the most generous. Not that they are, originally, better than the rich, but circumstances have fitted them to appreciate the misfortunes, the trials, the wrongs, that beset those a little lower down than themselves. But we have seen too many instances where those who were educated in luxury would cast aside with eagerness the sloth and selfishness that ensue when once awakened to better things, not to hope in appealing to the rich also.

And to all we appeal. To the poor, who will know how to sympathize with those who are not only poor but degraded, diseased, likely to be hurried onward to a shameful, hopeless death. To the rich, to equalize the advantages of which they have received more than their share. To men, to atone for the wrongs inflicted by men on that "weaker sex," who should, they say, be soft, confiding, dependent on them for protection. To women, to feel for those who have not been guarded either by social influence or inward strength from that first mistake which the opinion of the world makes irrevocable for women alone. Since their danger is so great, their fall so terrible, let mercies be multiplied when there is a chance of that partial restoration which society at present permits.

In New York we have come little into contact with that class of society who have a surplus of leisure at command; but in other cities we have found in that class many, some men, more women, who wanted only a decided object and clear light to fill the noble office of disinterested educators and guardians to their less fortunate fellows. It has been our happiness, in not a few instances, by merely apprising such persons of what was to be done, to rouse that generous spirit which relieved themselves from casual dejection, and a gradual ossification of the whole system, into a thoughtful, sympathetic and beneficent existence. Such no doubt are near us here, if we could but know it. A poet writes thus of the cities:

> Cities of proud hotels,
> Houses of rich and great,
> A stack of smoking chimneys,

> *A roof of frozen slate.*
> *It cannot conquer folly,*
> *Time and space conquering steam,*
> *And the light-outspeeding telegraph*
> *Bears nothing on its beam.*
>
> *The politics are base,*
> *The letters do not cheer,*
> *And't is far in the deeps of history*
> *The voice that speaketh clear;*
> *Trade and the streets ensnare us,*
> *Our bodies are weak and worn,*
> *We plot and corrupt each other,*
> *And we despoil the unborn.*
>
> *Yet there in the parlor sits*
> *Some figure of noble guise,*
> *Our angel in a stranger's form,*
> *Or woman's pleading eyes;*
> *Or only a flashing sunbeam*
> *In at the window-pane,*
> *Or music pours on mortals*
> *Its beautiful disdain."*

These pleading eyes, these angels in a stranger's form we meet or seem to meet as we pass through the thoroughfares of this great city. We do not know their names or homes. We cannot go to those still and sheltered homes and tell them the tales that would be sure to awaken the heart to a deep and active interest in this matter. But should these words meet their eyes, we would say, Have you entertained your leisure hours with the Mysteries of Paris or the pathetic story of Violet Woodville? Then you have some idea how innocence worthy of the brightest planet may be betrayed by want, or by the most generous tenderness; how the energies of a noble reformation may lie hidden beneath the ashes of a long burning, as in the case of La Louve. You must have felt that yourselves are not better, only more protected children of God than these. Do you want to link these fictions, which have made you weep, with facts around you where your pity might be of use? Go to the Penitentiary at Blackwell's Island. You may be repelled by seeing those who are in health, while at work together, keeping up one another's careless spirit and effrontery by bad association. But see them in the hospital where the worn features of the sick show the sad ruins of past loveliness, past gentleness. See in the eyes of the nurses the woman's spirit still, so kindly, so inspiring. See those little girls huddled in a corner, their neglected dress and hair contrasting with some ribbon of cherished finery held fast in a childish hand. Think what "sweet seventeen" was to you, and what it is to them, and see if you do not wish to aid in any enterprise that gives them a chance of better days. We assume no higher claim for this enterprise. The dreadful social malady which creates the need of it is one that imperatively demands deep-searching preventive measures; it is beyond cure. But, here and there, some precious soul may be saved from unwilling sin, unutterable woe. Is not the hope to save, here and there one, worthy of great and persistent exertion and sacrifice?

Although Hood's poem, "The Bridge of Sighs," has been printed once before in this paper, we are wont to make use of it again, as more touching than any thing that has been or is likely to be written on this subject. We think that many will be willing to give much time, thought, hope and money to save even one from falling from this

BRIDGE OF SIGHS

One more unfortunate,
Weary of breath,
Rashly importunate,
Gone to her death!

Take her up tenderly,
Lift her with care:
Fashioned so slenderly,
Young, and so fair!

Look at her garments
Clinging like cerements,
Whilst the wave constantly
Drips from her clothing;
Take her up instantly,
Loving, not loathing.

Touch her not scornfully;
Think of her mournfully,
Gently, and humanly:
Not of the stains of her:

All that remains of her,
Now, is pure womanly.

Make no deep scrutiny
Into her mutiny,
Rash and undutiful;
Past all dishonor.
Death has left on her
Only the beautiful.

Still, for all slips of hers,—
One of Eve's family.—
Wipe those poor lips of hers,
Oozing so clammily.

Loop up her tresses,
Escaped from the comb,—
Her fair auburn tresses;
Whilst wonderment guesses,
Where was her home?

Who was her father?
Who was her mother?
Had she a sister?
Had she a brother?
Or, was there a dearer one
Still, and a nearer one
Yet, than all other?

Alas, for the rarity
Of Christian charity
Under the sun!
O, it was pitiful,
Near a whole city full,
Home she had none.

Sisterly, brotherly,
Fatherly, motherly
Feelings had changed:
Love, by harsh evidence,
Thrown from its eminence;
Even God's providence
Seeming estranged.

Where the lamps quiver
So far in the river,
With many a light,
From window and casement,
From garret to basement,
She stood, with amazement,
Houseless, by night.

The bleak wind of March
Made her tremble and shiver;
But not the dark arch,
Or the black flowing river:
Mad from life's history,
Glad to death's mystery,
Swift to be hurled,—
Any where, any where
Out of the world!

In she plunged boldly,—
No matter how coldly
The rough river ran,—
Over the brink of it:
Picture it, think of it,
Dissolute man!
Lave in it, drink of it,
Then, if you can!

Take her up tenderly,
Lift her with care:
Fashioned so slenderly,
Young, and so fair!

Ere her limbs frigidly
Stiffen too rigidly,
Decently, kindly
Smooth and compose them;
And her eyes, close them,
Staring so blindly!

Dreadfully staring
Through muddy impurity,
As when with the daring

Last look of despairing
Fixed on futurity.

Perishing gloomily,
Spurred by contumely,
Cold inhumanity,
Burning insanity,
Into her rest!
Cross her hands humbly,
As if praying dumbly,
Over her breast!

Owning her weakness,
Her evil behaviour;
And leaving, with meekness,
Her sins to her Saviour!

WHAT FITS A MAN TO
BE A VOTER?
Is It to Be White Within, or
White Without

MARCH 31, 1846

THE COUNTRY HAD BEEN DENUDED of its forests, and men cried—"Come! we must plant anew, or there will be no shade for the homes of our children, or fuel for their hearths. Let us find the best kernels for a new growth."

And a basket of butternuts was offered.

But the planters rejected it with disgust. "What a black, rough coat it has," said they; "it is entirely unfit for the dishes on a nobleman's table, nor have we ever seen it in such places. It must have a greasy, offensive kernel; nor can fine trees grow up from such a nut."

"Friends," said one of the planters, "this decision may be rash. The chestnut has not a handsome outside; it is long encased in troublesome burrs, and, when disengaged, is almost as black as these nuts you despise. Yet from it grow trees of lofty stature, graceful form and long life. Its kernel is white and has furnished food to the most poetic and splendid nations of the older world."

"Don't tell me," says another, "brown is entirely different from black. I like brown very well; there is Oriental precedent for its respectability. Perhaps we will use some of your chestnuts, if we can get fine samples. But for the present I think we should use only English walnuts, such as our forefathers delighted to honor. Here are many basketsfull of them, quite enough for the present. We will plant them with a sprinkling between of the chestnut and acorn." "But," rejoined the other, "many butternuts are beneath the sod, and you cannot help a mixture of them being in your wood at any rate."

"Well! we will grub them up and cut them down wherever we find them. We can use the young shrubs for kindlings."

At that moment entered the council two persons of a darker complexion than most of those present, as if born beneath the glow of a more scorching sun. First came a Woman, beautiful in the mild, pure grandeur of her look; in whose large dark eye a prophetic intelligence was mingled with infinite sweetness. She looked at the assembly with an air of surprise, as if its aspect was strange to her. She threw quite back her veil, and stepping aside made room for her companion. His form was youthful, about the age of one we have seen in many a picture, produced by the thought of eighteen centuries, as of one "instructing the Doctors." I need not describe the features; all minds have their own impressions of such an image,

"Severe in youthful beauty."

In his hand he bore a little white banner on which was embroidered PEACE AND GOOD WILL TO MEN. And the words seemed to glitter and give out sparks, as he paused in the assembly.

"I came hither," said he, "an uninvited guest, because I read sculptured above the door—'All men born Free and Equal,' and in this dwelling hoped to find myself at home. What is the matter in dispute?"

Then they whispered one to another, and murmurs were heard— "He is a mere boy; young people are always foolish and extravagant;" or "He looks like a fanatic." But others said, "He looks like one whom we have been taught to honor. It will be best to tell him the matter in dispute."

When he heard it, he smiled and said, "It will be needful first to ascertain which of the nuts is soundest within." And with a hammer he broke one, two, and more of the English walnuts, and they were mouldy.

Then he tried the other nuts, but found most of them fresh within and white, for they were fresh from the bosom of the earth, while the others had been kept in a damp cellar.

And he said, "You had better plant them together, lest none or few of the walnuts be sound. And why are you so reluctant? Has not Heaven permitted them both to grow on the same soil? and does not that show what is intended about it?"

And they said, "But they are black and ugly to look upon." He replied, "They do not seem so to me. What my Father has fashioned in such guise offends not mine eye."

And they said, "But from one of these trees flew a bird of prey who has done great wrong. We meant, therefore, to suffer no such tree among us."

And he replied, "Amid the band of my countrymen and friends there was one guilty of the blackest crime, that of selling for a price the life of his dearest friend, yet all the others of his blood were not put under ban because of his guilt."

Then they said, "But in the Holy Book our teachers tell us, we are bid to keep in exile or distress whatsoever is black and unseemly in our eyes."

Then he put his hand to his brow and cried in a voice of the most penetrating pathos, "Have I been so long among ye and ye have not known me?"—And the Woman turned from them, the majestic hope of her glance, and both forms suddenly vanished, but the banner was left trailing in the dust.

The men stood gazing at one another. After which one mounted on high and said:

"Perhaps, my friends, we carry too far this aversion to objects merely because they are black. I heard, the other day, a wise man say that black was the color of evil—marked as such by God, and that whenever a white man struck a black man he did an act of worship to God.* I could not quite believe him. I hope, in what I'm about to add, I shall not be misunderstood. I am no Abolitionist. I respect above all things, divine or human, the Constitution framed by our forefathers, and the peculiar institutions hallowed by the usage of their sons. I have no sympathy with the black race in this country. I wish it to be understood that I feel toward negroes the purest personal antipathy.

---

* Fact, that this is affirmed.

It is a family trait with us. My little son, scarce able to speak, will cry out 'Nigger! Nigger!' whenever he sees one, and try to throw things at them. He made a whole omnibus load laugh the other day by his cunning way of doing this.* The child of my political antagonist, on the other hand, says 'he likes tullared children the best.'† You see he is tainted in his cradle by the loose principles of his parents, even before he can say nigger or pronounce the more refined appellation. But that is no matter. I merely mention this by the way: not to prejudice you against Mr. ———, but that you may appreciate the very different state of things in my family, and not misinterpret what I have to say. I was lately in one of our prisons where a somewhat injudicious indulgence had extended to one of the condemned felons, a lost and wretched outcast from society, the use of materials for painting, that having been his profession. He had completed at his leisure, a picture of the Lord's Supper. Most of the figures were well enough, but Judas he had represented as a black.‡ Now, gentlemen, I am of opinion that this is an unwarrantable liberty taken with the Holy Scriptures and shows too much prejudice in the community. It is my wish to be moderate and fair, and preserve a medium, neither, on the one hand, yielding the wholesome antipathies planted in our breasts as a safeguard against degradation, and our constitutional obligations, which, as I have before observed, are, with me, more binding than any other; nor on the other hand forgetting that liberality and wisdom which are the prerogative of every citizen of this free Commonwealth. I agree then with our young visitor. I hardly know, indeed, why a stranger and one so young was permitted to mingle in this council, but it was certainly thoughtful in him to crack and examine the nuts. I agree that it may be well to plant some of the black nuts among the others, so that, if many of the walnuts fail, we may make use of this inferior tree."

At this moment arose a hubbub, and such a clamor of "dangerous innovation," "political capital," "low-minded demagogue," "infidel who denies the Bible," "lower link in the chain of creation," &c. that it is impossible to say what was the decision.

---

* Fact
† Fact
‡ Fact

NEW-YORK DAILY TRIBUNE
DISPATCHES

In August of 1846, Fuller resigned her position as the New-York Daily Tribune's *literary editor and embarked on a journey to Europe. Now employed as one of Horace Greeley's foreign correspondents, she published a total of thirty-seven dispatches in the* Tribune *during the next three years. Initially, Fuller's dispatches were sent from England, Scotland, and France. Italy was her final destination. A resident of Rome during the Italian Revolution, Fuller offered the* Tribune's *readers a drama-filled record of the struggle for a unified and independent Italy. Aligned with the forces pressing for unification and independence, Fuller committed herself to the cause of the Roman Republic, an independent government established after Pope Pius IX's flight from Rome in November of 1848. Fuller's opening dispatches in the spring of 1848 were highly enthusiastic. The revolts that swept across Italy during that spring seemed a prelude to the Italy to which she had committed herself. Little more than a year later Fuller's hopes were dashed by a series of defeats, the most important of which involved the fall of the Roman Republic. Fuller's sympathy with the aspirations of the Italian revolutionaries endured. In her final dispatch, she declared, "Go where I may, a large part of my heart will ever remain in Italy."*

PARIS, NOV. 1846

I AM VERY SORRY to leave such a wide gap between my letters, but I was inevitably prevented from finishing one that was begun for the steamer of 4th November. I then hoped to prepare one after my arrival here in time for the Hibernia, but a severe cold, caught on the way, unfitted me for writing. It is now necessary to retrace my steps a long way, or lose sight of several things it has seemed desirable to mention to friends in America, though I shall make out my narrative more briefly than if nearer the time of action.

If I mistake not, my last closed just as I was looking back on the hill where I had passed the night in all the miserable chill and amid the ghostly apparitions of a Scotch mist, but which looked in the morning truly beautiful, and (had I not known it too well to be deceived) alluring, in its mantle of rich pink heath, the tallest and most full of blossoms we anywhere saw, and with the waterfall making music by its side, and sparkling in the morning sun.

Passing from Tarbet, we entered the grand and beautiful pass of Glencoe—sublime with purple shadows with bright lights between, and in one place an exquisitely silent and lonely little lake. The wildness of the scene was hightened by the black Highland cattle feeding here and there. They looked much at home, too, in the park at Inverary, where I saw them next day. In Inverary I was disappointed. I found, indeed, the position of every object the same as indicated in the "Legend of Montrose," but the expression of the whole seemed unlike what I had fancied. The present abode of the Argyle family is a modern structure, and it boasts very few vestiges of the old romantic history attached to the name. The park and look out upon the lake are beautiful, but except from a hasty pleasure in these, the old cross from Iona—that stands in the market-place—and the drone of the bagpipe which lulled me to sleep at night playing some melancholy air, there was nothing to make me feel that it was "a far cry to Lochaw," but, on the contrary, I seemed in the very midst of the prose —the civilized world.

Leaving Inverary, we left that day the Highlands too, passing through HELL GLEN, a very wild and grand defile. Taking boat then on Loch Levy, we passed down the Clyde, stopping an hour or two on our way at Dumbarton. Nature herself foresaw the era of picture when she made and placed this rock: there is every preparation for the artist's stealing a little piece from her treasures to hang on the walls of a room. Here I saw the sword of "Wallace wight," shown by a son of the 19th century, who said that his hero lived about fifty years ago, and who did not know the hight of this rock, in a cranny of which he lived, or at least ate and slept and "donned his clothes." From the top of the rock I saw sunset on the beautiful Clyde, animated that day by an endless procession of steamers, little skiffs, and boats. In one of the former, the Cardiff Castle, we embarked as the last light of day was fading, and that evening found ourselves in Glasgow.

I understand there is an intellectual society of high merit in Glasgow, but we were there only a few hours, and did not see any one. Certainly the place, as it may be judged of merely from the general aspect of the population and such objects as may be seen in the streets, more resembles an *Inferno* than any other we have yet visited. The people are more crowded together and the stamp of squalid, stolid misery and degradation more obvious and appalling. The English and Scotch do not take kindly to poverty like those of sunnier climes; it makes them fierce or stupid, and, life presenting no other cheap pleasure, they take refuge in drinking.

I saw here in Glasgow persons, especially women, dressed in dirty, wretched tatters, worse than none, and with an expression of listless, unexpecting woe upon their faces, far more tragic than the inscription over the gate of Dante's *Inferno*. To one species of misery suffered here to the last extent, I shall advert in speaking of London.

But from all these sorrowful tokens I by no means inferred the falsehood of the information that here was to be found a circle rich in intellect and in aspiration. The manufacturing and commercial towns, burning focuses of grief and vice, are also the centers of intellectual life, as in forcing beds the rarest flowers and fruits are developed by use of impure and repulsive materials. Where evil comes to an extreme, Heaven seems busy in providing means for the remedy. Need indeed is glaring throughout Scotland and England for the devoutest application of intellect and love to the cure of ills that cry aloud, and, without such application, *must* ere very long seek help by other means than words. Yet there is every reason to hope that those who ought to help are seriously, though slowly, becoming alive to the imperative nature of this duty, so we must not cease to hope, even in the streets of Glasgow and the gin palaces of Manchester, and the dreariest recesses of London.

From Glasgow we passed to Stirling, like Dumbarton endeared to the mind, which cherishes the memory of its childhood still more by Miss Porter's Scottish Chiefs than by association with "Snowdon's Knight and Scotland's King." We reached the town too late to see the Castle before the next morning, and I took up at the inn "The Scottish Chiefs," in which I had not read a word since ten or twelve years old. We are in the habit now of laughing when this book is named, as if it were a representative of what is most absurdly stilted or bombastic, but now, in reading, my maturer mind was differently impressed from what I expected, and the infatuation with which childhood and early youth regard this book and its companion, "Thaddeus of Warsaw," was justified. The characters and dialogue are, indeed, out of nature, but the sentiment that animates them is pure, true, and no less healthy than noble. Here is bad drawing, bad drama, but good music, to which the unspoiled heart will always echo, even when the intellect has learned to demand a better organ for its communication.

The Castle of Sterling is as rich as any place in romantic associations. We were shown its dungeons and its Court of Lions, where, says tradition, wild animals, kept in the grated cells adjacent, were brought out on festival occasions to furnish entertainment for the Court. So, while lords and ladies gay danced and sang above, prisoners pined and wild beasts starved below. This, at first blush looks like a very barbarous state of things, but, on reflection, one does not find that we have outgrown it in our present so-called state of refined civilization, only the present way of expressing the same facts is a little different. Still lords and ladies dance and sing above, unknowing or uncaring that the laborers who minister to their luxuries starve or are turned into wild beasts—below. Man need not boast his condition till he can weave his costly tapestry without the side that is kept under looking like that, methinks.

The Tournament Ground is still kept green and in beautiful order near Stirling Castle as a memento of the olden time, and as we passed away down the beautiful Firth, a turn of the river gave us a very advantageous view of it. So gay it looked, so festive in the bright sunshine, one almost seemed to see the graceful forms of knight and noble pricking their good steeds to the encounter, or the stalwart Douglas, vindicating his claim to be indeed a chief by conquest in the rougher sports of the yeomanry.

Passing along the Firth to Edinburgh we again passed two or three days in that beautiful city, which I could not be content to leave so imperfectly seen if I had not some hope of revisiting it when the bright lights that adorn it are concentrated there. In Summer almost every one is absent. I was very fortunate to see as many interesting persons as I did. On this second visit I saw James Simpson, a well known philanthropist, and leader in the cause of popular education. Infant schools have been an especial care of his, and America as well as Scotland has received the benefit of his thoughts on this subject. His last good work has been to induce the erection of public baths in Edinburgh, and the working people of that place, already deeply in his debt for the lectures he has been unwearied in delivering for their benefit, have signified their gratitude by presenting him with a beautiful model of a fountain in silver as an ornament to his study. Never was there a place where such a measure would be more important; if cleanliness be akin to godliness, Edinburgh stands at great disadvantage in her devotions. The impure air, the terrific dirt which surround the working people must make all progress in higher culture impossible, and I saw nothing which seemed to me so likely to have results of incalculable good, as this practical measure of the Simpsons, in support of the precept:

"Wash and be clean every whit."

We returned into England by the way of Melrose, not content to leave Scotland without making our pilgrimage to Abbotsford. The universal feeling, however, has made this pilgrimage so common that there is nothing left for me to say, yet, though I had read a hundred descriptions, everything seemed new as I went over this epitome of the mind and life of Scott, as what constitutes the great man is more commonly some extraordinary combination and balance of qualities, than the highest development of any one. So you cannot but here be struck anew by the singular combination in his mind of love for the picturesque and romantic with the commonest common sense, a delight in heroic excess, with the prudential habit of order. Here the most pleasing order pervades emblems of what men commonly esteem disorder and excess.

Amid the exquisite beauty of the ruins of Dryburgh, I saw with regret that his body rests in almost the only spot that is not green and cannot well be made so, for the light does not reach it.—That is not a fit couch for him who dressed so many dim and time-worn relics with living green.

Always cheerful and beneficent, Scott seemed to the common eye, in like measure, prosperous and happy up to the last years, and the chair in which, under the pressure of the sorrows which led to his death, he was propped up to write when brain and eye and hand refuse their aid, and the product remains only as a guide to the speculator as to the workings of the mind in case of insanity or approaching imbecility would by most persons be viewed as the only saddening relic of his career. Yet when I recall some passages in the Lady of the Lake, and the Address to his Harp, I cannot doubt that Scott had the full share of bitter in his cup, and feel the tender hope that we do about other gentle and generous guardians and benefactors of our youth, that in a nobler career they are now fulfilling still higher duties with serener mind, and trusting in us that we will try to fill their places with kindly deeds, ardent thoughts; nor leave the world in their absence,

> "A dim, vast vale of tears,
> Vacant and desolate."

PARIS [UNDATED]

WHEN I WROTE LAST I could not finish with London, and there remain yet two or three things I wish to speak of before passing to my impressions of this wonderful Paris.

I visited the model-prison at Pentonville but though in some respects an improvement upon others I have seen—though there was the appearance of great neatness and order in the arrangements of life—kindness and good judgement in the discipline of the prisoners—yet there was also an air of bleak forlornness about the place, and it fell short of what my mind demands of such abodes considered as redemption schools. But as the subject of prisons in now engaging the attention of many of the wisest and best, and the tendency is in what seems to me the true direction, I need not trouble myself to make crude and hasty suggestions; it is a subject to which persons who would be of use should give the earnest devotion of calm and leisurely thought.

The same day I went to see an establishment which gave me unmixed pleasure; it is a bathing establishment put at a very low rate to enable the poor to avoid one of the worst miseries of their lot, and which yet promises *to pay*. Joined with this is an establishment for washing clothes, where the poor can go and hire, for almost nothing, good tubs, water ready heated, the use of an apparatus for rinsing, drying and ironing, all so admirably arranged that a poor woman can in three hours get through an amount of washing and ironing that would, under ordinary circumstances, occupy three or four days. Especially the drying closets I contemplated with great satisfaction, and hope to see in our own country the same arrangements throughout the cities and even in the towns and villages.—Hanging out the clothes is a great exposure for women, even when they have a good place for it, but when, as is so common in cities, they must dry them in the house, how much they suffer! In New-York I know those poor women who take in washing endure a great deal of trouble and toil from this cause; I have suffered myself from being obliged to send back what had cost them so much toil, because it had been, perhaps inevitably, soiled in the drying or ironing, or filled with the smell of their miscellaneous cooking. In London it is much worse. An eminent physician told me he knew of two children whom he considered to have died because their mother, having but one room to live in, was obliged to wash and dry clothes close to their bed when they were ill. The poor people in London naturally do without washing all they can, and beneath that perpetual fall of soot the result may be guessed. All but the very poor in England put out their washing, and this custom ought to be universal in civilized countries, as it can be done much better and quicker by a few regular laundresses than by many families, and 'the washing day' is so malignant a foe to the peace and joy of households that it ought to be effaced from the calendar. But, as long as we are so miserable as to have any very poor people in this world, *they* cannot put out their washing, because they cannot earn enough money to pay for it, and, preliminary to something better, washing establishments like this of London are desirable.

One arrangement that they have here in Paris will be a good one, even when we cease to have any very poor people, and, please Heaven, also to have any very rich. These are the *Créches*—houses where poor women leave their children to be nursed during the day while they are at work. I have not yet been to see one of these, and must postpone speaking of them more fully to another letter.

I must mention that the superintendent of the washing establishment observed, with legitimate triumph, that it had been built without giving a single dinner or printing a single puff—an extraordinary thing, indeed, for England!

To turn to something a little gayer—the embroidery on this tattered coat of civilized life—I went into only two theatres, Old Drury —once the scene of great glories, now of execrable music and more execrable acting. If anything can be invented more excruciating than an English Opera, such as was the fashion at the time I was in London, I am sure no sin of mine deserves the punishment of bearing it.

At Sadler's Wells I saw a play which I had much admired in reading it, but found still better in actual representation; indeed, it seems to me there can be no better acting play: this is 'The Patrician's Daughter,' by J. W. Marston. The movement is rapid yet clear and free, the dialogue natural, dignified and flowing—the characters marked with few but distinct strokes. Where the tone of discourse rises with manly sentiment or passion, the audience applauded with bursts of generous feeling that gave me great pleasure, for this play is one that, in its scope and meaning, marks the new era in England; it is full of an experience which is inevitable to a man of talent there, and is harbinger of the day when the noblest commoner shall be the only noble possible in England.

But how different all this acting to what I find in France! Here the theatre is living; you see something really good, and good throughout. Not one touch of that stage strut and vulgar bombast of tone which the English actor fancies indispensable to scenic illusion is tolerated here. For the first time in my life I saw something represented in a style uniformly good, and should have found sufficient proof, if I had needed any, that all men will prefer what is good to what is bad, if only a fair opportunity for choice be allowed. When I came here, my first thought was to go and see Mademoiselle Rachel. I was sure that in her I should find a true genius, absolutely the diamond, and so it proved.—I went to see her seven or eight times, always in parts that required great force of soul and purity of taste even to conceive them, and only once had reason to find fault with her. On one single occasion I saw her violate the harmony of the character to produce effect at a particular moment; but almost invariably I found her a true artist, worthy of Greece, and worthy at many moments to have her conceptions immortalized in marble.

Her range even in high tragedy is limited. She can only express the darker passions, and grief in its most desolate aspects. Nature has not gifted her with those softer and more flowery attributes that lend to pathos its utmost tenderness. She does not melt to tears or calm or elevate the heart by the prescence of that tragic beauty that needs all the assaults of Fate to make it show its immortal sweetness. Her noblest aspect is when sometimes she expresses truth in some severe shape, and rises, simple and austere, above the mixed elements around her. On the dark side, she is very great in hatred and revenge, I admired her more in PHEDRE than in any other part in which I saw her, the guilty love inspired by the hatred of a goddess was expressed in all its symptoms with a force and terrible naturalness that almost suffocated the beholder. After she had taken the poison, the exhaustion and paralysis of the system—the sad, cold, calm submission to Fate— were still more grand.

I had heard so much about the power of her eye in one fixed look, and the expression she could concentrate in a single word, that the utmost results could only satisfy my expectations. It is, indeed, something magnificent to see the dark cloud give out such sparks, each one fit to deal a separate death, but it was not that I admired most in her.—It was the grandeur, truth and depth of her conception of each part, and the sustained purity with which she represented it.

For the rest, I shall write somewhere a detailed *critique* upon the parts in which I saw her. It is she who has made me acquainted with the true way of viewing French tragedy. I had no idea of its powers and symmetry till now, and received from the revelation high pleasure and a crowd of thoughts.

The French language from her lips is divine dialect; it is stripped of its national and personal peculiarities and becomes what any language must—moulded by such a genius—the pure music of the heart and soul. I never could remember her tone in speaking any word; it was too perfect; you had received the thought quite direct. Yet, had I never heard her speak a word, my mind could the genius of sculpture surpass her management of the antique drapery.

She has no beauty except in the intellectual severity of her outline, and bears marks of race that will grow stronger every year, and make her ugly before long. Still it will be a *grandiose,* gypsy or rather Sibyline ugliness, well adapted to the expression of some tragic part. Only it seems as if she could not live long; she expends force enough upon a part to furnish out a dozen common lives.

Though the French tragedy is well acted throughout, yet unhappily there is no male now with the spark of fire, and these men seem the meanest pigmies by the side of Rachel—so on the scene, beside the tragedy intended by the author, you see also that common tragedy, a woman of genius who throws away her precious heart, lives and dies for one unworthy of her. In parts this effect is productive of too much pain. I saw Rachel one night with her brother and sister. The sister imitated her so closely that you could not help seeing she had a manner, and an imitable manner. Her brother was in the play her lover; a wretched automaton, and presenting the most unhappy family likeness to herself. Since then I have hardly cared to go and see her. We could wish with geniuses as with the Phoenix—to see only one of the family at a time.

In the pathetic or sentimental drama Paris boasts another young actress, nearly as distinguished in that walk as Rachel in hers. This is Rose Cheny, whom we saw in her 98th personation of *Clarissa Harlowe*, and afterward in Genevieve and the *Protege sans le savoir*—a little piece written expressly for her by Scribe. The 'Miss Clarisse' of the French drama is a feeble and partial reproduction of the heroine of Richardson; indeed the original in all its force of intellect and character would have been too much for the charming Rose Cheny, but, to the purity and lovely tenderness of Clarissa she does full justice. In the other charters she was the true French girl, full of grace and a mixture of naïvete and cunning, sentiment and frivolity, that is winning and *piquant,* if not satisfying. Only grief seems very strange to those bright eyes; we do not find that they can weep much and bear the light of day, and the inhaling of charcoal seems near at hand to their brightest pleasures.

At the other little theatres you see excellent acting and a sparkle of wit unknown to the world out of France. The little pieces in which all the leading topics of the day are reviewed are full of drolleries that make you laugh at each instant. *Paudre-coton* is the only one of these I have seen; in this, among other jokes, Dumas, in the character of Monte-Christo and in costume half Oriental, half juggler, is made to pass the other theatres in review while seeking candidates for his new one.

Dumas appeared in court yesterday and defended his own cause against the editors who sue him for evading some of his engagements. I was very desirous to hear him speak and went there in what I was assured would be very good season, but a French audience, who knew the ground better, had slipped in before me, and I returned, as has been too often the case with me in Paris, having seen nothing but endless staircases, dreary vestibules, and *gens d'armes.* The hospitality of *le grande nation* to the stranger is, in many respects, admirable. Galleries, libraries, cabinets of coins, museums, are opened in the most liberal manner to the stranger, warmed, lighted, ay, and guarded, for him almost all days in the week; treasures of the past are at his service; but when anything is happening, in the present, the French run quicker, glide in more adroitly, and get possession of the ground. I find it not the most easy matter to get to places even when there is nothing going on—there is so much tiresome fuss of getting *billets* from one and another to be gone through; but when something is happening it is still worse. I missed hearing M Guizot in his speech on the Montpensier marriage, which would have given a very good idea of his manner, and which, like his defence of M Dumas, was a skillful piece of work as regards evasion of the truth. The good feeling toward England which had been fostered with so much care and toil seems to have been entirely dissipated by the mutual recriminations about this marriage, and the old dislike flames up more fiercely for having been hid awhile beneath the ashes. I saw the little Duchess, the innocent or ignorant topic of all this disturbance, when presented at Court. She went round the circle on the arm of the Queen. Though only fourteen she looks twenty, but has something fresh, engaging, and girlish about her. I fancy it will soon be rubbed out under the drill of the royal household.

I attended not only at the presentation but at the ball given at the Tuileries directly after; these are fine shows, as the suite of apartments is very handsome, brilliantly lighted, the French ladies surpassing all others in the art of dress; indeed, it gave me much pleasure to see them; certainly there are many ugly ones, but they are so well dressed and have such an air of graceful vivacity, that the general effect was of a flower-garden. As often happens, several American women were among the most distinguished for positive beauty; one from Philadelphia, who is by many persons considered the prettiest ornament of the dress circle at the Italian Opera, was especially marked by the attention of the King. However, these ladies, even if here a long time, do not attain the air and manner of French-women: the magnetic fluid that envelops them is less brilliant and exhilarating in its attractions.

It was pleasant to my eye, which has always been so wearied in our country by the sombre masses of men that overcloud our public assemblies, to see them now in so great variety of costume, color and decoration.

Among the crowd wandered Leverrier in the costume of Academician, looking as if he had lost, not found, his planet. French *savants* are more generally men of the world and even men of fashion than those of other climates; but, in his case, he seemed not to find it easy to exchange the music of the spheres for the music of fiddles.

Speaking of Leverrier leads to another of my disappointments. I went to the Sorbonne to hear him lecture, nothing dreaming that the old pedantic and theological character of those halls was strictly kept up in these days of light. An old guardian of the inner temple seeing me approach had his speech all ready, and, manning the entrance, said with a disdainful air, before we had time to utter a word, "Monsieur may enter if he pleases, but Madame must remain here," (*i.e.* in the court-yard). After some exclamations of surprise I found an alternative in the Hotel de Cluny, where I passed an hour very delightfully while waiting for my companion. The rich remains of other centuries are there so arranged that they can be seen to the best advantage; many of the works in ivory, china and carved wood are truly splendid or exquisite. I saw a dagger with jeweled hilt which talked whole poems to my mind. In the various 'Adorations of the Magi' I found constantly one of the wise men black, and with the marked African lineaments. Before I had half finished, my companion came and wished me at least to visit the lecture-rooms of the Sorbonne now that the talk, too good for female ears, was over. But the guardian again interfered to deny me entrance. "You can go, Madame," said he "to the College of France, you can go to this and t'other place, but you cannot enter here." "What, sir," said I, "is it your institution alone that remains in a state of barbarism?" "Que voulez vous, Madame," he replied, and, as he spoke, his little dog began to bark at me. "Que voulez vous, Madame, c'est la regle,"—"What would you have, Madame, IT IS THE RULE,"—a reply which makes me laugh even now, as I think how the satirical wits of former days might have used it against the bulwarks of learned dullness.

I was more fortunate in hearing Arago, and he justified all my expectations. Clear, rapid, full and equal, his discourse is worthy its celebrity, and I felt repaid for the four hours one is obliged to spend in going, in waiting and in hearing, for the lecture begins at half past one and you must be there before twelve to get a seat, so constant and animated is his popularity.

Generally the most celebrated lecturers are silent at this moment Michelet is ill. Mickiewicz, highly vaunted by discriminating hearers for a various and inspired eloquence, is absent. Sated with lectures in our own country, I have not felt willing to give my hours to the less distinguished, even although for me, as stranger and Columbian ignoramus, I know they would have many a kernel worth disengaging from the husks, if strength and time were more abundant.

I have attended with some interest two discussions at the Athenée—one on Suicide, the other on The Crusades. They are amateur affairs where, as always at such times, one hears much nonsense and vanity, much making of phrases and sentimental mental grimace; but there was one excellent speaker, adroit and rapid as only a Frenchman could be. With admirable readiness, skill and rhetorical polish, he examined the arguments of all the others and built upon their failures a triumph for himself. His management of the language, too, was masterly, and French is the best of languages for such a purpose—clear, flexible, full of sparkling points and quick, picturesque turns, with a subtle blandness that makes the dart tickle while it wounds. Truly he pleased the fancy, filled the ear and carried us pleasantly along over the smooth, swift waters; but then came from the crowd a gentleman, not one of the appointed orators of the evening, but who had really something in his heart to say—a grave, dark man, with Spanish eyes, and the simple dignity of honor and earnestness in all his gesture and manner. He said in few and unadorned words his say, and the sense of a real presence filled the room and those charms of rhetoric faded, as vanish the beauties of soap-bubbles from the eyes of astonished childhood.

I was present on one good occasion at the Academy the day that M. Rémusat was received there in the place of Royer Collard. I looked down from one of the tribunes upon the flower of the celebrities of France, that is to say, of the celebrities which are authentic, *comme il faut*. Among them were many marked faces, many fine heads; but, in reading the works of poets we always fancy them about the age of Apollo himself, and I found with pain some of my favorites quite old, and very unlike the company on Parnassus as represented by Raphael. Some however, were venerable, even noble, to behold. Indeed the literary dynasty of France is growing old, and here, as in England and Germany, there seems likely to occur a serious gap before the inauguration of another, if indeed another is coming.

However, it was an imposing sight; there are men of real distinction now in the Academy, and Molière would have a fair chance if he were proposed to-day. Among the audience I saw many ladies of fine expression and manner as well as one or two *Precieuses Ridicules,* a race which is never quite extinct.

M. Rémusat, as is the custom on these occasions painted the portrait of this predecessor; the discourse was brilliant and discriminating in the details, but the orator seemed to me to neglect drawing some obvious inferences which would have given a better point of view for his subject.

A *sceance* to me much more impressive and interesting was one which borrowed nothing from dress, decorations, or the presence of titled pomp. I went to call on La Mennais, to whom I had a letter. I found him in a little study; his secretary was writing in a larger room through which I passed. With him was a somewhat citizen-looking, but vivacious, elderly man, whom I was at first sorry to see, having wished for half an hour's undisturbed visit to the apostle of Democracy. But how quickly were those feelings displaced by joy when he named to me the great national lyrist of France, the unequaled Beranger. I had not expected to see him at all, for he is not one to be seen in any show place; he lives in the hearts of the people, and needs no homage from their eyes. I was very happy in that little study in presence of these two men, whose influence has been so great, so real. To me Beranger has been much; his wit, his pathos, his exquisite lyric grace, have made the most delicate strings vibrate, and I can feel, as well as see, what he is in his nation and his place. I have not personally received anything from La Mennais, as, born under other circumstances, mental facts to which he, once the pupil of Rome, has passed through such ordeals, are at the basis of all my thoughts. But I see well what he has been and is to Europe, and of what great force of nature and spirit. He seems suffering and pale, but in his eyes is the light of the future.

These are men who need no flourish of trumpets to announce their coming—no band of martial music upon their steps—no obsequious nobles in their train. They are the true kings, the theocratic kings, the judges in Israel. The hearts of men make music at their approach; the mind of the age is the historian of their passage; and only men of destiny like themselves shall be permitted to write their eulogies, or fill their vacant seat.

Wherever there is a genius like his own, a germ of the finest fruit still hidden beneath the soil, the "*Chante pauvre petit*" of Beranger shall strike, like a sunbeam, and give it force to emerge, and wherever there is the true Crusade—for the spirit, not the tomb of Christ—shall be felt an echo of the "*Que tes armes soient benis jeune soldat*" of La Mennais.

[UNDATED]

IN THE LAST DAYS AT PARIS I was fortunate in hearing some delightful music. A friend of Chopin's took me to see him, and I had the pleasure, which the delicacy of his health makes a rare one for the public, of hearing him play. All the impressions I had received from hearing his music imperfectly performed were justified, for it has marked traits which can be veiled but not travestied: but to feel it as it merits, one must hear himself; only a person as exquisitely organized as he can adequately express these subtle secrets of the creative spirit.

It was with very different sort of pleasure that I listened to the Chevalier Neukomm, the celebrated composer of "David," which has been so popular in our country. I heard him improvise on the *Orgue Expressif,* and afterward on a great organ which has just been built here by Cavaillé for the Cathedral of Ajaccio. Full, sustained, ardent, yet exact, the stream of his thought bears with it the attention of hearers of all characters, as his character, full of *bonhommie,* open, friendly, animated and sagacious, would seem to have something to present for the affection and esteem of all kinds of men. One was the minstrel, the other the orator of music: we want them both—the mysterious whispers and the resolute pleadings from the better world which calls us not to slumber here, but press daily onward to claim all our heritage.

Paris! I was sad to leave thee, thou wonderful focus, where ignorance ceases to be a pain, because there we find such means daily to lessen it. It is the only school where I ever found abundance of teachers who could bear being examined by the pupil in their special branches. I must go to this school more before I again cross the Atlantic, where often for years I have carried about some trifling question without finding the person who could answer it. Really deep questions we must all answer for ourselves—the more the pity not to get more quickly through with a crowd of details, where the experience of others might accelerate our progress.

Parting by *diligence,* we pursued our way from twelve o'clock on Thursday till twelve at night on Friday, thus having a large share of magnificent moonlight upon the unknown fields we were traversing. At Chalons we took a boat and reached Lyons betimes that afternoon. So soon as refreshed, we sailed out to visit some of the garrets of the weavers. As we were making inquiries about these, a sweet little girl who heard us offered to be our guide. She led us by a weary, winding way, whose pavement was much easier for her feet in their wooden *sabots* than for ours in Paris shoes, to the top of a hill from which we saw for the first time "the blue and arrowy Rhone." Entering the high buildings on this high hill, I found each chamber tenanted by a family of weavers, all weavers, wife, husband, sons, daughters—from nine years old upward—each was helping. On one side were the looms, nearer the door the cooking apparatus, the beds were shelves near the ceiling: they climbed up to them on ladders. My sweet little girl turned out to be a wife of six or seven years' standing, with two rather sickly looking children; she seemed to have the greatest comfort that is possible amid the perplexities of a hard and anxious lot, to judge by the proud and affectionate manner in which she always said "mon maré," and by the courteous gentleness of his manner toward her.—She seemed, indeed, to be one of those persons on whom "the Graces have smiled in their cradle" and to whom a natural loveliness of character makes the world as easy as it can be made while the evil spirit is still so busy choking the wheat with tares. I admired her graceful manner of introducing us into those dark little rooms, and she was affectionately received by all her acquaintance. But alas! that voice, by nature of such bird-like vivacity, repeated again and again, "Ah! we are all very unhappy now." "Do you sing together or go to evening schools?" "We have not the heart.—When we have a piece of work we do not stir till it is finished, and then we run to try and get another; but often we have to wait idle for weeks.—It grows worse and worse, and they say it is not likely to be any better. We can think of nothing but whether we shall be able to pay our rent. Ah! the work-people are very unhappy now." This poor, lovely little girl, at an age when the merchants' daughters of Boston and New-York are just making their first experiences of "society," knew the price of every article of food and clothing that is wanted by such a household to a farthing, her thought by day and her dream by night was, whether she should long be able to procure a scanty supply of these, and Nature had gifted her with precisely those qualities, which, unembarrassed by care, would have made her and all she loved really happy, and she was fortunate now, compared with many of her sex in Lyons—of whom a gentleman who knows the class well said to me, "When their work fails they have no resource except in the sale of their persons. There are but these two ways open to them, of weaving or prostitution to gain their bread." And there are those who dare to say that such a state of things is *well enough,* and what Providence intended for man—who call those who have hearts to suffer at the sight, energy and zeal to seek its remedy, visionaries and fanatics! To themselves be woe, who have eyes and see not, ears and hear not, the convulsions and sobs of injured Humanity!

My little friend told me she had nursed both her children—though almost all of her class are obliged to put their children out to nurse; "but," said she, "they are brought back so little, so miserable, that I resolved, if possible, to keep mine with me."—Next day in the steamboat I read a pamphlet by a physician of Lyons in which he recommends the establishment of *Crèches* not merely, like those of Paris to keep the children by day, but to provide wet nurses for them. Thus by the infants receiving nourishment from more healthy persons, and who, under the supervision of directors, would treat them well, he hopes to counteract the tendency to degenerate in this race of sedentary workers, and to save mothers from too heavy a burden of care and labor, without breaking the bond between them and their children, whom, under such circumstances, they could visit often and see them taken care of—as they, brought up to know nothing except how to weave, cannot take care of them.—Here, again, how is one reminded of Fourier's observations and plans, still more enforced by the recent developments at Manchester as to the habit of feeding children on opium, which has grown out of the position of things there.

Descending next day to Avignon, I had the mortification of finding the banks of the Rhone still sheeted with white, and there waded through melting snow to Laura's tomb. We did not see Mr. Dicken's Tower and Goblin; it was too late in the day—but we saw a snow-ball fight between two bands of the military in the Castle-yard that was gay enough to make a goblin laugh. And next day, on to Arles, still snow, snow and cutting blasts in the South of France, where everybody had promised us bird-songs and blossoms to console us for the dreary winter of Paris. At Arles, indeed, I saw the little saxifrage blossoming on the steps of the Amphitheatre, and fruit-trees in flower amid the tombs. Here was the first time I saw the great hand-writing of the Romans in its proper medium of stone, and I was content. It looked as grand and solid as I expected, as if life in those days was thought worth the having, the enjoying and the using. The sunlight was warm this day; it lay deliciously still and calm upon the ruins. One old woman sat knitting where twenty-five thousand persons once gazed down in fierce excitement on the fights of men and lions. Coming back, we were refreshed all through the streets by the sight of the women of Arles. They answered to their reputation for beauty; tall, erect and noble, with high and dignified features, and a full, earnest gaze of the eye, they looked as if the Eagle still waved its wings over their city. Even the very old women still have a degree of beauty, because when the colors are all faded and the skin wrinkled, the face retains this dignity of outline. The men do not share in these characteristics; some Priestess, well beloved of the powers of old religion, must have called down an especial blessing on her sex in this town.

Hence to Marseilles—where is little for the traveler to see, except the mixture of Oriental blood in the crowd of the streets. Thence by steamer to Genoa. Of this transit, he who has been on the Mediterranean in a stiff breeze well understands I can have nothing to say, except "I suffered." It was all one dull, tormented dream to me and, I believe, to most of the ship's company—a dream too of thirty hours' duration, instead of the promised sixteen.

The excessive beauty of Genoa is well known, and the impression upon the eye alone was correspondent with what I expected, but, alas! the weather was still so cold I could not realize that I had actually touched those shores to which I had looked forward all my life, where it seemed that the heart would expand, and the whole nature be turned to delight. Seen by a cutting wind, the marble palaces, the gardens, the magnificent water-view of Genoa failed to charm, "I *saw, not felt*, how beautiful they were." Only at Naples have I found *my* Italy, and here not till after a week's waiting—not till I began to believe that all I had heard in praise of the climate of Italy was fable, and that there is really no Spring anywhere except in the imagination of poets. For the first week was an exact copy of the miseries of a New-England Spring; a bright sun came for an hour or two in the morning just to flatter you forth without your cloak, and then—and then—came up a villanous, horrible wind, exactly like the worst East wind of Boston, breaking the heart, racking the brain and turning hope and fancy to an irrevocable green and yellow hue in lieu of their native rose.

However, here at Naples I *have* at last found *my* Italy; I have passed through the Grotto of Pausilippo, visited Cama, Baia, and Capre—ascended Vesuvius, and found all familiar, except the sense of enchantment, of sweet exhilaration this scene conveys.

> *"Behold how brightly breaks the morning!"*

and yet all new, as if never described, for Nature here, most prolific and exuberant in her gifts, has touched them all with a charm un-hackneyed, unhackneyable, which the boots of English dandies cannot trample out, nor the raptures of sentimental tourists daub or fade. Baia had still a hid divinity for me, Vesuvius a fresh baptism of fire, and Sorrento—oh Sorrento was beyond picture, beyond poesy, for the greatest Artist had been at work there in a temper beyond the reach of human art.

Beyond this, reader, my old friend and valued acquaintance on other themes, I shall tell you nothing of Naples, for it is a thing apart in the journey of life, and, if represented at all, should be so in a fairer form than offers itself at present. Now the actual life here is over, I am going to Rome, and expect to see that fane of thought the last day of this week.

At Genoa and Leghorn, I saw for the first time Italians in their homes. Very attractive I found them, charming women, refined men, eloquent and courteous. If the cold wind hid Italy, it could not the Italians. A little group of faces, each so full of character, dignity, and what is so rare in an American face, the capacity for pure, exalting passion, will live ever in my memory—the fulfillment of a hope!

We came from Leghorn in an English boat, highly recommended, and as little deserving of such praise as many another bepuffed article. In the middle of a fine, clear night, she was run into by the mail steamer, which all on deck perfectly saw coming upon her, for no reason that could be ascertained except that the man at the wheel said *he* had turned the right way, and it never seemed to occur to him that he could change when he found the other steamer had taken the same direction. To be sure the other steamer was equally careless, but as a change on our part would have prevented an accident that narrowly missed sending us all to the bottom, it hardly seemed worth while to persist for the sake of convicting them of error.

Neither the Captain nor any of his people spoke French, and we had been much amused before by the chambermaid acting out the old story of "Will you lend me the loan of a gridiron?" A Polish lady was on board with a French waiting-maid, who understood no word of English. The daughter of John Bull would speak to the lady in English, and, when she found it of no use, would say imperiously to the *suivante*—"Go and ask your mistress what she will have for breakfast." And now when I went on deck there was a parley between the two steamers, which the Captain was obliged to manage by such interpreters as he could find; it was a long and confused business. It ended at last in the Neapolitan steamer taking us in tow for an inglorious return to Leghorn. When she had decided upon this she swept round, her lights glancing like sagacious eyes, to take us. The sea was calm as a lake; the sky full of stars; she made a long detour with her black hull, her smoke and lights, which look so pretty at night, then came round to us like the bend of an arm embracing. It was a pretty picture, worth the stop and the fright—perhaps the loss of twenty-four hours, though I did not think so at the time. At Leghorn we changed the boat, and, retracing our steps, came now at last to Naples,—to this priest-ridden, misgoverned, full of dirty, degraded men and women, yet still most lovely Naples,—of which the most I can say is that the divine aspect of Nature *can* make you forget the situation of Man in this region, which was surely intended for him as a princely child, angelic in virtue, genius and beauty, and not as a begging, vermin-haunted, image-kissing Lazzarone.

[UNDATED]

THIS LETTER WILL REACH THE UNITED STATES about the 1st of January [1848]; and it may not be impertinent to offer a few New-Year's reflections. Every new year, indeed, confirms the old thoughts, but also presents them under some new aspects.

The American in Europe, if a thinking mind, can only become more American. In some respects it is a great pleasure to be here. Although we have an independent political existence, our position toward Europe, as to Literature and the Arts, is still that of a colony, and one feels the same joy here that is experienced by the colonist in returning to the parent home.

What was but picture to us becomes reality; remote allusions and derivations trouble no more: we see the pattern of the stuff, and understand the whole tapestry. There is a gradual clearing up on many points, and many baseless notions and crude fancies are dropped. Even the post-haste passage of the business American through the great cities, escorted by cheating couriers, and ignorant *valets de place,* unable to hold intercourse with the natives of the country, and passing all his leisure hours with his countrymen, who know no more than himself, clears his mind of some mistakes—lifts some mists from his horizon.

There are three species: first, the servile American—a being utterly shallow, thoughtless, worthless. He comes abroad to spend his money and indulge his tastes. His object in Europe is to have fashionable clothes, good foreign cookery, to know some titled persons, and furnish himself with coffee-house gossip, which he wins importance at home by retailing among those less traveled, and as uninformed as himself.

I look with unspeakable contempt on this class—a class which has all the thoughtlessness and partiality of the exclusive classes in Europe, without any of their refinement, or the chivalric feeling which still sparkles among them here and there. However, though these willing serfs in a free age do some little hurt, and cause some annoyance at present, it cannot last: our country is fated to a grand, independent existence, and as its laws develop, these parasites of a bygone period must wither and drop away.

Then there is the conceited American, instinctively bristling and proud of—he knows not what—He does not see, not he, that the history of Humanity for many centuries is likely to have produced results it requires some training, some devotion, to appreciate and profit by. With his great clumsy hands only fitted to work on a steam-engine, he seizes the old Cremona violin, makes it shriek with anguish in his grasp, and then declares he thought it was all humbug before he came, and now he knows it; that there is not really any music in these old things; that the frogs in one of our swamps make much finer, for *they* are young and alive. To him the etiquettes of courts and camps, the ritual of the Church, seem simply silly—and no wonder, profoundly ignorant as he is of their origin and meaning. Just so the legends which are the subjects of pictures, the profound myths which are represented in the antique marbles, amaze and revolt him; as, indeed, such things need to be judged of by another standard from that of the Connecticut Blue-Laws. He criticises severely pictures, feeling quite sure that his natural senses are better means of judgment than the rules of connoisseurs—not feeling that to see such objects mental vision as well as fleshly eyes are needed, and that something is aimed at in Art beyond the imitation of the commonest forms of Nature.

This is Jonathan in the sprawling state, the booby truant, not yet aspiring enough to be a good school-boy. Yet in his folly there is meaning; add thought and culture to his independence, and he will be a man of might: he is not a creature without hope, like the thick-skinned dandy of the class first specified.

The Artistes form a class by themselves. Yet among them, though seeking special aims by special means may also be found the lineaments of these two classes, as well as of the third, of which I am to speak.

3d. The thinking American—a man who, recognizing the immense advantage of being born to a new world and on a virgin soil, yet does not wish one seed from the Past to be lost. He is anxious to gather and carry back with him all that will bear a new climate and new culture. Some will dwindle; others will attain a bloom and stature unknown before. He wishes to gather them clean, free from noxious insects. He wishes to give them a fair trial in his new world. And that he may know the conditions under which he may best place them in that new world, he does not neglect to study their history in this.

The history of our planet in some moments seems so painfully mean and little, such terrible bafflings and failures to compensate some brilliant successes—such a crashing of the mass of men beneath the feet of a few, and these, too, of the least worthy—such a small drop of honey to each cup of gall, and, in many cases, so mingled, that it is never one moment in life purely tasted,—above all, so little achieved for Humanity as a whole, such tides of war and pestilence intervening to blot out the traces of each triumph, that no wonder if the strongest soul sometimes pauses aghast! No wonder if the many indolently console themselves with gross joys and frivolous prizes. Yes! those men *are* worthy of admiration who can carry this cross faithfully through fifty years; it is a great while for all the agonies that beset a lover of good, a lover of men; it makes a soul worthy of a speedier ascent, a more productive ministry in the next sphere. Blessed are they who ever keep that portion of pure, generous love with which they began life! How blessed those who have deepened the fountains, and have enough to spare for the thirst of others! Some such there are; and, feeling that, with all the excuses for failure, still only the sight of those who triumph gives a meaning to life or makes its pangs endurable, we must arise and follow.

Eighteen hundred years of this Christian culture in these European Kingdoms, a great theme never lost sight of, a mighty idea, an adorable history to which the hearts of men invariably cling, yet are genuine results rare as grains of gold in the river's sandy bed! Where is the genuine Democracy to which the rights of all men are holy? where the child-like wisdom learning all through life more and more of the will of God? where the aversion to falsehood in all its myriad disguises of cant, vanity, covetousness, so clear to be read in all the history of Jesus of Nazareth? Modern Europe is the sequel to that history, and see this hollow England, with its monstrous wealth and cruel poverty, its conventional life and low, practical aims; see this poor France, so full of talent, so adroit, yet so shallow and glossy still, which could not escape from a false position with all its baptism of blood; see that lost Poland and this Italy bound down by treacherous hands in all the force of genius; see Russia with its brutal Czar and innumerable slaves; see Austria and its royalty that represents nothing, and its people who, as people, are and have nothing! If we consider the amount of truth that has really been spoken out in the world, and the love that has beat in private hearts—how Genius has decked each spring-time with such splendid flowers, conveying each one enough of instruction in its life of harmonious energy, and how continually, unquenchably the spark of faith has striven to burst into flame and light up the Universe—the public failure seems amazing, seems monstrous.

Still Europe toils and struggles with her idea, and, at this moment, all things bode and declare a new outbreak of the fire, to destroy old palaces of crime! May it fertilize also many vineyards!—Here at this moment a successor of St. Peter, after the lapse of near two thousand years, is called "Utopian" by a part of this Europe, because he strives to get some food to the mouths of the *leaner* of his flock. A wonderful state of things, and which leaves as the best argument against despair that men do not, *cannot* despair amid such dark experiences—and thou, my country! will thou not be more true? does no greater success await thee? All things have so conspired to teach, to aid! A new world,

a new chance, with oceans to wall in the new thought against interference from the old!—Treasures of all kinds, gold, silver, corn, marble, to provide for every physical need! A noble, constant, starlike soul,
an Italian, led the way to its shores, and, in the first days, the strong,
the pure, those too brave, too sincere for the life of the Old World
hastened to people them. A generous struggle then shook off what was
foreign and gave the nation a glorious start for a worthy goal. Men
rocked the cradle of its hopes, great, firm, disinterested men who saw,
who wrote, as the basis of all that was to be done, a statement of the
rights, the inborn rights of men, which, if fully interpreted and acted
upon, leaves nothing to be desired.

Yet, oh Eagle, whose early flight showed this clear sight of the
Sun, how often dost thou near the ground, how show the vulture in
these later days! Thou wert to be the advance-guard of Humanity, the
herald of all Progress; how often hast thou betrayed this high commission! Fain would the tongue in clear triumphant accents draw example from the story, to encourage the hearts of those who almost
faint and die beneath the old oppressions. But we must stammer and
blush when we speak of many things. I take pride here that I may
really say the Liberty of the Press works well, and that checks and
balances naturally evolve from it which suffice to its government. I
may say the minds of our people are alert, and that Talent has a free
chance to rise. It is much. But dare I say that political ambition is not
as darkly sullied as in other countries? Dare I say that men of most
influence in political life are those who represent most virtue or even
intellectual power? Is it easy to find names in that career of which I
can speak with enthusiasm? Must I not confess in my country to a
boundless lust of gain? Must I not confess to the weakest vanity, which
bristles and blusters at each foolish taunt of the foreign press; and
must I not admit that the men who make these undignified rejoinders
seek and find popularity so? Must I not confess that there is as yet no
antidote cordially adopted that will defend even that great, rich country against the evils that have grown out of the commercial system in
the old world? Can I say our social laws are generally better, or show
a nobler insight into the wants of man and woman? I do, indeed, say
what I believe, that voluntary association for improvement in these
particulars will be the grand means for my nation to grow and give a
nobler harmony to the coming age. But it is only of a small minority
that I can say they as yet seriously take to heart these things; that
they earnestly meditate on what is wanted for their country,—for
mankind,—for our cause is, indeed, the cause of all mankind at pres-

ent. Could we succeed, really succeed, combine a deep religious love with practical development, the achievements of Genius with the happiness of the multitude, we might believe Man had now reached a commanding point in his ascent, and would stumble and faint no more. Then there is this horrible cancer of Slavery, and this wicked War, that has grown out of it. How dare I speak of these things here? I listen to the same arguments against the emancipation of Italy, that are used against the emancipation of our blacks; the same arguments in favor of the spoliation of Poland as for the conquest of Mexico. I find the cause of tyranny and wrong everywhere the same—and lo! my country the darkest offender, because with the least excuse, foresworn to the high calling with which she was called,—no champion of the rights of men, but a robber and a jailer; the scourge hid behind her banner; her eyes fixed, not on the stars, but on the possessions of other men.

How it pleases me here to think of the Abolitionists! I could never endure to be with them at home, they were so tedious, often so narrow, always so rabid and exaggerated in their tone.

But, after all, they had a high motive, something eternal in their desire and life; and, if it was not the only thing worth thinking of it was really something worth living and dying for to free a great nation from such a terrible blot, such a threatening plague. God strengthen them and make them wise to achieve their purpose!

I please myself, too, with remembering some ardent souls among the American youth who, I trust, will yet expand and help to give soul to the huge, over fed, too hastily grown-up body. May they be constant. "Were Man but constant he were perfect!" it has been said; and it is true that he who could be constant to those moments in which he has been truly human—not brutal, not mechanical—is on the sure path to his perfection and to effectual service of the Universe.

It is to the youth that Hope addresses itself, to those who yet burn with aspiration, who are not hardened in their sins. But I dare not expect too much of them. I am not very old, yet of those who, in life's morning, I saw touched by the light of a high hope, many have seceded. Some have become voluptuaries; some mere family men, who think it is quite life enough to win bread for half a dozen people and treat them decently; others are lost through indolence and vacillation. Yet some remain constant. "I have witnessed many a shipwreck, yet still beat noble hearts."

I have found many among the youth of England, of France—of Italy also—full of high desire, but will they have courage and purity to fight the battle through in the sacred, the immortal band? Of some of them I believe it and await the proof. If a few succeed amid the trial, we have not lived and loved in vain.

To these, the heart of my country, a Happy New Year! I do not know what I have written. I have merely yielded to my feelings in thinking of America; but something of true love must be in these lines—receive them kindly, my friends; it is, by itself, some merit for printed words to be sincere.

ROME, 29TH MARCH, 1848

IT IS LONG SINCE I HAVE WRITTEN; my health entirely gave way beneath the Roman Winter. The rain was constant, commonly falling in torrents from the 16th December to the 19th March. Nothing could surpass the dirt, the gloom, the desolation of Rome. Let no one fancy he has seen her who comes here only in the Winter. It is an immense mistake to do so. I cannot sufficiently rejoice that I did not first see Italy in the Winter.

The climate of Rome at this time of extreme damp I have found equally exasperating and weakening. I have had constant nervous headache without strength to bear it, nightly fever, want of appetite. Some constitutions bear it better, but the complaint of weakness and extreme dejection of spirits is general among foreigners in the wet season. The English say they become acclimated in two or three years and cease to suffer, though never so strong as at home.

Now this long dark dream—to me the most idle and most suffering season of my life—seems past. The Italian heavens wear again their deep blue; the sun shines gloriously; the melancholy lustres are stealing again over the Campagna, and hundreds of larks sing unwearied above its ruins.

Nature seems in sympathy with the great events that are transpiring; with the emotions which are swelling the hearts of men. The morning sun is greeted by the trumpets of the Roman Legions marching out once more, but now not to oppress but to defend. The stars look down on their jubilees over the good news which nightly reaches them from their brothers of Lombardy. This week has been one of nobler, sweeter feeling of a better hope and faith than Rome in her greatest days ever knew. How much has happened since I wrote!— First, the victorious resistance of Sicily and the revolution of Naples.

This has led us yet only to half measures, but even these have been of great use to the progress of Italy. The Neapolitans will, probably, have to get rid at last of the stupid crowned head who is at present their puppet, but their bearing with him has led to the wiser sovereigns granting these Constitutions, which, if eventually inadequate to the wants of Italy, will be so useful, are so needed, to educate her to seek better, completer forms of administration.

In the midst of all this serious work came the play of Carnival, in which there was much less interest felt than usual, but enough to dazzle and captivate a stranger. One thing, however, had been omitted in the description of the Roman Carnival; *i.e.* that it rains every day. Almost every day came on violent rain just as the tide of gay masks was fairly engaged in the Corso. This would have been well worth bearing once or twice for the sake of seeing the admirable good humor of this people. Those who had laid out all their savings in the gayest, thinnest dresses, on carriages and chairs for the Corso, and found themselves suddenly drenched, their finery spoiled, and obliged to ride and sit shivering all the afternoon. But they never murmured, never scolded, never stopped throwing their flowers. Their strength of constitution is wonderful. While I, in my shawl and boa, was coughing at the open window from the moment I inhaled the wet sepulchral air, the servant girls of the house had taken off their woolen gowns, and arrayed in white muslins and roses, sat in the drenched street beneath the drenching rain, quite happy, and have suffered nothing in consequence.

The Romans renounced the *moccaletti*, ostensibly as an expression of sympathy for the sufferings of the Milanese, but really because, at that time, there was great disturbance about the Jesuits, and the Government feared that difficulties would arise in the excitement of the evening. But, since, we have had this entertainment in honor of the Revolutions of France and Austria, and nothing could be more beautiful. The fun usually consists in all the people blowing one another's lights out; we had not this; all the little tapers were left to blaze, and the long Corso swarmed with tall fire-flies.—Lights crept out over the surface of all the houses, and such merry little twinkling lights, laughing and flickering with each slightest movement of those who held them. Up and down the Corso, they twinkled, they swarmed, they streamed, while a surge of gay triumphant sound ebbed and flowed beneath that glittering surface. Here and there danced men carrying aloft *moccoli*, and clanking chains, emblem of the tyrannic power now vanquished by the people. The people, sweet and noble, who, in the intoxication of their joy, were guilty of no rude or unkindly word or act, and who, no signal being given as usual for the termination of their diversion, closed, of their own accord and with one consent, singing the hymns for Pio, by nine o'clock, and retired peacefully to their homes, to dream of hopes they yet scarce understand.

This happened last week. The news of the dethronement of Louis Philippe reached us just after the close of the Carnival. It was just a year from my leaving Paris. I did not think, as I looked with such disgust on the empire of sham he had established in France, and saw the soul of the people imprisoned and held fast as in an iron vice, that it would burst its chains so soon. Whatever be the result, France has done gloriously; she has declared that she will not be satisfied with pretexts while there are facts in the world—that to stop her march is a vain attempt, though the onward path be dangerous and difficult. It is vain to cry Peace, peace, when there is no peace. The news from France, in these days, sounds ominous, though still vague; it would appear that the political is being merged in the social struggle: it is well; whatever blood is to be shed, whatever altars cast down. Those tremendous problems MUST be solved, whatever be the cost! That cost cannot fail to break many a bank, many a heart in Europe, before the good can bud again out of a mighty corruption. To you, people of America, it may perhaps be given to look on and learn in time for a preventive wisdom. You may learn the real meaning of the words FRATERNITY, EQUALITY: you may, despite the apes of the Past, who strive to tutor you, learn the needs of a true Democracy. You may in time learn to reverence, learn to guard, the true aristocracy of a nation, the only really noble—the LABORING CLASSES.

And Metternich, too, is crushed; the seed of the Woman has had his foot on the serpent. I have seen the Austrian arms dragged through the streets of Rome and burned in the Piazza del Popolo.—The Italians embraced one another and cried *Miracolo, Providenza!* the modern Tribune Ciceruacchio fed the flame with faggots; Adam Mickiewicz, the great Poet of Poland, long exiled from his country or the hopes of a country, looked on, while Polish women, exiled too, or who, perhaps, like one nun who is here, had been daily scourged by the orders of a tyrant, brought little pieces that had been scattered in the street and threw them into the flames—an offering received by the Italians with loud plaudits. It was a transport of the people, who found no way to vent their joy, but the symbol, the poesy, natural to the Italian mind; the ever-too-wise "upper classes" regret it, and the Germans choose to resent it as an insult to Germany; but it was nothing of the kind; the insult was to the prisons of Spielberg, to those who commanded the massacres of Milan; a base tyranny little congenial to the native German heart, as the true Germans of Germany are at this moment showing by their struggles, by their resolves.

When the double-headed eagle was pulled down from above the lofty portal of the Palazzo di Venezia, the people placed there in its stead one of white and gold inscribed with the name ALTA ITALIA, and quick upon the emblem followed the news that Milan was fighting against her tyrants—that Venice had driven them out and freed from their prisons the courageous Protestants in favor of truth, Tommaseo and Manin—that Manin, descendant of the last Doge, had raised the Republican banner on the Place St. Mark—and that Modena, that Parma, were driving out the unfeeling and imbecile creatures who had mocked Heaven and Man by the pretence of Government there.

With indescribable rapture these news were received in Rome. Men were seen dancing, women weeping with joy along the street. The youth rushed to enrol themselves in regiments to go to the frontier. In the Colosseum their names were received. Father Gavazzi, a truly patriotic monk, gave them the cross to carry on a new, a better, because defensive crusade. Sterbini, long exiled, addressed them; he said, "Romans, do you wish to go; do you wish to go with all your hearts? If so, you *may,* and those who do not wish to go themselves may give money. To those who will go, the government gives bread and fifteen baiocchi a day." The people cried "We too wish to go, but we do not wish so much; the Government is very poor; we can live on a paul a day." The princes answered by giving, one sixty thousand, others twenty, fifteen, ten thousand dollars. The people answered by giving at the benches which are opened in the piazzas literally everything; street-peddlers gave the gains of each day; women gave every ornament—from the splendid necklace and bracelet down to the poorest bit of coral; servant girls gave five pauls, two pauls, even half a paul, if they had no more; a man all in rags gave two pauls; "it is," said he, "all I have." "Then," said Torlonia, "take from me this dollar;" the man of rags thanked him warmly and handed that also to the bench, which refused to receive it. "No! *that* must stay with you," shouted all present. These are the people whom the traveler accuses of being unable to rise above selfish considerations. Nation, rich and glorious by nature as ever, capable, like all nations, all men, of being degraded by slavery, capable as are few nations, few men, of kindling into pure flame at the touch of a ray from the Sun of Truth, of Life.

The two or three days that followed, the troops were marching about by detachments, followed always by the people, to Ponte Malle, often farther. The women wept; for the habits of the Romans are so domestic, that it seemed a great thing to have their sons and lovers gone even for a few months. The English—or, at least those of the illiberal, bristling nature—too often met here, which casts out its porcupine quills against everything like enthusiasm (of the more generous Saxon blood I know some noble examples,) laughed at all this. They have said that this people would not fight; when the Sicilians, men and women, did so nobly they said, "Oh! the Sicilians are quite unlike the Italians; you will see when the struggle comes on in Lombardy, they cannot resist the Austrian force a moment." I said, "That force is only physical; do not you think a sentiment can sustain them?" They reply, "All stuff and poetry; it will fade the moment their blood flows." When news came that the Milanese, men and women, fight as the Sicilians did, they said, "Well, the Lombards are a better race, but these Romans are good for nothing; it is a farce for a Roman to try to walk even; they never walk a mile; they will not be able to support the first day's march of thirty miles, and not to have their usual minestra to eat either." Now the troops were not willing to wait for the Government to make the necessary arrangements for their march, so at the first night's station—Monterose—they did *not* find food or bedding, yet the second night, at Civita Castellana, they were so well alive as to remain dancing and vivaing Pio Nino in the piazza till after midnight. No, Messieurs, Soul is not quite nothing, if Matter be a clog upon its transports.

The Americans show a better, warmer feeling than they did; the meeting in New-York was of use in instructing the Americans abroad! The dinner given here on Washington's birthday, was marked by fine expressions of sentiment and a display of talent unusual on such occasions. There was a poem from Mr. Story of Boston, which gave great pleasure; a speech by Mr. Hillard, said to be very good, and one by Mr. Hedge of Bangor, exceedingly admired for the felicity of thought and image and the finished beauty of style.

Next week we shall have more news, and I shall try to write and mention also some interesting things want of time obliges me to omit in this letter. I annex a poem of Cranch's, descriptive of a picture he sends to Mr. Ogden Haggerty of your City, interesting in itself and not irrelevant to this present communication:

THE CASTLE OF THE COLONNAS

BY C. P. CRANCH

High on a rugged mountain, gray and old,
Gray like the rocks themselves—where heat and cold
For centuries with the battlements have striven.
As Man did once—its walls all bare and riven,
The castle stands—a mass of frowning stone,
With dark-green vines and ivy over-grown,
Through the gray rifts the deep Italian day
Smiles as it ever smiles on all decay.
Here in the olden days of feudal might
The proud Colonna donned his armor bright
And strode upon the ramparts, to survey
The vassal plains that far beneath him lay,
And mustering his brave knights, held them intent
To guard each oft-assaulted battlement.
Here bristling up the steep and narrow path

Host after host came flaming in fierce wrath.
Through the bright day and through the starlit night
Thundered the tempest of the bloody fight;
And those far Volscian mounta'ns, soft and blue,
Smiled through their purple haze, as now they do
On the deep stillness of this peaceful day,—
When nought is heard save—faint and far away,
Down by the vineyards green—the shepherd's song
Floating the vale and mountain side along;
Or cawing rooks that clamor hour by hour
Sailing around the Ruin's topmost tower.

Up the gray rocks no more the files advance;
No more the battle stern, the wild romance.
Peace hath her victories now, perchance as famed
As those in olden time the Warrior claimed.
All Italy hath breathed a freer air
Since good Mastai fills Saint Peter's chair:
More mildly seems to bend the Summer sky
Its infinite dome of blue, the morning's eye
Opens more hopefully, and evening closes
With tinted clouds like dropping leaves of roses,
Over the Roman streets and shrines and fountains,

O'er the Campagna and the purple mountains
Love, Freedom, Truth may yet extend their wing,
And all be realized that poets sing.

When great Colonna, driven from his home,
Landless, and stripped of all, went forth to roam,
"Where is thy fortress now?" they asked. With pride,
His hand upon his heart, the chief replied
" 'Tis here!"—And thou around whose onward course
Threaten the legions of tyrannic force,
Sovereign whom God hath surely blest and sent
To be of future good His instrument,
Though all desert thee in thine hour of need,
And leave thee houseless on the rocks to bleed,
Let thy soul's watchword be a truer light
Than even his who ruled by fear and might.
Thy Heart thy Fortress! An unfading youth
Shall yearly crown its battlements of truth.
In the bright panoply of God encased
No years shall molder and no tyrant waste.
No Ruin of the Past that heart shall be,
But a great Beacon-tower for the good and free.

Rome, February, 1848.

—APRIL 1.

Yesterday I passed at Ostia and Castle Fusano. A million birds sang; the woods teemed with blossoms: the sod grew green hourly over the graves of the mighty Past; the surf rushed in on a fair shore; the Tiber majestically retreated to carry inland her share from the treasures of the deep; the sea breezes burnt my face, but revived my heart; I felt the calm of thought, the sublime hopes of the Future, Nature, Man— so great, though so little—so dear, though incomplete. Returning to Rome, I find the news, pronounced official, that the viceroy Ranieri has capitulated at Verona; that Italy is free, independent, and One. I trust this will prove no April foolery, no premature news; it seems too good, too speedy a realization of hope, to have come on earth, and can only be answered in the words of the proclamation made yesterday by Pius IX.:

"The events which these two months past have seen rush after one another in so rapid succession, are no human work. Woe to him who in this wind, which shakes and tears up alike the lofty cedars and humble shrubs, hears not the voice of God! Woe to human pride, if to the fault or merit of any man whatsoever it refer these wonderful changes, instead of adoring the mysterious designs of Providence."

ROME, DECEMBER 2, 1848

Messrs. Greeley & McElrath:

EASY IS THE DESCENT TO ILL.

I have not written for six months, and within that time what changes have taken place on this side "the great water." Changes of how Great dramatic interest historically—of bearing infinitely important ideally.

I wrote last when Pius IX. had taken the first stride on the downward road. He had proclaimed himself the foe of farther Reform measures, when he implied that Italian independence was not important in his eyes, when he abandoned the crowd of heroic youth who had gone to the field with his benediction, to some of whom his own hand had given crosses. All the Popes, his predecessors, had meddled with, most frequently instigated, war; now came one who must carry out, literally, the doctrines of the Prince of Peace, when the war was not for mercy, or the aggrandizement of individuals, but to redeem national, to redeem human, rights from the grasp of foreign oppression.

I said some cried "traitor," some "imbecile," some "wept," but in the minds of all, I believe, at that time grief was finally predominant. They could no longer depend on him they had thought their best friend. They had lost their father.

Meanwhile his people would not submit to the inaction he urged. They saw it was not only ruinous to themselves, but base and treacherous to the rest of Italy. They said to the Pope, "This cannot be; you must follow up the pledges you have given, or, if you will not act to redeem them, you must have a Ministry that will." The Pope, after he had once declared to the contrary, ought to have persisted. He ought to have said, "I cannot thus belie myself, I cannot put my name to acts I have just declared to be against my conscience."

The Ministers of the people ought to have seen that the position they assumed was utterly untenable, that they could not advance with an enemy in the background cutting off all supplies. But some patriotism, and some vanity exhilarated them, and the Pope, having weakly yielded, they unwisely began their impossible task. Mamiani, their chief, I esteem a man, under all circumstances, unequal to such a position—a man of rhetoric, merely. But no man could have acted, unless the Pope had resigned his temporal power, the Cardinals been put under sufficient check, and the Jesuits and emissaries of Austria driven from their lurking-places.

A sad scene began. The Pope—shut up more and more in his palace, the crowd of selfish and insidious advisers darkening round, enslaved by a confessor—he who might have been the liberator of suffering Europe, permitted the most infamous treacheries to be practiced in his name. Private letters were written to the foreign powers denying the acts he outwardly sanctioned; the hopes of the people were evaded or dallied with; the Chamber of Deputies permitted to talk and pass measures which they never could get funds to put into execution; legions to form and maneuver, but never to have the arms and clothing they needed. Again and again the people went to the Pope for satisfaction. They got only—benediction.

Thus plotted and thus worked the scarlet men of sin, playing the hopes of Italy off and on, while *their* hope was of the miserable defeat consummated by a still worse traitor at Milan on the 6th August. But, indeed, what could be expected from the "SWORD OF PIUS IX." when Pius IX. himself had thus failed to his high vocation. The King of Naples bombarded his city and set on the lazzaroni to rob and murder the subjects he had deluded by his pretended gift of the Constitution. Pius proclaimed that he longed to embrace *all* the Princes of Italy. He talked of peace when all knew for a great part of the Italians there was no longer hope of peace except in the sepulchre, or Freedom.

The taunting manifestoes of Welden are a sufficient comment on the conduct of the Pope. "As the Government of His Holiness is too weak to control his subjects"—"As, singularly enough, a great number of Romans are found fighting against us, contrary to the expressed will of their Prince,"—such were the excuses for invasions of the Pontifical dominions and robbery and insult by which they were accompanied. Such invasions, it was said, made His Holiness very indignant; he remonstrated against these; but we find no word of remonstrance against the tyranny of the King of Naples—no word of sympathy for the victims of Lombardy, the sufferings of Verona, Vicenza, Padua, Mantua, Venice. In the affairs of Europe there are continued signs of the plan of the retrograde party to effect similar demonstrations in different places at the same hour. The 15th May was one of these marked days. On that day the King of Naples made use of the insurrection he had contrived to excite to massacre his people, and find an excuse for recalling his troops from Lombardy. The same day a similar crisis was hoped in Rome from the declarations of the Pope, but that did not work at the moment exactly as the foes of enfranchisement hoped.

However, the wounds were cruel enough. The Roman volunteers received the astounding news that they were not to expect protection or countenance from their Prince; all the army stood aghast that they were no longer to fight in the name of Pio. It had been so dear, so sweet to love and reverence really the Head of their Church, so inspiring to find their religion for once in accordance with the aspirations of the soul. They were to be deprived, too, of the aid of the disciplined Neapolitan troops and their artillery, on which they had counted. How cunningly all this was contrived to cause dissension and dismay may easily be seen.

The Neapolitan General Pepe nobly refused to obey, and called on the troops to remain with him. They wavered; but they are a pampered army, personally much attached to the King, who pays them well and indulges them at the expense of his people, that they may be his support against that people when in a throe of Nature it rises and strives for its rights. For the same reason, the sentiment of patriotism was little diffused among them in comparison with the other troops. And the alternative presented was one in which it required a very clear sense of higher duty to act against habit. Generally, after wavering a while, they obeyed and returned. The Roman States which had received them with so many testimonials of affection and honor were not slack to show a correspondent aversion and contempt on their retreat. The towns would not suffer their passage; the hamlets were unwilling to serve them even with fire and water. They were filled at once with shame and rage, one officer killed himself, unable to bear it; in the unreflecting minds of the soldiers, hate sprung up for the rest of Italy, and especially Rome, which will make them admirable tools of tyranny in case of civil war.

This was the first great calamity of the war. But apart from the treachery of the King of Naples and the dereliction of the Pope, it was impossible it should end thoroughly well. The people were in earnest, and have shown themselves so; brave, and able to bear privation. No one should dare, after the proofs of the Summer, to reiterate the taunt, so unfriendly frequent on foreign lips at the beginning of the contest, that the Italian can boast, shout, and fling garlands, but not *act*. The Italian always showed himself a noble and a brave, even in foreign service, and is doubly so in the cause of his country. But efficient heads were wanting. The Princes were not in earnest; they were looking at expediency. The Grand Duke, timid and prudent, wanted to do what was safest for Tuscany; his Ministry, "*Moderate*" and prudent, would have liked to win a great prize at small risk. They went no farther than the people pulled them. The King of Sardinia had taken the first bold step, and the idea that treachery on his part was premeditated cannot be sustained; it arises from the extraordinary aspect of his measures, and the knowledge that he is not incapable of treachery, as he proved in early youth. But now it was only his selfishness that worked to the same results. He fought and planned, not for Italy but the house of Savoy, which his Balbis and Giobertis had so long been prophesying was to reign supreme in the new great Era of Italy. These prophecies he more than half believed, because they chimed with his ambitious wishes; but he had not soul enough to realize them; he trusted only in his disciplined troops; he had not nobleness enough to believe he might rely at all on the sentiment of the people. For his troops he dared not have good Generals; conscious of meanness and timidity, he shrank from the approach of able and earnest men; he was only afraid they would, in helping Italy, take her and themselves out of his guardianship. Antonini was insulted, Garibaldi rejected; other experienced leaders, who had rushed to Italy at the first trumpet-sound, could never get employment from him. As to his generalship, it was entirely inadequate, even if he had made use of the first favorable moments. But his first thought was not to strike a blow at the Austrians before they recovered from the discomfiture of Milan, but to use the panic and need of his assistance to induce Lombardy and Venice to annex themselves to his kingdom. He did not even wish seriously to get the better till this was done, and when this was done, it was too late. The Austrian army was recruited, the Generals had recovered their spirits, and were burning to retrieve and avenge their past defeat. The conduct of Charles Albert had been shamefully evasive in the first months. The account given by Franzini, when challenged in the Chamber of Deputies at Turin, might be summed up thus: "Why, gentlemen, what would you have? Every one knows that the army is in excellent condition, and eager for action. They are often reviewed, hear speeches, and sometimes get medals. We take places always, if it is not difficult. I myself was present once when the troops advanced; our men behaved gallantly, and had the advantage in the first skirmish, but afterward the enemy pointed on us artillery from the hights, and naturally, we retired. But as to supposing that his Majesty Charles Albert is indifferent to the success of Italy in the war, that is absurd. He is the Sword of Italy; he is the most magnanimous of Princes! he is seriously occupied about the war; many a day I have been called into his tent to talk it over, before he was up in the morning!"

Sad was it that the heroic Milan, the heroic Venice, the heroic Sicily, should lean on such a reed as this, and by hurried acts, equally unworthy as unwise, sully the glory of their shields. Some names, indeed, stand out quite free from this blame. Mazzini, who kept up a combat against folly and cowardice, of day by day and hour by hour, with almost supernatural strength, warned the people constantly of the evils which their advisers were drawing upon them. He was heard then only by a few, but in this "Italia del Popolo" may be found many prophecies exactly fulfilled, as those of "the golden-haired love of Phoebus" during the struggles of Illium. He himself, in the last sad days of Milan, compared his lot to that of Cassandra. At all events, his hands are pure from all that ill. What could be done to arouse Lombardy he did, but the "Moderate" party unable to wean themselves from old habits, the pupils of the wordy Gioberti thought there could be no safety unless under the mantle of a Prince. They did not foresee that he would run away and throw that mantle on the ground.

Tommaseo and Manin also were clear in their aversion to these measures; and with them, as with all who were resolute in principle at that time, a great influence has followed.

It is said Charles Albert feels bitterly the imputations on his courage, and says they are most ungrateful when he has exposed the lives of himself and his sons in the combat. Indeed, there ought to be made a distinction between personal and mental courage. The former Charles Albert may possess, may have too much, of what this still aristocratic world calls "the feelings of a gentleman" to shun exposing himself to a chance shot now and then. And entire want of mental courage he has shown. His decisive battle was made so by giving up the moment Fortune turned against him. It is shameful to hear so many say this result was inevitable, just because the material advantages were in favor of the Austrians. Pray, was never a battle won against material odds? It is precisely such that a good leader, a noble man, may expect to win. Were the Austrians driven out of Milan because the Milanese had that advantage? The Austrians would again have suffered repulse from them, but for the baseness of this man, on whom they had been cajoled into relying: a baseness that deserves the pillory; and on a pillory will the "magnanimous," as he was meanly called in face of the crimes of his youth and the timid selfishness of his middle age, stand in the sight of posterity. He made use of his power only to betray Milan; he took from the citizens all means of defence, and then gave them up to the spoiler; he promised to defend them "to the last drop of his blood," and sold them the next minute; even the paltry terms he made he has not seen maintained. Had the people slain him in their rage, he well deserved it at their hands; and all his conduct since had confirmed that sudden verdict of passion.

Of all this great drama I have much to write, but elsewhere, in a more full form, and where I can duly sketch the portraits of actors little known in America. The materials are over-rich. I have bought my right in them by much sympathetic suffering; yet, amid the blood and tears of Italy, 't is joy to see some glorious new births.—the Italians are getting cured of mean adulation and hasty boasts; they are learning to prize and seek realities; the effigies of straw are getting knocked down, and living, growing men, take their places. Italy is being educated for the Future: her leaders are learning that the time is past for trust in Princes and precedents—that there is no hope except in Truth and God; her lower people are learning to shout less and think more.

Though my thoughts have been much with the public in this struggle for life, I have been away from it during the Summer months, in the quiet valleys, on the lonely mountains. There, personally undisturbed, I have seen the glorious Italian Summer wax and wane: the Summer of Southern Italy, which I did not see last year. On the mountains it was not too hot for me, and I enjoyed the great luxuriance of vegetation. I had the advantage of having visited the scene of the war minutely last Summer, so that, in mind, I could follow every step of the campaign; while around me were the glorious reliques of old times, the crumbling theater or temple of the Roman day; the bird's-nest village of the Middle Ages—on its purple hight shone the sun and moon of Italy in changeless lustre. It was great pleasure to me to watch the gradual growth and change of the seasons, so different from ours. Last year I had not leisure for this quiet acquaintance. Now I saw the fields first dressed in their carpets of grain, enameled richly with the red poppy and blue corn-flower—in that sunshine how resplendent! Then swelled the fig, the grape, the olive, the almond; and my food was of these products of this rich clime. For near three months I had grapes every day; the last four weeks enough daily for two persons for a cent! Exquisite salad for two persons' dinner and supper, a cent. All other products of the region in the same proportion. One who keeps still in Italy, and lives as the people do, may really have much simple luxury for very little money; though both travel and, to the inexperienced foreigner, life in the cities are expensive.

ROME, DECEMBER 2, 1848

Messrs. Greeley & McElrath:

NOT TILL I SAW THE SNOW on the mountains grow rosy in the Autumn sunset did I turn my steps again toward Rome. I was very ready to return. After three or four years of constant excitement this six months of seclusion had been welcome; but now I felt the need of meeting other eyes beside those, so bright and so shallow, of the Italian peasant. Indeed, I left what was most precious that I could not take with me, still it was a compensation that I was again to see Rome. Rome that almost killed me with her cold breath of last Winter, yet still with that cold breath whispered a tale of import so divine. Rome so beautiful, so great; her presence stupifies, and one has to withdraw to prize the treasures she has given. City of the Soul! yes, it is *that*; the very dust magnetizes you, and thousand spells have been chaining you in every careless, every murmuring moment. Yes! Rome, however seen, thou must be still adored; and every hour of absence or presence must deepen love with one who has known what it is to repose in thy arms.

Repose! for whatever be the revolutions, tumults, panics, hopes of the present day, still the temper of life here is Repose. The great Past enfolds us, and the emotions of the moment cannot here importantly disturb that impression. From the wild shout and throng of the streets the setting sun recalls us as it rests on a hundred domes and temples—rests on the Campagna, whose grass is rooted in departed human greatness. Burial-place so full of spirit that Death itself seems no longer cold; oh let me rest here, too! Rest, here, seems possible; meseems myriad lives still linger here, awaiting some one great summons.

The rivers had burst their bounds, and beneath the moon the fields round Rome lay, one sheet of silver. Entering the gate while the baggage was under examination I walked to the gate of a villa. Far

stretched its overarching shrubberies, its deep-green bowers; two statues with foot advanced and uplifted finger, seemed to greet me; it was
near the scene of great revels, great splendors in the old time; there
lay the gardens of Sallust, where were combined palace, theater, library, bath and villa. Strange things have happened now, the most
attractive part of which—the secret heart—lies buried or has fled to
animate other forms: for of that part historians have rarely given a
hint, more than they do now of the truest life of our day, that refuses
to be embodied by the pen; it craves forms more mutable, more eloquent than the pen can give.

I found Rome empty of foreigners: most of the English have fled
in affright—the Germans and French are wanted at home—the Czar
has recalled many of his younger subjects; he does not like the schooling they get here. That large part of the population which lives by the
visits of foreigners was suffering very much—trade, industry, for every
reason, stagnant. The people were every moment becoming more exasperated by the impudent measures of the Minister Rossi, and their
mortification at seeing Rome represented and betrayed by a foreigner.
And what foreigner? A pupil of Guizot and Louis Philippe. The news
had just reached them of the bombardment and storm of Vienna. Zuc-
chi, the Minister-of-War, left Rome to put down over-free manifesta-
tions in the Provinces, and impede the entrance of the troops of the
Patriot Chief, Garibaldi, into Bologna. From the Provinces came soldiery, called by Rossi to keep order at the opening of the Chamber of
Deputies. He reviewed them in the face of the Civic Guard; the Press
began to be restrained; men were arbitrarily seized and sent out of the
kingdom, the public indignation rose to its hight; the cup overflowed.

The 15th was a beautiful day and I had gone out for a long walk.
Returning at night, the old Padrona met me with her usual smile a
little clouded. "Do you know," said she, "that the Minister Rossi has
been killed?"

"Killed!"

"Yes—with a thrust in the back. A wicked man, surely, but is that
the way to punish CHRISTIANS?"

"I cannot," observed a Philosopher, "sympathize under any circumstances with so immoral a deed; but surely the manner of doing
it was *grandiose*."

The people at large was not so refined in their comments as either
the Padrona or the Philosopher; but soldiers and populace alike ran
up and down singing "Blessed the hand that rids the earth of a tyrant."

"Certainly, the manner *was* grandiose."

The Chamber was awaiting the entrance of Rossi. Had he lived to enter, he would have found the Assembly, without a single exception, ranged upon the Opposition benches. His carriage approached, attended by a howling, hissing multitude. He smiled, affected unconcern, but must have felt relieved when his horses entered the courtyard gate of the *Cancelleria*. He did not know he was entering the place of his execution. The horses stopped; he alighted in the midst of a crowd; it jostled him as if for the purpose of insult; he turned abruptly and received as he did so the fatal blow. It was dealt by a resolute, perhaps experienced, hand; he fell and spoke no word more.

The crowd, as if all previously acquainted with the plan, as no doubt most of them were, issued quietly from the gate and passed through the outside crowd—its members, among whom was he who dealt the blow, dispersing in all directions.—For two or three minutes this outside crowd did not know that anything special had happened.—When they did, the news was at the moment received in silence. The soldiers in whom Rossi had trusted, whom he had hoped to flatter and bribe, stood at their posts and said not a word.—Neither they nor any one asked "Who did this? Where is he gone?" The sense of the people certainly was that it was an act of summary justice on an offender whom the laws could not reach, but they felt it to be indecent to shout or exult on the spot where he was breathing his last. Rome, so long supposed the Capital of Christendom, certainly took a very pagan view of this act, and the piece represented on the occasion at the theaters was "The Death of Nero."

The next morning I went to the church of St. Andrea della Valle, where was to be performed a funeral service, with fine music, in honor of the victims of Vienna; for this they do here for the victims all round—"victims of Milan," "victims of Paris," "victims of Naples," and now "victims of Vienna." But today I found the church closed, the service put off—Rome was thinking about her own victims.

I passed into the church of *San Luigi dei Francesi*. The Republican flag was flying at the door; the young Sacristan said the fine musical service which this church gave formerly on St. Philip's day, in honor of Louis Philippe, would now be transferred to the Republican Anniversary, the 25th of February. I looked at the monument Chateaubriand erected when here, to a poor girl, who died last of her family, having seen all the others perish round her. I entered the Domenichino Chapel, and gazed anew on those magnificent representations of the Life and Death of St. Cecilia. She and St. Agnes are my favorite saints.

I love to think of those angel visits which her husband knew by the fragrance of roses and lilies left behind in the apartment. I love to think of his visit to the Catacombs, and all that followed. In this picture St. Cecilia, as she stretches out her arms toward the suffering multitude, seems as if an immortal fount of purest love sprung from her heart. She gives very strongly the sense of an inexhaustible love— the only love that is much worth thinking about.

Leaving the church I passed along, toward the *Piazza del Popolo,* "Yellow Tiber rose," but not high enough to cause "distress," as he does when in a swelling mood rather than "mantle" it. I heard the drums beating, and, entering the Piazza, I found the troops of the line already assembled, and the Civic Guard marching in by platoons; each *battaglione* saluted as it entered by trumpets and a fine strain from the hand of the Carbineers.

I climbed the Pincian to see better. There is no place so fine for anything of this kind as the Piazza del Popolo, it is so full of light, so fair and grand, the obelisk and fountain make so fine a center to all kinds of groups.

The object of the present meeting was for the Civic Guard and troops of the line to give pledges of sympathy preparatory to going to the Quirinal to demand a change of Ministry and of measures. The flag of the Union was placed in front of the obelisk; all present saluted it; some officials made addresses; the trumpets sounded, and all moved toward the Quirinal.

Nothing could be gentler than the disposition of the crowd. They were resolved to be played with no longer, but no threat was heard or thought—They believed that the Court would be convinced by the fate of Rossi that the retrograde movement it had attempted was impracticable. They knew the retrograde party were panic-struck, and hoped to use the occasion to free the Pope from their meshes. All felt that Pius IX. had fallen irrevocably from his high place of the friend of Progress and father of Italy: but still he was personally beloved, and still his name, so often shouted in hope and joy, had not quite lost its *prestige.*

I returned to the house, which is very near the Quirinal. On one side I could see the Palace and gardens of the Pope, on the other the Piazza Barberini and street of the Four Fountains. Presently I saw the carriage of Prince Barberini drive hurriedly into his court-yard gate, the footman signing to close it, a discharge of firearms was heard, and the drums of the Civic Guard beat to arms.

The Padrona ran up and down crying with every round of shot, "Jesu Maria, they are killing the Pope! O! poor Holy Father—Tita, Tita, (out of the window to her husband,) what *is* the matter?"

The lord of creation disdained to reply.

"Oh! Signora, pray, pray, ask Tita what is the matter?" I did so. "I don't know, Signora; nobody knows."

"Why don't you go on the mount and see?"

"It would be an imprudence, Signora; nobody will go."

I was just thinking to go myself when I saw a poor man borne by, badly wounded, and heard that the Swiss were firing on the people. Their doing so was the cause of whatever violence there was, and it was not much.

The people had assembled, as usual, at the Quirinal, only with more form and solemnity than usual. They had taken with them several of the Chamber of Deputies, and they sent an embassy, headed by Galetti, who had been in the late Ministry, to state their wishes. They received a peremptory negative. They then insisted on seeing the Pope, and pressed on the palace. The Swiss became alarmed, and fired from the windows, from the roof. They did this, it is said, without orders, but who could, at the time, suppose that? If it had been planned to exasperate the people to blood, what more could have been done? As it was, very little was shed; but the Pope, no doubt, felt great panic. He heard the report of fire-arms—heard that they tried to burn a door of the palace. I would lay my life that he could have shown himself without the slightest danger; nay, that the habitual respect for his presence would have prevailed, and hushed all tumult. He did not think so, and to still it once more degraded himself and injured his people, by making promises he did not mean to keep.

He protests now against those promises as extorted by violence, a strange plea, indeed, for the representative of St. Peter!

Rome is all full of effigies of those over whom violence had no power. There is an early Pope about to be thrown into the Tiber; violence had no power to make him say what he did not mean. Delicate girls, men in the prime of hope and pride of power—they were all alike about that. They could be done to death in boiling oil, roasted on coals, or cut to pieces; but they could not say what they did not mean. These formed the true Church; it was these who had power to disseminate the religion of Him, the Prince of Peace, who died a bloody death of torture between sinners, because He never could say what He did not mean.

A little church outside the gate of St. Sebastian commemorates this affecting tradition of the Church; Peter, alarmed at the persecution of the Christians, had gone forth to fly, when in this spot he saw a bright figure in his path and recognized his Master traveling toward Rome.

"Lord," he said, "whither goest thou?"

"I go," replied Jesus, "to die, with my people."

Peter comprehended the reproof. He felt that he must not a fourth time deny his Master, yet hope for salvation. He returned to Rome to offer his life in attestation of his faith.

The Roman Catholic Church has risen a monument to the memory of such facts. And has the present Head of that Church quite failed to understand their monition?

Not all the Popes have so failed, though the majority have been intriguing, ambitious men of the world. But even the mob of Rome— and in Rome there *is* a true mob of unheeding cabbage-sellers, who never had a thought before beyond contriving how to satisfy their animal instincts for the day—said, on hearing the protest, "There was another Pius, not long since, who talked in a very different style. When the French threatened him, he said, 'You may do with me as you see fit, but I cannot consent to act against my convictions.' "

In fact, the only dignified course for the Pope to pursue was to resign his temporal power. He could no longer hold it on his own terms; but to that he clung; and the counselors around him were men to wish him to regard *that* as the first of duties. When the question was of waging war for the independence of Italy, they regarded him solely the head of the Church; but when the demand was to satisfy the wants of his people, and ecclesiastical goods were threatened with taxes, then he was the Prince of the State, bound to maintain all the selfish prerogative of by-gone days for the benefit of his successors. Poor Pope! how has his mind been torn to pieces in these later days. It moves compassion. There can be no doubt that all his natural impulses are generous and kind, and in a more private station he would have died beloved and honored; but to this he was unequal; he has suffered bad men to surround; and by their misrepresentations and insidious suggestions, at last entirely to cloud his mind. I believe he really thinks now the Progress movement tends to anarchy, blood, all that looked worst in the first French Revolution. However that may be I cannot forgive him some of the circumstances of this flight. To fly to Naples to throw himself in the arms of the bombarding monarch, blessing him and thanking his soldiery for preserving that part of Italy from anarchy—to protest that all his promises at Rome were null and

void, when he thought himself in safety to choose a commission for
governing in his absence, composed of men of princely blood, but as
to character so null that everybody laughed and said he chose those
who could best be spared if they were killed; (but they all ran away
directly;) when Rome was thus left without any Government, to refuse
to see any deputation, even the Senator of Rome, whom he had so
gladly sanctioned,—these are the acts either of a fool or a foe. They
are not his acts, to be sure, but he is responsible, he lets them stand
as such in the face of the world, and weeps and prays for their success.

No more of him! His day is over. He has been made, it seems
unconsciously, an instrument of good his regrets cannot destroy. Nor
can he be made so important an instrument of ill. These acts have not
had the effect the foes of freedom hoped. Rome remained quite cool
and composed; all felt that they had not demanded more than was
their duty to demand, and were willing to accept what might follow.
In a few days all began to say, "Well, who would have thought it?
The Pope, the Cardinals, the Princes are gone, and Rome is perfectly
tranquil, and one does not miss anything, except that there are not so
many rich carriages and liveries."

The Pope may regret too late that he ever gave the people a chance
to make this reflection. Yet the best fruits of the movement may not
ripen for long. It is one which requires radical measures, clear-sighted,
resolute men: these last, as yet, do not show themselves in Rome. The
new Tuscan Ministry has three men of superior force in various ways:
Montanelli, Guerrazzi, D'Aguila; such are not as yet to be found in
Rome.

But should she fall this time, (and she must either advance with
decision and force, or fall—since to stand still is impossible,) the
people have learned much; ignorance and servility of thought are
lessened—the way is paving for final triumph.

And my country, what does she? You have chosen a new President
from a Slave State, representative of the Mexican War. But he seems
to be honest, a man that can be esteemed, and is one really known to
the people; which is a step upward after having sunk last time to
choosing a mere tool of party.

Pray send here a good Ambassador—one that has experience of
foreign life, that he may act with good judgment; and, if possible, a
man that has knowledge and views which extend beyond the cause of
party politics in the United States; a man of unity in principles, but
capable of understanding variety in forms. And send a man capable
to prize the luxury of living in, or knowing Rome: it is one that should

not be thrown away on a person who cannot prize or use it. Another century, and I might ask to be made Ambassador myself ('tis true, like other Ambassadors, I would employ clerks to do the most of the duty,) but woman's day has not come yet. They hold their clubs in Paris, but even George Sand will not act with women as they are. They say she pleads they are too mean, too treacherous. She should not abandon them for that, which is not nature but misfortune. How much I shall have to say on that subject if I live, which I hope I shall not, for I am very tired of the battle with giant wrongs, and would like to have some one younger and stronger arise to say what ought to be said, still more to do what ought to be done. Enough! if I felt these things in privileged America, the cries of mothers and wives beaten at night by sons and husbands for their diversion after drinking, as I have repeatedly heard them these past months, the excuse for falsehood, "I *dare not* tell my husband, he would be ready to kill me," have sharpened my perception as to the ills of Woman's condition and remedies that must be applied. Had I but genius, had I but energy, to tell what I know as it ought to be told! God grant them me, or some other more worthy woman, I pray.

But the hour of sending to the post approaches, and I must leave these great matters for some practical details. I wish to observe to my friends and all others, whom it may concern, that a banking-house here having taken Mr. Hooker, an American, into partnership, some facilities are presented for intercourse with Rome, which they may value. Mr. Hooker undertakes to have pictures copied, and to purchase those little objects of virtu peculiar to Rome, for those who cannot come themselves, as I suppose few would wish to at this time. He has the advantage of a general acquaintance with the artist to be employed, and an experience, that, no doubt, would enable him to do all this with better advantage than any stranger can for himself. It is also an excellent house to have to do with in money matters, reasonable, exact, and where none of the petty trickery or neglect so common at Torlonia's need be apprehended. They have now made arrangements with Livingston, Wells & Co. for the transmission of letters. Many addressed to me have been lost, I know not how; and I should like my friends to send to me when they can through this channel. Men who feel able can pay their letters through in this way, which has been impossible before. I have received many letters marked *paid through,* and I fear my friends in America have often paid what was quite useless, as no arrangements had been made for forwarding the letters post-paid to Rome. Those who write now can pay their letters to

Florence, if they have friends there, through *Livingston, Wells & Co.*
to care *Maquay, Pakenham & Co. Florence.* To us of Rome they can
be sent through the same, to care of *Pakenham, Hooker & Co.
Rome.*

Those of our friends, (I speak of the poor artists as well as myself,)
who cannot afford to pay, should at least forbear to write on thick
paper and under an envelop, the unnecessary use of which doubles the
expense of the letter. I am surprised to find even those who have been
abroad so negligent in these respects. I might have bought all the books
of reference I needed, and have been obliged to do without money that
could have been saved by attention from my friends to these particulars.

Write us two, three, four sheets if you will, on this paper, without
crossing. Then if one pays a couple of dollars for a letter, at least one
has something for the money: and letters are too important to happiness; we cannot afford to be without knowledge of your thoughts,
your lives; but it is hard, in people who can scarcely find bread, to
pay for coarse paper and an envelop the price of a beautiful engraving,
and know at the same time that they are doomed to leave Rome unable
to carry away a single copy of what they have most loved here, for
possession or for gift. So write, dear friends, much and often, but don't
ruin us for nothing.

Don Tirlone, the *Punch* of Rome, has just come in. This number
represents the Fortress of Gaeta; outside hangs a cage containing a
parrot (Pappagallo), the plump body of the bird is surmounted by a
noble large head with benign face and Papal head-dress. He sits on
the perch now with folded wings, but the cage door, in likeness of a
loggia, shows there is convenience to come forth for the purposes of
benediction, when wanted. Outside, the King of Naples, dressed as
Harlequin, plays the organ for instruction of the bird (unhappy penitent, doomed to penance,) and grinning with sharp teeth observes: "He
speaks in my way now." In the background a young Republican holds
ready the match for a barrel of gunpowder, but looks at his watch
waiting the moment to ignite it.

A happy New-Year to my country! may she be worthy of the
privileges she possesses, while others are lavishing their blood to win
them—that is all that need be wished for her at present.

ROME, EVENING OF FEB. 20, 1849

THE LEAGUE BETWEEN THE ITALIAN STATES, the Diet which was to establish it, had been the thought of Gioberti, had found its instrument at Rome in Mamiani. Its Deputies were to be named by Princes or Parliaments, their mandate to be limited by the then institutions of the several States, measures of mutual security and some modifications in the way of reform would be the utmost that could be hoped from it. The scope of this party did not go beyond more vigorous prosecution of the War for Independence, and the establishment of good Institutions for the several Principalities on a basis of assimilation.

Mazzini, the great radical thinker of Italy, was on the contrary persuaded that Unity not union was necessary to this country. He had taken for his motto GOD AND THE PEOPLE, and believed in no other powers. He wished an Italian Constitutional Assembly, selected directly by the People, and furnished with an unlimited mandate to decide what form was now required by the needs of the Peninsula. His own wishes, certainly, aimed at the Republic; but the decision remained with the Representatives of the People.

The thought of Gioberti had been at first the popular one, as he, in fact, was the seer of the so-called Moderate party. For myself I always looked upon him as entirely a charlatan, who covered his want of all real force by the thickest embroidered mantle of words. Still, for a time, he corresponded with the wants of the Italian mind. He assailed the Jesuits, and was of real use by embodying the distrust and aversion that brooded in the minds of men against these most insidious and inveterate foes to liberty and progress. This triumph, at least, he may boast: that sect has been obliged to yield, its extinction seems impossible, of such life-giving power was the fiery will of Loyola. In the *Primato* he had embodied the lingering hope of the Catholic Church; Pio IX. had answered to the appeal, had answered only to show its futility. He had run through Italy as courier for Charles Albert, when the so basely styled Magnanimous entered, pretending to save her from the stranger, really hoping to take her for himself. His own cowardice and treachery neutralized the hope, and Charles Albert, abject in his disgrace, took a retrograde Ministry. This the country would not suffer, and obliged him after a while to reassume at least the position of a year since by taking Gioberti for his Premier. But it soon became evident that the Ministry of Charles Albert was in the same position as had been that of Pio IX. The hand was powerless when the head was indisposed. Meantime the thought of Mazzini had echoed through Tuscany from the revered lips of Montanelli; it reached the Roman States, and, though at first propagated by foreign impulse, yet, as soon as understood, was welcomed as congenial. Montanelli had nobly said, addressing Florence, "We could not regret that the realization of this project should take place in a sister city, still more illustrious than ours." The Romans took him at his word; the Constitutional Assembly for the Roman States was elected with a double mandate, that the Deputies might sit in the Constitutional Assembly for all Italy whenever the other Provinces could send theirs. They were elected by universal suffrage. Those who listened to Jesuits and Moderates predicted that the project would fail of itself. The people were too ignorant to make use of the liberty of suffrage.

But ravens now-a-days are not the true prophetic birds. The Roman Eagle recommences her flight, and it is from its direction only that the High Priest may draw his augury. The people is certainly as ignorant as centuries of the worst government, the neglect of popular education, the enslavement of speech and the Press, could make it; yet it has an instinct to recognize measures that are good for it. A few weeks' schooling at some popular meetings, the clubs, the conversations of the National Guards in their quarters or on patrol, was sufficient to concert measures so well that the people voted in larger proportion than at contested elections in our country, and made a very good choice.

The opening of the Constitutional Assembly gave occasion for a fine procession. All the troops in Rome defiled from the Campidoglio; among them many bear the marks of suffering from the Lombard war. The banners of Sicily, Venice and Bologna waved proudly; that of Naples was veiled with crape. I was in a balcony in the Piazza Di Venezia; the Palazzo Di Venezia, that sternest feudal pile, so long the headquarters of Austrian machinations, seemed to frown as the bands each in passing struck up the *Marseillaise*. The nephew of Napoleon and Garibaldi, the hero of Montevideo, walked together, as Deputies. The Deputies, a grave band, mostly advocates or other professional men, walked without other badge of distinction than the tricolored scarf. I remembered the entrance of the Deputies to the Council only fourteen months ago, in the magnificent carriages lent by the Princes for the occasion, they too were mostly Nobles and their liveried attendants followed, carrying their scutcheons. Princes and Counselors have both fled or sunk into nothingness: in those Counselors was no Counsel.—Will it be found in the present? Let us hope it! What we see to-day has much more the air of reality than all that parade of scutcheons, or the pomp of dress and retinue with which the Ecclesiastical Court was wont to amuse the people.

A few days after followed the proclamation of the Republic. An immense crowd of people surrounded the *Palazzo della Cancelleria,* within whose courtyard Rossi fell, while the debate was going on within. At one o'clock in the morning of the 9th February, the Republic was resolved upon and the crowd rushed away to ring all the bells.

Early next morning I rose and went forth to seek the Republic. Over the Quirinal I went, through the Forum to the Capitol. There was nothing to be seen except the magnificent calm emperor, the tamers of horses, the fountain, the trophies, the lions, as usual; among the marbles for living figures, a few dirty, bold women, and Murillo boys in the sun just as usual. I passed into the Corso; there were men in the liberty cap; of course the lowest and vilest had been the first to assume it; all the horrible beggars persecuting as impudently as usual. I met some English; all their comfort was, "It would not last a month."—"They hoped to see all those fellows shot yet."—The English clergyman, more mild and legal, only hopes to see them (as the Ministry, Deputies, &c.) *hung.*

Mr. Carlyle would be delighted with his country men. They are entirely ready and anxious to see a Cromwell for Italy. They, too, think it is no matter what happens in "the back parlor," when the people starve. What signifies that, if there is "order" in the front? How dare they make a noise to disturb us yawning at billiards!

I met an American. He "had no confidence in the Republic." Why? Because he "had no confidence in the People." Why? Because "they were not like *our* People." Ah! Jonathan and John—excuse me, but I must say the Italian has a decided advantage over you in the power of quickly feeling generous sympathy, as well as some other things which I have not time now to particularize. *Mais nous nous reverrons.* I have memoranda from you both in my note-book.

At last the procession mounts the Campidoglio. It is all dressed with banners. The tricolor surmounts the Palace of the Senator; the Senator himself has fled. The Deputies mount the steps, and one of them reads, in a clear, friendly voice, the following words:

FUNDAMENTAL DECREE OF THE
CONSTITUTIONAL ASSEMBLY OF ROME.

ARTICLE I. The Papacy has fallen in fact and in right from the temporal Government of the Roman State.

ART. II. The Roman Pontifex shall have all the necessary guaranties for independence in the exercise of his spiritual power.

ART. III. The form of Government of the Roman State shall be a pure Democracy, and will take the glorious name of Roman Republic.

ART. IV. The Roman Republic will have with the rest of Italy the relations exacted by a common nationality.

Between each of these expressive sentences the speaker paused; the great bell of the Capitol gave forth its solemn melodies; the cannon answered; while the crowd shouted, *viva la Republica! viva Italia!*

The imposing grandeur of the spectacle to me gave new force to the thought that already swelled my heart; my nerves thrilled, and longed to see in some answering glance a spark of Rienzi, a little of that soul which made my country what she is. The American at my side remained impassive. Receiving all his birthright from a triumph of Democracy, he was quite indifferent to this manifestation on this consecrated spot. Passing the Winter in Rome to study Art, he was insensible to the artistic beauty of the scene—insensible to this new life of that spirit from which all the forms he gazes at in galleries emanated. He "did not see the *use* of these popular demonstrations."

Again, I must mention a remark of his as a specimen of the ignorance in which Americans usually remain during their flighty visits to these scenes, where they associate only with one another. And I do it the rather as this seemed a really thoughtful, intelligent man; no vain, vulgar trifler. He said—

"*The people* seem only to be looking on; they take no part."

"What people?" said I.

"Why, these round us; there is no other people."

There are a few beggars, errand-boys and nurse-maids.

"The others are only soldiers."

"Soldiers! The Civic Guard; all the decent men in Rome."

Thus it is that the American, on many points, becomes more ignorant for coming abroad, because he attaches some value to his crude impressions and frequent blunders. It is not thus that any seed-corn can be gathered from foreign gardens. Without modest scrutiny, patient study and observation, he spends his money and goes home with a new coat perhaps, but a mind befooled rather than instructed. It is necessary to speak the languages of these countries and know personally some of their inhabitants in order to form any accurate impressions.

The flight of the Grand Duke of Tuscany followed. In imitation of his great exemplar he promised and smiled to the last, deceiving Montanelli, the pure and sincere, at the very moment he was about to enter his carriage, into the belief that he persevered in his assent to the liberal movement. His position was certainly very difficult, but he might have left it like a gentleman, like a man of honor. 'T was pity to destroy so lightly the good opinion the Tuscans had of him. Now Tuscany meditates union with Rome.

Meanwhile, Charles Albert is filled with alarm. He is indeed betwixt two fires. Gioberti has published one of his prolix, weak addresses, in which he says that in the beginning of every revolution you must fix a limit beyond which you will not go; that, for himself, he has done it—others are surpassing his mark and he will not go any farther. Of the want of thought, of insight to historic and all other truths which distinguishes the "illustrious Gioberti," this assumption is a specimen. But it makes no difference; he and his Prince must go sooner or later, if the movement continues, nor is there any prospect of its being stayed unless by foreign intervention. This the Pope has not yet, it is believed, solicited, but there is little reason to hope he will be spared that crowning disgrace. He has already consented to the incitement of civil war. Should an intervention be solicited, all depends on France. Will she basely forfeit every pledge and every duty, to say nothing of her true interest? It seems that her President stands doubtful, intending to do what is for *his* particular interest; but if his interest proves opposed to the republican principle, will France suffer herself again to be hoodwinked and enslaved? It is impossible to know, she has already shown such devotion to the mere prestige of a name.

On England no dependence can be placed. She is guided by no great idea; her Parliamentary leaders sneer at sentimental policy, and the "jargon" of ideas. She will act, as always, for her own interest; and the interest of her present Government is becoming more and more the crushing of the democratic tendency. They are obliged to do it at home both in the back and the front parlor; it would not be decent as yet to have a Spielberg just at home for obstreperous patriots, but England has so many ships, it is just as easy to transport them to safe distance. Then the Church of England, so long an enemy to the Church of Rome, feels a decided interest with it on the subject of temporal possessions. The rich English traveler, fearing to see the Prince Borghese stripped of one of his palaces for a hospital or some such low use, thinks of his own twenty-mile park and the crowded village of beggars at its gate, and muses: "I hope to see them all shot yet, these rascally republicans."

How I wish my country would show some noble sympathy when an experience so like her own is going on. Politically she cannot interfere; but formerly when Greece and Poland were struggling, they were at least aided by private contributions. Italy, naturally so rich, but long racked and impoverished by her oppressors, greatly needs money to arm and clothe her troops. Some token of sympathy, too, from America would be so welcome to her now. If there were a circle of persons inclined to trust such to me, I might venture to promise the trust should be used to the advantage of Italy. It would make me proud to have my country show a religious faith in the progress of ideas, and make some small sacrifice of its own great resources in aid of a sister cause, now.

But I must close this letter, which it would be easy to swell to a volume from the material in my mind. One or two traits of the hour I must note. Mazzarelli, chief of the present Ministry, was a prelate, and named spontaneously by the Pope before his flight. He has shown entire and frank intrepidity. He has laid aside the title of Monsignor, and appears before the world as a layman.

Nothing can be more tranquil than has been the state of Rome all Winter. Every wile has been used by the obscurantists to excite the people, but their confidence in their leaders could not be broken. A little mutiny in the troops, stimulated by letters from their old leaders, was quelled in a moment. The day after the proclamation of the Republic, some zealous ignoramuses insulted the carriages that appeared with servants in livery. The Ministry published a grave admonition, that democracy meant liberty, not license, and that he who infringed upon an innocent freedom of action in others must be declared traitor to his country. Every act of the kind ceased instantly. An intimation that it was better not to throw large comfits or oranges during the Carnival, as injuries have thus been sometimes caused, was obeyed with equal docility.

On Sunday last placards affixed in the high places summoned the city to invest Giuseppe Mazzini with the rights of a Roman Citizen. I have not yet heard the result. The Pope made Rossi a Roman Citizen;

he was suffered to retain that title only one day. It was given him 14th Nov.; he died the 15th. Mazzini enters Rome at any rate for the first time in his life as deputy to the Constitutional Assembly; it would be a noble poetic justice, if he could enter also a Roman Citizen.

24th.—The Austrians have invaded Ferrara, taken $200,000 and six hostages and retired. This step is no doubt intended to determine whether France will resent the insult, or whether she will betray Italy. It shows also the assurance of the Austrian that the Pope will approve of an armed intervention. Probably before I write again these matters will reach some decided crisis.

ROME, 6TH MAY, 1849

I WRITE YOU from barricaded Rome. The Mother of Nations is now at bay against them all. Rome was suffering before. The misfortunes of other regions of Italy, the defeat at *Novara*, preconcerted in hope to strike the last blow at Italian independence, the surrender and painful condition of Genoa, the money difficulties—insuperable, unless the Government could secure confidence abroad as well as at home—prevented her people from finding that foot-hold for which they were ready. The vacillations of France agitated them, still they could not seriously believe she would ever act the part she has. We must say France, because, though many honorable men have washed their hands of all share in the perfidy, the Assembly voted funds to sustain the expedition to Civitá Vecchia, and the Nation, the Army have remained quiescent.

No one was, no one could be, deceived as to the scope of this expedition. It was intended to restore the Pope to the temporal sovereignty, from which the People, by the use of suffrage, had deposed him. No doubt the French, in case of success, proposed to temper the triumph of Austria and Naples, and stipulate for conditions that might soothe the Romans and make their act less odious. Also they were probably deceived by the representations of Gaeta, and believed that a large party, which had been intimidated by the republicans, would declare in favor of the Pope when they found themselves likely to be sustained. But this last pretext may in no way avail them. They landed at Civitá Vecchia, and no one declared for the Pope. They marched on Rome. Placards were affixed within the walls by hands unknown, calling upon the Papal party to rise within the town. Not a soul stirred.

The French had no excuse left for pretending to believe that the present Government was not entirely acceptable to the people. Notwithstanding, they assail the gates, they fire upon St. Peter's, and their balls pierced the Vatican. They were repulsed as they deserved, retired in quick and shameful defeat, as surely the brave French soldiery could not, if they had not been demoralized by a sense of what an infamous course they were pursuing. France, eager to destroy the last hope of Italian emancipation, France the alguazil of Austria, the soldiers of republican France, firing upon republican Rome! If there be angel as well as demon powers that interfere in the affairs of men, those bullets could scarcely fail to be turned back against their own breasts. Yet Roman blood has flowed also; I saw how it stained the walls of the Vatican Gardens on the 30th April—the first anniversary of the appearance of Pius IX's too famous encyclic letter. Shall he, shall any Pope ever again walk peacefully in these gardens. Impossible! The temporal sovereignty of the Popes was gone, by their shameless, merciless measures taken to restore it. The spiritual dominion falls too into irrevocable ruin.

What may be the issue, at this moment we cannot guess. The French have retired to Civitá Vecchia, but whether to re-embark or to await re-inforcements we know not. The Neapolitan force has halted within a few miles of the walls; it is not large, and they are undoubtedly surprised at the discomfiture of the French. Perhaps they wait for the Austrians, but we do not yet hear that these have entered Romana. Meanwhile Rome is strongly barricaded, and, though she cannot stand always against a world in arms, she means at least to try. Mazzini is at her head; she has now a guide "who understands his faith," and all there is of noble spirit will show itself. We all feel very sad, because the idea of bombs barbarously thrown in, and street-fight in Rome is peculiarly dreadful. Apart from all the blood and anguish inevitable at such times, the glories of Art may perish, and mankind be forever despoiled of the most beautiful inheritance. Yet I would defend Rome to the last moment. She must not be false to the higher hope that has dawned upon her. She must not fall back again into servility and corruption. And no one is willing. The interference of the French has roused the weakest to resistance. "From the Austrians, from the Neapolitans," they cried, "we expected this; but from the French, it is too infamous, it cannot be borne," and they all ran to arms and fought nobly.

The Americans here are not in a pleasant situation. Mr. Cass, the Chargé of the United States, stays here without recognizing the Government. Of course, he holds no position at the present moment that can enable him to act for us. Beside, it gives us pain that our country, whose policy it justly is to avoid physical interference with the affairs of Europe, should not use a moral influence. Rome has, as we did, thrown off a Government no longer tolerable; she has made use of the suffrage to form another; she stands on the same basis as ourselves. Mr. Rush did us great honor by his ready recognition of a principle as represented by the French Provisional Government; had Mr. Cass been empowered to do the same, our country would have acted nobly, and all that is most truly American in America would have spoken to sustain the sickened hopes of European democracy. But of this more when I write next. Who knows what I may have to tell another week?

ROME, MAY 27, 1849

I HAVE SUSPENDED WRITING in the expectation of some decisive event, but none such comes yet. The French, entangled in a web of falsehood, abashed by a defeat that Oudinot has vainly tried to gloss over, the expedition disowned by all honorable men at home, disappointed by Gaeta, because it dares not go the length the Papal infatuation demands, knows not what to do. The Neapolitans have been decidedly driven back, the last time in a most shameful rout; the King flying in front into their own borders. We have heard for several days that the Austrians were advancing, but they come not. They also, it is probable, meet with unexpected embarrassments. They find that the sincere movement of the Italian people is very unlike that of troops commanded by princes and generals who never wished to conquer and were always waiting to betray. Then their troubles at home are constantly increasing, and, should the Russian intervention quell them to-day, it is only to raise a storm far more terrible to-morrow.

The struggle is now fairly, thoroughly commenced between the principle of Democracy and the old powers, no longer legitimate. That struggle may last fifty years, and the earth be watered with the blood and tears of more than one generation, but the result is sure. All Europe, including Great Britain, where the most bitter resistance of all will be made, is to be under Republican Government in the next century.

"God works in a mysterious way."

Every struggle made by the old tyrannies, all their Jesuitical deceptions, their rapacity, their imprisonments and executions of the most generous men, only sow more Hydra teeth; the crop shoots up daily more and more plenteous.

When I first arrived in Italy, the vast majority of this people had no wish beyond limited monarchies, constitutional governments. They still respected the famous names of the nobility; they despised the priests, but were still fondly attached to the dogmas and ritual of the Roman Catholic Church. It required King Bomba, it required the triple treachery of Charles Albert, it required Pio IX. and the "illustrious Gioberti," it required the naturally kind-hearted, but, from the necessity of his position, cowardly and false Leopold of Tuscany, it required the vagabond "serene" meannesses of Parma and Modena, the "fatherly" Radetzky, and finally the imbecile Louis Bonaparte, "would-be Emperor of France," to convince this people that no transition is possible between the old and the new. The *work is done;* the revolution in Italy is now radical, nor can it stop till Italy become independent and united as a republic. Protestant she already is. The memory of saints and martyrs may continue to be revered, the ideal of Woman to be adored under the name of Maria.—Christ will now begin to be a little thought of; *his* idea was always kept carefully out of sight under the old regime; all the worship was for Madonna and Saints, who were to be well paid for interceding for sinners. An example which might make men cease to be such was no way to be coveted. Now the New Testament has been translated into Italian; copies are already dispersed far and wide; men calling themselves Christians will no longer be left entirely ignorant of the precepts and life of Jesus.

The people of Rome have burnt the Cardinals' carriages. They took the confessionals out of the churches, and made mock confessions in the piazzas, the scope of which was, "I have sinned, father, so and so." "Well, my son, how much will you pay to the church for absolution?" Afterward the people thought of burning the confessionals or using them for barricades, but at the request of the Triumvirate they desisted, and even put them back into the churches. But it was from no reaction of feeling that they stopped short, only from respect for the government. The "Tartuffe" of Moliére has been translated into Italian, and was last night performed with great applause at the Valle. Can all this be forgotten? Never! Should guns and bayonets replace the Pope on the throne, he will find its foundations, once deep as modern civilization, now so undermined that it falls with the least awkward movement.

But I cannot believe he will be replaced there. France alone could consummate that crime, that for her cruelest, most infamous treason. The Elections in France will decide. In three or four days we shall know whether the French nation at large be guilty or no—whether it be the will of the Nation to aid or strive to ruin a Government founded precisely on the same basis as their own.

I do not dare to trust that people. The peasant is yet very ignorant. The suffering workman is frightened as he thinks of the punishments that ensued on the insurrections of May and June. The man of property is full of horror, at the brotherly scope of Socialism. The aristocrat dreams of the guillotine always when he hears speak of the people. The influence of the Jesuits is still immense in France. Both in France and England the grossest falsehoods have been circulated with unwearied diligence about the state of things in Italy. An amusing specimen of what is still done in this line I find just now in a foreign journal, where it says there are red flags on all the houses of Rome, meaning to imply that the Romans are athirst for blood. Now, the fact is, that these flags are put up at the entrance of those streets where there is no barricade, as a signal to coachmen and horsemen that they can pass freely. There is one on the house where I am, in which is no person but myself who thirst for peace, and the *padrone* who thirsts for money.

Meanwhile the French troops are encamped at a little distance from Rome. Some attempts at fair and equal treaty when their desire to occupy Rome was firmly resisted, Oudinot describes in his dispatches as a readiness for *submission*. Having tried in vain to gain this point, he has sent to France for fresh orders. These will be decided by the turn the election takes. Meanwhile the French troops are much exposed to the Roman force where they are. Should the Austrians come up, what will they do? Will they shamelessly fraternize with them, after pretending and proclaiming that they came here as a check upon their aggressions? Will they oppose them in defence of Rome with which they are at war?

Ah! the way of falsehood, the way of treachery, how dark—how full of pitfalls and traps! Heaven defend from it all who are not yet engaged therein!

War near at hand seems to me even more dreadful than I had fancied it. True! it tries men's souls, lays bare selfishness in undeniable deformity. Here, it has produced much fruit of noble sentiment, noble act; but still it breeds vice, too, drunkenness, mental dissipation, tears asunder the tenderest ties, lavishes the productions of earth for which her starving poor stretch out their hands in vain, in the most unprofitable manner. And the ruin that ensues, how terrible. Let those who have ever passed happy days in Rome grieve to hear that the beautiful plantations of *Villa Borghese*—that chief delight and refreshment of citizens, foreigners, and little children, are laid low, as far as the obelisk. The fountain, singing alone amid the fallen groves, cannot be seen and heard without tears; it seems like some innocent infant calling and crowing amid dead bodies on a field which battle has strewn with the bodies of those that once cherished it. Also, the plantations of *Villa Salvage* on the Tiber, the beautiful avenue on the way from St. John Lateran to *La Maria Maggiore*, the trees of the Forum are fallen. Rome is shorn of the locks which lent grace to her venerable brow. She looks desolate, profaned. I feel what I never expected to, as if I might by and by be willing to leave Rome.

Then I have, for the first time, seen what wounded men suffer. The night of the 30th April I passed in the hospital, and saw the terrible agonies of those dying or who needed amputation, felt their mental pains, and longing for the loved ones who were away,—for many of these were Lombards, who had come from the field of Novara to fight upon a fairer chance—many were students of the University, who had enlisted and threw themselves into the front of the engagement. (N.B.—The impudent falsehoods of the French general's dispatches are incredible. The French were never decoyed on in any way. They were received with every possible mark of hostility. They were defeated in open field, the Garibaldi legion rushing out to them, and though they suffered much from the walls, they sustained themselves nowhere.—They never put up a white flag, till they wished to surrender. The vanity that strives to cover over these facts is unworthy men. The only excuse for the impudent conduct of the expedition is that they were deceived, not by the Romans here, but by the priests of Gaeta leading them to expect action in their favor within the walls. These priests themselves were deluded by their hopes and old habits of mind. The troops did not fight well, and Gen. Oudinot abandoned his wounded without proper care. All this says nothing against French valor, proved by ages of glory, beyond that doubt of their worst foes. They were demoralized because they fought in so bad a cause, and there was no sincere ardor or clear hope in any breast.)

But to return to the hospitals: these were put in order, and have been kept so by the Princess Belgiojoso. The Princess was born of one of the noblest families of the Milanese, a descendant of the great Trivulzio, and inherited a large fortune. Very early she compromised it in liberal movements, and, on their failure, was obliged to fly to Paris, where for a time she maintained herself by writing, and I think by painting also. A Princess so placed naturally excited great interest, and she drew around her a little court of celebrated men. After recovering her fortune, she still lived in Paris, distinguished for her talents and munificence, both toward literary men and her exiled countrymen. Later, on her estate, called Locate, between Pavia and Milan, she had made experiments in the Socialist direction with fine judgment and success. Association for education, for labor, for transaction of household affairs, had been carried on for several years; she had spared no devotion of time and money to this object, loved and was much beloved by those objects of her care, and said she hoped to die there. All is now despoiled and broken up, though it may be hoped that some seeds of peaceful reform have been sown which will spring to light when least expected. The Princess returned to Italy in 1847–48, full of hope in Pius IX. and Charles Albert. She showed her usual energy and truly princely heart, sustaining, at her own expense, a company of soldiers and a journal up to the last sad betrayal of Milan, August 6. These days undeceived all the people, but few of the noblesse; she was one of the few with mind strong enough to understand the lesson, and is now warmly interested in the Republican movement. From Milan she went to France, but, finding it impossible to effect anything serious there in behalf of Italy, returned, and has been in Rome about two months. Since leaving Milan she receives no income, her possessions being in the grasp of Radetzky, and cannot know when, if ever, she will again. But as she worked so largely and well with money, so can she without. She published an invitation to the Roman women to make lint and bandages and offer their services to the wounded; she put the hospitals in order; the central one, Trinita de Pellegrini, (once the abode where the Pilgrims were received during Holy week, and where foreigners were entertained by seeing their feet washed by the noble dames and dignitaries of Rome,) she has remained day and night since the wounded were first there, on the 30th of April. Some money she procured at first by going through Rome, accompanied by two other ladies veiled, to beg it. Afterward the voluntary contributions were generous; among the rest, I am proud to say, the Americans in Rome gave $250, of which a handsome portion came from Mr. Brown, the Consul.

I value this mark of sympathy more because of irritation and surprise occasioned here by the position of Mr. Cass, the Envoy. It is most unfortunate that we should have an envoy here for the first time, just to offend and disappoint the Romans. When all the other ambassadors are at Gaeta ours is in Rome, as if by his presence to discountenance the Republican Government which he does not recognize. Mr. Cass, it seems, is limited by his instructions not to recognize the Government till sure it can be sustained. Now, it seems to me the only dignified ground for our Government, the only legitimate ground for any Republican Government, is to recognize for any nation the Government chosen by itself. The suffrage had been correct here, and the proportion of votes to the whole population was much larger, it was said, by Americans here, than it is in our country at the time of contested elections. It had elected an Assembly, that Assembly had appointed, to meet the exigencies of this time, the Triumvirate. If any misrepresentations have induced America to believe, as France affects to have believed, that so large a vote could have been obtained by moral intimidation, the present unanimity of the population in resisting such immense odds, and the enthusiasm of their every expression in favor of the present Government, puts the matter beyond a doubt. The Roman people claims once more to have a national existence. It declines farther serfdom to an ecclesiastical court. It claims liberty of conscience, of action and of thought. Should it fall from its present position, it will not be from internal dissent, but from foreign oppression.

Since this is the case, surely our country, if no other, is bound to recognize the present Government *so long as it can sustain itself*. This position is that to which we have a right: being such, it is no matter how it is viewed by others. But I dare assert it is the only respectable one for our country, in the eyes of the Emperor of Russia himself.

The first best occasion is past, when Mr. Cass might, had he been empowered to act as Mr. Rush did in France, have morally strengthened the staggering Republic, which would have found sympathy where alone it is of permanent value on the basis of principle. Had it been in vain, what then? America would have acted honorably; as to his being compromised thereby with the Papal Government, that fear is idle. Pope and Cardinals have great hopes from America; the giant influence there is kept up with the greatest care; the number of Catholic writers in the United States, too, carefully counted. Had our Republican Government acknowledged this Republican Government, the Papal Camarilla would have respected us more, but not loved us less, for have we not the loaves and fishes to give as well as the precious souls to be saved? Ah! here, indeed, America might go straight forward with much to-be-deprecated impunity. Bishop Hughes himself need not be anxious. The first best occasion has passed, and the unrecognized, unrecognizing Envoy has given offense and not comfort, by a presence that seemed constantly to say, I do not think you can sustain yourselves. It has wounded both the heart and the pride of Rome. Some of the lowest people have asked me, "Is it not true that your country had a war to become free?"—"Yes." "Then why do they not feel for us?" Yet even now it is not too late. If America would only hail triumphant, if she would not sustain injured Rome, that would be something. "Can you suppose Rome will triumph," you say, "without money, and against so potent a league of foes?" I am not sure, but I hope, for I believe something in the heart of a people when fairly awakened. I have also a lurking confidence in what our fathers spoke of so constantly, a providential order of things, by which brute force and selfish enterprises are sometimes set at nought by aid which seems to descend from a higher sphere. Even old Pagans believed in that, you know, and I was born in America, Christianized by the Puritans—America, freed by eight years' patient suffering, poverty and struggle—America, so cheered in dark days by one spark of sympathy from a foreign shore—America, first "recognized" by Lafayette. I saw him in traversing our country, then great, rich, and free. Millions of men who owed in part their happiness to what, no doubt, was once sneered at as romantic sympathy, threw garlands on his path. It is natural that I should have some faith.

Send, dear America, a talisman to thy ambassadors, precious beyond all that boasted gold of California. Let it loose his tongue to cry "Long live the Republic, and may God bless the cause of the People, the brotherhood of nations and of men—the equality of rights for all." *Viva America!*

Hail to my country! May she live a free, a glorious, a loving life, and not perish, like the old dominions, from the leprosy of selfishness.

EVENING.

I am alone in the ghostly silence of a great house, not long since full of gay faces and echoing with gay voices, now deserted by every one but me—for almost all foreigners are gone now, driven by force either of the Summer heats or the foe. I hear all the Spaniards are going now, that twenty-one have taken passports to-day; why that is, I do not know.

I shall not go till the last moment, my only fear is of France. I cannot think in any case there would be found men willing to damn themselves to latest posterity by bombarding Rome. Other cities they may, careless of destroying the innocent and helpless, the babe and old grandsire who cannot war against them. But Rome, precious inheritance of mankind, will they run the risk of marring their shrined treasures? Would they dare do it?

Two of the balls that struck St. Peter's have been sent to Pio IX. by his children, who find themselves so much less "beloved" than were the Austrians.

These two days, days of solemn festivity in the kalends of the Church, have been duly kept, and the population looks cheerful as it swarms through the streets. The order of Rome, thronged as it is with troops, is amazing. I go from one end to the other, and where [go] the poorest and most barbarous of the population, (barbarously ignorant, I mean) alone and on foot. My friends send out their little children alone with their nurses. The amount of crime is almost nothing, what it was. The Roman, no longer pent in ignorance and crouching beneath espionage, no longer stabs in the dark. His energies have true vent; his better feelings are roused; he has thrown aside the stiletto. The power here is indeed miraculous, since no doubt still lurk within the walls many who are eager to incite brawls, if only to give an excuse for slander.

To-day I suppose twelve thousand Austrians marched into Florence. The Florentines have humbled and disgraced themselves in vain. They recalled the Grand Duke to ward off the entrance of the Austrians, but in vain went the deputation to Gaeta (in an American steamer!). Leopold was afraid to come till his dear cousins of Austria had put everything in perfect order; then the Austrians entered to take Leghorn, but the Florentines still kept on imploring they would not come there; Florence was as subdued, as good as possible already; they have had the answer they deserved. Now they crown their work by giving over Guerrazzi and Petracci to be tried by an Austrian Court Martial. Truly the cup of shame brims over.

I have been out on the *loggia* to look over the city. All sleeps with that peculiar air of serene majesty known to this city only.—This city that has grown, not out of the necessities of commerce nor the luxuries of wealth, but first out of heroism, then out of faith. Swelling domes, roofs softly tinted with yellow moss—what deep meaning, what deep repose, in your faintly seen outline!

The young Moon climbs among clouds—the clouds of a departing thunderstorm. Tender, smiling Moon! can it be that thy full orb may look down on a smoking, smoldering Rome, and see her best blood run along the stones without one in the world to defend, one to aid —scarce one to cry out a tardy "Shame?" We will wait, whisper the nations, and see if they can bear it. Rack them well to see if they are brave. *If they can do without us,* we will help them. Is it thus ye would be served in your turn? Beware!

ROME, JUNE 10, 1849

Messrs. Greeley & McElrath:

WHAT SHALL I WRITE of Rome in these sad but glorious days? Plain facts are the best; for my feelings I could not find fit words.

When I last wrote the second act of the French comedy was being played.

In the first, the French Government affected to consult the Assembly. The Assembly, or a majority of the Assembly, affected to believe the pretext it gave and voted funds for 12,000 men to go to Cività Vecchia. Arriving there, Oudinot proclaimed that he had come as a friend and brother. He was received as such. Immediately he took possession of the town, disarmed the Roman troops and published a manifesto in direct opposition to his first.

He sends to Rome that he is coming there as a friend; receives the answer that he is not wanted and cannot be trusted. This answer he chooses to consider as coming from a minority and advances on Rome. The pretended majority on which he counts never shows itself by a single motion within the walls. He makes an assault and is defeated. On this subject his dispatches to his Government are full of falsehoods that would disgrace the lowest pick-pocket, falsehoods which it is impossible he should not know to be such. The Assembly passes a vote of blame. M. Louis Bonaparte writes a letter of compliment and assurance that this course of violence shall be sustained. In conformity with this promise 12,000 more troops are sent. This time it is not thought necessary to consult the Assembly.

SECOND ACT

Now appears in Rome M. Ferdinand Lesseps, Envoy, &c. of the French Government. He declares himself clothed with full powers to treat with Rome. He cannot conceal his surprise at all he sees there, at the ability with which preparations have been made for defense, at the patriotic enthusiasm which pervaded the population. Nevertheless, in beginning his game of treaty-making he was not ashamed to insist on the French occupying the city. Again and again repulsed, he again and again returned to the charge on this point. And here I shall translate the letter addressed to him by the Triumvirate, both for its perfect candor of statement and to give an idea of the sweet and noble temper with which these treacherous aggressions have been met:

NOTE OF THE TRIUMVIRS TO MONSIEUR LESSEPS, MAY 25, 1849.

We have had the honor, Monsieur, to furnish you, in our note of the 16th, with some information as to the unanimous consent which was given to the formation of the Government of the Roman Republic. We, to-day, would speak to you of the actual question, such as it is debated in fact, if not by right, between the French Government and ours. You will allow us to do it with the frankness demanded by the urgency of the situation, as well as the sympathy which ought to govern all relations between France and Italy. Our diplomacy is the truth, and the character given to your mission is a guarantee that the best possible interpretation will be given to what we shall say to you.

With your permission we return for an instant, to the source of the present situation.

In consequence of conferences and arrangements which took place without the Government of the Roman Republic ever being called on to take part, it was sometime since decided by the Catholic Powers; 1st, That a modification should take place in the Government and institutions of the Roman States; 2d, That this modification should have for basis the return of Pius IX, not as Pope, for to that no obstacle is interposed by us, but as temporal sovereign; 3d, That if, to attain that aim, a continuous intervention was judged necessary, that intervention should take place.

We are willing to admit that while for some of the contracting Governments the only motive was the hope of a general restoration and absolute return to the treaties of 1815, the French Government was drawn into this agreement only

in consequence of erroneous information tending systematically to depict the Roman States as given up to anarchy and
governed by terror exercised in the name of an audacious
minority. We know also that in the modification proposed
the French Government intended to represent an influence
more or less liberal, opposed to the absolutist programme of
Austria and of Naples.—It does none the less remain true that
under the Apostolic or Constitutional form, with or without
liberal guarantees to the Roman people, the dominant
thought in all the negotiations to which we allude has been
some sort of return toward the past, a compromise between
the Roman people and Pius IX considered as a temporal
prince.

We cannot dissemble to ourselves, Monsieur, that the
French expedition has been planned and executed under the
inspiration of this thought. Its object was, on one side, to
throw the sword of France into the balance of negotiations
which were to be opened at Rome, on the other to guarantee
the Roman people from the excess of retrograde, but always
on condition that it should submit to constitutional monarchy
in favor of the Holy Father. This is assured to us partly from
informations which we believe we possess as to the concert
with Austria, from the proclamations of General Oudinot,
from the formal declarations made by successive envoys to
the Triumvirate, from the silence obstinately maintained always when we have sought to approach the political question
and obtain a formal declaration of the fact proved in our note
of the 16th that the institutions by which the Roman people
are governed at this moment are the free and spontaneous
expression of the wish of the people inviolable when legally
interrogated. For the rest, the vote of the French Assembly
sustains implicitly the fact that we affirm.

In presence of such a situation, under the menace of an
inadmissible compromise, and of negotiations which the state
of our people no way provoked, our part, Monsieur, could
not be doubtful. To resist,—we owed this to our country, to
France, to all Europe. We ought, in fulfillment of a mandate, loyally given, loyally accepted, to maintain to our country the inviolability, so far as that was possible to us, of its
territory, and of the institutions decreed by all the powers, by
all the elements, of the State. We ought to conquer the time

needed for appeal from France ill-informed to France better-informed, to save the sister Republic the disgrace and the remorse which must be hers if, rashly led on by bad suggestions from without, she became, before she was aware, accomplice of an act of violence to which we can find no parallel without going back to the first partition of Poland in 1772.—We owed to Europe to maintain, as far as we could, the fundamental principles of all international life, the independence of each people in all that concerns its internal administration. We say it without pride, for if it is with enthusiasm that we resist the attempts of the Neapolitan monarchy and of Austria, our eternal enemy, it is with profound grief that we are ourselves constrained to contend with the arms of France; we believe in following this line of conduct to have deserved well, not only of our country, but of all the people of Europe and of France herself.

We come to the actual question. You know, Monsieur, the events which have followed the French intervention. Our territory has been invaded by the King of Naples.

Four thousand Spaniards were to embark on the 17th for invasion of this country. The Austrians having surmounted the heroic resistance of Bologna have advanced into Romagna, are now marching on Ancona.

We have beaten and driven out of our territory the forces of the King of Naples. We believe we should do the same by the Austrian forces if the attitude of the French here did not fetter our action.

We are sorry to say it, but France must be informed that the expedition of Civitá Vecchia, said to be planned for protection, costs us very dear. Of all the interventions with which it is hoped to overwhelm us, that of the French has been the most perilous. Against the soldiers of Austria and the King of Naples we can fight, for God protects a good cause. But we *do not wish to fight* against the French. We are toward them in a state not of war but of simple defense. But this position, the only one we wish to take wherever we meet France, has for us all the inconveniences without any of the favorable chances of war.

The French expedition has, from the first, forced us to concentrate our troops, thus leaving our frontier open to Austrian invasion, Bologna and the cities of Romagna unsustained. The

Austrians have profited by this. After eight days of heroic resistance by the population Bologna was forced to yield. We had bought in France arms for our defense. Of these ten thousand fusils have been detained between Marseilles and Civitá Vecchia. These are in your hands. Thus with a single blow you deprive us of ten thousand soldiers. In every armed man is a soldier against the Austrians.

Your forces are disposed around our walls as if for a siege. They remain there without avowed aim or programme. They have forced us to keep the city in a state of defense which weighs upon our finances. They force us to keep here a body of troops who might be saving our cities from the occupation and ravages of the Austrians. They hinder our circulation, our provisions, our couriers. They keep minds in a state of excitement and distrust which might, if our population were less good and devoted, lead to sinister results. They do *not* engender anarchy nor reaction, for both are impossible at Rome, but they sow the seed of irritation against France and it is a misfortune for us who were accustomed to love and hope in her.

We are besieged, Monsieur, besieged by France, in the name of a protective mission, while some leagues off the King of Naples, flying, carries off our hostages, and the Austrian slays our brothers.

You have presented propositions. Those propositions have been declared inadmissible by the Assembly. To-day you add a fourth to the three already rejected.—This says that France will protect from foreign invasion all that part of our territory that may be occupied by her troops. You must yourself feel that this changes nothing in our position.

The parts of the territory occupied by your troops are in fact protected; but if only for the present, to what are they reduced? and if it is for the future, have we no other way to protect our territory than by giving it up entirely to you?

The root of the question is not true. It is in the occupation of Rome. This demand has constantly stood first in your list of propositions. Now we have had the honor to say to you, Monsieur, that is impossible. The people will never consent to it. If the occupation of Rome has for its aim only to protect it, the people thank you, but tell you at the same time that, able to defend Rome by its own forces, it would be dishonored even in your eyes by declaring itself insufficient, and needing the aid of some regiments of French soldiers. If the occupation has otherwise a political object, which God forbid, the people, which has given itself freely these institutions, cannot suffer it. Rome is its Capital, its Palladium, its Sacred City. It knows very well that apart from its principles, apart from its honor, there is civil war at the end of such an occupation. It is filled with distrust by your persistence. It foresees, once the troops admitted, changes in men and in intentions which would be fatal to its liberty. It knows that, in presence of foreign bayonets, the independence of its Assembly, of its Government, would be a vain word.—It has always Civitá Vecchia before its eyes.

On this point be sure its will is irrevocable. It will be massacred from barricade to barricade, before it will surrender. Can the soldiers of France wish to massacre a brother people whom they came to protect, because it does not wish to surrender to them its Capital?

There are for France only three parts to take in the Roman States. She ought to declare herself for us, against us, or neuter. To declare herself for us would be to recognize our Republic and fight side by side with us against the Austrians.

To declare against us is to crush without motive the liberty, the national life, of a friendly people, and fight side by side with the Austrians.

France *cannot* do that. She *will* not risk a European War to depress us her ally. Let her, then, rest neuter in this conflict between us and our enemies; only yesterday we hoped more from her, but to-day we demand only this.

The occupation of Civitá Vecchia is a fact accomplished; let it go. France thinks that, in the present state of things, she ought not to remain distant from the field of battle. She thinks that, vanquishers or vanquished, we may have need of her moderative action and of her protection. We do not think so; but we will not react against her. Let her keep Civitá Vecchia. Let her even extend her encampments, if the numbers of her troops require it in the healthy regions of Civitá Vecchia and Viterbo. Let her then wait the issue of the combats about to take place. All facilities will be offered her, every proof of frank and cordial sympathy given; her officers can visit Rome; her soldiers have all the solace possible. But let her neutrality

be sincere and without *arrière-penseé*. Let her declare herself
in explicit terms. Let her leave us free to use all our forces.
Let her restore our arms. Let her not by her cruisers drive
back from our ports the men who come to our aid from other
parts of Italy. Let her, above all, withdraw from before our
walls, and let even the appearance of hostilty cease between
two nations who, later, undoubtedly, are destined to unite in
the same international faith, as now they have adopted the
same form of Government.

In his answer, Lesseps appears moved by this statement, and particularly expresses himself thus:

> "One point appears above all to occupy you; it is the
> thought that we wish forcibly to impose upon you the ob-
> ligation of receiving us as friends. FRIENDSHIP AND
> VIOLENCE ARE INCOMPATIBLE. Thus it would be
> INCONSEQUENT on our part to begin by firing our cannon
> upon you to make you natural protectors. SUCH A CON-
> TRADICTION ENTERS NEITHER INTO MY INTEN-
> TIONS, NOR THOSE OF THE GOVERNMENT OF THE
> FRENCH REPUBLIC, NOR OF OUR ARMY AND ITS
> HONORABLE CHIEF."

These words were written at the headquarters of Oudinot, and of
course seen and approved by him. At the same time, in private conversation, "the honorable chief" would swear he would occupy Rome
by "one means or another." A few days after, Lesseps consented to
conditions such as the Romans would tolerate. He no longer insisted
on occupying Rome, but would content himself with good positions
in the country.—Oudinot protested that the Plenipotentiary had "ex-
ceeded his powers"—that he should not obey—that the Armistice was
at an end, and he should attack Rome on Monday. It was then
Friday—He proposed to leave these two days for the few foreigners
that remained to get out of town. Mr. Lesseps went off to Paris, in
great seeming indignation, to get *his* treaty ratified. Of course we could
not hear from him for eight or ten days. Meanwhile, the *honorable*
chief, alike in all his conduct, attacked on Sunday instead of Monday.
The attack began before sunrise and lasted all day. I saw it from my
window, which, though distant, commands the Gate St. Pancrazio.
Why the whole force was bent on that part, I do not know. If

they could take it, the town would be cannonaded and the barricades useless; but it is the same with the Pincian Gate. Small parties made feints in two other directions, but they were at once repelled. The French fought with great bravery, and this time it is said with beautiful skill and order, sheltering themselves in their advance by moveable barricades. The Italians fought like lions, and no inch of ground was gained by the assailant. The loss of the French is said to be very great: it could not be otherwise. Six or seven hundred Italians are dead or wounded, among them were many officers, those of Garibaldi especially, who are much exposed by their daring bravery, and whose red tunic makes them the natural mark of the enemy. It seems to me great folly to wear such a dress amid the dark uniforms, but Garibaldi has always done it. He has now been wounded twice here and seventeen times in Ancona.

All this week I have been much at the Hospitals where are these noble sufferers. They are full of enthusiasm; this time was no treason, no Vicenza, no Novara, no Milan. They had not been given up by wicked chiefs at the moment they were shedding their blood and they had conquered. All were only anxious to get out again and be at their posts. They seemed to feel that those who died so gloriously were fortunate; perhaps they were, for if Rome is obliged to yield, and how can she stand always unaided against the four powers? where shall these noble youths fly? They are the flower of the Italian youth, especially among the Lombards are some of the finest young men I have ever seen. If Rome falls, if Venice falls, there is no spot of Italian earth where they can abide more, and certainly no Italian will wish to take refuge in France. Truly you said, Mr. Lesseps, "Violence and friendship are incompatible."

A military funeral of the officer Ramorino was sadly picturesque and affecting. The white-robed priests went before the body singing, while his brothers in arms bore the lighted tapers. His horse followed, saddled and bridled. The horse hung his head and stepped dejectedly; he felt there was something strange and gloomy going on—felt that his master was laid low. Ramorino left a wife and children. A great proportion of those who run those risks are, happily, alone. Parents weep, but will not suffer long, their grief is not like that of widows and children.

Since the 3d we have only cannonade and skirmishes. The French are at their trenches, but cannot advance much; they are too much molested from the walls. The Romans have made one very successful sortie. The French availed themselves of a violent thunder-storm, when the walls were left more thinly guarded, to try to scale them, but were immediately driven back. It was thought by many that they never would be willing to throw bombs and shells into Rome, but they do whenever they can. That generous hope and faith in them as republicans and brothers, which put the best construction on their actions and believed in their truth, as far as possible, is now destroyed. The Government is false, and the people do not resist; the General is false, and the soldiers obey.

Meanwhile, frightful sacrifices are being made by Rome. All her glorious oaks, all her gardens of delight, her casinos, full of the monuments of genius and taste, are perishing in the defense. The houses, the trees which had been spared at gate St. Pancrazio, all afforded shelter to the foe, and caused so much loss of life, that the Romans have now fully acquiesced in destruction agonizing to witness. Villa Borghese is finally laid waste, the villa of Raphael has perished, the trees are all cut down at Villa Albani, and the house, that most beautiful ornament of Rome, must, I suppose, go too. The stately marble forms are already driven from their place in that portico where Winkelmann sat and walked with such delight. Villa Salvaze is burnt, with all its fine frescoes, and that bank of the Tiber, shorn of its lovely plantations.

Rome will never recover the cruel ravage of these days, perhaps only just begun. I had often thought of living a few months near St. Peter's that I might go as much as I liked to the Church and the Museum, have Villa Doria Pamfili and Monte Mario within the compass of a walk. It is not easy to find lodgings there, as it is a quarter foreigners never inhabit, but walking about to see what pleasant places there were, I had fixed my eye on a clean simple house near Ponte St. Angelo. It bore on a tablet that it was the property of Angela ———— *libera,* its little balconies with their old wooden rails, full of flowers in humble earthen vases, the many bird cages, the air of domestic quiet, and comfort marked it as the home of some vestal or widow, some lone woman, whose heart was centered in the ordinary and simplest pleasures of a home. I saw also she was one of the most limited income, and I thought "she will not refuse to let me a room for a few months, as I shall be as quiet as herself, and sympathize about the flowers and birds." Now the Villa Pamfili is all laid waste. The French encamp on Monte Mario, what they have done there is not known yet. The cannonade reverberates all day under the dome of St. Peter's, and the house of poor Angela is leveled with the ground. I hope her birds and the white peacocks of the Vatican gardens are in safety— but who cares for gentle, harmless creatures now?

I have been often interrupted while writing this letter, and suppose it is confused as well as incomplete. I hope my next may tell of something decisive one way or the other. News is not yet come from Lesseps, but the conduct of Oudinot, and the formation of the new French Ministry give reason to hope no good. Many seem resolved to force back Pius IX. among his bleeding flock, into the city ruined by him, where he cannot remain, and if he come all this struggle and sorrow is to be borne over again. Mazzini stands firm as a rock. I know not whether he hopes for a successful issue, but he *believes* in a God bound to protect men who do what they deem their duty. Yet how long, O Lord, shall the few trample on the many?

POSTSCRIPT.—I am surprised to see the air of perfect good faith with which articles from the London *Times,* upon the revolutionary movements, are copied into our papers. There exists not in Europe a paper more violently opposed to the cause of freedom than the *Times,* and neither its leaders nor its foreign correspondence are to be depended upon. It is said to receive money from Austria. I know not whether this be true, or whether it be merely subservient to the aristocratical feeling of England, which is far more opposed to Republican movements than is that of Russia; for in England fear embitters hate. It is droll to remember our reading in the class-book,

"Ay, down to the dust with them, slaves as they are."

To think how bitter the English were on the Italians who succumbed, and see how they hate those who resist; and their cowardice here in Italy, is ludicrous. It is they who run away at the least intimation of danger—it is they who invent all the "fe, fo, fum" stories about Italy,—it is they who write to the *Times* and elsewhere that they dare not for their lives stay in Rome, where I, a woman, walk everywhere alone, and all the little children do the same, with their nurses. More of this anon.

ROME, JULY 6, 1849

IF I MISTAKE NOT, I closed my last letter just as the news arrived here that the attempt of the Democratic party in France to resist the infamous proceedings of the Government had failed, and thus Rome, as far as human calculation went, had not a hope for her liberties left. An inland city cannot long sustain a siege when there is no hope of aid. Then followed the news of the surrender of Ancona, and Rome found herself quite alone—for, though Venice continued to hold out, all communication was cut off.

The Republican troops, almost to a man, left Ancona, but a long march separated them from Rome.

The extreme heat of these days was far more fatal to the Romans than their assailants, for, as fast as the French troops sickened, their place was taken by fresh arrivals. Ours also not only sustained the exhausting service by day, but were harrassed at night by attacks, feigned or real.—These commonly began about 11 or 12 o'clock at night, just when all who meant to rest were fairly asleep. I can imagine the harassing effect upon the troops, from what I feel in my sheltered pavilion, in consequence of not knowing a quiet night's sleep for a month.

The bombardment became constantly more serious. The house where I live was filled as early as the 20th with persons obliged to fly from the *Piazza di Gesù,* where the fiery rain fell thickest. The night of the 21st–22d, we were all alarmed about 2 o'clock A.M. by a tremendous cannonade. It was the moment when the breach was finally made by which the French entered.—They rushed in, and, I grieve to say, that by the only instance of defection known in the course of the siege, those companies of the regiment Union, which had in charge a casino on that point, yielded to panic and abandoned it. The French immediately entered and intrenched themselves. That was the fatal hour for the city. Every day afterward, though obstinately resisted, they gained, till at last, their cannon being well placed, the city was entirely commanded from the Janiculum, and all thought of further resistance was idle.

This was true policy to avoid the street fight, in which the Italian, an unpracticed soldier, but full of feeling and sustained from the houses, would have been no match for their disciplined troops. After the 22d, the slaughter of the Romans became every day more fearful. Their defenses were knocked down by the heavy cannon of the French, and, entirely exposed in their valorous onsets, great numbers perished on the spot. Those who were brought into the Hospitals were generally grievously wounded, very commonly subjects for amputation. My heart bled daily more and more at these sights, and I could not feel much for myself, though now the balls and bombs began to fall round me also. The night of the 28th the effect was truly fearful, as they whizzed and burst near me. As many as 30 fell upon or near the *Hotel de Russie,* where Mr. Cass has his temporary abode. The roof of the studio in the pavilion, tenanted by Mr. Stermer, well known to the visitors of Rome, for his highly-finished cabinet pictures, was torn to pieces. I sat alone in my much-exposed apartment thinking "if one strikes me, I only hope it will kill me at once, and that God will transport my soul to some sphere where Virtue and Love are not tyrannized over by egotism and brute force, as in this." However, that night passed; the next, we had reason to expect a still more fiery salute to the Pincian, as here alone remained three or four pieces of cannon which could be used. But the morning of the 30th, in a contest at the foot of the Janiculum, the line, old Papal troops, naturally not in earnest like the free corps, refused to fight against odds so terrible, the heroic Manara fell, with hundreds of his devoted Lombards. Garibaldi saw his best officers perish, and himself went in the afternoon to say to the Assembly that further resistance was unavailing.

The Assembly sent to Oudinot, but he refused any conditions, refused even to guarantee a safe departure to Garibaldi, his brave foe. Notwithstanding, a great number of men left the other regiments to follow the leader, whose courage had captivated them, whose habit of superiority to difficulties commanded their entire confidence. Toward the evening of Monday, 2d July, it was known that the French were preparing to cross the river and take possession of all the city. I went into the Corso with some friends; it was filled with citizens and military, the carriage was stopped by the crowd near the Doria palace; the lancers of Garibaldi galloped along in full career, I longed for Sir Walter Scott to be on earth again, and see them; all are light, athletic, resolute figures, many of the forms of the finest manly beauty of the South, all sparkling with its genius and ennobled by the resolute spirit, ready to dare, to do, to die. We followed them to the piazza of St. John Lateran. Never have I seen a sight so beautiful, so romantic, and so sad. Whoever knows Rome knows the peculiar solemn grandeur of that piazza, scene of the first triumph of Rienzi, the magnificence of the "mother of all churches," the Baptistery with its porphyry columns, the Santa Scala with its glittering mosaics of the early ages, the obelisk standing fairest of any of those most imposing monuments of Rome, the view through the gates of the Campagna, on that side so richly strewn with ruins. The sun was setting, the crescent moon rising, the flower of the Italian youth were marshalling in that solemn place. They had been driven from every other spot where they had offered their hearts as bulwarks of Italian Independence; in this last strong hold they had sacrificed hecatombs of their best and bravest in that cause; they must now go or remain prisoners and slaves. *Where* go, they knew not, for except distant Hungary there is not now a spot which would receive them, or where they can act as honor commands. They had all put on the beautiful dress of the Garibaldi legion, the tunic of bright red cloth, the Greek cap, or else round hat with Puritan plume, their long hair was blown back from resolute faces; all looked full of courage; they had counted the cost before they entered on this perilous struggle; they had weighed life and all its material advantages against Liberty, and made their election; they turned not back, nor flinched at this bitter crisis. I saw the wounded, all that could go, laden upon their baggage cars, some were already pale and fainting, still they wished to go. I saw many youths, born to rich inheritance, carrying in a handkerchief all their worldly goods; the women were ready, their eyes too were resolved, if sad. The wife of Garibaldi followed him horseback, he himself was distinguished by the white bournouse; his look was entirely that of a hero of the middle ages, his face still young, for the excitements of his life, though so many, have all been youthful, and there is no fatigue upon his brow or cheek. Fall or stand, one sees in him a man engaged in the career for which he is adapted by nature. He went upon the parapet and looked upon the road with a spy-glass, and, no obstruction being in sight, he turned his face for a moment back upon Rome, then led the way through the gate. Hard was the heart, stony and seared the eye that had no tear for that moment. Go! fated, gallant band, and if God care not indeed for men as for the sparrows, most of ye go forth to perish. And Rome, anew the Niobe! Must she lose also these beautiful and brave that promised her regeneration and would have given it, but for the perfidy, the overpowering force of the foreign intervention.

I know that many "respectable" gentlemen would be surprised to hear me speak in this way. Gentlemen who perform their "duties to society" by buying for themselves handsome clothes and furniture with the interest of their money, speak of Garibaldi and his men as "brigands" and "vagabonds." Such are they, doubtless, in the same sense as Jesus, Eneas and Moses were. To me men who can throw so slightly aside the ease of wealth, the joys of affection, for the sake of what they deem honor, in whatsoever form, are the "respectable." No doubt there are in these bands a number of men of lawless minds, and who follow this banner only because there is for them no other path. But the greater part are the noble youths who have fled from the Austrian conscription, or fly now from the renewal of Papal suffocation, darkened by the French protection.

As for the protectors, they entirely threw aside the mask, as it was always supposed they would, the moment they had possession of Rome.

I do not know whether they were really so bewildered by their priestly councilors as to imagine they would be well received in a city which they had bombarded, and where twelve hundred men were lying wounded by their assault. To say nothing of the justice or injustice of the matter, it could not be supposed that the Roman people, if it had any sense of dignity, would welcome them. However, I was not out, as what countenance I have would not give on such an occasion; but an English lady, my friend, told me they seemed to look expectingly for the strong party of friends they had always pretended to have within the walls. The French officers looked up to the windows for ladies, and she being the only one they saw, saluted her. She made no reply. They then passed into the Corso. Many were assembled, the softer Romans being unable to control a curiosity the Milanese would have disclaimed, but preserving an icy silence. In an evil hour, a foolish priest dared to break it by the cry of *Viva Pio Nono*. The populace, roused to fury, rushed on him with their knives. He was much wounded; one or two others were killed in the rush. The people howled, then, and hissed at the French, who advancing their bayonets, and clearing the way before them, fortified themselves in the piazzas. Next day the French troops were marched to and fro through Rome to inspire awe into the people, but it has only created a disgust amounting to loathing, to see that, with such an imposing force, and in great part fresh, the French were not ashamed to use bombs also, and kill women and children in their beds. Oudinot, then, seeing the feeling of the people, and finding they pursued as a spy any man who so much as showed the way to his soldiers—that the Italians went out of the cafés if Frenchmen entered; in short, that the people regarded him and his followers in the same light as the Austrians, has declared the state of siege in Rome—the Press is stifled—everybody is to be in the house at 9½ P.M. and, whoever in any way insults his men, or puts any obstacle in their way, is to be shot.

The fruits of all this will be the same as elsewhere: temporary repression will sow the seeds of perpetual resistance; and never was Rome in so fair a way to be educated for the Republican form of Government as now.

Especially could nothing be more irritating for an Italian population, in the month of July, than to drive them to their homes at half-past nine. After the insupportable heat of the day, their only enjoyment and refreshment is found in evening walks, and chats together as they sit before their cafés, or in groups outside some friendly door. Now they must hurry home when the drum beats at 9 o'clock. They are forbidden to stand or to sit in groups, and this by their bombarding *protector!* Comment is unnecessary.

French soldiers are daily missing; of some it is known that they have been killed by the Trasteverini for daring to make court to their women.—Of more than a hundred and fifty, it is only known that they cannot be found; and in two days of French "order" more acts of violence have been committed than in two months under the Triumvirate.

The French have taken up their quarters in the court-yards of the Quirinal and Venetian Palaces, which are full of the wounded, many of whom have been driven well nigh mad, and their burning wounds exasperated by the sound of their drums and trumpets—the constant sense of their insulting presence. The wounded have been warned to leave the Quirinal at the end of eight days, though there are many who cannot be moved from bed to bed without causing them great anguish and peril, nor is it known that any other place has been provided as a hospital for them. At the palace of Venice the French have searched for three emigrants that they wished to imprison, even in the apartments where the wounded were lying; they ran their bayonets into the matresses; they have taken for themselves beds given by the Romans to the hospital—not public property, but private gift. The hospital of Santo Spirito was a governmental establishment and, in using a part of it for the wounded, its director, Monsignore, had been retained, because he had the reputation of being honest and not illiberal. But as soon as the French entered he, with true priestly baseness, sent away the women nurses, saying he had no longer money to pay them—transported the wounded into a miserable, airless basement, that had before been used as a granary and appropriated the good apartments to the use of the French!

JULY 8

The report of this morning is that the French yesterday violated the domicile of our Consul, Mr. Brown, pretending to search for persons hidden there; that Mr. Brown, banner in one hand and sword in the other, repelled the assault, and fairly drove them down stairs; that then he made them an appropriate speech, though in a mixed language of English, French and Italian; that the crowd vehemently applauded Mr. Brown, who already was much liked for the warm sympathy he had shown the Romans in their aspirations and their distresses; that he then donned his uniform and went to Oudinot to make his protest. How this was received I know not, but understand Mr. B. departed with his family yesterday evening.

Will America look as coldly on the insult to herself as she has on the struggle of this injured people?

To-day an edict is out to disarm the National Guard. The generous "protectors" wish to take all the trouble upon themselves. Rome is full of them; at every step are met groups in the uniform of France, with faces bronzed in the African war, and so stultified by a life without enthusiasm and without thought, that I do not believe Napoleon would recognize them as French soldiers.—The effect of their appearance compared with that of the Italian free corps is that of body as compared with spirit. It is easy to see how they could be used to purposes so contrary to the legitimate policy of France, for they do not look more intellectual, more fitted to have opinions of their own, than the Austrian soldiery.

JULY 10

The plot thickens. The exact facts with regard to the invasion of Mr. Brown's house, I have not been able to ascertain. I suppose they will be published, as Oudinot has promised to satisfy Mr. Cass. I must add in reference to what I wrote sometime ago of the position of our envoy here, that the kind and sympathetic course of Mr. Cass toward the Republicans in these troubles, his very gentlemanly and courteous bearing, have from the minds of most removed all unpleasant feelings. They see that his position was very peculiar; sent to the Papal Government, finding here the Republican, and just at that moment violently assailed. Unless he had extraordinary powers he naturally felt obliged to communicate further with our Government before acknowledging this. I shall always regret, however, that he did not stand free to occupy the high position that belonged to the representative of the United States at that moment, and peculiarly because it was by a Republic that the Roman Republic was betrayed.—But, as I say, the plot thickens. Yesterday three families were carried to prison because a boy crowed like a cock at the French soldiery from the windows of the house they occupied. Another, because a man pursued took refuge in their court-yard. Yesterday, the city being most disarmed, came the edict to take down the arms of the Republic, "emblems of anarchy." But worst of all they have done is an edict commanding all foreigners who had been in the service of the Republican Government to leave Rome within twenty-four hours. This is the most infamous thing done yet, as it drives to desperation those who stayed because they had so many to go with and no place to go to, or because their relatives lie wounded here: no others wished to remain in Rome under present circumstances.

I am sick of breathing the same air with men capable of a part so utterly cruel and false. As soon as I can I shall take refuge in the mountains, if it be possible to find an obscure nook unpervaded by these convulsions. Let not my friends be surprised if they do not hear from me for some time. I may not feel like writing. I have seen too much sorrow, and alas! without power to aid. It makes me sick to see the palaces and streets of Rome full of these injurious foreigners, and to see the already changed aspect of her population. The men of Rome had begun, filled with new hopes, to develop unknown energy—they walked quick, their eyes sparkled, they delighted in duty, in responsibility; in a year of such life their effeminacy would have been vanquished—now, dejectedly, unemployed, they lounge along the streets, feeling that all the implements of labor, all the ensigns of hope, have been snatched from them. Their hands fall slack, their eyes rove aimless, the beggars begin to swarm again, and the black ravens who delight in the night of ignorance, the slumber of sloth, as the only sureties for their rule, emerge daily more and more frequent from their hiding places.

The following Address has been circulated from hand to hand:

TO THE PEOPLE OF ROME.

Misfortune, brothers, has fallen upon us anew. But it is trial of brief duration—it is the stone of the sepulcher which we shall throw away after three days, rising victorious and renewed, an immortal Nation. For with us are God and Justice—God and Justice, who cannot die, but always triumph, while Kings and Popes, once dead, revive no more.

As you have been great in the combat, be so in the days of sorrow—great in your conduct as citizens, of generous disdain, of sublime silence. Silence is the weapon we have now to use against the Cossacks of France and the Priests, their masters.

In the streets do not look at them; do not answer if they address you.

In the cafés, in the eating-houses, if they enter, rise and go out.

Let your windows remain closed as they pass.

Never attend their feasts, their parades.

The harmony of their musical bands be for you tones of slavery, and, when you hear them, fly.

Let the liberticide soldier be condemned to isolation; let him atone in solitude and contempt for having served priests and kings.

And you, Roman women—master-piece of God's work!— deign no look, no smile to those satellites of an abhorred Pope! Cursed be she who, before the odious satellites of Austria, forgets that she is Italian! Her name shall be published for the execration of all her people! And even the courtezans! let them show love for their country, and thus regain the dignity of citizens!

And our word of order, our cry of reunion and emancipation, be now and ever, VIVA LA REPUBLICA!

This incessant cry, which not even French slaves can dispute, shall prepare us to administer the bequest of our martyrs, shall be consoling dew to the immaculate and holy bones that repose, sublime holocaust of faith and of love, near our walls, and make doubly divine the Eternal City. In this cry we shall find ourselves always brothers, and we shall conquer. Viva Rome, the Capital of Italy! Viva the Italy of the People! Viva the Roman Republic!

A ROMAN.

Dated *Rome, July* 4, 1849.

For this day's anniversary, so joyously celebrated in our land, was that of the entrance of the French into Rome.

I know not whether the Romans will follow out this programme with constancy as the sterner Milanese have done. If they can, it will draw upon them endless persecutions, countless exactions, but at once educate and prove them worthy of a nobler life.

Yesterday I went over the scene of conflict. It was fearful even to *see* the casinos *Quattro Venti* and *Vascello* where the French and Romans had been several days near one another, all shattered to pieces, with fragments of rich stucco and painting still sticking to rafters between the great holes made by the cannonade, and think that men had stayed and fought in them when only a mass of ruins. The French, indeed, were entirely sheltered the last days; to my unpracticed eyes the extent and thoroughness of their works seemed miraculous, and gave me first clear idea of the incompetency of the Italians to resist organized armies. I saw their commanders had not even known enough of the art of war to understand how the French were conducting the siege.—It is true their resources were at any rate inadequate to resistance; only continual sorties would have arrested the progress of the foe, and to make them and man the wall their forces were inadequate. I was struck more than ever by the heroic valor of *ours*, let me say, as I have said all along, for go where I may, a large part of my heart will ever remain in Italy. I hope her children will always acknowledge me as a sister, though I drew not my first breath here. A contadini showed me where thirty-seven braves are buried beneath a heap of wall that fell upon them in the shock of one cannonade. A marble nymph, with broken arm, looked sadly that way from her sun-dried fountain, some roses were blooming still, some red oleanders amid the ruin. The sun was casting its last light on the mountains on the tranquil, sad Campagna, that sees one leaf turned more in the book of Woe. This was in the Vascello. I then entered the French ground, all mapped and hollowed like a honey-comb. A pair of skeleton legs protruding from a bank of one barricade; lower a dog scratched away its light covering of earth from the body of a man, and discovered it lying face upward all dressed; the dog stood gazing on it with an air of stupid amazement. I thought at that moment, recalling some letters received, "O men and women of America, spared these frightful sights, these sudden wrecks of every hope, what angel of Heaven do you suppose has time to listen to your tales of morbid woe? If any find leisure to work for men to-day, think you not they have enough to do to care for their victims here."

I see you have meetings, where you speak of the Italians, the Hungarians. I pray you *do something;* let it not end in a mere cry of sentiment. That is better than to sneer at all that is liberal, like the English; than to talk of the holy victims of patriotism as "anarchists" and "brigands,"—but it is not enough. It ought not to content your consciences. Do you owe no tithe to Heaven for the privileges it had showered on you, for whose achievement so many here suffer and perish daily? Deserve to retain them, by helping your fellow-men to acquire them. Our Government must abstain from interference, but private action is practicable, is due. For Italy, it is in this moment too late, but all that helps Hungary helps her also, helps all who wish the freedom of men from an hereditary yoke now become intolerable. Send money, send cheer—acknowledge as the legitimate leaders and rulers those men who represent the people, who understand its wants, who are ready to die or to live for its good. Kossuth I know not, but his people recognize him; Manin I know not, but with what firm nobleness, what persevering virtue, he has acted for Venice!—Mazzini I know, the man and his acts, great, pure and constant,—a man to whom only the next age can do justice, as it reaps the harvest of the seed he has sown in this.—Friends, countrymen, and lovers of virtue, lovers of freedom, lovers of truth!—be on the alert; rest not supine in your easier lives, but remember

> *"Mankind is one,*
> *And beats with one great heart."*

LETTERS

When Margaret Fuller was six years old, she embarked upon a program of instruction that her father had designed to educate his daughter as if she were a son preparing for college. Schooled in Latin and Greek, Fuller spent her days immersed in classical literature. Her evenings were devoted to reciting for her father. Simultaneously, she undertook the study of French and Italian. Roaming through her father's well-stocked library, Fuller read widely in European literature. Timothy Fuller continued to supervise his daughter's education after his election to Congress in 1819. Written to her father during the months he spent in Washington, Fuller's letters record the progress of her remarkable education. With their decision to send their daughter to Miss Prescott's Young Ladies' Seminary, Timothy and Margarett Fuller changed the trajectory of that education. Fuller's exclusive focus on an academic curriculum was now complemented by more typical training in social accomplishments.

Cambridge, 25 Dec 1819
My Dear Father
 I should have written to you immediately after the examination but mamma was out the two next days. But yesterday Uncle Elisha came here. He heard me recite and mended my pen. It is not at all a good one. He is coming to hear me recite Fridays and Tuesdays. I have been two afternoons to a writing school of which Mr Gould is the master. He is a most elegant writer. He keeps once in a week and his terms are one dollar a quarter. Mamma doubtless has written to you about the

473

Examination. I enclose you my composition and specimen of writing. I assure you I wrote the former off much better and made *almost* as many corrections as your critical self would were you at home. But Mr Dickinson kept the theme I corrected as he always does the theme which is written at the end of the quarter. I think this is the best theme I ever wrote. Write My Deserted Village goes on slowly. I have only translated a page and a half. However I am determined to finish it before New Years day which is about six days from this time—

Last night was very cold. The wind was very cold and keen and the ground was covered with snow.

William Henry the other day took his tier and having filled it with coals went around to ask us to eat some "tesnuts." Eugene has broke his bladder with kicking it about and now he has given up the sledge and skaits and wants a watch. This morning he asked mamma to give him a twenty cent piece. She told him he must earn it. He said if she would give it him he would earn it. Now he drinks sugar though mamma has offered to give him two cents a week if he will not drink it.

I have read papa that Zeluco is a very intelligent sensible book therefore as I assure you I have been a very good girl. I beg you will send me "carte blanche" to read Zeluco. Do not forget it dear papa. I have been reading a novel of the name of Hesitation. Do not let the name novel make you think it is either trifling or silly. A great deal of sentiment a great deal of reasoning is contained in it. In other words it is a moral-novel. Miss Argyle the principal heroine has not such superhuman wit beauty and sense as to make her an improbable character. Fitsroy earl of Montague is a sensible well informed man possessing a superior genius and deeply versed in the human character but improbably delicate in his ideas of love. Grosvenor a virtuous well bred youth but inexperienced and possessing ardent. Lady Clervaux a lady whose affections were withered and whose feelings were checked by being taught to believe that fashion is every thing. Sir Thomas has no character. Lord Percival Lorn is a person of very shallow judgement and very malignant feelings two things apparently incompatible. I can sketch no more at present you shall the rest in another letter. I am your affectionate daughter.

SARAH-MARGARET FULLER

Cambridge, 16 January 1820

My dear father

I received your letter of the 29th about a week ago. I should have written to you much sooner but have been very busy. I begin to be anxious about my letter of the 28th which you do not mention having received in any of your letters. If it has not miscarried it reached you a fortnight ago. Your letter to me was dated the day after mine was written but you do not mention it in any of your letters to Mamma.—

I attend a school which is kept by Aunt Abigail for *Eugene* and *myself* and my *cousins* which with writing and singing schools and my lessons to Uncle Elisha takes up *most* of my time—

I *have* not written to Miss *Kilshaw yet as* there is no opportunity of sending our letters. *Deep rooted* indeed is my affection for her. May it flourish an *ever* blooming flower till our kindred spirits absolved from earthly day mount together to those blissful regions where never again we shall be separated. I am not romantic, I am not making professions when I say I love Ellen better than my life. I love her better and reverence her more for her misfortunes. Why should I not she is as lovely as sweet tempered as before. These were what I loved before and as she possesses all these now why should my love diminish. Ought it not rather to increase as she has more need of it. It is for herself alone I grieve for the loss of fortune. She will be exposed to many a trial a temptation she would otherwise have escaped Not but I know she will go through them all No But I shall feel *all* her sorrows—

You will let me read Zeluco? will you not and no conditions. Have you been to the theatre this winter? Have they any oratorios at Washington?—I am writing a new tale called The young satirist. You must expect the remainder of this page to be filled with a series of unconnected intelligence. My beautiful pen now makes a large mark. I will write no farther. 17th January 1820.

Yesterday I threw by my pen for the reason mentioned above. Have you read Hesitation yet. I knew you would (though you are no novel reader) to see if they were rightly delineated for I am possessed of the greatest blessing of life a good and kind father. Oh I can never repay you for all the love you have shown me But I will do all I can.

We have had a dreadful snowstorm today. I never look around the room and behold all the comforts with which Heaven has blessed me without thinking of those *wretched* creatures who are wandering in all the snow without food or shelter. I am too young No I am not. In nine years a great part of my life I can remember but two good actions done those more out of selfishness than charity. There is a poor woman of the name of Wentworth in Boston she would willingly procure a subsistence but has not the means. My dear father a dollar would be a great sum to this poor woman. You remember the handsome dollar that I know your generosity would have bestowed on when I had finished my Deserted Village I shall finish it well and desire nothing but the pleasure of giving it to her. My dear father send it to me immediately I am going into town this week I have a thousand things to say but neither time or paper to say them in.

Farewell my dear Father I am Your affectionate daughter

MARGARET FULLER

P S I do not like Sarah, call me Margaret alone, pray do!

Boston March 13th 1822

My dear father,

On the day after tomorrow Dr Park will have an examination, which will I think go off with great splendour. Although I am immersed in the studies which are necessary to prepare me to support my part, I leave them for a moment to write to you. I received a letter from you a few days ago. Grandmamma had one to day, I did write to you in French, but Ma said the letter was too short. You shall soon have a longer one.—The reason that you have not had a letter from me, is that I promised to write to you in French. I shall have a vacation of a fortnight, which I shall spent at Canton, and I shall then have ample leisure to write to you. Indeed you must excuse my errors in every thing in this letter, I am surrounded by tasks and even now my maps which lie before me, seem to call for my attention and divide it with my letter. I am glad that you cannot witness my first Examination. I know what your feelings would be, mine are sufficient. My uncle Abraham will be there, he will acquaint you with my success, perhaps it may be a failure, but I hope not, be assured

that I will do my utmost to acquit myself well. I hardly dare trust that I shall be right in Geography, the numberless questions on the map quite disconcert me. History unless I am frightened quite out of my wits I am sure of and 'tis very improbable that I shall miss in parsing or Latin (by the bye I have learned to scan and parse) or French and I think my Italian will be right. I wonder if this is as interesting to any body else as it is to me, I think of nothing else. Goodbye my dear father, you will soon hear from me again
Your affectionate daughter

S M FULLER

Groton, May 21st. 1824
Dear [Father],

I received your letter, on Tuesday, with delight. I am much obliged to you for writing so soon, much sooner indeed than I had supposed you would; as I know how much you are engaged. I am happy to hear, that I have a fourth brother, though I hardly think he will rival my pet, Arthur in my affections. As to a name for him, I like Frank best, Frederick next, and I wish he might have three names.

By a letter from my uncle Elisha, I find that my uncle Henry is elected a Representative. If he wished for the dignity, I am happy that he has gained it, and beg that you will congratulate him in my name, as I think that I shall not very speedily find time to write to him, and should be sorry not to offer my felicitations on *such an accession of dignity*. I am contented here, which I think is as much as could be expected. Miss Prescott has about twenty boarders and from twenty to thirty day scholars. There are among the boarders six young ladies from Cambridge, Miss Chaplin, whom you know, Miss Warland, who is, I suppose, a sister of Mrs Manning, Miss Holmes, whose father is carpenter to the University, two Miss Frains, whose father has some office about the State Prison, and a Miss White from Lechmere Point. The others are Virginia Shaw, daughter to the late Commodore Shaw, who boards here with her stepmother, Miss Soley of Charlestown, Miss Nash, daughter to a sea captain in Boston, a Miss Prescott, and Miss Patten from—I know not where, and two Miss Fiskes, with Miss Hale, a ward of Mr *Amos* Lawrence's.

Miss Caroline James is my chum, and I have likewise in the room with me a Miss Wood, Miss Clarke of Princeton comes to the school and rooms at Mr Butler's. Among the Groton young ladies who attend the school I like Miss Butler and Miss Brasier best, Miss Lawrence and Miss Dana very well. I will describe them all sometime.

I study Hedge's Logick, Blair's Rhetorick and Colburn's Arithmetick. I feel myself rather degraded from Cicero's Oratory to One and two are how many. It *is* rather a change is it not? I do not believe the two former will do any good except as an exercise of the memory, but Miss Prescott knows best, of course. I wish you would write to Miss Prescott, for I do not know myself exactly what were your wishes with regard to the course of my studies.

The school hours are from half past eight to twelve in the morning, and from two to half past four in the afternoon. We have prayers at half past six in the morning and at eight in the evening. I walk every evening immediately after tea with some young ladies; I take a great deal of pleasure in these walks, for this part of the country is exceedingly beautiful.

I will give you a full length portrait of Miss Prescott, when I have more room. I dislike miniatures, they are seldom correct. Suffice it at present that I really love and admire her, though I did not intend to like her at all. She has two sisters, I like them both but prefer Miss Mary. I wish you would have the goodness to send me my Milton's Paradise Lost, my Hedge's Logick and Bible. I wish too that when it is convenient you would send me a newspaper. I shall depend on your writing directly to let me know how my dear mother is. I shall expect your June visit most impatiently, and hope my mother will then be well enough to accompany you. I hope by this time Aunt Fuller is safely returned from her journey, and that it was pleasant. Love to my brothers, sister if she is at home. I am, dearest father, your ever affectionate daughter
                                                     SARAH M. FULLER

After a year at Miss Prescott's Young Ladies' Seminary, Fuller returned to her family in Cambridge. Now fifteen and formal schooling behind her, Fuller began to take responsibility for her education. The extraordinary breadth of her reading is highlighted in the letters she sent to

Susan Prescott, the Seminary's headmistress. Philosophy, Italian po-
etry, French novels, and Castillian ballads filled her days. Engaged as
well in the stimulating world of Cambridge, Fuller's later youth was
rich indeed. All this abruptly changed with Timothy Fuller's decision
to settle the family in rural Groton, Massachusetts. Fuller's letters tes-
tify to her dissatisfaction. Groton constituted a painful exile during
which Fuller continued her studies, translated a drama of Goethe's,
and tutored her younger brothers.

[To Susan Prescott]
Cambridge, 11 July 1825

Having excused myself from accompanying my honored father to church, which I always do in the afternoon, when
possible, I devote to you the hours which Ariosto and Hel-
vetius ask of my eyes,—as, lying on my writing-desk, they
put me in mind that they must return this week to their
owner.

You keep me to my promise of giving you some sketch of
my pursuits. I rise a little before five, walk an hour, and then
practise on the piano, till seven, when we breakfast. Next I
read French,—Sismondi's Literature of the South of Europe,
—till eight, then two or three lectures in Brown's Philosophy.
About half-past nine I go to Mr. Perkin's school and study
Greek till twelve, when, the school being dismissed, I recite,
go home, and practise again till dinner, at two. Sometimes if
the conversation is very agreeable, I lounge for half an hour
over the dessert, though rarely so lavish of time. Then, when
I can, I read two hours in Italian, but I am often interrupted.
At six, I walk, or take a drive. Before going to bed, I play or
sing, for half an hour or so, to make all sleepy, and, about
eleven, retire to write a little while in my journal, exercises
on what I have read, or a series of characteristics which I am
filling up according to advice. Thus, you see, I am learning
Greek, and making acquaintance with metaphysics, and
French and Italian literature.

"How," you will say, "can I believe that my indolent, fanciful, pleasure-loving pupil, perseveres in such a course?" I
feel the power of industry growing every day, and, besides the
all-powerful motive of ambition, and a new stimulus lately
given through a friend. I have learned to believe that nothing,

no! not perfection, is unattainable. I am determined on distinction, which formerly I thought to win at an easy rate; but now I see that long years of labor must be given to secure even the *"succes de societe,"*—which, however, shall never content me. I see multitudes of examples of persons of genius, utterly deficient in grace and the power of pleasurable excitement. I wish to combine both. I know the obstacles in my way. I am wanting in that intuitive tact and polish, which nature has bestowed upon some, but which I must acquire. And, on the other hand, my powers of intellect, though sufficient, I suppose, are not well disciplined. Yet all such hindrances may be overcome by an ardent spirit. If I fail, my consolation shall be found in active employment.

[To Susan Prescott]
Cambridge, 14 May 1826
I am studying Madame de Stael, Epictetus, Milton, Racine, and Castillian ballads, with great delight. There's an assemblage for you. Now tell me, had you rather be the brilliant De Stael or the useful Edgeworth?—though De Stael is useful too, but it is on the grand scale, on liberalizing, regenerating principles, and has not the immediate practical success that Edgeworth has. I met with a parallel the other day between Byron and Rousseau, and had a mind to send it to you, it was so excellent.

[To Susan Prescott]
Cambridge, 10 January 1827
As to my studies, I am engrossed in reading the elder Italian poets, beginning with Berni, from whom I shall proceed to Pulci and Politian. I read very critically. Miss [Lydia Maria] Francis and I think of reading Locke, as introductory to a course of English metaphysics, and then De Stael on Locke's system. Allow me to introduce this lady to you as a most interesting woman, in my opinion. She is a natural person,— a most rare thing in this age of cant and pretension. Her conversation is charming,—she brings all her powers to bear upon it; her style is varied, and she has a very pleasant and spirited way of thinking. I should judge, too, that she pos-

sesses peculiar purity of mind. I am going to spend this evening with her, and wish you were to be with us.

[To Susan Prescott]
Cambridge, January 1830
You need not fear to revive painful recollections. I often think of those sad experiences. True, they agitate me deeply. But it was best so. They have had a most powerful effect on my character. I tremble at whatever looks like dissimulation. The remembrance of that evening subdues every proud, passionate impulse. My beloved supporter in those sorrowful hours, your image shines as fair to my mind's eye as it did in 1825, when I left you with my heart overflowing with gratitude for your singular and judicious tenderness. Can I ever forget that to your treatment in that crisis of youth I owe the true life,— the love of Truth and Honor?

[To James Freeman Clarke]
[September? 1833]
[Groton?]
Do you remember a conversation we had in the garden, one starlight evening, last summer, about the incalculable power which outward circumstances have over the character? You would not sympathize with the regrets I expressed, that mine had not been formed amid scenes and persons of nobleness and beauty, eager passions and dignified events; instead of those secret trials and petty conflicts which make my transition state so hateful to my memory and my tastes. You then professed the faith which I resigned with such anguish,—the faith which a Schiller could never attain,—a faith in the power of the human will. Yet now, in every letter, you talk to me of the power of circumstances. You tell me how changed you are. Every one of your letters is different from the one preceding, and all so altered from your former self. For are you not leaving all our old ground, and do you not apologize to me for all your letters? Why do you apologize? I think I know you very, very well; considering that we are both human, and have the gift of concealing our thoughts with words. Nay, further—I do not believe you will be able

to become anything which I cannot understand. I know I can sympathize with all who feel and think, from a Dryfesdale up to a Max Piccolomini. You say, you have become a machine. If so, I shall expect to find you a grand, high-pressure, wave-compelling one—requiring plenty of fuel. You might be a steam-engine, and move some majestic fabric at the rate of thirty miles an hour along the broad waters of the nineteenth century. None of your pendulum machines for me! I should, to be sure, turn away my head if I should hear you tick, and mark the quarters of hours; but the buzz and whiz of a good large life-endangerer would be music to mine ears. Oh no! sure there is no danger of your requiring to be set down quite on a level, kept in a still place, and wound up every eight days. Oh no, no! you are not one of that numerous company, who

> ————*live and die,*
> *Eat, drink, wake, sleep between,*
> *Walk, talk like clock-work too,*
> *So pass in order due,*
> > *Over the scene,*
> *To where the past—is past,*
> *The future—nothing yet, &c &c*

But we must all be machines: you shall be a steam-engine;— shall be a mill, with extensive water-privileges,—and I will be a spinning jenny. No! upon second thoughts, I will not be a machine. I will be an instrument not to be confided to vulgar hands—for instance, a chisel to polish marble, or a whetstone to sharpen steel!

[To Amelia Greenwood]
Groton 20th March 1834.
My always dear Amelia,
    . . . I have now been at home nearly five months—You know I had adopted the idea that the end of my little brothers and sister was my nearest duty—Circumstances not necessary to detail induced me to promise my father if he would allow William to come home this winter I would take charge of him also.

Four pupils are a serious and fatiguing charge for one of my some what ardent and impatient disposition. Five days in the week I have given daily lessons in three languages, in geography and history besides many other exercises on alternate days—This has consumed often eight, always five hours of my day—There has been a great deal of needle-work to-do, and is now nearly all finished and I shall not be obliged to pass my time about it when every-thing looks beautiful as I did las[t] summer—We have had very poor servants and for [some time past,] only one—My mother has been often [ill. My grand]mother (who passed the winter with [us) has been ill. Thus] you may imagine as I am the *only* [grown-up daughter, that] my time has been considerably [taxed.]

[But as, sad or merry, I must always be learning, I laid down a course of study at the beginning of winter, comprising certain] things about which I had always [felt deficient. These] were—The history and [Geography of] modern Europe, beginning the former in the fourteenth century The elements of Architecture—the works of Alfieri with his opinions on them—the hist and critical works of Goethe and Schiller and an outline of hist of our own country.

All this you see Dear, is might dry and would not interest you like the things I used to be learning. Thus I chose this time when I should have nothing to distract or dissipate my mind—I have nearly completed this course in the style I proposed (not minute or thorough, I confess) though I have had only three evenings in the week and chance hours in the day for it. I am very glad I have done it and feel the good effects already. I occasionally try my hand at composition but have not completed any thing to my satisfaction—I have sketched a number of plans but if ever accomplished they must be so in a season of more joyful energy, when my mind has been renovated and refreshed by change of scene or circumstance.—I have other plans but they are too undecided to be worth mentioning. My trans[lation] of Tasso cannot be published at present if ever—I regret this principally because I expected to have had a certain sum of money at my own disposal. . . .

I have done some good—I have trust that Providence will enable me to do more—My parents are *both* perfectly satisfied with me—I am *some what less dis*satisfied with myself

than heretofore—I am not absolutely without society—
Goethe!! says live a [ ] retired as we will we must soon become either d[ ] creditors. It has been so with me—There are
sev[ ] here to whom I am debtor for much kindness as [ ] of
considerable cultivation and enlargement. I do not however
esteem their characters worth drawing for *you.*

I have letters pretty frequently from Mrs Farrar, A
Higginson, A Barker, E Randall and James.—The latter seems
to anticipate seeing us again with much pleasure—He has had
many things to try him but has endured them as you and I
would expect—I had an extremely witty letter from Mrs Bar-
low yesterday which I should like to show you if you were
here—Mr B has had a call and they will remain—Present my
regards to Dr Bartlett love to your mother, Angy and Emma
and believe me silent or communicative your Friend as ever

M.F.

If there is news of M. Peabody I should like to hear of it.
I never he[ar]d she went but concluded she did.

*Timothy Fuller's sudden death from cholera in October of 1835 left
his family with few means of support. Timothy and Margarett Fuller's
eldest child did all she could to take her father's place, caring for her
mother, supervising the education of her younger brothers, and managing the family's affairs. Determined to provide for herself, Fuller also
began teaching at Bronson Alcott's Temple School in Boston. Moving
to Providence, Rhode Island's Greene Street School in the spring of
1837, she taught the school's young women courses ranging from natural history to English poetry. Fuller found teaching satisfying, but, as
she confessed to Ralph Waldo Emerson, "What grieves me too is to
find or fear my theory a cheat—I cannot serve two masters." Fuller
chose the master with which she identified most deeply. She set aside
teaching to pursue a career as a woman of letters.*

[To ?]
3 November 1835
[Groton?]
I thought I should be able to write ere now, how our affairs
were settled, but that time has not come yet. My father left
no will, and, in consequence, our path is hedged in by many

petty difficulties. He has left less property than we had anticipated, for he was not fortunate in his investments in real
estate. There will, however, be enough to maintain my
mother, and educate the children decently. I have often had
reason to regret being of the softer sex, and never more than
now. If I were an eldest son, I could be guardian to my brothers and sister, administer the estate, and really become the
head of my family. As it is, I am very ignorant of the management and value of property, and of practical details. I always hated the din of such affairs, and hoped to find a
life-long refuge from them in the serene world of literature
and the arts. But I am now full of desire to learn them, that
I may be able to advise and act, where it is necessary. The
same mind which has made other attainments, can, in time,
compass these, however uncongenial to its nature and habits.

[To ?]
[1836?]
The occupations of the coming six months I have settled.
Some duties come first to parents, brothers and sister but
these will not consume above one sixth of the time—The family is so small now Mother will have little need of my
sewing—We shall probably receive very little company—The
visits required of me by civility will be few—When the Farrars
return I hope to see them frequently—and E. Woodward I
may possibly know if she comes. But I shall not, of free-will
look out of door for a moment's pleasure—I shall have no
one to stay here for a[n]y time except Eliz—I love her and
she is never in the way—All hopes of travelling I have
dismissed—All youthful hopes of every kind I have pushed
from my thoughts—I will not, if I can help it, lose an hour
in castle-building and repining—Too much of that already! I
have now a pursuit of immediate importance to the German
language and literature I will give my undivided attention—I
have made rapid progress for one quite unassisted—I have
always hitherto been too constantly distracted by childish
feelings to acquire any thing properly but have snatched a
little here and there to feed my restless Fancy therewith—
Please God now to keep my mind composed, that I may store

it with all that may be conducive hereafter to the best good of others—

Oh! keep me steady in an honorable ambition. Favored by this calm, this obscurity of life I might learn every-thing, did not these feelings lavish away my strength—Let it be no longer thus—Teach me to think justly and act firmly—Stifle in my breast those feelings which pouring forth so aimlessly did indeed water but the desert and offend the sun's clear eye by producing weeds of rank luxuriance—Thou art my only Friend, thou has not seen fit to interpose one feeling, understanding breast between me and a rude, woful world. Vouchsafe then thy protection that I may "hold on in courage of soul." . . .

[To ?]
23 May, 1836
[Groton?]
I have just been reading Goethe's Lebensregel. It is easy to say "Do not trouble yourself with useless regrets for the past; enjoy the present, and leave the future to God." But it is *not* easy for characters, which are by nature neither *calm* nor *careless,* to act upon these rules. I am rather of the opinion of Novalis, that "Wer sich der hochsten Lieb ergeben Genest von ihnen Wunden nie."

But I will endeavor to profit by the instructions of the great philosopher who teaches, I think, what Christ did, to use without overvaluing the world.

Circumstances have decided that I must not go to Europe, and shut upon me the door, as I think, forever, to the scenes I could have loved. Let me now try to forget myself, and act for others' sakes. What I can do with my pen, I know not. At present, I feel no confidence or hope. The expectations so many have been led to cherish by my conversational powers, I am disposed to deem ill-founded. I do not think I can produce a valuable work. I do not feel in my bosom that confidence necessary to sustain me in such undertakings,—the confidence of genius. But I am now but just recovered from bodily illness, and still heart-broken by sorrow and disappointment. I may be renewed again, and feel differently. If I do not soon, I will make up my mind to teach. I can thus get money, which I will use for the benefit of my dear, gentle, suffering mother,—my brothers and sister. This will be the greatest consolation to me, at all events.

[To Bronson Alcott]
Groton 25th August 1836—
Dear Sir,

I am not quite sure that I understood your last words at Mr. Emerson's. *As* I understood, you had applied to some other person to assist you in your school before you thought of me and would write to me after receiving an answer from that person. A letter since received from Miss Peabody leads me to think that you may on your side be expecting to hear from me and, as I find it necessary to come to some decision about my employment for the winter, I think it best to write to you at any rate.

Will you have the kindness to answer this letter as soon as possible informing me whether you are desirous I should take Miss Peabody's place; whether, if I do take it, you expect me to reside in your family as she did; and whether any-thing would be expected from me beyond the instruction in Latin or other languages which you mentioned to me, with any other circumstances which you may think proper for me to know in order to [make] my decision. Also whether you could (if you wish me to come and I decide on doing so) dispense with my assistance till the 29th of September or the 1st of October. I could, if necessary, begin my lessons earlier, but my family affairs are so situated that it will be much more convenient to me to devote the coming month to their arrangement.

Every thing about me is in a state of uncertainty but I suppose, if I do not hear from you before Friday of next week, that I shall on that day set out on a journey which will occupy ten days or a fortnight. I should, however, leave directions for any letter from you to be forwarded to me.

My acquaintance with your views and character is not sufficiently thorough to give me a confidence that I could satisfy you. But I think as far as I understand your plan I might carry it into execution as successfully as most persons, and I should like to become more conversant with your method of teaching. It would be but an experiment on both sides, for, as I have never yet been subordinate to any one, I cannot tell how I should please or be pleased. But your proposal has attracted me more than any which has yet been made to me.

If I was right in my first supposition and you did *not* make me any direct proposal but only spoke of the possibility of doing so, do not let this letter embarrass you. You have only to say how it was.—

With much regard yours

S. M. FULLER

I am sorry that I have forgotten your first name and have no present means of ascertaining it so as to direct my letter properly. I am not usually so inaccurate; but I hope that, being directed to the street where you live, my letter will not fail to reach you.

[To ?]
[ca. Summer 1837]
[Providence]
I am still quite unwell, and all my pursuits and propensities have a tendency to make my head worse. It is but a bad head,—as bad as if I were a great man! I am not entitled to so bad a head by anything I have done; but I flatter myself it is very interesting to suffer so much, and a fair excuse for not writing pretty letters, and saying to my friends the good things I think about them.

I was so desirous of doing all I could, that I took a great deal more upon myself than I was able to bear. Yet now that the twenty-five weeks of incessant toil are over, I rejoice in it all, and would not have done an iota less. I have fulfilled all my engagements faithfully; have acquired more power of attention, self-command, and fortitude; have acted in life as I thought I would in my lonely meditations; and I have gained some knowledge of means. Above all,—blessed be the Father of our spirits!—my aims are the same as they were in the happiest flight of youthful fancy. I have learned too, at last, to rejoice in all past pain, and to see that my spirit has been judiciously tempered for its work. In future I may sorrow, but can I ever despair?

The beginning of the winter was forlorn. I was always ill; and often thought I might not live, though the work was but just begun. The usual disappointments, too, were about me. Those from whom aid was expected failed, and others who aided did not understand my aims. Enthusiasm for the things loved best fled when I seemed to be buying and selling them. I could not get the proper point of view, and could not keep a healthful state of mind. Mysteriously a gulf seemed to have opened between me and most intimate friends, and for the first time for many years I was entirely, absolutely, alone. Finally, my own character and designs lost all romantic interest, and I felt vulgarized, profaned, forsaken,—though obliged to smile brightly and talk wisely all the while. But these clouds at length passed away.

And now let me try to tell you what has been done. To one class I taught the German language, and thought it good success, when, at the end of three months, they could read twenty pages of German at a lesson, and very well. This class, of course, was not interesting, except in the way of observation and analysis of language.

With more advanced pupils I read, in twenty-four weeks, Schiller's Don Carlos, Artists, and Song of the Bell, besides giving a sort of general lecture on Schiller; Goethe's Hermann and Dorothea, Goetz von Berlichingen, Iphigenia, first part of Faust,—three weeks of thorough study this, as valuable to me as to them,—and Clavigo,—thus comprehending samples of all his efforts in poetry, and bringing forward some of his prominent opinions; Lessing's Nathan, Minna, Emilia Galeotti; parts of Tieck's Phantasus, and nearly the whole first volume of Richter's Titan.

With the Italian class, I read parts of Tasso, Petrarch,— whom they came to almost adore,—Ariosto, Alfieri, and the whole hundred cantos of the Divina Commedia, with the aid of the fine Athenaeum copy, Flaxman's designs, and all the best commentaries. This last piece of work was and will be truly valuable to myself.

I had, besides, three private pupils, Mrs. ———, who became very attractive to me, ———, and little ———, who had not the use of his eyes. I taught him Latin orally, and read the History of England and Shakespeare's historical plays in connection. This lesson was given every day for ten weeks, and was very interesting, though very fatiguing. The labor in Mr. Alcott's school was also quite exhausting. I, however, loved the children, and had many valuable thoughts suggested, and Mr. A's society was much to me.

As you may imagine, the Life of Goethe is not yet written; but I have studied and thought about it much. It grows in my mind with everything that does grow there. My friends in Europe have sent me the needed books on the subject, and I am now beginning to work in good earnest. It is very possible that the task may be taken from me by somebody in England, or that in doing it I may find myself incompetent; but I go in hope, secure, at all events, that it will be the means of the highest culture.

[To Ralph Waldo Emerson?]
Providence R I July 3d 1837
I was fully persuaded in my own mind that I shld never recover, and was only kept up by the conviction that till it was time for me to die, I ought to act as if I hoped to live.

I cannot yet say whether I shall stay here, at first I was much disappointed on examining my field of action. It seemed to me that I could not work at all on subjects so unprepared as I found here. However I tried and think I already perceive that it is not in vain. There is room here, if I mistake not, for a great move in the cause of education, but whether it is I who am to help move, I cannot yet tell. I some times think *yes,* because the plan is becoming so complete in my mind, ways and means are continually occurring to me, and so far as I have tried them, they seem to succeed. I am left almost as much at liberty as if no other person were concerned with me. The arrangements I have made in the school are satisfactory to me for the present. I am sure I shall do good in the way of clearing the ground either for myself or somebody else. About sixty pupils, I should think, are under my care more or less, and they many of them begin already to attempt to walk in the ways I point but which are unknown indeed to most of them. Activity of mind, accuracy in processes, constant looking for principles, and search after the good and beautiful, "that's the ground I go upon" as Mr S says in Vivian Gray, and many of those who have never studied any thing but words seem much pleased with their new prospects—However I am aware that if there is difficulty, there is charm too to them in all this novelty, and am prepared to see new obstacles constantly rising up. Besides, my own progress in any of those acquirements, wh[ic]h I have most loved will be no wise aided by staying here. I must work years to get ready a hill side for my vineyard [   ]. As to Goethe I scarce know how to answer you. I should think after hearing me say so much about him, you wld be aware that I do not consider him from that point of view you wish me to take. I do not go to him as a guide or friend but as a great thinker, who makes me think, a wonderful artist who gratifies my tastes—As far as he had religion or morality, I sh[ou]ld say they were expressed in this poem of his "Eins und Alles," of wh[ic]h I send you a rude translation.

[To Ralph Waldo Emerson]
Providence 1st March 1838—
My dear friend,

Many a Zelterian epistle have I mentally addressed to you full of sprightly scraps about the books I have read, the spectacles I have seen, and the attempts at men and women with whom I have come in contact. But I have not been able to put them on paper, for even when I have attempted it, you have seemed so busy and noble, and I so poor and dissipated that I have not felt worthy to address you.

At present I am not at all Zelterian in my mood but very sombre and sullen. I have shut the door for a few days and tried to do something—You have *really* been doing something! And that is why I write—I want to see you and still more to hear you. I must kindle my torch again. Why have I not heard you this winter? I feel very humble just now yet I dare to say that being lives not who would have received from your lectures as much as I should. There are noble books but one wants the breath of life sometimes. And I see no divine person. I myself am more divine than any I see—I think that is enough to say about them—I know Dr Wayland now, but I shall not care for him. He would never understand me, and, if I met him, it must be by those means of suppression and accommodation which I at present hate to my hearts core. I hate every-thing that is reasonable just now, "wise limitations" and all. I have behaved much too well for some time past; it has spoiled my peace. What grieves me too is to find or fear my theory a cheat—I cannot serve two masters, and I fear all the hope of being a worldling and a literary existence also must be resigned—Isolation is necessary to me as to others. Yet I keep on "fulfilling all my duties" as the technical phrase is except to myself.—But why do I write thus to you who like nothing but what is good ie cheerfulness and fortitude? Is it partly because yours is an image of my oratory. I suppose you will not know what this means. [A]nd if I do not jest when I write to you I must *pray*. And partly as a preliminary to asking you, unsympathizing, unhelpful, wise good, man that you are to do several things for me. I hear you are to deliver one of your lectures again in Boston. I would have you do it while I am there. I shall come on Wednesday next and stay till the following Monday. Perhaps you will come to see me, for though I am not as good as I was, yet as I said before, I am better than most persons *I* see and, I dare say, better than most persons *you* see. But perhaps you do not need to see anybody, for you are acting and nobly—If so you need not come yourself, but send me your two lectures on Holiness and Heroism to read while in Boston. Let me have these two lectures to read *at any rate,* whether you come or no. Do not disappoint me. I will treat them well and return them safe. I shall be at Mr Sturgis's all the time. I shall come out on Thursday to hear you at Cambridge, but they wrote me that lecture would be on the Heart and not so fine as some of yours.

I have not read any books except what every body reads, Gardiner on Music (thank *you* for that; it was a great deal to me.) Carlyle as noble as I hoped, absorbing me quite for a fortnight, Lamb's letters, Whately's Rhetoric.

Lately I have been amusing myself with looking at you through two pair of spectacles of very dissimilar construction in Brownson's review and the Democratic [Review]. I have a disciple of yours in my German class—a very lovely young man. He has never seen you but gets regular bulletins of you from some friend in Boston—I suppose I could get them animated into inviting you to speak to the Larvae here if you would come. Several gentlemen promised me their aid, if there was a chance of getting you. Adieu Sanctissime. Tell Lidian that the thought of her holiness is very fragrant to me. Tell your son that if he has grown less like Raphael's cherubs I will never forgive him. Tell my dear Elizabeth that I love her just as I did last August, but shall probably never write to her—

Devoutly if not worthily yours

S. M. FULLER

[To Almira P. Barlow]
Providence, Nov 8. 1838.

I am sorry on some accounts you will not come to Groton, yet I fear the seclusion of the place would be too much for you. For me, it is what I most covet. I shall go home about Christmas and stay till April, and never set foot out of doors unless to take exercise; and see no human face, divine or otherwise, out of my own family. But I am wearied out; I have gabbled and simpered, and given my mind to the public view these two years back, till there seems to be no good left in me.

Pray Heaven I may find some in those vestal solitudes.

M.F.—

Having committed herself to a career as a woman of letters, Fuller still found herself in need of an income. Beginning a series of classes, or "Conversations" between herself and other highly educated women, she led members of Boston's female elite in explorations of Greek mythology, development of the arts, and female intellectual potential. She told Sophia Ripley that she hoped "to systematize thought and give a precision in which our sex are so deficient, chiefly, I think because they have so few inducements to test and classify what they receive." The twenty dollars that Fuller received from each of the participants provided her with an income for the next five years. Simultaneously, Fuller took responsibility for the Dial, *a Transcendentalist periodical that she edited from 1840 until 1842. Convinced that her nation needed to reform itself intellectually and spiritually, Fuller told William Henry Channing that the* Dial *should challenge Americans "to think more deeply and more nobly by letting them see how some minds are kept alive by a wise self-trust." Fuller's translations, essays*

on critical theory, poems, and commentaries on Goethe appeared in
the pages of the Dial *during these years. Her final contribution, "The*
Great Lawsuit: Man versus *Men.* Woman *versus* Women," *served as*
the basis for Woman in the Nineteenth Century.

[To Sophia Ripley?]
Jamaica Plain,
27th August, 1839—
My dear friend,

I find it more difficult to give on paper a complete outline
of my plan for the proposed conversations than I expected.
There is so much to say that I cannot make any statement
satisfactory to myself within such limits as would be convenient for your purpose. As no one will wish to take the trouble
of reading a long manuscript, I shall rather suggest than tell
what I wish to do, and defer a full explanation to the first
meeting. I wish you to use this communication according to
your own judgement; if it seems to you too meagre to give
any notion of any plan, lay it aside and interpret for me to
whomsoever it may concern.

The advantages of such weekly meeting might be great
enough to repay the trouble of attendance if they consisted
only in supplying a point of union to well-educated and thinking women in a city which, with great pretensions to mental
refinement, boasts at present nothing of the kind and where
I have heard many of mature age wish for some such means
of stimulus and cheer, and these people for a place where they
could state their doubts and difficulties with hope of gaining
aid from the experience or aspirations of others. And if my
office were only to suggest topicks which would lead to conversation of a better order than is usual at social meetings and
to turn back the current when digressing into personalities or
commonplaces so that—what is invaluable in the experience
of each might be brought to bear upon all. I should think the
object not unworthy of an effort. But my own ambition goes
much farther. Thus to pass in review the departments of
thought and knowledge and endeavor to place them in due
relation to one another in our minds. To systematize thought
and give a precision in which our sex are so deficient, chiefly,
I think because they have so few inducements to test and

classify what they receive. To ascertain what pursuits are best suited to us in our time and state of society, and how we may make best use of our means for building up the life of thought upon the life of action.

Could a circle be assembled in earnest desirous to answer the great questions. What were we born to do? How shall we do it? which so few ever propose to themselves 'till their best years are gone by. I should think the undertaking a noble one, and if my resources should prove sufficient to make me its moving spring, I should be willing to give it a large portion of those coming years which will as I hope be my best. I look upon it with no blind enthusiasm, nor unlimited faith, but with a confidence that I have attained a distinct perception of means which if there are persons competent to direct them, can supply a great want and promote really[?] high objects. So far as I have tried them yet they have met with success so much beyond my hopes, that my faith will not be easily shaken, or my earnestness chilled.

Should I however be disappointed in Boston I could hardly hope that such a plan could be brought to bear upon general society in any other city of the U.S. But I do not fear if a good beginning can be had, I am confident that twenty persons cannot be brought together for better motives than those of vanity or pedantry to talk upon such subjects as we propose without finding in themselves great deficiencies which they will be very desirous to supply. Should the enterprize fail, it will be either from incompetence in me or that sort of vanity in others which wears the garb of modesty. On the first of these points I need not speak. I can scarcely have felt the wants of others so much without feeling my own still more deeply. And from the depth of my feeling and the earnestness it gave such power as I have thus far exerted has come. Of course those who propose to meet me feel a confidence in me. And should they be disappointed I shall regret it not solely or most on my own account. I have not given my gage without weighing my capacity to sustain defeat. For the other I know it is very hard to lay aside the shelter of vague generalities, the cant of coterie criticism and the delicate disdains of *good society* and fearless meet the light although it flow from the sun of truth. Yet, as without such generous courage nothing can be done, or learned I cannot but hope to see many capable of it. Willing that others should think their sayings crude, shallow or tasteless if by such unpleasant means they may secure real health and vigor which may enable them to see their friends undefended by rouge or candlelight.

Since I saw you I have been told that several persons are desirous to join, if only they need not talk. I am so sure that the success of the whole depends on conversation being general that I do not wish any one to join who does not intend, *if possible,* to take an active part. No one will be forced, but those who do not talk will not derive the same advantages with those who openly state their impressions and consent to learn by blundering as is the destiny of Man here below. And general silence or side talks would paralyze me. I should feel coarse and misplaced if I were to be haranguing too much. In former instances I have been able to make it easy and even pleasant to twenty five out of thirty to bear their part, to question, to define, to state and examine their opinions. If I could not do as much now I should consider myself unsuccessful and should withdraw. But I should expect communication to be effected by degrees and to do a great deal myself at the first meetings.

My method has been to open a subject as for instance *Poetry* as

> expressed in
> External nature,
> The Life of man
> Literature
> The Fine Arts
> or History of a nation to be studied in
> Its religious and civil institutions
> Its literature and arts,
> The characters of its great men

and after as good a general statement as I know how to make select a branch of the subject and lead others to give their thoughts upon it.

When they have not been successful in verbal utterance of their thoughts I have asked for them in writing. At the next meeting I read these aloud and canvassed their adequacy without mentioning the names of the writers. I found this less and less necessary as I proceeded and my companions acquired greater command both of thoughts and language, but for a time it was useful. I hope it may not be necessary now, but if it should great advantages may be derived from even this limited use of the pen.

I do not wish at present to pledge myself to any course of subjects. Except generally that they will be such as literature and the arts present in endless profusion. Should a class be brought together, I should wish first to ascertain our common ground and in a few meetings should see whether it be practicable to follow up the design in my mind which would look as yet too grand on paper. Let us see whether there will be any organ and if so note down the music to which it may give breath.

I believe I have said as much as any one will wish to read. I am ready to answer any question which may be proposed meanwhile. I will add nothing more here except always yours truly

S. M. Fuller

[To Ralph Waldo Emerson]
Nov 12 1839
Had the first meeting with my class last Wednesday and gave them a brief statement of my views and aims apparently not without success for they were intent and many (some strangers to me) said words of faith and cheer to me afterwards. But tomorrow comes the real trial of whether they will talk themselves. There are some fine faces.

[To ?]
[ca. Autumn? 1839?]
[Jamaica Plain?]
The circle I meet interests me. So even devoutly thoughtful seems their spirit, that, from the very first I took my proper place, and never had the feeling I dreaded, of display, of a paid Corinne. I feel as I would, truly a teacher and a guide.

All are intelligent; five or six have talent. But I am never driven home for ammunition; never put to any expense; never truly called out. What I have is always enough; though I feel how superficially I am treating my subject.

[To ?]
25 Nov 1839
M[y] class is singularly prosperous I think. I was so fortunate as to rouse at once the tone of simple earnestness which can scarcely, when once awakened, cease to vibrate. All seem in a glow and quite as receptive as I wish. They question and examine, yet follow leadings; and thoughts (not opinions) have been trumps every time. There are about 25 members, and every one, I believe full of interest. The first time, ten took part in the conversation; the last still more. Mrs Bancroft came out in a way that surprized me. She seems to have shaken off a wonderful number of films. She showed pure vision, sweet sincerity, and much talent. Mrs Josiah Quincy keeps us in good order and takes care yet "Xy" and "morality" are not forgotten. The first time was the genealogy of heaven and earth, then the will (Jupiter), the Understanding (Mercury).

Second, the celestial inspiration of genius, perception and transmission of divine law (Apollo) the terrene inspiration the impassioned abandonment of Genius (Bacchus) of the thunderbolt, the Caduceus, the ray, and the grape having disposed of as well as might be, we came to the wave, and the seashell it moulds; to Beauty, and Love, her parent her child.

I assure you there is more Greek than Bostonian spoken at the meetings, and we may have pure honey of Hymettus to give you yet. I have been happy *a mourir*. Four hundred and seventy designs of Raffalle in my possession for a week.

[To William Henry Channing ?]
1840
Since the Revolution, there has been little, in the circumstances of this country, to call out the higher sentiments. The effect of continued prosperity is the same on nations as on individuals,—it leaves the nobler faculties undeveloped. The

need of bringing out the physical resources of a vast extent of country, the commercial and political fever incident to our institutions, tend to fix the eyes of men on what is local and temporary, on the external advantages of their condition. The superficial diffusion of knowledge, unless attended by a correspondent deepening of its sources, is likely to vulgarize rather than to raise the thought of a nation, depriving them of another sort of education through sentiments of reverence, and leading the multitude to believe themselves capable of judging what they but dimly discern. They see a wide surface, and forget the difference between seeing and knowing. In this hasty way of thinking and living they traverse so much ground that they forget that not the sleeping railroad passenger, but the botanist, the geologist, the poet, really see the country, and that, to the former, "a miss is as good as a mile." In a word, the tendency of circumstances has been to make our people superficial, irreverent, and more anxious to get a living than to live mentally and morally. This tendency is no way balanced by the slight literary culture common here, which is mostly English, and consists in a careless reading of publications of the day, having the same utilitarian tendency with our own proceedings. The infrequency of acquaintance with any of the great fathers of English lore marks this state of things.

New England is now old enough,—some there have leisure enough,—to look at all this; and the consequence is a violent reaction, in a small minority, against a mode of culture that rears such fruits. They see that political freedom does not necessarily produce liberality of mind, nor freedom in church institutions—vital religion; and, seeing that these changes cannot be wrought from without inwards, they are trying to quicken the soul, that they may work from within outwards. Disgusted with the vulgarity of a commercial aristocracy, they become radicals; disgusted with the materialistic working of "rational" religion, they become mystics. They quarrel with all that is, because it is not spiritual enough. They would, perhaps, be patient if they thought this the mere sensuality of childhood in our nation, which it might outgrow; but they think that they see the evil widening, deepening,—not only debasing the life, but corrupting the thought of our people, and they feel that if they know not well what should be done, yet that the duty of every good man is to utter a protest against what is done amiss.

Is this protest undiscriminating? are these opinions crude? do these proceedings threaten to sap the bulwarks on which men at present depend? I confess it all, yet I see in these men promise of a better wisdom than in their opponents. Their hope for man is grounded on his destiny as an immortal soul, and not as a mere comfort-loving inhabitant of earth, or as a subscriber to the social contract. It was not meant that the soul should cultivate the earth, but that the earth should educate and maintain the soul. Man is not made for society, but society is made for man. No institution can be good which does not tend to improve the individual. In these principles I have confidence so profound, that I am not afraid to trust those who hold them, despite their partial views, imperfectly developed characters, and frequent want of practical sagacity. I believe, if they have opportunity to state and discuss their opinions, they will gradually sift them, ascertain their grounds and aims with clearness, and do the work this country needs. I hope for them as for "the leaven that is hidden in the bushel of meal, till all be leavened." The leaven is not good by itself, neither is the meal; let them combine, and we shall yet have bread.

Utopia is impossible to build up. At least, my hopes for our race on this one planet are more limited than those of most of my friends. I accept the limitations of human nature, and believe a wise acknowledgement of them one of the best conditions of progress. Yet every noble scheme, every poetic manifestation, prophesies to man his eventual destiny. And were not man ever more sanguine than facts at the moment justify, he would remain torpid, or be sunk in sensuality. It is on this ground that I sympathize with what is called the "Transcendental party," and that I feel their aim to be the true one. They acknowledge in the nature of man an arbiter for his deeds,—a standard transcending sense and time,—and are, in my view, the true utilitarians. They are but at the beginning of their course, and will, I hope, learn how to make use of the past, as well as to aspire for the future, and to be true in the present moment.

My position as a woman, and the many private duties which have filled my life, have prevented my thinking deeply on several of the great subjects which these friends have at heart. I suppose, if ever I become capable of judging, I shall differ from most of them on important points. But I am not afraid to trust any who are true, and in intent noble, with their own course nor to aid in enabling them to express their thoughts, whether I coincide with them or not.

On the subject of Christianity, my mind is clear. If Divine, it will stand the test of any comparison. I believe the reason it has so imperfectly answered to the aspirations of its Founder is, that men have received it on external grounds. I believe that a religion, thus received, may give the life an external decorum, but will never open the fountains of holiness in the soul.

One often thinks of Hamlet as the true representative of idealism in its excess. Yet if, in his short life, man be liable to some excess, should we not rather prefer to have the will palsied like Hamlet, by a deep-searching tendency and desire for poetic perfection, than to have it enlightened by worldly sagacity, as in the case of Julius Caesar, or made intense by pride alone, as in that of Coriolanus?

After all, I believe it is absurd to attempt to speak on these subjects within the limits of a letter. I will try to say what I mean in print some day. Yet one word as to "the material," in man. Is it not the object of all philosophy, as well as of religion and poetry, to prevent its prevalence? Must not those who see most truly be ever making statements of the truth to combat this sluggishness, or worldliness? What else are sagas, poets, preachers, born to do? Men go an undulating course, —sometimes on the hill, sometimes in the valley. But he only is in the right who in the valley forgets not the hill-prospect, and knows in darkness that the sun will rise again. That is the real life which is subordinated to, not merged in, the ideal; he is only wise who can bring the lowest act of his life into sympathy with its highest thought. And this I take to be the one only aim of our pilgrimage here. I agree with those who think that no true philosophy will try to ignore or annihilate the material part of man, but will rather seek to put it in its place, as servant and minister to the soul.

[To Frederic Henry Hedge]
Jamaica Plain
1st Jany 1840.
My dear Henry,

I write this new years day to wish you all happiness and to say that there is reason to expect the new journal (in such dim prospect when you were here) may see the light next April. And we depend on you for the first No. and for solid bullion too. Mr Emerson will write every number and so will you if you are good and politic, for it is the best way to be heard from your sentry box there in Bangor.—My friend, I really hope you will make this the occasion for assailing the public ear with such a succession of melodies that all the stones will advance to form a city of refuge for the just. I think with the greatest pleasure of working in company with you. But what will it be? will you give us poems or philosophy or criticism, and how much, for we are planning out our first No. by the yard. Let me hear from you directly.

Except one scrap of a letter to Mr Ripley I have seen no word from you since you left us. But in the journal you will write to us constantly and of your best life.—I have little taste, myself, for this epistolary medium. It does not refresh like conversation, it does not stimulate, like good serious study or writing.

Were we near I should have a vast deal to tell you, but my life is rather a subject for a metaphysical romance than a gazette. I waste much time in sickness and am now again under medical care. Also I have a good deal of domestic care which I like quite as little. I have three young ladies with me to be carved into roses "with flowers and foliage over-wrought." My class in town succeeds very well I think, but it breaks up my time a good deal. They talk as much as I could expect and seem deeply interested in the subjects. I think also of giving readings in Boston from Goethe's Miscellanies, if they collect a circle large enough to make it worth my while.—When I am at home I write all I can, to what purpose time will show!

Mr Emerson is lecturing well; his introductory was noble. He makes statements much nearer completeness than ever before; this all the audience feel.

The world is somewhat occupied with Mr Norton and Mr

Ripley. The seeming mildness of Mr N's late rejoinder gives him at present the advantage, but Mr R. comes out again this week.

I write in haste pray you write at leisure and forth with. With best wishes of the new year to Lucy, believe me in hope, trust, and love always your friend

Margaret F.

[To William Henry Channing]
Jamaica Plain,
22d March, 1840—
My dear friend,

This eveg is not a very good time to answer your letter, but I must take it, *faute de mieux,* because I want to say to you. Though your plan be a brave one, and I would wish to become acquainted with Ernest as speedily as possible, yet if you be not ready at once to commence your pilgrimage with him, send some short pieces. I do not ask as James was wont for "bundles" of fine original compositions but make use of the modester words *some* or *several* and I pray you heed my request, for with this first number we want room for choice. I have myself a great deal written but as I read it over scarce a word seems pertinent to the place or time. When I meet people I can adapt myself to them, but when I write, it is into another world, not a better one perhaps, but one with very dissimilar habits of thought to this where I am domesticated. How much those of us who have been much formed by the European mind have to unlearn and lay aside, if we would act here. I would fain do something worthily that belonged to the country where I was born, but most times I fear it may not be.

What others can do, whether all that has been said is the mere restlessness of discontent, or there are thoughts really struggling for utterance will I think be tested now. A perfectly free organ is to be offered for the expression of individual thought and character. There are no party measures to be carried, no particular standard to be set up. A fair calm tone, a recognition of universal principles will, I hope pervade the essays in every form. I hope there will neither be a spirit of dogmatism nor of compromise. That this periodical will not aim at leading public opinion, but at stimulating each man to think for himself, to think more deeply and more nobly by letting them see how some minds are kept alive by a wise self-trust. I am not sanguine as to the amount of talent which will be brought to bear on this publication. I find all concerned rather indifferent, and see no great promise for the present. I am sure we cannot show high culture, and I doubt about vigorous thought. But I hope we shall show free action as far as it goes and a high aim. It were much if a periodical could be kept upon to accomplish no outward object, but merely to afford an avenue for what of free and calm thought might be originated among us by the wants of individual minds.

James promises nothing but if I can get him here I shall expect some sound rough fruit of American growth. From Mr Emerson we may hope good literary criticisms, but his best thoughts must, I suppose take the form of lectures for the present.

But you will see I wish you were here that I might talk with you once. I cannot write well to any one to whom I do not write constantly. But we shall write constantly to our friends in print now. When I have finished "Ernest" I will seal and send a letter I wr[ote] you last summer provided it seems fit for an appendix to the record of your search.

My dear friend, you speak of your sense of "unemployed force."—I feel the same. I never, never in life have had the happy feeling of really doing any thing. I can only console myself for these semblances of actions by seeing that others seem to be in some degree aided by them. But Oh! really to feel the glow of action, without its weariness, what heaven it must be! I cannot think, can you, that all men in all ages have suffered thus from an unattained Ideal. The race must have been worn out ere now by such corrosion. May you be freed from it! for me, my constant ill-health makes me daily more inadequate to my desires and my life now seems but a fragment. At such hours we take refuge in the All, we know that somewhere in Nature this vitality stifled here is manifesting itself. But individuality is so dear we would fain sit beneath our own vines and fig trees.

Farewell, pray write to me again if it suits you so to do. I should answer all the letters, a compliment I do not always pay. My respects to Miss Channing. Mother and sister are not near me now, but they think of you ever with respect and love.

    Yours

                                 S. Margaret Fuller.

[To Ralph Waldo Emerson]
29 Sept 1840
I have felt the impossibility of meeting far more than you; so much, that, if you ever know me well, you will feel that the fact of my abiding by you thus far, affords a strong proof that we are to be much to one another. How often have I left you despairing and forlorn. How often have I said, this light will never understand my fire; this clear eye will never discern the law by which I am filling my circle; this simple force will never interpret my need of manifold being.

    Dear friend on one point misunderstand me less. I do not love power other than every vigorous nature delights to feel itself living. To violate the sanctity of relations, I am as far from it as you can be. I make no claim. I have no wish which is not dictated by a feeling of truth. Could I lead the highest Angel captive by a look, that look I would not give, unless prompted by true love. I am no usurper. I ask only mine own inheritance. If it be found that I have mistaken its boundaries, I will give up the choicest vineyard, the fairest flowergarden, to its lawful owner.

    In me I did not think you saw the purity, the singleness, into which, I have faith that all this darting motion, and restless flame shall yet be attempered and subdued. I felt that you did not for me the highest office of friendship, by offering me the clue of the labyrinth of my own being. Yet I thought you appreciated the fearlessness which shrinks from no truth in myself and others, and trusted me, believing that I knew the path for myself. O it must be that you have felt the worth of that truth which has never hesitated to infringe our relation, or aught else, rather than not vindicate itself. If you have not seen this stair on which God has been so untiringly leading me to himself, you have indeed been wholly ignorant of me. Then indeed, when my soul, in its childish agony of prayer, stretched out its arms to you as a father, did you not see what was meant by this crying for the moon; this sullen rejection of playthings which had become unmeaning? Did you then say 'I know not what this means; perhaps this will trouble me; the time will come when I shall hide my eyes from this mood;'—then you are not the friend I seek.

But did not you ask for a "foe" in your friend? Did not you ask for a "large formidable nature"? But a beautiful foe, I am not yet, to you. Shall I ever be? I know not. My life is now prayer. Through me sweetest harmonies are momently breathing. Shall they not make me beautiful,—Nay, beauty! Shall not all vehemence, all eccentricity, be purged by these streams of divine light? I have, in these hours, but one pain; the sense of the infinite exhausts and exalts: it cannot therefore possess me wholly; else, were I also one wave of gentlest force. Again I shall cease to melt and flow; again I shall seek and pierce and rend asunder.

But oh, I am now full of such sweet certainty, never never more can it be utterly shaken. All things have I given up to the central power, myself, you also; yet, I cannot forbear adding, dear friend. I am now so at home, I know not how again to wander and grope, seeking my place in another Soul. I need to be recognized. After this, I shall be claimed, rather than claim, yet if I speak of facts, it must be as I see them.

To L. my love. In her, I have always recognized the saintly element. *That,* better than a bible in my hand, shows that it cannot be to me wholly alien. Yet am I no saint, no anything, but a great soul born to know all, before it can return to the creative fount.

Yesterday, I saw Mr R. He had, on reflection, taken my frankness in the true way; we are much nearer, and, I think, shall go on better and better. Say no word of this or of aught personal to ———. His vanity makes him perfidious, without his intending it.

[To Ralph Waldo Emerson]
[17? March 1842]
My dear Waldo,

I requested Miss P to write to you, but, after looking over her letter, I want to add some lines myself. I hoped they would get at these particulars before you returned from N. York, that you might hear them on your way and not be teased as soon as you arrived at your quiet home, but you came earlier than I had expected. Yesterday I found myself so unwell, and really exhausted, letters recd from the family made my stay here so uncertain that I wrote the little notice with regard to the possibility of suspending the Dial for a time, feeling that I must draw back from my promise that I would see to the summer no.—But this morng after J. Clarke and Miss P. had at last the means of almost entirely examining the accounts, they give me the result you find in her letter to you, which makes it impossible for me to go on at all.

I could not do it, in future, if I have the same burden on me as I have had before, even as well as I have done. There is a perceptible diminution of my strength, and this winter which has been one of so severe labor I shall not recover fully from for two or three months. Then if I must take up a similar course next winter and have this tie upon me for the summer I think I should sink under it entirely.

I grieve to disappoint you after all the trouble you have taken. I am also sorry myself, for if I could have received a maintenance from this Dial, I could have done my duties to it well, which I never have all this time, and my time might have been given to my pen, while now for more than three months I have been able to write no line except letters. But it cannot be helped. It has been a sad business.

I think perhaps Mr Parker would like to carry it on even under these circumstances. For him, or for you it would be much easier than for me, for you have quiet homes, and better health. Of course if you do carry it on, I should like to do any thing I can to aid you.

There must be prompt answer as the press will wait.

Your affectionate

MARGARET

[To William Henry Channing ?]
25 August 1842
Concord
Beneath this roof of peace, beneficence, and intellectual activity, I find just the alternation of repose and satisfying pleasure that I need.

Do not find fault with the hermits and scholars. The true
text is:—

> *"Mine own Telemachus*
> *He does his work—I mine."*

All do the work, whether they will or no; but he is "mine
own Telemachus" who does it in the spirit of religion, never
believing that the last results can be arrested in any one measure or set of measures, listening always to the voice of the
Spirit,—and who does this more than [Waldo]?

After the first excitement of intimacy with him,—when
I was made so happy by his high tendency, absolute purity,
the freedom and infinite graces of an intellect cultivated much
beyond any I had known,—came with me the questioning
season. I was greatly disappointed in my relation to him.
I was, indeed, always called on to be worthy,—this benefit was sure in our friendship. But I found no intelligence
of my best self; far less was it revealed to me in new modes;
for not only did he seem to want the living faith which
enables one to discharge this holiest office of a friend, but
he absolutely distrusted me in every region of my life with
which he was unacquainted. The same trait I detected in his
relations with others. He had faith in the Universal, but not
in the Individual Man; he met men, not as a brother, but as
a critic. Philosophy appeared to chill instead of exalting the
poet.

But now I am better acquainted with him. His "accept" is
true; the "I shall learn," with which he answers every accu-
sation, is no less true. No one can feel his limitations, in fact,
more than he, though he always speaks confidently from his
present knowledge as all he has yet, and never qualifies or
explains. He feels himself "shut up in a crystal cell," from
which only "a great love or a great task could release me,"
and hardly expects either from what remains in this life. But
I already see so well how these limitations have fitted him for
his peculiar work, that I can no longer quarrel with them;
while from his eyes looks out the angel that must sooner or
later break every chain. Leave him in his cell affirming absolute truth; protesting against humanity, if so he appears to

do; the calm observer of the courses of things. Surely, "he keeps true to this thought, which is the great matter." He has already paid his debt to his time; how much more he will give we cannot know; but already I feel how invaluable is a cool mind, like his, amid the warring elements around us. As I look at him more by his own law, I understand him better; and as I understand him better, differences melt away. My inmost heart blesses the fate that gave me birth in the same clime and time, and that has drawn me into such a close bond with him as, it is my hopeful faith, will never be broken, but from sphere to sphere ever more hallowed.

What did you mean by saying I had imbibed much of his way of thought? I do indeed feel his life stealing gradually into mine; and I sometimes think that my work would have been more simple, and my unfolding to a temporal activity more rapid and easy, if we had never met. But when I look forward to eternal growth, I am always aware that I am far larger and deeper for him. His influence has been to me that of lofty assurance and sweet serenity. He says, I come to him as the European to the Hindoo, or the gay Trouvére to the Puritan in his steeple hat. Of course this implies that our meeting is partial. I present to him the many forms of nature and solicit with music; he melts them all into spirit and reproves performance with prayer. When I am with God alone, I adore in silence. With nature I am filled and grow only. With most men I bring words of now past life, and do actions suggested by the wants of their natures rather than my own. But he stops me from doing anything, and makes me think.

In the spring of 1844, Fuller completed another series of "Conversations," her fifth in as many years. That summer she published her first book, Summer on the Lakes. *Fuller seemed poised for change. Horace Greeley, the editor of the* New-York Daily Tribune, *offered her a radical possibility, asking Fuller to take a position as his newspaper's literary editor. She said yes. Preparing* Woman in the Nineteenth Century *for publication during the fall, she joined Greeley at the end of 1844. Between December of 1844 and August of 1846, Fuller offered readers her opinion on an astonishing variety of subjects, including a defense of the controversial French novelist George Sand, a sharply worded condemnation of slavery, and an analysis of the Swedish philosopher Emanuel Swedenborg.*

[To William Henry Channing]
Cambridge, 28 Apr 1844
It was the last meeting of my class. We had a most animated meeting. On bidding me goodbye, they all and always show so much goodwill and love, that I feel I must really have become a friend to them. I was then loaded with beautiful gifts, accompanied with those little delicate poetic traits of which I shd delight to tell you, if we were near. Last, came a beautiful bunch of flowers, passion flowers, heliotrope, and soberer flowers. Then I went to take my repose on C's sofa, and we had a most sweet afternoon together.—

[To ?]
[Summer] 1844
Every day, I rose and attended to the many little calls which are always on me, and which have been more of late. Then, about eleven, I would sit down to write, at my window, close to which is the appletree lately full of blossoms, and now of yellow birds. Opposite me was Del Sarto's Madonna; behind me Silenus, holding in his arms the infant Pan. I felt very content with my pen, my daily bouquet, and my yellow birds. About five I would go out and walk till dark; then would arrive my proofs, like crabbed old guardians, coming to tea every night. So passed each day. The 23d of May, my birthday, about one o'clock, I wrote the last line of my little book [Summer on the Lakes]; then I went to Mount Auburn, and walked gently among the graves.

[To William Henry Channing]
[June? 1844]
I think I have written too sweetly or in too fair words, hush the moral voice with mindfulness that such is always the Poetry of Truth.

I want to send you an eagle's feather from the Eagle's nest at Oregon [Illinois]. Sarah [Clarke] gave me three the other day; one I have given to Cary [Sturgis], one I keep, one is for you. I never expect to use mine, but perhaps you will write me *the* letter sometime with yours. I may not have opportunity to send it soon; eagles' feathers won't go into parcels of a common shape.

As to my book, there are complimentary notices, in the papers and I receive good letters about it. It is much read already, and esteemed "very entertaining"! Little and Brown take the risk and allow a percentage. My bargain with them is only for one edition; if this succeeds, I shall make a better. They take their own measures about circulating the work, but any effort from my friends helps, of course. Short notices by you, distributed at Phila[delphia], New York and even Cincinnati would attract attention and buyers!! Outward success in this way is very desirable to me, not so much on account of present profit to be derived, as because it would give me advantage in making future bargains, and open the way to ransom more time for writing.

The account of the Seeress pleases many, and it is amusing to see how elderly routine gentlemen, such as Dr Francis and Mr Farrar, are charmed with the little story of Mariana. They admire, at poetic distance, that powerful nature that would alarm them so in real life. How canst thou be willing that any should see me as Mariana?—I shall always do so—I feel that the inmost passages are only from God, music, and love. Imagine prose eyes, with glassy curiosity, looking out for Mariana. Nobody dreams of its being like me; they all thought Miranda was, in the Great Lawsuit. People seem to think that not more than one phase of character can be shown in one life.

Sylvain is only a suggested picture, you would not know the figure by which it is drawn, if you could see it. Have no desire, I pray thee, ever to realize these ideals. The name I took from Fanny Elser's partner.

In the bridal dance, after movements of a birdlike joy, and overflowing sweetness, when he comes forward, she retires with a proud, timid grace, so beautiful; it said "see what a man I am happy enough to love." And then came forward this *well-taught dancer,* springing and pirouetting without one

tint of genius, one ray of soul; it was very painful and symbolized much, far more than I have expressed with Sylvain
and Mariana.

Write me anything more that strikes you, then will the book
become very interesting to me.

Have you begun the memoir? I hope next Sunday to write
out what I have to say about your uncle, and then will send
it. They have built a mean house close to his willows. I wish
they had waited for me to be gone.

Cary has been staying with me for near a fortnight, pleasant
is our independent life in the still house. There are many
things I might tell you, but must wait for time is not abundant
with me just now. With blessing Farewell.

If you dislike my version of your visions, will not you burn
it and write them out for me yourself.

[To William Henry Channing]
Sunday eveg
17th Novr 1844.
At last, my dear William, I have finished the pamphlet
[*Woman in the Nineteenth Century*]. The last day it kept
spinning out beneath my hand. After taking a long walk
early on one of the most noble exhilarating sort of morn-
ings I sat down to write and did not put the last stroke till
near nine in the evening. Then I felt a delightful glow as if
I had put a good deal of my true life in it, as if, suppose I
went away now, the measure of my foot-print would be left
on the earth. That was several days ago, and I do not know
how it will look on revision, for I must leave several days
more between me and it before I undertake that, but think
it will be much better than if it had been finished at Cambridge, for here has been no headach, and leisure to choose
my hours.

It will make a pamphlet rather larger than a number of the
Dial, and would take a fortnight or more to print. Therefore
I am anxious to get the matter *en train* before I come to N.Y.
that I may begin the 1st Decr for I want to have it out by
Christmas. Will you then see Mr Greeley about it the latter

part of this week or the beginning of next? He is absent now, but will be back by that time and I will write to him about it. Perhaps he will like to undertake it himself.

The estimate you sent me last summer was made expecting an edition of fifteen hundred, but I think a thousand will be enough. The writing, though I have tried to make my meaning full and clear, requires, shall I say? too much culture in the reader to be quickly or extensively diffused. I shall be satisfied if it moves a mind here and there and through that others; shall be well satisfied if an edition of a thousand is disposed of in the course of two or three years

If the expense of publication should not exceed a hundred or even a hundred and fifty dollars, I should not be unwilling to undertake it, if thought best by you and Mr G. But I suppose you would not think that the favorable way as to securing a sale.

If given to a publisher I wish to dispose of it only for one edition. I should hope to be able to make it constantly better while I live and should wish to retain full command of it, in case of subsequent editions. [   ] to be made up before coming here. If Mr. G. really did expect him to write whig editorials, that, I agree with you, he could not do, but I do not think he has ascertained Mr. G's design, and he will go home without doing so. . . .

Adieu dear friend.

Less than two years after she had left New England for New York City, Fuller departed for Europe early in the fall of 1846. She told her friends Samuel and Anna Barker Ward that the journey which had been deferred a decade could no longer have a significant impact on her. "My mind and character are too much formed," she insisted prior to her departure. Fuller could not have been more mistaken. The next four years were the most decisive of her life. A resident of Rome during the Revolution of 1848, she made an impassioned commitment to the cause of Italian unification and independence. With a passion that was equally strong, she pledged herself to Giovanni Ossoli, an Italian nobleman who shared her engagement with the Italian Revolution. Their son, Angelo, was born two months before the establishment of the Roman Republic in November of 1848. This victory was followed by a

*series of devastating defeats that culminated in the fall of the Roman
Republic only seven months later. Little wonder that Fuller told Samuel and Anna in a later letter that "so great has been the passion of
my life since you knew me, it is difficult to speak."*

[To Samuel and Anna Barker Ward]
New York.
3d March, 1846.
My ever dear friend,

I was glad, indeed, to get your and Anna's letters after the
long silence. Indeed, of your health and outward life I had
heard in other ways, but my heart had often turned towards
you and wished for sight of your handwriting at least.

Yet I do not feel able to answer the good part of your letter,
I mean the thinking part, unless I do so in the Tribune. I may,
very likely, take it as text, if I can find a suitable form for my
reflections.

At present I am not fit to write a good letter. I cannot spare
time or feeling. All the month of January I was sick in a way
that unfitted me for any serious effort. Ever since I have been
toiling in vain to make up at the same time for my forced
derelictions and to meet new demands. *Now* I am on the
point, in addition to my usual work of getting out two vols
of my Miscellanies (pieces from Dial and Tribune wh will
require a good deal of revision; they are to be published in
Wiley and Putnam's series) and getting ready to go to Europe
in August, wh will be hard work, as Mr Greeley is to be
absent most of the summer and I have promised to stay by
the Tribune till the last. Add to this the perplexity and
grief as to home affairs that Ellery's last freak has brought
upon me—

But it is not of this I want to speak, but of my going to
Europe. It is now ten years, since I was forced to abandon
the hope of going at the time when I felt that my health and
mind required it as they never could again. Still more I felt
that in not going with you at the time when our minds were
so in unison, and when I was drawn so strongly towards your
peculiar province, I lost what life could never replace. I feel
so still.

At every step I have missed the culture I sought in going,

for with me it [was] no scheme of pleasure but the means of needed development. It was what I wanted after my painful youth, and what I was ready to use and be nourished by. It would have given my genius wings and I should have been, not in idea indeed, but in achievement far superior to what I can be now. Fate or Heaven, or whatever we may call it, did not will it so, and in entering other and less congenial paths, I do feel that I have tried to make the best of life in every sense I could. Many sweet fruits has it brought me, fruits of spiritual knowledge and a liberal communion with the woful struggling crowd of fellow men. I have accepted my lot, such as it was, and while I have not cast over it any veil of commonplace resignations I have not complained inwardly or outwardly. I have, indeed, had my periods of morbid suffering, because the perpetual stress upon me has been beyond my strength to bear, and at this present time I feel threatened with one, because the day is thronged a great deal too thick with tasks and perplexities and I have not the chance for repose that I ought.

I hope however to avoid it, for I have grown wise and now seek physical remedies for irritated nerves, rather than struggle with them mentally, which I formerly augmented the ill by doing.

I do not look forward to seeing Europe now as so very important to me. My mind and character are too much formed. I shall not modify them much but only add to my stores of knowledge. Still, even in this sense, I wish much to go. It is important to me, almost needful in the career I am now engaged in. I feel that, if I persevere, there is nothing to hinder my having an important career even now. But it must be in the capacity of a journalist, and for that I need this new field of observation.

I want to go in a way not too laborious for my strength and it is with this view that I apply to you. I have about a thousand dollars secured for my absence. But from all calculations I seem likely to want five hundred more. Can I through you or your father have a credit abroad to that amount, in case I need it. I wish to be in debt to a friend, that in case I live and return, I may pay it gradually as I earn it and not feel oppressed by it. I should like it to be a debt in regular form, and pay suitable interest for the use of the money. If I live I could probably earn that sum soon, if I die, the lender would not eventually be a loser, as seven or eight hundred dollars will come to me when Mother leaves this world from which she seems likely to be driven prematurely, though truly I wish I might go first.

I think I remember something of your saying you never meant to *lend* money. If you have any vow or resolution of that kind that will interfere, or if I am mistaken in thinking that y[ou]r fathers relations abroad would make this easier to you than any one else, write soon, dear Sam, and say so, and I shall apply elsewhere. If I cannot get it otherwise I can take upon me correspondences with periodicals here, only too much of that will give me so much labor as in good measure to deprive me of the benefit of the journey. Dearest Anna, I thank much for the sweet picture of your life. It will be repose to think of it, in dust and rush of a different one. I have no time to answer except about my visit. I wish *very* much, to come but do not feel sure of being able and if I am, the visit must be short. I should like much however to come, if I can, and should be glad to meet Cary [Sturgis] as else I cannot see her again. Will you ask her for the last of June or first of July and I will come then, if possible. I am glad we saw so much of each other last summer, we may not meet much again for a good or bad while.

I feel sorry not to have the books you name, they came out in my sick time and not being noticed by my hand do not belong to me by rules of the office. I send such as I have.

Dear Sam I look to see you. Shall be here 4 Amity place, Mrs Elwell's till 12th March, after that time inquire at Tribune office. I have been interrupted forty times while writing and now am so again, but ever yours

MARGARET.

[To Elizabeth Hoar]
Paris, 18 January 1847
You wished to hear of George Sand, or, as they say in Paris, "Madame Sand." I find that all we had heard of her was true in the outline; I had supposed it might be exaggerated. She

had every reason to leave her husband,—a stupid, brutal man, who insulted and neglected her. He afterwards gave up their child to her for a sum of money. But the love for which she left him lasted not well, and she has had a series of lovers, and I am told has one now, with whom she lives on the footing of combined means, independent friendship! But she takes rank in society like a man, for the weight of her thoughts, and has just given her daughter in marriage. Her son is a grown-up young man, an artist. Many women visit her, and esteem it an honor. Even an American here, and with the feelings of our country on such subjects, Mrs.———, thinks of her with high esteem. She has broken with La Mennais, of whom she was once a disciple.

I observed to Dr. François, who is an intimate of hers, and loves and admires her, that it did not seem a good sign that she breaks with her friends. He said it was not so with her early friends; that she has chosen to buy a chateau in the region where she passed her childhood, and that the people there love and have always loved her dearly. She is now at the chateau, and, I begin to fear, will not come to town before I go. Since I came, I have read two charming stories recently written by her. Another longer one she has just sold to *La Presse* for fifteen thousand francs. She does not receive nearly as much for her writings as Balzac, Dumas, or Sue. She has a much greater influence than they, but a less circulation.

She stays at the chateau, because the poor people there were suffering so much, and she could help them. She has subscribed *twenty thousand francs* for their relief, in the scarcity of the winter. It is a great deal to earn by one's pen: a novel of several volumes sold for only fifteen thousand francs, as I mentioned before.

[To Ralph Waldo Emerson]
Naples, 15 March 1847
Mickiewicz, the Polish poet, first introduced the Essays to an acquaintance in Paris. I did not meet him anywhere, and, as I heard a great deal of him which charmed me, I sent him your poems, and asked him to come and see me. He came,

and I found in him the man I had long wished to see, with the intellect and passions in due proportion for a full and healthy human being, with a soul constantly inspiring. Unhappily, it was a very short time before I came away. How much time had I wasted on others which I might have given to this real and important relation. In France, among the many persons that brought me some good thing, it was only with Mickiewicz, that I felt any deep founded mental connection.

After hearing music from Chopin and Neukomm, I quitted Paris on the 25th February, and came, *via* Chalons, Lyons, Avignon, (where I waded through melting snow to Laura's tomb,) Arles, to Marseilles; thence, by steamer, to Genoa, Leghorn, and Pisa. Seen through a cutting wind, the marble palaces, the gardens, the magnificent water-view of Genoa, failed to charm. Only at Naples have I found *my* Italy. Between Leghorn and Naples, our boat was run into by another, and we only just escaped being drowned.

[To Caroline Sturgis Tappan]
Rome
11th Jany 1848
My dear Caroline,

Your letter came today and did me good. I wept long over it and now I can hardly write for tears, but these relieve me more than anything, and in these days I cannot have them much.

I have begun to feel very sad at having no letter from you; it was a year since I had one; all that time I had no line from William Channing; the friendships I had paid for with so much heart's blood, so many thoughts in the long past seemed to flee from me, and I lost courage for the ties of the present. Now comes your letter and gives me the dear certainty that there is love, is realization, hope and faith in your life. At present you have really cast your lot with another person, live in a house I suppose; sleep and wake in unison with humanity; an island flowers in the river of your life.

I cannot say anything about it from my present self. Yet permanent love for the same object does not seem to me impossible, though once I thought, I felt it and have ceased to feel. At any rate the union of two natures for a time is so great.

The shells I got for you in Venice they *are* the same Consuelo used to gather; that was one reason I sent them. I wrote in a hurry a few lines for the person who unexpectedly offered; he must have lost them. The little necklace with the cross I meant for Greta. I did not think of it for you, supposing it too little and besides, it did not match the chain and bracelet, being set with different beads. But if you like it; keep it. I can get her something she will like as well.

But these are fragile things. I should like to give you something that may last and will send Raphael's Poesy. I have two copies one of which I keep at the head of my bed; perhaps you will put yours in the same place. I will send, also, a little rosary to hang beside it; red I think. I suppose you like red still.

At the time you dreamt of me I was in Venice, very ill, very suffering, but I could not have hated anything. I was very weary of the good friends who were with me, because they never knew what I was feeling, and always brought forward what I wanted to leave behind. I wanted to forget myself in Italy, and, while with them, it was impossible. Yet I was unreasonable enough to feel some bitterness at the indifference with which they left me, alone in a foreign land, and to see that they were seemingly impatient to be delayed two or three days by the state of my health. Yet as I felt bitterness it was not against them, but the destiny which placed me with them, instead of those who fancied they loved me; to be sure I had not put their love to the proof.

My life in Lombardy and Switzerland was a series of beautiful pictures, dramatic episodes, not without some noble genuine life in my own soul. The time when I wrote to you from Como was a peaceful external existence. I floated on the lake with my graceful Polish countess, hearing her stories of heroic sorrow, and I walked in the delicious gardens of the villas with many another summer friend. Red banners floated; children sang and shouted; the lakes of Venus and Diana glittered in the sweetest sunshine. The pretty girls of Bellaggio, with their coral necklaces, all brought flowers to "the American Countess" and "hoped she would be as happy as she deserved." Whether this cautious wish is fulfilled I know not, but certainly I left all this glitter of life behind at Como.

My days at Milan were not unmarked. I have known some happy hours; but they all lead to sorrow, and not only the cups of wine but of milk seem drugged with poison for me. It does not seem to be my fault,—this destiny: I do not court these things, they come. I am a poor magnet with power to be wounded by the bodies I attract.

Leaving Milan, I had a brilliant day in Parma. I had not known Correggio before; he deserves all his fame. I stood in the parlor of the Abbess, the person for whom all was done, and Paradise seemed opened by the nymph, upon her car of light, and the divine children peeping through the vines. Sweet soul of love! I should weary of you too; but it was glorious that day.

I had another good day, too, crossing the Apennines. The young crescent moon rose in orange twilight, just as I reached the highest peak. I was alone on foot; I heard no sound; I prayed.

At Florence, I was very ill. For three weeks, my life hung upon a thread. The effect of the Italian climate on my health is not favorable. I feel as if I had received a great injury. I am tired and woe-worn; often, in the bed, I wish I could weep my life away. However, they brought me gruel, I took it, and after a while rose up again. In the time of the vintage, I went alone to Sienna. This is a real untouched Italian place. This excursion, and the grapes, restored me at that time.

When I arrived in Rome, I was at first intoxicated to be here. The weather was beautiful, and many circumstances combined to place me in a kind of passive, childlike well-being. That is all over now, and, with this year, I enter upon a sphere of my destiny so difficult, that I, at present, see no way out, except through the gate of death. It is useless to write of it; you are of a distance and cannot help me;— whether accident or angel will, I have no intimation. I have no reason to hope I shall not reap what I have sown, and do not. Yet how I shall endure it I cannot guess; it is all a dark, sad enigma. The beautiful forms of art charm no more, and a love, in which there is all fondness, but no help, flatters in vain. I am all alone; nobody around me sees any of this. My numerous friendly acquaintances are troubled if they see me ill, and who so affectionate and kind as Mr. and Mrs. S.? but kindness did me good at the time. Write, too, your new address. I have to write still to that which I have known; indeed it will be very strange to me to call you by another name, but I suppose it will be necessary. Ever dear Carrie yours in love

MARGARET.

I have found just such another shell necklace for Greta, so keep that one in peace

[To Ralph Waldo Emerson]
Rome, 10 June 1849

I received your letter amid the round of cannonade and musketry. It was a terrible battle fought here from the first till the last light of day. I could see all its progress from my balcony. The Italians fought like lions. It is a truly heroic spirit that animates them. They make a stand here for honor and their rights, with little ground for hope that they can resist, now they are betrayed by France.

Since the 30th April, I go almost daily to the hospitals, and, though I have suffered,—for I had no idea before, how terrible gunshot-wounds and wound-fever are,—yet I have taken pleasure, and great pleasure, in being with the men; there is scarcely one who is not moved by a noble spirit. Many, especially among the Lombards, are the flower of Italian youth. When they begin to get better, I carry them books, and flowers; they read, and we talk.

The palace of the Pope, on the Quirinal, is now used for convalescents. In those beautiful gardens, I walk with them, —one with his sling, another with his crutch. The gardener plays off all his waterworks for the defenders of the country, and gathers flowers for me, their friend.

A day or two since, we sat in the Pope's little pavilion, where he used to give private audience. The sun was going gloriously down over Monte Mario, where gleamed the white tents of the French lighthorse among the trees. The cannonade was heard at intervals. Two bright-eyed boys sat at our feet, and gathered up eagerly every word said by the heroes of the day. It was a beautiful hour, stolen from the midst of ruin and sorrow; and tales were told as full of grace and pathos as in the gardens of Boccaccio, only in a very different spirit,—with noble hope for men, with reverence for woman.

The young ladies of the family, very young girls, were filled with enthusiasm for the suffering, wounded patriots, and they wished to go to the hospital to give their services. Excepting the three superintendents, none but married ladies were permitted to serve there, but their services were accepted. Their governess then wished to go too, and, as she could speak several languages, she was admitted to the rooms of the wounded soldiers, to interpret for them, as the nurses knew nothing but Italian, and many of these poor men were suffering, because they could not make their wishes known. Some are French, some German, and many Poles. Indeed, I am afraid it is too true that there were comparatively but few Romans among them. This young lady passed several nights there.

Should I never return,—and sometimes I despair of doing so, it seems so far off, so difficult, I am caught in such a net of ties here,—if ever you know of my life here, I think you will only wonder at the constancy with which I have sustained myself; the degree of profit to which, amid great difficulties, I have put the time, at least in the way of observation. Meanwhile, love me all you can; let me feel, that, amid the fearful agitations of the world, there are pure hands, with healthful, even pulse, stretched out toward me, if I claim their grasp.

I feel profoundly for Mazzini; at moments I am tempted to say, "Cursed with every granted prayer,"—so cunning is the daemon. He is become the inspiring soul of his people. He saw Rome, to which all his hopes through life tended, for the first time as a Roman citizen, and to become in a few days its ruler. He has animated, he sustains her to a glorious effort, which, if it fails, this time, will not in the age. His country will be free. Yet to me it would be so dreadful to cause all this bloodshed, to dig the graves of such martyrs.

Then Rome is being destroyed; her glorious oaks; her villas, haunts of sacred beauty, that seemed the possession of the world forever,—the villa of Raphael, the villa of Albani, home of Winkelmann, and the best expression of the ideal of modern Rome, and so many other sanctuaries of beauty,— all must perish, lest a foe should level his musket from their shelter. *I* could not, could not!

I know not, dear friend, whether I ever shall get home across that great ocean, but here in Rome I shall no longer wish to live. O, Rome, *my* country! could I imagine that the triumph of what I held dear was to heap such desolation on thy head!

[To Constanza Arconati Visconti]
[August, 1849]

Reading a book called "The Last Days of the Republic in Rome," I see that my letter, giving my impressions of that period, may well have seemed to you strangely partial. If we can meet as once we did, and compare notes in the same spirit of candor, while making mutual allowance for our different points of view, your testimony and opinions would be invaluable to me. But will you have patience with my democracy,—my revolutionary spirit? Believe that in thought I am more radical than ever. The heart of Margaret you know,—it is always the same. Mazzini is immortally dear to me,—a thousand times dearer for all the trial I saw made of him in Rome;—dearer for all he suffered. Many of his brave friends perished there. We who, less worthy, survive, would fain make up for the loss, by our increased devotion to him, the purest, the most disinterested of patriots, the most affectionate of brothers. You will not love me less that I am true to him.

Then, again, how will it affect you to know that I have united my destiny with that of an obscure young man,— younger than myself; a person of no intellectual culture, and in whom, in short, you will see no reason for my choosing; yet more, that this union is of long standing; that we have with us our child, of a year old, and that it is only lately I acquainted my family with the fact.

If you decide to meet with me as before, and wish to say something about the matter to your friends, it will be true to

say that there have been pecuniary reasons for this concealment. But *to you* in confidence I add, this is only half the
truth; and I cannot explain or satisfy my dear friend farther
—I should wish to meet her independent of all relations; but
as we live in the midst of "society," she would have to enquire
for me now as *Margaret Ossoli;* that being done, I should like
to say nothing farther on the subject.

However you may feel about all this, dear Madame Arconati, you will always be the same in my eyes. I earnestly wish
you may not feel estranged, but only, if you do, I would rather
for you to act upon it. Let us meet as friends, or not at all—
In all events I remain ever yours,

                                                    MARGARET

[To Samuel and Anna Barker Ward]
Florence
21st Octr 1849
My dear Sam,

I saw with great pleasure your writing on one of the letters
brought by Mr Mozier and opened that one first; it was a
disappointment to find only a few lines about the money,
though I thank you much for your affectionate thoughtfulness
of me which induced your sending that; it was welcome at
this period, though I am sorry to need such aid and should
not but for the violation of pledges in those who had not only
promised but offered to secure me employment ample for my
maintenance in remaining abroad. But I will not stain this
brief page with any notice of the bitter cares and disappointments I have been made to suffer at a time when a little peace
would have been so precious. Ere reading this you will know
that I am married and that my husband is not better situated
than myself; indeed worse for he must be for the present separated from his natural friends and career. He will have by
and by a little money from the paternal estate, but, in the
present condition of the Roman dominion, it is not easy to
raise, we may have to wait several years. Every thing has
turned against us; we are not disposed to complain amid the
desolation of other homes, and the deep griefs the noblest we

know are suffering, yet our causes for anxiety are great, the rather as we have a little tender one to care for, and I confess I do not feel much courage when I think of privation for him. I would wish him the shelter of a secure roof, good care and a serene environment in his earliest days. I thought I had loved the children of others as much as I could love a child, but find the thrill far more vital with my own; you may perhaps look for me to say something of my companion and to you I should like to, but it is too difficult; you are among the very few of my friends who I think may be able to see why we can live together, and may appreciate the unspoiled nature and loveliness of his character; he is entirely without what is commonly called culture, educated by a tutor and that tutor an old priest, he knows readin ritin and rithmetic, but the first I think he never used to go through with a book; nature has been his book; of that some lines he has spelled thoroughly. To me the simplicity, the reality, the great tenderness and refinement of his character make a domestic place in this world and as it is for my heart that he loves me, I hope he may always be able to feel the same, but that is as God pleases. It seems to us now that, if we were sure of a narrow competency, we could have a good deal of happiness together in what remains of life; however it is not worth-while to trouble much, life itself is so uncertain; we both had a narrow escape during the seige of Rome; our little one has since been very near death, and now the Cholera is as near as Bolgona.

I will now turn to Anna from whom I have a letter since receiving yours—you speak dear Anna of my not having answered some letter, probably some one has been lost, as many were in the more convulsed days; here five have come to me that have been *perdus* in some corner for more than a year but none was from you; it was I know not how long since I had heard. Now I thank you for this one which gives me the real facts as to your health, Sam's new life &c. I had heard before that you bore your imprisonment beautifully but had been led to fear you would not be able to walk any more, but lose the benefit and joy of free motion entirely as Mrs Spring did when I knew her; you do not say positively, but I infer from your letter it is nothing so, for you talk of climbing the hills with me. Your hills and all objects in America look very far off to me; at times I cannot realize that I shall ever see the old familiar faces again; very dear and lovely they seem in the distance, especially now as in the sad reflux of that great tide of life in which my heart had gone forward with as much force as was left it I have more time to think of lang syne. It makes me weep to think of it; life was so fatiguing then and is so now, beyond my strength; happy are those who have a childhood of play beneath the trees; I hope your little ones will have it in their mountain home, and that if I do not see you or them there we shall meet in Elysium— But perhaps we shall meet in some very different place; I have some vague idea of returning next summer, though ways means and prospects are yet to be discovered. At present we are moored in Florence, I hope till April or May. I wrote to you the day I recd [received] your letter, but before finishing, the Police began to trouble us, and I have been uncertain if we should not have to go away. Now we have permission to stay for two months and I supposed they will make no difficulty about renewing it. So I hope you will write here to Margaret Ossoli, care J. Mozier Esq. Although a green retirement and still country life seem now to me so sweet, I felt glad to hear that Sam is to leave it for a time; it is better to mix often with the struggling suffering crowd; it is a more generous life and culture. Happy those who can alternate the two lives at pleasure. I like to see Dante as he stands here on the wall of the Cathedral. Heaven and Hell are in the near view, he touches the walls of Florence. Yet it is not Florence I would have chosen to touch. Florence is a kind of Boston: it has not the poetic greatness of the other Italian cities; it is a place to work and study in; simple life does not seem so great. I feel reconciled to be here now as the place most economical and convenient and where I still have two or three friends. I begin to feel interested again in looking at Art and I like walking on the heights, beside the air agrees with the baby; who seems to grow better every day; still this place will never charm me as have (I do not speak of Rome, which was my *home*) but Venice, Milan, Bologna, Brescia, in fact almost all Italian towns. The end of my sheet bids me come to an end; you asked me to write a *real* letter. I fear this will give you no satisfaction, if so, pardon dear Anna, so great has been the passion of my life since you knew me, it is difficult to speak. My friends remain in their place. I seem to have more clue to their state than they to mine. Across the stream I see them; they look fair and tall, but I must go to them; they cannot come to me. Farewell.

SUGGESTED
READING

The variety of subjects addressed in these readings reflects Margaret Fuller's exceptionally broad interests. German culture, women's rights, Transcendentalism, classical literature all engaged Fuller. Edited by Robert Hudspeth, the five volumes of Fuller's letters provide a wealth of insights into her richly textured life. Joel Myerson's valuable *Descriptive Bibliography* guides readers through Fuller's writings.

Allen, Margaret Vanderhaar. *The Achievement of Margaret Fuller.* University Park: Pennsylvania State University Press, 1979.

Blackwell, Jeannine, and Suzanne Zantop. *Bitter Healing: German Women Writers From 1700 to 1830.* Lincoln: University of Nebraska Press, 1990.

Blanchard, Paula. *Margaret Fuller: From Transcendentalism to Revolution.* New York: Delacorte Press, 1978.

Buell, Lawrence. *New England Literary Culture.* Cambridge: Cambridge University Press, 1986.

Buell, Lawrence. *Literary Transcendentalism: Style and Vision in the American Renaissance.* Ithaca: Cornell University Press, 1973.

Capper, Charles. *Margaret Fuller: The Private Years.* New York: Oxford University Press, 1992.

Cayton, Mary Kupiec. *Emerson's Emergence: Self and Society in the Transformation of New England, 1800–1845.* Chapel Hill: University of North Carolina Press, 1989.

Chai, Leon. *The Romantic Foundations of the American Renaissance.* Ithaca: Cornell University Press, 1987.

Chevigny, Belle Gale. *The Woman and the Myth.* Old Westbury, N.Y.: The Feminist Press, 1976. Revised edition. Boston: Northeastern University Press, 1993.

Chevigny, Bell Gale. "The Long Arm of Censorship: Mythmaking in Margaret Fuller's Time and Our Own." *Signs: Journal of Women in Culture and Society* 2 (Winter 1976): 450–460.

Deiss, Joseph Jay. *The Roman Years of Margaret Fuller: A Biography.* New York: Crowell, 1969.

DuBois, Ellen. *Feminism and Suffrage: The Emergence of an Independent Women's Movement in America, 1848–1869.* Ithaca: Cornell University Press, 1978.

Ellison, Julie. *Delicate Subjects: Romanticism, Gender, and the Ethics of Understanding.* Ithaca: Cornell University Press, 1990.

Emerson, Ralph Waldo, William Henry Channing, and James Freeman Clarke. *Memoirs of Margaret Fuller Ossoli,* 2 vols. Boston: Phillips, Sampson, 1852.

Flexner, Eleanor. *Century of Struggle: The Woman's Rights Movement in the United States.* Cambridge: Harvard University Press, 1975.

Hatfield, Henry. *Goethe: A Critical Introduction.* Cambridge: Harvard University Press, 1964.

Higginson, Thomas Wentworth. *Margaret Fuller Ossoli.* Boston: Houghton, Mifflin & Company, 1884.

Higham, John. *From Boundlessness to Consolidation: The Transformation of American Culture, 1848–1860.* Ann Arbor: University of Michigan Press, 1969.

Hudspeth, Robert, ed. *The Letters of Margaret Fuller,* 5 vols. Ithaca: Cornell University Press, 1983–1988.

Kolodny, Annette. *The Land Before Her: Fantasy and Experience of the American Frontiers, 1630–1860.* Chapel Hill: University of North Carolina Press, 1984.

Kolodny, Annette. "Inventing a Feminist Discourse: Rhetoric and Resistance in Margaret Fuller's *Woman in the Nineteenth Century.*" *New Literary History* 25 (Spring 1994): 355–382.

Kornfeld, Eve and Melissa Marks. "Margaret Fuller: Minerva and the Muse." *Journal of American Culture* 3 (Fall 1990): 47–59.

Myerson, Joel. *Critical Essays on Margaret Fuller.* Boston: G.K. Hall, 1980.

Myerson, Joel. *Margaret Fuller: A Descriptive Bibliography.* Pittsburgh: University of Pittsburgh Press, 1978.

Myerson, Joel. *Margaret Fuller: An Annotated Secondary Bibliography.* New York: Burt Franklin & Company, 1977.

Pochman, Henry A. *German Culture in America.* Madison: University of Wisconsin Press, 1957.

Reynolds, Larry J., and Susan Belasco Smith. *"These Sad But Glorious*

Days": *Dispatches From Europe, 1846–1850.* New Haven: Yale University Press, 1991.

Reynolds, Larry J. *European Revolutions and the American Literary Renaissance.* New Haven: Yale University Press, 1988.

Riasanovsky, Nicholas V. *The Emergence of Romanticism.* New York: Oxford University Press, 1992.

Robertson, Priscilla. *Revolutions of 1848: A Social History.* Princeton: Princeton University Press, 1952.

Robinson, David. "Margaret Fuller and the Transcendental Ethos: *Woman in the Nineteenth Century.*" *Publications of the Modern Language Association of America* 97 (January 1982): 83–98.

Rose, Anne C. *Transcendentalism as a Social Movement, 1830–1850.* New Haven: Yale University Press, 1981.

Rosowski, Susan J. "Margaret Fuller, an Engendered West, and *Summer on the Lakes.*" *Western American Literature* 25 (August 1990): 125–145.

Showalter, Elaine. *Sister's Choice: Tradition and Change in American Women's Writing.* Oxford: Oxford University Press, 1991.

Urbanski, Marie Mitchell Olesen, ed. *Margaret Fuller: Visionary of the New Age.* Orono: Northern Lights, 1994.

Urbanski, Marie Mitchell Olesen. *Margaret Fuller's* Woman in the Nineteenth Century: *A Study of Form and Content, of Sources and Influence.* Westport, Conn.: Greenwood, 1980.

Wade, Mason. *Margaret Fuller: Whetstone of Genius.* New York: Viking, 1940.

Ziff, Lazar. *Literary Democracy: The Declaration of Cultural Independence in America.* New York: Viking, 1981.

Zwang, Christina. *Feminist Conversations: Fuller, Emerson, and the Task of Reading.* Ithaca: Cornell University Press, 1994.

THE VIKING PORTABLE LIBRARY

FOR THE BEST IN PAPERBACKS, LOOK FOR THE

In every corner of the world, on every subject under the sun, Penguin represents quality and variety—the very best in publishing today.

For complete information about books available from Penguin—including Pelicans, Puffins, Peregrines, and Penguin Classics—and how to order them, write to us at the appropriate address below. Please note that for copyright reasons the selection of books varies from country to country.

In the United Kingdom: For a complete list of books available from Penguin in the U.K., please write to *Dept E.P., Penguin Books Ltd, Harmondsworth, Middlesex, UB7 0DA*.

In the United States: For a complete list of books available from Penguin in the U.S., please write to *Consumer Sales, Penguin USA, P.O. Box 999— Dept. 17109, Bergenfield, New Jersey 07621-0120*. Visa and MasterCard holders call 1-800-253-6476 to order all Penguin titles.

In Canada: For a complete list of books available from Penguin in Canada, please write to *Penguin Books Canada Ltd, 10 Alcorn Avenue, Suite 300, Toronto, Ontario, Canada M4V 3B2*.

In Australia: For a complete list of books available from Penguin in Australia, please write to the *Marketing Department, Penguin Books Ltd, P.O. Box 257, Ringwood, Victoria 3134*.

In New Zealand: For a complete list of books available from Penguin in New Zealand, please write to the *Marketing Department, Penguin Books (NZ) Ltd, Private Bag, Takapuna, Auckland 9*.

In India: For a complete list of books available from Penguin, please write to *Penguin Overseas Ltd, 706 Eros Apartments, 56 Nehru Place, New Delhi, 110019*.

In Holland: For a complete list of books available from Penguin in Holland, please write to *Penguin Books Nederland B.V., Postbus 195, NL-1380AD Weesp, Netherlands*.

In Germany: For a complete list of books available from Penguin, please write to *Penguin Books Ltd, Friedrichstrasse 10-12, D-6000 Frankfurt Main 1, Federal Republic of Germany*.

In Spain: For a complete list of books available from Penguin in Spain, please write to *Longman, Penguin España, Calle San Nicolas 15, E-28013 Madrid, Spain*.

In Japan: For a complete list of books available from Penguin in Japan, please write to *Longman Penguin Japan Co Ltd, Yamaguchi Building, 2-12-9 Kanda Jimbocho, Chiyoda-Ku, Tokyo 101, Japan*.